THE INFERNAL DEVICES

Clockwork
PRINCE

Also by Cassandra Clare

THE MORTAL INSTRUMENTS

City of Bones

City of Ashes

City of Glass

City of Fallen Angels

City of Lost Souls

City of Heavenly Fire

THE INFERNAL DEVICES

Clockwork Angel

Clockwork Prince

Clockwork Princess

THE DARK ARTIFICES

Lady Midnight

The Shadowhunter's Codex

With Joshua Lewis

The Bane Chronicles

With Sarah Rees Brennan
and Maureen Johnson

THE INFERNAL DEVICES

Clockwork
ANGEL

Also by Cassandra Clare

THE MORTAL INSTRUMENTS

City of Bones

City of Ashes

City of Glass

City of Fallen Angels

City of Lost Souls

City of Heavenly Fire

THE INFERNAL DEVICES

Clockwork Angel

Clockwork Prince

Clockwork Princess

THE DARK ARTIFICES

Lady Midnight

The Shadowhunter's Codex
With Joshua Lewis

The Bane Chronicles
With Sarah Rees Brennan
and Maureen Johnson

THE INFERNAL DEVICES

Clockwork ANGEL

Book One

CASSANDRA CLARE

Margaret K. McElderry Books
NEW YORK LONDON TORONTO SYDNEY NEW DELHI

MARGARET K. McELDERRY BOOKS

An imprint of Simon & Schuster Children's Publishing Division

1230 Avenue of the Americas, New York, New York 10020

MARGARET K. McELDERRY BOOKS is a trademark of Simon & Schuster, Inc.

For information about special discounts for bulk purchases, please contact Simon & Schuster Special Sales at 1-866-506-1949 or business@simonandschuster.com.

The Simon & Schuster Speakers Bureau can bring authors to your live event. For more information or to book an event, contact the Simon & Schuster Speakers Bureau at 1-866-248-3049 or visit our website at www.simonspeakers.com.

Also available in a Margaret K. McElderry Books hardcover edition

Cover design by Russell Gordon

Interior design by Mike Rosamilia

Map illustration by Drew Willis

The text for this book is set in Dolly.

Manufactured in the United States of America

This Margaret K. McElderry Books paperback edition September 2015

12 14 16 18 20 19 17 15 13

The Library of Congress has cataloged the hardcover edition as follows:

Clare, Cassandra.

Clockwork angel / Cassandra Clare.

p. cm.—(The infernal devices ; bk. 1)

Summary: When sixteen-year-old orphan Tessa Gray's older brother suddenly vanishes, her search for him leads her into Victorian-era London's dangerous supernatural underworld, and when she discovers that she herself is a Downworlder, she must learn to trust the demon-killing Shadowhunters if she ever wants to learn to control her powers and find her brother.

ISBN 978-1-4169-7586-1 (hc)

ISBN 978-1-4424-0946-0 (eBook)

[1. Supernatural—Fiction. 2. Demonology—Fiction. 3. Orphans—Fiction. 4. Secret societies—Fiction. 5. London (England)—History—19th century—Fiction. 6. Great Britain—History—Victoria, 1837–1901—Fiction.] I. Title.

PZ7.C5265Cl 2010

[Fic]—dc22

2010008616

ISBN 978-1-4814-5602-9 (repackaged pbk)

For Jim and Kate

1 Tessa and Jem's meeting place

2 The *yin fen* house

3 The Institute

4 Mortmain's warehouses

13 The Dark Sisters' House

11 Entrance to the Council chambers

12 Cross Bones Graveyard

CHISWICK

6

13 To the Dark Sisters' House

5 The Argent Rooms

6 Lightwood House

7 Woolsey's house

8 Hatchards bookshop

9 The Devil Tavern

10 Entrance to the Faerie Courts

ST. JOHN'S WOOD

REGENT'S PARK

MARYLEBONE

SOHO

HOLBORN

SPITALFIELDS

NOTTING HILL

HYDE PARK

MAYFAIR

KENSINGTON

BELGRAVIA

WESTMINSTER

LONDON

SOUTHWARK

LAMBETH

CHELSEA

River Thames

BATTERSEA PARK

FULHAM

CAMBERWELL

BRIXTON

Foreword

For many years during the time I've been a writer, people have asked me if I get inspiration for my books from my dreams.

My response has always been that I wish that I did. It seems like such a fun way to get story ideas—dream something and wake up compelled to put the story to paper. Unfortunately, the only real dreams I ever have about my characters and stories are nonsensical: all my characters are in front of me in line at the grocery store and have too many items in their carts.

Which makes the genesis of the idea I had for the Infernal Devices pretty unusual. It wasn't a dream, but it was a daydream.

I was in London, on a trip to promote *City of Bones*, the first book of the Shadowhunters chronicles. I was crossing Blackfriars Bridge, which is a lovely old bridge in the City of London over the river Thames. It was a gray cloudy day, and mist was drifting along the bridge. I leaned against the parapet and looked down at the water.

I thought about how the bridge had stood for so many years, and of all that it must have witnessed. Slowly the image of a girl with brown hair and a boy dressed in Victorian clothing came into my mind, and as I pictured them there on the bridge, I imagined a strange army of clockwork monsters hidden in the shadows, waiting to pounce.

I went home feeling unsettled and inspired. Slowly the story of Tessa, Jem, and Will began to take shape in my mind—I chose the location of the London Institute for its proximity to Blackfriars Bridge, for I always knew the bridge would be central to the tale.

After much wandering around London (using a map dated 1879, which led to a lot of getting lost) I decided the Institute would be Saint Bride's Church off Fleet Street, a gorgeous church gutted by firebombs during the Blitz.

I chose 1878 because it was a time of transition from an old England to a new England: there was regular train service, there was gas light, there were sewers, and yet the time period retained the graciousness and beauty of the past. It seemed like a wonderful era in which to set a story about three young people learning who they are and all they are capable of, especially when it came to the story of a young girl learning she is destined for more than an arranged marriage—that she is destined for an extraordinary love.

I believe that historical fiction is the closest thing we have to time travel. I wanted to feel as much as I could that I was living and breathing the time period of the Infernal Devices, so I set myself a project: for six months I read nothing but books set in the mid and late Victorian era.

It was research by immersion. Soon I started to imagine that I was seeing horse-drawn carriages instead of cars, that I could smell the Thames River and hear the Bow Bells. I wanted my readers to feel that the past was accessible, so the characters of a bygone time's pain and joy would seem real and true. It was a time obsessed with death, in which diseases which are now cured easily were rife, and sicknesses we now understand seemed as mysterious as the corrupting touch of a demon. The real world as it was then slotted neatly into my already-imagined world of the Shadowhunters, demon-hunters, and magic users and gave it new depth and richness: creating a hero who could see and talk to imploring ghosts and another who was condemned to die young of a fatal demonic illness, no matter how desperate the efforts to save him, just as in reality victims of consumption sickened and died without penicillin. The Brontë family, who produced *Wuthering Heights* and *Jane Eyre*, were decimated by consumption, and to mark my respect for and debt to their work I named the head of the London Institute—Charlotte Branwell—after two of the Brontë siblings. It was a difficult time for a woman to have authority in the Shadowhunter world and the mundane world, but Charlotte manages it. Tessa, Charlotte, Sophie, and Jessamine are all heroines who I adore, coping with the prejudice of a time more difficult for women than our own in a way that I hoped would also resonate with the oppression women still face today.

I immersed myself in books to write this series, and in this series two of the characters also find inspiration and comfort in books. Tessa and Will bond over Charles Dickens's *A Tale of Two Cities*, in which one of the heroes considers himself a soul doomed to wickedness. Will thinks he too is doomed to be corrupt and unloved; over the course of the books he learns how wrong he was. His best friend, James Carstairs, who is dying, believes that he is fated to die without love, like the poet Keats, whom his character is partially based on. Both Will and Jem love each other—they are blood brothers—but despite that love, they have no hope. In Tessa they both find their salvation, because Tessa believes in hope—not just because she is stalwart and a heroine, but also because she has discovered hope in books.

Tessa is a bookworm: she doesn't only love classics by the Brontës and Dickens, but the many novels of her time that I read during my months-long reading project. She reads voraciously, in the same way I did, books considered both high- and lowbrow, and she gains enjoyment from both kinds. She learns she has the power to shapeshift, reflecting our real-life ability to slip inside the skin of fictional characters when we read.

I wanted to write a heroine who was invested in books as much as I was and as I knew my readers were: a girl who learned that adventure was possible from books, that romance was potentially as wonderful as it was painful, that courage and kindness would carry her through, and that she could be marvelously transformed. I wanted every girl reading the Infernal Devices to feel that she could be the heroine of a novel—maybe even this one.

Thames River Song

A note of salt
slips in and the river rises,
darkening to the color of tea,
swelling to meet the green.
Above its banks the cogs and wheels
of monstrous machines
clank and spin, the ghost within
vanishes into its coils,
whispering mysteries.
Each tiny golden cog has teeth,
each great wheel moves
a pair of hands which take
the water from the river,
devour it, convert it into steam,
coerce the great machine to run
on the force of its dissolution.
Gently, the tide is rising,
corrupting the mechanism.
Salt, rust and silt
slowing the gears.
Down at the banks
the iron tanks
sway into their moorings
with the hollow boom
of a gigantic bell,
of drum and cannon
which cry out in a tongue of thunder
and the river rolls under.

—Elka Cloke

PROLOGUE

London, April 1878.

The demon exploded in a shower of ichor and guts.

William Herondale jerked back the dagger he was holding, but it was too late. The viscous acid of the demon's blood had already begun to eat away at the shining blade. He swore and tossed the weapon aside; it landed in a filthy puddle and commenced smoldering like a doused match. The demon itself, of course, had vanished—dispatched back to whatever hellish world it had come from, though not without leaving a mess behind.

"Jem!" Will called, turning around. "Where are you? Did you see that? Killed it with one blow! Not bad, eh?"

But there was no answer to Will's shout; his hunting partner had been standing behind him in the damp and crooked street a few moments before, guarding his back, Will was positive, but now Will was alone in the shadows. He frowned in annoyance—it was much less fun showing off without Jem to show off *to*. He glanced behind him, to where the street narrowed into a passage that gave onto the black, heaving water of the Thames in the distance. Through the gap Will could see the dark outlines of docked ships, a forest of masts like a leafless orchard. No Jem there; perhaps he had gone back to Narrow Street in search of better illumination. With a shrug Will headed back the way he had come.

Narrow Street cut across Limehouse, between the docks beside the river and the cramped slums spreading west toward Whitechapel. It was as narrow as its name suggested, lined with warehouses and lopsided wooden buildings. At the moment it was deserted; even the drunks staggering home from the Grapes up the road had found somewhere to collapse for the night. Will liked Limehouse, liked the feeling of being on the edge of the world, where ships left each day for unimaginably far ports. That the area was a sailor's haunt, and consequently full of gambling hells, opium dens, and brothels, didn't hurt either. It was easy to lose yourself in a place like this. He didn't even mind the smell of it—smoke and rope and tar, foreign spices mixed with the dirty riverwater smell of the Thames.

Looking up and down the empty street, he scrubbed the sleeve of his coat across his face, trying to rub away the ichor that stung and burned his skin. The cloth came away stained green and black. There was a cut on the back of his hand too, a nasty one. He could use a healing rune. One of Charlotte's, preferably. She was particularly good at drawing *iratzes*.

A shape detached itself from the shadows and moved toward Will. He started forward, then paused. It wasn't Jem, but rather a mundane policeman wearing a bell-shaped helmet, a heavy overcoat, and a puzzled expression. He stared at Will, or rather *through* Will. However accustomed Will had become to glamour, it was always strange to be looked through as if he weren't there. Will was seized with the sudden urge to grab the policeman's truncheon and watch while the man flapped around, trying to figure out where it had gone; but Jem had scolded him the few times he'd done that before, and while Will never really could understand Jem's objections to the whole enterprise, it wasn't worth making him upset.

With a shrug and a blink, the policeman moved past Will, shaking his head and muttering something under his breath about swearing off the gin before he truly started seeing things. Will stepped aside to let the man pass, then raised his voice to a shout: "James Carstairs! Jem! Where *are* you, you disloyal bastard?"

This time a faint reply answered him. "Over here. Follow the witchlight."

Will moved toward the sound of Jem's voice. It seemed to be coming from a dark opening between two warehouses; a faint gleam was visible within the shadows, like the darting light of a will-o'-the-wisp. "Did you hear me before? That Shax demon thought it could get me with its bloody great pincers, but I cornered it in an alley—"

"Yes, I heard you." The young man who appeared at the mouth of the alley was pale in the lamplight—paler even than he usually was, which was quite pale indeed. He was bareheaded, which drew the eye immediately to his hair. It was an odd bright silver color, like an untarnished shilling. His eyes were the same silver, and his fine-boned face was angular, the slight curve of his eyes the only clue to his heritage.

There were dark stains across his white shirtfront, and his hands were thickly smeared with red.

Will tensed. "You're bleeding. What happened?"

Jem waved away Will's concern. "It's not my blood." He turned his head back toward the alley behind him. "It's hers."

Will glanced past his friend, into the thicker shadows of the alley. In the far corner of it was a crumpled shape—only a shadow in the darkness, but when Will looked closely, he could make out the shape of a pale hand, and a wisp of fair hair.

"A dead woman?" Will asked. "A mundane?"

"A girl, really. Not more than fourteen."

At that, Will cursed with great volume and expression. Jem waited patiently for him to be done.

"If we'd only happened along a little earlier," Will said finally. "That bloody demon —"

"That's the peculiar thing. I don't think this is the demon's work." Jem frowned. "Shax demons are parasites, brood parasites. It would have wanted to drag its victim back to its lair to lay eggs in her skin while she was still alive. But this girl—she was stabbed, repeatedly. And I don't think it was here, either. There simply isn't enough blood in the alley. I think she was attacked elsewhere, and she dragged herself here to die of her injuries."

"But the Shax demon—"

"I'm telling you, I don't think it *was* the Shax. I think the Shax was pursuing her—hunting her down for something, or someone, else."

"Shaxes have a keen sense of scent," Will allowed. "I've heard of warlocks using them to follow the tracks of the missing. And it did seem to be moving with an odd sort of purpose." He looked past Jem, at the pitiful smallness of the crumpled shape in the alley. "You didn't find the weapon, did you?"

"Here." Jem drew something from inside his jacket—a knife, wrapped in white cloth. "It's a sort of misericord, or hunting dagger. Look how thin the blade is."

Will took it. The blade was indeed thin, ending in a handle made of polished bone. The blade and hilt both were stained with dried blood. With a frown he wiped the flat of the knife across the rough fabric of his sleeve, scraping it clean until a symbol, burned into the blade, became visible. Two serpents, each biting the other's tail, forming a perfect circle.

"*Ouroboros*," Jem said, leaning in close to stare at the knife. "A double one. Now, what do you think that means?"

"The end of the world," said Will, still looking at the dagger, a small smile playing about his mouth, "and the beginning."

Jem frowned. "I understand the symbology, William. I meant, what do you think its presence on the dagger signifies?"

The wind off the river was ruffling Will's hair; he brushed it out of his eyes with an impatient gesture and went back to studying the knife. "It's an alchemical symbol, not a warlock or Downworlder one. That usually means humans—the foolish mundane sort who think trafficking in magic is the ticket for gaining wealth and fame."

"The sort who usually end up a pile of bloody rags inside some pentagram." Jem sounded grim.

"The sort who like to lurk about the Downworld parts of our fair city." After wrapping the handkerchief around the blade carefully, Will slipped it into his jacket pocket. "D'you think Charlotte will let me handle the investigation?"

"Do *you* think you can be trusted in Downworld? The gambling hells, the dens of magical vice, the women of loose morals . . ."

Will smiled the way Lucifer might have smiled, moments before he fell from Heaven. "Would tomorrow be too early to start looking, do you think?"

Jem sighed. "Do what you like, William. You always do."

Southampton, May.

Tessa could not remember a time when she had not loved the clockwork angel. It had belonged to her mother once, and her mother had been wearing it when she died. After that it had sat in her mother's jewelry box, until her brother, Nathaniel, took it out one day to see if it was still in working order.

The angel was no bigger than Tessa's pinky finger, a tiny statuette made of brass, with folded bronze wings no larger than a cricket's. It had a delicate metal face with shut crescent eyelids, and hands crossed over a sword in front. A thin chain that looped beneath the wings allowed the angel to be worn around the neck like a locket.

Tessa knew the angel was made out of clockwork because if she lifted it to her ear she could hear the sound of its machinery, like the sound of a watch. Nate had exclaimed in surprise that it was still working after so many years, and he had looked in vain for a knob or a screw, or some other method by which the angel might be wound. But there had been nothing to find. With a shrug he'd given the angel to Tessa. From that moment she had never taken it off; even at night the angel lay against her chest as she slept, its constant *ticktock, ticktock* like the beating of a second heart.

She held it now, clutched between her fingers, as the *Main* nosed its way between other massive steamships to find a spot at the Southampton dock. Nate had insisted that she come to Southampton instead of Liverpool, where most transatlantic steamers arrived. He had claimed it was because Southampton was a much pleasanter place to arrive at, so Tessa couldn't help being a little disappointed by this, her first sight of England. It was drearily gray. Rain drummed down onto the spires of a distant church, while black smoke rose from the chimneys of ships and stained the already dull-colored sky. A crowd of people in dark clothes, holding umbrellas, stood on the docks. Tessa strained to see if her brother was among them, but the mist and spray from the ship were too thick for her to make out any individual in great detail.

Tessa shivered. The wind off the sea was chilly. All of Nate's letters had claimed that London was beautiful, the sun shining every day. Well, Tessa thought, hopefully the weather there was better than it was here, because she had no warm clothes with her, nothing more substantial than a woolen shawl that had belonged to Aunt Harriet, and a pair of thin gloves. She had sold most of her clothes to pay for her aunt's funeral, secure in the knowledge that her brother would buy her more when she arrived in London to live with him.

A shout went up. The *Main*, its shining black-painted hull gleaming wet with rain, had anchored, and tugs were plowing their way through the heaving gray water, ready to carry baggage and passengers to the shore. Passengers streamed off the ship, clearly desperate to feel land under their feet. So different from their departure from New York. The sky had been blue then, and a brass band had been playing. Though, with no one there to wish her good-bye, it had not been a merry occasion.

Hunching her shoulders, Tessa joined the disembarking crowd. Drops of rain stung her unprotected head and neck like pinpricks from icy little needles, and her hands, inside their insubstantial gloves, were clammy and wet with rain. Reaching the quay, she looked around eagerly, searching for a sight of Nate. It had been nearly two weeks since she'd spoken to a soul, having kept almost entirely to herself on board the *Main*. It would be wonderful to have her brother to talk to again.

He wasn't there. The wharves were heaped with stacks of luggage and all sorts of boxes and cargo, even mounds of fruit and vegetables wilting and dissolving in the rain. A steamer was departing for Le Havre nearby, and damp-looking sailors swarmed close by Tessa, shouting in French. She tried to move aside, only to be almost trampled by a throng of disembarking passengers hurrying for the shelter of the railway station.

But Nate was nowhere to be seen.

"You are Miss Gray?" The voice was guttural, heavily accented. A man had moved to stand in front of Tessa. He was tall, and was wearing a sweeping black coat and a tall hat, its brim collecting rainwater like a cistern. His eyes were peculiarly bulging, almost protuberant, like a frog's, his skin as rough-looking as scar tissue. Tessa had to fight the urge to cringe away from him. But he knew her name. Who here would know her name except someone who knew Nate, too?

"Yes?"

"Your brother sent me. Come with me."

"Where is he?" Tessa demanded, but the man was already walking away. His stride was uneven, as if he had a limp from an old injury. After a moment Tessa gathered up her skirts and hurried after him.

He wound through the crowd, moving ahead with purposeful speed. People jumped aside, muttering about his rudeness as he shouldered past, with Tessa nearly running to keep up. He turned abruptly around a pile of boxes, and came to a halt in front of a large, gleaming black coach. Gold letters had been painted across its side, but the rain and mist were too thick for Tessa to read them clearly.

The door of the carriage opened and a woman leaned out. She wore an enormous plumed hat that hid her face. "Miss Theresa Gray?"

Tessa nodded. The bulging-eyed man hurried to help the woman out of the carriage—and then another woman, following after her. Each of them immediately opened an umbrella and raised it, sheltering themselves from the rain. Then they fixed their eyes on Tessa.

They were an odd pair, the women. One was very tall and thin, with a bony, pinched face. Colorless hair was scraped back into a chignon at the back of her head. She wore a dress of brilliant violet silk, already spattered here and there with splotches of rain, and matching violet gloves. The other woman was short and plump, with small eyes sunk deep into her head; the bright pink gloves stretched over her large hands made them look like colorful paws.

"Theresa Gray," said the shorter of the two. "What a delight to make your acquaintance at last. I am Mrs. Black, and this is my sister, Mrs. Dark. Your brother sent us to accompany you to London."

Tessa—damp, cold, and baffled—clutched her wet shawl tighter around herself. "I don't understand. Where's Nate? Why didn't he come himself?"

"He was unavoidably detained by business in London. Mortmain's couldn't spare him. He sent ahead a note for you, however." Mrs. Black held out a rolled-up bit of paper, already dampened with rain.

Tessa took it and turned away to read it. It was a short note from her brother apologizing for not being at the docks to meet her, and letting her know that he trusted Mrs. Black and Mrs. Dark—*I call them the Dark Sisters, Tessie, for obvious reasons, and they seem to find the name agreeable!*—to bring her safely to his house in London. They were, his note said, his landladies as well as trusted friends, and they had his highest recommendation.

That decided her. The letter was certainly from Nate. It was in his handwriting, and no one else ever called her Tessie. She swallowed hard and slipped the note into her sleeve, turning back to face the sisters. "Very well," she said, fighting down her lingering sense of disappointment—she had been so looking forward to seeing her brother. "Shall we call a porter to fetch my trunk?"

"No need, no need." Mrs. Dark's cheerful tone was at odds with her pinched gray features. "We've already arranged to have it sent on ahead." She snapped her fingers at the bulging-eyed man, who swung himself up into the driver's seat at the front of the carriage. She placed her hand on Tessa's shoulder. "Come along, child; let's get you out of the rain."

As Tessa moved toward the carriage, propelled by Mrs.

Dark's bony grip, the mist cleared, revealing the gleaming golden image painted on the side of the door. The words "The Pandemonium Club" curled intricately around two snakes biting each other's tails, forming a circle. Tessa frowned. "What does that mean?"

"Nothing you need worry about," said Mrs. Black, who had already climbed inside and had her skirts spread out across one of the comfortable-looking seats. The inside of the carriage was richly decorated with plush purple velvet bench seats facing each other, and gold tasseled curtains hanging in the windows.

Mrs. Dark helped Tessa up into the carriage, then clambered in behind her. As Tessa settled herself on the bench seat, Mrs. Black reached to shut the carriage door behind her sister, closing out the gray sky. When she smiled, her teeth gleamed in the dimness as if they were made out of metal. "Do settle in, Theresa. We've a long ride ahead of us."

Tessa put a hand to the clockwork angel at her throat, taking comfort in its steady ticking, as the carriage lurched forward into the rain.

SIX WEEKS LATER

1

The Dark House

Beyond this place of wrath and tears
Looms but the Horror of the shade
—William Ernest Henley, "Invictus"

"The Sisters would like to see you in their chambers, Miss Gray."

Tessa set the book she had been reading down on the bed-side table, and turned to see Miranda standing in the doorway of her small room—just as she did at this time every day, delivering the same message she delivered every day. In a moment Tessa would ask her to wait in the corridor, and Miranda would leave the room. Ten minutes later she'd return and say the same thing again. If Tessa didn't come obediently after a few of these attempts, Miranda would seize her and drag her, kicking and screaming, down the stairs to the hot, stinking room where the Dark Sisters waited.

It had happened every day of the first week that Tessa had been in the Dark House, as she had come to call the place they kept her prisoner, until eventually Tessa had realized that the screaming and kicking didn't do much good and simply wasted her energy. Energy that was probably better saved for other things.

"One moment, Miranda," Tessa said. The maid bobbed an awkward curtsy and went out of the room, shutting the door behind her.

Tessa rose to her feet, glancing around the small room that had been her prison cell for six weeks. It was small, with flowered wallpaper, and sparsely furnished—a plain deal table with a white lace cloth over it where she ate her meals; the narrow brass bed where she slept; the cracked washstand and porcelain jug for her ablutions; the windowsill where she stacked her books, and the small chair where she sat each night and wrote letters to her brother—letters she knew she could never send, letters she kept hidden under her mattress where the Dark Sisters would not find them. It was her way of keeping a diary and of assuring herself, somehow, that she would see Nate again someday and be able to give them to him.

She crossed the room to the mirror that hung against the far wall, and smoothed down her hair. The Dark Sisters, as they in fact seemed to wish to be called, preferred her not to look messy, although they didn't appear to mind her appearance one way or the other past that—which was fortunate, because her reflection made her wince. There was the pale oval of her face dominated by hollow gray eyes—a shadowed face without color in its cheeks or hope in its expression. She wore the unflattering black schoolmarmish dress that the Sisters had given her once she'd arrived; her trunk had never followed her, despite their promises, and this was now the only piece of clothing she owned. She looked away quickly.

She hadn't always flinched from her reflection. Nate, with his fair good looks, was the one in the family generally agreed to have inherited her mother's beauty, but Tessa had always been perfectly content with her own smooth brown hair and steady gray eyes. Jane Eyre had had brown hair, and plenty of other heroines besides. And it wasn't so bad being tall, either—taller than most of the boys her own age, it was true, but Aunt Harriet had always said that as long as a tall woman carried herself well, she would forever look regal.

She didn't look regal now, though. She looked pinched and bedraggled and altogether like a frightened scarecrow. She wondered if Nate would even recognize her if he saw her today.

At that thought her heart seemed to shrink inside her chest. *Nate.* He was the one she was doing all this for, but sometimes she missed him so much it felt like she'd swallowed broken glass. Without him, she was completely alone in the world. There was no one at all for her. No one in the world who cared whether she lived or died. Sometimes the horror of that thought threatened to overwhelm her and plunge her down into a bottomless darkness from which there would be no return. If no one in the entire world cared about you, did you really exist at all?

The click of the lock cut her thoughts off abruptly. The door opened; Miranda stood on the threshold.

"It is time to come with me now," she said. "Mrs. Black and Mrs. Dark are waiting."

Tessa looked at her in distaste. She couldn't guess how old

Miranda was. Nineteen? Twenty-five? There was something ageless about her smooth round face. Her hair was the color of ditch water, pulled back harshly behind her ears. Exactly like the Dark Sisters' coachman, she had eyes that protruded like a frog's and made her look like she was permanently surprised. Tessa thought they must be related.

As they went downstairs together, Miranda marching along with her graceless, clipped gait, Tessa raised her hand to touch the chain around her throat where the clockwork angel hung. It was habit—something she did each time she was forced to see the Dark Sisters. Somehow the feel of the pendant around her neck reassured her. She kept hold of it as they passed landing after landing. There were several levels of corridors to the Dark House, though Tessa had seen nothing of it but the Dark Sisters' chambers, the halls and stairs, and her own room. Finally they reached the shadowed cellar. It was dank down here, the walls clammy with unpleasant moisture, though apparently the Sisters didn't mind. Their office was ahead, through a set of wide double doors. A narrow corridor led away in the other direction, vanishing into darkness; Tessa had no idea what lay down that hallway, but something about the thickness of the shadows made her glad she had never found out.

The doors to the Sisters' office were open. Miranda didn't hesitate, but clomped inside, Tessa following after her with great reluctance. She hated this room more than any other place on earth.

To begin with, it was always hot and wet inside, like a swamp, even when the skies outside were gray and rainy. The walls seemed to seep moisture, and the upholstery on the seats and sofas was always blooming with mold. It smelled strange as well, like the banks of the Hudson on a hot day: water and garbage and silt.

The Sisters were already there, as they always were, seated behind their enormous raised desk. They were their usual colorful selves, Mrs. Black in a dress of vibrant salmon pink and Mrs. Dark in a gown of peacock blue. Above the brilliantly colored satins, their faces were like deflated gray balloons. They both wore gloves despite how hot the room was.

"Leave us now, Miranda," said Mrs. Black, who was spinning the heavy brass globe they kept on the desk with one plump, white-gloved finger. Tessa had many times tried to get a better look at the globe—something about the way the continents were laid out had never looked quite right to her, especially the space in the center of Europe—but the sisters always kept her away from it. "And shut the door behind you."

Expressionless, Miranda did as asked. Tessa tried not to wince as the door shut behind her, closing off what little breeze there was in this airless place.

Mrs. Dark tilted her head to the side. "Come here, Theresa." Of the two women, she was the more kind—more likely to wheedle and persuade than her sister, who liked to convince with slaps and hissed threats. "And take this."

She held something out: a dilapidated bit of pink fabric tied in a bow, the sort that might be used as a girl's hair ribbon.

She was used to being handed things by the Dark Sisters now. Things that had once belonged to people: tie pins and watches, mourning jewelry, and children's toys. Once the laces of a boot; once a single earring, stained with blood.

"Take this," said Mrs. Dark again, a hint of impatience in her voice. "And Change."

Tessa took the bow. It lay in her hand, as light as a moth's wing, and the Dark Sisters stared impassively at her. She remembered books she had read, novels in which characters were on trial, standing quaking in the dock at the Old Bailey and praying for a verdict of not guilty. She often felt she was on trial herself in this room, without knowing of what crime she stood accused.

She turned the bow over in her hand, remembering the first time the Dark Sisters had handed an object to her—a woman's glove, with pearl buttons at the wrist. They had shouted at her to Change, had slapped her and shaken her as she'd told them over and over again with rising hysteria that she had no idea what they were talking about, no idea what they were asking her to do.

She hadn't cried, even though she'd wanted to. Tessa hated to cry, especially in front of people she didn't trust. And of the only two people in the world she trusted, one was dead and the other imprisoned. They had told her that, the Dark Sisters, had told her that they had Nate, and if she didn't do what they said, he would die. They'd showed her his ring, the one that had been her father's—stained with blood now—to prove it. They hadn't let her hold it or touch it, had snatched it back as she'd reached for it, but she'd recognized it. It was Nate's.

After that she had done everything they'd asked. Had drunk the potions they'd given her, done the hours of agonizing exercises, forced herself to think the way they wanted her to. They'd told her to imagine herself as clay, being shaped and molded on the potter's wheel, her form amorphous and changeable. They'd told her to reach down into the objects they'd given her, to imagine them as living things, and to draw out the spirit that animated them.

It had taken weeks, and the first time she had Changed, it had been so blindingly painful that she'd vomited and passed out. When she'd woken, she'd been lying on one of the moldering chaises in the Dark Sisters' rooms, a damp towel being sponged across her face. Mrs. Black had been leaning down over her, her breath as bitter as vinegar, her eyes alight. "You did well today, Theresa," she had said. "Very well."

That evening when Tessa had gone up to her room, there had been gifts for her, two new books on her bedside table. Somehow the Dark Sisters had realized that reading and novels were Tessa's passion. There was a copy of *Great Expectations* and—of all things—*Little Women*. Tessa had hugged the books to herself and, alone and unwatched in her room, had let herself cry.

It had grown easier since then, the Changing. Tessa still didn't understand what happened inside her to make it possible, but she had memorized the series of steps the Dark Sisters had taught her, the way a blind person might memorize the number of paces it takes to walk from their bed to the door of their room. She didn't know what was around her in the strange dark place they asked her to journey to, but she knew the pathway through it.

She drew on those memories now, tightening her grip on the ragged bit of pink fabric she held. She opened her mind and let the darkness come down, let the connection that bound her to the hair ribbon and the spirit inside it—the ghostly echo of the person who had once owned it—unravel like a golden thread leading through the shadows. The room she was in, the oppressive heat, the noisy breathing of the Dark Sisters, all of it fell away as she followed the thread, as the light grew more intense around her and she wrapped herself in it as if she were wrapping herself in a blanket.

Her skin began to tingle and to sting with thousands of tiny shocks. This had been the worst part, once—the part that had convinced her she was dying. Now she was used to it, and bore it stoically as she shuddered all over, from her scalp to her toes. The clockwork angel around her throat seemed to tick faster, as if in rhythm with her speeding heart. The pressure inside her skin built—Tessa gasped—and her eyes, which had been closed, flew open as the sensation built to a crescendo—and then vanished.

It was over.

Tessa blinked dizzily. The first moment after a Change was always like blinking water out of your eyes after submerging yourself in a bath. She looked down at herself. Her new body was slight, almost frail, and the fabric of her dress hung loose, pooling on the floor at her feet. Her hands, clasped in front of her, were pale and thin, with chapped tips and bitten nails. Unfamiliar, alien hands.

"What is your name?" Mrs. Black demanded. She had risen to her feet and was looking down at Tessa with her pale eyes burning. She looked almost hungry.

Tessa didn't have to answer. The girl whose skin she wore answered for her, speaking through her the way spirits were said to speak through their mediums—but Tessa hated to think about it that way; the Change was so much more intimate, so much more frightening, than that. "Emma," the voice that came from Tessa said. "Miss Emma Bayliss, ma'am."

"And who are you, Emma Bayliss?"

The voice replied, words tumbling out of Tessa's mouth,

bringing strong images with them. Born in Cheapside, Emma had been one of six children. Her father was dead, and her mother sold peppermint water from a cart in the East End. Emma had learned to sew to bring in money when she was still a small child. Nights, she spent sitting at the little table in her kitchen, sewing seams by the light of a tallow candle. Sometimes, when the candle burned down and there was no money for another, she would go out into the streets and sit below one of the municipal gas lamps, using its light to sew by. . . .

"Is that what you were doing out on the street the night you died, Emma Bayliss?" asked Mrs. Dark. She was smiling thinly now, running her tongue over her lower lip, as if she could sense what the answer would be.

Tessa saw narrow, shadowy streets, wrapped in thick fog, a silver needle working by faint yellow gaslight. A step, muffled in the fog. Hands that reached out of the shadows and took hold of her shoulders, hands that dragged her, screaming, into the darkness. The needle and thread falling from her hands, the bows ripped from her hair as she struggled. A harsh voice shouting something angry. And then the silver blade of a knife flashing down through the dark, slicing into her skin, drawing out the blood. Pain that was like fire, and terror like nothing else she'd ever known. She kicked out at the man holding her, succeeding in knocking the dagger from his hand; she caught the blade and ran, stumbling as she weakened, the blood draining out of her fast, so fast. She crumpled in an alley, hearing the hissing scream of *something* behind her. She knew it was following her, and she was hoping to die before it reached her—

The Change shattered like glass. With a cry Tessa fell to her knees, the torn little bow falling from her hand. It was *her* hand again—Emma had gone, like a cast-off skin. Tessa was once more alone inside her own mind.

Mrs. Black's voice came from far away. "Theresa? Where is Emma?"

"She's dead," Tessa whispered. "She died in an alley—bled to death."

"Good." Mrs. Dark exhaled, a sound of satisfaction. "Well done, Theresa. That was very good."

Tessa said nothing. The front of her dress was splotched with blood, but there was no pain. She knew it was not her blood; it wasn't the first time this had happened. She closed her eyes, spinning in the darkness, willing herself not to faint.

"We should have had her do this before," said Mrs. Black. "The matter of the Bayliss girl has been bothering me."

Mrs. Dark's reply was curt. "I wasn't sure she was up to it. You remember what happened with the Adams woman."

Tessa knew immediately what they were talking about. Weeks ago she had Changed into a woman who had died of a gunshot wound to the heart; blood had poured down her dress and she had Changed back immediately, screaming in hysterical terror until the Sisters had made her see that she herself was unharmed.

"She's advanced wonderfully since then, don't you think, Sister?" Mrs. Black said. "Given what we had to work with in the beginning—she didn't even know what she *was*."

"Indeed, she was absolutely unformed *clay*," Mrs. Dark agreed. "We have truly worked a miracle here. I can't see how the Magister could fail to be pleased."

Mrs. Black gave a little gasp. "Does that mean—Do you think it's *time*?"

"Oh, absolutely, my dear sister. She's as ready as she'll ever be. It's time for our Theresa to meet her master." There was a gloating note in Mrs. Dark's voice, a sound so unpleasant that it cut through Tessa's blinding dizziness. What were they talking about? Who was the Magister? She watched through lowered eyelashes as Mrs. Dark jerked the silk bellpull that would summon Miranda to come and take Tessa back to her room. It appeared that the lesson was over for today.

"Perhaps tomorrow," Mrs. Black said, "or even tonight. If we told the Magister she was ready, I cannot imagine he would not hurry here without delay."

Mrs. Dark, stepping out from behind the desk, chuckled. "I understand that you're eager to be paid for all our work, dear sister. But Theresa must not be simply *ready*. She must be . . . presentable as well as able. Don't you agree?"

Mrs. Black, following her sister, muttered a response that was cut short as the door opened and Miranda came in. She wore the same dull look as ever. The sight of Tessa crouched and bloody on the floor seemed to occasion no surprise in her. Then again, Tessa thought, she had probably seen far worse in this room.

"Take the girl back up to her room, Miranda." The eagerness was gone from Mrs. Black's voice, and she was all brusqueness again. "Get the things—you know, the ones we showed you—and get her dressed and ready."

"The things . . . you showed me?" Miranda sounded blank.

Mrs. Dark and Mrs. Black exchanged a disgusted look, and approached Miranda, blocking Tessa's view of the girl. Tessa heard them whispering to her, and caught a few words— "dresses" and "wardrobe room" and "do what you can to make her look pretty," and then finally, Tessa heard the rather cruel,

"I'm not sure Miranda is *clever* enough to obey vague instructions of that sort, sister."

Make her look pretty. But what did they care whether she looked pretty or not, when they could force her to look any way they wanted? What did it matter what her true appearance was? And why would the Magister care? Though, it was very clear from the Sisters' behavior that they believed he would.

Mrs. Black swept from the room, her sister following behind her, as she always did. At the door Mrs. Dark paused, and looked back at Tessa. "Do remember, Theresa," she said, "that this day—this very night—is what all of our preparation has been for." She took hold of her skirts in both bony hands. "Do *not* fail us."

She let the door bang shut behind her. Tessa flinched at the noise, but Miranda, as always, seemed utterly unaffected. In all the time that she had passed in the Dark House, Tessa had never been able to startle the other girl, or surprise an unguarded expression out of her.

"Come," Miranda said. "We must go upstairs now."

Tessa rose to her feet, slowly. Her mind was whirling. Her life in the Dark House had been horrible, but she had—she realized now—grown almost used to it. She had known what to expect each day. She had known the Dark Sisters were preparing her for something, but she had not known what that something was. She had believed—naively, perhaps—that they wouldn't kill her. Why waste all this training on her if she was only going to die?

But something in Mrs. Dark's gloating tone gave her pause. Something had changed. They had achieved what they wanted with her. They were going to be "paid." But who was going to do the paying?

"Come," Miranda said again. "We must get you ready for the Magister."

"Miranda," Tessa said. She spoke softly, the way she might have spoken to a nervous cat. Miranda had never answered a question of Tessa's before, but that didn't mean it wasn't worth trying. "Who is the Magister?"

There was a long silence. Miranda stared straight ahead, her doughy face impassive. Then, to Tessa's surprise, she spoke. "The Magister is a very great man," she said. "It will be an honor for you when you are married to him."

"*Married?*" Tessa echoed. The shock was so intense that she could suddenly see the whole room more clearly—Miranda, the blood-splattered rug on the floor, the heavy brass globe on the desk, still tilted in the position Mrs. Black had left it in. "Me? But—who is he?"

"He is a very great man," Miranda said again. "It will be an honor." She moved toward Tessa. "You must come with me now."

"No." Tessa backed away from the other girl, retreating until the small of her back struck painfully against the desk. She looked around desperately. She could run, but she'd never get past Miranda to the door; there were no windows, no doors to other rooms. If she hid behind the desk, Miranda would simply drag her out and haul her to her room. "Miranda, *please.*"

"You must come with me now," Miranda repeated; she had almost reached Tessa. Tessa could see herself reflected in the black pupils of the other girl's eyes, could smell the faint, bitter, almost charred smell that clung to Miranda's clothes and skin. "You must —"

With a strength she didn't know she possessed, Tessa seized the base of the brass globe on the desk, lifted it, and swung it with all her might at Miranda's head.

It connected with a sickening sound. Miranda reeled back—and then straightened. Tessa shrieked and dropped the globe, staring—the whole left side of Miranda's face was crushed in, like a paper mask that had been smashed flat on one side. Her cheekbone was flattened, her lip mashed against her teeth. But there was no blood, no blood at all.

"You must come with me now," Miranda said, in the same flat tone she always used.

Tessa gaped.

"You must come—you m-must—you—you—you—yyyyyyyyyyyyy—" Miranda's voice shuddered and broke, degenerating into a stream of gibberish. She moved toward Tessa, then jerked to the side, twitching and stumbling. Tessa turned from the desk and began to back away as the injured girl spun, faster and faster. She reeled across the room like a staggering drunk, still shrieking, and crashed into the far wall—which seemed to stun her. She collapsed to the ground and lay still.

Tessa raced to the door and out into the corridor beyond, pausing only once, just outside the room, to look back. It seemed, in that brief moment, as if a thread of black smoke were rising from Miranda's prone body, but there was no time to stare. Tessa darted down the hall, leaving the door hanging open behind her.

She dashed for the stairs and hurtled up them, nearly tripping over her skirts and banging her knee painfully on one of the steps. She cried out and scrambled on, up to the first landing, where she dashed into the corridor. It stretched out ahead of her, long and curving, disappearing into shadows. As she raced down it, she saw that it was lined with doors. She paused and tried one, but it was locked, and so was the next one, and the next after that.

Another set of stairs led down at the end of the hallway. Tessa raced down them and found herself in an entryway. It looked as if it had once been grand—the floor was cracked and stained marble, and high windows on either side were shielded with curtains. A little bit of light spilled through the lace, illuminating an enormous front door. Tessa's heart leaped. She dived for the knob, seized it, and flung the door open.

There was a narrow cobblestoned street beyond, with rows of terraced houses lining either side. The smell of the city hit Tessa like a blow—it had been so long since she'd breathed outside air. It was close to dark, the sky the dimming blue of twilight, obscured by smudges of fog. In the distance she could hear voices, the cries of children playing, the clop of horses' hooves. But here the street was nearly deserted, save for a man leaning against a nearby gas lamp, reading a newspaper by its light.

Tessa dashed down the steps and toward the stranger, catching him by the sleeve. "Please, sir—if you could help me—"

He turned, and looked down at her.

Tessa stifled a scream. His face was as white and waxy as it had been the first time she'd seen him, at the dock in Southampton; his bulging eyes still reminded her of Miranda's, and his teeth gleamed like metal when he grinned.

It was the Dark Sisters' coachman.

Tessa turned to run, but it was already too late.

2
HELL IS COLD

Between two worlds life hovers like a star,
'Twixt night and morn, upon the horizon's verge.
How little do we know that which we are!
How less what we may be!
—Lord Byron, *Don Juan*

"You stupid little girl," Mrs. Black spat as she jerked tight the knots holding Tessa's wrists to her bed frame. "What did you think you were going to accomplish, running away like that? Where did you think you could *possibly* go?"

Tessa said nothing, simply set her chin and looked toward the wall. She refused to let Mrs. Black, or her horrible sister, see how close she was to tears, or how much the ropes binding her ankles and wrists to the bed hurt.

"She is entirely insensible of the honor being done to her," said Mrs. Dark, who was standing by the door as if to make sure

Tessa didn't rip free of her bonds and rush out through it. "It is disgusting to behold."

"We have done what we can for her to make her ready for the Magister," Mrs. Black said, and sighed. "A pity we had such dull clay to work with, despite her talent. She is a deceitful little fool."

"Indeed," agreed her sister. "She does realize, doesn't she, what will happen to her brother if she tries to disobey us again? We might be willing to be lenient this time, but the next . . ." She hissed through her teeth, a sound that made the hairs rise up on the back of Tessa's neck. "Nathaniel will not be so fortunate."

Tessa couldn't stand it anymore; even knowing she shouldn't speak, shouldn't give them the satisfaction, she couldn't hold the words back. "If you told me who the Magister was, or what he wants with me—"

"He wants to marry you, you little fool." Mrs. Black, finished with the knots, stepped back to admire her handiwork. "He wants to give you *everything*."

"But why?" Tessa whispered. "Why me?"

"Because of your talent," Mrs. Dark said. "Because of what you are and what you can do. What we trained you to do. You should be *grateful* to us."

"But my brother." Tears burned behind Tessa's eyes. *I will not cry, I will not cry, I will not cry*, she told herself. "You told me that if I did everything you said, you'd let him go—"

"Once you marry the Magister, he'll give you whatever you want. If that's your brother, he'll give it to you." There was no remorse or emotion in Mrs. Black's voice.

Mrs. Dark chuckled. "I know what she's thinking. She's

thinking that if she could have whatever she wanted, she'd have us killed."

"Don't waste your energy even imagining the possibility." Mrs. Black chucked Tessa under the chin. "We have an ironclad contract with the Magister. He can never harm us, nor would he want to. He owes us everything, for giving him you." She leaned in closer, dropping her voice to a whisper. "He wants you healthy and intact. If he didn't, I'd have you beaten bloody. If you dare disobey us again, I'll defy his wishes and have you whipped until your skin peels off. Do you understand?"

Tessa turned her face to the wall.

There had been a night on the *Main*, as they'd passed Newfoundland, when Tessa had not been able to sleep. She had gone out on the deck to get a breath of air, and had seen the night sea ablaze with white glittering mountains—icebergs, one of the sailors had told her as he'd passed, broken loose from the ice sheets of the north by the warmer weather. They had drifted slowly on the dark water, like the towers of a drowned white city. Tessa had thought that she'd never seen such a lonely sight.

She had only begun to imagine loneliness, she knew now. Once the Sisters left, Tessa discovered, she no longer felt like she wanted to cry. The pressure at the backs of her eyes was gone, replaced by a dull feeling of hollow despair. Mrs. Dark had been right. If Tessa could have killed them both, she would have.

She pulled experimentally at the ropes tying her legs and arms to the bedposts. They didn't budge. The knots were tight; tight enough to dig into her flesh and make her hands and feet tingle and shiver with pins and needles. She had a few minutes, she estimated, before her extremities went dead entirely.

Part of her—and not a small part—wanted to stop struggling, to lie there limply until the Magister came to take her away. The sky was already darkening outside the small window; it couldn't be much longer now. Perhaps he really did want to marry her. Perhaps he truly wanted to give her everything.

Suddenly she heard Aunt Harriet's voice in her head: *When you find a man you wish to marry, Tessa, remember this: You will know what kind of man he is not by the things he says, but by the things he* does.

Aunt Harriet had been right, of course. No man she would ever want to marry would have arranged to have her treated like a prisoner and a slave, imprisoned her brother, and had her tortured in the name of her "talent." It was a travesty and a joke. Heaven only knew what the Magister wanted to do with her once he had his hands on her. If it was something she could survive, she imagined she would soon enough wish she hadn't.

God, what a useless talent she had! The power to change her appearance? If only she had the power to set things on fire, or shatter metal, or cause knives to grow out of her fingers! Or if she only had the power to make herself invisible, or shrink herself to the size of a mouse—

She went suddenly still, so still that she could hear the ticking of the clockwork angel against her chest. She didn't have to shrink herself down to the size of a mouse, did she? All she had to do was make herself small enough that the ties around her wrists would be loose.

It was possible for her to Change into someone a second

time, without touching something that had belonged to them—as long as she'd done it before. The Sisters had made her memorize how to do it. For the first time, she was glad of something they'd forced her to learn.

She pressed herself back against the hard mattress and made herself remember. The street, the kitchen, the movement of the needle, the glow of the gaslight. She willed it on, willed the Change to come. *What's your name? Emma. Emma Bayliss . . .*

The Change bore down on her like a train, almost knocking the breath out of her—reshaping her skin, reforming her bones. She choked back her screams and arched her back—

And it was done. Blinking, Tessa stared up at the ceiling, then glanced sideways, staring at her wrist, at the rope around it. There were her hands—Emma's hands—thin and frail, the circle of the rope loose around her small wrists. Triumphantly Tessa jerked her hands free and sat up, rubbing at the red marks where the rope had burned her skin.

Her ankles were still tied. She leaned forward, her fingers working quickly at the knots. Mrs. Black, it turned out, could tie knots like a sailor. Tessa's fingers were bloodied and sore by the time the rope fell away and she sprang to her feet.

Emma's hair was so thin and fine that it had slipped free of the clips holding Tessa's own hair back. Tessa pushed her hair back impatiently over her shoulders and shook herself free of Emma, letting the Change wash away from her until her hair slid through her fingers, thick and familiar to the touch. Glancing at the mirror across the room, she saw that little Emma Bayliss was gone and she was herself again.

A noise behind her made her whirl. The knob of the bedroom door was turning, twisting back and forth as if the person on the other side were having difficulty getting it open.

Mrs. Dark, she thought. The woman was back, to whip her until she was bloody. Back, to take her to the Magister. Tessa hurried across the room, seized the porcelain jug from the washstand, and then scuttled to the side of the door, the jug gripped hard in her whitened fist.

The knob turned; the door opened. In the dimness all Tessa could see was shadows as someone stepped into the room. She lunged forward, swinging the jug with all her strength—

The shadowy figure moved, as quick as a whip, but not quite quick enough; the jug slammed into the figure's outstretched arm before flying from Tessa's grasp to crash into the far wall. Broken crockery rained down onto the floor as the stranger yelled.

The yell was undeniably a masculine one. So was the flood of cursing that followed.

She backed away, then dashed for the door—but it had slammed shut, and tug as she would on the knob, it wouldn't budge. Bright light blazed through the room as if the sun had risen. Tessa spun, blinking away the tears in her eyes—and stared.

There was a boy standing in front of her. He couldn't have been much older than she was—seventeen or possibly eighteen. He was dressed in what looked like workman's clothes—a frayed black jacket, trousers, and tough-looking boots. He wore no waistcoat, and thick leather straps crisscrossed his waist and chest. Attached to the straps were weapons—daggers and folding knives and things that looked like blades of ice. In his right hand he held a sort of glowing stone—it was shining, providing the light in the room that had nearly blinded Tessa.

His other hand—slim and long-fingered—was bleeding where she had gashed the back of it with her pitcher.

But that wasn't what made her stare. He had the most beautiful face she had ever seen. Tangled black hair and eyes like blue glass. Elegant cheekbones, a full mouth, and long, thick lashes. Even the curve of his throat was perfect. He looked like every fictional hero she'd ever conjured up in her head. Although she'd never imagined one of them cursing at her while shaking his bleeding hand in an accusing fashion.

He seemed to realize she was staring at him, because the cursing stopped. "You cut me," he said. His voice was pleasant. British. Very ordinary. He looked at his hand with critical interest. "It might be fatal."

Tessa looked at him with wide eyes. "Are you the Magister?"

He tilted his hand to the side. Blood ran down it, spattering the floor. "Dear me, massive blood loss. Death could be imminent."

"*Are you the Magister?*"

"Magister?" He looked mildly surprised by her vehemence. "That means 'master' in Latin, doesn't it?"

"I . . ." Tessa was feeling increasingly as if she were trapped in a strange dream. "I suppose it does."

"I've mastered many things in my life. Navigating the streets of London, dancing the quadrille, the Japanese art of flower arranging, lying at charades, concealing a highly intoxicated state, delighting young women with my charms . . ."

Tessa stared.

"Alas," he went on, "no one has ever actually referred to me as 'the master,' or 'the magister,' either. More's the pity . . ."

"Are you highly intoxicated at the moment?" Tessa meant

the question in all seriousness, but realized the moment the words were out of her mouth that she must have sounded awfully rude—or worse, flirtatious. He seemed too steady on his feet to really be drunk, anyway. She'd seen Nate intoxicated enough times to know the difference. Perhaps he was merely insane.

"How very direct, but I suppose all you Americans are, aren't you?" The boy looked amused. "Yes, your accent gives you away. What's your name, then?"

Tessa looked at him in disbelief. "What's *my* name?"

"Don't you know it?"

"You—you've come bursting into my room, scared me nearly to death, and now you demand to know my name? What on earth's *your* name? And who are you, anyway?"

"My name is Herondale," the boy said cheerfully. "William Herondale, but everyone calls me Will. Is this really your room? Not very nice, is it?" He wandered toward the window, pausing to examine the stacks of books on her bedside table, and then the bed itself. He waved a hand at the ropes. "Do you often sleep tied to the bed?"

Tessa felt her cheeks flame and was amazed, under the circumstances, that she still had the capacity to be embarrassed. Should she tell him the truth? Was it at all possible that he was the Magister? Though anyone who looked like that wouldn't need to tie girls up and imprison them in order to get them to marry him.

"Here. Hold this." He handed her the glowing stone. Tessa took it, half-expecting it to burn her fingers, but it was cool to the touch. The moment it struck her palm, its light dimmed to a shimmering flicker. She looked toward him in dismay, but he had made his way to the window and was looking out, seemingly unconcerned. "Pity we're on the third floor. I could manage the jump, but it would probably kill you. No, we must go through the door and take our chances in the house."

"Go through the— What?" Tessa, feeling mired in a semi-permanent state of confusion, shook her head. "I don't understand."

"How can you not understand?" He pointed at her books. "You read novels. Obviously, I'm here to rescue you. Don't I look like Sir Galahad?" He raised his arms dramatically. "'*My strength is as the strength of ten, Because my heart is pure—*'"

Something echoed, far away inside the house—the sound of a door slamming.

Will said a word Sir Galahad would never have said, and sprang away from the window. He landed with a wince, and glanced ruefully down at his injured hand. "I'll need to take care of this later. Come along . . ." He looked at her pointedly, a question in his eyes.

"Miss Gray," she said faintly. "Miss Theresa Gray."

"Miss Gray," he repeated. "Come along, then, Miss Gray." He sprang past her, moved toward the door, found the knob, turned it, yanked—

Nothing happened.

"It won't work," she said. "The door cannot be opened from the inside."

Will grinned ferociously. "Can't it?" He reached for his belt, for one of the objects that hung on it. He chose what looked like a long, slender twig, picked clean of smaller branches, and made of a whitish-silver material. He placed the end of it against the door and *drew*. Thick black lines spiraled out from the tip of the flexible cylinder, making an audible hissing noise as they spread across the wooden surface like a directed spill of ink.

"You're *drawing?*" Tessa demanded. "I don't really see how that can possibly—"

There was a noise like cracking glass. The doorknob, untouched, spun—fast, then faster, and the door sprang open, a faint puff of smoke rising from the hinges.

"Now you do," Will said, and, pocketing the strange object, gestured for Tessa to follow him. "Let's go."

Inexplicably, she hesitated, looking back toward the room that had been her prison for nearly two months. "My books—"

"I'll get you more books." He urged her into the corridor ahead of him, and pulled the door shut behind them. After catching hold of her wrist, he drew her down the hallway and around a corner. Here were the stairs that she had descended so many times with Miranda. Will took them two at a time, pulling her after him.

From above them Tessa heard a scream. It was unmistakably Mrs. Dark's.

"They've found you missing," Will said. They had reached the first landing, and Tessa slowed her pace—only to be jerked ahead by Will, who seemed disinclined to stop.

"Aren't we going out the front door?" she demanded.

"We can't. The building's surrounded. There's a line of carriages pulled up out front. I appear to have arrived at an unexpectedly exciting time." He started down the stairs again, and Tessa followed. "Do you know what the Dark Sisters had planned for this evening?"

"No."

"But you were expecting someone called the Magister?" They were in the cellar now, where the plaster walls gave way suddenly to damp stone. Without Miranda's lantern it was quite dark. Heat rose to meet them like a wave. "By the Angel, it's like the ninth circle of Hell down here—"

"The ninth circle of Hell is cold," Tessa said automatically.

Will stared at her. "What?"

"In the *Inferno*," she told him. "Hell is cold. It's covered in ice."

He stared at her for another long moment, the corners of his mouth twitching, then held out his hand. "Give me the witchlight." At her blank expression he made an impatient noise. "The stone. Give me the stone."

The moment his hand closed about the stone, light blazed up from it again, raying out through his fingers. For the first time Tessa saw that he had a design on the back of his hand, drawn there as if in black ink. It looked like an open eye. "As for the temperature of Hell, Miss Gray," he said, "let me give you a piece of advice. The handsome young fellow who's trying to rescue you from a hideous fate is *never* wrong. Not even if he says the sky is purple and made of hedgehogs."

He really is mad, Tessa thought, but didn't say so; she was too alarmed by the fact that he had started toward the wide double doors of the Dark Sisters' chambers.

"No!" She caught at his arm, pulling him back. "Not that way. There's no way out. It's a dead end."

"Correcting me again, I see." Will turned and strode the other way, toward the shadowy corridor Tessa had always feared. Swallowing hard, she followed him.

The corridor narrowed as they went along it, the walls

pressing in on either side. The heat was even more intense here, making Tessa's hair spring into curls and paste itself to her temples and neck. The air felt thick and was hard to breathe. For a while they walked in silence, until Tessa could stand it no longer. She had to ask, even though she knew the answer would be no.

"Mr. Herondale," she said, "did my brother send you to find me?"

She half-feared he'd make some mad comment in response, but he simply looked at her curiously. "Never heard of your brother," he said, and she felt the dull ache of disappointment gnaw at her heart. She'd known Nate couldn't have sent him— he'd have known her name, then, wouldn't he?—but it still hurt. "And outside of the past ten minutes, Miss Gray, I'd never heard of you, either. I've been following the trail of a dead girl for near on two months. She was murdered, left in an alley to bleed to death. She'd been running from . . . something." The corridor had reached a forking point, and after a pause Will headed to the left. "There was a dagger beside her, covered in her blood. It had a symbol on it. Two snakes, swallowing each other's tails."

Tessa felt a jolt. *Left in an alley to bleed to death. There was a dagger beside her.* Surely the body had been Emma's. "That's the same symbol that's on the side of the Dark Sisters' carriage— That's what I call them, Mrs. Dark and Mrs. Black, I mean—"

"You're not the only one who calls them that; the other Downworlders do the same," said Will. "I discovered that fact while investigating the symbol. I must have carried that knife through a hundred Downworld haunts, searching for someone who might recognize it. I offered a reward for information.

Eventually the name of the Dark Sisters came to my ears."

"Downworld?" Tessa echoed, puzzled. "Is that a place in London?"

"Never mind that," said Will. "I'm boasting of my investigative skills, and I would prefer to do it without interruption. Where was I?"

"The dagger—" Tessa broke off as a voice echoed down the corridor, high and sweet and unmistakable.

"*Miss Gray.*" Mrs. Dark's voice. It seemed to drift between the walls like coiling smoke. "*Oh, Miss Graaaay. Where are you?*"

Tessa froze. "Oh, God, they've caught up with—"

Will seized her wrist again, and they were off running, the witchlight in his other hand throwing a wild pattern of shadows and light against the stone walls as they hurtled down the twisting corridor. The floor sloped down, the stones underfoot growing gradually more slick and damp as the air around them grew hotter and hotter. It was as if they were racing down into Hell itself as the voices of the Dark Sisters echoed off the walls. "*Miss Graaaaaay! We shan't let you run, you know. We shan't let you hide! We'll find you, poppet. You know we will.*"

Will and Tessa careened around a corner, and came up short—the corridor ended at a pair of high metal doors. Releasing Tessa, Will flung himself against them. They burst open and he tumbled inside, followed by Tessa, who spun to slam them shut behind her. The weight of them was almost too much for her to manage, and she had to throw her back against them to force them, finally, closed.

The only illumination in the room was Will's glowing stone, its light sunk down now to an ember between his fingers. It lit him in the darkness, like limelight on a stage, as he reached around her to slam the bolt home on the door. The bolt was heavy and flaking with rust, and, standing as close to him as she was, she could feel the tension in his body as he dragged it home and let it fall into place.

"Miss Gray?" He was leaning against her, her back against the closed doors. She could feel the driving rhythm of his heart—or was it her heart? The odd white illumination cast by the stone shimmered against the sharp angle of his cheeks, the faint sheen of sweat on his collarbones. There were marks there, too, she saw, rising from the unbuttoned collar of his shirt—like the mark on his hand, thick and black, as if someone had inked designs onto his skin.

"Where are we?" she whispered. "Are we safe?"

Without answering he drew away, raising his right hand. As he lifted it, the light blazed up higher, illuminating the room.

They were in a sort of cell, though it was very large. The walls, floor, and ceiling were stone, sloping down to a large drain in the middle of the floor. There was only one window, very high up in the wall. There were no doors save the ones they had come through. But none of that was what made Tessa draw in her breath.

The place was a slaughterhouse. There were long wooden tables running the length of the room. Bodies lay on one of them—human bodies, stripped and pale. Each had a black incision in the shape of a Y marking its chest, and each head dangled back over the edge of the table, the hair of the women sweeping the floor like brooms. On the center table were piles of bloodstained knives and machinery—copper cogs and brass gears and sharp-toothed silver hacksaws.

Tessa crammed a hand into her mouth, stifling a scream. She tasted blood as she bit down on her own fingers. Will didn't seem to notice; he was white-faced as he looked around, mouthing something under his breath that Tessa couldn't make out.

There was a crashing noise and the metal doors shuddered, as if something heavy had flung itself against them. Tessa lowered her bleeding hand and cried out, "Mr. Herondale!"

He turned, as the doors shuddered again. A voice echoed from the other side of them: "Miss Gray! Come out now, and we won't hurt you!"

"They're lying," Tessa said quickly.

"Oh, do you really think so?" Having packed as much sarcasm into the question as was humanly possible, Will pocketed his glowing witchlight and leaped onto the center table, the one covered in bloodied machinery. He bent down and caught up a heavy-looking brass cog, and weighed it in his hand. With a grunt of effort he hurled it toward the high window; the glass shattered, and Will raised his voice. "Henry! Some assistance, please! Henry!"

"Who's Henry?" Tessa demanded, but at that moment the doors shuddered a third time, and thin cracks appeared in the metal. Clearly, they weren't going to hold much longer. Tessa dashed to the table and seized a weapon, almost at random—this one was a ragged-toothed metal hacksaw, the kind butchers used to cut through bone. She whirled around, clutching it, as the doors burst open.

The Dark Sisters stood in the doorway—Mrs. Dark, as tall and bony as a rake in her shining lime green gown, and Mrs. Black, red-faced, her eyes narrowed to slits. A bright corona of blue sparks surrounded them, like tiny fireworks. Their gazes slid over Will—who, still standing on the table, had drawn one of his icy blades from his belt—and came to rest on Tessa. Mrs. Black's mouth, a red slash in her pale face, stretched into a grin. "Little Miss Gray," she said. "You ought to know better than to run. We told you what would happen if you ran again. . . ."

"Then do it! Whip me bloody. Kill me. I don't care!" Tessa shouted, and was gratified to see that the Dark Sisters looked at least a little taken aback by her outburst; she'd been too terrified to raise her voice to them before. "I won't let you give me to the Magister! I'd rather die!"

"What an unexpectedly sharp tongue you have, Miss Gray, my dear," said Mrs. Black. With great deliberation she reached to draw the glove from her right hand, and for the first time, Tessa saw her bare hand. The skin was gray and thick, like an elephant's hide, her nails long dark talons. They looked as sharp as knives. Mrs. Black gave Tessa a fixed grin. "Perhaps if we cut it out of your head, you'd learn to mind your manners."

She moved toward Tessa—and was blocked by Will leaping down from the table to put himself between them. "*Malik*," he said, and his ice-white blade blazed up like a star.

"Get out of my way, little Nephilim warrior," said Mrs. Black. "And take your seraph blades with you. This is not your battle."

"You're wrong about that." Will narrowed his eyes. "I've heard some things about you, my lady. Whispers that run through Downworld like a river of black poison. I've been told you and your sister will pay handsomely for the bodies of dead humans, and you don't much mind how they get that way."

"Such a fuss over a few mundanes." Mrs. Dark chuckled and moved to stand beside her sister, so that Will, with his blazing sword, was between Tessa and both ladies. "We have no quarrel with you, Shadowhunter, unless you choose to pick one. You have invaded our territory and broken Covenant Law in doing so. We could report you to the Clave—"

"While the Clave disapproves of trespassers, oddly they take an even darker view of beheading and skinning people. They're peculiar that way," Will said.

"People?" Mrs. Dark spat. "*Mundanes.* You care no more about them than we do." She looked toward Tessa then. "Has he told you what he really is? He isn't human—"

"You're one to talk," Tessa said in a trembling voice.

"And has she told *you* what *she* is?" Mrs. Black demanded of Will. "About her talent? What she can do?"

"If I were to venture a guess," Will replied, "I would say it has something to do with the Magister."

Mrs. Dark looked suspicious. "You know of the Magister?" She glanced at Tessa. "Ah, I see. Only what she has told you. The Magister, little boy angel, is more dangerous than you could ever imagine. And he has waited a long time for someone with Tessa's ability. You might even say he is the one who caused her to be born—"

Her words were swallowed up in a colossal crash as the whole east wall of the room suddenly caved in. It was like the walls of Jericho tumbling down in Tessa's old Bible stories picture book. One moment the wall was there, and the next it wasn't; there was a huge gaping rectangular hole instead, steaming with choking swirls of plaster dust.

Mrs. Dark gave a thin scream and seized her skirts with her

bony hands. Clearly she hadn't expected the wall to collapse, any more than Tessa had.

Will caught hold of Tessa's hand and pulled her toward him, blocking her with his body as chunks of stone and plaster rained down on them. As his arms went around her, she could hear Mrs. Black screaming.

Tessa twisted in Will's grip, trying to see what was happening. Mrs. Dark stood, pointing with one gloved, trembling finger toward the dark hole in the wall. The dust was beginning to settle, barely—enough so that the figures moving toward them through the wreckage slowly began to take shape. The shadowy outlines of two human figures became visible; each was holding a blade, and each blade shone with the same blue-white light as Will's. *Angels*, Tessa thought, wondering, but she didn't say it. That light, so bright—what else could they be?

Mrs. Black gave a screech and lunged forward. She threw her hands out, and sparks shot from them like exploding fireworks. Tessa heard someone yell—a very human yell—and Will, releasing Tessa, spun and flung his bright-burning sword at Mrs. Black. It whipped through the air, end over end, and drove into her chest. Screaming and twisting, she staggered backward and fell, crashing down onto one of the horrible tables, which collapsed in a mess of blood and splintering wood.

Will grinned. It wasn't a pleasant sort of grin. He turned to look at Tessa then. For a moment they stared at each other, silently, across the space that separated them—and then his other companions flooded in around him, two men in close-fitting dark coats, brandishing shining weapons, and moving so fast that Tessa's vision blurred.

Tessa backed toward the far wall, trying to avoid the chaos

in the center of the room, where Mrs. Dark, howling imprecations, was holding off her attackers with the burning sparks of energy that flew from her hands like fiery rain. Mrs. Black was writhing on the floor, sheets of black smoke rising from her body as if she were burning from the inside out.

Tessa moved toward the open door that led to the corridor—and strong hands seized her and yanked her backward. Tessa shrieked and twisted, but the hands circling her upper arms were as strong as iron. She turned her head to the side and sank her teeth into the hand gripping her left arm. Someone yelled and let go of her; spinning, she saw a tall man with a shock of untidy ginger hair staring at her with a reproachful expression, his bleeding left hand cradled against his chest. "Will!" he shouted. "Will, she bit me!"

"Did she, Henry?" Will, looking amused as usual, appeared like a summoned spirit from the chaos of smoke and flames. Behind him, Tessa could see the second of his companions, a muscular brown-haired young man, holding a struggling Mrs. Dark. Mrs. Black was a dark humped shape on the ground. Will raised an eyebrow in Tessa's direction. "It's bad form to bite," he informed her. "Rude, you know. Hasn't anyone ever told you that?"

"It's also rude to go about grabbing at ladies you haven't been introduced to," Tessa said stiffly. "Hasn't anyone told you *that*?"

The ginger-haired man whom Will had called Henry shook his bleeding hand with a rueful smile. He had a nice sort of face, Tessa thought; she almost felt guilty for having bitten him.

"Will! Look out!" the brown-haired man shouted. Will

spun as something flew through the air, narrowly missed Henry's head, and crashed into the wall behind Tessa. It was a large brass cog, and it hit the wall with such force that it stuck there like a marble wedged into a bit of pastry. Tessa whirled—and saw Mrs. Black advancing toward them, her eyes burning like coal in her crumpled white face. Black licks of flame sprayed up around the hilt of the sword that protruded from her chest.

"Damn—" Will reached for the hilt of another blade wedged through the belt at his waist. "I thought we'd put that thing down—"

Baring her teeth, Mrs. Black lunged. Will leaped out of the way, but Henry wasn't quite as fast; she struck him and knocked him backward. Clinging on like a tick, she rode him to the ground, snarling, her claws sinking into his shoulders as he yelled. Will whirled, the blade now in his hand; raising it, he shouted "*Uriel!*" and it flared up suddenly in his grip like a blazing torch. Tessa fell back against the wall as he whipped the blade downward. Mrs. Black reared back, her claws out, reaching for him—

And the blade sheared neatly through her throat. Completely severed, her head struck the ground, rolling and bumping, as Henry, yelling in disgust and soaked in blackish blood, shoved the remains of her body off him and scrambled to his feet.

A terrible scream tore through the room. "*Nooooo!*"

The cry had come from Mrs. Dark. The brown-haired man holding her let go with a sudden cry as blue fire shot from her hands and eyes. Yelling in pain, he fell to the side as she tore away from him and advanced on Will and Tessa, Mrs. Dark's eyes flaming like black torches. She was hissing words in a language that Tessa had never heard. It sounded like crackling flames. Raising a hand, the woman flung what looked like a bolt of lightning toward Tessa. With a cry Will sprang in front of her, his glowing blade extended. The lightning ricocheted off the blade and struck one of the stone walls, which glowed with a sudden strange light.

"Henry," Will shouted, without turning, "if you could remove Miss Gray to a place of safety—*soon*—"

Henry's bitten hand came down on Tessa's shoulder, as Mrs. Dark flung another sheet of lightning toward her. *Why is she trying to kill me?* Tessa thought dizzily. *Why not Will?* And then, as Henry pulled her toward him, more light sheared off Will's blade, refracting into a dozen blazing shards of brightness. For a moment Tessa stared, caught by the unlikely beauty of it—and then she heard Henry shout, telling her to drop to the floor, but it was too late. One of the blazing shards had caught her shoulder with incredible force. It was like being struck by a hurtling train. She was knocked free of Henry's grasp, lifted, and flung backward. Her head struck the wall with blinding force. She was conscious only briefly of Mrs. Dark's high screeching laughter, before the world went away.

3

THE INSTITUTE

Love, hope, fear, faith—these make humanity;
These are its sign and note and character
—Robert Browning, *Paracelsus*

In the dream Tessa lay once again tied to the narrow brass bed in the Dark House. The Sisters leaned over her, clacking pairs of long knitting needles and laughing in shrill high-pitched voices. As Tessa watched, their features changed, their eyes sinking into their heads, their hair falling out, and stitches appearing across their lips, sewing them shut. Tessa shrieked voicelessly, but they did not seem to hear.

The Sisters vanished entirely then, and Aunt Harriet was standing over Tessa, her face flushed with fever as it had been during the terrible illness that had killed her. She looked at Tessa with great sadness. "I tried," she said. "I tried to love you. But it isn't easy to love a child that isn't human in the least...."

"Not human?" said an unfamiliar female voice. "Well, if she isn't human, Enoch, what is she?" The voice sharpened in impatience. "What do you mean, you don't know? Everyone's something. This girl can't be nothing at all...."

Tessa woke with a cry, her eyes flying open, and found herself staring at shadows. Darkness clustered about her thickly. She could barely hear the murmur of voices through her panic, and struggled into a sitting position, kicking away blankets and pillows. Dimly, she recognized that the blanket was thick and heavy, not the thin, braided one that belonged to the Dark House.

She was in a bed, just as she had dreamed, in a great stone room, and there was hardly any light. She heard the rasp of her own breath as she turned, and a scream forced its way out of her throat. The face from her nightmare hovered in the darkness before her—a great white moon of a face, its head shaved bald, smooth as marble. Where the eyes should have been there were only indentations in the flesh—not as if the eyes had been ripped out, but as if they had never grown there at all. The lips were banded with black stitches, the face scrawled with black marks like the ones on Will's skin, though these looked as if they had been cut there with knives.

She screamed again and scrabbled backward, half-falling off the bed. She hit the cold stone floor, and the fabric of the white nightdress she was wearing—someone must have put it on her while she was unconscious—ripped at the hem as she scrambled to her feet.

"Miss Gray." Someone was calling her name, but in her panic, she knew only that the voice was unfamiliar. The speaker was *not* the monster who stood staring at her from the bedside, its scarred face impassive; it had not moved when she did, and though it showed no signs of pursuing her, she began to back away, carefully, feeling behind herself for a door. The room was so dim, she could see only that it was roughly oval, the walls and floor all of stone. The ceiling was high enough to be in black shadow, and there were long windows across the opposite wall, the sort of arched windows that might have belonged in a church. Very little light filtered through them; it looked as if the sky outside was dark. "Theresa Gray—"

She found the door, the metal handle; turning, she seized on it thankfully, and pulled. Nothing happened. A sob rose up in her throat.

"Miss Gray!" the voice said again, and suddenly the room was flooded with light—a sharp, white-silver light that she recognized. "Miss Gray, I am sorry. It was not our intention to frighten you." The voice was a woman's: still unfamiliar, but youthful and concerned. "Miss Gray, please."

Tessa turned slowly and put her back against the door. She could see clearly now. She was in a stone room whose central focus was a large, four-poster bed, its velvet coverlet now rucked and hanging sideways where she had dragged it off the mattress. Tapestry curtains were pulled back, and there was an elegant tapestry rug on the otherwise bare floor. In fact, the room itself was fairly bare. There were no pictures or photographs hanging on the wall, no ornaments cluttering the surfaces of the dark wood furniture. Two chairs stood facing each other near the bed, with a small tea table between them. A Chinese screen in one corner of the room hid what were probably a bathtub and washstand.

Beside the bed stood a tall man who wore robes like a monk's, of a long, coarse, parchment-colored material. Red-brown runes circled the cuffs and hem. He carried a silver staff, its head carved in the shape of an angel and runes decorating its length. The hood of his robe was down, leaving bare his scarred, white, blinded face.

Beside him stood a very small woman, almost child-size, with thick brown hair knotted at the nape of her neck, and a neat, clever little face with bright, dark eyes like a bird's. She wasn't pretty exactly, but there was a calm, kindly look on her face that made the ache of panic in Tessa's stomach ease slightly, though she couldn't have said exactly why. In her hand she held a glowing white stone like the one Will had held at the Dark House. Its light blazed out between her fingers, illuminating the room.

"Miss Gray," she said. "I am Charlotte Branwell, head of the London Institute, and this beside me is Brother Enoch—"

"What kind of monster is he?" Tessa whispered.

Brother Enoch said nothing. He was entirely expressionless.

"I know there are monsters on this earth," said Tessa. "You cannot tell me otherwise. I have seen them."

"I would not want to tell you otherwise," said Mrs. Branwell. "If the world were not full of monsters, there would be no need for Shadowhunters."

Shadowhunter. What the Dark Sisters had called Will Herondale.

Will. "I was—Will was with me," said Tessa, her voice shaking. "In the cellars. Will said—" She broke off and cringed inwardly. She should not have called Will by his Christian name; it implied an intimacy between them that did not exist. "Where is Mr. Herondale?"

"He's here," Mrs. Branwell said calmly. "In the Institute."

"Did he bring me here as well?" Tessa whispered.

"Yes, but there is no need to look betrayed, Miss Gray. You had struck your head quite hard, and Will was concerned about you. Brother Enoch, though his looks might frighten you, is a skilled practitioner of medicine. He has determined that your head injury is slight, and in the main you are suffering from shock and nervous anxiety. In fact, it might be for the best if you sat down now. Hovering barefoot by the door like that will only give you a chill, and do you little good."

"You mean because I can't run," Tessa said, licking her dry lips. "I can't get away."

"If you demand to get away, as you put it, after we have talked, I will let you go," said Mrs. Branwell. "The Nephilim do not trap Downworlders under duress. The Accords forbid it."

"The Accords?"

Mrs. Branwell hesitated, then turned to Brother Enoch and said something to him in a low voice. Much to Tessa's relief, he drew up the hood of his parchment-colored robes, hiding his face. A moment later he was moving toward Tessa; she stepped back hurriedly and he opened the door, pausing only for a moment on the threshold.

In that moment, he spoke to Tessa. Or perhaps "spoke" was not the word for it: She heard his voice inside her head, rather than outside it. *You are Eidolon, Theresa Gray. Shape-changer. But not of a sort that is familiar to me. There is no demon's mark on you.*

Shape-changer. He knew what she was. She stared at him, her heart pounding, as he went through the door and closed it behind him. Tessa knew somehow that if she were to run to the door and try the handle she would once again find it locked, but the urge to escape had left her. Her knees felt as if they had turned to water. She sank down in one of the large chairs by the bed.

"What is it?" Mrs. Branwell asked, moving to sit in the chair opposite Tessa's. Her dress hung so loosely on her small frame, it was impossible to tell if she wore a corset beneath it, and the bones in her small wrists were like a child's. "What did he say to you?"

Tessa shook her head, gripping her hands together in her lap so that Mrs. Branwell could not see her fingers trembling.

Mrs. Branwell looked at her keenly. "First," she said, "please call me Charlotte, Miss Gray. Everyone in the Institute does. We Shadowhunters are not so formal as most."

Tessa nodded, feeling her cheeks flush. It was hard to tell how old Charlotte was; she was so small that she looked quite young indeed, but her air of authority made her seem older, old enough that the idea of calling her by her Christian name seemed very odd. Still, as Aunt Harriet would have said, when in Rome . . .

"Charlotte," Tessa said, experimentally.

With a smile, Mrs. Branwell—Charlotte—leaned back slightly in her chair, and Tessa saw with some surprise that she had dark tattoos. A *woman* with tattoos! Her marks were like the ones Will bore: visible on her wrists below the tight cuffs of her dress, with one like an eye on the back of her left hand. "Second, let me tell you what I already know about you, Theresa Gray." She spoke in the same calm tone she'd had before, but her eyes, though still kind, were sharp as pins. "You're American. You came here from New York City because you were following your brother, who had sent you a steam-ship ticket. His name is Nathaniel."

Tessa sat frozen. "How do you know all this?"

"I know that Will found you in the Dark Sisters' house," Charlotte said. "I know that you claimed someone named the Magister was coming for you. I know that you have no idea who the Magister is. And I know that in a battle with the Dark Sisters, you were rendered unconscious and brought here."

Charlotte's words were like a key unlocking a door. Suddenly Tessa remembered. Remembered running with Will down the corridor; remembered the metal doors and the room full of blood on the other side; remembered Mrs. Black, her head sev-ered; remembered Will flinging his knife—

"Mrs. Black," she whispered.

"Dead," said Charlotte. "Very." She settled her shoulders against the back of the chair; she was so slight that the chair rose up high above her, as if she were a child sitting in a par-ent's chair.

"And Mrs. Dark?"

"Gone. We searched the whole house, and the nearby area, but found no trace of her."

"The whole house?" Tessa's voice shook, very slightly. "And there was no one in it? No one else alive, or . . . or dead?"

"We did not find your brother, Miss Gray," Charlotte said. Her tone was gentle. "Not in the house, nor in any of the sur-rounding buildings."

"You—were looking for him?" Tessa was bewildered.

"We did not find him," Charlotte said again. "But we did find your letters."

"My letters?"

"The letters you wrote to your brother and never sent," said Charlotte. "Folded under your mattress."

"You *read* them?"

"We had to read them," said Charlotte in the same gentle tone. "I apologize for that. It is not often that we bring a Downworlder into the Institute, or anyone who is not a Shadowhunter. It represents a great risk to us. We had to know that you were not a danger."

Tessa turned her head to the side. There was something horribly violating about this stranger having read her inmost thoughts, all the dreams and hopes and fears she'd poured forth, not thinking anyone would ever see them. The backs of her eyes stung; tears were threatening, and she willed them back, furious with herself, with everything.

"You're trying not to cry," Charlotte said. "I know that when I do that myself, it sometimes helps to look at a bright light directly. Try the witchlight."

Tessa moved her gaze to the stone in Charlotte's hand and gazed at it fixedly. The glow of it swelled up in front of her eyes like an expanding sun. "So," she said, fighting past the tightness in her throat, "you have decided I am not a danger, then?"

"Perhaps only to yourself," said Charlotte. "A power such as yours, the power of shape-shifting—it is no wonder the Dark Sisters wanted to get their hands on you. Others will as well."

"Like you do?" Tessa said. "Or are you going to pretend that you've let me into your precious Institute simply out of charity?"

A look of hurt flashed across Charlotte's face. It was brief, but it was real, and it did more to convince Tessa that she might have been wrong about Charlotte than anything the other woman could have said. "It is not charity," she said. "It is my vocation. Our vocation."

Tessa simply looked at her blankly.

"Perhaps," Charlotte said, "it would be better if I explained to you what we are—and what we do."

"*Nephilim*," said Tessa. "That's what the Dark Sisters called Mr. Herondale." She pointed at the dark markings on Charlotte's hand. "You're one as well, aren't you? Is that why you have those—those markings?"

Charlotte nodded. "I am one of the Nephilim—the Shadowhunters. We are . . . a race, if you will, of people, people with special abilities. We are stronger and swifter than most humans. We are able to conceal ourselves with magics called glamours. And we are especially skilled at killing demons."

"Demons. You mean—like Satan?"

"Demons are evil creatures. They travel great distances to come to this world and feed upon it. They would ravage it into ashes and destroy its inhabitants if we did not prevent it." Her voice was intent. "As it is the job of the human police to protect the citizenry of this city from one another, it is our job to protect them from demons and other supernatural dangers. When there are crimes that affect the Shadow World, when the Law of our world is broken, we must investigate. We are bound by the Law, in fact, to make inquiries even into the *rumor* of Covenant Law being contravened. Will told you about the dead girl he found in the alley; she was the only *body*, but there have been other disappearances, dark rumors of mundane boys and girls vanishing off the city's poorer streets. Using magic to murder human beings is against the Law, and therefore a matter for our jurisdiction."

"Mr. Herondale seems awfully young to be a sort of policeman."

"Shadowhunters grow up quickly, and Will did not investigate alone." Charlotte didn't sound as if she wished to elaborate. "That is not all we do. We safeguard the Covenant Law and uphold the Accords—the laws that govern peace among Downworlders."

Will had used that word as well. "Downworld? Is that a place?"

"A Downworlder is a being—a *person*—who is part supernatural in origin. Vampires, werewolves, faeries, warlocks—they are all Downworlders."

Tessa stared. Faeries were a children's tale, and vampires the stuff of penny dreadfuls. "Those creatures exist?"

"*You* are a Downworlder," Charlotte said. "Brother Enoch confirmed it. We simply don't know of what sort. You see, the kind of magic you can do—your ability—it isn't something an ordinary human being could do. Neither is it something one of us, a Shadowhunter, could do. Will thought you were most likely a warlock, which is what I would have guessed myself, but all warlocks have some attribute that marks them as warlocks. Wings, or hooves, or webbed toes, or, as you saw in the case of Mrs. Black, taloned hands. But you, you're completely human in appearance. And it is clear from your letters that you know, or believe, both of your parents to be human."

"*Human?*" Tessa stared. "Why wouldn't they have been human?"

Before Charlotte could answer, the door opened, and a slender, dark-haired girl in a white cap and apron came in, carrying a tea tray, which she set down on the table between them. "Sophie," Charlotte said, sounding relieved to see the girl. "Thank you. This is Miss Gray. She will be a guest of ours this evening."

Sophie straightened, turned to Tessa, and bobbed a curtsy. "Miss," she said, but the novelty of being curtsied to was lost on Tessa as Sophie raised her head and her full face became visible. She ought to have been very pretty—her eyes were a luminous dark hazel, her skin smooth, her lips soft and delicately shaped—but a thick, silvery ridged scar slashed from the left corner of her mouth to her temple, pulling her face sideways and distorting her features into a twisted mask. Tessa tried to hide the shock on her own face, but she could see as Sophie's eyes darkened that it hadn't worked.

"Sophie," Charlotte said, "did you bring in that dark red dress earlier, as I asked? Can you have it brushed and sponged for Tessa?" She turned back to Tessa as the maid nodded and went to the wardrobe. "I took the liberty of having one of our Jessamine's old dresses made over for you. The clothes you were wearing were ruined."

"Much obliged," Tessa said stiffly. She hated having to be grateful. The Sisters had pretended they were doing her favors, and look how that had turned out.

"Miss Gray." Charlotte looked at her earnestly. "Shadowhunters and Downworlders are not enemies. Our accord may be an uneasy one, but it is my belief that Downworlders are to be trusted—that, indeed, they hold the key to our eventual success against the demon realms. Is there something I can do to show you that we do not plan to take advantage of you?"

"I . . ." Tessa took a deep breath. "When the Dark Sisters first told me about my power, I thought they were mad," she said. "I told them such things didn't exist. Then I thought I was trapped in some sort of nightmare where they did. But then Mr. Herondale came, and he knew of magic, and had that glowing stone, and I thought, *Here is someone who might help me*." She looked up at Charlotte. "But you do not seem to know why I am the way I am, or even *what* I am. And if even you do not . . ."

"It can be . . . difficult to learn how the world truly is, to see it in its true shape and form," Charlotte said. "Most human beings never do. Most could not bear it. But I have read your letters. And I know that you are strong, Miss Gray. You have withstood what might have killed another young girl, Downworlder or not."

"I didn't have a choice. I did it for my brother. They would have murdered him."

"Some people," Charlotte said, "would have let that happen. But I know from reading your own words that you never even considered that." She leaned forward. "Have you any idea where your brother is? Do you think he is most likely dead?"

Tessa sucked in a breath.

"Mrs. Branwell!" Sophie, who had been attending to the hem of a wine-red dress with a brush, looked up and spoke with a reproachful tone that surprised Tessa. It was not the place of servants to correct their employers; the books she'd read had made that very clear.

But Charlotte only looked rueful. "Sophie is my good angel," she said. "I tend to be a little too blunt. I thought there might be something you knew, something that wasn't in your letters, that might give us knowledge of his whereabouts."

Tessa shook her head. "The Dark Sisters told me he was

imprisoned in a safe location. I assume he is still there. But I have no idea how to find him."

"Then you should stay here at the Institute until he can be located."

"I don't want your charity." Tessa said mulishly. "I can find another lodging place."

"It would not be charity. We are bound by our own laws to help and aid Downworlders. To send you away with nowhere to go would break the Accords, which are important rules we must abide by."

"And you wouldn't ask for anything in return?" Tessa's voice was bitter. "You won't ask me to use my—my ability? You won't require me to Change?"

"If," Charlotte said, "you do not wish to use your power, then no, we will not force you to. Though I do believe you your-self might benefit from learning how it might be controlled and used—"

"No!" Tessa's cry was so loud that Sophie jumped and dropped her brush. Charlotte glanced over at her and then back at Tessa. She said, "As you wish, Miss Gray. There are other ways you could assist us. I'm sure there is much that you know that was not contained in your letters. And in return, we could help you to search for your brother."

Tessa's head went up. "You would do that?"

"You have my word." Charlotte stood up. Neither of them had touched the tea on its tray. "Sophie, if you could help Miss Gray dress? Then I will bring her in to dinner."

"Dinner?" After hearing such a deal about Nephilim, and Downworld, and faeries and vampires and demons, the pros-pect of dinner was almost shocking in its ordinariness.

"Certainly. It's nearly seven o'clock. You've already met Will; you can meet everyone else. Perhaps you'll see that we're to be trusted."

And with a brisk nod, Charlotte left the room. As the door closed after her, Tessa shook her head mutely. Aunt Harriet had been bossy, but she'd had nothing on Charlotte Branwell.

"She has a strict manner, but she's really very kind," Sophie said, laying out on the bed the dress Tessa was meant to wear. "I've never known anyone with a better heart."

Tessa touched the sleeve of the dress with the tip of her finger. It was dark red satin, as Charlotte had said, with black moiré ribbon trim around the waist and hem. She had never worn anything so nice.

"Would you like me to help you get dressed for dinner, miss?" Sophie asked. Tessa remembered something Aunt Harriet had always said—that you could know a man not by what his friends said about him, but by how he treated his servants. If Sophie thought Charlotte had a good heart, then perhaps she did.

She raised her head. "Much obliged, Sophie. I believe I would."

Tessa had never had anyone assist her in getting dressed before, other than her aunt. Though Tessa was slender, the dress had clearly been made for a smaller girl, and Sophie had to lace Tessa's stays tightly to make it fit. She clucked under her breath while she did it. "Mrs. Branwell doesn't believe in tight lacing," she explained. "She says it causes nervous headaches and weakness, and a Shadowhunter can't afford to be weak. But Miss Jessamine likes the waists of her dresses *very* small, and she does insist."

"Well," said Tessa, a little breathless, "I'm not a Shadow-hunter, anyway."

"There is that," Sophie agreed, doing up the back of the dress with a clever little buttonhook. "There. What do you think?"

Tessa looked at herself in the mirror, and was taken aback. The dress was too small on her, and had clearly been designed to be fitted closely to the body as it was. It clung almost shockingly to her figure down to the hips, where it swelled into gathers in the back, draped over a modest bustle. The sleeves were turned back, showing frills of champagne lace at the cuffs. She looked—older, she thought, not the tragic scarecrow she had looked in the Dark House, but not someone entirely familiar to herself either. *What if one of the times I Changed, when I turned back into myself, I didn't do it quite right? What if this isn't even my true face?* The thought sent such a bolt of panic through her that she felt as if she might faint.

"You *are* a little pale," Sophie said, examining Tessa's reflection with a judicious gaze. She didn't appear particularly shocked by the dress's tightness, at least. "You could try pinching your cheeks a bit to bring the color. That's what Miss Jessamine does."

"It was awfully kind of her—Miss Jessamine, I mean—to lend me this dress."

Sophie chuckled low in her throat. "Miss Jessamine's never worn it. Mrs. Branwell gave it to her as a gift, but Miss Jessamine said it made her look sallow and tossed it in the back of her wardrobe. Ungrateful, if you ask me. Now, go on then and pinch your cheeks a bit. You're pale as milk."

Having done so, and having thanked Sophie, Tessa emerged from the bedroom into a long stone corridor. Charlotte was there, waiting for her. She set off immediately, with Tessa behind her, limping slightly—the black silk shoes, which did not quite fit, were not kind to her bruised feet.

Being in the Institute was a bit like being inside a castle— the ceiling disappearing up into gloom, the tapestries hanging on the walls. Or at least it was what Tessa imagined the inside of a castle might look like. The tapestries bore repeating motifs of stars, swords, and the same sort of designs she'd seen inked on Will and Charlotte. There was a single repeating image too, of an angel rising out of a lake, carrying a sword in one hand and a cup in the other. "This place used to be a church," Charlotte said, answering Tessa's unasked question. "The Church of All-Hallows-the-Less. It burned down during the Great Fire of London. We took over the land after that and built the Institute on the ruins of the old church. It's useful for our purposes to remain on consecrated ground."

"Don't people think it's odd, you building on the site of an old church like this?" Tessa asked, hurrying to keep up.

"They don't know about it. Mundanes—that's what we call ordinary people—aren't aware of what we do," Charlotte explained. "To them, from the outside the place looks like an empty patch of land. Beyond that, mundanes aren't really very interested in what doesn't affect them directly." She turned to usher Tessa through a door and into a large brightly lit dining room. "Here we are."

Tessa stood blinking in the sudden illumination. The room was huge, big enough for a table that could have seated twenty people. An immense gasolier hung down from the ceiling, filling the room with a yellowish glow. Over a sideboard loaded with expensive-looking china, a gilt-framed mirror ran the length of the room. A low glass bowl of white flowers decorated the table's center. Everything was tasteful, and very ordinary. There was nothing unusual about the room, nothing that might hint at the nature of the house's occupants.

Though the entire long dining table was draped with white linen, only one end was set, with places for five people. Only two people were already sitting—Will and a fair-haired girl about Tessa's age in a shimmering low-necked gown. They appeared to be studiously ignoring each other; Will looked up in apparent relief when Charlotte and Tessa came in. "Will," Charlotte said. "You remember Miss Gray?"

"My recollection of her," said Will, "is most vivid indeed." He was no longer wearing the odd black clothes he'd been wearing the day before, but an ordinary pair of trousers and a gray jacket with a black velvet collar. The gray made his eyes look bluer than ever. He grinned at Tessa, who felt herself flush and looked quickly away.

"And Jessamine—Jessie, do look up. Jessie, this is Miss Theresa Gray; Miss Gray, this is Miss Jessamine Lovelace."

"So pleased to make your acquaintance," Jessamine murmured. Tessa couldn't help staring at her. She was almost ridiculously pretty, what one of Tessa's novels would have called an English rose—all silvery fair hair, soft brown eyes, and creamy complexion. She wore a very bright blue dress, and rings on almost every one of her fingers. If she had the same black skin markings that Will and Charlotte did, they weren't visible.

Will cast Jessamine a look of plain loathing, and turned to Charlotte. "Where's your benighted husband, then?"

Charlotte, taking a seat, gestured for Tessa to sit opposite her, in the chair beside Will. "Henry is in his workroom. I've sent Thomas to fetch him. He'll be up in a moment."

"And Jem?"

Charlotte's look was warning, but "Jem is unwell" was all she said. "He's having one of his days."

"He's *always* having one of his days." Jessamine sounded disgusted.

Tessa was about to inquire as to who Jem might be, when Sophie entered, followed by a plump woman of middle age whose gray hair was escaping from a bun at the back of her head. The two of them began to serve food from the sideboard. There was roast pork, potatoes, savory soup, and fluffy dinner rolls with creamy yellow butter. Tessa felt suddenly lightheaded; she had forgotten how hungry she was. She bit into a roll, only to check herself when she saw Jessamine staring.

"You know," Jessamine said airily, "I don't believe I've ever seen a warlock eat before. I suppose you needn't ever bant, do you? You can just use magic to make yourself slender."

"We don't know for certain that she's a warlock, Jessie," said Will.

Jessamine ignored him. "Is it dreadful, being so evil? Are you worried you'll go to Hell?" She leaned closer to Tessa. "What do you think the Devil's *like*?"

Tessa set her fork down. "Would you like to meet him? I could summon him up in a trice if you like. Being a warlock, and all."

Will let out a whoop of laughter. Jessamine's eyes narrowed. "There's no call to be rude," she began—then broke off as Charlotte sat bolt upright with an astonished shriek.

"*Henry!*"

A man was standing in the dining room's arched doorway— a familiar-looking tall man, with a shock of ginger hair and hazel eyes. He wore a torn tweed Norfolk jacket over a shockingly bright striped waistcoat; his trousers were covered in what looked peculiarly like coal dust. But none of that was what had made Charlotte scream; it was the fact that his left arm appeared to be on fire. Little flames licked up his arm from a point above his elbow, releasing tendrils of black smoke.

"Charlotte, darling," Henry said to his wife, who was staring at him in gape-mouthed horror. Jessamine, beside her, was wide eyed. "Sorry I'm late. You know, I think I might nearly have the Sensor working—"

Will interrupted. "Henry," he said, "you're on fire. You do know that, don't you?"

"Oh, yes," Henry said eagerly. The flames were now nearly to his shoulder. "I've been working like a man possessed all day. Charlotte, did you hear what I said about the Sensor?"

Charlotte dropped her hand from her mouth. "Henry!" she shrieked. "Your *arm!*"

Henry glanced down at his arm, and his mouth dropped open. "Bloody *hell*" was all he had time to say before Will, exhibiting a startling presence of mind, stood up, seized the vase of flowers off the table, and hurled the contents over Henry. The flames went out, with a faint protesting sizzle, leaving Henry standing soaking wet in the doorway, one sleeve of his jacket blackened and a dozen damp white flowers strewn at his feet.

Henry beamed and patted the burned sleeve of his jacket with a look of satisfaction. "You know what this means?"

Will set the vase down. "That you set yourself on fire and didn't even notice?"

"That the flame-retardant mixture I developed last week works!" Henry said proudly. "This material must have been burning for a good ten minutes, and it isn't even half burned through!" He squinted down at his arm. "Perhaps I ought to set the other sleeve on fire and see how long—"

"Henry," said Charlotte, who appeared to have recovered from her shock, "if you set yourself on fire deliberately, I will institute divorce proceedings. Now sit down and eat your supper. And say hello to our guest."

Henry sat, glanced across the table at Tessa—and blinked in surprise. "I know you," he said. "You bit me!" He sounded pleased about it, as if recollecting a pleasant memory they'd both shared.

Charlotte shot a despairing look at her husband.

"Have you asked Miss Gray about the Pandemonium Club yet?" Will asked.

The Pandemonium Club. "I know the words. They were written on the side of Mrs. Dark's carriage," Tessa said.

"It's an organization," Charlotte said. "A rather old organization of mundanes who have interested themselves in the magical arts. At their meetings they do spells and try to summon up demons and spirits." She sighed.

Jessamine snorted. "I can't imagine why they bother," she said. "Messing about with spells and wearing hooded robes and setting little fires. It's ridiculous."

"Oh, they do more than that," said Will. "They're more powerful in Downworld than you might think. Many rich and important figures in mundane society are members—"

"That only makes it sillier." Jessamine tossed her hair. "They have money and power. Why are they playing around with magic?"

"A good question," said Charlotte. "Mundanes who involve

themselves in things they know nothing about are likely to meet unpleasant ends."

Will shrugged. "When I was trying to track down the source of the symbol on that knife Jem and I found in the alley, I was directed to the Pandemonium Club. The members of it in turn directed me to the Dark Sisters. It's their symbol—the two serpents. They supervised a set of secret gambling dens frequented by Downworlders. They existed to lure mundanes in and trick them into losing all their money in magical games, then, when the mundanes fell into debt, the Dark Sisters would extort the money back at ruinous rates." Will looked over at Charlotte. "They ran some other businesses as well, most unsavory ones. The house in which they kept Tessa, I had been told, was a Downworlder brothel catering to mundanes with unusual tastes."

"Will, I'm not at all sure—," Charlotte began dubiously.

"Hmph," Jessamine said. "No wonder you were so keen to go there, William."

If she had hoped to annoy Will, it didn't work; she might as well not have spoken, for all the attention he paid her. He was looking at Tessa across the table, his eyebrows arched slightly. "Have I offended you, Miss Gray? I imagined that after all you've seen, you would not be easily shocked."

"I am not offended, Mr. Herondale." Despite her words, Tessa felt her cheeks flame. Well-brought-up young ladies didn't know what a brothel was, and certainly wouldn't say the word in mixed company. Murder was one thing, but this . . . "I, ah, don't see how it could have been a . . . place like that," she said as firmly as she could. "No one ever came or went, and other than the maidservant and the coachman, I never saw anyone else who lived there."

"No, by the time I got there, it was quite deserted," Will agreed. "Clearly they had decided to suspend business, perhaps in the interests of keeping you isolated." He glanced over at Charlotte. "Do you think Miss Gray's brother has the same ability she does? Is that, perhaps, why the Dark Sisters captured him in the first place?"

Tessa interjected, glad for the change of subject. "My brother never showed any sign of such a thing—but, then, neither did I until the Dark Sisters found me."

"What *is* your ability?" Jessamine demanded. "Charlotte won't say."

"Jessamine!" Charlotte scowled at her.

"I don't believe she has one," Jessamine went on. "I think she's simply a little sneak who knows that if we believe she's a Downworlder, we'll have to treat her well because of the Accords."

Tessa set her jaw. She thought of her Aunt Harriet saying *Don't lose your temper, Tessa,* and *Don't fight with your brother simply because he teases you.* But she didn't care. They were all looking at her—Henry with curious hazel eyes, Charlotte with a gaze as sharp as glass, Jessamine with thinly veiled contempt, and Will with cool amusement. What if they all thought what Jessamine thought? What if they all thought she was angling for charity? Aunt Harriet would have hated accepting charity even more than she'd disapproved of Tessa's temper.

It was Will who spoke next, leaning forward to look intently into her face. "You can keep it a secret," he said softly. "But secrets have their own weight, and it can be a very heavy one."

Tessa raised her head. "It needn't be a secret. But it would be easier for me to show you than to tell you."

"Excellent!" Henry looked pleased. "I enjoy being shown things. Is there anything you require, like a spirit lamp, or—"

"It's not a séance, Henry," Charlotte said wearily. She turned to Tessa. "You don't need to do this if you don't want to, Miss Gray."

Tessa ignored her. "Actually, I do require something." She turned to Jessamine. "Something of yours, please. A ring, or a handkerchief—"

Jessamine wrinkled her nose. "Dear me, it sounds to me rather as if your special power is pickpocketing!"

Will looked exasperated. "Give her a ring, Jessie. You're wearing enough of them."

"*You* give her something, then." Jessamine set her chin.

"No." Tessa spoke firmly. "It must be something of yours." *Because of everyone here, you're the closest to me in size and shape. If I transform into tiny Charlotte, this dress will simply fall off me*, Tessa thought. She had considered trying to use the dress itself, but since Jessamine had never worn it, Tessa wasn't sure the Change would work and didn't want to take any chances.

"Oh, very well then." Petulantly Jessamine detached from her smallest finger a ring with a red stone set in it, and passed it across the table to Tessa. "This had better be worth the trouble."

Oh, it will be. Unsmiling, Tessa put the ring in the palm of her left hand and closed her fingers around it. Then she shut her eyes.

It was always the same: nothing at first, then the flicker of something at the back of her mind, like someone lighting a candle in a dark room. She groped her way toward it, as the Dark Sisters had taught her. It was hard to strip away the fear and the shyness, but she had done it enough times now to know what to expect—the reaching forward to touch the light at the center of the darkness; the sense of light and enveloping warmth, as if she were drawing a blanket, something thick and heavy, around herself, covering every layer of her own skin; and then the light blazing up and surrounding her—and she was inside it. Inside someone else's skin. Inside their mind.

Jessamine's mind.

She was only at the edge of it, her thoughts skimming the surface of Jessamine's like fingers skimming the surface of water. Still, it took her breath away. Tessa had a sudden, flashing image of a bright piece of candy with something dark at its center, like a worm at the core of an apple. She felt resentment, bitter hatred, anger—a terrible fierce longing for *something*—

Her eyes flew open. She was still sitting at the table, Jessamine's ring clutched in her hand. Her skin zinged with the sharp pins and needles that always accompanied her transformations. She could feel the oddness that was the different weight of another body, not her own; could feel the brush of Jessamine's light hair against her shoulders. Too thick to be held back by the pins that had clasped Tessa's hair, it had come down around her neck in a pale cascade.

"By the Angel," breathed Charlotte. Tessa looked around the table. They were all staring at her—Charlotte and Henry with their mouths open; Will speechless for once, a glass of water frozen halfway to his lips. And Jessamine—Jessamine was gazing at her in abject horror, like someone who has seen a vision of their own ghost. For a moment Tessa felt a stab of guilt.

It lasted only a moment, though. Slowly Jessamine lowered her hand from her mouth, her face still very pale. "*Goodness*, my nose is enormous," she exclaimed. "Why didn't anyone tell me?"

4

WE ARE SHADOWS

Pulvis et umbra sumus.
—Horace, *Odes*

The moment Tessa transformed back to her own shape, she had
to suffer a barrage of questions. For people who lived in a shadow
world of magic, the assembled Nephilim seemed surprisingly
awed by her ability, which only served to underline what Tessa
had already begun to suspect—that her shape-changing talent
was exceedingly unusual. Even Charlotte, who had known about
it before Tessa's demonstration, seemed fascinated.

"So you must be holding something that belongs to the person you're transforming into?" Charlotte asked for the second
time. Sophie and the older woman, who Tessa suspected was
the cook, had already taken away the dinner plates and had

served fancy cake and tea, but none of the diners had touched it yet. "You can't simply *look* at someone and—"

"I explained that already." Tessa's head was beginning to hurt. "I must be holding something that belongs to them, or a bit of hair or an eyelash. Something that's *theirs*. Otherwise nothing happens."

"Do you think a vial of blood would do the trick?" Will asked, in a tone of academic interest.

"Probably—I don't know. I've never tried it." Tessa took a sip of her tea, which had grown cold.

"And you're saying that the Dark Sisters *knew* this was your talent? They knew you had this ability before you did?" Charlotte asked.

"Yes. It's why they wanted me in the first place."

Henry shook his head. "But *how* did they know? I don't quite understand that part."

"I don't *know*," Tessa said, not for the first time. "They never explained it to me. All I know is what I told you—that they seemed to know exactly what it was I could do, and how to train me to do it. They spent hours with me, every day . . ." Tessa swallowed against the bitterness in her mouth. Memories of how it had been rose up in her mind—the hours and hours in the cellar room at the Dark House, the way they had screamed at her that Nate would die if she couldn't Change as they wanted her to, the agony when she finally learned to do it. "It *hurt*, at first," she whispered. "As if my bones were snapping, melting inside my body. They would force me to Change two, three, then a dozen times a day, until I would finally lose consciousness. And then, the next day, they'd start at it again. I was locked in that room, so I couldn't try to leave. . . ." She took a ragged breath. "That last day, they tested me by asking me to Change into a girl who had died. She had memories of being attacked with a dagger, being stabbed. Of some *thing* chasing her into an alley—"

"Perhaps it was the girl Jem and I found." Will sat up straight, his eyes shining. "Jem and I guessed she must have escaped from an attack and run out into the night. I believe they sent the Shax demon after her to bring her back, but I killed it. They must have wondered what happened."

"The girl I changed into was named Emma Bayliss," Tessa said, in a half whisper. "She had very fair hair—tied in little pink bows—and she was only a little thing."

Will nodded as if the description were familiar to him.

"Then they did wonder what had happened to her. That's why they had me Change into her. When I told them she was dead, they seemed relieved."

"The poor soul," Charlotte murmured. "So you can Change into the dead? Not only the living?"

Tessa nodded. "Their voices speak in my mind when I Change too. The difference is that many of them can remember the moment they died."

"Ugh." Jessamine shuddered. "How *morbid.*"

Tessa looked over at Will. *Mr. Herondale,* she chided herself silently, but it was hard to think of him that way. She felt somehow as if she knew him better than she really did. But that was foolishness. "You found me because you were looking for the murderer of Emma Bayliss," she said. "But she was only one dead human girl. One dead—what do you call it?—mundane. Why so much time and effort to find out what happened to her?"

For a moment Will's eyes met hers, his own a very dark

blue. Then his expression changed—only a slight change, but she saw it, though she could not have said what the change meant. "Oh, I wouldn't have bothered, but Charlotte insisted. She felt there was something larger at work. And once Jem and I infiltrated the Pandemonium Club, and heard rumors of the other murders, we realized there was more going on than the death of one girl. Whether or not we like mundanes particularly, we can't allow them to be systematically slaughtered. It's the reason we exist."

Charlotte leaned forward across the table. "The Dark Sisters never mentioned what use they intended to make of your abilities, did they?"

"You know about the Magister," Tessa said. "They said they were preparing me for him."

"For him to do what?" Will asked. "Eat you for dinner?"

Tessa shook her head. "To—to marry me, they said."

"To marry you?" Jessamine was openly scornful. "That's ridiculous. They were probably going to blood sacrifice you and didn't want you to panic."

"I don't know about that," Will said. "I looked in several rooms before I found Tessa. I remember one that was done up surprisingly like a wedding chamber. White hangings on an enormous bed. A white dress hanging in the wardrobe. It looked about your size." He eyed Tessa thoughtfully.

"Ceremonial marriage can be a very powerful thing," Charlotte said. "Performed properly, it could allow someone access to your ability, Tessa, even the power to control you." She drummed her fingertips thoughtfully on the tabletop. "As for 'the Magister,' I've researched the term in the archives. It is often used to denote the head of a coven or other group of magicians. The sort of group the Pandemonium Club imagines itself to be. I can't help but feel that the Magister and the Pandemonium Club are connected."

"We've investigated them before and never managed to catch them doing anything dodgy," Henry pointed out. "It isn't against the Law to be an idiot."

"Lucky for you," Jessamine said under her breath.

Henry looked hurt, but said nothing. Charlotte cast Jessamine a freezing look.

"Henry is right," said Will. "It isn't as if Jem and I didn't catch them doing the odd illegal thing—drinking absinthe laced with demon powders, and so forth. As long as they were only hurting themselves, it hardly seemed worth involving ourselves. But if they've graduated to harming others . . ."

"Do you know who any of them are?" Henry asked curiously.

"The mundanes, no," Will said dismissively. "There never seemed a reason to find out, and many of them went masked or disguised at club events. But I recognized quite a few of the Downworlders. Magnus Bane, Lady Belcourt, Ragnor Fell, de Quincey—"

"De Quincey? I hope he wasn't breaking any laws. You know how much trouble we've had finding a head vampire we can see eye to eye with," fretted Charlotte.

Will smiled into his tea. "Whenever I saw him, he was being a perfect angel."

After a hard look at him, Charlotte turned to Tessa. "Did the servant girl you mentioned—Miranda—have your ability? Or what about Emma?"

"I don't think so. If Miranda did, they would have been

training her as well, wouldn't they, and Emma didn't remember anything like that."

"And they never mentioned the Pandemonium Club? Some larger purpose to what they were doing?"

Tessa racked her brain. What was it the Dark Sisters had talked about when they'd thought she wasn't listening? "I don't think they ever said the name of the club, but they would talk sometimes about meetings they were planning on attending, and how the other members would be pleased to see how they were getting on with me. They did say a name once. . . ." Tessa screwed her face up, trying to remember. "Someone else who was in the club. I don't remember, though I recall thinking the name sounded foreign. . . ."

Charlotte leaned forward across the table. "Can you *try*, Tessa? Try to remember?"

Charlotte meant no harm, Tessa knew, and yet her voice called up other voices in Tessa's head—voices urging her to *try*, to reach into herself, to draw out the power. Voices that could turn hard and cold at the slightest provocation. Voices that wheedled and threatened and lied.

Tessa drew herself upright. "First, what about my brother?"

Charlotte blinked. "Your brother?"

"You said that if I gave you information about the Dark Sisters, you'd help me find my brother. Well, I told you what I knew. And I still don't have any idea where Nate is."

"Oh." Charlotte sat back, looking almost startled. "Of course. We'll start investigating his whereabouts tomorrow," she reassured Tessa. "We'll start with his workplace—speak to his employer and find out if he knows anything. We have contacts in all sorts of places, Miss Gray. Downworld runs on gossip like the mundane world does. Eventually we'll turn up someone who knows something about your brother."

The meal ended not long after that, and Tessa excused herself from the table with a feeling of relief, declining Charlotte's offer to guide her back to her room. All she wanted was to be alone with her thoughts.

She made her way down the torchlit corridor, remembering the day she had stepped off the boat at Southampton. She had come to England knowing no one but her brother, and had let the Dark Sisters force her into serving them. Now she had fallen in with the Shadowhunters, and who was to say they would treat her any better? Like the Dark Sisters, they wanted to use her—use her for the information she knew—and now that they were all aware of her power, how long would it be before they wanted to use her for that, too?

Still lost in thought, Tessa nearly walked directly into a wall. She brought herself up short—and looked around, frowning. She had been walking for much longer than it had taken her and Charlotte to reach the dining room, and still she hadn't found the room she remembered. In fact, she wasn't even sure she had found the *corridor* she remembered. She was in a hallway now, lined with torches and hung with tapestries, but was it the same one? Some of the corridors were very bright, some very dim, the torches burning with varying shades of brightness. Sometimes the torches flared up and then faded as she passed, as if responding to some peculiar stimulus she couldn't see. This particular corridor was fairly dim. She picked her way to the end of it carefully, where it branched into two more, each identical to this one.

"Lost?" inquired a voice behind her. A slow, arrogant voice, immediately familiar.

Will.

Tessa turned and saw that he was leaning carelessly against the wall behind her, as if he were lounging in a doorway, his feet in their scuffed boots crossed in front of him. He held something in his hand: his glowing stone. He pocketed it as she looked at him, dousing its light.

"You ought to let me show you around the Institute a bit, Miss Gray," he suggested. "You know, so you don't get lost again."

Tessa narrowed her eyes at him.

"Of course, you can simply continue wandering about on your own if you really wish to," he added. "I ought to warn you, though, that there are at least three or four doors in the Institute that you really shouldn't open. There's the one that leads to the room where we keep trapped demons, for instance. They can get a bit nasty. Then there is the weapons room. Some of the weapons have a mind of their own, and they *are* sharp. Then there are the rooms that open onto empty air. They're meant to confuse intruders, but when you're as high as the top of a church, you don't want to accidentally slip and—"

"I don't believe you," Tessa said. "You're an awful liar, Mr. Herondale. Still—" She bit her lip. "I don't like wandering about. You can show me around if you promise no tricks."

Will promised. And, to Tessa's surprise, he was true to his word. He guided her down a succession of identical-looking corridors, talking as they walked. He told her how many rooms the Institute had (more than you could count), told her how many Shadowhunters could live in it at once (hundreds), and displayed for her the vast ballroom in which was held an annual Christmas party for the Enclave—which, Will explained, was their term for the group of Shadowhunters who lived in London. (In New York, he added, the term was "Conclave." American Shadowhunters, it seemed, had their own lexicon.)

After the ballroom came the kitchen, where the middle-aged woman Tessa had seen in the dining room was introduced as Agatha, the cook. She sat sewing in front of a massive kitchen range and was, to Tessa's intense mystification, also smoking an enormous pipe. She smiled indulgently around it as Will took several chocolate tarts from the plate where they had been left to cool on the table. Will offered one to Tessa.

She shuddered. "Oh, no. I *hate* chocolate."

Will looked horrified. "What kind of monster could possibly hate chocolate?"

"He eats *everything*," Agatha told Tessa with a placid smile. "Since he was twelve, he has. I suppose it's all the training that keeps him from getting fat."

Tessa, amused at the idea of a fat Will, complimented the pipe-puffing Agatha on her mastery of the enormous kitchen. It looked like a place you could cook for hundreds, with row upon row of jarred preserves and soups, spice tins, and a huge haunch of beef roasting on a hook over the open fireplace.

"Well done," Will said after they'd left the kitchen. "Complimenting Agatha like that. Now she'll like you. It's no good if Agatha doesn't like you. She'll put stones in your porridge."

"Oh, dear," Tessa said, but she couldn't hide the fact that she was entertained. They went from the kitchen to the music room, where there were harps and a great old piano, gathering dust. Down a set of stairs was the drawing room, a pleasant place where the walls, instead of being bare stone, were papered with a bright print of leaves and lilies. A fire was going in a large grate, and several comfortable armchairs were pulled up near it. There was a great wooden desk in the room too, which Will explained was the place where Charlotte did much of the work of running the Institute. Tessa couldn't help wondering what it was that Henry Branwell did, and where he did it.

After that there was the weapons room, finer than anything Tessa imagined you might see in a museum. Hundreds of maces, axes, daggers, swords, knives, and even a few pistols hung on the walls, as well as a collection of different kinds of armor, from greaves worn to protect the shins to full suits of chain mail. A solid-looking young man with dark brown hair sat at a high table, polishing a set of short daggers. He grinned when they came in. "Evenin', Master Will."

"Good evening, Thomas. You know Miss Gray." He indicated Tessa.

"You were at the Dark House!" Tessa exclaimed, looking more closely at Thomas. "You came in with Mr. Branwell. I thought—"

"That I was a Shadowhunter?" Thomas grinned. He had a sweet, pleasant, open sort of face, and a lot of curling hair. His shirt was open at the neck, showing a strong throat. Despite his obvious youth, he was extremely tall and muscular, the width of his arms straining against his sleeves. "I'm not, miss—only trained like one."

Will leaned back against the wall. "Did that order of misericord blades come in, Thomas? I've been running into a certain amount of Shax demons lately, and I need something narrow that can pierce armored carapaces."

Thomas started to say something to Will about shipping being delayed due to weather in Idris, but Tessa's attention had been distracted by something else. It was a tall box of golden wood, polished to a high shine, with a pattern burned into the front—a snake, swallowing its own tail.

"Isn't that the Dark Sisters' symbol?" she demanded. "What's it doing here?"

"Not quite," said Will. "The box is a Pyxis. Demons don't have souls; their consciousness comes from a sort of energy, which can sometimes be trapped and stored. The Pyxis contains them safely—oh, and the design is an *ouroboros*—the 'tail devourer.' It's an ancient alchemical symbol meant to represent the different dimensions—our world, inside the serpent, and the rest of existence, outside." He shrugged. "The Sisters' symbol is the first time I've seen anyone draw an *ouroboros* with two snakes— Oh, no you don't," he added as Tessa reached for the box. He deftly stepped in front of her. "The Pyxis can't be touched by anyone who isn't a Shadowhunter. Nasty things will happen. Now let's go. We've taken up enough of Thomas's time."

"I don't mind," Thomas protested, but Will was already on his way out. Tessa glanced back at Thomas from the doorway. He'd gone back to polishing the weaponry, but there was something about the set of his shoulders that made Tessa think he seemed a little bit lonely.

"I didn't realize you let mundanes fight with you," she said to Will after they'd left the weapons room behind. "Is Thomas a servant, or—"

"Thomas has been with the Institute for almost his entire life," Will said, guiding Tessa around a sharp turn in the corridor. "There are families who have the Sight in their veins, families who have always served Shadowhunters. Thomas's parents served Charlotte's parents in the Institute, and now Thomas serves Charlotte and Henry. And his children will serve theirs. Thomas does everything—drives, cares for Balios and Xanthos—those are our horses—and helps with the weapons. Sophie and Agatha manage the rest, though Thomas assists them on occasion. I suspect he's sweet on Sophie and doesn't like to see her work too hard."

Tessa was glad to hear it. She'd felt awful about her reaction to Sophie's scar, and the thought that Sophie had a male admirer—and a handsome one at that—eased her conscience slightly. "Perhaps he's in love with Agatha," she said.

"I hope not. I intend to marry Agatha myself. She may be a thousand years old, but she makes an incomparable jam tart. Beauty fades, but cooking is eternal." He paused in front of a door—big and oak, with thick brass hinges. "Here we are, now," he said, and the door swung open at his touch.

The room they entered was bigger even than the ballroom she had seen before. It was longer than it was wide, with rectangular oak tables set down the middle of it, vanishing up to the far wall, which was painted with an image of an angel. Each table was illuminated by a glass lamp that flickered white. Halfway up the walls was an interior gallery with a wooden railing running around it that could be reached by means of spiral staircases on either side of the room. Rows upon rows of bookshelves stood at intervals, like sentries forming alcoves on either side of the room. There were more bookshelves upstairs as well; the books inside were hidden behind screens of fretted metal, each screen stamped with a pattern of four Cs. Huge, outward-curving stained-glass windows, lined with worn stone benches, were set at intervals between the shelves.

A vast tome had been left out on a stand, its pages open and inviting; Tessa moved toward it, thinking it must be a dictionary, only to find that its pages were scrawled with illegible, illuminated script and etched with unfamiliar-looking maps.

"This is the Great Library," said Will. "Every Institute has a library, but this one is the largest of them all—the largest in the West, at any rate." He leaned against the door, his arms crossed over his chest. "I said I would get you more books, didn't I?"

Tessa was so startled that he remembered what he had said, that it took her several seconds to respond. "But the books are all behind bars!" she said. "Like a literary sort of prison!"

Will grinned. "Some of these books are dangerous," he said. "It's wise to be careful."

"One must always be careful of books," said Tessa, "and what is inside them, for words have the power to change us."

"I'm not sure a book has ever changed me," said Will. "Well, there is one volume that promises to teach one how to turn oneself into an entire flock of sheep—"

"Only the very weak-minded refuse to be influenced by literature and poetry," said Tessa, determined not to let him run wildly off with the conversation.

"Of course, why one would want to be an entire flock of sheep is another matter entirely," Will finished. "Is there something you want to read here, Miss Gray, or is there not? Name it, and I shall attempt to free it from its prison for you."

"Do you think the library has *The Wide, Wide World*? Or *Little Women*?"

"Never heard of either of them," said Will. "We haven't many novels."

"Well, I want novels," said Tessa. "Or poetry. Books are for reading, not for turning oneself into livestock."

Will's eyes glittered. "I think we may have a copy of *Alice's Adventures in Wonderland* about somewhere."

Tessa wrinkled her nose. "Oh, that's for little children, isn't it?" she said. "I never liked it much—seemed like so much nonsense."

Will's eyes were very blue. "There's plenty of sense in nonsense sometimes, if you wish to look for it."

But Tessa had already spied a familiar volume on a shelf and went over to greet it like an old friend. "*Oliver Twist!*" she cried. "Have you any other of Mr. Dickens's novels?" She clasped her hands together. "Oh! Do you have *A Tale of Two Cities*?"

"That silly thing? Men going around getting their heads chopped off for love? Ridiculous." Will unpeeled himself from the door and made his way toward Tessa where she stood by the bookshelves. He gestured expansively at the vast number of volumes all around him. "No, here you'll find all sorts of advice about how to chop off someone's *else's* head if you need to; much more useful."

"I don't!" Tessa protested. "Need to chop off anyone's head, that is. And what's the point of a lot of books no one actually wants to *read*? Haven't you really any other novels?"

"Not unless *Lady Audley's Secret* is that she slays demons in her spare time." Will bounded up onto one of the ladders and yanked a book off the shelf. "I'll find you something else to read. Catch." He let it fall without looking, and Tessa had to dart forward to seize it before it hit the floor.

It was a large squarish volume bound in dark blue velvet. There was a pattern cut into the velvet, a swirling symbol reminiscent of the marks that decorated Will's skin. The title was stamped on the front in silver: *The Shadowhunter's Codex*. Tessa glanced up at Will. "What is this?"

"I assumed you'd have questions about Shadowhunters, given that you're currently inhabiting our sanctum sanctorum, so to speak. That book ought to tell you anything you want to know—about us, about our history, even about Downworlders like you." Will's face turned grave. "Be careful with it, though. It's six hundred years old and the only copy of its kind. Losing or damaging it is punishable by death under the Law."

Tessa thrust the book away from her as if it were on fire. "You can't be serious."

"You're right. I'm not." Will leaped down from the ladder and landed lightly in front of her. "You do believe everything I say, though, don't you? Do I seem unusually trustworthy to you, or are you just a naïve sort?"

Instead of replying, Tessa scowled at him and stalked across the room toward one of the stone benches inside a window alcove. Throwing herself down onto the seat, she opened the *Codex* and began to read, studiously ignoring Will even as he moved to sit beside her. She could feel the weight of his gaze on her as she read.

The first page of the Nephilim book showed the same image she'd grown used to seeing on the tapestries in the corridors: the angel rising out of the lake, holding a sword in one hand

and a cup in the other. Underneath the illustration was a note: *The Angel Raziel and the Mortal Instruments.*

"That's how it all began," Will said cheerfully, as if oblivious to the fact that she was ignoring him. "A summoning spell here, a bit of angel blood there, and you've a recipe for indestructible human warriors. You'll never understand us from reading a book, mind you, but it's a start."

"Hardly human—more like avenging angels," Tessa said softly, turning the pages. There were dozens of pictures of angels—tumbling out of the sky, shedding feathers as a star might shed sparks as it fell. There were more images of the Angel Raziel, holding open a book on whose pages runes burned like fire, and there were men kneeling around him, men on whose skin Marks could be seen. Images of men like the one she'd seen in her nightmare, with missing eyes and sewed-shut lips; images of Shadowhunters brandishing flaming swords, like warrior angels out of Heaven. She looked up at Will. "You are, then, aren't you? Part angel?"

Will didn't answer. He was looking out the window, through a clear lower pane. Tessa followed his gaze; the window gave out onto what had to be the front of the Institute, for there was a rounded courtyard below them, surrounded by walls. Through the bars of a high iron gate surmounted by a curved arch, she could glimpse a bit of the street beyond, lit by dim yellow gaslight. There were iron letters worked into the wrought arch atop the gate; when looked at from this direction, they were backward, and Tessa squinted to decipher them.

"*Pulvis et umbra sumus.* It's a line from Horace. 'We are dust and shadows.' Appropriate, don't you think?" Will said. "It's not a long life, killing demons; one tends to die young, and then they burn your body—dust to dust, in the literal sense. And then we vanish into the shadows of history, nary a mark on the page of a mundane book to remind the world that once we existed at all."

Tessa looked at him. He was wearing that look she found so odd and compelling—that amusement that didn't seem to pass beyond the surface of his features, as if he found everything in the world both infinitely funny and infinitely tragic all at the same time. She wondered what had made him this way, how he had come to find darkness amusing, for it was a quality he didn't appear to share with any of the other Shadowhunters she had met, however briefly. Perhaps it was something he had learned from his parents—but what parents?

"Don't you ever worry?" she said softly. "That what's out there—might come in here?"

"Demons and other unpleasantness, you mean?" Will asked, though Tessa wasn't sure if that was what she had meant, or if she had been speaking of the evils of the world in general. He placed a hand against the wall. "The mortar that made these stones was mixed with the blood of Shadowhunters. Every beam is carved of rowan wood. Every nail used to hammer the beams together is made of silver, iron, or electrum. The place is built on hallowed ground surrounded by wards. The front door can be opened only by one possessing Shadowhunter blood; otherwise it remains locked forever. This place is a fortress. So no, I am *not* worried."

"But why live in a fortress?" At his surprised look she elaborated. "You clearly aren't related to Charlotte and Henry, they're hardly old enough to have adopted you, and not all

Shadowhunter children must live here or there would be more than you and Jessamine—"

"And Jem," Will reminded her.

"Yes, but—you see what I mean. Why don't you live with your family?"

"None of us *have* parents. Jessamine's died in a fire, Jem's—well Jem came from quite a distance away to live here, after his parents were murdered by demons. Under Covenant Law, the Clave is responsible for parentless Shadowhunter children under the age of eighteen."

"So you are one another's family."

"If you must romanticize it, I suppose we are—all brothers and sisters under the Institute's roof. You as well, Miss Gray, however temporarily."

"In that case," Tessa said, feeling hot blood rise to her face, "I think I would prefer it if you called me by my Christian name, as you do with Miss Lovelace."

Will looked at her, slow and hard, and then smiled. His blue eyes lit when he smiled. "Then you must do the same for me," he said. "Tessa."

She had never thought about her name much before, but when he said it, it was as if she were hearing it for the first time. Her own breath was very short when she said, softly, "Will."

"Yes?" Amusement glittered in his eyes.

With a sort of horror Tessa realized that she had simply said his name for the sake of saying it; she hadn't actually had a question. Hastily she said, "How do you learn—to fight like you do? To draw those magical symbols, and the rest of it?"

Will smiled. "We had a tutor who provided our schooling

and physical training—though he's left for Idris, and Charlotte's looking for a replacement—along with Charlotte, who takes care of teaching us history and ancient languages."

"So she's your governess?"

A look of dark mirth passed across Will's features. "You could say that. But I wouldn't call Charlotte a governess if I were you, not if you want to preserve your limbs intact. You wouldn't think it to look at her, but she's quite skilled with a variety of weapons, our Charlotte."

Tessa blinked in surprise. "You don't mean—Charlotte doesn't *fight*, does she? Not the way you and Henry do."

"Certainly she does. Why wouldn't she?"

"Because she's a woman," Tessa said.

"So was Boadicea."

"Who?"

"'*So the Queen Boadicea, standing loftily charioted,/Brandishing in her hand a dart and rolling glances lioness-like*—'" Will broke off at Tessa's look of incomprehension, and grinned. "Tennyson? If you were English, you'd know. Remind me to find a book about her for you. Regardless, she was a powerful warrior queen. When she was finally defeated, she took poison rather than let herself be captured by the Romans. She was braver than any man. I like to think Charlotte is much in the same mold, if somewhat smaller."

"But she can't be any good at it, can she? I mean, women don't have those sort of feelings."

"What kind of feelings are those?"

"Bloodlust, I suppose," Tessa said after a moment. "Fierceness. Warrior feelings."

"I saw you waving that hacksaw at the Dark Sisters," Will

pointed out. "And if I recall correctly, Lady Audley's secret was, in fact, that she was a murderer."

"So you've read it!" Tessa couldn't hide her delight.

He looked amused. "I prefer *The Trail of the Serpent*. More adventure, less domestic drama. Neither is as good as *The Moonstone*, though. Have you read Collins?"

"I *adore* Wilkie Collins," Tessa cried. "Oh—*Armadale*! And *The Woman in White* . . . Are you laughing at me?"

"Not *at* you," said Will, grinning, "more *because* of you. I've never seen anyone get so excited over books before. You'd think they were diamonds."

"Well, they are, aren't they? Isn't there anything *you* love like that? And don't say 'spats' or 'lawn tennis' or something silly."

"Good Lord," he said with mock horror, "it's like she knows me already."

"Everyone has something they can't live without. I'll find out what it is for you, never you fear." She meant to speak lightly, but at the look on his face, her voice trailed off into uncertainty. He was looking at her with an odd steadiness; his eyes were the same dark blue as the velvet binding of the book she held. His gaze passed over her face, down her throat, to her waist, before rising back up to her face, where it lingered on her mouth. Tessa's heart was pounding as if she had been running up stairs. Something in her chest ached, as if she were hungry or thirsty. There was something she *wanted*, but she didn't know what—

"It's late," Will said abruptly, looking away from her. "I should show you back to your room."

"I—" Tessa wanted to protest, but there was no reason to do

so. He was right. It *was* late, the pinprick light of stars visible through the clear panes of the window. She rose to her feet, cradling the book to her chest, and went with Will out into the corridor.

"There are a few tricks to learning your way around the Institute that I ought to teach you," he said, still not looking at her. There was something oddly diffident in his attitude now that hadn't been there moments before, as if Tessa had done something to offend him. But what could she have done? "Ways to identify the different doors and turn—"

He broke off, and Tessa saw that someone was coming down the corridor toward them. It was Sophie, a basket of laundry tucked under one of her arms. Seeing Will and Tessa, she paused, her expression growing more guarded.

"Sophie!" Will's diffidence turned to mischief. "Have you finished putting my room in order yet?"

"It's done." Sophie didn't return his smile. "It was filthy. I hope that in future you can refrain from tracking bits of dead demon through the house."

Tessa's mouth fell open. How could Sophie talk to Will like that? She was a servant, and he—even if he *was* younger than she was—was a gentleman.

And yet Will seemed to take it in stride. "All part of the job, young Sophie."

"Mr. Branwell and Mr. Carstairs seem to have no problem cleaning their boots," Sophie said, looking darkly from Will to Tessa. "Perhaps you could learn from their example."

"Perhaps," said Will. "But I doubt it."

Sophie scowled, and started off along the corridor again, her shoulders tightly set with indignation.

Tessa looked at Will in amazement. "What was that?"

Will shrugged lazily. "Sophie enjoys pretending she doesn't like me."

"Doesn't like you? She *hates* you!" Under other circumstances, she might have asked if Will and Sophie had had a falling out, but one didn't fall out with *servants*. If they were unsatisfactory, one ceased to employ them. "Did—did something happen between you?"

"Tessa," Will said with exaggerated patience. "Enough. There are things you can't hope to understand."

If there was one thing Tessa hated, it was being told that there were things she couldn't understand. Because she was young, because she was a girl—for any of a thousand reasons that never seemed to make any real sense. She set her chin stubbornly. "Well, not if you won't tell me. But then I'd have to say that it looks a great deal like she hates you because you did something awful to her."

Will's expression darkened. "You can think what you like. It's not as if you know anything about me."

"I know you don't like giving straightforward answers to questions. I know you're probably around seventeen. I know you like Tennyson—you quoted him at the Dark House, and again just now. I know you're an orphan, as I am—"

"I *never* said I was an orphan." Will spoke with unexpected savagery. "And I loathe poetry. So, as it happens, you really don't know anything about me at all, do you?"

And with that, he spun on his heel and walked away.

5

THE SHADOWHUNTER'S CODEX

Dreams are true while they last, and do we not live in dreams?
—Alfred, Lord Tennyson, "The Higher Pantheism"

It took an age of wandering glumly from corridor to identical corridor before Tessa, by lucky chance, recognized a rip in yet another of the endless tapestries and realized that the door to her bedroom must be one of the ones lining that particular hallway. A few minutes of trial and error later, and she was gratefully shutting the correct door behind her and sliding the bolt home in the lock.

The moment she was back in her nightgown and had slipped under the covers, she opened *The Shadowhunter's Codex* and began to read. *You'll never understand us from reading a book,* Will had said, but that wasn't the point really. He didn't know what books meant to her, that books were symbols of truth and meaning, that this one acknowledged that she existed and that there were others like her in the world. Holding it in her hands made Tessa feel that everything that had happened to her in the past six weeks was real—more real even than living through it had been.

Tessa learned from the *Codex* that all Shadowhunters descended from an archangel named Raziel, who had given the first of them a volume called the Gray Book, filled with "the language of Heaven"—the black runic Marks that covered the skin of trained Shadowhunters such as Charlotte and Will. The Marks were cut into their skin with a styluslike tool called a stele—the odd penlike object she'd seen Will use to draw on the door at the Dark House. The Marks provided Nephilim with all sorts of protection: healing, superhuman strength and speed, night vision, and even allowed them to hide themselves from mundane eyes with runes called glamours. But they were not a gift anyone could use. Cutting Marks into the skin of a Downworlder or human—or even a Shadowhunter who was too young or improperly trained—would be torturously painful and result in madness or death.

The Marks were not the only way they protected themselves—they wore tough, enchanted leather garments called gear when they went into battle. There were sketches of men in the gear of different countries. To Tessa's surprise, there were also sketches of women in long shirts and trousers—not bloomers, such as the sort she'd seen ridiculed in newspapers, but real men's trousers. Turning the page, she shook her head, wondering if Charlotte and Jessamine really wore such outlandish getups.

The next pages were devoted to the other gifts Raziel had

given the first Shadowhunters—powerful magical objects called the Mortal Instruments—and a home country: a tiny piece of land sliced out of what was then the Holy Roman Empire, surrounded with wardings so that mundanes could not enter it. It was called Idris.

The lamp flickered low as Tessa read, her eyelids slipping lower and lower. Downworlders, she read, were supernatural creatures such as faeries, werewolves, vampires, and warlocks. In the case of vampires and werewolves, they were humans infected with demon disease. Faeries, on the other hand, were half-demon and half-angel, and therefore possessed both great beauty and an evil nature. But warlocks—warlocks were the direct offspring of humans and demons. No wonder Charlotte had asked if both her parents were human. *But they were*, she thought, *so I can't possibly be a warlock, thank God*. She stared down at an illustration showing a tall man with shaggy hair, standing in the center of a pentagram chalked onto a stone floor. He looked completely normal, save for the fact that he had eyes with slit pupils like a cat's. Candles burned at each of the star's five points. The flames seemed to slide together, blurring as Tessa's own vision blurred in exhaustion. She closed her eyes—and was instantly dreaming.

In the dream she danced through whirling smoke down a corridor lined with mirrors, and each mirror she passed showed her a different face. She could hear lovely, haunting music. It seemed to come from some distance away, and yet was all around. There was a man walking ahead of her—a boy, really, slender and youthful—but though she felt that she knew him, she could neither see his face nor recognize him. He might have been her brother, or Will, or someone else entirely. She followed, calling to him, but he receded down the

*corridor as if the smoke carried him with it. The music rose and rose
to a crescendo—*

And Tessa woke, breathing hard, the book sliding off her
lap as she sat up. The dream was gone, but the music remained,
high and haunting and sweet. She made her way to the door
and peered out into the hallway.

The music was louder in the corridor. In fact, it was coming
from the room across the hall. The door was ajar slightly, and
notes seemed to pour through the opening like water through
the narrow neck of a vase.

A dressing gown hung on a hook by the door; Tessa drew
it down and slipped it on over her nightclothes, stepping out
into the hallway. As if in a dream, she crossed the corridor
and put her hand gently to the door; it swung open under her
touch. The room within was dark, lit only by moonlight. She
saw that it was not unlike her own bedroom across the hall, the
same large four-poster bed, the same dark heavy furniture. The
curtains had been pulled back from one tall window, and pale
silver light poured into the room like a rain of needles. In the
square patch of moonlight before the window, someone was
standing. A boy—he seemed too slight to be a grown man—
with a violin propped against his shoulder. His cheek rested
against the instrument, and the bow sawed back and forth over
the strings, wringing notes out of it, notes as fine and perfect
as anything Tessa had ever heard.

His eyes were closed. "Will?" he said, without opening his
eyes or ceasing to play. "Will, is that you?"

Tessa said nothing. She could not bear to speak, to interrupt the music—but in a moment the boy broke it off himself,
lowering his bow and opening his eyes with a frown.

"Will—," he started, and then, seeing Tessa, his lips parted in surprise. "You're not Will." He sounded curious, but not at all annoyed, despite the fact that Tessa had barged into his bedroom in the middle of the night and surprised him playing the violin in his nightclothes, or what Tessa assumed were his nightclothes. He wore a light loose-fitting set of trousers and a collarless shirt, with a black silk dressing gown tied loosely over them. She had been right. He was young, probably the same age as Will, and the impression of youth was heightened by his slightness. He was tall but very slender, and disappearing below the collar of his shirt, she could see the curling edges of the black designs that she had earlier seen on Will's skin, and on Charlotte's.

She knew what they were called now. Marks. And she knew what they made him. Nephilim. The descendant of men and angels. No wonder that in the moonlight his pale skin seemed to shine like Will's witchlight. His hair was pale silver as well, as were his angular eyes.

"I'm so sorry," she said, clearing her throat. The noise sounded terribly harsh to her, and loud in the silence of the room; she wanted to cringe. "I—I didn't mean to come in here like this. It's— My room is across the hall, and . . ."

"That's all right." He lowered the violin from his shoulder. "You're Miss Gray, aren't you? The shape-changer girl. Will told me a bit about you."

"Oh," Tessa said.

"Oh?" The boy's eyebrows rose. "You don't sound terribly pleased that I know who you are."

"It's that I think Will is angry with me," Tessa explained. "So whatever he told you—"

He laughed. "Will is angry with everyone," he said. "I don't let it color my judgment."

Moonlight spilled off the polished surface of the boy's violin as he turned to lay it down on top of the wardrobe, the bow beside it. When he turned back to her, he was smiling. "I should have introduced myself earlier," he said. "I'm James Carstairs. Please call me Jem—everyone does."

"Oh, you're Jem. You weren't at dinner," Tessa recalled. "Charlotte said you were ill. Are you feeling better?"

He shrugged. "I was tired, that's all."

"Well, I imagine it must be tiring, doing what you all do." Having just read the *Codex*, Tessa felt herself burning up with questions about Shadowhunters. "Will said you came from a long way away to live here—were you in Idris?

He raised his eyebrows. "You know of Idris?"

"Or did you come from another Institute? They're in all the big cities, aren't they? And why to London—"

He interrupted her, bemused. "You ask a lot of questions, don't you?"

"My brother always says curiosity is my besetting sin."

"As sins go, it isn't the worst one." He sat down on the steamer trunk at the foot of the bed, and regarded her with a curious gravity. "So go ahead; ask me whatever you want. I can't sleep anyway, and distractions are welcome."

Immediately Will's voice rose up in the back of Tessa's head. Jem's parents had been killed by demons. *But I can't ask him about that*, Tessa thought. Instead she said, "Will told me you came from very far away. Where did you live before?"

"Shanghai," Jem said. "You know where that is?"

"China," said Tessa with some indignation. "Doesn't everyone know that?"

Jem grinned. "You'd be surprised."

"What were you doing in China?" Tessa asked, with honest interest. She couldn't quite picture the place Jem was from. When she thought of China, all that came to mind was Marco Polo and tea. She had the sense that it was very, very far, as if Jem had come from the ends of the earth—east of the sun and west of the moon, Aunt Harriet would have said. "I thought no one went there but missionaries and sailors."

"Shadowhunters live all over the world. My mother was Chinese; my father was British. They met in London and moved to Shanghai when he was offered the position of running the Institute there."

Tessa was startled. If Jem's mother had been Chinese, then so was he, wasn't he? She knew there were Chinese immigrants in New York—they mostly worked in laundries or sold hand-rolled cigars from stands on the street. She had never seen one of them who looked anything like Jem, with his odd silvery hair and eyes. Perhaps it had something to do with him being a Shadowhunter? But she couldn't think of a way to ask that didn't seem horrendously rude.

Fortunately, Jem didn't seem to be waiting for her to continue the conversation. "I apologize for asking, but—your parents are dead, aren't they?"

"Did Will tell you that?"

"He didn't need to. We orphans learn to recognize one another. If I might ask—were you very young when it happened?"

"I was three when they died in a carriage accident. I hardly remember them at all." *Only in tiny flashes—the scent of tobacco smoke, or the pale lilac of my mother's dress.* "My aunt raised me. And my brother, Nathaniel. My aunt, though—" At this, to her surprise, her throat began to tighten. A vivid picture of Aunt Harriet came to her mind, lying in the narrow brass bed in her bedroom, her eyes bright with fever. Not recognizing Tessa at the end and calling her by her mother's name, Elizabeth. Aunt Harriet had been the only mother Tessa had really ever known. Tessa had held her thin hand while she'd died, there in the room with the priest. She remembered thinking that now she truly was alone. "She died recently. She took a fever unexpectedly. She never had been very strong."

"I'm sorry to hear that," Jem said, and he genuinely did sound sorry.

"It was terrible because my brother was already gone by then. He'd left for England a month before. He'd even sent us back presents—tea from Fortnum and Mason, and chocolates. And then Aunt took sick and died, and I wrote to him over and over, but my letters came back. I was in despair. And then the ticket arrived. A ticket for a steamship to Southampton, and a note from Nate saying he'd meet me at the docks, that I must come live with him in London now that Aunt was gone. Except now I don't think he ever wrote that note at all—" Tessa broke off, her eyes stinging. "I'm sorry. I'm maundering on. You don't need to hear all this."

"What sort of man is your brother? What is he like?"

Tessa looked at Jem with a little surprise. The others had asked her what he might have done to get himself into his current situation, if she knew where the Dark Sisters might be keeping him, if he had the same power she did. But no one had ever asked what he was *like*.

"Aunt used to say he was a dreamer," she said. "He always lived in his head. He never cared about how things were, only how they would be, someday, when he had everything he wanted. When *we* had everything *we* wanted," she corrected herself. "He used to gamble, I think because he couldn't imagine losing—it wasn't part of his dreams."

"Dreams can be dangerous things."

"No—no." She shook her head. "I'm not saying it right. He was a wonderful brother. He . . ." Charlotte was right; it was easier to fight back tears if she found something, some object, to fix her gaze on. She stared at Jem's hands. They were slender and long, and he had the same design on the back of his hand that Will did, the open eye. She pointed at it. "What's that meant to do?"

Jem seemed not to notice she had changed the subject. "It's a Mark. You know what those are?" He held his hand out to her, palm down. "This one is the Voyance. It clears our Sight. Helps us to see Downworld." He turned his hand over, and drew up the sleeve of his shirt. All along the pale inside of his wrist and inner arm were more of the Marks, very black against his white skin. They seemed to thread with the pattern of his veins, as if his blood ran through the Marks, too. "For swiftness, night vision, angelic power, to heal quickly," he read out loud. "Though their names are more complex than that, and not in English."

"Do they hurt?"

"They hurt when I received them. They don't hurt at all now." He drew his sleeve down and smiled at her. "Now, don't tell me that's all the questions you have."

Oh, I have more than you think. "Why can't you sleep?"

She saw that she had caught him off guard; a look of hesitancy flashed across his face before he spoke. *But why hesitate?* she thought. He could always lie, or simply deflect, as Will would have. But Jem, she sensed instinctively, wouldn't lie. "I have bad dreams."

"I was dreaming too," she said. "I dreamed about your music."

He grinned. "A nightmare, then?"

"No. It was lovely. The loveliest thing I've heard since I came to this horrible city."

"London isn't horrible," Jem said equably. "You simply have to get to know it. You must come with me out into London someday. I can show you the parts of it that are beautiful—that I love."

"Singing the praises of our fair city?" a light voice inquired. Tessa whirled, and saw Will, leaning against the frame of the doorway. The light from the corridor behind him outlined his damp-looking hair with gold. The hem of his dark overcoat and his black boots were edged with mud, as if he had just come from outdoors, and his cheeks were flushed. He was bareheaded as always. "We treat you well here, don't we, James? I doubt I'd have that kind of luck in Shanghai. What do you call us there, again?"

"*Yang guizi,*" said Jem, who appeared unsurprised by Will's sudden appearance. "'Foreign devils.'"

"Hear that, Tessa? I'm a devil. So are you." Will unhitched himself from the doorway and sauntered into the room. He flung himself down onto the edge of the bed, unbuttoning his coat. It had a shoulder cape attached to it, very elegant, lined in blue silk.

"Your hair's wet," Jem said. "Where have you been?"

"Here, there, and everywhere." Will grinned. Despite his usual grace, there was something about the way he moved—the flush on his cheeks and the glitter in his eyes—

"Boiled as an owl, are you?" Jem said, not without affection.

Ah, Tessa thought. *He's drunk.* She'd seen her own brother under the influence of alcohol enough times to recognize the symptoms. Somehow, she felt obscurely disappointed.

Jem grinned. "Where have you been? The Blue Dragon? The Mermaid?"

"The Devil Tavern, if you must know." Will sighed and leaned against one of the posts of the bed. "I had such plans for this evening. The pursuit of blind drunkenness and wayward women was my goal. But alas, it was not to be. No sooner had I consumed my third drink in the Devil than I was accosted by a delightful small flower-selling child who asked me for two-pence for a daisy. The price seemed steep, so I refused. When I told the girl as much, she proceeded to rob me."

"A little girl robbed you?" Tessa said.

"Actually, she wasn't a little girl at all, as it turns out, but a midget in a dress with a penchant for violence, who goes by the name of Six-Fingered Nigel."

"Easy mistake to make," Jem said.

"I caught him in the act of slipping his hand into my pocket," Will said, gesturing animatedly with his scarred, slender hands. "I couldn't let that stand, of course. A fight broke out almost immediately. I had the upper hand until Nigel leaped onto the bar and struck me from behind with a pitcher of gin."

"Ah," said Jem. "That does explain why your hair's wet."

"It was a fair fight," Will said. "But the proprietor of the Devil didn't see it that way. Threw me out. I can't go back for a fortnight."

"Best thing for you," Jem said unsympathetically. "Glad to hear it's business as usual, then. I was worried for a moment there that you'd come home early to see if I was feeling better."

"You seem to be doing perfectly well without me. In fact, I see you've met our resident shape-shifting mystery woman," Will said, glancing toward Tessa. It was the first time he'd acknowledged her presence since he'd appeared in the doorway. "Do you normally turn up in gentlemen's bedrooms in the middle of the night? If I'd known that, I would have campaigned harder to make sure Charlotte let you stay."

"I don't see how what I do is your concern," Tessa replied. "Especially since you abandoned me in the corridor and left me to find my own way back to my room."

"And you found your way to Jem's room instead?"

"It was the violin," Jem explained. "She heard me practicing."

"Ghastly wailing noise, isn't it?" Will asked Tessa. "I don't know how all the cats in the neighborhood don't come running every time he plays."

"I thought it was pretty."

"That's because it was," Jem agreed.

Will pointed a finger accusingly in their direction. "You're ganging up on me. Is this how it's going to be from now on? I'll be odd man out? Dear God, I'll have to befriend Jessamine."

"Jessamine can't stand you," Jem pointed out.

"Henry, then."

"Henry will set you on fire."

"Thomas," Will suggested.

"Thomas," Jem began—and doubled up, suddenly racked with an explosive fit of coughing so violent that he slid from the steamer trunk to crouch on his knees. Too shocked to move, Tessa could only stare as Will—his expansive drunkenness seeming to vanish in a split second—sprang off the bed and knelt down by Jem, placing a hand on his shoulder.

"James," he said quietly. "Where is it?"

Jem held up a hand to ward him off. Racking gasps shook his thin frame. "I don't need it—I'm all right—"

He coughed again, and a fine spray of red splattered the floor in front of him. Blood.

Will's hand tightened on his friend's shoulder; Tessa saw the knuckles whiten. "Where is it? Where did you put it?"

Jem waved his hand feebly toward the bed. "On—," he gasped. "On the mantel—in the box—the silver one—"

"I'll get it, then." It was as gently as Tessa had ever heard Will say anything. "Stay here."

"As if I'd go anywhere." Jem scrubbed the back of his hand across his mouth; it came away with red streaking the open-eye Mark.

Standing up, Will turned—and saw Tessa. For a moment he looked purely startled, as if he'd forgotten she was there at all.

"Will—," she whispered. "Is there anything—"

"Come with me." Catching her by the arm, Will marched her, gently, toward the open door. He thrust her out into the corridor, moving to block her view of the room. "Good night, Tessa."

"But he's coughing blood," Tessa protested in a low voice. "Perhaps I should get Charlotte—"

"No." Will glanced over his shoulder, then back at Tessa. He leaned toward her, his hand on her shoulder. She could feel every one of his fingers pressing into the flesh. They were close enough that she could smell the night air on his skin, the scent of metal and smoke and fog. Something about the way he smelled was strange, but she couldn't place exactly what it was.

Will spoke in a low voice. "He has medicine. I'll get it for him. There's no need for Charlotte to know about this."

"But if he's ill—"

"Please, Tessa." There was a pleading urgency in Will's blue eyes. "It would be better if you said nothing about it."

Somehow Tessa found she could not say no. "I—all right."

"Thank you." Will released her shoulder, and raised his hand to touch her cheek—so lightly she thought she might almost have imagined it. Too startled to say anything, she stood in silence as he closed the door between them. As she heard the lock slide home, she realized why she had thought something was odd when Will had leaned toward her.

Though Will had said he'd been out all night drinking— though he'd even claimed to have had a pitcher of gin smashed over his head—there had been no smell of alcohol on him at all.

It was a long time before Tessa could sleep again. She lay awake, the *Codex* open at her side, the clockwork angel ticking at her chest, and she watched the lamplight trace patterns across the ceiling.

Tessa stood looking at herself in the mirror over the vanity table as Sophie did up the buttons on the back of her dress. In the morning light that streamed through the high windows, she looked very pale, the gray shadows under her eyes standing out in splotches.

She had never been one to stare in mirrors. A quick glance to see that her hair was all right and that there were no spots on her clothes. Now she could not stop looking at that thin, pale face in the glass. It seemed to ripple as she looked at it, like a reflection seen in water, like the vibration that took her just before the Change. Now that she had worn other faces, seen through other eyes, how could she ever say any face was really her own, even if it was the face she had been given at birth? When she Changed back to herself, how was she to know there wasn't some slight shift in her very self, something that made her not who she was anymore? Or did it matter what she looked like at all? Was her face nothing but a mask of flesh, irrelevant to her true self?

She could see Sophie reflected in the mirror as well; her face was turned so that her scarred cheek was to the mirror. It looked even more awful in daylight. It was like seeing a lovely painting slashed to ribbons with a knife. Tessa itched to ask her what had happened, but knew she shouldn't. Instead she said, "I'm much obliged to you for helping me with the dress."

"Pleased to be of service, miss." Sophie's tone was flat.

"I only wanted to ask," Tessa began. Sophie stiffened. *She thinks I'm going to ask her about her face*, Tessa thought. Out loud she said, "The way you talked to Will in the corridor last night—"

Sophie laughed. It was a short laugh, but a real one. "I am permitted to speak to Mr. Herondale however I like, whenever I like. It's one of the conditions of my employment."

"Charlotte lets you make your own conditions?"

"It's not simply anyone who can work at the Institute," Sophie explained. "You need to have a touch of the Sight. Agatha has it, and so does Thomas. Mrs. Branwell wanted me right away when she knew I had it, said she'd been looking for a maid for Miss Jessamine for simply ages. She warned me about Mr. Herondale, though, said he'd likely be rude to me, and familiar. She said I could be rude right back, that nobody would mind."

"Someone ought to be rude to him. He's rude enough to everyone else."

"I'd warrant that's what Mrs. Branwell thought." Sophie shared a grin with Tessa in the mirror; she was absolutely lovely when she smiled, Tessa thought, scar or no scar.

"You like Charlotte, don't you?" she said. "She does seem awfully kind."

Sophie shrugged. "In the old house I was in service in, Mrs. Atkins—that was the housekeeper—she would keep track of every candle we used, every bit of soap we had. We had to use the soap down to a sliver before she'd give us a new bit. But Mrs. Branwell gives me new soap whenever I want it." She said this as if it were a firm testament to Charlotte's character.

"I suppose they have a lot of money here at the Institute." Tessa thought of the gorgeous furnishings and the grandeur of the place.

"Perhaps. But I've made over enough dresses for Mrs. Branwell to know she doesn't buy them new."

Tessa thought of the blue gown Jessamine had worn to dinner the night before. "What about Miss Lovelace?"

"She has her own money," said Sophie darkly. She stepped back from Tessa. "There. You're fit to be seen now."

Tessa smiled. "Thank you, Sophie."

***

When Tessa came into the dining room, the others were already midway through breakfast—Charlotte in a plain gray dress, spreading jam onto a piece of toast; Henry half-hidden behind a newspaper; and Jessamine picking daintily at a bowl of porridge. Will had a pile of eggs and bacon on his plate and was digging into them industriously, which Tessa couldn't help noting was unusual for someone who claimed to have been out drinking all night.

"We were just talking about you," Jessamine said as Tessa found a seat. She pushed a silver toast rack across the table toward Tessa. "Toast?"

Tessa, picking up her fork, looked around the table anxiously. "What about me?"

"What to do with you, of course. Downworlders can't live in the Institute forever," said Will. "I say we sell her to the Gypsies on Hampstead Heath," he added, turning to Charlotte. "I hear they purchase spare women as well as horses."

"Will, stop it." Charlotte glanced up from her breakfast. "That's ridiculous."

Will leaned back in his chair. "You're right. They'd never buy her. Too scrawny."

"That's enough," Charlotte said. "Miss Gray shall remain. If for no other reason than because we're in the middle of an investigation that requires her assistance. I've already dispatched a message to the Clave telling them that we're keeping her here until this Pandemonium Club matter is cleared up and her brother is found. Isn't that right, Henry?"

"Quite," Henry said, setting the newspaper down. "The Pandemonium thingie is a top priority. Absolutely."

"You'd better tell Benedict Lightwood, too," said Will. "You know how he is."

Charlotte blanched slightly, and Tessa wondered who Benedict Lightwood might be. "Will, today I'd like you to revisit the site of the Dark Sisters' house; it's abandoned now, but it's still worth a final search. And I want you to take Jem with you—"

At that, the amusement left Will's expression. "Is he well enough?"

"He is quite well enough." The voice wasn't Charlotte's. It was Jem's. He had come into the room quietly and was standing by the sideboard, his arms folded across his chest. He was much less pale than he had been the previous night, and the red waistcoat he wore brought a slight tinge of color to his cheeks. "In fact, he's ready when you are."

"You should have some breakfast first," Charlotte fretted, pushing the plate of bacon toward him. Jem sat, and smiled at Tessa across the table. "Oh, Jem—this is Miss Gray. She's—"

"We've met," Jem said quietly, and Tessa felt a rush of heat in her face. She couldn't help staring at him as he picked up a piece of bread and applied butter to it. It seemed hard to imagine that anyone quite so ethereal-looking could possibly eat toast.

Charlotte looked puzzled. "You have?"

"I encountered Tessa in the corridor last night and introduced myself. I think I may have given her something of a fright." His silver eyes met Tessa's across the table, sparkling with amusement.

Charlotte shrugged. "Very well, then. I'd like you to go with Will. In the meantime, today, Miss Gray—"

"Call me Tessa," Tessa said. "I would prefer it if everyone did."

"Very well, Tessa," said Charlotte with a little smile. "Henry and I will be paying a call on Mr. Axel Mortmain, your brother's employer, to see if he, or any of his employees, might have any information as to your brother's whereabouts."

"Thank you." Tessa was surprised. They had said they were going to look for her brother, and they were actually doing it. She hadn't expected that they would.

"I've heard of Axel Mortmain," said Jem. "He was a taipan, one of the big business heads in Shanghai. His company had offices on the Bund."

"Yes," said Charlotte, "the newspapers say he made his fortune in imports of silk and tea."

"Bah." Jem spoke lightly, but there was an edge to his voice. "He made his fortune in opium. All of them did. Buying opium in India, sailing it to Canton, trading it for goods."

"He wasn't breaking the law, James." Charlotte pushed the newspaper across the table toward Jessamine. "Meanwhile, Jessie, perhaps you and Tessa can go through the paper and make note of anything that might pertain to the investigation, or be worth a second look—"

Jessamine recoiled from the paper as if it were a snake. "A lady does not read the newspaper. The society pages, perhaps, or the theater news. Not this filth."

"But you are not a lady, Jessamine—," Charlotte began.

"Dear me," said Will. "Such harsh truths so early in the morning cannot be good for the digestion."

"What I mean," Charlotte said, correcting herself, "is that you are a Shadowhunter first, and a lady second."

"Speak for yourself," Jessamine said, pushing her chair back. Her cheeks had turned an alarming shade of red. "You know," she said, "I wouldn't have expected you to notice, but it seems clear that the only thing Tessa has to put on her back is that awful old red dress of mine, and it doesn't fit her. It doesn't even fit me anymore, and she's taller than I am."

"Can't Sophie . . . ," Charlotte began vaguely.

"You can take a dress in. It's another thing to make it twice as big as it was to start with. Really, Charlotte." Jessamine blew out her cheeks in exasperation. "I think you ought to let me take poor Tessa into town to get some new clothes. Otherwise, the first time she takes a deep breath, that dress will fall right off her."

Will looked interested. "I think she should try that out now and see what happens."

"Oh," Tessa said, thoroughly confused. Why was Jessamine being so kind to her suddenly when she'd been so unpleasant only the day before? "No, really it's not necessary—"

"It is," Jessamine said firmly.

Charlotte was shaking her head. "Jessamine, as long as you live in the Institute, you are one of us, and you have to contribute—"

"You're the one who insists we have to take in Downworlders who are in trouble, and feed and shelter them," Jessamine said. "I'm quite sure that includes clothing them as well. You see, I will be contributing—to Tessa's upkeep."

Henry leaned across the table toward his wife. "You'd better let her do it," he advised. "Remember the last time you tried to get her to sort the daggers in the weapons room, and she used them to cut up all the linens?"

"We needed new linens," said Jessamine, unabashed.

"Oh, all right," Charlotte snapped. "Honestly, sometimes I despair of the lot of you."

"What've I done?" Jem inquired. "I only just arrived."

Charlotte put her face into her hands. As Henry began to pat her shoulders and make soothing noises, Will leaned across Tessa toward Jem, ignoring her completely as he did so. "Should we leave now?"

"I need to finish my tea first," Jem said. "Anyway, I don't see what you're so fired up about. You said the place hadn't been used as a brothel in ages?"

"I want to be back before dark," Will said. He was leaning nearly across Tessa's lap, and she could smell that faint boy-smell of leather and metal that seemed to cling to his hair and skin. "I have an assignation in Soho this evening with a certain attractive someone."

"Goodness," Tessa said to the back of his head. "If you keep seeing Six-Fingered Nigel like this, he'll expect you to declare your intentions."

Jem choked on his tea.

Spending the day with Jessamine began as badly as Tessa had feared. The traffic was dreadful. However crowded New York might have been, Tessa had never seen anything like the snarling mess of the Strand at midday. Carriages rolled side by side with costermongers' carts piled high with fruit and vegetables; women shawled and carrying shallow baskets full of flowers dived madly in and out of traffic as they tried to interest the occupants of various carriages in their wares; and cabs came to a full stop in the midst of traffic so that the cabdrivers could scream at one another out their windows. This noise added to the already awesome din—ice cream peddlers shouting "Hokey-pokey, penny a lump," newspaper boys hawking the day's latest headline, and someone somewhere playing a barrel organ. Tessa wondered how everyone living and working in London wasn't deaf.

As she stared out the window, an old woman carrying a large metal cage full of fluttering colorful birds stepped out alongside their coach. The old woman turned her head, and Tessa saw that her skin was as green as a parrot's feathers, her eyes wide and all black like a bird's, her hair a shock of multicolored feathers. Tessa started, and Jessamine, following her gaze, frowned. "Close the curtains," she said. "It keeps out the dust." And, reaching past Tessa, Jessamine did just that.

Tessa looked at her. Jessamine's small mouth was set in a thin line. "Did you see—?" Tessa began.

"No," Jessamine said, shooting Tessa what she had often seen referred to in novels as a "killing" look. Tessa glanced hastily away.

Things did not improve when they finally reached the fashionable West End. Leaving Thomas patiently waiting with the horses, Jessamine dragged Tessa in and out of various dressmakers' salons, looking at design after design, standing by while the prettiest shop assistant was chosen to model a sample. (No real lady would let a dress that might have been worn by a stranger touch her skin.) In each establishment she gave a different false name and a different story; in each establishment the owners seemed enchanted by her looks and obvious wealth and couldn't help her fast enough. Tessa, mostly ignored, lurked on the sidelines, half-dead from boredom.

In one salon, posing as a young widow, Jessamine even examined the design for a black mourning dress of crepe and lace. Tessa had to admit it would have set off her blond pallor well.

"You would look absolutely beautiful in this, and could not possibly fail to make an advantageous remarriage." The dressmaker winked in a conspiratorial fashion. "In fact, do you know what we call this design? 'The Trap Rebaited.'"

Jessamine giggled, the dressmaker smiled limpidly, and Tessa considered racing out into the street and ending it all by throwing herself under a hansom cab. As if conscious of her annoyance, Jessamine glanced toward her with a condescending smile. "I'm also looking for a few dresses for my cousin from America," she said. "The clothes there are simply horrible. She's as plain as a pin, which doesn't help, but I'm sure you can do something with her."

The dressmaker blinked as if this were the first time she'd noticed Tessa, and perhaps it was. "Would you like to choose a design, ma'am?"

The following whirlwind of activity was something of a revelation for Tessa. In New York her clothes had been bought by her aunt—ready-made pieces that had had to be altered to fit, and always cheap material in drab shades of dark gray or navy. She had never before learned, as she did now, that blue was a color that suited her and brought out her gray-blue eyes, or that she should wear rose pink to put color in her cheeks. As her measurements were taken amidst a blur of discussion of princess sheaths, cuirass bodices, and someone named Mr. Charles Worth, Tessa stood and stared at her face in the mirror, half-waiting for the features to begin to slip and change, to reform themselves. But she remained herself, and at the end of it all she had four new dresses on order to be delivered later in the week—one pink, one yellow, one striped blue and white with bone buttons, and a gold and black silk—as well as two smart jackets, one with darling beaded tulle adorning the cuffs.

"I suspect you may actually look pretty in that last outfit," Jessamine said as they climbed back up into the carriage. "It's amazing what fashion can do."

Tessa counted silently to ten before she replied. "I'm awfully obliged to you for everything, Jessamine. Shall we return to the Institute now?"

At that, the brightness went out of Jessamine's face. *She truly hates it there,* Tessa thought, puzzled more than anything else. What was so dreadful about the Institute? Of course its whole reason for existing was peculiar enough, certainly, but Jessamine had to be used to that by now. She was a Shadowhunter like the rest.

"It's such a lovely day," Jessamine said, "and you've hardly seen anything of London. I think a walk in Hyde Park is in order. And after that, we could go to Gunter's and have Thomas get ices for us!"

Tessa glanced out the window. The sky was hazy and gray, shot through with lines of blue where the clouds briefly drifted apart from one another. In no way would this be considered a lovely day in New York, but London seemed to have different standards for weather. Besides, she owed Jessamine something now, and the last thing in the world the other girl wanted to do, clearly, was go home.

"I adore parks," said Tessa.

Jessamine almost smiled.

* * *

"You didn't tell Miss Gray about the cogs," Henry said.

Charlotte looked up from her notes and sighed. It had always been a sore point for her that, however often she had requested a second, the Clave only allowed the Institute one carriage. It was a fine one—a town coach—and Thomas was an excellent driver. But it did mean that when the Institute's Shadowhunters went their separate ways, as they were doing today, Charlotte was forced to borrow a carriage from Benedict Lightwood, who was far from her favorite person. And the only carriage he was willing to lend her was small and uncomfortable. Poor Henry, who was so very tall, was bumping his head against the low roof.

"No," she said. "The poor girl, she seemed so dazed already. I couldn't tell her that the mechanical devices we found in the cellar had been manufactured by the company that employed her brother. She's so worried about him. It seemed more than she'd be able to bear."

"It might not mean anything, darling," Henry reminded her. "Mortmain and Company manufactures most of the machine tools used in England. Mortmain is really something of a genius. His patented system for producing ball bearings—"

"Yes, yes." Charlotte tried to keep the impatience out of her voice. "And perhaps we should have told her. But I thought it best that we speak to Mr. Mortmain first and gather what impressions we can. You're correct. He may know nothing at all, and there may be little connection. But it would be quite a coincidence, Henry. And I am very wary of coincidence."

She glanced back down at the notes she'd made about Axel Mortmain. He was the only (and likely, though the notes did not specify, illegitimate) son of Dr. Hollingworth Mortmain, who in a matter of years had risen from the humble position of ship's surgeon on a trading vessel bound for China to wealthy private trader, buying and selling spices and sugar, silk and tea, and—it wasn't stated, but Charlotte was in agreement with Jem on the matter—probably opium. When Dr. Mortmain had died, his son, Axel, at barely twenty years of age, had inherited his fortune, which he'd promptly invested in building a fleet of ships faster and sleeker than any others plying the seas. Within a decade the younger Mortmain had doubled, then quadrupled, his father's riches.

In more recent years he had retired from Shanghai to London, had sold his trading ships, and had used the money to buy a large company that produced the mechanical devices needed to make timepieces, everything from pocket watches to grandfather clocks. He was a very wealthy man.

The carriage drew up in front of one of a row of white terraced houses, each with tall windows looking out over the square. Henry leaned out of the carriage and read the number off a brass plaque affixed to a front gatepost. "This must be it." He reached for the carriage door.

"Henry," said Charlotte, placing a hand on his arm. "Henry, do keep in mind what we talked about this morning, won't you?"

He smiled ruefully. "I will do my best not to embarrass you or trip up the investigation. Honestly, sometimes I wonder why you bring me along on these things. You know I'm a bumbler when it comes to people."

"You're not a bumbler, Henry," Charlotte said gently. She longed to reach out and stroke his face, push his hair back and reassure him. But she held herself back. She knew—she had been advised enough times—not to force on Henry affection he probably did not want.

Leaving the carriage with the Lightwoods' driver, they mounted the stairs and rang the bell; the door was opened by a footman wearing dark blue livery and a dour expression. "Good morning," he said brusquely. "Might I inquire as to your business here?"

Charlotte glanced sideways at Henry, who was staring past the footman with a dreamy sort of expression. Lord knew what his mind was on—cogs, gears, and gadgets, no doubt—but it certainly wasn't on their present situation. With an inward sigh she said, "I am Mrs. Gray, and this is my husband, Mr. Henry Gray. We're seeking a cousin of ours—a young man named Nathaniel Gray. We haven't heard from him in nearly six weeks. He is, or was, one of Mr. Mortmain's employees—"

For a moment—it might have been her imagination—she thought she saw something, a flicker of uneasiness, in the footman's eyes. "Mr. Mortmain owns quite a large company. You can't expect him to know the whereabouts of everyone who works for him. That would be impossible. Perhaps you should inquire with the police."

Charlotte narrowed her eyes. Before they had left the Institute, she had traced the insides of her arms with persuasion runes. It was the rare mundane who was totally unsusceptible to their influence. "We have, but they don't seem to have progressed at all with the case. It's so dreadful, and we're so concerned about Nate, you see. If we could see Mr. Mortmain for a moment . . ."

She relaxed as the footman nodded slowly. "I'll inform Mr.

Mortmain of your visit," he said, stepping back to allow them inside. "Please wait in the vestibule." He looked startled, as if surprised at his own acquiescence.

He swung the door wide, and Charlotte followed him in, Henry behind her. Though the footman failed to offer Charlotte a seat—a failure of politesse she attributed to the confusion brought on by the persuasion runes—he did take Henry's coat and hat, and Charlotte's wrap, before leaving the two of them to stare curiously around the entryway.

The room was high ceilinged but not ornate. It was also absent the expected pastoral landscapes and family portraits. Instead, hanging from the ceiling were long silk banners painted with the Chinese characters for good luck; an Indian platter of hammered silver propped in one corner; and pen-and-ink sketches of famous landmarks lining the walls. Charlotte recognized Mount Kilimanjaro, the Egyptian pyramids, the Taj Mahal, and a section of China's Great Wall. Mortmain clearly was a man who traveled a great deal and was proud of the fact.

Charlotte turned to look at Henry to see if he was observing what she was, but he was staring vaguely off toward the stairs, lost in his own mind again; before she could say anything, the footman rematerialized, a pleasant smile on his face. "Please come this way."

Henry and Charlotte followed the footman to the end of the corridor, where he opened a polished oak door and ushered them before him.

They found themselves in a grand study, with wide windows looking out onto the square. Dark green curtains were pulled back to let in the light, and through the windowpanes

Charlotte could see their borrowed carriage waiting for them at the curb, the horse with its head dipped into a nose-bag, the driver reading a newspaper on his high seat. The green branches of trees moved on the other side of the street, an emerald canopy, but it was noiseless. The windows blocked all sound, and there was nothing audible in this room at all save the faint ticking of a wall clock with MORTMAIN AND COMPANY engraved on the face in gold.

The furniture was dark, a heavy black-grained wood, and the walls were lined with animal heads—a tiger, an antelope, and a leopard—and more foreign landscapes. There was a great mahogany desk in the center of the room, neatly arranged with stacks of paper, each pile weighted down with a heavy copper gear. A brass-bound globe bearing the legend WYLD'S GLOBE OF THE EARTH, WITH THE LATEST DISCOVERIES! anchored one corner of the desk, the lands under the rule of the British empire picked out in pinkish red. Charlotte always found the experience of examining mundane globes a strange one. Their world was not the same shape as the one she knew.

Behind the desk sat a man, who rose to his feet as they entered. He was a small energetic-looking figure, a middle-aged man with hair graying suitably at the sideburns. His skin looked windburned, as if he had often been outside in rough weather. His eyes were a very, very light gray, his expression pleasant; despite his elegant, expensive-looking clothes, it was easy to imagine him on the deck of a ship, peering keenly into the distance. "Good afternoon," he said. "Walker gave me to understand that you are looking for Mr. Nathaniel Gray?"

"Yes," Henry said, to Charlotte's surprise. Henry rarely, if ever, took the lead in conversations with strangers. She wondered if it had anything to do with the intricate-looking blueprint on the desk. Henry was looking at it as yearningly as if it were food. "We're his cousins, you know."

"We do appreciate you taking this time to talk to us, Mr. Mortmain," Charlotte added hastily. "We know he was only an employee of yours, one of dozens—"

"Hundreds," said Mr. Mortmain. He had a pleasant baritone voice, which at the moment sounded very amused. "It is true I can't keep track of them all. But I do remember Mr. Gray. Though I must say, if he ever mentioned that he had cousins who were Shadowhunters, I can't say I recall it."

6

STRANGE EARTH

We must not look at goblin men,
We must not buy their fruits:
Who knows upon what soil they fed
Their hungry thirsty roots?
—Christina Rossetti, "Goblin Market"

"You know," said Jem, "this isn't at all what I thought a brothel would look like."

The two boys stood at the entrance to what Tessa called the Dark House, off Whitechapel High Street. It looked dingier and darker than Will remembered, as if someone had swabbed it with a coating of extra dirt. "What were you imagining exactly, James? Ladies of the night waving from the balconies? Nude statues adorning the entranceway?"

"I suppose," Jem said mildly, "I was expecting something that looked a bit less drab."

Will had thought rather the same thing the first time he had been there. The overwhelming sensation one had inside the Dark House was that it was a place no one had ever really thought of as a home. The latched windows looked greasy, the drawn curtains dingy and unwashed.

Will rolled up his sleeves. "We'll probably have to knock down the door—"

"Or," said Jem, reaching out and giving the knob a twist, "not."

The door swung open onto a rectangle of darkness.

"Now, that's simply laziness," said Will. Taking a hunting dagger from his belt, he stepped cautiously inside, and Jem followed, keeping tight hold of his jade-headed walking stick. They tended to take turns going first into dangerous situations, though Jem preferred to be rear guard much of the time—Will always forgot to look behind him.

The door swung shut behind them, prisoning them in the half-lit gloom. The entryway looked almost the same as it had the first time Will had been there—the same wooden staircase leading up, the same cracked but still elegant marble flooring, the same air thick with dust.

Jem raised his hand, and his witchlight flared into life, frightening a group of blackbeetles. They scurried across the floor, causing Will to grimace. "Nice place to live, isn't it? Let's hope they left something behind other than filth. Forwarding addresses, a few severed limbs, a prostitute or two . . ."

"Indeed. Perhaps, if we're fortunate, we can still catch syphilis."

"Or demon pox," Will suggested cheerfully, trying the door under the stairs. It swung open, unlocked as the front door had been. "There's always demon pox."

"Demon pox does not exist."

"Oh ye of little faith," said Will, disappearing into the darkness under the stairs.

Together they searched the cellar and the ground-floor rooms meticulously, finding little but rubbish and dust. Everything had been stripped from the room where Tessa and Will had fought off the Dark Sisters; after a long search Will discovered something on the wall that looked like a smear of blood, but there seemed no source for it, and Jem pointed out it could just as well be paint.

Abandoning the cellar, they moved upstairs, and found a long corridor lined with doors that was familiar to Will. He had raced down it with Tessa behind him. He ducked into the first room on the right, which had been the room he'd found her in. No sign lingered of the wild-eyed girl who'd hit him with a flowered pitcher. The room was empty, the furniture having been taken away to be searched inside the Silent City. Four dark indentations on the floor indicated where a bed had once stood.

The other rooms were much the same. Will was trying the window in one when he heard Jem shout that he should come quickly; he was in the last room on the left. Will made haste and found Jem standing in the center of a large square room, his witchlight shining in his hand. He was not alone. There was one piece of furniture remaining here—an upholstered armchair, and seated in it was a woman.

She was young—probably no older than Jessamine—and wore a cheap-looking printed dress, her hair gathered up at the nape of her neck. It was dull-brown mousy hair, and her hands were bare and red. Her eyes were wide open and staring.

"Gah," said Will, too surprised to say anything else. "Is she—"

"She's dead," said Jem.

"Are you certain?" Will could not take his eyes off the woman's face. She was pale, but not with a corpse's pallor, and her hands lay folded in her lap, the fingers softly curved, not stiff with the rigor of death. He moved closer to her and placed a hand on her arm. It was rigid and cold beneath his fingers. "Well, she's not responding to my advances," he observed more brightly than he felt, "so she *must* be dead."

"Or she's a woman of good taste and sense." Jem knelt down and looked up into the woman's face. Her eyes were pale blue and protuberant; they stared past him, as dead-looking as painted eyes. "Miss," he said, and reached for her wrist, meaning to take a pulse.

She moved, jerking under his hand, and let out a low inhuman moan.

Jem stood up hastily. "What in—"

The woman raised her head. Her eyes were still blank, unfocused, but her lips moved with a grinding sound. "Beware!" she cried. Her voice echoed around the room, and Will, with a yell, jumped back.

The woman's voice sounded like gears grating against one another. "Beware, Nephilim. As you slay others, so shall you be slain. Your angel cannot protect you against that which neither God nor the devil has made, an army born neither of Heaven nor Hell. Beware the hand of man. Beware." Her voice rose to a high, grinding shriek, and she jerked back and forth in the chair like a puppet being yanked on invisible strings. "BEWARE BEWAREBEWAREBEWARE—"

"Good God," muttered Jem.

"BEWARE!" the woman shrieked one last time, and toppled

forward to sprawl on the ground, abruptly silenced. Will stared, openmouthed.

"Is she . . . ?" he began.

"Yes," Jem said. "I think she's *quite* dead this time."

But Will was shaking his head. "Dead. You know, I don't *think* so."

"What do you think, then?"

Instead of answering, Will went and knelt down by the body. He put two fingers to the side of the woman's cheek and turned her head gently until she faced them. Her mouth was wide, her right eye staring at the ceiling. The left dangled halfway down her cheek, attached to its socket by a coil of copper wire.

"She's not alive," said Will, "but not dead, either. She may be . . . like one of Henry's gadgets, I think." He touched her face. "Who could have done this?"

"I can hardly guess. But she called us Nephilim. She knew what we are."

"Or someone did," said Will. "I don't imagine she *knows* anything. I think she's a machine, like a clock. And she has run down." He stood up. "Regardless, we had best get her back to the Institute. Henry will want to have a look at her."

Jem did not reply; he was looking down at the woman on the floor. Her feet were bare beneath the hem of her dress, and dirty. Her mouth was open and he could see the gleam of metal inside her throat. Her eye dangled eerily on its bit of copper wire as somewhere outside the windows a church clock chimed the midday hour.

Once inside the park, Tessa found herself beginning to relax. She hadn't been in a green, quiet place since she'd come to

London, and she found herself almost reluctantly delighted by the sight of grass and trees, though she thought the park nowhere near as fine as Central Park in New York. The air was not as hazy here as it was over the rest of the city, and the sky overhead had achieved a color that was almost blue.

Thomas waited with the carriage while the girls made their promenade. As Tessa walked beside Jessamine, the other girl kept up a constant stream of chatter. They were making their way down a broad thoroughfare that, Jessamine informed her, was inexplicably called Rotten Row. Despite the inauspicious name, it was apparently *the* place to see and be seen. Down the center of it paraded men and women on horseback, exquisitely attired, the women with their veils flying, their laughter echoing in the summer air. Along the sides of the avenue walked other pedestrians. Chairs and benches were set up under the trees, and women sat twirling colorful parasols and sipping peppermint water; beside them bewhiskered gentlemen smoked, filling the air with the smell of tobacco mixed with cut grass and horses.

Though no one stopped to talk to them, Jessamine seemed to know who everyone was—who was getting married, who was seeking a husband, who was having an affair with so-and-so's wife and everyone knew all about it. It was a bit dizzying, and Tessa was glad when they stepped off the row and onto a narrower path leading into the park.

Jessamine slid her arm through Tessa's and gave her hand a companionable squeeze. "You don't know what a relief it is to finally have another girl around," she said cheerfully. "I mean, Charlotte's all right, but she's boring and married."

"There's Sophie."

Jessamine snorted. "Sophie's a servant."

"I've known girls who were quite companionable with their ladies' maids," Tessa protested. This was not precisely true. She had read about such girls, though she had never known one. Still, according to novels, the main function of a ladies' maid was to listen to you as you poured your heart out about your tragic love life, and occasionally to dress in your clothes and pretend to be you so you could avoid being captured by a villain. Not that Tessa could picture Sophie participating in anything like that on Jessamine's behalf.

"*You've* seen what her face looks like. Being hideous has made her bitter. A ladies' maid is meant to be pretty, and speak French, and Sophie can't manage either. I told Charlotte as much when she brought the girl home. Charlotte didn't listen to me. She never does."

"I can't imagine why," said Tessa. They had turned onto a narrow path that wound between trees. The glint of the river was visible through them, and the branches above knotted together into a canopy, blocking the brightness of the sun.

"I know! Neither can I!" Jessamine raised her face, letting what sun broke through the canopy dance across her skin. "Charlotte never listens to anyone. She's always henpecking poor Henry. I don't know why he married her at all."

"I assume because he loved her?"

Jessamine snorted. "No one thinks that. Henry wanted access to the Institute so he could work on his little experiments in the cellar and not have to fight. And I don't think he *minded* marrying Charlotte—I don't think there was anyone else he wanted to marry—but if someone else had been running the Institute, he would have married them instead."

She sniffed. "And then there's the boys—Will and Jem. Jem's pleasant enough, but you know how foreigners are. Not really trustworthy and basically selfish and lazy. He's always in his room, pretending to be ill, refusing to do anything to help out," Jessamine went on blithely, apparently forgetting the fact that Jem and Will were off searching the Dark House right now, while she promenaded in the park with Tessa. "And *Will*. Handsome enough, but behaves like a lunatic half the time; it's as if he were brought up by savages. He has no respect for anyone or anything, no concept of the way a gentleman is supposed to behave. I suppose it's because he's Welsh."

Tessa was baffled. "Welsh?" *Is that a bad thing to be?* she was about to add, but Jessamine, thinking that Tessa was doubting Will's origins, went on with relish.

"Oh, yes. With that black hair of his, you can absolutely tell. His mother was a Welshwoman. His father fell in love with her, and that was that. He left the Nephilim. Maybe she cast a spell on him." Jessamine laughed. "They have all kinds of odd magic and things in Wales, you know."

Tessa did not know. "Do you know what happened to Will's parents? Are they dead?"

"I suppose they must be, mustn't they, or they would have come looking for him?" Jessamine furrowed her brow. "Ugh. Anyway. I don't want to talk about the Institute anymore." She swung around to look at Tessa. "You must be wondering why I've been being so nice to you."

"Er . . ." Tessa had been wondering, rather. In novels girls like herself, girls whose families had once had money but who had fallen on hard times, were often taken in by kindly wealthy protectors and were furnished with new clothes and a good education. (Not, Tessa thought, that there had been anything wrong with her education. Aunt Harriet had been as learned as any governess.) Of course, Jessamine did not in any way resemble the saintly older ladies of such tales, whose acts of generosity were totally selfless. "Jessamine, have you ever read *The Lamplighter?*"

"Certainly not. Girls shouldn't read novels," said Jessamine, in the tone of someone reciting something she'd heard somewhere else. "Regardless, Miss Gray, I have a proposition to put to you."

"Tessa," Tessa corrected automatically.

"Of course, for we are already the best of friends," Jessamine said, "and shall soon be even more so."

Tessa regarded the other girl with bafflement. "What do you mean?"

"As I am sure horrid Will has told you, my parents, my dear papa and mama, are dead. But they left me a not inconsiderable sum of money. It was put aside in trust for me until my eighteenth birthday, which is only in a matter of months. You see the problem, of course."

Tessa, who did not see the problem, said, "I do?"

"I am not a Shadowhunter, Tessa. I despise everything about the Nephilim. I have never wanted to be one, and my dearest wish is to leave the Institute and never speak to a single soul who resides there ever again."

"But I thought that your parents were Shadowhunters. . . ."

"One does not have to be a Shadowhunter if one does not wish to," Jessamine snapped. "My parents did not. They left the Clave when they were young. Mama was always perfectly clear. She never wanted the Shadowhunters near me. She said she would never wish that life on a girl. She wanted other things for me. That I would make my debut, meet the Queen, find a good husband, and have darling little babies. An *ordinary life*." She said the words with a savage sort of hunger. "There are other girls in this city right now, Tessa, other girls my age, who aren't as pretty as me, who are dancing and flirting and laughing and catching husbands. They get lessons in French. I get lessons in horrid demon languages. It's not *fair*."

"You can still get married." Tessa was puzzled. "Any man would—"

"I could marry a *Shadowhunter*." Jessamine spat out the word. "And live like Charlotte, having to dress like a man and fight like a man. It's disgusting. Women aren't meant to behave like that. We are meant to graciously preside over lovely homes. To decorate them in a manner that is pleasing to our husbands. To uplift and comfort them with our gentle and angelic presence."

Jessamine sounded neither gentle nor angelic, but Tessa forbore mentioning this. "I don't see how I . . ."

Jessamine caught Tessa's arm fiercely. "Don't you? I can leave the Institute, Tessa, but I cannot live alone. It wouldn't be respectable. Perhaps if I were a widow, but I am only a girl. It just isn't done. But if I had a companion—a sister—"

"You wish me to pretend to be your *sister*?" Tessa squeaked.

"Why not?" Jessamine said, as if this were the most reasonable suggestion in the world. "Or you could be my cousin from America. Yes, that would work. You do see," she added, more practically, "that it isn't as if you have anywhere else to go, is it? I'm quite positive we would catch husbands in no time at all."

Tessa, whose head had begun to ache, wished Jessamine would cease to speak of "catching" husbands the way one might catch a cold, or a runaway cat.

"I could introduce you to all the best people," Jessamine continued. "There would be balls, and dinner parties—" She broke off, looking around in sudden confusion. "But—where are we?"

Tessa glanced around. The path had narrowed. It was now a dark trail leading between high twisted trees. Tessa could no longer see the sky, nor hear the sound of voices. Beside her, Jessamine had come to a halt. Her face creased with sudden fear. "We've wandered off the path," she whispered.

"Well, we can find our way back, can't we?" Tessa spun around, looking for a break in the trees, a patch of sunlight. "I think we came from that way—"

Jessamine caught suddenly at Tessa's arm, her fingers claw-like. Something—no, someone—had appeared before them on the path.

The figure was small, so small that for a moment Tessa thought they were facing a child. But as the form stepped forward into the light, she saw that it was a man—a hunched, wizened-looking man, dressed like a peddler, in ragged clothes, a battered hat pushed back on his head. His face was wrinkled and white, like a mold-covered old apple, and his eyes were gleaming black between thick folds of skin.

He grinned, showing teeth as sharp as razors. "Pretty girls."

Tessa glanced at Jessamine; the other girl was rigid and

staring, her mouth a white line. "We ought to go," Tessa whispered, and pulled at Jessamine's arm. Slowly, as if she were in a dream, Jessamine allowed Tessa to turn her so they faced back the way they had come—

And the man was before them once again, blocking the way back to the park. Far, far in the distance, Tessa thought she could see the park, a sort of clearing, full of light. It looked impossibly far away.

"You wandered off the path," said the stranger. His voice was singsong, rhythmic. "Pretty girls, you wandered off the path. You know what happens to girls like you."

He took a step forward.

Jessamine, still rigid, was clutching her parasol as though it were a lifeline. "Goblin," she said, "hobgoblin, whatever you are—we have no quarrel with any of the Fair Folk. But if you touch us—"

"You wandered from the path," sang the little man, coming closer, and as he did, Tessa saw that his shining shoes were not shoes after all but gleaming hooves. "Foolish Nephilim, to come to this place un-Marked. Here is land more ancient than any Accords. Here there is strange earth. If your angel blood should fall upon it, golden vines will grow from the spot, with diamonds at their tips. And I claim it. I claim your blood."

Tessa tugged at Jessamine's arm. "Jessamine, we should—"

"Tessa, be *quiet*." Shaking her arm free, Jessamine pointed her parasol at the goblin. "You don't want to do this. You don't want—"

The creature sprang. As he hurtled toward them, his mouth seemed to peel wide, his skin splitting, and Tessa saw the face beneath—fanged and vicious. She screamed and stumbled backward, her shoe catching on a tree root. She thumped to the ground as Jessamine raised her parasol, and with a flick of Jessamine's wrist, the parasol burst open like a flower.

The goblin screamed. He screamed and fell back and rolled on the ground, still screaming. Blood streamed from a wound in his cheek, staining his ragged gray jacket.

"I told you," Jessamine said. She was breathing hard, her chest rising and falling as if she had been racing through the park. "I told you to leave us alone, you filthy creature—" She struck at the goblin again, and now Tessa could see that the edges of Jessamine's parasol gleamed an odd gold-white, and were as sharp as razors. Blood was splattered across the flowered material.

The goblin howled, throwing up his arms to protect himself. He looked like a little old hunched man now, and though Tessa knew it was an illusion, she couldn't help feeling a pang of pity. "Mercy, mistress, mercy—"

"Mercy?" Jessamine spat. "You wanted to grow flowers out of my blood! Filthy goblin! Disgusting creature!" She slashed at him again with the parasol, and again, and the goblin screamed and thrashed. Tessa sat up, shaking the dirt out of her hair, and staggered to her feet. Jessamine was still screaming, the parasol flying, the creature on the ground spasming with each blow. "I hate you!" Jessamine shrieked, her voice thin and trembling. "I hate you, and everything like you—Downworlders—disgusting, *disgusting*—"

"Jessamine!" Tessa ran to the other girl and threw her arms around her, pinning Jessamine's arms against her body. For a moment Jessamine struggled, and Tessa realized there was no way she could hold her. She was *strong*, the muscles under her soft feminine skin coiled and as tense as a whip. And then Jessamine went suddenly limp, sagging back against Tessa, her breath hitching as the parasol drooped in her hand. "No," she wailed. "No. I didn't want to. I didn't mean to. *No—*"

Tessa glanced down. The goblin's body was humped and motionless at their feet. Blood spread across the ground from the place where he lay, running across the earth like dark vines. Holding Jessamine as she sobbed, Tessa could not help but wonder what would grow there now.

It was, unsurprisingly, Charlotte who recovered from her astonishment first. "Mr. Mortmain, I'm not sure what you could possibly mean—"

"Of course you are." He was smiling, his lean face split from ear to ear by an impish grin. "Shadowhunters. The Nephilim. That's what you call yourselves, isn't it? The by-blows of men and angels. Strange, since the Nephilim in the Bible were hideous monsters, weren't they?"

"You know, that's not necessarily true," Henry said, unable to restrain his inner pedant. "There's an issue of translation from the original Aramaic—"

"Henry," Charlotte said warningly.

"Do you really trap the souls of the demons you kill in a gigantic crystal?" Mortmain went on, wide eyed. "How magnificent!"

"D'you mean the Pyxis?" Henry looked baffled. "It's not a crystal, more like a wooden box. And they aren't so much souls—demons don't *have* souls. They have energy—"

"Be *quiet*, Henry," Charlotte snapped.

"Mrs. Branwell," Mortmain said. He sounded dreadfully

cheerful. "Please do not concern yourself. I already know every-thing about your kind, you see. You're Charlotte Branwell, aren't you? And this is your husband, Henry Branwell. You run the London Institute from the site of what was once the church of All-Hallows-the-Less. Did you honestly think I wouldn't know who you were? *Especially* once you tried to glamour my footman? He can't bear being glamoured, you know. Gives him a rash."

Charlotte narrowed her eyes. "And how have you come by all this information?"

Mortmain leaned forward eagerly, templing his hands. "I am a student of the occult. Since my time in India as a young man, when I first learned of them, I have been fascinated with the shadow realms. For a man in my position, with sufficient funds and more than sufficient time, many doors are open. There are books one may purchase, information that can be paid for. Your knowledge is not as secret as you might think."

"Perhaps," said Henry, looking deeply unhappy, "but— It is *dangerous*, you know. Killing demons—it's not like shooting tigers. They can hunt you as well as you can hunt them."

Mortmain chuckled. "My boy, I have no intention of racing out to fight demons bare-handed. Of course this sort of information is dangerous in the hands of the flighty and the hotheaded, but mine is a careful and sensible mind. I seek only an expansion of my knowledge of the world, nothing more." He looked about the room. "I must say, I've never had the honor of talking to Nephilim before. Of course, mention of you is frequent in the literature, but to read about something and to truly experience it are two very different things, I'm sure you'll agree. There is so very much you could teach me—"

"That," Charlotte said in a freezing tone, "will be quite enough of that."

Mortmain looked at her, puzzled. "Pardon me?"

"Since you seem to know so much about Nephilim, Mr. Mortmain, might I ask if you know what our mandate is?"

Mortmain looked smug. "To destroy demons. To protect humans—mundanes, as I understand you call us."

"Yes," said Charlotte, "and a great deal of the time what we are protecting humans from is their own very foolish selves. I see that you are no exception to this rule."

At that, Mortmain looked actually astonished. His glance went to Henry. Charlotte knew that look. It was a look only exchanged between men, a look that said, *Can you not control your wife, sir?* A look, she knew, that was quite wasted on Henry, who seemed to be trying to read the upside-down blueprints on Mortmain's desk and was paying very little attention to the conversation.

"You think the occult knowledge you have acquired makes you very clever," said Charlotte. "But I have seen my share of dead mundanes, Mr. Mortmain. I cannot count the times we have attended to the remains of some human who fancied himself expert in magical practices. I remember, when I was a girl, being summoned to the home of a barrister. He belonged to some silly circle of men who believed themselves to be magicians. They spent their time chanting and wearing robes and drawing pentagrams on the ground. One evening he determined that his skill was sufficient to attempt the raising of a demon."

"And was it?"

"It was," Charlotte said. "He raised the demon Marax. It

proceeded to slaughter him, and all of his family." Her tone was matter-of-fact. "We found most of them hanging headless, upside down in the carriage house. The youngest of his children was roasting on a spit over the fire. We never did find Marax."

Mortmain had paled, but retained his composure. "There are always those who overreach their abilities," he said. "But I—"

"But you would never be so foolish," Charlotte said. "Save that you are, at this very moment, being that foolish. You look at Henry and myself and you are not afraid of us. You are amused! A fairy tale come to life!" She slammed her hand down hard on the edge of his desk, making him jump. "The might of the Clave stands behind us," she said, in as cold a tone as she could muster. "Our mandate is to protect humans. Such as Nathaniel Gray. He has vanished, and something occult is clearly behind that vanishing. And here we find his erstwhile employer, clearly steeped in matters of the occult. It beggars belief that the two facts are not connected."

"I—He—Mr. Gray has vanished?" Mortmain stammered.

"He has. His sister came to us, searching for him; she had been informed by a pair of warlocks that he was in grave danger. While you, sir, are amusing yourself, he may be dying. And the Clave does not look kindly on those who stand in the way of its mandate."

Mortmain passed a hand over his face. When he emerged from behind it, he looked gray. "I shall, of course," he said, "tell you whatever you want to know."

"Excellent." Charlotte's heart was beating fast, but her voice betrayed no anxiety.

"I used to know his father. Nathaniel's father. I employed him almost twenty years ago when Mortmain's was mainly a shipping concern. I had offices in Hong Kong, Shanghai, Tianjin—" He broke off as Charlotte tapped her fingers impatiently on the desk. "Richard Gray worked for me here in London. He was my head clerk, a kind and clever man. I was sorry to lose him when he moved his family to America. When Nathaniel wrote to me and told me who he was, I offered him a job on the spot."

"Mr. Mortmain." Charlotte's voice was steely. "This is not germane—"

"Oh, but it is," the small man insisted. "You see, my knowledge of the occult has always been of assistance to me in business matters. Some years ago, for instance, a well-known Lombard Street bank collapsed—destroyed dozens of large companies. My acquaintance with a warlock helped me avoid disaster. I was able to withdraw my funds before the bank dissolved, and that saved my company. But it raised Richard's suspicions. He must have investigated, for eventually he confronted me with his knowledge of the Pandemonium Club."

"You are a member, then," Charlotte murmured. "Of course."

"I offered Richard membership in the club—even took him to a meeting or two—but he was uninterested. Shortly after that he moved his family to America." Mortmain spread his hands wide. "The Pandemonium Club is not for everyone. Traveling widely as I have, I heard stories of similar organizations in many cities, groups of men who know of the Shadow World and wish to share their knowledge and advantages, but one pays the heavy price of secrecy for membership."

"One pays a heavier price than that."

"It isn't an evil organization," Mortmain said. He sounded almost wounded. "There were many great advancements, many great inventions. I saw a warlock create a silver ring that could transport the wearer to another location whenever he twisted one around his finger. Or a doorway that could bring you anywhere in the world you wanted to go. I've seen men brought back from the brink of death—"

"I'm aware of magic and what it can do, Mr. Mortmain." Charlotte glanced at Henry, who was examining a blueprint for some sort of mechanical gadget, mounted on a wall. "There is one question that concerns me. The warlocks who appear to have kidnapped Mr. Gray are somehow associated with the club. I have always heard it called a club for mundanes. Why would there be Downworlders in it?"

Mortmain's forehead creased. "Downworlders? You mean the supernatural folk—warlocks and lycanthropes and the like? There are levels and levels of membership, Mrs. Branwell. A mundane such as myself can become a member of the club. But the chairmen—those who run the enterprise—they are Downworlders. Warlocks, lycanthropes, and vampires. The Fair Folk shun us, though. Too many captains of industry— railroads, factories, and the like—for them. They hate such things." He shook his head. "Lovely creatures, faeries, but I do fear progress will be the death of them."

Charlotte was uninterested in Mortmain's thoughts on faeries; her mind was whirling. "Let me guess. You introduced Nathaniel Gray to the club, exactly as you had introduced his father."

Mortmain, who had seemed to be regaining a bit of his old confidence, wilted again. "Nathaniel had worked in my office in London for only a few days before he confronted me. I gath- ered he had learned of his father's experience at the club, and it had given him a fierce desire to know more. I couldn't refuse. I brought him to a meeting and thought that would be the end of it. But it wasn't." He shook his head. "Nathaniel took to the club like a duck to water. A few weeks after that first meeting, he was gone from his lodging house. He sent a letter for me, terminating his employment and saying he was going to work for another Pandemonium Club member, someone who apparently was willing to pay him enough to sustain his gambling habits." He sighed. "Needless to say, he left no forwarding address."

"And that's all?" Charlotte's voice rose in disbelief. "You didn't try to look for him? Find out where he had gone? Who his new employer was?"

"A man can take employment where he likes," Mortmain said, blustering. "There was no reason to think—"

"And you haven't seen him since?"

"No. I told you—"

Charlotte cut him off. "You say he took to the Pandemonium Club like a duck to water, yet you haven't seen him at a single meeting since he left your employment?"

A look of panic flickered in Mortmain's eyes. "I . . . I have not been to a meeting since then myself. Work has kept me extremely busy."

Charlotte looked hard at Axel Mortmain across his massive desk. She was a good judge of character, she had always thought. It wasn't as if she hadn't come across men like Mortmain before. Bluff, genial, confident men, men who believed that their success in business or some other worldly pursuit meant that they would have the same success should they choose to pursue the magical arts. She thought of the barrister again, the walls of his Knightsbridge house painted scarlet with the blood of his family. She thought what his terror might have been like, in those last moments of his life. She could see the beginnings of a similar fear in Axel Mortmain's eyes.

"Mr. Mortmain," she said, "I am not a fool. I know there is something you are concealing from me." She took from her reticule one of the cogs that Will had retrieved from the Dark Sisters' house, and set it on the desk. "This looks like something your factories might produce."

With a distracted look Mortmain glanced down at the small piece of metal on his desk. "Yes—yes, that's one of my cogs. What of it?"

"Two warlocks calling themselves the Dark Sisters—both members of the Pandemonium Club—they've been murdering humans. Young girls. Barely more than children. And we found this in the cellar of their home."

"I've nothing to do with any murders!" Mortmain exclaimed. "I never—I thought—" He had begun to sweat.

"What did you think?" Charlotte's voice was soft.

Mortmain picked up the cog in shaking fingers. "You can't imagine . . ." His voice trailed off. "A few months ago one of the club's board members—a Downworlder, and very old and powerful—came to me and asked me to sell him some mechanical equipment cheaply. Cogs and cams and the like. I didn't ask what it was for—why would I? There seemed nothing remarkable about the request."

"By any chance," Charlotte said, "was this the same man whose employment Nathaniel joined after he left yours?"

Mortmain dropped the cog. As it rolled across the table,

he slammed his hand down on top of it, halting its progress. Though he said nothing, Charlotte could tell by the flicker of fear in his eyes that her guess was correct. A tingle of triumph ran through her nerves.

"His name," she said. "Tell me his name."

Mortmain was staring at the desk. "It would be worth my life to tell you."

"What about Nathaniel Gray's life?" said Charlotte.

Without meeting her eyes Mortmain shook his head. "You've no idea how powerful this man is. How dangerous."

Charlotte straightened up. "Henry," she said. "Henry, bring me the Summoner."

Henry turned away from the wall and blinked at her in confusion. "But, darling—"

"Bring me the device!" Charlotte snapped. She loathed snapping at Henry; it was like kicking a puppy. But sometimes it had to be done.

The look of confusion didn't leave Henry's face as he joined his wife before Mortmain's desk, and drew something from his jacket pocket. It was a dark metal oblong, with a series of peculiar-looking dials across the face of it. Charlotte took it and brandished it at Mortmain.

"This is a Summoner," she told him. "It will allow me to summon the Clave. Inside of three minutes they will surround your house. Nephilim will drag you from this room, screaming and kicking. They will perform upon you the most exquisite tortures until you are forced to speak. Do you know what happens to a man when demon blood is dripped into his eyes?"

Mortmain gave her a ghastly look, but said nothing.

"Please don't test me, Mr. Mortmain." The device in

Charlotte's hand was slippery with sweat, but her voice was even. "I would hate to watch you die."

"Good Lord, man, tell her!" Henry burst out. "Really, there's no need for this, Mr. Mortmain. You're only making it harder on yourself."

Mortmain covered his face with his hands. He had always wanted to meet real Shadowhunters, Charlotte thought, looking at him. And now he had.

"De Quincey," he said. "I don't know his first name. Just de Quincey."

By the Angel. Charlotte exhaled slowly, lowering the device to her side. "De Quincey? It can't be . . ."

"You know who he is?" Mortmain's voice was dull. "Well, I suppose you would."

"He's the head of a powerful London vampire clan," Charlotte said almost reluctantly, "a very influential Downworlder, and an ally of the Clave. I can't imagine that he would—"

"He's the head of the club," said Mortmain. He looked exhausted, and a little gray. "Everyone else answers to him."

"The head of the club. Has he a title?"

Mortmain looked faintly surprised to be asked. "The Magister."

With a hand that shook only slightly, Charlotte slipped the device she had been holding into her sleeve. "Thank you, Mr. Mortmain. You've been most helpful."

Mortmain looked at her with a sort of drained resentment. "De Quincey will find out that I've told you. He'll have me killed."

"The Clave will see that he does not. And we will keep your name out of this. He shall never know you spoke to us."

"You would do that?" Mortmain said softly. "For what was it—a foolish mundane?"

"I have hopes for you, Mr. Mortmain. You seem to have realized your own folly. The Clave will be watching you—not only for your own protection, but to see that you stay away from the Pandemonium Club and organizations like it. For your own sake, I hope you will regard our meeting as a warning."

Mortmain nodded. Charlotte moved to the door, Henry behind her; she already had it open and was standing on the threshold when Mortmain spoke again. "They were only cogs," he said softly. "Only gears. Harmless."

It was Henry, to Charlotte's surprise, who replied, without turning, "Inanimate objects are harmless indeed, Mr. Mortmain. But one cannot always say the same of the men who use them."

Mortmain was silent as the two Shadowhunters left the room. A few moments later they were out in the square, breathing fresh air—as fresh as the air of London ever was. It might be thick with coal smoke and dust, Charlotte thought, but at least it was free of the fear and desperation that had hung like a haze in Mortmain's study.

Drawing the device from her sleeve, Charlotte offered it to her husband. "I suppose I ought to ask you," she said as he received it with a grave expression, "what *is* that object, Henry?"

"Something I've been working on." Henry looked at it fondly. "A device that can sense demon energies. I was going to call it a Sensor. I haven't got it working yet, but when I do!"

"I'm sure it will be splendid."

Henry transferred his fond expression from the device

to his wife, a rare occurrence. "What pure genius, Charlotte. Pretending you could summon the Clave on the spot, just to frighten that man! But how did you know I'd have a device you could put to your uses?"

"Well, you did, darling," said Charlotte. "Didn't you?"

Henry looked sheepish. "You are as terrifying as you are wonderful, my dear."

"Thank you, Henry."

The ride back to the Institute was a silent one; Jessamine stared out the window of the cab at the snarling London traffic and refused to say a word. She held her parasol across her lap, seemingly indifferent to the fact that the blood on its edges was staining her taffeta jacket. When they reached the churchyard, she let Thomas help her down from the carriage before reaching to grip Tessa's hand.

Surprised at the contact, Tessa could only stare. Jessamine's fingers in hers were icy. "Come *along*," Jessamine snapped impatiently, and pulled her companion toward the Institute doors, leaving Thomas staring after them.

Tessa let the other girl draw her up the stairs, into the Institute proper, and down a long corridor, this one almost identical to the one outside Tessa's bedroom. Jessamine located a door, pushed Tessa through it, and followed, shutting the door behind them. "I want to show you something," she said.

Tessa looked around. It was another of the large bedrooms of which the Institute seemed to have an infinite number. Jessamine's, though, had been decorated somewhat to her taste. Above the wooden wainscoting the walls were papered in rose silk, and the coverlet on the bed was printed with flowers. There was a white vanity table too, its surface covered with an expensive-looking dressing table set: a ring stand, a bottle of flower water, and a silver-backed hairbrush and mirror.

"Your room is lovely," Tessa said, more in hopes of calming Jessamine's evident hysteria than because she meant it.

"It's much too small," Jessamine said. "But come—over here." And flinging the bloodied parasol down onto her bed, she marched across the room to a corner by the window. Tessa followed with some puzzlement. There was nothing in the corner but a high table, and on the table was a dollhouse. Not the sort of two-room cardboard Dolly's Playhouse that Tessa had had as a child. This was a beautiful miniature reproduction of a real London town house, and when Jessamine touched it, Tessa saw that the front of it swung open on tiny hinges.

Tessa caught her breath. There were beautiful tiny rooms perfectly decorated with miniature furniture, everything built to scale, from the little wooden chairs with needlepoint cushions to the cast-iron stove in the kitchen. There were small dolls, too, with china heads, and real little oil paintings on the walls.

"This was my house." Jessamine knelt down, bringing herself to eye level with the dollhouse rooms, and gestured for Tessa to do the same.

Awkwardly, Tessa did, trying not to kneel on Jessamine's skirts. "You mean this was the dollhouse you had when you were a little girl?"

"No." Jessamine sounded irritated. "This was my *house*. My father had this made for me when I was six. It's modeled exactly on the house we lived in, on Curzon Street. This was the wallpaper we had in the dining room"—she pointed—"and those are exactly the chairs in my father's study. You see?"

She looked at Tessa intently, so intently that Tessa felt sure she was supposed to be seeing something here, something beyond an extremely expensive toy that Jessamine should have long ago grown out of. She simply didn't know what that could be. "It's very pretty," she said finally.

"See, here in the parlor is Mama," said Jessamine, touching one of the tiny dolls with her finger. The doll wobbled in its plush armchair. "And here in the study, reading a book, is Papa." Her hand glided over the little porcelain figure. "And upstairs in the nursery is Baby Jessie." Inside the little crib there was indeed another doll, only its head visible above tiny coverlets. "Later they'll have dinner here, in the dining room. And then Mama and Papa will sit in the drawing room by the fire. Some nights they go to the theater, or to a ball or a dinner." Her voice had grown hushed, as if she were reciting a well-remembered litany. "And then Mama will kiss Papa good night, and they will go to their rooms, and they will sleep *all night long*. There will be no calls from the Clave that drive them out in the middle of the night to fight demons in the dark. There will be no one tracking blood into the house. No one will lose an arm or an eye to a werewolf, or have to choke down holy water because a vampire attacked them."

Dear God, Tessa thought.

As if Jessamine could read Tessa's mind, her face twisted. "When our house burned, I had nowhere else to go. It wasn't as if there were relations that could take me in; all of Mama and Papa's relations were Shadowhunters and hadn't spoken to them since they'd broken with the Clave. Henry is the one who made me that parasol. Did you know that? I thought it was quite pretty until he told me that the fabric is edged with electrum, as sharp as a razor. It was always meant to be a weapon."

"You saved us," Tessa said. "In the park today. I can't fight at all. If you hadn't done what you did—"

"I shouldn't have done it." Jessamine stared into the dollhouse with empty eyes. "I will not have this life, Tessa. I *will not have it.* I don't care what I have to do. I won't live like this. I'd rather die."

Alarmed, Tessa was about to tell her not to talk like that, when the door opened behind them. It was Sophie, in her white cap and neat dark dress. Her eyes, when they rested on Jessamine, were wary. She said, "Miss Tessa, Mr. Branwell very much wants to see you in his study. He says it's important."

Tessa turned to Jessamine to ask her if she would be all right, but Jessamine's face had closed like a door. The vulnerability and anger were gone; the cold mask was back. "Go along, then, if Henry wants you," she said. "I'm quite tired of you already, and I think I'm getting a headache. Sophie, when you return, I'll need you to massage my temples with eau de cologne."

Sophie's eyes met Tessa's across the room with something like amusement. "As you like, Miss Jessamine."

7

THE CLOCKWORK
GIRL

But helpless Pieces of the Game He plays
Upon this chequer-board of Nights and Days
Hither and thither moves, and checks and slays.
—"The Rubaiyat of Omar Khayyam,"
translated by Edward FitzGerald, 1859

It had grown dark outside the Institute, and Sophie's lantern cast strange dancing shadows on the walls as she led Tessa down one flight of stone stairs after another. The steps were old, concave in the centers, where generations of feet had worn them down. The walls were roughly textured stone, the tiny windows set into them at intervals giving way eventually to blankness that seemed to indicate that they had passed belowground.

"Sophie," Tessa said finally, her nerves rubbed raw by the darkness and silence, "are we going down into the church *crypt*, by any chance?"

Sophie chuckled, and the lights of the lantern flickered on the walls. "It used to be the crypt, before Mr. Branwell had it fixed up into a laboratory for himself. He's always down there, tinkering with his toys and his experiments. It doesn't half drive Mrs. Branwell wild."

"What's he making?" Tessa nearly tripped over an uneven stair, and had to grab for the wall to right herself. Sophie didn't appear to notice.

"All sorts of things," Sophie said, her voice echoing strangely off the walls. "Inventing new weapons, protective gear for the Shadowhunters. He loves clockwork and mechanisms and that sort of thing. Mrs. Branwell sometimes says she thinks he'd love her better if she ticked like a clock." She laughed.

"It sounds," Tessa said, "as if you're fond of them. Mr. and Mrs. Branwell, I mean."

Sophie said nothing, but the already proud set of her back seemed to harden slightly.

"Fonder of them than you are of Will, anyway," Tessa said, hoping to soften the other girl's mood with humor.

"*Him.*" The disgust was plain in Sophie's voice. "He's— Well, he's a bad sort, isn't he? Reminds me of the son of my last employer. He was proud just like Mr. Herondale. And whatever he wanted, he got, from the day he was born. And if he didn't get it, well . . ." She reached up then, almost unconsciously, and touched the side of her face, where the scar ran from mouth to temple.

"Then what?"

But Sophie's brusque manner was back. "Then he'd be like to pitch a fit, that's all." Transferring her glowing lantern from one hand to the other, she peered down into the shadowy darkness. "Be careful here, miss. The stairs can get awfully damp and slippery toward the bottom."

Tessa moved closer to the wall. The stone was cold against her bare hand. "Do you think it's simply because Will's a Shadowhunter?" she inquired. "And they— Well, they rather think they're superior, don't they? Jessamine, too—"

"But Mr. Carstairs is *not* like that. He isn't at all like the others. And neither are Mr. and Mrs. Branwell."

Before Tessa could say anything else, they came to an abrupt stop at the foot of the stairs. There was a heavy oak door there with a barred grille set into it; Tessa could see nothing through the grille but shadows. Sophie reached for the wide iron bar across the door and pushed it down, hard.

The door swung open onto an enormous brightly lit space. Tessa moved into the room with wide eyes; this had clearly been the crypt of the church that had originally stood on this spot. Squat pillars held up a roof that disappeared into darkness. The floor was made up of great stone slabs darkened with age; some were carved with words, and Tessa guessed that she stood on the gravestones—and the bones—of those who had been buried in the crypt. There were no windows, but the bright white illumination that Tessa had come to know as witchlight shone down from brass fixtures fastened to the pillars.

In the center of the room were a number of large wooden tables, their surfaces covered with all manner of mechanical objects—gears and cogs made of dully shining brass and iron; long strings of copper wire; glass beakers filled with liquids of different colors, some of them giving off wisps of smoke or bitter odors. The air smelled metallic and sharp, like the air before a storm. One table was entirely covered with a scatter of weapons, the blades shining under the witchlight. There was a half-finished suit of what looked like thinly scaled metal armor, hanging on a wire frame by a great stone table whose surface was concealed by a lumpy cluster of thick woolen blankets.

Behind the table stood Henry, and beside him, Charlotte. Henry was showing his wife something he held in his hand—a copper wheel, perhaps a gear—and was speaking to her in a low voice. He wore a loose canvas shirt over his clothes, like a fisherman's smock, and it was smeared with dirt and dark fluid. Still, what struck Tessa most about him was the assurance with which he spoke to Charlotte. There was none of his usual diffidence. He sounded confident and direct, and his hazel eyes, when he raised them to look at Tessa, were clear and steady.

"Miss Gray! So Sophie showed you the way down here, did she? Very good of her."

"Why, yes, she—," Tessa began, glancing behind her, but Sophie was not there. She must have turned at the door and gone soundlessly back up the stairs. Tessa felt foolish for not having noticed. "She did," she finished. "She said that you wanted to see me?"

"Indeed," Henry said. "We could use your help with something. Could you come over here for a moment?"

He gestured for her to join him and Charlotte by the table. As Tessa approached, she saw that Charlotte's face was white and pinched, her brown eyes shadowed. She looked at Tessa, bit her lip, and glanced down toward the table, where the heaped fabric—*moved.*

Tessa blinked. Had she imagined it? But no, there had been a flicker of movement—and now that she was closer, she saw that what was on the table was not so much a pile of fabric as fabric *covering* something—something approximately the size and shape of a human body. She stopped in her tracks, as Henry reached out, took hold of a corner of the fabric, and drew it away, revealing what lay beneath.

Tessa, feeling suddenly dizzy, reached to grasp the edge of the table. "*Miranda.*"

The dead girl lay on her back on the table, her arms flung out to either side, her dull brown hair straggling down around her shoulders. The eyes that had so unnerved Tessa were gone. Now there were hollow black sockets in her white face. Her cheap dress had been cut open down the front, baring her chest. Tessa winced, looked away—and then looked back quickly, in disbelief. For there was no naked flesh, and no blood, despite the fact that Miranda's chest had been sliced open down the front, her skin peeled back on either side like the skin of an orange. Beneath the grotesque mutilation gleamed the brightness of—metal?

Tessa moved forward until she was standing across from Henry at the table where Miranda lay. Where there should have been blood, torn flesh, and mutilation, there were only the two sheets of white skin folded back, and beneath them a carapace of metal. Sheets of copper, intricately fitted together, made up her chest, flowing smoothly down into a jointed cage of copper and flexible brass that was Miranda's waist. A square of copper, about the size of Tessa's palm, was missing from the center of the dead girl's chest, revealing a hollow space.

"Tessa." Charlotte's voice was soft but insistent. "Will and

Jem found this—this body in the house where you were kept. The house was completely empty except for her; she'd been left in a room, alone."

Tessa, still staring in fascination, nodded. "Miranda. The Sisters' maidservant."

"Do you know anything about her? Who she might be? Her history?"

"No. No. I thought . . . I mean, she hardly ever spoke, and then she only repeated things the Sisters had said."

Henry hooked a finger into Miranda's lower lip and pulled her mouth open. "She has a rudimentary metal tongue, but her mouth was never really constructed for speech, or for consuming food. She has no gullet, and I would guess no stomach. Her mouth ends in a sheet of metal behind her teeth." He turned her head from side to side, his eyes narrowing.

"But what *is* she?" Tessa asked. "A sort of Downworlder, or demon?"

"No." Henry let go of Miranda's jaw. "She is not precisely a *living* creature at all. She is an automaton. A mechanical creature, made to move and appear as a human being moves and appears. Leonardo da Vinci designed one. You can find it in his drawings—a mechanical creature that could sit up, walk, and turn its head. He was the first to suggest that human beings are only complex machines, that our insides are like cogs and pistons and cams made of muscle and flesh. So why could they not be replaced with copper and iron? Why couldn't you *build* a person? But *this*. Jaquet Droz and Maillardet could never have dreamed of this. A true biomechanical automaton, self-moving, self-directing, wrapped in human flesh." His eyes shone. "It's beautiful."

"Henry." Charlotte's voice was tight. "That flesh you're admiring. It came from *somewhere*."

Henry passed the back of his hand across his forehead, the light dying out of his eyes. "Yes—those bodies in the cellar."

"The Silent Brothers have examined them. Most are missing organs—hearts, livers. Some are missing bones and cartilage, even hair. We cannot but assume the Dark Sisters were harvesting these bodies for parts to create their mechanical creatures. Creatures like Miranda."

"And the coachman," Tessa said. "I think he was one as well. But why would anyone do such a thing?"

"There is more," Charlotte said. "The mechanical tools in the Dark Sisters' cellar were manufactured by Mortmain and Company. The company your brother worked for."

"Mortmain!" Tessa tore her gaze from the girl on the table. "You went to see him, didn't you? What did he say about Nate?"

For a moment Charlotte hesitated, glancing at Henry. Tessa knew that glance. It was the sort of glance people gave each other when they were preparing to engage in a joint falsehood. The sort of look she and Nathaniel had given each other, once, when they'd been concealing something from Aunt Harriet.

"You're hiding something from me," she said. "Where's my brother? What does Mortmain know?"

Charlotte sighed. "Mortmain is deeply involved in the occult underworld. He's a member of the Pandemonium Club, which seems to be run by Downworlders."

"But what has that to do with my brother?"

"Your brother found out about the club and was fascinated by it. He went to work for a vampire named de Quincey. A very influential Downworlder. De Quincey is in fact the head of the

Pandemonium Club." Charlotte sounded bitterly disgusted. "There is a title to go with the job, it seems."

Feeling suddenly dizzy, Tessa braced her hand against the edge of the table. "The Magister?"

Charlotte looked at Henry, who had his hand inside the creature's chest panel. He reached in and drew something out—a human heart, red and fleshy, but hard and shiny-looking as if it had been lacquered. It had been bound around with copper and silver wires. Every few moments it would give a listless thump. Somehow it was still beating. "Would you like to hold it?" he asked Tessa. "You'd have to be careful. These copper tubes wind throughout the creature's body, carrying oil and other flammable liquids. I have yet to identify them all."

Tessa shook her head.

"Very well." Henry looked disappointed. "There was something I wished you to see. If you'll simply look here—" He turned the heart carefully in his long fingers, revealing a flat metal panel on the opposite side of it. The panel had been etched with a seal—a large Q, a small D inside it.

"De Quincey's mark," said Charlotte. She looked bleak. "I've seen it before, on correspondence from him. He's always been an ally of the Clave, or so I thought. He was there at the Accords when they were signed. He's a powerful man. He controls all the Night Children in the western part of the city. Mortmain says that de Quincey bought mechanical parts from him, and this would seem to bear that out. It looks as if you weren't the only thing in the Dark Sisters' house that was being prepared for the Magister's use. These clockwork creatures were as well."

"If this vampire is the Magister," Tessa said slowly, "then he is the one who had the Dark Sisters capture me, and he is the one who forced Nate to write me that letter. He must know where my brother is."

Charlotte almost smiled. "You *are* single-minded, aren't you."

Tessa's voice was hard. "Don't imagine that I don't want to know what the Magister wants with me. Why he had me captured and trained. How on earth he knew I had my—my ability. And don't think I wouldn't want revenge if I could have it." She took a shuddering breath. "But my brother is all I have. I must find him."

"*We* will find him, Tessa," Charlotte said. "Somehow all of this—the Dark Sisters, your brother, your own ability, and de Quincey's involvement—fits together like a puzzle. We simply haven't found all the missing bits of it yet."

"I must say, I hope we find them soon," Henry said, casting a sad glance at the body on the table. "What could a vampire want with a lot of half-mechanical people? None of this makes any sense."

"Not yet," said Charlotte, and she set her small chin. "But it will."

Henry remained in his laboratory even after Charlotte had announced that it was past time for them to return upstairs for supper. Insisting that he would be along in five minutes, he waved them off absently as Charlotte shook her head.

"Henry's laboratory—I've never seen anything like it," Tessa said to Charlotte when they were halfway up the stairs. She was already out of breath, though Charlotte was moving with a steady, purposeful gait and looked as if she would never tire.

"Yes," Charlotte replied a little sadly. "Henry would spend all day and all night there if I allowed it."

If I allowed it. The words surprised Tessa. It was the husband, wasn't it, who decided what was and was not allowed, and how his home should be run? The wife's duty was simply to carry out his wishes, and to provide him with a calm and stable refuge from the chaos of the world. A place he might retreat. But the Institute was hardly that. It was part home, part boarding school, and part battle station. And whoever might be in charge of it, it clearly wasn't Henry.

With an exclamation of surprise, Charlotte stopped short on the step above Tessa. "Jessamine! What on earth's the matter?"

Tessa looked up. Jessamine stood at the head of the stairs, framed in the open doorway. She still wore her day clothes, though her hair, now in elaborate ringlets, had clearly been arranged for evening, no doubt by the ever-patient Sophie. There was an immense scowl on her face.

"It's Will," she said. "He's being absolutely ridiculous in the dining room."

Charlotte looked puzzled. "How is this different from his being totally ridiculous in the library or the weapons room or any of the other places he's usually ridiculous?"

"Because," Jessamine said, as if this should be obvious, "we have to *eat* in the dining room." She turned and flounced off down the hallway, glancing back over her shoulder to make sure that Tessa and Charlotte were following her.

Tessa couldn't help but smile. "It is a bit like they're your children, isn't it?"

Charlotte sighed. "Yes," she said. "Except for the part where they're required to love me, I suppose."

Tessa could think of nothing to say in reply to that.

* * *

Since Charlotte insisted that there was something she had to do in the drawing room before supper, Tessa made her way to the dining room by herself. Once she had arrived there—quite proud of herself for not having lost her way—she found that Will was standing on one of the sideboards, tinkering with something attached to the ceiling.

Jem was seated in a chair, looking up at Will with a dubious expression. "It serves you right if you break it," he said, and inclined his head as he caught sight of Tessa. "Good evening, Tessa." Following her stare, he grinned. "I was hanging the gasolier crookedly, and Will is endeavoring to straighten it."

Tessa could see nothing wrong with the gasolier, but before she could say so, Jessamine stalked into the room and shot a glare at Will. "Really! Can't you get Thomas to do that? A gentleman needn't—"

"Is that blood on your sleeve, Jessie?" Will inquired, glancing down.

Jessamine's face tightened. Without another word she turned on her heel and stalked to the far end of the table, where she set herself down in a chair and stared stonily ahead.

"Did something happen while you and Jessamine were out?" It was Jem, looking genuinely worried. As he turned his head to look at Tessa, she saw something green gleam against the base of his throat.

Jessamine looked over at Tessa, a look of near panic on her face. "No," Tessa began. "It was nothing—"

"I've done it!" Henry entered the room triumphantly, brandishing something in his hand. It looked like a copper tube with a black button on one side. "I'll wager you didn't think I could, did you?"

Will abandoned his efforts with the gasolier to glare at Henry. "None of us have the slightest idea what you're on about. You do know that?"

"I've gotten my Phosphor to work at last." Henry proudly brandished the object. "It functions on the principle of witchlight but is five times more powerful. Merely press a button, and you will see a blaze of light the like of which you have never imagined."

There was a silence. "So," said Will finally, "it's a very, very bright witchlight, then?"

"Exactly," Henry said.

"Is that useful, precisely?" Jem inquired. "After all, witchlight is just for illumination. It's not as if it's dangerous. . . ."

"Wait till you see it!" Henry replied. He held up the object. "Watch."

Will moved to object, but it was too late; Henry had already pressed the button. There was a blinding flare of light and a whooshing sound, and the room was plunged into blackness. Tessa gave a yelp of surprise, and Jem laughed softly.

"Am I blind?" Will's voice floated out of the darkness, tinged with annoyance. "I'm not going to be at all pleased if you've blinded me, Henry."

"No." Henry sounded worried. "No, the Phosphor seems to— Well, it seems to have turned all the lights in the room *off.*"

"It's not supposed to do that?" Jem sounded mild, as always.

"Er," said Henry, "no."

Will muttered something under his breath. Tessa couldn't quite hear him, but was fairly sure she'd caught the words "Henry" and "fatheaded." A moment later there was an enormous crash.

"Will!' someone cried out in alarm. Bright light filled the room, sending Tessa into a fit of blinking. Charlotte was standing in the doorway, holding a witchlight lamp aloft in one hand, and Will was lying on the floor at her feet in a welter of broken crockery from the sideboard. "What on earth . . ."

"I was trying to straighten the gasolier," Will said crossly, sitting up and brushing crockery bits off his shirt.

"Thomas could have done that. And now you've gone and wrecked half the plates."

"And much obliged to your idiot husband for that." Will looked down at himself. "I think I've broken something. The pain is quite agonizing."

"You seem quite intact to me." Charlotte was remorseless. "Get up. I suppose we'll be eating by witchlight tonight."

Jessamine, down at the end of the table, sniffed. It was the first noise she'd made since Will had asked her about the blood on her jacket. "I *hate* witchlight. It makes my complexion look absolutely green."

Despite Jessamine's greenness, Tessa found she rather liked the witchlight. It laid a diffuse white glow over everything and made even the peas and onions look romantic and mysterious. As she buttered a dinner roll with a heavy silver knife, she couldn't help but think of the small apartment in Manhattan where she, her brother, and her aunt had eaten their meager suppers around a plain deal table by the light of a few candles. Aunt Harriet had always been careful to keep everything so scrupulously clean, from the white lace curtains at the front windows to the shining copper kettle on the stove. She had always said that the less you had, the more careful you had to be about everything you *did* have. Tessa wondered if the Shadowhunters were careful about everything they had.

Charlotte and Henry were recounting what they had learned from Mortmain; Jem and Will listened attentively while Jessamine gazed in boredom at the window. Jem seemed especially interested in the description of Mortmain's house, with its artifacts from all over the globe. "I told you," he said. "Taipan. They all think of themselves as very important men. Above the law."

"Yes," Charlotte said. "He had that manner about him, as if he were used to being listened to. Men like that are often easy marks for those who want to draw them into the Shadow World. They are used to having power and expect to be able to get more power easily and with little cost to themselves. They have no idea how high the price for power in Downworld is." She turned, frowning, to Will and Jessamine, who seemed to be quarreling about something in snappish tones. "What is the matter with you two?"

Tessa took the opportunity to turn to Jem, who was sitting on her right side. "Shanghai," she said in a low voice. "It sounds so fascinating. I wish I could travel there. I've always wanted to travel."

As Jem smiled at her, she saw that gleam again at his throat. It was a pendant carved out of dull green stone. "And now you have. You're here, aren't you?"

"I've only ever traveled before in books. I know that sounds silly, but—"

Jessamine interrupted them by slamming her fork down onto the table. "Charlotte," she demanded shrilly, "make Will let me *alone*."

Will was leaning back in his chair, his blue eyes glittering. "If she'd say why she has blood on her clothes, I *would* leave her alone. Let me guess, Jessie. You ran across some poor woman in the park who had the misfortune of wearing a gown that clashed with yours, so you slit her throat with that clever little parasol of yours. Do I have it right?"

Jessamine bared her teeth at him. "You're being ridiculous."

"You are, you know," Charlotte told him.

"I mean, I'm wearing blue. Blue goes with *everything*," Jessamine went on. "Which, really, you ought to know. You're vain enough about your own clothes."

"Blue does not go with everything," Will told her. "It does not go with red, for instance."

"I have a red and blue striped waistcoat," Henry interjected, reaching for the peas.

"And if *that* isn't proof that those two colors should never be seen together under Heaven, I don't know what is."

"Will," Charlotte said sharply. "Don't speak to Henry like that. Henry—"

Henry raised his head. "Yes?"

Charlotte sighed. "That's Jessamine's plate you're spooning peas onto, not yours. Do pay attention, darling."

As Henry looked down in surprise, the dining room door opened and Sophie came in. Her head was down, her dark hair shining. As she bent to speak softly to Charlotte, the witchlight cast its harsh glow over her face, making her scar gleam like silver against her skin.

A look of relief spread over Charlotte's face. A moment later she had risen to her feet and hurried out of the room, pausing only to touch Henry lightly on the shoulder as she went.

Jessamine's brown eyes widened. "Where's she going?"

Will looked at Sophie, his gaze sliding over her in that way that Tessa knew was like fingertips stroking over your skin. "Indeed, Sophie, my dear. Where *did* she go?"

Sophie shot him a venomous look. "If Mrs. Branwell had wanted you to know, I'm sure she would have told you," she snapped, and hurried out of the room after her mistress.

Henry, having set down the peas, attempted a genial smile. "Well, then," he said. "What was it we were discussing?"

"None of that," Will said. "We want to know where Charlotte's gone. Did something happen?"

"No," Henry said. "I mean, I don't *think* so—" He glanced around the room, saw four pairs of eyes fixed on him, and sighed. "Charlotte doesn't always tell me what she's doing. You know that." He smiled a little painfully. "Can't blame her, really. Can't count on me to be sensible."

Tessa wished she could say something to comfort Henry. Something about him made her think of Nate when he was younger, gawkish and awkward and easily hurt. Reflexively she put up her hand to touch the angel at her throat, seeking reassurance in its steady ticking.

Henry looked over at her. "That clockwork object you wear around your neck—might I see it for a moment?"

Tessa hesitated, then nodded. It was only Henry, after all. She unhooked the clasp of the chain, drew off the necklace, and handed it to him.

"This is a clever little object," he said, turning it over in his hands. "Where did you get it?"

"It was my mother's."

"Like a sort of talisman." He glanced up. "Would you mind if I examined it in the laboratory?"

"Oh." Tessa couldn't hide her anxiety. "If you're very careful with it. It's all I have of my mother's. If it were broken . . ."

"Henry won't break or damage it," Jem reassured her. "He's really very good with this sort of thing."

"It's true," said Henry, so modest and matter-of-fact about it that there seemed nothing conceited about the statement. "I'll return it to you in pristine condition."

"Well . . ." Tessa hesitated.

"I don't see what the fuss is," said Jessamine, who had looked bored throughout this exchange. "It's not like it has diamonds in it."

"Some people value sentiment over diamonds, Jessamine." It was Charlotte, standing in the doorway. She looked troubled. "There is someone here who wants to speak with you, Tessa."

"With *me*?" Tessa demanded, the clockwork angel forgotten for the moment.

"Well, who *is* it?" Will said. "Must you keep us all in suspense?"

Charlotte sighed. "It's Lady Belcourt. She's downstairs. In the Sanctuary Room."

"Now?" Will frowned. "Did something happen?"

"I contacted her," said Charlotte. "About de Quincey. Just before supper. I hoped she would have some information, and she does, but she insists on seeing Tessa first. It seems that despite all our precautions, rumors about Tessa have leaked into Downworld, and Lady Belcourt is . . . interested."

Tessa set her fork down with a clatter. "Interested in what?"

She looked around the table, realizing that four pairs of eyes were now fixed on *her*. "Who is Lady Belcourt?" When no one replied, she turned to Jem as the likeliest to give her an answer. "Is she a Shadowhunter?"

"She's a vampire," Jem said. "A vampire *informant*, actually. She gives information to Charlotte and keeps us apprised of what's going on in the Night community."

"You needn't speak to her if you don't want to, Tessa," Charlotte said. "I can send her away."

"No." Tessa pushed her plate away. "If she's well informed about de Quincey, perhaps she knows something about Nate as well. I can't risk her being sent off if she might have information. I'll go."

"Don't you even want to know what she wants from you?" Will asked.

Tessa looked at him measuredly. The witchlight made his skin paler, his eyes more intently blue. They were the color of the water of the North Atlantic, where the ice drifted on its blue-black surface like snow clinging to the dark glass pane of a window. "Aside from the Dark Sisters, I've never really met another Downworlder," she said. "I think—that I would like to."

"Tessa—," Jem began, but she was already on her feet. Not looking back at anyone at the table, she hurried out of the room after Charlotte.

8

CAMILLE

Fruits fail and love dies and time ranges;
Thou art fed with perpetual breath,
And alive after infinite changes,
And fresh from the kisses of death;
Of langours rekindled and rallied,
Of barren delights and unclean,
Things monstrous and fruitless, a pallid
And poisonous queen.
—Algernon Charles Swinburne, "Dolores"

Tessa was only halfway down the corridor when they caught up to her—Will and Jem, walking on either side of her. "You didn't *really* think we weren't going to come along, did you?" Will asked, raising his hand and letting the witchlight flare up between his fingers, lighting the corridor to daylight brightness. Charlotte, hurrying along ahead of them, turned and frowned, but said nothing.

"I know *you* can't leave anything well enough alone," Tessa replied, looking straight ahead. "But I thought better of Jem."

"Where Will goes, I go," Jem said good-naturedly. "And besides, I'm as curious as he is."

"That hardly seems a subject for boasting. Where *are* we going?" Tessa added, startled, as they reached the end of the corridor and turned left. The next hall stretched away behind them into unprepossessing shadow. "Have we turned the wrong way?"

"Patience is a virtue, Miss Gray," said Will. They had reached a long corridor that sloped precipitously downward. The walls were bare of tapestries or torches, and the dimness made Tessa realize why Will had carried his witchlight stone.

"This corridor leads to our Sanctuary," said Charlotte. "It is the only part of the Institute that is not on hallowed ground. It is where we meet with those who, for whatever reason, cannot enter hallowed ground: those who are cursed, vampires, and the like. It is also often a place we choose to shelter Downworlders who are in danger from demons or other denizens of the Shadow World. For that reason, there are many protections placed on the doors, and it is difficult to enter or exit the room without possessing either a stele or the key."

"Is it a curse? Being a vampire?" Tessa asked.

Charlotte shook her head. "No. We think it is a sort of demon disease. Most diseases that affect demons are not transmissible to human beings, but in some cases, usually through a bite or a scratch, the disease can be passed on. Vampirism. Lycanthropy—"

"Demon pox," said Will.

"Will, there's no such thing as demon pox, and you know it," Charlotte said. "Now, where was I?"

"Being a vampire isn't a curse. It's a disease," Tessa filled in. "But they still can't enter hallowed ground, then? Does that mean they're damned?"

"That depends on what you believe," said Jem. "And whether you even believe in damnation at all."

"But you hunt demons. You must believe in damnation!"

"I believe in good and evil," said Jem. "And I believe the soul is eternal. But I don't believe in the fiery pit, the pitchforks, or endless torment. I do not believe you can threaten people into goodness."

Tessa looked at Will. "What about you? What do you believe?"

"*Pulvis et umbra sumus*," said Will, not looking at her as he spoke. "I believe we are dust and shadows. What else is there?"

"Whatever you believe, please don't suggest to Lady Belcourt that you think she's damned," said Charlotte. She had come to a halt where the corridor ended in a set of high iron doors, each carved with a curious symbol that looked like two pairs of back-to-back Cs. She turned and looked at her three companions. "She has very kindly offered to help us, and there's no purpose in offering her such insults. That applies to you especially, Will. If you can't be polite, I'll send you out of the Sanctuary. Jem, I trust you to be your charming self. Tessa . . ." Charlotte turned her grave, kind eyes on Tessa. "Try not to be frightened."

She drew an iron key from a pocket of her dress, and slid it into the lock of the door. The head of the key was in the shape of an angel with outspread wings; the wings gleamed out once, briefly, as Charlotte turned the key, and the door swung open.

The room beyond was like the vault of a treasure-house. There were no windows, and no doors save the one they had entered through. Enormous stone pillars held up a shadowed roof, illuminated by the light of a row of burning candelabras. The pillars were carved all around with loops and scrolls of runes, forming intricate patterns that teased the eye. Huge tapestries hung down from the walls, each one slashed with the figure of a single rune. There was a great gilt-framed mirror, too, making the place seem twice as large. A massive stone fountain rose in the middle of the room. It had a circular base, and in the center was the statue of an angel with folded wings. Rivers of tears poured from its eyes and plashed into the fountain below.

Beside the fountain, between two of the massive pillars, stood a group of chairs upholstered in black velvet. The woman who sat in the tallest of the chairs was slender and stately. A hat was tipped forward on her head, balancing a massive black plume at its top. Her dress was of rich red velvet, her icy white skin swelling gently over the fitted bodice, though her chest never rose or fell with a breath. A rope of rubies wound her throat like a scar. Her hair was thick and pale blond, clustered in delicate icy curls around her nape; her eyes were a luminous green that shone like a cat's.

Tessa caught her breath. So Downworlders could be beautiful.

"Douse your witchlight, Will," Charlotte said under her breath, before hurrying forward to greet her guest. "So good of you to wait for us, Baroness. I trust you have found the Sanctuary comfortable enough for your tastes?"

"As always, Charlotte." Lady Belcourt sounded bored; she had a faint accent that Tessa couldn't identify.

"Lady Belcourt. Please let me introduce you to Miss Theresa Gray." Charlotte indicated Tessa, who, not knowing what else to do, inclined her head politely. She was trying to remember how one addressed baronesses. She rather thought it had something to do with whether they were married to barons or not, but she couldn't exactly recall. "Beside her is Mr. James Carstairs, one of our young Shadowhunters, and with him is—"

But Lady Belcourt's green eyes were already resting on Will. "William Herondale," she said, and smiled. Tessa tensed, but the vampire's teeth seemed absolutely normal; no sign of sharpened incisors. "Fancy you coming to greet me."

"You *know* each other?" Charlotte looked astonished.

"William won twenty pounds from me at faro," said Lady Belcourt, her green gaze lingering on Will in a way that made Tessa's neck prickle. "A few weeks ago, in a Downworld gambling house run by the Pandemonium Club."

"He did?" Charlotte looked at Will, who shrugged.

"It was part of the investigation. I was disguised as a foolish mundane who had come to the place to partake in vice," explained Will. "It would have aroused suspicion had I refused to gamble."

Charlotte set her chin. "Nevertheless, Will, that money you won was evidence. You should have given it to the Clave."

"I spent it on gin."

"*Will.*"

Will shrugged. "The spoils of vice are a burdensome responsibility."

"Yet one you seem strangely able to bear," observed Jem, with an amused flash of his silvery eyes.

Charlotte threw up her hands. "I will deal with you later, William. Lady Belcourt, am I to understand that you also are a member of the Pandemonium Club?"

Lady Belcourt made a dreadful face. "Certainly not. I was at the gambling house that night because a warlock friend of mine was hoping to win a little easy money at cards. The club's events are open to most Downworlders. The members like us to appear there; it impresses the mundanes and opens their pocketbooks. I know there are Downworlders running the enterprise, but I would never become one of them. The entire business seems so déclassé."

"De Quincey is a member," said Charlotte, and behind her large brown eyes, Tessa could see the light of her fierce intelligence. "I have been told he is the head of the organization, in fact. Did you know that?"

Lady Belcourt shook her head, clearly uninterested in this piece of information. "De Quincey and I were close years ago, but no longer, and I have been direct with him about my lack of interest in the club. I suppose he could be the head of the club; it's a ridiculous organization, if you ask me, but doubtless very lucrative." She leaned forward, folding her slim gloved hands in her lap. There was something oddly fascinating about her movements, even the smallest ones. They had a strange animal grace. It was like watching a cat as it slunk through the shadows. "The first thing you must understand about de Quincey," she said, "is that he is the most dangerous vampire in London. He has made his way to the top of the city's most powerful clan. Any vampire living within London is subject to his whim." Her scarlet lips thinned. "The second thing you must understand is that de Quincey is old—old even for one of the Night Children. He lived most of his life before the Accords, and he loathes them, and loathes living beneath the yoke of the Law. And most of all, he hates the Nephilim."

Tessa saw Jem lean in and whisper something to Will, whose mouth quirked up at the corner in a smile. "Indeed," Will said. "How could anyone despise us when we are so charming?"

"I am sure you know that you are not loved by most Downworlders."

"But we thought de Quincey was an ally." Charlotte rested her thin nervous hands on the back of one of the velvet chairs. "He has always cooperated with the Clave."

"Pretense. It is in his interest to cooperate with you, so he does. But he would happily see you all sunk fathoms below the sea."

Charlotte had gone pale, but rallied. "And you know nothing of his involvement with two women called the Dark Sisters? Nothing of his interest in automatons—mechanical creatures?"

"Ugh, the Dark Sisters." Lady Belcourt shuddered. "Such ugly, unpleasant creatures. Warlocks, I believe. I avoided them. They were known to provide for the members of the club who might have less . . . savory interests. Demon drugs, Downworld prostitutes, that sort of thing."

"And the automatons?"

Lady Belcourt fluttered her delicate hands in a bored fashion. "If de Quincey has some fascination with watch parts, I know nothing of it. In fact, when you first contacted me about de Quincey, Charlotte, I had no intention of coming forward with *any* information at all. It is one thing to share a few Downworld secrets with the Clave, another thing entirely to betray the most powerful vampire in London. That was, until I heard about your little shape-shifter." Her green eyes came to rest on Tessa. The red lips smiled. "I can see the family resemblance."

Tessa stared. "The resemblance to whom?"

"Why, to Nathaniel, of course. To your brother."

Tessa felt as if ice water had been dumped down the back of her neck, shocking her to full alertness. "You've seen my brother?"

Lady Belcourt smiled, the smile of a woman who knows she holds a room in the palm of her hand. "I saw him a few times at various Pandemonium Club occasions," she said. "He had that hapless look about him, poor creature, of a mundane under a spell. Probably gambled away everything he had. They always do. Charlotte told me the Dark Sisters took him; that doesn't surprise me. They love to drive a mundane into the ground with debt and then collect in the most shocking ways. . . ."

"But he's alive?" Tessa said. "You've seen him alive?"

"It was some time ago, but yes." Lady Belcourt gave a wave of her hand. Her gloves were scarlet, and her hands looked as if they had been dipped in blood. "To return to the matter at hand," she said. "We were speaking of de Quincey. Tell me, Charlotte, did you know he holds parties at his town house in Carleton Square?"

Charlotte took her hands off the chair back. "I've heard it mentioned."

"Unfortunately," said Will, "it seems he neglected to invite us. Perhaps our invitations went astray in the post."

"At these parties," Lady Belcourt went on, "humans are

tortured and killed. I believe their bodies are dumped into the Thames for the mudlarks to pick over. Now, did you know *that*?"

Even Will looked taken aback. Charlotte said, "But the murder of humans by the Night Children is forbidden under the Law—"

"And de Quincey despises the Law. He does this as much to mock the Nephilim as because he enjoys the killing. Though he does enjoy that, make no mistake about it."

Charlotte's lips were bloodless. "How long has this been going on, Camille?"

So that was her name, Tessa thought. *Camille.* It was a French-sounding name; perhaps that explained her accent.

"At least a year. Perhaps longer." The vampire's tone was cool, indifferent.

"And you are telling me this only now because . . ." Charlotte sounded hurt.

"The price for revealing the secrets of the Lord of London is death," Camille said, her green eyes darkening. "And it would have done you no good, even if I had told you. De Quincey is one of your allies. You have no reason and no excuse to burst into his home as if he were a common criminal. Not with no evidence of wrongdoing on his part. My understanding is that, under these new Accords, a vampire must actually be observed harming a human before the Nephilim can take action?"

"Yes," said Charlotte reluctantly, "but if we had been able to attend one of the parties—"

Camille let out a short laugh. "De Quincey would never let that happen! At the first sight of a Shadowhunter, he would have locked the place up tightly. You would never have been permitted to enter."

"But *you* could," Charlotte said. "You could have brought one of us with you—"

The plume on Camille's hat trembled as she tossed her head. "And risk my own life?"

"Well, you're not precisely *alive*, are you?" said Will.

"I value my existence as much as you do, Shadowhunter," said Lady Belcourt, narrowing her eyes. "A lesson you would do well to learn. It could hardly hurt the Nephilim to cease thinking that all those who do not live exactly as they do must therefore not truly *live* at all."

It was Jem who spoke then, for what seemed like the first time since they had entered the room. "Lady Belcourt—if you'll pardon my asking—what is it exactly that you want from Tessa?"

Camille looked directly at Tessa then, her green eyes as brilliant as jewels. "You can disguise yourself as anyone, is that correct? A perfect disguise—appearance, voice, and manner? That's what I have heard." Her lip curled. "I have my sources."

"Yes," Tessa said hesitantly. "That is, I have been told the disguise is identical."

Camille looked at her narrowly. "It would have to be perfect. If you were to disguise yourself as me—"

"As *you*?" Charlotte said. "Lady Belcourt, I don't see—"

"I see," said Will immediately. "If Tessa were disguised as Lady Belcourt, she could make her way into one of de Quincey's parties. She could observe him breaking the Law. Then the Clave could attack, without shattering the Accords."

"Quite the little strategist, you are." Camille smiled, revealing her white teeth once again.

"And it would also provide a perfect opportunity to search de Quincey's residence," said Jem. "See what we can discover about his interest in these automatons. If he really has been murdering mundanes, there's no reason to think that it wasn't for more purposes than mere sport." He gave Charlotte a meaningful look, and Tessa knew that he was thinking, as she was, of the bodies in the cellar of the Dark House.

"We would have to figure out some way to signal the Clave from inside de Quincey's," Will mused, his blue eyes already alight. "Perhaps Henry could devise something. It would be invaluable to have a blueprint of the house's construction—"

"Will," Tessa protested. "I don't—"

"And of course you wouldn't be going alone," Will said impatiently. "I would go with you. I wouldn't let anything happen to you."

"Will, no," Charlotte said. "You and Tessa alone, in a house full of vampires? I forbid it."

"Then who would you send in with her, if not me?" Will demanded. "You know I can protect her, and you know I'm the right choice—"

"I could go. Or Henry—"

Camille, who had been watching all this with a look of mixed boredom and amusement, said, "I'm afraid I agree with William. The only individuals admitted to these parties are de Quincey's close friends, vampires, and the human subjugates of vampires. De Quincey has seen Will before, passing as a mundane fascinated by the occult; he won't be surprised to find that he's graduated to vampiric servitude."

Human subjugate. Tessa had read of them in the *Codex*: Subjugates, or darklings, were mundanes who had sworn themselves to the service of a vampire. For the vampire, they provided companionship and food, and in return received small transfusions of vampire blood at intervals. This blood kept them bound to their vampire master, and also ensured that when they died, they would become vampires as well.

"But Will is only seventeen," Charlotte protested.

"Most human subjugates *are* young," said Will. "Vampires like to acquire their subjugates when they're youthful—prettier to look at, and less chance of diseased blood. And they'll live a bit longer, though not much." He looked pleased with himself. "Most of the rest of the Enclave wouldn't be able to pass convincingly as a handsome young human subjugate—"

"Because the rest of us all are hideous, are we?" Jem inquired, looking amused. "Is that why I can't do it?"

"No," Will said. "You know why it can't be you." He said it without any inflection, and Jem, after looking at him for a moment, shrugged and looked away.

"I'm truly not sure about this," Charlotte said. "When is the next of these events set to happen, Camille?"

"Saturday night."

Charlotte took a deep breath. "I'll have to speak to the Enclave, before I can agree. And Tessa would have to agree as well."

Everyone looked at Tessa.

She licked her dry lips nervously. "You believe," she said to Lady Belcourt, "that there's a chance my brother might be there?"

"I cannot promise he will be there. He might. But *someone* there will likely know what has happened to him. The Dark Sisters were regulars at de Quincey's parties; doubtless they or their cohorts, if captured and interrogated, will yield you some answers."

Tessa's stomach churned. "I'll do it," she said. "But I want to be promised that *if* Nate is there, we'll get him out, and if he isn't, we'll find out where he is. I want to make sure it's not all about catching de Quincey. It must be about saving Nate, too."

"Of course," Charlotte said. "But I don't know, Tessa. It will be very dangerous—"

"Have you ever Changed yourself into a Downworlder?" Will inquired. "Do you even know if it's something that would be possible?"

Tessa shook her head. "I've never done anything like that. But . . . I could try." She turned to Lady Belcourt. "Could I have something of yours? A ring, or a handkerchief perhaps."

Camille reached her hands behind her head, brushing aside the thick coils of silver-blond hair that lay against her neck, and unclasped her necklace. Letting it dangle from her slender fingers, she held it out to Tessa. "Here. Take this."

With a frown Jem stepped forward to take the necklace, and then held it out to Tessa. She felt the weight of it as she took it from him. It was heavy, and the square ruby pendant the size of a bird's egg felt cold to the touch, as cold as if it had been lying in snow. Closing her hand around it was like closing her fingers around a shard of ice. She took a sharp breath, and closed her eyes.

It was strange, different this time as the transformation took hold. The darkness rose quickly, wrapping itself around her, and the light she saw in the distance was a cold silver glow. The chill that flowed from the light was scalding. Tessa drew the light toward her, surrounding herself with its icy burning light, pushing herself through to the core of it. The light rose in shimmering white walls around her—

She felt a sharp pain then, in the center of her chest, and for a moment her vision went red—deep scarlet, the color of blood. Everything was blood-colored, and she began to panic, fighting her way free, her eyelids flying open—

And she was there again, in the Sanctuary Room, with all the others staring at her. Camille was smiling slightly; the others looked startled, if not as thunderstruck as they had when she had transformed into Jessamine.

But something was terribly wrong. There was a great hollow emptiness inside her—not pain, but a cavernous sense of something *missing*. Tessa choked, and a searing shock went through her. She sank down into an armchair, her hands pressed against her chest. She was trembling all over.

"Tessa?" Jem sank down onto his heels beside the chair, taking one of her hands. She could see herself in the mirror that hung on the opposite wall—or more accurately, she could see the image of Camille. Camille's shimmering pale hair, unpinned, rained down over her shoulders, and her white skin swelled and spilled over the bodice of Tessa's now too-tight dress in a way that would have made Tessa flush—if she could have flushed. But blushing required blood actually running in one's veins, and she remembered, with a dawning terror, that vampires did not breathe, did not get hot or cold, and did not have hearts that beat in their chests.

So *that* was the hollowness, the strangeness that she felt. Her heart was still, in her chest like a dead thing. She took another sobbing breath. It hurt, and she realized that while she *could* breathe, her new body did not want or need to.

"Oh, God," she said in a soft whisper to Jem. "I—my heart's not beating. I feel as if I've died. Jem—"

He stroked her hand, carefully, soothingly, and looked up at her with his silver eyes. The expression in them had not changed with the change in her; he looked at her as he had before, as if she were still Tessa Gray. "You're alive," he said, in a voice so soft only she could hear it. "You're wearing a different skin, but you're Tessa, and you're alive. Do you know how I know that?"

She shook her head.

"Because you said the word 'God' just now to me. No vampire could say that." He squeezed her hand. "Your soul is still the same."

She closed her eyes and sat still for a moment, concentrating on the pressure of his hand on hers, his warm skin against hers that was icy cold. Slowly the trembling that shook her body began to fade; she opened her eyes, and gave Jem a faint, shaky smile.

"Tessa," said Charlotte. "Are you— Is everything all right?"

Tessa drew her eyes away from Jem's face and looked at Charlotte, who was watching her with an anxious gaze. Will, beside Charlotte, wore an unreadable expression.

"You will have to practice a bit, moving and holding yourself, if you wish to convince de Quincey that you are me," Lady Belcourt said. "I would never slump in a chair like that." She tilted her head to the side. "Still, overall, an impressive showing. Someone trained you well."

Tessa thought of the Dark Sisters. Had they trained her well? Had they done her a favor, unlocking this dormant power inside her, despite how much she had hated them and it? Or would it have been better if she had never known that she was different?

Slowly she let go, let the Camille skin slip away from her. It felt as if she were rising up out of icy water. Her hand tightened on Jem's as the chill ran through her, head to toe, a freezing cascade. Something leaped inside her chest then. Like a bird that has lain stunned and motionless after flying into a window, only to gather its strength and leap from the ground to soar into the air, her heart began suddenly to beat again. Air filled her lungs, and she released Jem, her hands flying to her chest, her fingers pressed against the skin to feel the soft rhythm beneath.

She looked in the mirror across the room. She was herself again: Tessa Gray, not a miraculously beautiful vampire. She felt an overwhelming relief.

"My necklace?" Lady Belcourt said coolly, and held out her slender hand. Jem took the ruby pendant from Tessa to bring it to the vampire; as he lifted it, Tessa saw that there were words etched on the silver frame of the pendant: AMOR VERUS NUMQUAM MORITUR.

She looked across the room at Will, she wasn't sure why, only to find that he was looking back at her. They both glanced hastily away. "Lady Belcourt," Will said, "since none of us have ever been in de Quincey's home, do you think it would be possible for you to provide a floor plan, or even a sketch of the grounds and rooms?"

"I shall provide you with something better." Lady Belcourt raised her arms to clasp the necklace around her throat. "Magnus Bane."

"The warlock?" Charlotte's eyebrows rose.

"Indeed," said Lady Belcourt. "He knows the town house as well as I do and is often invited to de Quincey's social events.

Though, like me, he has formerly eschewed the parties at which murder is committed."

"Noble of him," muttered Will.

"He will meet you there, and guide you through the house. No one there will be surprised to see us together. Magnus Bane is my lover, you see."

Tessa's mouth opened slightly. This was not the sort of thing ladies said in polite company, or any company. But perhaps it was different for vampires? Everyone else looked as stunned as she did, except Will, who as usual looked as if he were trying not to laugh.

"How nice," Charlotte said at last, after a pause.

"Indeed it is," Camille said, and rose to her feet. "And now, if someone will escort me out. It grows late, and I have not yet fed."

Charlotte, who was regarding Tessa with concern, said, "Will, Jem, if you'll go?"

Tessa watched as the two boys flanked Camille like soldiers—which, she supposed, was what they were—and followed her from the room. Last through the door, the vampire paused and looked back over her shoulder. Her pale blond curls brushed her cheeks as she smiled; she was so beautiful that Tessa felt a sort of pang, looking at her, overriding her instinctive feeling of aversion.

"If you do this," said Camille, "and you succeed—whether or not you find your brother—I can promise you, little shapeshifter, that you won't regret it."

Tessa frowned, but Camille was already gone. She moved so fast that it was as though she had vanished between one breath and the next. Tessa turned toward Charlotte. "What do you think she meant by that? That I won't regret it?"

Charlotte shook her head. "I don't know." She sighed. "I'd like to think that she meant that the knowledge of a good deed done would console you, but it's Camille, so . . ."

"Are all vampires like that?" Tessa asked. "Cold like that?"

"Many of them have been alive a long time," Charlotte said diplomatically. "They don't see things the way we do."

Tessa put her fingers to her aching temples. "Indeed, they don't."

Of all the things that bothered Will about vampires—the way they moved soundlessly, the low and inhuman timbre of their voices—it was the way they smelled that bothered him most. Or rather, the way they didn't smell. All human beings smelled like *something*—sweat, soap, perfume—but vampires had no scent, like wax mannequins.

Ahead of him, Jem was holding the last of the doors that led from the Sanctuary to the outer foyer of the Institute. All these spaces had been deconsecrated so that vampires and others of their ilk could use them, but Camille could never come any farther into the Institute than that. Escorting her out was more than a courtesy. They were making sure she didn't accidentally wander onto consecrated ground, which would be dangerous for everyone involved.

Camille brushed by Jem, hardly looking at him, and Will followed, pausing only long enough to mutter "She doesn't smell like anything" to Jem under his breath.

Jem looked alarmed. "You've been *smelling* her?"

Camille, who was waiting by the next doorway for them, turned her head at this and smiled. "I can hear everything you say, you know," she said. "It is true, vampires have no scent. It makes us better predators."

"That, and excellent hearing," Jem said, and let the door swing shut behind Will. They were standing in the small square entryway with Camille now, her hand on the knob of the front door as if she meant to hurry out, but there was nothing hurried in her expression as she looked them over.

"Look at you both," she said, "all black and silver. You could be a vampire," she said to Jem, "with your pallor, and your looks. And you," she said to Will, "well, I don't think anyone at de Quincey's will doubt that you could be my human sub-jugate."

Jem was looking at Camille, with that look that Will always thought could cut glass. He said:

"Why are you doing this, Lady Belcourt? This plan of yours, de Quincey, all of it—why?"

Camille smiled. She was beautiful, Will had to admit—but then, a lot of vampires were beautiful. Their beauty had always seemed to him like the beauty of pressed flowers—lovely, but dead. "Because the knowledge of what he was doing weighed on my conscience."

Jem shook his head. "Perhaps you are the sort who would sacrifice yourself on the altar of principle, but I doubt it. Most of us do things for reasons that are more purely personal. For love, or for hate."

"Or for revenge," Will said. "After all, you've known about what was going on for a year now, and you only just came to us."

"That was because of Miss Gray."

"Yes, but that's not all it is, is it?" Jem said. "Tessa is your opportunity, but your reason, your motive, is something else."

He cocked his head to the side. "Why do you hate de Quincey so much?"

"I don't see what business it is of yours, little silver Shadowhunter," Camille said, and her lips had drawn back from her teeth, leaving her fangs visible, like bits of ivory against the red of her lips. Will knew that vampires could show their fangs at will, but it was still unnerving. "Why does it matter what my motives are?"

Will filled in the answer for Jem, already knowing what the other boy had been thinking. "Because otherwise we can't trust you. Perhaps you're sending us into a trap. Charlotte wouldn't want to believe it, but that doesn't make it not possible."

"Lead you into a trap?" Camille's tone was mocking. "And incur the terrifying wrath of the Clave? Hardly likely!"

"Lady Belcourt," said Jem, "whatever Charlotte might have promised you, if you want our help, you will answer the question."

"Very well," she said. "I can see you will not be satisfied unless I give you an explanation. You," she said, nodding toward Will, "are correct. And you seem to know a curious amount about love and revenge for one so young; we must discuss them someday, together." She smiled again, but the smile did not reach her eyes. "I had a lover, you see," she said. "He was a shape-changer, a lycanthrope. It is forbidden for the Night Children to love or to lie with the Moon's Children. We were careful, but de Quincey found us out. Found us out and murdered him, in much the way he will be murdering some poor mundane prisoner at his next party." Her eyes shone like green lamps as she looked at them both. "I loved him, and de

Quincey murdered him, and the others of my kind helped and abetted him. I will not forgive them for it. Kill them all."

The Accords, now ten years old, marked a historic moment for both Nephilim and Downworlders. No longer would the two groups strive to destroy each other. They would be united against a common foe, the demon. There were fifty men at the signing of the Accords in Idris: ten of the Night Children; ten of Lilith's Children, known as warlocks; ten of the Fair Folk; ten of the Moon's Children; and ten of Raziel's blood—

Tessa jerked awake at the sound of a knock on her door; she had been half-drowsing on the pillow, her finger still keeping a place in *The Shadowhunter's Codex*. After setting the book down, she barely had time to sit up and draw the covers about herself before the door opened.

In came lamplight, and Charlotte with it. Tessa felt an odd twinge, almost disappointment—but who else had she been expecting? Despite the late hour, Charlotte was dressed as if she planned to go out. Her face was very serious, and there were lines of tiredness below her dark eyes. "You're awake?"

Tessa nodded, and lifted the book she had been reading. "Reading."

Charlotte said nothing, but crossed the room and sat down at the foot of Tessa's bed. She held out her hand. Something gleamed in her palm; it was Tessa's angel pendant. "You left this with Henry."

Tessa set her book down and took the pendant. She slipped the chain over her head, and felt reassured as the familiar weight settled against the hollow of her throat. "Did he learn anything from it?"

"I'm not sure. He said it was all clogged up on the inside with years of rust, that it was a wonder it was working at all. He cleaned out the mechanism, though it doesn't seem to have resulted in much of a change. Perhaps it ticks more regularly now?"

"Perhaps." Tessa didn't care; she was just happy to have the angel, the symbol of her mother and her life in New York, back in her possession.

Charlotte folded her hands in her lap. "Tessa, there is something I haven't told you."

Tessa's heart began to beat faster. "What is it?"

"Mortmain . . ." Charlotte hesitated. "When I said that Mortmain introduced your brother to the Pandemonium Club, that was true, but not the whole truth. Your brother already knew about the Shadow World, before Mortmain ever told him. It seems he learned about it from your father."

Stunned, Tessa was silent.

"How old were you when your parents died?" Charlotte asked.

"It was an accident," Tessa said, a little dazed. "I was three. Nate was six."

Charlotte frowned. "So young for your father to confide in your brother, but . . . I suppose it's possible."

"No," Tessa said. "No, you don't understand. I had the most ordinary, the most human, upbringing imaginable. Aunt Harriet, she was the most practical woman in the world. And she would have known, wouldn't she? She was mother's younger sister; they brought her with them from London when they came to America."

"People keep secrets, Tessa, sometimes even from the ones they love." Charlotte brushed her fingers across the cover of the *Codex*, with its embossed seal. "And you must admit, it does make sense."

"Sense? It doesn't make any kind of sense!"

"Tessa . . ." Charlotte sighed. "We don't know why you have the ability that you do. But if one of your parents was connected in some way to the magical world, doesn't it make sense that that connection might have something to do with it? If your father was a member of the Pandemonium Club, isn't that how de Quincey might have known about you?"

"I suppose." Tessa spoke grudgingly. "It's only . . . I believed so strongly when I first came to London that everything that was happening to me was a dream. That my life before had been real and this was a dreadful nightmare. I thought that if only I could find Nate, we could go back to the life we had before." She raised her eyes to Charlotte's. "But now I cannot help but wonder if perhaps the life I had before was the dream and all this was the truth. If my parents knew of the Pandemonium Club—if they were part of the Shadow World too—then there is no world I can go back to that will be clean of all this."

Charlotte, her hands still folded in her lap, looked at Tessa steadily. "Have you ever wondered why Sophie's face is scarred?"

Caught off guard, Tessa could only stammer. "I—I wondered, but I—didn't like to ask."

"Nor should you," said Charlotte. Her voice was cool and firm. "When I first saw Sophie, she was crouched in a doorway, filthy, with a bloody rag clutched to her cheek. She *saw* me as I went by, even though I was glamoured at the time. That's what drew my attention to her. She has a touch of the Sight, as do Thomas and Agatha. I offered her money, but she wouldn't take it. I wheedled her into accompanying me to a tea shop, and she told me what had happened to her. She had been a parlor maid, in a fine house in St. John's Wood. Parlor maids, of course, are chosen for their looks, and Sophie was beautiful—which turned out to be both a great advantage and a great disadvantage for her. As you might imagine, the son of the house took an interest in seducing her. She turned him away repeatedly. In a rage, he took a knife and cut open her face, saying that if he couldn't have her, he'd make sure no one ever wanted her again."

"How awful," Tessa whispered.

"She went to her mistress, the boy's mother, but he claimed that she'd tried to seduce *him*, and he'd taken up the knife to fight her off and protect *his* virtue. Of course, they threw her out on the street. By the time I found her, her cheek was badly infected. I brought her here and had the Silent Brothers see to her, but while they cured the infection, they couldn't heal the scar."

Tessa put her hand to her own face in a gesture of unconscious sympathy. "Poor Sophie."

Charlotte cocked her head to the side and looked at Tessa out of her bright brown eyes. She had such a strong presence, Tessa thought, that it was hard to remember sometimes how physically small she was, how birdlike and tiny. "Sophie has a gift," she said. "She has the Sight. She can see what others do not. In her old life she often wondered if she was mad. Now she knows that she is not mad but special. There, she was only a parlor maid, who would likely have lost her position once her looks had faded. Now she is a valued member of our household, a gifted girl with much to contribute." Charlotte leaned forward. "You look back on the life you had, Tessa, and it seems safe to you in comparison to this one. But you and your aunt were very poor, if I am not mistaken. If you had not come to London, where would you have gone once she died? What would you have done? Would you have found yourself weeping in an alley like our Sophie?" Charlotte shook her head. "You have a power of incalculable value. You need ask nothing of anyone. You need depend on no one. You are free, and that freedom is a gift."

"It is hard to think of something as a gift when you have been tormented and imprisoned for it."

Charlotte shook her head. "Sophie said to me once that she was glad she had been scarred. She said that whoever loved her now would love her true self, and not her pretty face. This is your true self, Tessa. This power is who you are. Whoever loves you now—and you must also love yourself—will love the truth of you."

Tessa picked up the *Codex* and hugged it against her chest. "So you are saying I am right. This is what is real, and the life I had before was the dream."

"That is correct." Gently Charlotte patted Tessa's shoulder; Tessa almost jumped at the contact. It had been a long time, she thought, since anyone had touched her in such a motherly fashion; she thought of Aunt Harriet, and her throat hurt. "And now it is time to wake up."

9

The Enclave

May make my heart as a millstone, set my face as a flint,
Cheat and be cheated, and die: who knows? we are ashes and dust.
—Alfred, Lord Tennyson, "Maud"

"Try it again," Will suggested. "Simply walk from one end of the room to the other. We'll tell you if you look convincing."

Tessa sighed. Her head throbbed, as did the backs of her eyes. It was exhausting learning how to pretend to be a vampire.

It had been two days since Lady Belcourt's visit, and Tessa had spent almost every moment since then attempting to convincingly transform herself into the vampire woman, without enormous success. She still felt as if she were sliding around on the surface of Camille's mind, unable to reach through and grasp hold of thoughts or personality. It made it difficult to know how to walk, how to talk, and what sort of expressions she ought to be wearing when she met the vampires at de Quincey's party—whom, no doubt, Camille knew very well, and whom Tessa would be expected to know too.

She was in the library now, and had spent the last few hours since lunch practicing walking with Camille's odd gliding walk, and speaking with her careful drawling voice. Pinned at her shoulder was a jeweled brooch that one of Camille's human subjugates, a wrinkled little creature called Archer, had brought over in a trunk. There had been a dress, too, for Tessa to wear to de Quincey's, but it was much too heavy and elaborate for daytime. Tessa made do with her own new blue and white dress, which was bothersomely too tight in the bosom and too loose in the waist whenever she changed into Camille.

Jem and Will had set up camp on one of the long tables in the back of the library, ostensibly to help and advise her, but more likely, it seemed, to mock and be amused by her consternation. "You point your feet out too much when you walk," Will went on. He was busy polishing an apple on his shirtfront, and appeared not to notice Tessa glaring at him. "Camille walks delicately. Like a faun in the woods. Not like a duck."

"I do not walk like a duck."

"I like ducks," Jem observed diplomatically. "Especially the ones in Hyde Park." He glanced sideways at Will; both boys were sitting on the edge of the high table, their legs dangling over the side. "Remember when you tried to convince me to feed a poultry pie to the mallards in the park to see if you could breed a race of cannibal ducks?"

"They ate it too," Will reminisced. "Bloodthirsty little beasts. Never trust a duck."

"Do you mind?" Tessa demanded. "If you're not going to help me, you might as well both leave. I didn't let you stay here so that I could listen to you nattering on about ducks."

"Your impatience," said Will, "is most unladylike." He grinned at her around the apple. "Perhaps Camille's vampire nature is asserting itself?"

His tone was playful. It was so odd, Tessa thought. Only a few days ago he had snarled at her about his parents, and later had begged her to help him hide Jem's bloody coughing, his face burning with intensity as he did so. And now he was teasing her as if she were a friend's little sister, someone whom he knew casually, perhaps thought of with affection, but for whom he had no complex feelings at all.

Tessa bit her lip—and winced at the unexpected sharp pain. Camille's vampire teeth—*her* teeth—were ruled by an instinct she couldn't understand. They seemed to slide forward without warning or prompting, alerting her to their presence only by sudden bursts of pain as they punctured the fragile skin of her lip. She tasted blood in her mouth—her own blood, salty and hot. She pressed her fingertips to her mouth; when she drew her hand away, her fingers were spotted with red.

"Leave it alone," said Will, setting down his apple and rising to his feet. "You'll find you heal very quickly."

Tessa poked at her left incisor with her tongue. It was flat again, an ordinary tooth. "I don't understand what makes them come out like that!"

"Hunger," said Jem. "Were you thinking about blood?"
"No."
"Were you thinking about eating me?" Will inquired.
"No!"

"No one would blame you," said Jem. "He's very annoying."

Tessa sighed. "Camille is so *difficult*. I don't understand the first thing about her, much less *being* her."

Jem looked at her closely. "Are you able to touch her thoughts? The way you said you could touch the thoughts of those you transformed into?"

"Not yet. I've been trying, but all I get are occasional flashes, images. Her thoughts seem very well protected."

"Well, hopefully you can break through that protection before tomorrow night," said Will. "Or I wouldn't say much about our chances."

"Will," Jem chided. "Don't say that."

"You're right," Will said. "I shouldn't underestimate my own skills. Should Tessa make a mess of things, I'm sure I'll be able to fight our way through the slavering vampire masses to freedom."

Jem—as was his habit, Tessa was starting to realize—simply ignored this. "Perhaps," he said, "you can only touch the thoughts of the dead, Tessa? Perhaps most of the objects given to you by the Dark Sisters were taken from people they had murdered."

"No. I touched Jessamine's thoughts when I Changed into her. So that can't be it, thankfully. What a morbid talent that would be."

Jem was looking at her with thoughtful silver eyes; something about the intensity of his gaze made her feel almost uncomfortable. "How clearly can you see the thoughts of the dead? For instance, if I gave you an item that had once belonged to my father, would you know what he was thinking when he died?"

It was Will's turn to look alarmed. "James, I don't think—," he began, but broke off as the door to the library opened and Charlotte entered the room. She wasn't alone. There were at least a dozen men following her, strangers whom Tessa had never seen before.

"The Enclave," Will whispered, and gestured for Jem and Tessa to duck behind one of the ten-foot bookcases. They observed from their hiding place as the room filled with Shadowhunters—most of them men. But Tessa saw, as they filed into the room, that among them were two women.

She could not help staring at them, remembering what Will had said about Boadicea, that women could be warriors as well. The taller of the women—and she must have been nearly six feet in height—had powder white hair wound into a crown at the back of her head. She looked as if she were well into her sixties, and her presence was regal. The second of the women was younger, with dark hair, catlike eyes, and a secretive demeanor.

The men were a more mixed group. The eldest was a tall man dressed all in gray. His hair and skin were gray as well, his face bony and aquiline, with a strong, thin nose and a sharp chin. There were hard lines at the corners of his eyes and dark hollows under his cheekbones. His eyes were rimmed with red. Beside him stood the youngest of the group, a boy probably no more than a year older than Jem or Will. He was handsome in an angular sort of way, with sharp but regular features, tousled brown hair, and a watchful expression.

Jem made a noise of surprise and displeasure. "Gabriel Lightwood," he muttered to Will under his breath. "What's he doing here? I thought he was in school in Idris."

Will hadn't moved. He was staring at the brown-haired boy with his eyebrows raised, a faint smile playing about his lips.

"Just don't get into a fight with him, Will," Jem added hastily. "Not here. That's all I ask."

"Rather a lot to ask, don't you think?" Will said without looking at Jem. Will had leaned out from behind the bookcase, and was watching Charlotte as she ushered everyone toward the large table at the front of the room. She seemed to be urging everyone to settle themselves into seats around it.

"Frederick Ashdown and George Penhallow, here, if you please," Charlotte said. "Lilian Highsmith, if you'd sit over there by the map—"

"And where is Henry?" asked the gray-haired man with an air of brusque politeness. "Your husband? As one of the heads of the Institute, he really ought to be here."

Charlotte hesitated for only a fraction of a second before plastering a smile onto her face. "He's on his way, Mr. Lightwood," she said, and Tessa realized two things—one, that the gray-haired man was most likely the father of Gabriel Lightwood, and two, that Charlotte was lying.

"He'd better be," Mr. Lightwood muttered. "An Enclave meeting without the head of the Institute present—most irregular." He turned then, and though Will moved to duck back behind the tall bookcase, it was too late. The man's eyes narrowed. "And who's back there, then? Come out and show yourself!"

Will glanced toward Jem, who shrugged eloquently. "No point hiding till they drag us out, is there?"

"Speak for yourself," Tessa hissed. "I don't need Charlotte angry at me if we're not supposed to be in here."

"Don't work yourself into a state. There's no reason you'd have had any idea about the Enclave meeting, and Charlotte's perfectly well aware of that," Will said. "She always knows exactly who to blame." He grinned. "I'd turn yourself back into yourself, though, if you take my meaning. No need to give too much of a shock to their hoary old constitutions."

"Oh!" For a moment Tessa had nearly forgotten she was still disguised as Camille. Hastily she went to work stripping away the transformation, and by the time the three of them stepped out from behind the bookshelves, she was her own self again.

"Will." Charlotte sighed on seeing him, and shook her head at Tessa and Jem. "I told you the Enclave would be meeting here at four o'clock."

"Did you?" Will said. "I must have forgotten that. Dreadful." His eyes slid sideways, and he grinned. "'Lo there, Gabriel."

The brown-haired boy returned Will's look with a furious glare. He had very bright green eyes, and his mouth, as he stared at Will, was hard with disgust. "William," he said finally, and with some effort. He turned his gaze on Jem. "And James. Aren't you both a little young to be lurking around Enclave meetings?"

"Aren't you?" Jem said.

"I turned eighteen in June," Gabriel said, leaning so far back in his chair that the front legs came off the ground. "I have every right to participate in Enclave activities now."

"How fascinating for you," said the white-haired woman Tessa had thought looked regal. "So is this her, Lottie? The warlock girl you were telling us about?" The question was directed at Charlotte, but the woman's gaze rested on Tessa. "She doesn't look like much."

"Neither did Magnus Bane the first time I saw him," said Mr. Lightwood, bending a curious eye on Tessa. "Let's have it then. Show us what you can do."

"I'm not a warlock," Tessa protested angrily.

"Well, you're certainly something, my girl," said the older woman. "If not a warlock, then what?"

"That will do." Charlotte drew herself up. "Miss Gray has already proved her bona fides to me and Mr. Branwell. That will have to be good enough for now—at least until the Enclave makes the decision that they wish to utilize her talents."

"Of course they do," said Will. "We haven't a hope of succeeding in this plan without her—"

Gabriel brought his chair forward with such force that the front legs slammed into the stone floor with a cracking noise. "Mrs. Branwell," he said furiously, "is William, or is he not, too young to be participating in an Enclave meeting?"

Charlotte's gaze went from Gabriel's flushed face to Will's expressionless one. She sighed. "Yes, he is. Will, Jem, if you'll please wait outside in the corridor with Tessa."

Will's expression tightened, but Jem bent a warning look on him, and he remained silent. Gabriel Lightwood looked triumphant. "I will show you out," he announced, springing to his feet. He ushered the three of them out of the library, then swung out into the corridor after them. "You," he spat at Will, pitching his voice low so that those in the library couldn't overhear him. "You disgrace the name of Shadowhunters everywhere."

Will leaned against the corridor wall and regarded Gabriel with cool blue eyes. "I didn't realize there was much of a name left to disgrace, after your father—"

"I will thank you *not* to speak of my family," Gabriel snarled, reaching behind himself to pull the library door shut.

"How unfortunate that the prospect of your gratitude is not a tempting one," Will said.

Gabriel stared at him, his hair disarrayed, his green eyes brilliant with rage. He reminded Tessa of someone in that moment, though she could not have said who. "What?" Gabriel growled.

"He means," Jem clarified, "that he doesn't care for your thanks."

Gabriel's cheeks darkened to a dull scarlet. "If you weren't underage, Herondale, it would be *monomachia* for us. Just you and me, to the death. I'd chop you into bloody carpet rags—"

"Stop it, Gabriel," Jem interrupted, before Will could reply. "Goading Will into single combat—that's like punishing a dog after you've tormented it into biting you. You know how he is."

"Much obliged, James," Will said, without taking his eyes off Gabriel. "I appreciate the testament to my character."

Jem shrugged. "It is the truth."

Gabriel shot Jem a dark glare. "Stay out of this, Carstairs. This doesn't concern you."

Jem moved closer to the door, and to Will, who was standing perfectly still, matching Gabriel's cold stare with one of his own. The hairs on the back of Tessa's neck had begun to prickle. "If it concerns Will, it concerns me," Jem said.

Gabriel shook his head. "You're a decent Shadowhunter, James," he said, "and a gentleman. You have your—disability, but no one blames you for that. But this—" He curled his lip, jabbing a finger in Will's direction. "This filth will only drag you down. Find someone else to be your *parabatai*. No one expects Will Herondale to live past nineteen, and no one will be sorry to see him go, either—"

That was too much for Tessa. Without thinking about it she burst out indignantly, "What a thing to say!"

Gabriel, interrupted midrant, looked as shocked as if one of the tapestries had suddenly started talking. "Pardon me?"

"You heard me. Telling someone you wouldn't be sorry if they died! It's inexcusable!" She took hold of Will by the sleeve. "Come along, Will. This—this person—obviously isn't worth wasting your time on."

Will looked hugely entertained. "So true."

"You—you—" Gabriel, stammering slightly, looked at Tessa in an alarmed sort of way. "You haven't the slightest idea of the things he's done—"

"And I don't care, either. You're all Nephilim, aren't you? Well, aren't you? You're supposed to be on the same side." Tessa frowned at Gabriel. "I think you owe Will an apology."

"I," said Gabriel, "would rather have my entrails yanked out and tied in a knot in front of my own eyes than apologize to such a worm."

"Gracious," said Jem mildly. "You can't mean that. Not the Will being a worm part, of course. The bit about the entrails. That sounds dreadful."

"I do mean it," said Gabriel, warming to his subject. "I would rather be dropped into a vat of Malphas venom and left to dissolve slowly until only my bones were left."

"Really," said Will. "Because I happen to know a chap who could sell us a vat of—"

The door of the library opened. Mr. Lightwood stood on the threshold. "Gabriel," he said in a freezing tone. "Do you plan to attend the meeting—your first Enclave meeting, if I must remind you—or would you rather play out here in the corridor with the rest of the children?"

No one looked particularly pleased by that comment, especially Gabriel, who swallowed hard, nodded, shot one last glare at Will, and followed his father back into the library, slamming the door shut behind them.

"Well," said Jem after the door had closed behind Gabriel. "That was about as bad as I had expected it would be. Is this the first time you've seen him since last year's Christmas party?" he asked, addressing the question to Will.

"Yes," said Will. "Do you think I should have told him I missed him?"

"No," said Jem.

"Is he always like that?" Tessa asked. "So awful?"

"You should see his older brother," said Jem. "Makes Gabriel look sweeter than gingerbread. Hates Will even more than Gabriel, too, if that's possible."

Will grinned at that, then turned and began making his way down the corridor, whistling as he went. After a moment's hesitation, Jem went after him, gesturing for Tessa to follow.

"Why would Gabriel Lightwood hate you, Will?" Tessa asked as they went. "What did you do to him?"

"It wasn't anything I did to him," Will said, stalking along at a rapid pace. "It was something I did to his sister."

Tessa looked sideways at Jem, who shrugged. "Where there's our Will, there's a half-dozen angry girls claiming he's compromised their virtue."

"Did you?" Tessa asked, hurrying to keep up with the boys. There was simply only so fast you could walk in heavy skirts that swished around your ankles as you went. The delivery of dresses from Bond Street had come the day before, and she was only just beginning to get used to wearing such expensive stuff. She remembered the light dresses she'd worn as a little girl, when she'd been able to run up to her brother, kick him in the ankle, and dart away without him being able to catch her. She wondered briefly what would happen if she tried to do that to Will. She doubted it would work out to her advantage, though the thought had a certain appeal. "Compromise her virtue, I mean."

"You have a lot of questions," Will said, veering sharply to the left and up a set of narrow stairs. "Don't you?"

"I do," Tessa said, the heels of her boots clicking loudly on the stone steps as she followed Will upward. "What's *parabatai*? And what did you mean about Gabriel's father being a disgrace to Shadowhunters?"

"*Parabatai* in Greek is just a term for a soldier paired with a chariot driver," said Jem, "but when Nephilim say it, we mean a matched team of warriors—two men who swear to protect each other and guard each other's backs."

"Men?" said Tessa. "There couldn't be a team of women, or a woman and a man?"

"I thought you said women didn't have bloodlust," Will said without turning around. "And as for Gabriel's father, let's say that he has something of a reputation for liking demons and Downworlders more than he should. I would be surprised if some of the elder Lightwood's nocturnal visits to certain houses in Shadwell haven't left him with a nasty case of demon pox."

"Demon pox?" Tessa was horrified and fascinated at the same time.

"He's made that up," Jem hastily reassured her. "Really, Will. How many times do we have to tell you there's no such thing as demon pox?"

Will had stopped in front of a narrow door at a bend in the staircase. "I think this is it," he said, half to himself, and jiggled the knob. When nothing happened, he took his stele out of his jacket and scrawled a black Mark on the door. It swung open, with a puff of dust. "This ought to be a storeroom."

Jem followed him inside, and after a moment so did Tessa. She found herself in a small room whose only illumination was from an arched window set high in the wall above. Watery light poured through, showing a square space filled with trunks and boxes. It could have been any spare storage room anywhere, if it hadn't been for what looked like piles of old weapons stacked in the corners—heavy rusty-looking iron things with broad blades and chains connected to spiked chunks of metal.

Will took hold of one of the trunks and moved it sideways to create a clear square of space on the floor. More dust puffed up. Jem coughed and shot him a reproachful look. "One would think you brought us here to murder us," he said, "if it weren't that your motivations for doing so seem cloudy at best."

"Not murder," Will said. "Hold on. I need to move one more trunk."

As he pushed the heavy thing toward the wall, Tessa cast a sidelong look at Jem. "What did Gabriel mean," she asked, pitching her voice too low for Will to hear, "'your disability'?"

Jem's silvery eyes widened fractionally, before he said, "My ill health. That's all."

He was lying, Tessa knew. He had the same sort of look Nate did when he lied—a little too clear-eyed a gaze to be a truthful one. But before she could say anything else, Will straightened up and announced, "There we are. Come sit down."

He then proceeded to seat himself on the dusty stained floor; Jem went to sit beside him, but Tessa hung back for a moment, hesitant. Will, who had his stele out, looked up at her with a crooked smile. "Not going to join us, Tessa? I suppose you don't want to ruin the pretty dress Jessamine bought you."

It was the truth, actually. Tessa had no desire to wreck the nicest item of clothing she had ever owned. But Will's mocking tone was more annoying than the thought of destroying the dress. Setting her jaw, she went and sat down opposite the boys, so that they formed a triangle between them.

Will placed the tip of the stele against the dirty floor, and began to move it. Broad dark lines flowed from the tip, and Tessa watched in fascination. There was something particular and beautiful about the way the stele scrawled—not like ink flowing from a pen, but more as if the lines had always been there, and Will was uncovering them.

He was halfway through when Jem made a noise of realization, clearly recognizing the Mark that his friend was drawing. "What do you—," he began, but Will held up the hand he wasn't drawing with, shaking his head.

"Don't," Will said. "If I make a mess of this, we could well fall through the floor."

Jem rolled his eyes, but it didn't seem to matter: Will was already finished, and was lifting the stele away from the design he had drawn. Tessa gave a little cry as the warped floorboards between them seemed to shimmer—and then became as transparent as a window. Scooting forward, forgetting entirely about her dress, she found herself staring through it as if through a pane of glass.

She was looking down into what she realized was the library. She could see the large round table and the Enclave seated at it, Charlotte between Benedict Lightwood and the elegant white-haired woman. Charlotte was easily recognizable, even from above, by the neat knotting of her brown hair and the quick movements of her small hands as she spoke.

"Why up here?" Jem asked Will in a low voice. "Why not the weapons room? It's next to the library."

"Sound radiates," said Will. "Just as easy to listen from up here. Besides which, who's to say one of them wouldn't decide to pay a visit to the weapons room halfway through the meeting to see what we've in stock? It's happened before."

Tessa, staring down in fascination, realized that indeed she could hear the murmur of voices. "Can they hear us?"

Will shook his head. "The enchantment is strictly one-way." He frowned, leaning forward. "What are they talking about?"

The three of them fell silent, and in the quiet the sound of Benedict Lightwood's voice rose clearly to their ears. "I don't know about this, Charlotte," he said. "This whole plan seems very risky."

"But we cannot simply let de Quincey go on as he has," Charlotte argued. "He's the head vampire of the London clans. The rest of the Night Children look to him for guidance. If we allow him to cavalierly break the Law, what message does that send to Downworld? That the Nephilim have grown lax in their guardianship?"

"Just so I understand," Lightwood said, "you're willing to take Lady Belcourt's word that de Quincey, a longtime ally of the Clave, is actually murdering mundanes in his own house?"

"I don't know why you're surprised, Benedict." There was an edge to Charlotte's voice. "Is it your suggestion that we *ignore* her report, despite the fact that she has given us nothing but reliable information in the past? And despite the fact that if she is once again telling the truth, the blood of everyone that de Quincey murders from this point onward will be on our hands?"

"And despite the fact that we are bound by the Law to investigate any report of the Covenant being broken," said a slender dark-haired man at the far end of the table. "You know that as well as the rest of us, Benedict; you're simply being stubborn."

Charlotte exhaled as Lightwood's face darkened. "Thank you, George. I appreciate that," she said.

The tall woman who had earlier called Charlotte Lottie gave a low, rumbling laugh. "Don't be so dramatic, Charlotte," she said. "You must admit, the whole business is bizarre. A shape-changing girl who may or may not be a warlock, brothels full of dead bodies, and an informant who swears he sold de Quincey some machine tools—a fact that you seem to regard as a piece of the most consummate evidence, despite refusing to tell us your informant's name."

"I swore I wouldn't involve him," Charlotte protested. "He fears de Quincey."

"Is he a Shadowhunter?" Lightwood demanded. "Because if not, he isn't reliable."

"Really, Benedict, your views are most antiquated," said the woman with the catlike eyes. "One might believe, talking to you, that the Accords had never happened."

"Lilian is correct; you're being ridiculous, Benedict," said George Penhallow. "Looking for an entirely reliable informant is like looking for a chaste mistress. If they were virtuous, they would be little use to you in the first place. An informant merely provides information; it is our job to *verify* that information, which is what Charlotte is suggesting that we do."

"I would simply hate to see the powers of the Enclave misused in this instance," Lightwood said in a silky tone. It was very odd, Tessa thought, hearing this group of elegant adults addressing one another without honorifics, simply by their first names. But it seemed to be Shadowhunter custom. "If, for instance, there were a vampire who had a grudge against the head of her clan, and perhaps wanted to see him removed from power, what better way than to get the Clave to do her dirty work for her?"

"Hell," Will muttered, exchanging a glance with Jem. "How does he know about that?"

Jem shook his head, as if to say *I don't know.*

"Know about what?" Tessa whispered, but her voice was drowned out by Charlotte and the white-haired woman both talking at once.

"Camille would *never* do that!" Charlotte protested. "She isn't a fool, for one thing. She knows what the punishment for lying to us would be!"

"Benedict has a point," said the older woman. "It would be better if a Shadowhunter had seen de Quincey breaking the Law—"

"But that's the point of this whole enterprise," Charlotte said. There was a tinge to her voice—of nervousness, a strained desire to prove herself. Tessa felt a flicker of sympathy for her. "To observe de Quincey breaking the Law, Aunt Callida."

Tessa made a startled noise.

Jem looked up. "Yes, she's Charlotte's aunt," he said. "It was her brother—Charlotte's father—who used to run the Institute. She likes to tell people what to do. Although, of course *she* always does whatever she wants."

"She does at that," Will agreed. "Did you know she propositioned me once?"

Jem did not look as if he believed this even slightly. "She did not."

"She did," Will insisted. "It was all very scandalous. I might have acceded to her demands too, if she didn't frighten me so much."

Jem simply shook his head and turned his attention back to the scene unfolding in the library. "There is also the matter of de Quincey's seal," Charlotte was saying, "which we found inside the body of the clockwork girl. There is simply too much evidence linking him to these events, too much evidence not to investigate."

"I agree," said Lilian. "I for one am concerned about this matter of the clockwork creatures. Making clockwork girls is one thing, but what if he's making a clockwork army?"

"That's pure speculation, Lilian," said Frederick Ashdown.

Lilian dismissed this with a wave of her hand. "An automaton is neither seraph nor demon in its alliance; it is not one of the children of God or of the Devil. Would it be vulnerable to our weapons?"

"I think you're imagining a problem that does not exist,"

said Benedict Lightwood. "There have been automatons for years now; mundanes are fascinated with the creatures. None has posed a threat to us."

"None has been made using magic before," said Charlotte.

"That you know of." Lightwood looked impatient.

Charlotte straightened her back; only Tessa and the others, looking down upon her, could see that her hands were knotted tightly together in her lap. "Your concern, Benedict, seems to be that we will unfairly punish de Quincey for a crime he has not committed, and in doing so jeopardize the relationship between the Night Children and the Nephilim. Am I correct?"

Benedict Lightwood nodded.

"But all that Will's plan calls for is for us to *observe* de Quincey. If we do not see him breaking the Law, we will not act against him, and the relationship will not be threatened. If we do see him breaking the Law, then the relationship is a lie. We cannot allow abuse of Covenant Law, however . . . convenient it might be for us to ignore."

"I agree with Charlotte," said Gabriel Lightwood, speaking up for the first time, and much to Tessa's surprise. "I think her plan is a sound one. Except in one part—sending the shape-shifter girl in there with Will Herondale. He isn't even old enough to be at this meeting. How can he be trusted with a mission of this gravity?"

"Smarmy little prig," Will snarled, leaning farther forward, as if he longed to reach through the magical portal and strangle Gabriel. "When I get him alone . . ."

"I ought to go in with her instead," Gabriel went on. "I can look out for her a bit more. Instead of simply looking out for myself."

"Hanging's too good for him," agreed Jem, who looked as if he were trying not to laugh.

"Tessa knows Will," protested Charlotte. "She *trusts* Will."

"I wouldn't go that far," muttered Tessa.

"Besides," Charlotte said, "it's Will who devised this plan, Will who de Quincey will recognize from the Pandemonium Club. It's Will who knows what to search for inside de Quincey's town house to tie him to the clockwork creatures and the murdered mundanes. Will's an excellent investigator, Gabriel, and a good Shadowhunter. You have to give him that."

Gabriel sat back in his chair, crossing his arms over his chest. "I don't have to give him anything."

"So Will and your warlock girl enter the house, endure de Quincey's party until they observe some contravention of the Law, and then signal to the rest of us—how?" inquired Lilian.

"With Henry's invention," Charlotte said. There was a slight—only very slight—tremble to her voice as she said it. "The Phosphor. It will send up a flare of extremely bright witchlight, illuminating all the windows in de Quincey's house, just for a moment. That will be the signal."

"Oh, good Lord, not one of Henry's inventions again," said George.

"There were some complications with the Phosphor at first, but Henry demonstrated it for me last night," Charlotte protested. "It works perfectly."

Frederick snorted. "Remember the last time Henry offered us the use of one of his inventions? We were all cleaning fish guts off our gear for days."

"But it wasn't supposed to be used near water—," Charlotte began, still in the same quavering voice, but the others had already begun talking over her, chattering excitedly about Henry's failed inventions and the dreadful consequences thereof, while Charlotte lapsed into silence. *Poor Charlotte,* Tessa thought. Charlotte, whose sense of her own authority was so important, and so dearly bought.

"Bastards, talking over her like that," muttered Will. Tessa looked at him in astonishment. He was staring intently down at the scene before him, his fists tight at his sides. So he was fond of Charlotte, she thought, and she was surprised how pleased she was to realize it. Perhaps it meant Will actually did have feelings after all.

Not that it had anything to do with her, whether he did or not, of course. She looked hastily away from Will, at Jem, who seemed equally out of countenance. He was biting his lip. "Where is Henry? Shouldn't he have arrived by now?"

As if in answer, the door to the storage room banged open with a crash, and the three of them spun around to see Henry standing wild-eyed and wild-haired in the doorway. He was clutching something in his hand—the copper tube with the black button on the side that had nearly caused Will to break his arm falling off the sideboard in the dining room.

Will eyed it fearfully. "Get that blasted object away from me."

Henry, who was red-faced and sweating, stared at them all in horror. "Hell," he said. "I was looking for the library. The Enclave—"

"Is meeting," said Jem. "Yes, we know. It's a flight down from here, Henry. Third door on the right. And you'd better go. Charlotte's waiting for you."

"I know," Henry wailed. "Blast, blast, blast. I was just trying to get the Phosphor right, is all."

"Henry," Jem said, "Charlotte *needs* you."

"Right." Henry turned as if to dart out of the room, then swung around and stared at them, a look of confusion passing over his freckled face, as if he had only now had cause to wonder why Will, Tessa, and Jem might be crouching together in a mostly disused storage room. "What are you three doing in here, anyway?"

Will tilted his head to the side and smiled at Henry. "Charades," he said. "Massive game."

"Ah. Right, then," said Henry, and dashed out the door, letting it swing shut behind him.

"Charades." Jem snorted in disgust, then leaned forward again, elbows on his knees, as Callida's voice drifted up from below. "Honestly, Charlotte," she was saying, "when will you admit that Henry hasn't anything to do with running this place, and that you're doing it all by yourself? Perhaps with help from James Carstairs and Will Herondale, but neither of them is any older than seventeen. How much help can they be?"

Charlotte made a murmured noise of deprecation.

"It's too much for one person, especially someone your age," said Benedict. "You're only twenty-three years old. If you'd like to step down—"

Only twenty-three! Tessa was astonished. She'd thought Charlotte was much older, probably because she exuded such an air of competence.

"Consul Wayland assigned the running of the Institute to me and my husband five years ago," Charlotte replied sharply, apparently having found her voice again. "If you have some issue with his choice, you should take it up with him. In the meantime I shall direct the Institute as I see fit."

"I hope that means that plans such as the one you're suggesting are still up for a vote?" said Benedict Lightwood. "Or are you governing by fiat now?"

"Don't be ridiculous, Lightwood, of course it's up for a vote," said Lilian crossly, without giving Charlotte a chance to answer. "All in favor of moving on de Quincey, say aye."

To Tessa's surprise, there was a chorus of ayes, and not a single nay. The discussion had been contentious enough that she'd been certain at least one of the Shadowhunters would try to back out. Jem caught her startled look and smiled. "They're always like this," he murmured. "They like to jockey for power, but none of them would vote no on an issue like this. They'd be branded a coward for doing so."

"Very well," said Benedict. "Tomorrow night it is, then. Is everyone sufficiently prepared? Are there—"

The door to the library banged open, and Henry charged in—looking, if possible, even more wild-eyed and wild-haired than before. "I'm here!" he announced. "Not too late, am I?"

Charlotte covered her face with her hands.

"Henry," said Benedict Lightwood dryly. "How pleasant to see you. Your wife was just briefing us on your newest invention. The Phosphor, is it?"

"Yes!" Henry held the Phosphor up proudly. "This is it. And I can promise it works as advertised. See?"

"Now, there's no need for a demonstration," Benedict began hastily, but it was too late. Henry had already pressed the button. There was a bright flash, and the lights in the library winked out suddenly, leaving Tessa staring at an unlit black square in the floor. Gasps rose up from below. There was a shriek, and something crashed to the ground and shattered. Rising above it all was the sound of Benedict Lightwood, swearing fluently.

Will looked up and grinned. "Bit awkward for Henry, of course," he remarked cheerfully, "and yet, somehow quite satisfying, don't you think?"

Tessa couldn't help but agree, on both counts.

10

PALE KINGS AND PRINCES

I saw pale kings and princes too,
Pale warriors, death-pale were they all
—John Keats, "La Belle Dame Sans Merci"

As the coach rattled along the Strand, Will raised a black-gloved hand and drew one of the velvet curtains back from the window, letting a splash of yellow gaslight find its way into the carriage's dark interior. "It rather looks," he said, "as if we might be in for rain tonight."

Tessa followed his gaze; out the window the sky was a cloudy steel gray—the usual for London, she thought. Men in hats and long dark coats hurried along the pavement on either side of the street, their shoulders hunched against a brisk wind that carried coal dust, horse manure, and all sorts of eye-stinging rubbish in its wake. Once again Tessa thought she could smell the river.

"Is that a *church* directly in the middle of the street?" she wondered aloud.

"It's St. Mary le Strand," said Will, "and there's a long story about it, but I'm not going to tell it to you now. Have you been listening to anything I've been saying?"

"I was," Tessa said, "until you started on about rain. Who cares about rain? We're on our way to some sort of—vampire society event, and I've no idea how I'm supposed to behave, and so far you haven't helped me much at all."

The corner of Will's mouth twitched upward. "Just be careful. When we arrive at the house, you can't look to me for help or instruction. Remember, I am your human subjugate. You keep me about you for blood—blood whenever you want it—and nothing else."

"So you're not going to speak tonight," Tessa said. "At all."

"Not unless you instruct me to," said Will.

"This evening sounds as if it might be better than I thought."

Will seemed not to have heard her. With his right hand he was tightening one of the metal knife-bearing cuffs on his left wrist. He was staring off toward the window, as if seeing something that wasn't visible to her. "You might be thinking of vampires as feral monsters, but these vampires are not like that. They are as cultured as they are cruel. Sharpened knives to humanity's dull blade." The line of his jaw was set hard in the dim light. "You will have to try to keep up. And for God's sake, if you can't, don't say anything at all. They have a tortuous and opaque sense of etiquette. A serious social gaffe could mean instant death."

Tessa's hands tightened on each other in her lap. They were cold. She could feel the cold of Camille's skin, even through her gloves. "Are you joking? The way you were in the library, about dropping that book?"

"No." His voice was remote.

"Will, you're frightening me." The words came out of Tessa's mouth before she could stop them; she tensed, expecting mockery.

Will drew his gaze away from the window and looked at her as if some realization had dawned on him. "Tess," he said, and Tessa felt a momentary jolt; no one had ever called her Tess. Sometimes her brother had called her Tessie, but that was all. "You know you don't have to do this if you don't want to."

She took a breath, one she didn't need. "And then what? We would turn the carriage around and go home?"

He put his hands out, and took hers. Camille's hands were so small that Will's capable dark-gloved ones seemed to swallow them up. "One for all, and all for one," he said.

She smiled at that, weakly. *"The Three Musketeers?"*

His steady gaze held hers. His blue eyes were very dark, uniquely so. She had known people before with blue eyes, but they had always been light blue. Will's were the color of the sky just on the edge of night. His long lashes veiled them as he said, "Sometimes, when I have to do something I don't want to do, I pretend I'm a character from a book. It's easier to know what *they* would do."

"Really? Who do you pretend you are? D'Artagnan?" Tessa asked, naming the only one of the Three Musketeers that she could remember.

"'It is a far, far better thing that I do, than I have ever done,'" Will quoted. *"'It is a far, far better rest that I go to than I have ever known.'"*

"Sydney Carton? But you said you hated *A Tale of Two Cities*!"

"I don't really." Will seemed unabashed by his lie.

"And Sydney Carton was a dissipated alcoholic."

"Exactly. There was a man who was worthless, and knew he was worthless, and yet however far down he tried to sink his soul, there was always some part of him capable of great action." Will lowered his voice. "What is it he says to Lucie Manette? That though he is weak, he can still burn?"

Tessa, who had read *A Tale of Two Cities* more times than she could count, whispered, "*And yet I have had the weakness, and have still the weakness, to wish you to know with what a sudden mastery you kindled me, heap of ashes that I am, into fire.*" She hesitated. "But that was because he loved her."

"Yes," said Will. "He loved her enough to know she was better off without him." His hands were still on hers, the heat of them burning through her gloves. The wind was brisk outside, and had ruffled his ink black hair as they had crossed the Institute courtyard to the carriage. It made him look younger, and more vulnerable—and his eyes, too, were vulnerable, open like a door. The way he was looking at her, she would not have thought Will could, or would, look at anyone like that. If she could blush, she thought, how she would be blushing now.

And then she wished she had not thought of that. For that thought led, inevitably and unpleasantly, to another: Was he looking at her now, or at Camille, who was, indeed, exquisitely beautiful? Was that the reason for his change in expression? Could he see Tessa through the disguise, or only the shell of her?

She drew back, taking her hands from his, though his were closed tightly around hers. It took her a moment to disengage them.

"Tessa—," he began, but before he could say more, the carriage came to a jerking stop that set the velvet curtains swaying. Thomas called, "We're here!" from the driver's seat. Will, after taking a deep breath, swung the door open and leaped down to the pavement, lifting his hand to help her down after him.

Tessa bent her head as she exited the carriage to avoid crushing any of the roses on Camille's hat. Though Will wore gloves, as she did, she could almost imagine she felt the pulsing of blood under his skin, even through the double layer of fabric that separated them. He was flushed, the color high in his cheeks, and she wondered if it was the cold whipping the blood into his face, or something else.

They were standing in front of a tall white house with a white-pillared entrance. It was surrounded by similar houses on either side, like rows of pale dominoes. Up a row of white steps was a pair of double doors painted black. They were ajar, and Tessa could see the glimmer of candlelight from within, shimmering like a curtain.

Tessa turned to look at Will. Behind him Thomas was seated at the front of the carriage, his hat tipped forward to hide his face. The silver-handled pistol tucked into his waistcoat pocket was entirely hidden from view.

Somewhere in the back of her head, she felt Camille laugh, and she knew, without knowing how she knew, that she was sensing the vampire woman's amusement at her admiration of Will. *There you are*, Tessa thought, relieved despite her annoyance. She had begun to fear that Camille's inner voice would never come to her.

She drew away from Will, lifting her chin. The haughty pose wasn't natural to her—but it was to Camille. "You will address me not as Tessa but as a servant would," she said, her lip curling. "Now come." She jerked her head imperiously toward the steps, and started off without looking back to see if he followed.

An elegantly dressed footman awaited her at the top of the steps. "Your Ladyship," he murmured, and as he bowed, Tessa saw the two fang punctures in his neck, just above the collar. She turned her head to see Will behind her, and was about to introduce him to the footman when Camille's voice whispered in the back of her head, *We do not introduce our human pets to each other. They are our nameless property, unless we choose to give them names.*

Ugh, Tessa thought. In her disgust, she hardly noticed as the footman guided her down a long corridor and into a large marble-floored room. He bowed again and departed; Will moved to her side, and for a moment they both stood staring.

The space was lit only by candles. Dozens of gold candelabras dotted the room, fat white candles blazing in the holders. Hands carved of marble reached from the walls, each gripping a scarlet candle, drips of red wax blooming like roses along the sides of the carved marble.

And among the candelabras moved vampires, their faces as white as clouds, their movements graceful and liquid and strange. Tessa could see their similarities to Camille, the features they shared—the poreless skin, the jewel-colored eyes, the pale cheeks splotched with artificial rouge. Some looked more human than others; many were dressed in the fashions of bygone ages—knee breeches and cravats, skirts as full as Marie Antoinette's or gathered into trains at the back, lace cuffs and linen frills. Tessa's gaze scanned the room frantically, searching for a familiar fair-haired figure, but Nathaniel was nowhere to be seen. Instead she found herself trying not to stare at a tall skeletal woman, dressed in the heavily wigged and powdered fashion of a hundred years ago. Her face was stark and dreadful, whiter than the white powder dusting her hair. Her name was Lady Delilah, Camille's voice whispered in Tessa's mind. Lady Delilah held a slight figure by the hand, and Tessa's mind recoiled—a child, in this place?—but when the figure turned, she saw that it was a vampire as well, sunken dark eyes like pits in its rounded childish face. It smiled at Tessa, showing bared fangs.

"We must look for Magnus Bane," Will said under his breath. "He is meant to guide us through this mess. I shall point him out if I see him."

She was about to tell Will that Camille would recognize Magnus for her, when she caught sight of a slender man with a shock of fair hair, wearing a black swallowtail coat. Tessa felt her heart leap—and then fall in bitter disappointment as he turned. It was not Nathaniel. This man was a vampire, with a pale, angular face. His hair was not yellow like Nate's but was almost colorless under the candlelight. He dropped Tessa a wink and began to move toward her, pushing through the crowd. There were not only vampires among them, Tessa saw, but human subjugates as well. They carried gleaming serving trays, and on the trays were sets of empty glasses. Beside the glasses lay an array of silver utensils, all sharp-pointed. Knives, of course, and thin tools like the awls shoemakers used to punch holes in leather.

As Tessa stared in confusion, one of the subjugates was stopped by the woman in the white powdered wig. She snapped her fingers imperiously, and the darkling—a pale boy in a gray jacket and trousers—turned his head to the side obediently. After plucking a thin awl from the tray with her skinny fingers, the vampire drew the sharp tip across the skin of the boy's throat, just below his jaw. The glasses rattled on the tray as his hand shook, but he didn't drop the tray, not even when the woman lifted a glass and pressed it against his throat so that the blood ran down into it in a thin stream.

Tessa's stomach tightened with a sudden mixture of revulsion—and hunger; she could not deny the hunger, even though it belonged to Camille and not her. Stronger than the thirst, though, was her horror. She watched as the vampire woman lifted the glass to her lips, the human boy beside her standing gray-faced and trembling as she drank.

She wanted to reach for Will's hand, but a vampire baroness would never hold the hand of her human subjugate. She straightened her spine, and beckoned Will to her side with a quick snap of her fingers. He looked up in surprise, then moved to join her, clearly fighting to hide his annoyance. But hide it he must. "Now, don't go wandering off, William," she said with a meaningful glance. "I don't want to lose you in the crowd."

Will's jaw set. "I'm getting the oddest feeling that you're enjoying this," he said under his breath.

"Nothing odd about it." Feeling unbelievably bold, Tessa chucked him under the chin with the tip of her lace fan. "Simply behave yourself."

"They are *so* hard to train, aren't they?" The man with the colorless hair emerged out of the crowd, inclining his head toward Tessa. "Human subjugates, that is," he added, mistaking her startled expression for confusion. "And then once you have them properly trained, they die of something or other. Delicate creatures, humans. All the longevity of butterflies."

He smiled. The smile showed teeth. His skin had the bluish paleness of hardened ice. His hair was nearly white and hung arrow-straight to his shoulders, just brushing the collar of his elegant dark coat. His waistcoat was gray silk, figured with a pattern of twisting silver symbols. He looked like a Russian prince out of a book. "It's good to see you, Lady Belcourt," he said, and there was an accent to his voice too, not French— more Slavic. "Did I catch a glimpse of a new carriage through the window?"

This is de Quincey, Camille's voice breathed in Tessa's mind. Images rose up suddenly in her brain, like a fountain turned on, pouring forth visions instead of water. She saw herself dancing with de Quincey, her hands on his shoulders; she stood by a black stream under the white sky of a northern night, watching as he fed on something pale and sprawled in the grass; she sat motionless at a long table of other vampires, de Quincey at the head of it, as he shouted and screamed at her and brought his fist down so hard that the marble top of the table shivered into cracks. He was shouting at her, something about a werewolf and a relationship she would live to regret. Then she was sitting alone in a room, in the dark, and weeping, and de Quincey came in and knelt by her chair and took her hand, wanting to comfort her, though he had been the one to cause her pain. *Vampires can weep?* Tessa thought first, and then, *They have known each other a long time, Alexei de Quincey and Camille Belcourt. They were friends once, and he thinks they are friends still.*

"Indeed, Alexei," she said, and as she said it, she knew this was the name she had been trying to recall at the dinner table the other night—the foreign name the Dark Sisters had spoken. *Alexei.* "I wanted something a bit . . . roomier." She held her hand out, and stood still while he kissed it, his lips cold on her skin.

De Quincey's eyes slid past Tessa to Will, and he licked his lips. "And a new subjugate as well, I see. This one is quite fetching." He reached out a thin pale hand, and drew his forefinger down the side of Will's cheek to his jaw. "Such unusual coloring," he mused. "And these eyes."

"Thank you," said Tessa, in the manner of one being complimented on an especially tasteful choice of wallpaper. She watched nervously as de Quincey moved even closer to Will, who looked pale and strained. She wondered if he was having trouble holding himself back when surely every one of his nerves was screaming *Enemy! Enemy!*

De Quincey trailed his finger from Will's jaw to his throat, to the point at his collarbone where his pulse beat. "There," he said, and this time when he smiled, his white fangs were visible. They were sharp and fine at the points, like needles. His eyelids drooped, languorous and heavy, and his voice when he spoke was thick. "You wouldn't mind, Camille, would you, if I just had a little bite. . . ."

Tessa's vision went white. She saw de Quincey again, the front of his white shirt scarlet with blood—and she saw a body hanging upside down from a tree at the dark stream's edge, pale fingers dangling in the black water. . . .

Her hand whipped out, faster than she'd ever imagined she could have moved, and caught de Quincey's wrist. "My darling, no," she said, a wheedling tone in her voice. "I'd so like to keep him to myself for just a little while. You know how your appetite runs away with you sometimes." She lowered her eyelids.

De Quincey chuckled. "For you, Camille, I will exercise my restraint." He drew his wrist away, and for a moment, under the flirtatious poise, Tessa thought she saw a flash of anger in his eyes, quickly masked. "In honor of our long acquaintance."

"Thank you, Alexei."

"Have you given any further thought, my dear," he said, "to my offer of a membership in the Pandemonium Club? I know the mundanes bore you, but they are a source of funds, nothing more. Those of us on the board are on the verge of some very . . . exciting discoveries. Power beyond your wildest dreams, Camille."

Tessa waited, but Camille's inner voice was silent. Why? She fought down panic and managed to smile at de Quincey. "My dreams," she said, and hoped he would think the hoarseness in her voice was from amusement and not fear, "may be more wild already than you imagine."

Beside her, she could tell that Will had shot her a surprised look; he quickly schooled his features to blandness, though, and glanced away. De Quincey, his eyes gleaming, only smiled.

"I ask only that you consider my offer, Camille. And now I must attend to my other guests. I trust I will see you at the ceremony?"

Dazed, she simply nodded. "Of course."

De Quincey bowed, turned, and vanished into the crowd. Tessa let her breath out. She hadn't realized she'd been holding it.

"Don't," said Will softly at her side. "Vampires don't need to breathe, remember."

"My God, Will." Tessa realized she was shaking. "He would have bitten you."

Will's eyes were dark with rage. "I would have killed him first."

A voice spoke at Tessa's elbow. "And then you would both be dead."

She whirled and saw that a tall man had appeared just behind her, as soundlessly as if he had drifted there like smoke. He wore an elaborate brocade jacket, like something out of the previous century, with a riot of white lace at his collar and cuffs. Below the long jacket Tessa glimpsed knee breeches, and high buckled shoes. His hair was like rough black silk, so dark it had a bluish sheen to it; his skin was brown, the cast of his features like Jem's. She wondered if perhaps, like Jem, he was of foreign extraction. In one ear he sported a silver loop from which dangled a diamond pendant the size of a finger, which sparkled brilliantly under the lights, and there were diamonds set into the head of his silver walking stick. He seemed to gleam all over, like witchlight. Tessa stared; she had never seen anyone dressed in such a mad fashion.

"*This* is Magnus," said Will quietly, sounding relieved. "Magnus Bane."

"My darling Camille," Magnus said, bending to kiss her gloved hand. "We have been parted too long."

The moment he touched her, Camille's memories came rushing up in a flood—memories of Magnus holding her, kissing her, touching her in a distinctly intimate and personal manner. Tessa jerked her hand back with a squeak.

And now *you reappear,* she thought resentfully in Camille's direction.

"I see," he murmured, straightening. His eyes, when he raised them to Tessa's, nearly made her lose her composure: They were gold-green with slit pupils, the eyes of a cat set in a distinctly human face. They were full of shimmering amusement. Unlike Will, whose eyes held a trace of sadness even when he was amused, Magnus's eyes were full of a surprising joy. They darted sideways, and he jerked his chin toward the far side of the room, indicating that Tessa should follow him. "Come along, then. There's a private room where we can talk."

In a daze Tessa followed him, Will at her side. Was she imagining it, or did the white faces of the vampires turn to follow her as she passed? A redheaded female vampire in an elaborate blue dress glared at her as she went; Camille's voice whispered that the woman was jealous of de Quincey's regard for her. Tessa was grateful when Magnus finally reached a door—so cleverly set into the paneled wall that she didn't realize it was a door until the warlock had produced a key. He slid the door open with a soft click. Will and Tessa followed him inside.

The room was a library, obviously rarely used; though volumes lined the walls, they were grimed with dust, as were the velvet curtains that hung across the windows. When the door shut behind them, the light in the room dimmed; before Tessa could say anything, Magnus snapped his fingers and twin fires leaped up in the fireplaces on either side of the room. The flames of the fire were blue, and the fire itself had a strong scent, like burning joss sticks.

"Oh!" Tessa could not stop a small exclamation of surprise from passing her lips.

With a grin Magnus flung himself onto the great marble-topped table in the center of the room, and lay down on his side, his head propped on his hand. "Have you never seen a warlock do magic before?"

Will gave an exaggerated sigh. "Please refrain from teasing her, Magnus. I expect Camille told you she knows very little of the Shadow World."

"Indeed," Magnus said unrepentantly, "but it's hard to believe, considering what she can do." His eyes were on Tessa. "I saw your face when I kissed your hand. You knew who I was immediately, didn't you? You know what Camille knows. There are some warlocks and demons who can shift—take on any shape. But I have never heard of one who could do what you do."

"It cannot be said for certain that I'm a warlock," Tessa said. "Charlotte says I'm not marked like a warlock would be marked."

"Oh, you're a warlock. Depend on it. Just because you don't have bat ears . . ." Magnus saw Tessa frown, and raised his eyebrows. "Oh, you don't *want* to be a warlock, do you? You despise the idea."

"I just never thought . . . ," Tessa said in a whisper. "That I was anything other than human."

Magnus's tone was not unsympathetic. "Poor thing. Now that you know the truth, you can never go back."

"Leave her alone, Magnus." Will's tone was sharp. "I must search the room. If you won't help, at least try not to torment Tessa while I do it." He moved toward the big oak desk in the corner of the room and began rummaging among the papers atop it.

Magnus glanced toward Tessa and winked. "I think he's jealous," he said in a conspiratorial whisper.

Tessa shook her head and moved toward the nearest bookshelf. There was a book propped open on the middle shelf as if to display it. The pages were covered with bright, intricate figures, some parts of the illustrations gleaming as if they had been painted onto the parchment with gold. Tessa exclaimed in surprise. "It's a Bible."

"Does that astonish you?" Magnus inquired.

"I thought vampires couldn't touch holy things."

"It depends on the vampire—how long they've been alive, what kind of faith they have. De Quincey actually collects old Bibles. He says there's hardly another book out there with so much blood on the pages."

Tessa glanced toward the closed door. The faint swell of voices on the other side was audible. "Won't we excite some sort of comment, hiding in here like this? The others—the vampires—I'm sure they were staring at us as we came in."

"They were staring at Will." In some ways Magnus's smile was as unnerving as a vampire's, even though he didn't have fangs. "Will looks wrong."

Tessa glanced over at Will, who was rummaging through the desk drawers with gloved hands. "I find that hard to credit coming from someone dressed as you are," Will said.

Magnus ignored this. "Will doesn't behave like the other human subjugates. He doesn't stare at his mistress with blind adoration, for instance."

"It's that monstrous hat of hers," said Will. "Puts me off."

"Human subjugates are never 'put off,'" said Magnus. "They adore their vampire masters, whatever they wear. Of course,

the guests were also staring because they know of my relationship with Camille, and are wondering what we might be doing
here in the library . . . alone." He wiggled his eyebrows at Tessa.

Tessa thought back to her visions. "De Quincey . . . He
said something to Camille about regretting her relationship
with a werewolf. He made it sound as if it were a crime she
committed."

Magnus, who was now lying on his back and twirling his
walking stick over his head, shrugged. "To him it would be.
Vampires and werewolves despise each other. They claim it has
something to do with the fact that the two races of demons that
spawned them were involved in a blood feud, but if you ask me,
it's simply that they're both predators, and predators always
resent incursions into their territory. Not that vampires are all
that fond of the fey, or my kind either, but de Quincey rather
likes me. He thinks we're friends. In fact, I suspect he'd like to
be more than friends." Magnus grinned, to Tessa's confusion.
"But I despise him, though he doesn't know it."

"Then, why spend time with him at all?" asked Will, who
had moved to a tall secretary between two of the windows and
was examining its contents. "Why come to his house?"

"Politics," said Magnus with another shrug. "He is the head
of the clan; for Camille not to come to his parties when invited
would be construed as an insult. And for me to allow her to go
alone would be . . . careless. De Quincey is dangerous, and no
less to those of his own kind. Especially those who have dis-
pleased him in the past."

"Then you should—," Will began, and broke off, his voice
altering. "I've found something." He paused. "Perhaps you
should have a look at this, Magnus." Will came over to the

table and set down on it what looked like a long sheet of rolled paper. He gestured for Tessa to join him, and unrolled the paper across the table's surface. "There was little of interest in the desk," he said, "but I did find this, hidden in a false drawer in the cabinet. Magnus, what do you think?"

Tessa, who had moved to stand beside Will at the table, gazed down at the paper. It was covered with a rough blueprint drawing of a human skeleton made up of pistons, cogs, and plates of hammered metal. The skull had a hinged jaw, open sockets for eyes, and a mouth that ended just behind the teeth. There was a panel in the chest too, just like Miranda's. All along the left side of the page were scrawled what looked like notes, in a language Tessa could not decipher. The letters were utterly unfamiliar.

"Blueprint for an automaton," said Magnus, cocking his head to the side. "An artificial human being. Humans have always been fascinated by the creatures—I suppose because they are humanoid but cannot die or be hurt. Have you ever read *The Book of Knowledge of Ingenious Mechanical Devices*?"

"I've never even heard of it," said Will. "Are there any bleak moors in it, shrouded in mysterious mists? Ghostly brides wandering the halls of ruined castles? A handsome fellow rushing to the rescue of a beauteous yet penniless maiden?"

"No," said Magnus. "There's a rather racy bit about cogs halfway through, but really most of it is rather dry."

"Then Tessa won't have read it, either," said Will.

Tessa glared at him, but said nothing; she *hadn't* read it, and she wasn't in the mood to let Will get to her.

"Well, then," said Magnus. "It was written by an Arab scholar, two centuries before Leonardo da Vinci, and described how machines could be built that would mimic the actions of human beings. Now, there is nothing alarming about that in and of itself. But it is this"—Magnus's long finger brushed gently across the writing on the left side of the page—"that concerns me."

Will leaned closer. His sleeve brushed Tessa's arm. "Yes, that was what I wanted to ask you about. Is it a spell?"

Magnus nodded. "A binding spell. Meant to infuse demonic energy into an inanimate object, thus giving that object a sort of life. I've seen the spell used. Before the Accords vampires liked to amuse themselves by creating little demonic mechanisms like music boxes that would play only at night, mechanical horses that could ride only after sundown, that sort of silliness." He tapped thoughtfully on the head of his walking stick. "One of the great problems of creating convincing automatons, of course, has always been their appearance. No other material quite gives the semblance of human flesh."

"But what if one were to use it—human flesh, I mean?" Tessa asked.

Magnus paused delicately. "The problem there, for human designers, is, ah, obvious. Preserving the flesh destroys its appearance. One would have to use magic. And then magic again, to bind the demon energy to the mechanical body."

"And what would that achieve?" Will asked, an edge to his voice.

"Automatons have been built that can write poems, draw landscapes—but only those they are directed to create. They have no individual creativity or imagination. Animated by a demon energy, however, an automaton would have a measure of thought and will. But any bound spirit is enslaved. It would inevitably be entirely obedient to whoever had done the binding."

"A clockwork army," Will said, and there was a sort of bitter humor in his voice. "Born of neither Heaven nor Hell."

"I wouldn't go that far," Magnus said. "Demon energies are hardly an easy item to come by. One must summon demons up, then bind them, and you know what a difficult process that is. Obtaining enough demon energies to create an army would be well-nigh impossible and extraordinarily risky. Even for an evil-minded bastard like de Quincey."

"I see." And with that, Will rolled up the paper and slipped it into his jacket. "Much obliged for your help, Magnus."

Magnus looked faintly puzzled, but his response was courteous: "Of course."

"I gather you wouldn't be sorry to see de Quincey gone and another vampire in his place," said Will. "Have you actually observed him breaking the Law?"

"Once. I was invited here to witness one of his 'ceremonies.' As it turned out—" Magnus looked uncharacteristically grim. "Well, let me show you."

He turned and moved toward the bookshelf that Tessa had been examining earlier, gesturing for them to join him. Will followed, Tessa beside him. Magnus snapped his fingers again, and as blue sparks flew, the illustrated Bible slid to the side, revealing a small hole that had been cut into the wood at the back of the shelf. As Tessa leaned forward in surprise, she saw that it offered a view into an elegant music room. At least, that was what she thought at first, seeing the chairs set up in rows facing the back of the room; it made a sort of theater. Rows of lit candelabras were set up for illumination. Red satin floor-length curtains blocked off the back walls, and the floor was slightly raised, creating a sort of makeshift stage. There was nothing on it but a single chair with a high wooden back.

Steel manacles were attached to the arms of the chair, glittering like insect carapaces in the candlelight. The wood of the chair was blotched, here and there, with dark red stains. The legs of the chair, Tessa saw, were nailed to the floor.

"This is where they have their little . . . performances," said Magnus, an undertone of distaste in his voice. "They bring out the human and lock him—or her—to the chair. Then they take turns draining their victim slowly, while the crowd watches and applauds."

"And they enjoy that?" Will said. The disgust in his voice was more than an undertone. "The mundanes' pain? Their fear?"

"Not all the Night Children are like this," Magnus said quietly. "These are the worst of them."

"And the victims," said Will, "where do they find them?"

"Criminals, mostly," said Magnus. "Drunkards, addicts, whores. The forgotten and lost. Those who will not be missed." He looked squarely at Will. "Would you like to elaborate on your plan?"

"We begin when we see the Law being broken," said Will. "The moment a vampire moves to harm a human, I will signal the Enclave. They'll attack."

"Really," Magnus said. "How will they get in?"

"Don't worry about that." Will was unfazed. "Your job is to take Tessa at that point and get her safely out of here. Thomas is waiting outside with the carriage. Bundle yourselves into it and he'll take you back to the Institute."

"Seems a waste of my talents, assigning me to look after one moderately sized girl," Magnus observed. "Surely you could use me—"

"This is a Shadowhunter affair," said Will. "We make the Law, and we uphold the Law. The assistance you've given us so far has been invaluable, but we require no more from you."

Magnus met Tessa's eyes over Will's shoulder; his look was wry. "The proud isolation of the Nephilim. They have use for you when they have use for you, but they cannot bring themselves to share a victory with Downworlders."

Tessa turned to Will. "You're sending me away as well, before the fighting starts?"

"I must," said Will. "It would be best for Camille not to be seen to be cooperating with Shadowhunters."

"That's nonsense," said Tessa. "De Quincey will know I— she—brought you here. He'll know she lied about where she found you. Does she think that after this, the rest of the clan won't know she's a traitor?"

Somewhere in the back of her head, Camille's soft laughter purred. She did not sound afraid.

Will and Magnus exchanged a look. "She does not expect," said Magnus, "that a single vampire who is here tonight will survive the evening to accuse her."

"The dead can tell no tales," said Will softly. The flickering light in the room painted his face in alternating shades of black and gold; the line of his jaw was hard. He looked toward the peephole, eyes narrowing. "Look."

The three of them jostled to get close to the peephole, through which they saw the pocket doors at one end of the music room slide open. Through them was the large candlelit drawing room; vampires began to stream through the doors, taking their places in the seats before the "stage."

"It's time," Magnus said softly, and slid the peephole closed.

* * *

The music room was nearly full. Tessa, arm in arm with Magnus, watched as Will threaded his way through the crowd, looking for three seats together. He was keeping his head bowed, his eyes on the floor, but even so—

"They're still looking at him," she said to Magnus under her breath. "At Will, I mean."

"Of course they are," said Magnus. His eyes reflected light like a cat's as they surveyed the room. "Look at him. The face of a bad angel and eyes like the night sky in Hell. He's very pretty, and vampires like that. I can't say I mind either." Magnus grinned. "Black hair and blue eyes are my favorite combination."

Tessa reached up to pat Camille's pale blond curls.

Magnus shrugged. "Nobody's perfect."

Tessa was spared answering; Will had found a set of chairs together, and was beckoning them over with a gloved hand. She tried not to pay attention to the way the vampires were looking at him as she let Magnus lead her toward the seats. It was true that he was beautiful, but what did they care? Will was just food to them, wasn't he?

She sat down with Magnus on one side of her and Will on the other, her silk taffeta skirts rustling like leaves in a stiff wind. The room was cool, not like a room crowded with human beings, who would have been giving off body heat. Will's sleeve slid up his arm as he reached to pat the pocket of his waistcoat, and she saw that his arm was dotted with goose bumps. She wondered if the human companions of vampires were always cold.

A rustle of whispers went through the room, and Tessa tore

her eyes from Will. The light of the candelabras did not reach the far recesses of the room; portions of the "stage"—the back of the room—were blotched with shadows, and even Tessa's vampire eyes could not discern what was moving within the darkness until de Quincey appeared suddenly from the shadows.

The audience was silent. Then de Quincey grinned. It was a manic grin, showing fangs, and it transformed his face. He looked wild and savage now, wolflike. A murmur of hushed appreciation went through the room, the way a human audience might show appreciation for an actor with a particularly good stage presence.

"Good evening," said de Quincey. "Welcome, friends. Those of you who have joined me here"—and he smiled directly at Tessa, who was too nervous to do anything but stare back— "are proud sons and daughters of the Night Children. We do not bend our necks beneath the oppressive yoke called the Law. We do not answer to Nephilim. Nor shall we abandon our ancient customs at their whim."

It was impossible not to notice the effect de Quincey's speech was having on Will. He was as taut as a bow, his hands clenched in his lap, the veins standing out in his neck.

"We have a prisoner," de Quincey went on. "His crime is betraying the Night Children." He swept his gaze across the audience of waiting vampires. "And what is the punishment for such treason?"

"It is death!" cried a voice, the vampire woman Delilah. She was straining forward in her seat, a terrible eagerness on her face.

The other vampires took up her cry. "Death! Death!"

More shadowy forms slipped between the curtains that

formed the makeshift stage. Two male vampires, holding between them the struggling form of a human man. A black hood concealed the man's features. All Tessa could see was that he was slender, probably young—and filthy, his fine clothes torn and ragged. His bare feet left bloody smears on the boards as the men dragged him forward and flung him into the chair. A faint gasp of sympathy escaped Tessa's throat; she felt Will tense beside her.

The man continued to thrash feebly, like an insect on the end of a pin, as the vampires strapped his wrists and ankles to the chair, and then stepped back. De Quincey grinned; his fangs were out. They shone like ivory pins as he surveyed the crowd. Tessa could sense the vampires' restlessness—and more than their restlessness, their hunger. No longer did they resemble a well-bred audience of human theatergoers. They were as avid as lions scenting prey, lurching forward in their chairs, their eyes wide and glowing, their mouths open.

"When can you summon the Enclave?" Tessa said to Will in an urgent whisper.

Will's voice was tight. "When he draws blood. We must *see* him do it."

"Will—"

"Tessa." He whispered her real name, his fingers gripping hers. "Be *quiet*."

Reluctantly Tessa returned her attention to the stage, where de Quincey was approaching the shackled prisoner. He paused by the chair—reached out—and his thin pale fingers brushed the man's shoulder, as light as a spider's touch. The prisoner convulsed, jerking in desperate terror as the vampire's hand slid from his shoulder to his neck. De Quincey laid two white fingers to the man's pulse point, as if he were a doctor checking a patient's heartbeat.

De Quincey wore a silver ring on one finger, Tessa saw, one side of which sharpened to a needle point that protruded when he tightened his hand into a fist. There was a flash of silver, and the prisoner screamed—the first sound he had made. There was something familiar about the sound.

A thin line of red appeared on the prisoner's throat, like a loop of red wire. Blood welled and spilled down into the hollow of his collarbone. The prisoner thrashed and struggled as de Quincey, his face now a rictus mask of hunger, reached to touch two fingers to the red liquid. He lifted the stained fingertips to his mouth. The crowd was hissing and moaning, barely able to stay in their seats. Tessa glanced toward a woman in a white-plumed hat. Her mouth was open, her chin wet with drool.

"Will," Tessa murmured. "Will, *please*."

Will glanced past her, at Magnus. "Magnus. Take her out of here."

Something in Tessa rebelled at the idea of being sent away. "Will, no, I'm all right here—"

Will's voice was quiet, but his eyes blazed. "We've been over this. Go, or I won't summon the Enclave. Go, or that man will die."

"Come." It was Magnus, his hand on her elbow, guiding her to stand. Reluctantly she allowed the warlock to draw her to her feet, and then toward the doors. Tessa glanced around anxiously to see if anyone noticed their departure, but no one was looking at them. All attention was riveted on de Quincey and the prisoner, and many vampires were already on their feet, hissing and cheering and making inhuman hungry sounds.

Among the seething crowd, Will was still seated, leaning forward like a hunting dog yearning to be released from the leash. His left hand slid into his waistcoat pocket, and emerged with something copper held between his fingers.

The Phosphor.

Magnus swung the door open behind them. "Hurry."

Tessa hesitated, looking back at the stage. De Quincey was standing behind the prisoner now. His grinning mouth was smeared with blood. He reached out and took hold of the prisoner's hood.

Will rose to his feet, the Phosphor held aloft. Magnus swore and pulled at Tessa's arm. She half-turned as if to go with him, then froze as de Quincey whipped off the black hood to reveal the prisoner beneath.

His face was swollen and bruised with beatings. One of his eyes was black and swelled shut. His blond hair was pasted to his skull with blood and sweat. But none of that mattered; Tessa would have known him anyway, anywhere. She knew now why his cry of pain had sounded so familiar to her.

It was Nathaniel.

11

FEW ARE ANGELS

We all are men,
In our own natures frail, and capable
Of our flesh; few are angels
—Shakespeare, *King Henry VIII*

Tessa screamed.

Not a human scream but a vampire scream. She barely recognized the sound that came from her own throat—it sounded like shattering glass. Only later did she even realize that she was screaming words. She would have thought she'd cry her brother's name, but she didn't.

"Will!" she screamed. "Will, now! Do it now!"

A gasp ran through the room. Dozens of white faces swung toward Tessa. Her scream had broken through their bloodlust. De Quincey was motionless on the stage; even Nathaniel was looking at her, dazed and staring, as if wondering if her screams were a dream born out of his agony.

Will, his finger on the button of the Phosphor, hesitated. His eyes met Tessa's across the room. It was only for a split second, but de Quincey saw their glance. As if he could read it, the look on his face changed, and he swung his hand up to point directly at Will.

"The boy," he spat. "Stop him!"

Will tore his gaze from Tessa's. The vampires were already rising to their feet, moving toward him, their eyes glittering with rage and hunger. Will looked past them, at de Quincey, who was staring at Will with fury. There was no fear on Will's face as his gaze met the vampire's—no hesitation, and no surprise.

"I am not a boy," he said. "I am Nephilim."

And he pressed the button.

Tessa braced herself for a flare of white witchlight. Instead there was a great *whoosh* of sound as the flames of the candelabras shot toward the ceiling. Sparks flew, scattering the floor with glowing embers, catching in the curtains, in the skirts of women's dresses. Suddenly the room was full of billowing black smoke and screams—high-pitched and horrible.

Tessa could no longer see Will. She tried to dart forward, but Magnus—she had nearly forgotten he was there—caught her firmly by the wrist. "Miss Gray, no," he said, and when she responded by pulling away harder, he added, "Miss Gray! You're a vampire now! If you catch fire, you'll go up like kindling wood—"

As if to illustrate his point, at that moment a stray spark landed atop Lady Delilah's white wig. It burst into flames. With a cry she tried to rip it from her head, but as her hands came in contact with the flames, they, too, caught fire as if they were made of paper instead of skin. In less than a second both her arms were burning like torches. Howling, she raced toward the door, but the fire was faster than she was. Within seconds a bonfire raged where she had stood. Tessa could just see the outline of a blackened screaming creature writhing inside it.

"Do you see what I mean?" Magnus shouted in Tessa's ear, struggling to make himself heard over the howls of the vampires, who were diving this way and that, trying to avoid the flames.

"Let me go!" Tessa shrieked. De Quincey had leaped into the melee; Nathaniel was slumped alone onstage, apparently unconscious, only his manacles holding him to the chair. "That's my brother up there. My *brother!*"

Magnus stared at her. Taking advantage of his confusion, Tessa jerked her arm free and began to run toward the stage. The room was chaos: vampires rushing to and fro, many of them stampeding toward the doorway. The vampires who had reached the door were pushing and shoving to get through it first; others had turned course and were streaming toward the French doors that looked out over the garden.

Tessa veered to avoid a fallen chair, and nearly ran headlong into the redheaded vampire in the blue dress who had glared at her earlier. She looked terrified now. She plunged toward Tessa—then seemed to stumble. Her mouth opened in a scream, and blood poured from it like a fountain. Her face crumpled, folding in on itself, the skin resolving into dust and raining down from the bones of her skull. Her red hair shriveled and turned gray; the skin of her arms melted and turned to powder, and with a last despairing shriek the vampire woman collapsed into a stringy heap of bones and dust lying atop an empty satin dress.

Tessa gagged, tore her eyes away from the remains, and saw Will. He stood directly in front of her, holding a long silver knife; the blade was smeared with scarlet blood. His face was bloody too, his eyes wild. "What the *hell* are you still doing here?" he shouted at Tessa. "You *unbelievably* stupid—"

Tessa heard the noise before Will did, a thin whining sound, like a piece of broken machinery. The fair-haired boy in the gray jacket—the human servant Lady Delilah had drunk from earlier—was rushing at Will, a high-pitched wailing sound coming from his throat, his face smeared with tears and blood. He was carrying a torn-off chair leg in one hand; the end of it was ragged and sharp.

"Will, look *out!*" Tessa shouted, and Will spun. He moved *fast*, Tessa saw, like a dark blur, and the knife in his hand was a flash of silver in the smoky dimness. When he stopped moving, the boy was lying on the ground, the blade protruding from his chest. Blood welled around it, thicker and darker than vampire blood.

Will, staring down, was ashen. "I thought . . ."

"He would have killed you if he could," Tessa said.

"You know nothing of it," Will said. He shook his head, once, as if clearing it of her voice, or of the sight of the boy on the ground. The subjugate looked very young, his twisted face softer in death. "I told you to go—"

"That's my brother," Tessa said, pointing toward the back of the room. Nathaniel was still unconscious, limp in his manacles. If it weren't for the blood still flowing from the wound in his neck, she would have thought he was dead. "Nathaniel. In the chair."

Will's eyes widened in astonishment. "But how—?" he began. He didn't get a chance to finish his question. At that moment the sound of shattering glass filled the room. The French windows burst inward, and the room was suddenly flooded with Shadowhunters in their dark fighting gear. They were driving before them in a screaming, ragged group the vampires who had fled into the garden. As Tessa stared, more Shadowhunters began flooding in from the other doors as well, herding more vampires in front of them, like dogs herding sheep into a pen. De Quincey staggered before the other vampires, his pale face smeared with black ash, his teeth bared.

Tessa saw Henry among the Nephilim, easily recognizable by his ginger hair. Charlotte was there too, dressed like a man all in dark fighting gear, like the women pictured in Tessa's Shadowhunter book. She looked small and determined and surprisingly fierce. And then there was Jem. His gear made him appear all the more startlingly pale, and the black Marks on his skin stood out like ink on paper. In the crowd she recognized Gabriel Lightwood; his father, Benedict; slim black-haired Mrs. Highsmith; and behind them all strode Magnus, blue sparks flying from his hands as he gestured.

Will exhaled, some of the color returning to his face. "I wasn't sure they'd come," he muttered, "not with the Phosphor malfunctioning." He tore his eyes away from his friends and looked at Tessa. "Go attend to your brother," he said. "That'll get you out of the worst of it. I hope."

He turned and walked away from her without a backward glance. The Nephilim had herded the remaining vampires, those who had not been killed by the fire—or by Will—into the center of a makeshift circle of Shadowhunters. De Quincey towered among the group, his pale face twisted in rage; his shirt was stained with blood—his own or someone else's, she couldn't tell. The other vampires huddled behind him like children behind a parent, looking both fierce and wretched at the same time.

"The Law," de Quincey growled, as Benedict Lightwood advanced on him, a shining blade in his right hand, its surface scored with black runes. "The Law protects us. We surrender to you. The Law—"

"You have broken the Law," snarled Benedict. "Therefore its protection no longer extends to you. The sentence is death."

"One mundane," said de Quincey, sparing a glance toward Nathaniel. "One mundane who has *also* broken Covenant Law—"

"The Law does not extend to mundanes. They cannot be expected to follow the laws of a world they know nothing of."

"He is worthless," de Quincey said. "You do not know how worthless. Do you really desire to shatter our alliance over one worthless mundane?"

"It is more than just one mundane!" Charlotte cried, and from her jacket she drew the paper Will had taken from the library. Tessa had not seen Will pass it to Charlotte, but he must have. "What of these spells? Did you think we would not discover them? This—this black sorcery is absolutely forbidden by the Covenant!"

De Quincey's still face betrayed only a hint of his surprise. "Where did you find that?"

Charlotte's mouth was a hard thin line. "That doesn't matter."

"Whatever it is you think you know—," de Quincey began.

"We know enough!" Charlotte's voice was full of passion. "We know you hate and despise us! We know your alliance with us has been a sham!"

"And have you made it against Covenant Law now to dislike Shadowhunters?" de Quincey said, but the sneer was gone from his voice. He sounded ragged.

"Do not play your games with us," spat Benedict. "After all we've done for you, after we passed the Accords into Law— Why? We've tried to make you equal to ourselves—"

De Quincey's face twisted. "*Equal?* You don't know what the word means. You cannot let go of your own conviction, let go of your belief in your inherent superiority, for long enough to even *consider* what that would mean. Where are our seats on the Council? Where is our embassy in Idris?"

"But that—that's ridiculous," Charlotte said, though she had blanched.

Benedict shot Charlotte an impatient look. "And irrelevant. None of this excuses your behavior, de Quincey. While you sat in council with us, pretending you were interested in peace, behind our backs you broke the Law and mocked our power. Surrender yourself, tell us what we want to know, and we might let your clan survive. Otherwise, there will be no mercy."

Another vampire spoke. It was one of the men who had strapped Nathaniel to his chair, a big flame-haired man with an angry face. "If we needed any further proof that the Nephilim have never meant their promises of peace, here it is. Dare to attack us, Shadowhunters, and you'll have a war on your hands!"

Benedict only grinned. "Then let the war begin here," he

said, and flung the blade at de Quincey. It whipped through the air—and plunged hilt-deep into the chest of the redheaded vampire, who had flung himself in front of his clan leader. He exploded in a shower of blood as the other vampires shrieked. With a howl de Quincey rushed Benedict. The other vampires seemed to awaken from their panicked stupor, and swiftly followed suit. Within seconds the room was a melee of screams and chaos.

The sudden chaos unfroze Tessa as well. Catching up her skirts, she ran for the stage, and dropped to her knees next to Nathaniel's chair. His head lolled to the side, his eyes closed. The blood from the wound in his neck had flowed to a slow trickle. Tessa caught at his sleeve. "Nate," she whispered. "Nate, it's me."

He moaned, but made no other reply. Biting her lip, Tessa went to work on the manacles that fastened his wrists to the chair. They were hard iron, fastened to the sturdy chair arms with rows of nails—clearly designed to withstand even vampire strength. She pulled at them until her fingers bled, but they didn't budge. If only she had one of Will's knives.

She glanced out over the room. It was still dark with smoke. In among the swirls of blackness, she could see the bright flashes of weapons, the Shadowhunters brandishing the brilliant white daggers Tessa knew now were called seraph blades, each one brought into shimmering life by the name of an angel. Vampire blood flew from the blades' edges, as bright as a scatter of rubies. She realized—with a shock of surprise, for the vampires at first had terrified her—that the vampires were clearly overmatched here. Though the Night Children were vicious and fast, the Shadowhunters were nearly as fast, and had weapons and training on their side. Vampire after vampire fell under the onslaught of the seraph blades. Blood ran in sheets across the floor, soaking the edges of the Persian rugs.

The smoke cleared in a spot, and Tessa saw Charlotte dispatching a burly vampire in a gray morning jacket. She slashed the blade of her knife across his throat, and blood sprayed across the wall behind them. He sank, snarling, to his knees, and Charlotte finished him with a thrust of her blade to his chest.

A blur of motion exploded behind Charlotte; it was Will, followed by a wild-eyed vampire brandishing a silver pistol. He pointed it at Will, aimed, and fired. Will dived out of the way and skidded across the bloody floor. He rolled to his feet, and bounded up onto a velvet-seated chair. Ducking another shot, he leaped again, and Tessa watched with amazement as he ran lightly along the *backs* of a row of chairs, leaping down from the last of them. He whirled to face the vampire, now a distance from him across the room. Somehow a short-bladed knife gleamed in his hand, though Tessa had not seen him draw it. He threw it. The vampire ducked aside, but was not quite fast enough; the knife sank into his shoulder. He roared in pain and was reaching for the knife when a slim, dark shadow reared up out of nowhere. There was a flash of silver, and the vampire blew apart in a shower of blood and dust. As the mess cleared, Tessa saw Jem, a long blade still raised in his fist. He was grinning, but not at her; he kicked the silver pistol—now lying abandoned among the vampire's remains—hard, and it skidded across the floor, fetching up at Will's feet. Will nodded toward Jem with a return of his grin, swept the pistol off the floor, and shoved it through his belt.

"Will!" Tessa called to him, though she wasn't sure if he could hear her over the din. "Will—"

Something seized her by the back of her dress and hauled her up and backward. It was like being caught in the talons of an enormous bird. Tessa screamed once, and found herself flung forward, skidding across the floor. She hit the stack of chairs. They crashed to the floor in a deafening mass, and Tessa, sprawled among the mess, looked up with a shout of pain.

De Quincey stood over her. His black eyes were wild, rimmed with red; his white hair straggled over his face in matted clumps, and his shirt was slashed open across the front, the edges of the tear soaked with blood. He must have been cut, though not deeply enough to kill him, and had healed. The skin under the torn shirt looked unmarked now. "*Bitch*," he snarled at Tessa. "Lying traitorous bitch. You brought that boy in here, Camille. That Nephilim."

Tessa scrambled backward; her back hit the wall of fallen chairs.

"I welcomed you back to the clan, even after your disgusting little—interlude—with the lycanthrope. I tolerate that ridiculous warlock of yours. And this is how you repay me. Repay *us*." He held his hands out to her; they were streaked with black ash. "You see this," he said. "The dust of our dead people. Dead *vampires*. And you betrayed them for *Nephilim*." He spat the word as if it were poison.

Something bubbled up out of Tessa's throat. Laughter. Not her laughter; Camille's. "*'Disgusting interlude'*?" The words came out of Tessa's mouth before she could stop them. It was as if she had no control over what she was saying. "I loved him— like you never loved me—like you've never loved anything.

And you killed him just to show the clan that you could. I want you to know what it is like to lose everything that matters to you. I want you to know, as your home burns and your clan is brought to ashes and your own miserable life ends, that *I am the one who is doing this to you.*"

And Camille's voice was gone just as quickly as it had come, leaving Tessa feeling drained and shocked. That didn't stop her, though, from using her hands, behind her, to scrabble among the smashed chairs. Surely there had to be *something*, some broken-off piece that she could use as a weapon. De Quincey was staring at her in shock, his mouth open. Tessa imagined that no one had ever talked to him like that. Certainly not another vampire.

"Perhaps," he said. "Perhaps I underestimated you. Perhaps you will destroy me." He advanced on her, his hands out, reaching. "But I will bring you with me—"

Tessa's fingers closed around the leg of a chair; without even thinking about it, she swung the chair up and over and brought it crashing down on de Quincey's back. She felt elated as he yelled and staggered back. She scrambled to her feet as the vampire straightened up, and she swung the chair at him again. This time a jagged bit of broken chair arm caught him across the face, opening up a long red cut. His lips curled back from his teeth in a silent snarl, and he *sprang*—there was no other word for it. It was like the silent spring of a cat. He struck Tessa to the ground, landing on top of her and knocking the chair from her hand. He lunged at her throat, teeth bared, and she raked her clawed hand across his face. His blood, where it dripped on her, seemed to burn, like acid. She screamed and struck out at him harder, but he only laughed; his pupils had disappeared into the black of his eyes, and he looked entirely inhuman, like some sort of monstrous predatory serpent.

He caught her wrists in his grasp and forced them down on either side of her, hard against the floor. "Camille," he said, leaning down over her, his voice thick. "Be still, little Camille. It will be over in moments—"

He threw his head back like a striking cobra. Terrified, Tessa struggled to free her trapped legs, meaning to kick him, kick him as hard as she could—

He yelled. Yelled and writhed, and Tessa saw that there was a hand caught in his hair, yanking his head up and back, dragging him to his feet. A hand inked all over with swirling black Marks.

Will's hand.

De Quincey was hauled screaming to his feet, his hands clamped to his head. Tessa struggled upright, staring, as Will flung the howling vampire contemptuously away from him. Will wasn't smiling anymore, but his eyes were glittering, and Tessa could see why Magnus had described their color as the sky in Hell.

"*Nephilim.*" De Quincey staggered, righted himself, and spat at Will's feet.

Will drew the pistol from his belt and aimed it at de Quincey. "One of the Devil's own abominations, aren't you? You don't even deserve to live in this world with the rest of us, and yet when we let you do so out of pity, you throw our gift back in our faces."

"As if we need your pity," de Quincey replied. "As if we could ever be less than you. You Nephilim, thinking you are—" He stopped abruptly. He was so smeared with filth that it was hard to tell, but it looked as if the cut on his face had already healed.

"Are what?" Will cocked the pistol; the click was loud even above the noise of the battle. "Say it."

The vampire's eyes burned. "Say what?"

"'God,'" said Will. "You were going to tell me that we Nephilim play at God, weren't you? Except you can't even say the word. Mock the Bible all you want with your little collection, you still can't say it." His finger was white on the trigger of the gun. "Say it. Say it, and I'll let you live."

The vampire bared his teeth. "You cannot kill me with that—that stupid human toy."

"If the bullet passes through your heart," Will said, his aim unwavering, "you'll die. And I am a very good shot."

Tessa stood, frozen, staring at the tableau before her. She wanted to step backward, to go to Nathaniel, but she was afraid to move.

De Quincey raised his head. He opened his mouth. A thin rattle came out as he tried to speak, tried to shape a word his soul would not let him say. He gasped again, choked, and put a hand to his throat. Will began to laugh—

And the vampire sprang. His face twisted in a mask of rage and pain, he launched himself at Will with a howl. There was a blur of movement. Then the gun went off and there was a spray of blood. Will hit the floor, the pistol skidding from his grip, the vampire on top of him. Tessa scrambled to retrieve the pistol, caught it, and turned to see that de Quincey had seized Will from the back, his forearm jammed against Will's throat.

She raised the pistol, her hand shaking—but she had never used a pistol before, had never shot anything, and how to shoot the vampire without injuring Will? Will was clearly choking, his face suffused with blood. De Quincey snarled something and tightened his grip—

And Will, ducking his head, sank his teeth into the vampire's forearm. De Quincey yelled and jerked his arm away; Will flung himself to the side, retching, and rolled to his knees to spit blood onto the stage. When he looked up, glittering red blood was smeared across the lower half of his face. His teeth shone red too when he—Tessa couldn't believe it—*grinned*, actually grinned, and looking at de Quincey, said, "How do *you* like it, vampire? You were going to bite that mundane earlier. Now you know what it's like, don't you?"

De Quincey, on his knees, stared from Will to the ugly red hole in his own arm, which was already beginning to close up, though dark blood still trickled from it thinly. "For that," he said, "you will die, Nephilim."

Will spread his arms wide. On his knees, grinning like a demon, blood dripping from his mouth, he barely looked human himself. "Come and get me."

De Quincey gathered himself to spring—and Tessa pulled the trigger. The gun kicked back, hard, into her hand, and the vampire fell sideways, blood streaming from his shoulder. She had missed the heart. *Damn it.*

Howling, de Quincey began to pull himself to his feet. Tessa raised her arm, pulled the trigger on the pistol again—nothing. A soft click let her know the gun was empty.

De Quincey laughed. He was still clutching his shoulder, though the blood flow had already slowed to a trickle. "*Camille*," he spat at Tessa. "I will be back for you. I will make you sorry you were ever reborn."

Tessa felt a chill at the pit of her stomach—not just *her* fear. Camille's. De Quincey bared his teeth one last time and whirled with incredible speed. He raced across the room and flung himself into a high glass window. It shattered outward in an explosion of glass, carrying him forward as if his body were being carried on a wave, vanishing into the night.

Will swore. "We can't lose him—," he began, and started forward. Then he spun as Tessa screamed. A ragged-looking male vampire had risen up behind her like a ghost appearing out of the air, and had snatched her by the shoulders. She tried to pull free, but his grip was too strong. She could hear him murmuring in her ear, horrible words about how she was a traitor to the Night Children, and how he would tear her open with his teeth.

"Tessa," Will shouted, and she wasn't sure if he sounded angry, or something else. He reached for the gleaming weapons at his belt. His hand closed around the hilt of a seraph blade, just as the vampire spun Tessa around. She caught sight of his leering white face, the blood-tipped fangs out, ready to tear. The vampire lunged forward—

And exploded in a shower of dust and blood. He dissolved, the flesh melting away from his face and hands, and Tessa caught sight for a moment of the blackened skeleton beneath before it, too, crumbled, leaving an empty pile of clothes behind. Clothes, and a gleaming silver blade.

She looked up. Jem stood a few feet away, looking very pale. He held the blade in his left hand; his right was empty. There was a long cut along one of his cheeks, but he seemed otherwise uninjured. His hair and eyes gleamed a brutal silver in the light of the dying flames. "I think," he said, "that that was the last of them."

Surprised, Tessa glanced around the room. The chaos had subsided. Shadowhunters moved here and there in the wreckage—some were seated on chairs, being attended to by stele-wielding healers—but she could not see a single vampire. The smoke of the burning had subsided as well, though white ash from the torched curtains still floated down over the room like unexpected snow.

Will, blood still dripping from his chin, looked at Jem with his eyebrows raised. "Nice throw," he said.

Jem shook his head. "You bit de Quincey," he said. "You fool. He's a *vampire*. You know what it means to bite a vampire."

"I had no choice," said Will. "He was choking me."

"I know," Jem said. "But really, Will. *Again?*"

It was Henry, in the end, who freed Nathaniel from the torture chair by the simple expedient of smashing it apart with the flat side of a sword until the manacles came free. Nathaniel slid to the floor, where he lay moaning, Tessa cradling him. Charlotte fussed a bit, bringing wet cloths to clean Nate's face, and a ragged bit of curtain to throw over him, before she raced off to engage Benedict Lightwood in an energetic conversation— during which she alternated between pointing back at Tessa and Nathaniel and waving her hands in a dramatic manner. Tessa, utterly dazed and exhausted, wondered what on earth Charlotte could be doing.

It hardly mattered, really. Everything seemed to be going on in a dream. She sat on the floor with Nathaniel as the Shadowhunters moved around her, drawing on one another with their steles. It was incredible to watch their injuries vanishing as the healing Marks went onto their skin. They all seemed equally able to draw the Marks. She watched as Jem, wincing, unbuttoned his shirt to show a long cut along one pale shoulder; he looked away, his mouth tight, as Will drew a careful Mark below the injury.

It wasn't until Will, having finished with Jem, came sauntering over to her that she realized why she was so tired.

"Back to yourself, I see," he said. He had a damp towel in one hand but hadn't yet bothered to clean the blood off his face and neck.

Tessa glanced down at herself. It was true. At some point she had lost Camille and become herself again. She must have been dazed indeed, she thought, not to have noticed the return of her own heartbeat. It pulsed inside her chest like a drum.

"I didn't know you knew how to use a pistol," Will added.

"I don't," Tessa said. "I think Camille must have. It was—instinctive." She bit her lip. "Not that it matters, since it didn't work."

"We rarely use them. Etching runes into the metal of a gun or bullet prevents the gunpowder from igniting; no one knows why. Henry has tried to address the problem, of course, but not with any success. Since you can't kill a demon without a runed weapon or a seraph blade, guns aren't much use to us. Vampires die if you shoot them through the heart, admittedly, and werewolves can be injured if you have a silver bullet, but if you miss the vitals, they'll just come at you angrier than ever. Runed blades simply work better for our purposes. Get a vampire with a runed blade and it's much harder for them to recover and heal."

Tessa looked at him, her gaze steady. "Isn't it hard?"

Will tossed the damp cloth aside. It was scarlet with blood. "Isn't *what* hard?"

"Killing vampires," she said. "They may not be people, but they *look* like people. They feel as people do. They scream and bleed. Isn't it hard to slaughter them?"

Will's jaw tightened. "No," he said. "And if you really knew anything about them—"

"Camille feels," she said. "She loves and hates."

"And *she* is still alive. Everyone has choices, Tessa. Those vampires would not have been here tonight if they hadn't made theirs." He glanced down at Nathaniel, limp in Tessa's lap. "Nor, I imagine, would your brother have been."

"I don't know why de Quincey wanted him dead," Tessa said softly. "I don't know what he could have done to incur the wrath of vampires."

"Tessa!" It was Charlotte, darting up to Tessa and Will like a hummingbird. She still seemed so tiny, and so harmless, Tessa thought—despite the fighting gear she wore and the black Marks that laced her skin like curling snakes. "We've been given permission to bring your brother back to the Institute with us," she announced, gesturing at Nathaniel with a small hand. "The vampires may well have drugged him. He's certainly been bitten, and who knows what else? He could turn darkling—or worse, if we don't prevent it. In any case, I doubt they'll be able to help him in a mundane hospital. With us, at least the Silent Brothers can see to him, poor thing."

"Poor thing?" echoed Will rather rudely. "He rather got himself into this, didn't he? No one told him to run off and get himself involved with a bunch of Downworlders."

"Really, Will." Charlotte eyed him coldly. "Can't you have a little empathy?"

"Dear God," said Will, looking from Charlotte to Nate and

back again. "Is there anything that makes women sillier than the sight of a wounded young man?"

Tessa slitted her eyes at him. "You might want to clean the rest of the blood off your face before you continue arguing in *that* vein."

Will threw his arms up into the air and stalked off. Charlotte looked at Tessa, a half smile curving the side of her mouth. "I must say, I rather like the way you manage Will."

Tessa shook her head. "No one manages Will."

It was quickly decided that Tessa and Nathaniel would go with Henry and Charlotte in the town coach; Will and Jem would ride home in a smaller carriage borrowed from Charlotte's aunt, with Thomas as their driver. The Lightwoods and the rest of the Enclave would stay behind to search de Quincey's house, leaving no evidence of their battle for the mundanes to find in the morning. Will had wanted to stay and take part in the search, but Charlotte had been firm. He had ingested vampire blood and needed to return to the Institute as soon as possible to begin the cure.

Thomas, however, would not allow Will into the carriage as covered in blood as he was. After announcing that he would return in "half a tick," Thomas had gone off to find a damp piece of cloth. Will leaned against the side of the carriage, watching as the Enclave rushed in and out of de Quincey's house like ants, salvaging papers and furniture from the remains of the fire.

Returning with a soapy rag, Thomas handed it over to Will, and leaned his big frame against the side of the carriage. It rocked under his weight. Charlotte had always encouraged

Thomas to join Jem and Will for the physical parts of their training, and as the years had gone by, Thomas had grown from a scrawny child to a man so large and muscular that tailors despaired over his measurements. Will might have been the better fighter—his blood made him that—but Thomas's commanding physical presence was not easy to ignore.

Sometimes Will could not help remembering Thomas as he had first come to the Institute. He belonged to a family that had served the Nephilim for years, but he had been born so frail they'd thought he wouldn't live. When he'd reached twelve years of age, he'd been sent to the Institute; at that time he'd still been so small that he'd looked barely nine. Will had made fun of Charlotte for wanting to employ him, but had secretly hoped he would stay so that there might be another boy his own age in the house. And they had been friends of a sort, the Shadowhunter and the servant boy—until Jem had come and Will had forgotten Thomas almost completely. Thomas had never seemed to hold it against him, treating Will always with the same friendliness with which he treated everyone else.

"Always rum to see this sort of thing goin' on, and none of the neighbors out for so much as a gander," Thomas said now, glancing up and down the street. Charlotte had always demanded that the Institute servants speak "proper" English within its walls, and Thomas's East End accent tended to come and go depending on whether he remembered.

"There are heavy glamours at work here." Will scrubbed at his face and neck. "And I would imagine there are quite a few on this street who are not mundanes, who know to mind their own business when Shadowhunters are involved."

"Well, you are a terrifying lot, that's true," Thomas said, so equably that Will suspected he was being made fun of. Thomas pointed at Will's face. "You'll have a stunner of a mouse tomorrow, if you don't get an *iratze* on there."

"Maybe I *want* a black eye," said Will peevishly. "Did you think of that?"

Thomas just grinned and swung himself up into the driver's box at the front of the carriage. Will went back to scrubbing dried vampire blood off his hands and arms. The task was absorbing enough that he was able to almost completely ignore Gabriel Lightwood when the other boy appeared out of the shadows and sauntered over to Will, a superior smile plastered on his face.

"Nice work in there, Herondale, setting the place on fire," Gabriel observed. "Good thing we were there to clean up after you, or the whole plan would have gone down in flames, along with the shreds of your reputation."

"Are you implying that shreds of my reputation remain intact?" Will demanded with mock horror. "Clearly I have been doing something wrong. Or *not* doing something wrong, as the case may be." He banged on the side of the carriage. "Thomas! We must away at once to the nearest brothel! I seek scandal and low companionship."

Thomas snorted and muttered something that sounded like "bosh," which Will ignored.

Gabriel's face darkened. "Is there *anything* that isn't a joke to you?"

"Nothing that comes to mind."

"You know," Gabriel said, "there was a time I thought we could be friends, Will."

"There was a time I thought I was a ferret," Will said, "but that turned out to be the opium haze. Did you know it had that effect? Because I didn't."

"I think," Gabriel said, "that perhaps you might consider whether jokes about opium are either amusing or tasteful, given the . . . situation of your friend Carstairs."

Will froze. Still in the same tone of voice, he said, "You mean his disability?"

Gabriel blinked. "What?"

"That's what you called it. Back at the Institute. His 'disability.'" Will tossed the bloody cloth aside. "And you wonder why we aren't friends."

"I just wondered," Gabriel said, in a more subdued voice, "if perhaps you have ever had enough."

"Enough of what?"

"Enough of behaving as you do."

Will crossed his arms over his chest. His eyes glinted dangerously. "Oh, I can never get enough," he said. "Which, incidentally, is what your sister said to me when—"

The carriage door flew open. A hand shot out, grabbed Will by the back of the shirt, and hauled him inside. The door banged shut after him, and Thomas, sitting bolt upright, seized the reins of the horses. A moment later the carriage had lurched forth into the night, leaving Gabriel staring, infuriated, after it.

"What were you thinking?" Jem, having deposited Will onto the carriage seat opposite him, shook his head, his silvery eyes shining in the dimness. He held his cane between his knees, his hand resting lightly atop the dragon's-head carving. The cane had belonged to Jem's father, Will knew, and had been designed for him by a Shadowhunter weapons maker in

Beijing. "Baiting Gabriel Lightwood like that—why do you do it? What's the point?"

"You heard what he said about you—"

"I don't care what he says about me. It's what everyone thinks. He just has the nerve to say it." Jem leaned forward, resting his chin on his hand. "You know, I cannot function as your missing sense of self-preservation forever. Eventually you will have to learn to manage without me."

Will, as he always did, ignored this. "Gabriel Lightwood is hardly much of a threat."

"Then forget Gabriel. Is there a particular reason you keep biting vampires?"

Will touched the dried blood on his wrists, and smiled. "They don't expect it."

"Of course they don't. They know what happens when one of us consumes vampire blood. *They* probably expect you to have more sense."

"That expectation never seems to serve them very well, does it?"

"It hardly serves you, either." Jem looked at Will thoughtfully. He was the only one who never fell out of temper with Will. Whatever Will did, the most extreme reaction he seemed to be able to provoke in Jem was mild exasperation. "What happened in there? We were waiting for the signal—"

"Henry's bloody Phosphor didn't work. Instead of sending up a flare of light, it set the curtains on fire."

Jem made a choked noise.

Will glared at him. "It's not funny. I didn't know whether the rest of you were going to show up or not."

"Did you really think we wouldn't come after you when the

whole place went up like a torch?" Jem asked reasonably. "They could have been roasting you over a spit, for all we knew."

"And Tessa, the silly creature, was supposed to be out the door with Magnus, but she wouldn't leave—"

"Her brother *was* manacled to a chair in the room," Jem pointed out. "I'm not sure I would have left either."

"I see you're determined to miss my point."

"If your point is that there was a pretty girl in the room and it was distracting you, then I think I've taken your point handily."

"You think she's pretty?" Will was surprised; Jem rarely opined on this sort of thing.

"Yes, and you do too."

"I hadn't noticed, really."

"Yes, you have, and I've noticed you noticing." Jem was smiling. Despite the stress of the battle, he looked healthy tonight. There was color in his cheeks, and his eyes were a dark and steady silver. There were times, when the illness was at its worst, when all the color drained even from his eyes, leaving them horribly pale, nearly white, with that black speck of pupil in the center like a speck of black ash on snow. It was times like that when he also became delirious. Will had held Jem down while he'd thrashed about and cried out in another language and his eyes had rolled back into his head, and every time it happened, Will thought that this was it, and Jem was really going to die this time. He sometimes then thought about what he would do afterward, but he couldn't imagine it, any more than he could look back and remember his life before he had come to the Institute. Neither bore thinking about for very long.

But then there were other times, like this, when he looked at Jem and saw no mark of illness on him, and wondered what it would be like in a world where Jem was not dying. And that did not bear thinking about either. It was a terrible black place in himself that the fear came from, a dark voice he could only silence with anger, risk, and pain.

"Will." Jem's voice cut into Will's unpleasant reverie. "Have you heard a single word I've said in the past five minutes?"

"Not really."

"We needn't talk about Tessa if you don't want to, you know."

"It's not Tessa." This was true. Will hadn't been thinking about Tessa. He was getting good at not thinking about her, really; all it took was determination and practice. "One of the vampires had a human servant who rushed me. I killed him," said Will. "Without even thinking about it. He was just a stupid human boy, and I killed him."

"He was a darkling," said Jem. "He was Turning. It would have been a matter of time."

"He was just a boy," Will said again. He turned his face toward the window, though the brightness of the witchlight in the carriage meant that all he could see was his own face, reflected back at him. "I'm going to get drunk when we get home," he added. "I think I'm going to have to."

"No, you won't," said Jem. "You know exactly what will happen when we get home."

Because he was right, Will scowled.

Ahead of Will and Jem, in the first carriage, Tessa sat on the velvet bench seat across from Henry and Charlotte; they were talking in murmurs about the night and how it had gone.

Tessa let the words wash over her, barely caring. Only two Shadowhunters had been killed, but de Quincey's escape was a disaster, and Charlotte was worried that the Enclave would be angry with her. Henry made soothing noises, but Charlotte seemed inconsolable. Tessa would have felt bad for her, if she'd had the energy to feel much at all.

Nathaniel lay across Tessa, his head in her lap. She bent over him, stroking his filthy matted hair with her gloved fingers. "Nate," she said, so softly that she hoped Charlotte couldn't hear her. "It's all right now. Everything's all right."

Nathaniel's lashes fluttered and his eyes opened. His hand came up—the fingernails broken, his joints swollen and twisted—and he took tight hold of her hand, lacing his fingers through hers. "Don't go," he said thickly. His eyes fluttered shut again; he was clearly drifting in and out of consciousness, if he was really conscious at all. "Tessie—stay."

No one else ever called her that; she shut her eyes, willing the tears back. She did not want Charlotte—or any Shadowhunter—to see her cry.

12

BLOOD AND WATER

I dare not always touch her, lest the kiss
Leave my lips charred. Yea, Lord, a little bliss,
Brief bitter bliss, one hath for a great sin;
Nathless thou knowest how sweet a thing it is.
—Algernon Charles Swinburne, "Laus Veneris"

When they reached the Institute, Sophie and Agatha were waiting at the open doors with lanterns. Tessa stumbled with tiredness as she left the carriage, and was surprised—and grateful—when Sophie came to help her up the steps. Charlotte and Henry half-carried Nathaniel. Behind them the carriage with Will and Jem in it rattled through the gates, Thomas's voice carrying on the cool night air as he called out a greeting.

Jessamine, not to Tessa's surprise, was nowhere to be seen.

They installed Nathaniel in a bedroom much like Tessa's—

the same dark heavy wood furniture, the same grand bed and wardrobe. As Charlotte and Agatha settled Nathaniel into the bed, Tessa sank into the chair beside it, half-feverish with worry and exhaustion. Voices—soft sickroom voices—swirled around her. She heard Charlotte say something about the Silent Brothers, and Henry answered in a subdued voice. At some point Sophie appeared at her elbow and urged her to drink something hot and sweet-sour that brought energy slowly flooding back into her veins. Soon enough she was able to sit up and look around her a bit, and she realized to her surprise that except for herself and her brother, the room was empty. Everyone had gone.

She glanced down at Nathaniel. He lay corpse-still, his face lividly bruised, his matted hair tangled against the pillows. Tessa could not help but recall with a pang the beautifully dressed brother of her memories, his fair hair always so carefully brushed and arranged, shoes and cuffs spotless. This Nathaniel did not look like someone who had ever spun his sister around the living room in a dance, humming to himself under his breath for the sheer joy of being alive.

She leaned forward, meaning to look more closely at his face, and saw a flicker of movement out of the corner of her eye. Turning her head, she saw it was only herself, reflected in the mirror on the far wall. In Camille's dress, she looked to her own eyes like a child playing dress-up. She was too slight for the sophisticated style of it. She looked like a child—a silly child. No wonder Will had—

"Tessie?" Nathaniel's voice, weak and frail, broke her instantly out of her thoughts of Will. "Tessie, don't leave me. I think I'm ill."

"Nate." She reached for his hand, seized it between her gloved palms. "You're all right. You'll be all right. They've sent for doctors. . . ."

"Who are 'they'?" His voice was a thin cry. "Where are we? I don't know this place."

"This is the Institute. You'll be safe here."

Nathaniel blinked. There were dark rings, almost black, around each of his eyes, and his lips were crusted with what looked like dried blood. His eyes wandered from side to side, not fixing on anything. "Shadowhunters." He sighed the word on an exhale of breath. "I didn't think they really existed. . . . The Magister," Nathaniel whispered suddenly, and Tessa's nerves jumped. "He said they were the Law. He said they were to be feared. But there is no law in this world. There is no punishment—just killing or being killed." His voice rose. "Tessie, I'm so sorry—about everything—"

"The Magister. Do you mean de Quincey?" Tessa demanded, but Nate made a choking sound then, and stared behind her with a look of terrible fear. Releasing his hand, Tessa turned to see what he was staring at.

Charlotte had come into the room almost noiselessly. She was still wearing her men's clothes, though she had thrown an old-fashioned long cloak on over them, with a double clasp at the throat. She looked very small, in part because Brother Enoch stood beside her, casting a vast shadow across the floor. He wore the same parchment robes he had before, though now his staff was black, its head carved in the shape of dark wings. His hood was up, casting his face in shadow.

"Tessa," Charlotte said. "You remember Brother Enoch. He is here to help Nathaniel."

With an animal howl of terror, Nate caught at Tessa's wrist. She looked down at him in bewilderment. "Nathaniel? What's wrong?"

"De Quincey told me about them," Nathaniel gasped. "The Gregori—the Silent Brothers. They can kill a man with a thought." He shuddered. "Tessa." His voice was a whisper. "Look at his *face*."

Tessa looked. While she had been talking to her brother, Brother Enoch had soundlessly drawn back his hood. The smooth pits of his eyes reflected the witchlight, the glare unforgiving on the black, scarred stitching around his mouth.

Charlotte took a step forward. "If Brother Enoch might examine Mr. Gray—"

"No!" Tessa cried. Wrenching her arm from Nate's grasp, she put herself between her brother and the other two occupants of the room. "Don't touch him."

Charlotte paused, looking troubled. "The Silent Brothers are our best healers. Without Brother Enoch, Nathaniel . . ." Her voice trailed off. "Well, there isn't much we can do for him."

Miss Gray.

It took her a moment to realize that the word, her name, hadn't been spoken out loud. Instead, like a snatch of a half-forgotten song, it had echoed inside her own head—but not in the voice of her own thoughts. This thought was alien, inimical—*other*. Brother Enoch's voice. It was the way he had spoken to her as he had left the room on her first day at the Institute.

It is interesting, Miss Gray, Brother Enoch went on, *that you are a Downworlder, and yet your brother is not. How did such a thing come to pass?*

Tessa went still. "You—you can tell that just by looking at him?"

"Tessie!" Nathaniel pushed himself upright against the pillows, his pale face flushed. "What are you doing, talking to the Gregori? He's dangerous!"

"It's all right, Nate," Tessa said, not taking her eyes off Brother Enoch. She knew she ought to be frightened, but what she really felt was a stab of disappointment. "You mean there's nothing unusual about Nate?" she asked, in a low voice. "Nothing supernatural?"

Nothing at all, said the Silent Brother.

Tessa hadn't realized how much she was half-hoping that her brother was like her until this moment. Disappointment sharpened her voice. "I don't suppose, since you know so much, that you know what I am? Am I a warlock?"

I cannot tell you. There is that about you that marks you as one of Lilith's Children. Yet there is no demon's sign on you.

"I did notice that," Charlotte said, and Tessa realized that she could hear Brother Enoch's voice as well. "I thought perhaps she wasn't a warlock. Some humans are born with some slight power, like the Sight. Or she could have faerie blood—"

She isn't human. She is something else. I will study on it. Perhaps there is something in the archives to guide me. Eyeless as he was, Brother Enoch seemed to be searching Tessa's face with his gaze. *There is a power I sense you have. A power no other warlock does.*

"The Changing, you mean," said Tessa.

No. I do not mean that.

"Then what?" Tessa was astonished. "What could I—?" She broke off at a noise from Nathaniel. Turning, she saw that he had fought free of his blankets and was lying half-off the bed, as if he'd attempted to get up; his face was sweaty and deathly white. Guilt stabbed at her. She'd been caught up in what Brother Enoch had been saying and had forgotten her brother.

She darted to the bed, and with Charlotte's assistance she wrestled Nate back onto the pillows, pulling the blanket up around him. He seemed much worse than he had been moments before. As Tessa tucked the blanket around him, he caught at her wrist again, his eyes wild. "Does he know?" he demanded. "Does he know where I am?"

"Who do you mean? De Quincey?"

"Tessie." He squeezed her wrist tightly, pulling her down to hiss a whisper into her ear. "You must forgive me. He told me you would be the queen of them all. He said they were going to kill me. I don't want to die, Tessie. I don't *want* to die."

"Of course not," she soothed, but he didn't seem to hear her. His eyes, fixed on her face, went suddenly wide, and he screamed.

"Keep it away from me! Keep it away from me!" he howled. He pushed at her, thrashing his head back and forth on the pillows. "Dear God, don't let it touch me!"

Frightened, Tessa snatched her hand back, turning to Charlotte—but Charlotte had moved away from the bed, and Brother Enoch stood in her place, his eyeless face immobile. *You must let me help your brother. Or he will likely die*, he said.

"What is he raving about?" Tessa demanded wretchedly. "What's wrong with him?"

The vampires gave him a drug, to keep him calm while they fed. If he is not cured, the drug will drive him mad and then kill him. Already he has begun to hallucinate.

"It's not my fault!" Nathaniel shrieked. "I had no choice! It's not my fault!" He turned his face toward Tessa; she saw to her horror that his eyes had gone entirely black, like an insect's eyes. She gasped, backing away.

"Help him. Please help him." She caught at Brother Enoch's sleeve, and immediately regretted it; the arm beneath the sleeve was as hard as marble, and freezing to the touch. She dropped her hand in horror, but the Silent Brother did not seem to even notice her presence. He had stepped past her, and now put his scarred fingers against Nathaniel's forehead. Nathaniel sank back against the pillows, his eyes closing.

You must leave. Brother Enoch spoke without turning from the bed. *Your presence will only slow his healing.*

"But Nate asked me to stay—"

Go. The voice in Tessa's mind was icy.

Tessa looked at her brother; he was still against the pillows, his face gone slack. She turned toward Charlotte, meaning to protest, but Charlotte met her glance with a small shake of the head. Her eyes were sympathetic, but unyielding. "As soon as your brother's condition changes, I will find you. I promise."

Tessa looked at Brother Enoch. He had opened the pouch at his waist and was setting objects down on the bedside table, slowly and methodically. Glass vials of powder and liquid, bunches of dried plants, sticks of some black substance like soft coal. "If anything happens to Nate," Tessa said, "I shall never forgive you. Never."

It was like speaking to a statue. Brother Enoch did not respond to her with so much as a twitch.

Tessa fled from the room.

After the dimness of Nate's sickroom, the brightness of the sconces in the corridor stung Tessa's eyes. She leaned against the wall by the door, willing her tears back. It was the second time that evening she had nearly cried, and she was annoyed with herself. Clenching her right hand into a fist, she slammed it against the wall behind her, hard, sending a shock wave of pain up her arm. *That* cleared the tears, and her head.

"That looked like it hurt."

Tessa turned. Jem had come up behind her in the corridor, as silent as a cat. He had changed out of his gear. He wore loose dark trousers tied at the waist, and a white shirt only a few shades lighter than his skin. His fine bright hair was damp, curling against his temples and the nape of his neck.

"It did." Tessa cradled her hand against her chest. The glove she wore had softened the blow, but her knuckles still ached.

"Your brother," Jem said. "Is he going to be all right?"

"I don't know. He's in there with one of those—those monk creatures."

"Brother Enoch." Jem regarded her with sympathetic eyes. "I know how the Silent Brothers look, but they're really very good doctors. They set great store by healing and medicinal arts. They live a long time, and know a great deal."

"It hardly seems worth living a long time if you're going to look like *that*."

The corner of Jem's mouth twitched. "I suppose it depends on what you're living for." He looked at her more closely. There was something about the *way* Jem looked at her, she thought. Like he could see into and through her. But nothing inside her, nothing he saw or heard, could bother or upset or disappoint him.

"Brother Enoch," she said suddenly. "Do you know what he

said? He told me that Nate isn't like me. He's fully human. No special powers at all."

"And that upsets you?"

"I don't know. On the one hand I wouldn't wish this—this *thing* I am—on him, or anyone. But if he isn't like me, then it means he isn't completely my brother. He's my parents' son. But whose daughter am I?"

"You can't concern yourself with that. Certainly it would be wonderful if we all knew exactly who we were. But that knowledge doesn't come from outside, but from inside. '*Know thyself*,' as the oracle says." Jem grinned. "My apologies if that sounds like sophistry. I'm only telling you what I've learned from my own experience."

"But I *don't* know myself." Tessa shook her head. "I'm sorry. After the way you fought at de Quincey's, you must think I'm a terrible coward, crying because my brother *isn't* a monster and I don't have the courage to be a monster all by myself."

"You're not a monster," said Jem. "Or a coward. On the contrary, I was quite impressed by the way you shot at de Quincey. You would almost certainly have killed him if there'd been any more bullets in the gun."

"Yes, I think I would have. I *wanted* to kill them all."

"That's what Camille asked us to do, you know. *Kill them all.* Perhaps it was her emotions you were feeling?"

"But Camille has no reason to care about Nate, or what happens to him, and that was when I felt most murderous. When I saw Nate there, when I realized what they were planning to do—" She took a shuddering breath. "I don't know how much of that was me and how much was Camille. And I don't even know if it's right to have those sort of feelings—"

"You mean," asked Jem, "for a girl to have those feelings?"

"For anyone to have them, maybe—I don't know. Maybe I mean for a girl to have them."

Jem seemed to look through her then, as if he were seeing something beyond her, beyond the corridor, beyond the Institute itself. "Whatever you are physically," he said, "male or female, strong or weak, ill or healthy—all those things matter less than what your heart contains. If you have the soul of a warrior, you are a warrior. Whatever the color, the shape, the design of the shade that conceals it, the flame inside the lamp remains the same. *You* are that flame." He smiled then, seeming to have come back to himself, slightly embarrassed. "That's what I believe."

Before Tessa could reply, Nate's door opened, and Charlotte came out. She responded to Tessa's questioning look with an exhausted-looking nod. "Brother Enoch has helped your brother a great deal," she said, "but there is much left to be done, and it will be morning before we know more. I suggest you go to sleep, Tessa. Exhausting yourself won't help Nathaniel."

With an effort of will Tessa forced herself simply to nod, and not to fling herself at Charlotte with a barrage of questions she knew she wouldn't get answers to.

"And Jem." Charlotte turned to him. "If I could talk to you for a few moments? Will you walk with me to the library?"

Jem nodded. "Of course." He smiled at Tessa, inclining his head. "Tomorrow, then," he said, and followed Charlotte down the corridor.

The moment they vanished around the corner, Tessa tried the door of Nate's room. It was locked. With a sigh she turned and headed the other way down the corridor. Perhaps Charlotte was right. Perhaps she ought to get some sleep.

Halfway down the corridor she heard a commotion. Sophie, a metal pail in each of her hands, suddenly appeared in the hallway, banging a door shut behind her. She looked livid. "His Highness is in a particularly fine temper this evening," she announced as Tessa approached. "He threw a pail at my head, he did."

"Who?" Tessa asked, and then realized. "Oh, you mean Will. Is he all right?"

"Well enough to throw pails," Sophie said crossly. "And to call me a nasty name. I don't know what it meant. I think it was in French, and that usually means someone's calling you a whore." She tightened her lips. "I'd best run and get Mrs. Branwell. Maybe *she* can get him to take the cure, if I can't."

"The cure?"

"He must drink this." Sophie thrust a pail toward Tessa; Tessa couldn't quite see what was in it, but it looked like ordinary water. "He *has* to. Or I wouldn't like to say as what'll happen."

A mad impulse took hold of Tessa. "*I'll* get him to do it. Where is he?"

"Upstairs, in the attic." Sophie's eyes were large. "But I wouldn't if I was you, miss. He's downright nasty when he's like this."

"I don't care," Tessa said, reaching for the pail. Sophie handed it to her with a look of relief and apprehension. It was surprisingly heavy, filled to the brim with water and slopping over. "Will Herondale needs to learn to take his medicine like a man," Tessa added, and pushed open the door to the attic,

Sophie looking after her with an expression that clearly said she thought Tessa had gone out of her head.

Beyond the door was a narrow flight of stairs going up. She held the pail in front of her as she went; it slopped water onto the bodice of her dress, raising goose bumps on her skin. By the time she had reached the top of the steps, she was damp and breathless.

There was no door at the head of the stairs; they ended abruptly at the attic, a huge room whose roof was so steeply gabled that it gave the impression of being low-ceilinged. Rafters just above Tessa's head ran the length of the room, and there were very low square windows set at intervals in the walls, through which Tessa could see the gray dawn light. The floor was bare polished boards. There was no furniture at all, and no light beyond the pale illumination that came from the windows. A set of even narrower stairs led to a closed trapdoor in the ceiling.

In the center of the room lay Will, barefoot, flat on his back on the floor. A number of pails surrounded him—and the floor around him, Tessa saw as she approached, was soaked with water. Water ran in rivulets down the boards and pooled in the uneven hollows of the floor. Some of the water was tinged reddish, as if it had been mixed with blood.

Will had an arm thrown over his face, hiding his eyes. He was not lying still, but moving restlessly, as if he were in some pain. As Tessa neared, he said something in a low voice, something that sounded like a name. *Cecily*, Tessa thought. Yes, it sounded very much as if he had said the name Cecily.

"Will?" she said. "Who are you talking to?"

"Back, are you, Sophie?" Will replied without raising his

head. "I told you if you brought me another one of those infernal pails, I'd—"

"It's not Sophie," Tessa said. "It's me. Tessa."

For a moment Will was silent—and motionless, save for the rise and fall of his chest as he breathed. He wore only a pair of dark trousers and a white shirt, and like the floor around him, he was soaking wet. The fabric of his clothes clung to him, and his black hair was pasted to his head like wet cloth. He must have been freezing cold.

"They sent *you?*" he said finally. He sounded incredulous, and something else, too.

"Yes," answered Tessa, though this was not strictly true.

Will opened his eyes and turned his head toward her. Even in the dimness she could see the intensity of his eye color. "Very well, then. Leave the water and go."

Tessa glanced down at the pail. For some reason her hands did not seem to want to let go of the metal handle. "What is it, then? I mean to say—what am I bringing you, exactly?"

"They didn't tell you?" He blinked at her in surprise. "It's holy water. To burn out what's in me."

It was Tessa's turn to blink. "You mean—"

"I keep forgetting everything you don't know," Will said. "Do you recall earlier this evening when I bit de Quincey? Well, I swallowed some of his blood. Not much, but it doesn't take much to do it."

"To do what?"

"To turn you into a vampire."

At that, Tessa nearly did drop the pail. "You're turning into a *vampire?*"

Will grinned at that, propping himself up on one elbow.

"Don't alarm yourself unduly. It requires days for the transformation to occur, and even then, I would have to die before it took hold. What the blood *would* do is make me irresistibly drawn to vampires—drawn to them in the hopes that they'd make me one of them. Like their human subjugates."

"And the holy water . . ."

"Counteracts the effects of the blood. I must keep drinking it. It makes me sick, of course—makes me cough up the blood and everything else in me."

"Good Lord." Tessa thrust the pail toward him with a grimace. "I suppose I had better give it to you, then."

"I suppose you had." Will sat up, and put his hands out to take the pail from her. He scowled down at the contents, then held it up and tipped it toward his mouth. After swallowing a few mouthfuls, he grimaced and dumped the rest unceremoniously over his head. Finished, he tossed the bucket aside.

"Does that help?" Tessa asked with honest curiosity. "Pouring it over your head like that?"

Will made a strangled noise that was only somewhat of a laugh. "The questions you ask . . ." He shook his head, flinging droplets of water from his hair onto Tessa's clothes. Water soaked the collar and front of his white shirt, turning it transparent. The way it clung to him, showing the lines of him underneath—the ridges of hard muscle, the sharp line of collarbone, the Marks burning through like black fire—it made Tessa think of the way one might lay thin paper down over a brass engraving, brushing charcoal over it to bring the shape through. She swallowed, hard. "The blood makes me feverish, makes my skin burn," Will said. "I can't get cool. But, yes, the water helps."

Tessa just stared at him. When he had come into her room at the Dark House, she had thought he was the most beautiful boy she'd ever seen, but just now, looking at him—she had never looked at a boy like that, not in this way that brought blood hot to her face, and tightened her chest. More than anything else she wanted to touch him, to touch his wet hair, to see if his arms, corded with muscle, were as hard as they looked, or if his callused palms were rough. To put her cheek against his, and feel his eyelashes brush her skin. Such long lashes . . .

"Will," she said, and her voice sounded thin to her own ears. "Will, I want to ask you . . ."

He looked up at her. The water made his lashes cling to one another, so that they formed starlike sharp points. "What?"

"You act like you don't care about anything," she said on an exhale of breath. She felt as if she had been running, and had crested a hill and was racing down the other side, and there was no stopping now. Gravity was taking her where she had to go. "But—everyone cares about *something*. Don't they?"

"Do they?" Will said softly. When she didn't answer, he leaned back on his hands. "Tess," he said. "Come over here and sit by me."

She did. It was cold and damp on the floor, but she sat, gathering her skirts up around her so only the tips of her boots showed. She looked at Will; they were very close together, facing each other. His profile in the gray light was cold and clean; only his mouth had any softness.

"You never laugh," she said. "You behave as if everything is funny to you, but you never laugh. Sometimes you smile when you think no one is paying attention."

For a moment he was silent. Then, "You," he said, half-reluctantly. "You make me laugh. From the moment you hit me with that bottle."

"It was a jug," she said automatically.

His lips quirked up at the corners. "Not to mention the way that you always correct me. With that funny look on your face when you do it. And the way you shouted at Gabriel Lightwood. And even the way you talked back to de Quincey. You make me . . ." He broke off, looking at her, and she wondered if she looked the way she felt—stunned and breathless. "Let me see your hands," he said suddenly. "Tessa?"

She gave them to him, palms up, hardly looking at them herself. She could not look away from his face.

"There's still blood," he told her. "On your gloves." And, looking down, she saw it was true. She had not taken off Camille's white leather gloves, and they were streaked with blood and dirt, shredded near the fingertips where she had pried at Nate's manacles.

"Oh," she said, and began to draw her hands back, meaning to take the gloves off, but Will let go of only her left hand. He continued to hold the right one, lightly, by the wrist. There was a heavy silver ring on his right index finger, she saw, carved with a delicate design of birds in flight. His head was bent, his damp black hair falling forward; she couldn't see his face. He brushed his fingers lightly over the surface of the glove. There were four pearl buttons fastening it closed at the wrist, and as he ran his fingertips over them, they sprang open and the pad of his thumb brushed against the bare skin of her inner wrist, where the blue veins pulsed.

She nearly jumped out of her skin. "Will."

"Tessa," he said. "What do you want from me?"

He was still stroking the inside of her wrist, his touch doing odd delicious things to her skin and nerves. Her voice shook when she spoke. "I—I want to understand you."

He looked up at her, through his lashes. "Is that really necessary?"

"I don't know," Tessa said. "I'm not sure anyone *does* understand you, except possibly Jem."

"Jem doesn't understand me," Will said. "He cares for me—like a brother might. It's not the same thing."

"Don't you *want* him to understand you?"

"Dear God, no," he said. "Why should he need to know my reasons for living my life as I do?"

"Maybe," Tessa said, "he simply wants to know that there *is* a reason."

"Does it matter?" Will asked softly, and with a swift motion he slipped her glove entirely off her hand. The chilly air of the room struck the bare skin of her fingers with a shock, and a shiver passed over Tessa's entire body, as if she had found herself suddenly naked in the cold. "Do reasons matter when there's nothing that can be done to change things?"

Tessa reached for an answer, and found none. She was shivering, almost too hard to speak.

"Are you cold?" Lacing his fingers with hers, Will took her hand and pressed it to his cheek. She was startled by the feverish heat of his skin. "Tess," he said, his voice thick and soft with desire, and she leaned toward him, swaying like a tree whose branches were weighted by snow. Her whole body ached; *she* ached, as if there were a terrible hollow emptiness inside her. She was more conscious of Will than she had ever been of anything or anyone else in her life, of the faint shine of blue beneath his half-closed lids, of the shadow of light stubble across his jaw where he hadn't shaved, of faint white scars that dotted the skin of his shoulders and throat—and more than anything else of his mouth, the crescent shape of it, the slight dent in the center of his bottom lip. When he leaned toward her and brushed his lips across hers, she reached for him as if she would otherwise drown.

For a moment their mouths pressed hotly together, Will's free hand tangling in her hair. Tessa gasped when his arms went around her, her skirts snagging on the floor as he pulled her hard against him. She put her hands lightly around his neck; his skin was burning hot to the touch. Through the thin wet material of his shirt, she could feel the muscles of his shoulders, hard and smooth. His fingers found her jeweled hair clasp and pulled at it, and her hair spilled down around her shoulders, the comb rattling to the floor, and Tessa gave a little cry of surprise against his mouth. And then, without warning, he ripped his hands from her and pushed hard against her shoulders, shoving her away from him with such force that she nearly fell backward, and only stopped herself awkwardly, her hands braced on the floor behind her.

She sat with her hair hanging down around her like a tangled curtain, staring at him in amazement. Will was on his knees, his chest hitching up and down as if he had been running incredibly fast and far. He was pale, except for two fever splotches of red across his cheeks. "God in Heaven," he whispered. "What was that?"

Tessa felt her cheeks turn scarlet. Wasn't Will the one who

was supposed to know exactly what *that* was, and wasn't she the one who was supposed to have pushed him away?

"I *can't*." His hands were fists at his sides; she could see them trembling. "Tessa, I think you had better go."

"*Go?*" Her mind whirled; she felt as if she had been in a warm, safe place and without warning had been cast out into a freezing, empty darkness. "I . . . I should not have been so forward. I'm sorry—"

A look of intense pain flashed across his face. "God. Tessa." The words seemed dragged out of him. "Please. Just leave. I can't have you here. It's—not possible."

"Will, please—"

"*No.*" He jerked his gaze away from hers, averting his face, his eyes fixed on the floor. "I'll tell you anything you want to know tomorrow. Anything. Just leave me alone now." His voice broke unevenly. "Tessa. I'm begging you. Do you understand? I'm *begging you.* Please, *please* leave."

"Very well," Tessa said, and saw with a mixture of amazement and pain that the lines of tension went out of his shoulders. Was it that much of a horror having her there, and that much of a relief that she was leaving? She rose to her feet, her dress damp and cold and heavy, her feet nearly slipping on the wet floor. Will didn't move or look up, but stayed where he was on his knees, staring at the ground as Tessa made her way across the room and down the stairs, without looking back.

Some time later, her room half-lit with the wan glow of the London sunrise, Tessa lay on the bed, too exhausted to change out of Camille's clothes—too exhausted, even, to sleep. It had been a day of firsts. The first time she had used her power at her own wish and discretion, and had felt good about it. The first time she had fired a pistol. And—the only first she had ever dreamed of, for years—her first kiss.

Tessa rolled over, burying her face in the pillow. For so many years she had wondered what her first kiss would be like—if he would be handsome, if he would love her, if he would be kind. She had never imagined that the kiss would be so brief and desperate and wild. Or that it would taste of holy water. Holy water and blood.

13

SOMETHING DARK

Tessa woke the next day to Sophie lighting the lamp by her bedside. With a moan Tessa made a move to cover her aching eyes.

"Now, then, miss." Sophie addressed Tessa with her usual briskness. "You've gone and slept the day away. It's past eight o'clock in the evening, and Charlotte said to wake you."

"Past eight? At *night*?" Tessa threw back her blankets, only to realize, to her surprise, that she was still wearing Camille's gown, now crushed and crumpled, not to mention stained. She must have collapsed into bed still entirely dressed. Memories of the night before began to flood into her mind—the white faces of vampires, the fire eating its way up the curtains, Magnus Bane laughing, de Quincey, Nathaniel, and Will. *Oh, God,* she thought. *Will.*

She pushed the thought of him from her mind and sat up, looking anxiously at Sophie. "My brother," she said. "Is he . . ."

Sophie's smile wavered. "No worse, really, but no better, either." Seeing Tessa's stricken expression, she said, "A hot bath and food, miss, that's what you need. It won't make your brother any better for you to starve and let yourself get filthy."

Tessa looked down at herself. Camille's dress was ruined, that was evident—torn and stained with blood and ash in a dozen places. Her silk stockings were ripped, her feet filthy, her hands and arms streaked with grime. She hesitated to think about the state of her hair. "I suppose you're right."

The bathtub was an oval claw-footed affair hidden behind a Japanese screen in a corner of the room. Sophie had filled it with hot water that was already beginning to cool. Tessa slid behind the screen, undressed, and lowered herself into the bath. The hot water came up to her shoulders, warming her. For a moment she sat motionless, letting the heat soak into her chilled bones. Slowly she began to relax, and closed her eyes—

Memories of Will flooded in on her. Will, the attic, the way he had touched her hand. The way he had kissed her, then ordered her away.

She ducked under the surface of the water as if she could hide from the humiliating memory. It didn't work. *Drowning yourself won't help,* she told herself sternly. *Now, drowning Will, on the other hand . . .* She sat up, reached for the cake of lavender soap on the edge of the bath, and scrubbed her skin and hair with it until the water turned black with ash and dirt. Perhaps it wasn't actually possible to scrub away your thoughts of someone, but she could try.

Sophie was waiting for Tessa when she emerged from behind the screen. There was a tray of sandwiches and tea at the ready. In front of the mirror, she helped Tessa dress in her yellow gown trimmed with dark braid; it was fussier than Tessa would have preferred, but Jessamine had liked the design very much in the shop and had insisted that Tessa have it made for her. *I can't wear yellow, but it's ever so suitable for girls with dull brown hair like yours,* she'd said.

The feeling of the brush going through her hair was very pleasant; it reminded Tessa of when she had been a small girl and Aunt Harriet had brushed her hair for her. It was soothing enough that when Sophie spoke next, it jolted her slightly.

"Did you manage to get Mr. Herondale to take his medicine last night, miss?"

"Oh, I—" Tessa scrambled to collect herself, but it was too late; scarlet color had flooded up her neck into her face. "He didn't want to," she finished lamely. "But I convinced him in the end."

"I see." Sophie's expression didn't change, but the rhythmic strokes of the brush through Tessa's hair began to come faster. "I know it's not my place, but—"

"Sophie, you can say anything you want to me, truly."

"It's just—Master Will." Sophie's words came out in a rush. "He isn't someone you should care for, Miss Tessa. Not like that. He isn't to be trusted, or relied on. He—he isn't what you think he is."

Tessa clasped her hands in her lap. She felt a vague sense of unreality. Had things really gone so far that she needed to be warned off Will? And yet it was good to have someone to talk to about him. She felt a bit like a starving person being offered food. "I don't know what I think he is, Sophie. He's like one thing sometimes, and then he can change completely, like the wind changing, and I don't know why, or what's happened—"

"Nothing. Nothing's happened. He just doesn't care about anyone but himself."

"He cares about Jem," Tessa said quietly.

The brush went still; Sophie had paused, frozen. There was something she wanted to say, Tessa thought, something she was holding herself back from saying. But what was it?

The brush began to move again. "That's not enough, though."

"You mean that I shouldn't wring my heart out over some boy who will never care for me—"

"No!" Sophie said. "There are worse things than that. It's all right to love someone who doesn't love you back, as long as they're worth you loving them. As long as they *deserve* it."

The passion in Sophie's voice surprised Tessa. She twisted around to look at the other girl. "Sophie, is there someone you care for? Is it Thomas?"

Sophie looked astonished. "*Thomas?* No. What ever gave you that idea?"

"Well, because I think he cares for you," Tessa said. "I've seen him looking at you. He watches you when you're in the room. I suppose I thought . . ."

Her voice trailed off at Sophie's flabbergasted look.

"Thomas?" Sophie said again. "No, that couldn't be. I'm sure he hasn't any such thoughts about me."

Tessa didn't move to contradict her; clearly, whatever

feelings Thomas might have had, Sophie didn't return them. Which left . . .

"Will?" Tessa said. "Do you mean you cared for Will once?" *Which would explain the bitterness and the dislike*, she thought, considering how Will treated girls who fancied him.

"*Will?*" Sophie sounded absolutely horrified—horrified enough to forget to call Will Mr. Herondale. "Are you asking me if I was ever in love with *him?*"

"Well, I thought— I mean, he's awfully handsome." Tessa realized she sounded rather feeble.

"There's more to someone being lovable than the way they *look*. My last employer," Sophie said, her careful accent slipping with her excitement as she spoke, so that "last" sounded more like "larst," "he was always off on safari in Africa and India, shooting tigers and things. And he told me that the way you can tell if a bug or a snake is poisonous, like, is if it's got really lovely, bright markings. The more beautiful its skin is, the more deadly it is. That's what Will's like. All that pretty face and whatnot just hides how twisted up and rotten he is on the inside."

"Sophie, I don't know—"

"There's something dark in him," Sophie said. "Something black and dark that he's hiding. He's got some sort of secret, the kind that eats you up inside." She set the silver-haired brush down on the vanity, and Tessa saw with surprise that her hand was shaking. "You mark my words."

After Sophie left, Tessa took the clockwork angel from her bedside table and strung it around her neck. As it settled against her chest, she felt immediately reassured. She had missed it while she'd been disguised as Camille. Its presence was a comfort, and—though it was foolish, she knew—she thought perhaps that if she visited Nate while wearing it, he might feel its presence and be reassured as well.

She kept her hand on it as she shut the bedroom door behind her, made her way down the corridor, and knocked on his door softly. When there was no answer, she took hold of the knob and pushed the door open. The curtains in the room were drawn back, the room half-filled with light, and she could see Nate asleep on his back against a mound of pillows. He had one arm flung across his forehead, and his cheeks were bright with fever.

He wasn't alone, either. In the armchair by the head of the bed sat Jessamine, a book open on her lap. She met Tessa's surprised look with a cool and level stare.

"I—," Tessa began, and collected herself. "What are you doing here?"

"I thought I would read to your brother for a while," Jessamine said. "Everyone's been asleep half the day, and he was being cruelly neglected. Just Sophie checking in on him, and you can't count on *her* for decent conversation."

"Nate's unconscious, Jessamine; he doesn't *want* conversation."

"You can't be sure," Jessamine said. "I've heard that people can hear what you say to them even if they're quite unconscious, or even dead."

"He's not *dead*, either."

"Certainly not." Jessamine gave him a lingering look. "He's far too handsome to die. Is he married, Tessa? Or is there a girl back in New York who has a claim on him?"

"On *Nate*?" Tessa stared. There had always been girls, all sorts of girls, who'd been interested in Nate, but he had the attention span of a butterfly. "Jessamine, he isn't even conscious. Now is hardly the time—"

"He'll get better," Jessamine announced. "And when he does, he'll know I'm the one who nursed him back to health. Men always fall in love with the woman who nurses them back to health. 'When pain and anguish wring the brow, / A ministering angel thou!'" she finished, with a self-satisfied smirk. Seeing Tessa's horrified look, she scowled. "What's wrong? Am I not good enough for your precious brother?"

"He doesn't have any money, Jessie—"

"I have enough money for both of us. I just need someone to take me away from this place. I told you that."

"In fact, you asked me if I'd be the one to do it."

"Is *that* what's putting you out of countenance?" Jessamine asked. "Really, Tessa, we can still be the best of friends once we're sisters-in-law, but a man is always better than a woman for this sort of thing, don't you think?"

Tessa could think of nothing to say in reply.

Jessamine shrugged. "Charlotte wishes to see you, by the way. In the drawing room. She wanted me to tell you. You don't need to worry about Nathaniel. I've been checking his temperature every quarter hour and putting cold compresses on his forehead besides."

Tessa wasn't sure she believed any of this, but as Jessamine was patently uninterested in giving up her place by Nathaniel's side, and it hardly seemed worth a battle, she turned with a disgusted sigh and left the room.

The door to the drawing room, when she reached it, was

slightly ajar; she could hear raised voices from the other side. She hesitated, her hand half-lifted to knock—then she heard the sound of her own name and she froze.

"This isn't the London Hospital. Tessa's brother shouldn't be here!" It was Will's voice, raised to a shout. "He's not a Downworlder, just a stupid, venal mundane who found himself mixed up in something he couldn't manage—"

Charlotte replied, "He can't be treated by mundane doctors. Not for what's wrong with him. Be reasonable, Will."

"He already knows about Downworld." The voice was Jem's: calm, logical. "In fact, he may know quite a bit of important information that we don't know. Mortmain claimed Nathaniel was working for de Quincey; he might have information about de Quincey's plans, the automatons, the whole Magister business—all of it. De Quincey wanted him dead, after all. Perhaps it was because he knew something he shouldn't."

There was a long silence. Then, "We can call in the Silent Brothers again, then," said Will. "They can claw through his mind, see what they find. We needn't wait for him to wake up."

"You know that sort of process is delicate with mundanes," protested Charlotte. "Brother Enoch has already said that the fever has driven Mr. Gray into hallucinations. It's impossible for him to sort through what in the boy's mind is the truth and what is feverish delirium. Not without damaging his mind, possibly permanently."

"I doubt it was that much of a mind to begin with." Tessa heard Will's tone of disgust even through the door and felt her stomach tighten with rage.

"You know nothing about the man." Jem spoke more coldly than Tessa had ever heard him speak before. "I can't imagine what's driving this mood of yours, Will, but it does you no credit."

"I know what it is," Charlotte said.

"You do?" Will sounded appalled.

"You're as upset as I am about how last night went. We had only two fatalities, true, but de Quincey's escape doesn't reflect well on us. It was my plan. I pushed it on the Enclave, and now they will blame me for anything that went wrong. Not to mention that Camille has had to go into hiding since we've no idea where de Quincey is, and by now he probably has a blood price on her head. And Magnus Bane, of course, is furious with us that Camille has vanished. So our best informant and our best warlock are lost to us at the moment."

"But we did stop de Quincey from murdering Tessa's brother and who knows how many more mundanes," Jem said. "That should count for something. Benedict Lightwood didn't want to believe in de Quincey's betrayal at first; now he has no choice. He knows you were right."

"That," said Charlotte, "is likely only going to make him angrier."

"Perhaps," said Will. "And perhaps if you hadn't insisted on tying the success of *my* plan to the functionality of one of Henry's ridiculous inventions, we wouldn't be having this conversation now. You can dance around it all you like, but the reason everything went wrong last night is because the Phosphor didn't work. Nothing Henry invents ever works. If you'd just admit your husband's a useless fool, we'd all be a lot better off."

"*Will.*" Jem's voice held cold fury.

"No. James, don't." Charlotte's voice shook; there was a sort of thump, as if she'd sat herself down very suddenly in a chair. "Will," she said, "Henry is a good, kind man and he loves you."

"Don't be maudlin, Charlotte." Will's voice held only scorn.

"He's known you since you were a boy. He cares for you like you were his own younger brother. As do I. All I've ever done is love you, Will—"

"Yes," said Will, "and I wish you wouldn't."

Charlotte made a pained noise, like a kicked puppy. "I know you don't mean that."

"I mean everything I say," said Will. "Especially when I tell you that we're better off sifting through Nathaniel Gray's mind now rather than later. If you're too sentimental to do it—"

Charlotte began to interrupt, but it didn't matter. This was too much for Tessa. She hurled the door open and stalked inside. The inside of the room was lit by a roaring fire, in contrast to the squares of dark gray glass that let in what there was of the cloudy twilight. Charlotte sat behind the large desk, Jem in a chair beside her. Will, on the other hand, was leaning against the fireplace mantel; he was flushed with obvious anger, his eyes blazing, his shirt collar askew. His eyes met Tessa's for a moment of pure astonishment. Any hope she had entertained that he might have magically forgotten what had happened in the attic the night before vanished. He flushed at the sight of her, his fathomless blue eyes darkening—and looked away, as if he couldn't stand to hold her gaze.

"I suppose you've been eavesdropping, then?" he asked. "And now you're here to give me a piece of your mind about your precious brother?"

"At least I have a mind to give you a piece of, which Nathaniel won't, if you have your way." Tessa turned to

Charlotte. "I won't let Brother Enoch go pawing through Nate's mind. He's sick enough already; it would probably kill him."

Charlotte shook her head. She looked exhausted, her face gray, her eyelids drooping. Tessa wondered if she'd slept at all. "Most assuredly, we will allow him to heal before we think about questioning him."

"What if he's ill for weeks? Or months?" Will said. "We might not have that much time."

"Why not? What's so urgent you want to risk my brother's life on it?" Tessa snapped.

Will's eyes were slivers of blue glass. "All you've ever cared about is finding your brother. And now you've found him. Good for you. But that was never *our* goal. You do realize that, don't you? We don't usually go quite this far out of our way for the sake of one delinquent mundane."

"What Will is trying to say," Jem interjected, "though failing at civility, is—" He broke off, and sighed. "De Quincey said that your brother was someone he had trusted. And now de Quincey is gone, and we have no idea where he's hiding. The notes we found in his office hint that de Quincey believed there would soon be a war between Downworlders and Shadowhunters, a war those clockwork creatures he was working on doubtless figured into prominently. You can see why we want to know where he is, and what else your brother might know."

"Maybe *you* want to know those things," Tessa said, "but it's not my fight. I'm not a Shadowhunter."

"Indeed," said Will. "Don't think we don't know that."

"Be quiet, Will." Charlotte's tone held more than its usual asperity. She turned from him to Tessa, her brown eyes beseeching. "We trust you, Tessa. You need to trust us, too."

"No," Tessa said. "No, I don't." She could feel Will's gaze on her and was suddenly filled with a startling rage. How *dare* he be cold to her, angry at her? What had she done to deserve it? She'd let him kiss her. That was all. Somehow, it was as if that alone had erased everything else she had done that evening— as if now that she'd kissed Will, it no longer mattered that she had also been brave. "You wanted to use me—just like the Dark Sisters did—and the moment you had a chance to, the moment Lady Belcourt came along and you needed what I could do, you wanted me to do it. Never mind how danger- ous it was! You behave as if I have some responsibility to your world, your laws and your Accords, but it's your world, and you're the ones meant to govern it. It's not my fault if you're doing a rotten job!"

Tessa saw Charlotte whiten and sit back. She felt a sharp twinge in her chest. It wasn't Charlotte she had meant to hurt. Still, she went on. She couldn't help herself, the words coming out in a flood, "All your talk about Downworlders and how you don't hate them. That's all nothing, isn't it? Just words. You don't mean them. And as for mundanes, have you ever thought maybe you'd be better at protecting them if you didn't despise them all so much?" She looked at Will. He was pale, his eyes blazing. He looked—she wasn't sure she could describe his expression. Horrified, she thought, but not at her; the horror ran deeper than that.

"Tessa," Charlotte protested, but Tessa was already fum- bling for the door. She turned at the last moment, on the threshold, to see them all staring at her.

"Stay away from my brother," she snapped. "And *don't* fol- low me."

* * *

Anger, Tessa thought, was satisfying in its own way, when you gave in to it. There was something peculiarly gratifying about shouting in a blind rage until your words ran out.

Of course, the aftermath was less pleasant. Once you'd told everyone you hated them and not to come after you, where exactly did you *go?* If she went back to her own room, it was as much as saying she was just having a tantrum that would wear off. She couldn't go to Nate and bring her black mood into his sickroom, and lurking anywhere else meant risking being found sulking by Sophie or Agatha.

In the end she took the narrow, winding stairs that led down through the Institute. She made her way through the witch-lit nave and came out onto the broad front steps of the church, where she sank down on the top stair and wrapped her arms around herself, shivering in the unexpectedly cold breeze. It must have rained sometime during the day, for the steps were damp, and the black stone of the courtyard shone like a mirror. The moon was out, darting in between racing scuds of cloud, and the huge iron gate gleamed blackly in the fitful light. *We are dust and shadows.*

"I know what you're thinking." The voice that came from the doorway behind Tessa was soft enough that it could almost have been part of the wind that rattled the leaves on the tree branches.

Tessa turned. Jem stood in the arch of the doorway, the white witchlight behind him lighting his hair so that it shone like metal. His face, though, was hidden in shadow. He held his cane in his right hand; the dragon's eyes gleamed watchfully at Tessa.

"I don't think you do."

"You're thinking, *If they call this damp nastiness summer, what must winter be like?* You'd be surprised. Winter's actually much the same." He moved away from the door and sat down on the step beside Tessa, though not too close. "It's spring that's really lovely."

"Is it?" Tessa said, without much real interest.

"No. It's actually quite foggy and wet as well." He looked sideways at her. "I know you said not to follow you. But I was rather hoping you just meant Will."

"I did." Tessa twisted round to look up at him. "I shouldn't have shouted like that."

"No, you were quite right to say what you did," said Jem. "We Shadowhunters have been what we are for so long, and are so insular, that we often forget to look at any situation from someone else's point of view. It is only ever about whether something is good for the Nephilim or bad for the Nephilim. Sometimes I think we forget to ask whether it is good or bad for the world."

"I never meant to hurt Charlotte."

"Charlotte is very sensitive about the way the Institute is run. As a woman, she must fight to be heard, and even then her decisions are second-guessed. You heard Benedict Lightwood at the Enclave meeting. She feels she has no freedom to make a mistake."

"Do any of us? Do any of *you*? Everything is life and death to you." Tessa took a long breath of the foggy air. It tasted of city, metal and ashes and horses and river water. "I just—I feel sometimes as if I can't bear it. Any of it. I wish I'd never learned what I was. I wish Nate had stayed home and none of this had ever happened!"

"Sometimes," Jem said, "our lives can change so fast that the change outpaces our minds and hearts. It's those times, I think, when our lives have altered but we still long for the time before everything was altered—that is when we feel the greatest pain. I can tell you, though, from experience, you grow accustomed to it. You learn to live your new life, and you can't imagine, or even really remember, how things were before."

"You're saying I'll get used to being a warlock, or whatever it is that I am."

"You've always been what you are. That's not new. What you'll get used to is knowing it."

Tessa took a deep breath, and let it out slowly. "I didn't mean what I said upstairs," she said. "I don't think the Nephilim are as dreadful as all that."

"I know you didn't mean it. If you had, you wouldn't be here. You'd be at your brother's side, guarding him against our dire intentions."

"Will didn't really mean what he said, either, did he," Tessa said after a moment. "He wouldn't hurt Nate."

"Ah." Jem looked out toward the gate, his gray eyes thoughtful. "You're correct. But I'm surprised you know it. *I* know it. But I have had years to understand Will. To know when he means what he says and when he doesn't."

"So you don't ever get angry at him?"

Jem laughed out loud. "I would hardly say *that*. Sometimes I want to strangle him."

"How on earth do you prevent yourself?"

"I go to my favorite place in London," said Jem, "and I stand and look at the water, and I think about the continuity of life, and how the river rolls on, oblivious of the petty upsets in our lives."

Tessa was fascinated. "Does that work?"

"Not really, but after that I think about how I could kill him while he slept if I really wanted to, and then I feel better."

Tessa giggled. "So where is it, then? This favorite place of yours?"

For a moment Jem looked pensive. Then he bounded to his feet, and held out the hand that did not clasp the cane. "Come along, and I'll show you."

"Is it far?"

"Not at all." He smiled. He had a lovely smile, Tessa thought—and a contagious one. She couldn't help smiling back, for what felt like the first time in ages.

Tessa let herself be pulled to her feet. Jem's hand was warm and strong, surprisingly reassuring. She glanced back at the Institute once, hesitated, and let him draw her through the iron gate and out into the shadows of the city.

14

BLACKFRIARS
BRIDGE

Twenty bridges from Tower to Kew
Wanted to know what the River knew,
For they were young and the Thames was old,
And this is the tale that the River told.
—Rudyard Kipling, "The River's Tale"

Stepping through the Institute's iron gate, Tessa felt a bit like Sleeping Beauty leaving her castle behind its wall of thorns. The Institute was in the center of a square, and streets left the square in each cardinal direction, plunging into narrow labyrinths between houses. Still with his hand courteously on her elbow, Jem led Tessa down a narrow passage. The sky overhead was like steel. The ground was still damp from the rain earlier in the day, and the sides of the buildings that seemed to press in on either side were streaked with damp and stained with black residues of dust.

Jem talked as they went, not saying much of import but keeping up a soothing chatter, telling her what he had thought of London when he had first come here, how everything had seemed to him a uniform shade of gray—even the people! He had been unable to believe it could rain so much in one place, and so unceasingly. The damp had seemed to come up from the floors and into his bones, so that he'd thought he would eventually sprout mold, in the manner of a tree. "You *do* get used to it," he said as they came out from the narrow passage and into the broadness of Fleet Street. "Even if sometimes you feel as if you ought to be able to be wrung out like a washrag."

Remembering the chaos of the street during the day, Tessa was comforted to see how much quieter it was in the evening, the thronging crowds reduced to the occasional figure striding along the pavement, head down, keeping to the shadows. There were still carriages and even single riders in the road, though none seemed to notice Tessa and Jem. A glamour at work? Tessa wondered, but didn't ask. She was enjoying just listening to Jem talk. This was the oldest part of the city, he told her, where London had been born. The shops that lined the street were closed, their blinds drawn, but advertisements still blared from every surface, advertisements for everything from Pears soap to hair tonic to announcements urging people to attend a lecture on spiritualism. As Tessa walked, she caught glimpses of the spires of the Institute between the buildings, and couldn't help but wonder if anyone else could see them. She remembered the parrot woman with the green skin and feathers. Was the Institute really hidden in plain sight? Curiosity getting the better of her, she asked Jem as much.

"Let me show you something," he said. "Stop here." He took Tessa by the elbow and turned her so that she was facing across the street. He pointed. "What do you see there?"

She squinted across the street; they were near the intersection of Fleet Street and Chancery Lane. There seemed nothing remarkable about where they stood. "The front of a bank. What else is there to see?"

"Now let your mind wander a bit," he said, still in the same soft voice. "Look at something else, the way you might avoid looking directly at a cat so as not to frighten it. Glance at the bank again, out of the corner of your eye. Now look at it, directly, and very fast!"

Tessa did as directed—and stared. The bank was gone; in its place was a half-timbered tavern, with great diamond-paned windows. The light within the windows was tinted with a reddish glow, and through the open front door more red light poured out onto the pavement. Through the glass dark shadows moved—not the familiar shadows of men and women, but shapes too tall and thin, too oddly elongated or many-limbed to be human. Bursts of laughter interrupted a high, sweet, thin music, haunting and seductive. A sign hanging over the door showed a man reaching to tweak the nose of a horned demon. Lettered below the image were the words THE DEVIL TAVERN.

This is where Will was the other night. Tessa looked toward Jem. He was staring at the tavern, his hand light on her arm, his breathing slow and soft. She could see the red light of the pub reflected in his silvery eyes like sunset on water. "Is *this* your favorite place?" she asked.

The intensity went out of his gaze; he looked at her, and

laughed. "Lord, no," he said. "Just something I wanted you to see."

Someone came out the tavern door then, a man in a long black overcoat, an elegant watered silk hat placed firmly on his head. As he glanced up the street, Tessa saw that his skin was an inky dark blue, his hair and beard as white as ice. He moved east toward the Strand as Tessa watched, wondering if he would garner curious stares, but his passage was no more noted by passersby than that of a ghost would be. In fact, the mundanes who passed in front of the Devil Tavern seemed barely to notice it at all, even when several spindly, chittering figures exited and nearly knocked over a tired-looking man wheeling an empty cart. He paused to look around for a moment, puzzled, then shrugged and went on.

"There was a very ordinary tavern there once," said Jem. "As it grew more and more infested with Downworlders, the Nephilim became concerned about the intertwining of the Shadow World with the mundane world. They barred mundanes from the place by the simple expedient of using a glamour to convince them that the tavern had been knocked down and a bank erected in its place. The Devil is a nearly exclusively Downworlder haunt now." Jem glanced up at the moon, a frown crossing his face. "It's growing late. We'd better move on."

After a single glance back at the Devil, Tessa moved after Jem, who continued to chat easily as they went, pointing out things of interest—the Temple Church, where the law courts were now, and where once the Knights Templar had sustained pilgrims on their route to the Holy Land. "They were friends of the Nephilim, the knights. Mundanes, but not without their own knowledge of the Shadow World. And of course," he added, as they came out from the network of streets and onto Blackfriars Bridge itself, "many think that the Silent Brothers are the original Black Friars, though no one can prove it. This is it," he added, gesturing before him. "My favorite place in London."

Looking out over the bridge, Tessa couldn't help but wonder what Jem liked so much about the place. It stretched from one bank of the Thames to the other, a low granite bridge with multiple arches, the parapets painted dark red and gilded with gold and scarlet paint that gleamed in the moonlight. It would have been pretty if it hadn't been for the railway bridge that ran along the east side of it, silent in the shadows but still an ugly latticework of iron railings stretching away to the river's opposite bank.

"I know what you're thinking," Jem said again, just as he had outside the Institute. "The railway bridge, it's hideous. But it means people rarely come here to admire the view. I enjoy the solitude, and just the look of the river, silent under the moon."

They walked to the center of the bridge, where Tessa leaned against a granite parapet and looked down. The Thames was black in the moonlight. The expanse of London stretched away on either bank, the great dome of St. Paul's looming up behind them like a white ghost, and everything shrouded in the softening fog that laid a gently blurring veil over the harsh lines of the city.

Tessa glanced down at the river. The smell of salt and dirt and rot came off the water, mixing with the fog. Still there was something portentous about London's river, as if it carried the weight of the past in its currents. A bit of old poetry came into her head. "'*Sweet Thames, run softly till I end my song*,'" she said, half under her breath. Normally she would never have quoted poetry aloud in front of anyone, but there was something about Jem that made her feel that whatever she did, he wouldn't pass judgment on her.

"I've heard that bit of rhyme before," was all he said. "Will's quoted it at me. What is it?"

"Spenser. 'Prothalamion.'" Tessa frowned. "Will does seem to have an odd affinity for poetry for someone so . . . so . . ."

"Will reads constantly, and has an excellent memory," said Jem. "There is very little he does not remember." There was something in his voice that lent weight to his assertion beyond the mere statement of fact.

"You like Will, don't you?" said Tessa. "I mean, you're fond of him."

"I love him as if he were my brother," said Jem matter-of-factly.

"You can say that," Tessa said. "However horrid he is to everyone else, he loves *you*. He's kind to you. What did you ever do, to make him treat you so differently from all the rest?"

Jem leaned sideways against the parapet, his gaze on her but still faraway. He tapped his fingers thoughtfully against the jade top of his cane. Taking advantage of his clear distraction, Tessa let herself stare at him, marveling a little at his strange beauty in the moonlight. He was all silver and ashes, not like Will's strong colors of blue and black and gold.

Finally he said, "I don't know, really. I used to think it was because we were both without parents, and therefore he felt we were the same—"

"I'm an orphan," Tessa pointed out. "So is Jessamine. He doesn't think he is like us."

"No. He doesn't." Jem's eyes were guarded, as if there were something he wasn't saying.

"I don't understand him," Tessa said. "He can be kind one moment and absolutely awful the next. I cannot decide if he is kind or cruel, loving or hateful—"

"Does it matter?" Jem said. "Is it required that you make such a decision?"

"The other night," she went on, "in your room, when Will came in. He said he had been drinking all night, but then, later, when you—later he seemed to become instantly sober. I've seen my brother drunk. I know it doesn't vanish like that in an instant; even my aunt throwing a pail of cold water in Nate's face wouldn't have roused him from stupor, not if he were truly intoxicated. And Will didn't smell of alcohol, or seem ill the next morning. But why would he lie and say he was drunk if he wasn't?"

Jem looked resigned. "And there you have the essential mystery of Will Herondale. I used to wonder the same thing myself. How anyone could drink as much as he claimed and survive, much less fight as well as he does. So one night I followed him."

"You *followed* him?"

Jem grinned crookedly. "Yes. He went out, claiming an assignation or some such, and I followed him. If I'd known what to expect, I would have worn sturdier shoes. All night he walked through the city, from St. Paul's to Spitalfields Market to Whitechapel High Street. He went down to the river and wandered about the docks. Never did he stop to speak to a single soul. It was like following a ghost. The next morning he was ready with some ribald tale of false adventures, and I never demanded the truth. If he wishes to lie to me, then he must have a reason."

"He lies to you, and yet you trust him?"

"Yes," Jem said. "I trust him."

"But—"

"He lies consistently. He always invents the story that will make him look the worst."

"Then, has he told you what happened to his parents? Either the truth or lies?"

"Not entirely. Bits and pieces," Jem said after a long pause. "I know that his father left the Nephilim. Before Will was ever born. He fell in love with a mundane girl, and when the Council refused to make her a Shadowhunter, he left the Clave and moved with her to a very remote part of Wales, where they thought they wouldn't be interfered with. The Clave was furious."

"Will's mother was a mundane? You mean he is only half a Shadowhunter?"

"Nephilim blood is dominant," said Jem. "That's why there are three rules for those who leave the Clave. First, you must sever contact with any and all Shadowhunters you have ever known, even your own family. They can never speak to you again, nor can you speak to them. Second, you cannot call upon the Clave for help, no matter what your danger. And the third . . ."

"What's the third?"

"Even should you leave the Clave," said Jem, "they can still lay claim to your children."

A little shiver went through Tessa. Jem was still staring out at the river, as if he could see Will in its silvered surface. "Every six years," he said, "until the child is eighteen, a representative of the Clave comes to your family and asks the child if they would like to leave their family and join the Nephilim."

"I can't imagine anyone would," Tessa said, appalled. "I mean, you'd never be able to speak to your family again, would you?"

Jem shook his head.

"And Will agreed to that? He joined the Shadowhunters regardless?"

"He refused. Twice, he refused. Then, one day—Will was twelve or so—there was a knock on the Institute door and Charlotte answered it. She would have been eighteen then, I think. Will was standing there on the steps. She told me he was covered in road dust and dirt as if he'd been sleeping in hedge-rows. He said, 'I am a Shadowhunter. One of you. You have to let me in. I have nowhere else to go.'"

"He said that? Will? 'I have nowhere else to go'?"

He hesitated. "You understand, all this is information I heard from Charlotte. Will's never mentioned a word of any of it to me. But that's what she claims he said."

"I don't understand. His parents—they're dead, aren't they? Or they would have come looking for him."

"They did," Jem said quietly. "A few weeks after Will arrived, Charlotte told me, his parents followed. They came to the front door of the Institute and banged on it, calling for him. Charlotte went into Will's room to ask him if he wanted to see them. He had crawled under the bed and had his hands over his ears. He wouldn't come out, no matter what she did, and he wouldn't see them. I think Charlotte finally went down and sent them away, or they left of their own accord, I'm not sure—"

"Sent them away? But their child was inside the Institute. They had a right—"

"They had no right." Jem spoke gently enough, Tessa thought, but there was something in his tone that put him as far away from her as the moon. "Will chose to join the Shadowhunters. Once he made that choice, they had no more claim on him. It was the right and responsibility of the Clave to turn them away."

"And you've never asked him why?"

"If he wanted me to know, he'd tell me," Jem said. "You asked why I think he tolerates me better than other people. I'd imagine it's precisely *because* I've never asked him why." He smiled at her, wryly. The cold air had whipped color into his cheeks, and his eyes were bright. Their hands were close to each other's on the parapet. For a brief, half-confused moment Tessa thought that he might be about to put his hand over hers, but his gaze slid past her and he frowned. "Bit late for a walk, isn't it?"

Following his gaze, she saw the shadowy figures of a man and a woman coming toward them across the bridge. The man wore a workman's felt hat and a dark woolen coat; the woman had her hand on his arm, her face inclined toward his. "They probably think the same thing about us," Tessa said. She looked up into Jem's eyes. "And you, did you come to the Institute because you had nowhere else to go? Why didn't you stay in Shanghai?"

"My parents ran the Institute there," said Jem, "but they were murdered by a demon. He—it—was called Yanluo." His voice was very calm. "After they died, everyone thought that the safest thing for me would be to leave the country, in case the demon or its cohorts came after me as well."

"But why here, why England?"

"My father was British. I spoke English. It seemed reasonable." Jem's tone was as calm as ever, but Tessa sensed there was something he wasn't telling her. "I thought I would feel more at home here than I would in Idris, where neither of my parents had ever been."

Across the bridge from them the strolling couple had paused at a parapet; the man seemed to be pointing out features of the railway bridge, the woman nodding as he spoke. "And did you—feel more at home, that is?"

"Not precisely," Jem said. "Almost the first thing I realized when I came here was that my father never thought of himself as British, not the way an Englishman would. Real Englishmen are British first, and gentlemen second. Whatever else it is they might be—a doctor, a magistrate or landowner—comes third. For Shadowhunters it's different. We are Nephilim, first and foremost, and only after that do we make a nod to whatever country we might have been born and bred in. And as for third, there is no third. We are only ever Shadowhunters. When other Nephilim look at me, they see only a Shadowhunter. Not like mundanes, who look at me and see a boy who is not entirely foreign but not quite like them either."

"Half one thing and half another," Tessa said. "Like me. But *you* know you're human."

Jem's expression softened. "As are you. In all the ways that matter."

Tessa felt the backs of her eyes sting. She glanced up and saw that the moon had passed behind a cloud, giving it a pearlescent luster. "I suppose we should go back. The others must be worried."

Jem moved to offer her his arm—and paused. The strolling

couple Jem had noted before were suddenly in front of them, blocking their way. Though they must have moved very swiftly to reach the far side of the bridge so fast, they stood eerily still now, their arms linked. The woman's face was concealed in the shadow of a plain bonnet, the man's hidden beneath the brim of his felt hat.

Jem's hand tightened on Tessa's arm, but his voice was neutral when he spoke. "Good evening. Is there something we can help you with?"

Neither of them spoke, but they moved a step closer, the woman's skirt rustling in the wind. Tessa looked around, but there was no one else on the bridge, no one visible at either embankment. London seemed utterly deserted under the blurring moon.

"Pardon me," Jem said. "I'd appreciate it if you'd let me and my companion go by." He took a step forward, and Tessa followed. They were close enough now to the silent couple that when the moon came out from behind its cloud, flooding the bridge with silvery light and illuminating the face of the man in the felt hat, Tessa recognized him instantly.

The tangled hair; the wide once-broken nose and scarred chin; and most of all the protruding, popping eyes, the same eyes as the woman who stood beside him, her blank stare fixed on Tessa in a manner terribly reminiscent of Miranda's.

But you're dead. Will killed you. I saw your body. Tessa whispered, "It's him, the coachman. He belongs to the Dark Sisters."

The coachman chuckled. "I *belong*," he said, "to the Magister. While the Dark Sisters served him, I served them. Now I serve him alone."

The coachman's voice sounded different from how Tessa

remembered—less thick, more articulate, with an almost sinister smoothness. Beside Tessa, Jem had gone very still. "Who are you?" he demanded. "Why are you following us?"

"The Magister has directed us to follow you," the coachman said. "You are Nephilim. You are responsible for the destruction of his home, the destruction of his people, the Children of the Night. We are here to deliver a declaration of war. And we are here for the girl." He turned his eyes to Tessa. "She is the property of the Magister, and he will have her."

"The Magister," said Jem, his eyes very silver in the moonlight. "Do you mean de Quincey?"

"The name you give him does not matter. He is the Magister. He has told us to deliver a message. That message is war."

Jem's hand tightened on the head of his cane. "You serve de Quincey but are not vampires. What are you?"

The woman standing beside the coachman made a strange sighing noise, like the high whistle of a train. "Beware, Nephilim. As you slay others, so shall you be slain. Your angel cannot protect you against that which neither God nor the Devil has made."

Tessa began to turn toward Jem, but he was already in motion. His hand swung up, the jade-headed cane in it. There was a flash. A wickedly sharp and shimmering blade shot from the end of the cane. With a swift turn of his body, Jem plunged the blade forward and slashed it into the coachman's chest. The man staggered back, a high whirring sound of surprise issuing from his throat.

Tessa drew in her breath. A long slash across the coachman's shirt gaped open, and beneath it was visible neither flesh nor blood but shining metal, raggedly scored by Jem's blade.

Jem drew his blade back, letting out a breath, satisfaction mixed with relief. "I knew it—"

The coachman snarled. His hand darted into his coat and withdrew a long serrated knife, the kind butchers used to cut through bone, while the woman, snapping into action, moved toward Tessa, her ungloved hands outstretched. Their movements were jerky, uneven—but very, very fast, much faster than Tessa would have guessed they could move. The coachman's companion advanced on Tessa, her face expressionless, her mouth half-open. Something metallic gleamed inside it— metal, or copper. *She has no gullet, and I would guess, no stomach. Her mouth ends in a sheet of metal behind her teeth.*

Tessa retreated until her back hit the parapet. She looked for Jem, but the coachman was advancing on him again. Jem slashed away at him with the blade, but it seemed only to slow the man down. The coachman's coat and shirt hung away from his body now in ragged strips, clearly showing the metal carapace beneath.

The woman grabbed for Tessa, who darted aside. The woman lumbered forward and crashed into the parapet. She seemed to feel no more pain than the coachman did; she drew herself stiffly upright and turned to move toward Tessa again. The impact seemed to have damaged her left arm, though, for it hung bent at her side. She swung toward Tessa with her right arm, fingers grasping, and seized her by the wrist. Her grip was tight enough to make Tessa scream as the small bones in her wrist flared with pain. She clawed at the hand that held her, her fingers sinking deep into slick, soft skin. It peeled away like the skin of a fruit, Tessa's nails scraping against the metal beneath with a harshness that sent shivers up her spine.

She tried to jerk her hand back, but she only succeeded in pulling the woman toward her; she was making a whirring, clicking noise in her throat that sounded unpleasantly insectile, and up close her eyes were pupil-less and black. Tessa pulled her foot back to kick out—

And there was the sudden clang of metal on metal; Jem's blade flashed down with a clean slice, cutting the woman's arm in half at the elbow. Tessa, released, fell back, the bodiless hand falling from her wrist, striking the ground at her feet; the woman was jerking around toward Jem, *whir-click*, *whir-click*. He moved forward, striking at the woman hard with the flat of the cane, knocking her back a step, and then another and another until she hit the railing of the bridge so hard that she overbalanced. Without a cry she fell, plunging toward the water below; Tessa raced to the railing just in time to see her slip beneath the surface. No bubbles rose to show where she had vanished.

Tessa spun back around. Jem was clutching his cane, breathing hard. Blood ran down the side of his face from a cut, but he seemed otherwise unharmed. He held his weapon loosely in one hand as he gazed at a dark humped shape on the ground at his feet, a shape that moved and jerked, flashes of metal showing between the ribbons of its torn clothing. When Tessa moved closer she saw that it was the body of the coachman, writhing and jerking. His head had been sliced cleanly away, and a dark oily substance pumped from the stump of his neck, staining the ground.

Jem reached up to push his sweat-dampened hair back, smearing the blood across his cheek. His hand shook. Hesitantly Tessa touched his arm. "Are you all right?"

His smile was faint. "I should be asking *you* that." He shuddered slightly. "Those mechanical *things*, they unnerve me. They—" He broke off, staring past her.

At the south end of the bridge, moving toward them with sharp staccato motions, were at least a half dozen more of the clockwork creatures. Despite the jerkiness of their movements, they were approaching swiftly, almost hurtling forward. They were already a third of the way across the bridge.

With a sharp *click* the blade vanished back into Jem's cane. He seized Tessa's hand, his voice breathless. *"Run."*

They ran, Tessa clutching his hand, glancing behind only once, in terror. The creatures had made it to the center of the bridge and were moving toward them, gathering speed. They were male, Tessa saw, dressed in the same kind of dark woolen coats and felt hats as the coachman had been. Their faces gleamed in the moonlight.

Jem and Tessa reached the steps at the end of the bridge, and Jem kept a tight grip on Tessa's hand as they hurtled down the stairs. Her boots slipped on the damp stone, and he caught her, his cane clattering awkwardly against her back; she felt his chest rise and fall against hers, hard, as if he were gasping. But he couldn't be out of breath, could he? He was a Shadowhunter. The *Codex* said they could run for miles. Jem pulled away, and she saw that his face was tight, as if he were in pain. She wanted to ask him if he'd been hurt, but there was no time. They could hear clattering footsteps on the stairs above them. Without a word Jem took hold of her wrist again and pulled her after him.

They passed the Embankment, lit by the glow of its dolphin lamps, before Jem turned aside and plunged between two buildings into a narrow alley. The alley sloped up, away from the river. The air between the buildings was dank and close, the cobblestones slick with filth. Washing flapped like ghosts from windows overhead. Tessa's feet were screaming in their fashionable boots, her heart slamming against her chest, but there was no slowing down. She could *hear* the creatures behind them, hear the *whir-click* of their movements, closer and closer.

The alley opened out into a wide street, and there, rising up before them, was the looming edifice of the Institute. They dashed through the entrance, Jem releasing her as he whirled to slam and lock the gates behind them. The creatures reached them just as the bolts slid home; they crashed against the gate like windup toys unable to stop themselves, rattling the iron with a tremendous crash.

Tessa backed up, staring. The clockwork creatures were pressed up against the gates, their hands reaching through the gaps in the iron. She looked around wildly. Jem stood beside her. He was as white as paper, one hand pressed to his side. She reached for his hand, but he stepped back, out of her reach. "Tessa." His voice was uneven. "Get into the Institute. You need to get inside."

"Are you hurt? Jem, are you injured?"

"No." His voice was muffled.

A rattle from the gate made Tessa look up. One of the clockwork men had his hand through a gap in the gate and was pulling at the iron chain that held it closed. As she stared in fascinated horror, she saw that he was dragging at the loops of metal with such force that the skin was peeling away from his fingers, showing the jointed metal hands beneath. There was obviously tremendous strength in those hands. The metal was warping and twisting in his grip; it was clearly a matter of minutes before the chain split and broke.

Tessa seized hold of Jem's arm. His skin was burning hot to the touch; she could feel it through his clothes. "Come *on*."

With a groan he let her pull him toward the front door of the church; he was staggering, and leaning on her heavily, his breath rattling in his chest. They lurched up the stairs, Jem sliding out of her grip almost the moment they reached the top step. He hit the ground on his knees, choking coughs ripping through him, his whole body spasming.

The gate burst open. The clockwork creatures spilled through into the drive, led by the one who had torn the chain apart, his skin-stripped hands gleaming in the moonlight.

Remembering what Will had said, that one had to have Shadowhunter blood to open the door, Tessa reached for the bellpull that hung beside it and yanked it, hard, but heard no sound. Desperate, she whirled back to Jem, still crouched on the ground. "Jem! Jem, please, you have to open the door—"

He raised his head. His eyes were open, but there was no color to them. They were all white, like marbles. She could see the moon reflected in them.

"*Jem!*"

He tried to rise to his feet, but his knees gave out; he slumped to the ground, blood running from the corners of his mouth. The cane had rolled from his hand, almost to Tessa's feet.

The creatures had reached the foot of the steps; they began to surge upward, lurching a little, the one with the skinned hands in the lead. Tessa flung herself against the doors of the Institute, pounding her fists against the oak. She could hear the hollow reverberations of her blows echoing on the other side, and despaired. The Institute was so huge, and there was no *time*.

At last she gave up. Turning away from the door, she was horrified to see that the leader of the creatures had reached Jem; it was bending over him, its skinned metal hands on his chest.

With a cry she seized up Jem's cane and brandished it. "Get away from him!" she cried.

The creature straightened up, and in the moonlight, for the first time, she saw its face clearly. It was smooth, almost featureless, only indentations where the eyes and mouth should have been, and no nose. It raised its skinned hands; they were stained dark with Jem's blood. Jem himself lay very still, his shirt torn, blood pooling blackly around him. As Tessa stared in horror, the clockwork man wiggled his bloody fingers at her, in a sort of grotesque parody of a wave—then turned and sprang away down the steps, almost scuttling, like a spider. He dashed through the gates and was lost to view.

Tessa moved toward Jem, but the other automatons moved swiftly to block her way. They were *all* as blank-faced as their leader, a matching set of faceless warriors, as if there had not quite been time to *finish* them.

With a *whir-click* a pair of metal hands reached for her, and she swung the cane, almost blindly. It connected with the side of a clockwork man's head. She felt the impact of wood against metal ringing up her arm, and he staggered to the side, but only for a moment. His head whipped back around with incredible speed. She swung again, the cane slamming against his shoulder this time; he lurched, but other hands flashed out, seizing the cane, yanking it from her grasp with such force that the skin of her hand burned. She remembered the painful strength of Miranda's grip on her, as the automaton who had snatched the cane from her brought it down across his knee with stunning force.

It snapped in half with an awful sound. Tessa whirled to run, but metal hands clamped down on her shoulders, yanking her back. She struggled to pull free—

And the doors of the Institute burst open. The light that poured from them blinded her momentarily, and she could see nothing but the outline of dark figures, ringed in light, spilling from the church's interior. Something whistled by her head, grazing her cheek. There was the grinding sound of metal on metal, and then the clockwork creature's arms relaxed and she fell forward onto the steps, choking.

Tessa looked up. Charlotte stood above her, her face pale and set, a sharp metal disc in one hand. Another, matching, disc was buried in the chest of the mechanical man who had held her. He was twisting and spasming in a circle, like a malfunctioning toy. Blue sparks flew from the gash in his neck.

Around him the rest of the creatures were spinning and lurching as the Shadowhunters converged on them, Henry bringing his seraph blade down in an arc, slicing open the chest of one of the automatons, sending it reeling and jerking into the shadows. Beside him was Will, swinging what looked like a sort of scythe, over and over, chopping another of the creatures to bits with such fury that it sent up a fountain of blue sparks. Charlotte, darting down the steps, threw the second of her disks; it sheared through the head of a metal monster with a sickening noise. He crumpled to the ground, leaking more sparks and black oil.

The remaining two creatures, seeming to think better

of the situation, turned and sprang toward the gates. Henry darted after them with Charlotte on his heels, but Will, dropping his weapon, turned and raced back toward the steps. "What happened?" he shouted at Tessa. She stared, too dazed to answer. His voice rose, tinged with furious panic. "Are you hurt? Where's Jem?"

"I'm not hurt," she whispered. "But Jem, he collapsed. There." She pointed to where Jem lay, crumpled in the shadows beside the door.

Will's face went blank, like a slate wiped clean of chalk. Without looking at her again he raced up the stairs and dropped down by Jem, saying something in a low voice. When there was no reply, Will raised his head, shouting for Thomas to come help him carry Jem, and shouting something else, something Tessa couldn't make out through her dizziness. Perhaps he was shouting at her. Perhaps he thought this was all her fault? If she hadn't grown so angry, if she hadn't run away and made Jem follow her—

A dark shadow loomed in the lit doorway. It was Thomas, tousle-haired and serious, who went without a word to kneel down by Will. Together they lifted Jem to his feet, an arm slung around each of their shoulders. They hurried inside without a backward glance.

Dazed, Tessa looked out over the courtyard. Something was strange, different. It was the sudden silence after all the clamor and noise. The destroyed clockwork creatures lay in shattered pieces about the courtyard, the ground was slick with viscous fluid, the gates hung open, and the moon shone blankly down on everything just as it had shone down on her and Jem on the bridge, when he had told her that she was human.

15

FOREIGN MUD

Ah God, that love were as a flower or flame,
That life were as the naming of a name,
That death were not more pitiful than desire,
That these things were not one thing and the same!
—Algernon Charles Swinburne, "Laus Veneris"

"Miss Tessa." The voice was Sophie's. Tessa turned and saw her framed in the doorway, a lantern swinging from her hand. "Are you all right?"

Tessa felt pitifully grateful to see the other girl. She had been feeling so alone. "I'm not hurt. Henry has gone after the creatures, though, and Charlotte—"

"They'll be just fine." Sophie put a hand on Tessa's elbow. "Come, let's get you inside, miss. You're bleeding."

"I am?" Puzzled, Tessa put her fingers up to touch her

forehead; they came away stained red. "I must have struck my head when I fell against the steps. I didn't even feel it."

"Shock," Sophie said calmly, and Tessa thought how many times in her employment here Sophie must have done these things—bandaged up cuts, wiped away blood. "Come along, and I'll get a compress for your head."

Tessa nodded. With a last glance over her shoulder at the destruction in the courtyard, she let Sophie guide her back inside the Institute. The next short while was something of a blur. After Sophie helped her upstairs and into an armchair in the drawing room, she bustled off and returned moments later with Agatha, who pressed a cup of something hot into Tessa's hand.

Tessa knew what it was the moment she smelled it—brandy and water. She thought of Nate and hesitated, but once she'd had a few mouthfuls, things began to swim back into focus. Charlotte and Henry returned, bringing with them the smell of metal and fighting. Tight-lipped, Charlotte set her weapons down on a table and called for Will. He didn't respond, but Thomas did, hurrying down the corridor, his coat stained with blood, to tell her that Will was with Jem, and that Jem was going to be all right.

"The creatures injured him, and he lost some blood," Thomas said, running a hand through his tangled brown hair. He looked at Sophie as he said it. "But Will gave him an *iratze*—"

"And his medicine?" Sophie asked quickly. "Has he had some of that?"

Thomas nodded, and the tight set of Sophie's shoulders relaxed just a bit. Charlotte's gaze softened as well. "Thank you, Thomas," she said. "Perhaps you can see if he requires anything else?"

Thomas nodded, and set off back down the corridor with a last glance over his shoulder at Sophie, who did not seem to notice. Charlotte sank down onto the ottoman opposite Tessa. "Tessa, can you tell us what happened?"

Clutching the cup, her fingers cold despite its heat, Tessa shuddered. "Did you catch the ones that escaped? The— whatever they are. The metal monsters?"

Charlotte shook her head gravely. "We pursued them through the streets, but they disappeared once we reached Hungerford Bridge. Henry thinks there was some magic involved."

"Or a secret tunnel," Henry said. "I did also suggest a secret tunnel, my dear." He looked at Tessa. His friendly face was streaked with blood and oil, his brightly striped waistcoat slashed and torn. He looked like a schoolboy who'd been in a bad scrape of some sort. "Did you see them coming out of a tunnel, perhaps, Miss Gray?"

"No," Tessa said, her voice half a whisper. To clear her throat, she took another sip of the drink Agatha had given her, and set the cup down before running through it all—the bridge, the coachman, the chase, the words the creature had spoken, the way they had burst through the Institute gates. Charlotte listened with a pinched white face; even Henry looked grim. Sophie, sitting quietly on a chair, attended to the story with the grave intensity of a schoolgirl.

"They said it was a declaration of war," Tessa finished. "That they were coming to wreak revenge on us—on you, I suppose—for what happened to de Quincey."

"And the creature referred to him as the Magister?" Charlotte asked.

Tessa pressed her lips together firmly to keep them from trembling. "Yes. He said the Magister wanted me and that he had been sent to retrieve me. Charlotte, this is my fault. If it weren't for me, de Quincey wouldn't have sent those creatures tonight, and Jem—" She looked down at her hands. "Maybe you should just let him have me."

Charlotte was shaking her head. "Tessa, you heard de Quincey last night. He hates Shadowhunters. He would strike at the Clave regardless of you. And if we gave you to him, all we would be doing is placing a potentially valuable weapon in his hands." She looked at Henry. "I wonder why he waited this long. Why not come for Tessa when she was out with Jessie? Unlike demons, these clockwork creatures can go out during the day."

"They *can*," said Henry, "but not without alarming the populace—not yet. They don't look enough like ordinary human beings to pass without exciting comment." He took a shining gear from his pocket and held it up. "I examined the remains of the automatons down in the courtyard. These ones de Quincey sent after Tessa on the bridge are not like the one in the crypt. They're more sophisticated, made of tougher metals, and with a more advanced jointure. Someone's been working on the design in those blueprints Will found, refining it. The creatures are faster now, and deadlier."

But how refined? "There was a spell," Tessa said quickly. "On the blueprint. Magnus deciphered it. . . ."

"The binding spell. Meant to tie a demon energy to an automaton." Charlotte looked at Henry. "Did de Quincey—?"

"Succeed in performing it?" Henry shook his head. "No. Those creatures are simply configured to follow a pattern, like music boxes. But they are not animate. They do not have intelligence or will or life. And there is nothing demonic about them."

Charlotte exhaled in relief. "We *must* find de Quincey before he succeeds in his goal. Those creatures are difficult enough to kill as it is. The Angel knows how many of them he's made, or how difficult they'd be to kill if they had the cunning of demons."

"An army born neither of Heaven nor Hell," said Tessa softly.

"Exactly," said Henry. "De Quincey must be found and stopped. And in the meantime, Tessa, you must stay in the Institute. Not that we want to keep you a prisoner here, but it would be safer if you remained inside."

"But for how long—?" Tessa began—and broke off, as Sophie's expression changed. She was looking at something over Tessa's shoulder, her hazel eyes suddenly wide. Tessa followed her gaze.

It was Will. He stood in the doorway of the drawing room. There was a streak of blood across his white shirt; it looked like paint. His face was still, almost masklike, his gaze fixed on Tessa. As their eyes met across the room, she felt the pulse jump in her throat.

"He wants to talk to you," Will said.

There was a moment of silence as everyone in the drawing room looked at him. There was something forbidding about the intensity of Will's gaze, the tension of his stillness. Sophie had her hand at her throat, her fingers nervously fluttering at her collar.

"Will," Charlotte said finally. "Do you mean Jem? Is he all right?"

"He's awake and talking," Will said. His gaze slid momentarily to Sophie, who had glanced down, as if to hide her expression. "And now he wants to speak to Tessa."

"But . . ." Tessa looked toward Charlotte, who seemed troubled. "Is he all right? Is he well enough?"

Will's expression didn't change. "He wants to talk to you," he said, enunciating each word very clearly. "So you will get up, and you will come with me, and you will talk to him. Do you understand?"

"Will," Charlotte began sharply, but Tessa was already rising, smoothing down her rumpled skirts with the flat of her hands. Charlotte looked worriedly at her, but said nothing more.

Will was utterly silent as they made their way down the corridor, witchlight sconces throwing their shadows against the far walls in spindly patterns. There was blackish oil as well as blood splattered on his white shirt, smudging his cheek; his hair was tangled, his jaw set. She wondered if he had slept at all since dawn, when she had left him in the attic. She wanted to ask him, but everything about him—his posture, his silence, the set of his shoulders—said that no questions would be welcome.

He pushed open the door of Jem's room and ushered her in ahead of him. The only light in the room came from the window and from a taper of witchlight on the bedside table. Jem lay half-under the covers of the high carved bed. He was as white as his nightshirt, the lids of his closed eyes dark blue. Leaning against the side of the bed was his jade-headed cane.

Somehow it had been repaired and was whole again, gleaming as if new.

Jem turned his face toward the sound of the door, not opening his eyes. "Will?"

Will did something then that amazed Tessa. He forced his face into a smile, and said, in a passably cheerful tone, "I brought her, like you asked."

Jem's eyes flicked open; Tessa was relieved to see that they had returned to their usual color. Still, they had the look of shadowed holes in his pale face.

"Tessa," he said, "I'm so sorry."

Tessa looked at Will—for permission or guidance, she wasn't sure, but he was staring straight ahead. Clearly he would be no help. Without another glance at him she hurried across the room and sank down in the chair by the side of Jem's bed. "Jem," she said in a low voice, "you shouldn't be sorry, or be apologizing to me. I should be the one apologizing. You didn't do anything wrong. I was the target of those clockwork things, not you." She patted the coverlet gently; wanting to touch his hand but not daring to. "If it wasn't for me, you never would have been hurt."

"Hurt." Jem spoke the word on an exhale of breath, almost with disgust. "I wasn't hurt."

"James." Will's tone held a warning note.

"She should know, William. Otherwise she'll think this was all her fault."

"You were ill," Will said, not looking at Tessa as he spoke. "It's nobody's fault." He paused. "I just think you should be careful. You're not well still. Talking will just tire you out."

"There are more important things than being careful." Jem

struggled to sit up, the cords in his neck straining as he lifted himself, propping his back against the pillows. When he spoke again, he was slightly breathless. "If you don't like it, Will, you don't have to stay."

Tessa heard the door open and close behind her with a soft click. She knew without looking that Will had gone. She couldn't help it—a slight pang went through her, the way it always seemed to do when he left a room.

Jem sighed. "He's so stubborn."

"He was right," Tessa said. "At least, he was right that you don't need to tell me anything you don't want to. I know none of it was your fault."

"Fault has nothing to do with it," Jem said. "I just think you might as well have the truth. Concealing it rarely helps anything." He looked toward the door for a moment, as if his words were half-meant for the absent Will. Then he sighed again, raking his hands through his hair. "You know," he said, "that for most of my life I lived in Shanghai with my parents? That I was raised in the Institute there?"

"Yes," Tessa said, wondering if he was still a little dazed. "You told me, on the bridge. And you told me that a demon had killed your parents."

"*Yanluo*," said Jem. There was hatred in his voice. "The demon had a grudge against my mother. She'd been responsible for the death of a number of its demon offspring. They'd had a nest in a small town called Lijiang, where they'd been feeding on local children. She burned the nest out and escaped before the demon found her. Yanluo bided its time for years—Greater Demons live forever—but it never forgot. When I was eleven, Yanluo found a weak spot in the ward that protected the Institute, and tunneled inside. The demon killed the guards and took my family prisoner, binding us all to chairs in the great room of the house. Then it went to work.

"Yanluo tortured me in front of my parents," Jem went on, his voice empty. "Over and over it injected me with a burning demon poison that scorched my veins and tore at my mind. For two days I went in and out of hallucinations and dreams. I saw the world drowned in rivers of blood, and I heard the screams of all the dead and dying throughout history. I saw London burning, and great metal creatures striding here and there like huge spiders—" He caught his breath. He was very pale, his nightshirt stuck to his chest with sweat, but he waved away Tessa's expression of concern. "Every few hours I would come back to reality long enough to hear my parents screaming for me. Then on the second day, I came back and heard only my mother. My father had been silenced. My mother's voice was raw and cracked, but she was still saying my name. Not my name in English, but the name she had given me when I was born: Jian. I can still hear her sometimes, calling out for me."

His hands were tight on the pillow he held, tight enough that the fabric had begun to tear.

"Jem," Tessa said softly. "You can stop. You needn't tell me all of it now."

"You remember when I said that Mortmain had probably made his money smuggling opium?" he asked. "The British bring opium into China by the ton. They have made a nation of addicts out of us. In Chinese we call it 'foreign mud' or 'black smoke.' In some ways Shanghai, my city, is built on opium. It wouldn't exist as it does without it. The city is full of dens where hollow-eyed men starve to death because all they want is the drug, more of the drug. They'll give anything for it. I used to despise men like that. I couldn't understand how they were so weak."

He took a deep breath.

"By the time the Shanghai Enclave became worried at the silence from the Institute and broke in to save us, both my parents were already dead. I don't remember any of it. I was screaming and delirious. They took me to the Silent Brothers, who healed my body as well as they could. There was one thing they couldn't fix, though. I had become addicted to the substance the demon had poisoned me with. My body was dependent on it the way an opium addict's body is dependent on the drug. They tried to wean me off it, but going without it caused terrible pain. Even when they were able to block the pain with warlock spells, the lack of the drug pushed my body to the brink of death. After weeks of experimentation they decided that there was nothing to be done: I could not live without the drug. The drug itself meant a slow death, but to take me off it would mean a very quick one."

"Weeks of experimentation?" Tessa echoed. "When you were only eleven years old? That seems cruel."

"Goodness—real goodness—has its own sort of cruelty to it," said Jem, looking past her. "There, beside you on the bedside table, is a box. Can you give it to me?"

Tessa lifted the box. It was made of silver, its lid inlaid with an enamel scene that depicted a slim woman in white robes, barefoot, pouring water out of a vase into a stream. "Who is she?" she asked, handing the box to Jem.

"Kwan Yin. The goddess of mercy and compassion. They say she hears every prayer and every cry of suffering and does what she can to answer it. I thought perhaps if I kept the cause of my suffering in a box with her image on it, it might make that suffering a little less." He flicked open the clasp on the box, and the lid slid back. Inside was a thick layer of what Tessa thought at first was ash, but the color was too bright. It was a layer of thick silvery powder almost the same bright silver color as Jem's eyes.

"This is the drug," he said. "It comes from a warlock dealer we know in Limehouse. I take some of it every day. It's why I look so—so ghostly; it's what drains the color from my eyes and hair, even my skin. I wonder sometimes if my parents would even recognize me. . . ." His voice trailed off. "If I have to fight, I take more. Taking less weakens me. I had taken none today before we went out to the bridge. That's why I collapsed. Not because of the clockwork creatures. Because of the drug. Without any in my system, the fighting, the running, was too much for me. My body started feeding on itself, and I collapsed." He shut the box with a snap, and handed it back to Tessa. "Here. Put it back where it was."

"You don't need any?"

"No. I've had enough tonight."

"You said that the drug meant a slow death," Tessa said. "So do you mean the drug is killing you?"

Jem nodded, strands of bright hair falling across his forehead.

Tessa felt her heart skip a painful beat. "And when you fight, you take more of it? So, why don't you stop fighting? Will and the others—"

"Would understand," Jem finished for her. "I know they would. But there is more to life than not dying. I am a

Shadowhunter. It is what I am, not just what I do. I can't live without it."

"You mean you don't want to."

Will, Tessa thought, would have been angry if she'd said that to him, but Jem just looked at her intently. "I mean I don't want to. For a long time I searched for a cure, but eventually I stopped, and asked Will and the rest to stop as well. I am not this drug, or its hold on me. I believe that I am better than that. That my life is about more than that, however and whenever it might end."

"Well, I don't want you to die," Tessa said. "I don't know why I feel it so strongly—I've just met you—but I don't want you to die."

"And I trust you," he said. "I don't know why—I've just met you—but I do." His hands were no longer clutching the pillow, but lying flat and still on the tasseled surface. They were thin hands, the knuckles just slightly too big for the rest of them, the fingers tapering and slender, a thick white scar running across the back of his right thumb. Tessa wanted to slide her own hand over his, wanted to hold his tightly and comfort him—

"Well, this is all very touching." It was Will, of course, having come soundlessly into the room. He had changed his bloody shirt, and he seemed to have washed up hastily. His hair looked damp, his face scrubbed, though the crescents of his nails were still black with dirt and oil. He looked from Jem to Tessa, his face carefully blank. "I see that you told her."

"I did." There was nothing challenging in Jem's tone; he never looked at Will with anything but affection, Tessa thought, no matter how provoking Will was. "It's done. There's no more need for you to fret about it."

"I disagree," said Will. He gave Tessa a pointed look. She remembered what he had said about not tiring Jem out, and rose from her chair.

Jem gave her a wistful look. "Must you go? I was rather hoping you'd stay and be a ministering angel, but if you must go, you must."

"I'll stay," Will said a bit crossly, and threw himself down in the armchair Tessa had just vacated. "I can minister angelically."

"None too convincingly. And you're not as pretty to look at as Tessa is," Jem said, closing his eyes as he leaned back against the pillow.

"How rude. Many who have gazed upon me have compared the experience to gazing at the radiance of the sun."

Jem still had his eyes closed. "If they mean it gives you a headache, they aren't wrong."

"Besides," Will said, his eyes on Tessa, "it's hardly fair to keep Tessa from her brother. She hasn't had a chance to look in on him since this morning."

"That's true." Jem's eyes fluttered open for a moment; they were silvery black, dark with sleep. "My apologies, Tessa. I nearly forgot."

Tessa said nothing. She was too busy being horrified that Jem wasn't the only one who had nearly forgotten about her brother. *It's all right*, she wanted to say, but Jem's eyes were shut again, and she thought he might be asleep. As she watched, Will leaned forward and drew up the blankets, covering Jem's chest.

Tessa turned around and let herself out as quietly as she could.

The light in the corridors was burning low, or perhaps it had simply been brighter in Jem's room. Tessa stood for a moment, blinking, before her eyes adjusted. She gave a start. "Sophie?"

The other girl was a series of pale smudges in the dimness—her pale face, and the white cap dangling from her hand by one of its ties.

"Sophie?" Tessa said. "Is something wrong?"

"Is he all right?" Sophie demanded, a strange small hitch in her voice. "Is he going to be all right?"

Too startled to make sense of her question, Tessa said, "Who?"

Sophie stared at her, her eyes mutely tragic. "Jem."

Not Master Jem, or Mr. Carstairs. Jem. Tessa looked at her in utter astonishment, suddenly remembering. *It's all right to love someone who doesn't love you back, as long as they're worth you loving them. As long as they deserve it.*

Of course, Tessa thought. *I'm so stupid. It's Jem she's in love with.*

"He's fine," she said as gently as she could. "He's resting, but he was sitting up and talking. He'll be quite recovered soon, I'm sure. Perhaps if you wanted to see him—"

"No!" Sophie exclaimed at once. "No, that wouldn't be right or proper." Her eyes were shining. "I'm much obliged to you, miss. I—"

She turned then, and hurried away down the corridor. Tessa looked after her, troubled and perplexed. How could she not have seen it earlier? How could she have been so blind? How strange to have the power to literally transform yourself into other people, and yet be so unable to put yourself in their place.

* * *

The door to Nate's room was slightly ajar; Tessa pushed it open the rest of the way as quietly as she could, and peered inside.

Her brother was a heaped mound of blankets. The light from the guttering candle on the bedside table illuminated the fair hair spread across his pillow. His eyes were closed, his chest rising and falling regularly.

In the armchair beside the bed sat Jessamine. She, too, was asleep. Her blond hair was coming out of its carefully arranged chignon, the curls tumbling down onto her shoulders. Someone had thrown a heavy woolen blanket over her, and her hands clutched it, drawing it up against her chest. She looked younger than Tessa had ever seen her look, and vulnerable. There was nothing about her of the girl who had slaughtered the faerie in the park.

It was so odd, Tessa thought, what brought out tenderness in people. It was never what you would have expected. As quietly as she could, she turned away, shutting the door behind her.

Tessa slept fitfully that night, waking often amid dreams of clockwork creatures coming for her, reaching out their spindly metal-jointed hands to catch and tear at her skin. Eventually that dissolved into a dream of Jem, who lay asleep in a bed while silver powder rained down on him, burning where it struck the coverlet he lay under, until eventually the whole bed burned, and Jem slept peacefully on, oblivious to Tessa's warning cries.

Finally she dreamed of Will, standing at the apex of the dome of St. Paul's, alone under the light of a white, white moon. He wore a black frock coat, and the Marks on his skin were plain to be seen on his neck and hands under the glow of the sky. He looked down on London like a bad angel pledged to save the city from its own worst dreams, while below him London slept on, indifferent and unknowing.

Tessa was torn from her dream by a voice in her ear, and a hand vigorously shaking her shoulder. "Miss!" It was Sophie, her voice sharp. "Miss Gray, you simply *must* wake. It's your brother."

Tessa shot upright, scattering pillows. Afternoon light poured through the bedroom windows, illuminating the room—and Sophie's anxious face. "Nate's awake? He's all right?"

"Yes—I mean, no. I mean, I don't know, miss." There was a little catch in Sophie's voice. "You see, he's gone missing."

16

The Binding Spell

And once, or twice, to throw the dice
Is a gentlemanly game,
But he does not win who plays with Sin
In the secret House of Shame.
—Oscar Wilde, "The Ballad of Reading Gaol"

"Jessamine! Jessamine, what's going on? Where's Nate?"

Jessamine, who was standing just outside Nate's room, whirled to face Tessa as she hurried up the corridor. Jessamine's eyes were red-rimmed, her expression angry. Loose curls of blond hair were coming out of the usually neatly arranged knot at the back of her head. "I don't *know*," she snapped. "I fell asleep in the chair beside the bed, and when I woke up, he was gone— just gone!" She narrowed her eyes. "Gracious, you look ghastly."

Tessa glanced down at herself. She hadn't bothered with

a crinoline, or even shoes. She'd just thrown on a dress and slid her bare feet into slippers. Her hair was straggling down around her shoulders, and she imagined she likely resembled the madwoman Mr. Rochester kept in his attic in *Jane Eyre*. "Well, Nate can't have gone very far, not as ill as he is," Tessa said. "Isn't anyone *looking* for him?"

Jessamine threw up her hands. "Everyone's looking for him. Will, Charlotte, Henry, Thomas, even Agatha. I don't suppose you want us to roust poor Jem out of bed and make him part of the search party too?"

Tessa shook her head. "Honestly, Jessamine—" She broke off, turning away. "Well, I'm going to look as well. You can stay here if you like."

"I do like." Jessamine tossed her head as Tessa spun away and stalked off down the corridor, her mind whirling. Where on earth could Nate have gone? Had he been feverish, delirious? Had he gotten out of bed not knowing where he was and staggered off to look for her? The thought made her heart clench. The Institute was a baffling maze, she thought as she turned yet another blind corner into yet another tapestry-lined corridor. If she could barely find her way around it even now, how could Nate possibly—

"Miss Gray?"

Tessa turned and saw Thomas emerging from one of the doors along the hall. He was in shirtsleeves, his hair tousled as usual, his brown eyes very serious. She felt herself go very still. *Oh, God, it's bad news.* "Yes?"

"I've found your brother," Thomas said, to Tessa's astonishment.

"You *have*? But where was he?"

"In the drawing room. Got himself a bit of a hiding place, behind the curtains, he had." Thomas spoke hastily, looking sheepish. "Minute he saw me, he went right off his chump. Started screamin' and yellin'. Tried to bolt right past me, an' I nearly had to give him one over the gash to keep him quiet—" At Tessa's look of incomprehension, Thomas paused, and cleared his throat. "That is to say, I'm afraid I may have frightened him, miss."

Tessa put her hand over her mouth. "Oh, dear. But he's all right?"

It seemed that Thomas did not know quite where to look. He was embarrassed to have found Nate cowering behind Charlotte's curtains, Tessa thought, and she felt a wave of indignation on Nate's behalf. Her brother wasn't a Shadowhunter; he hadn't grown up killing things and risking his life. Of course he was terrified. And he was probably delirious with fever, on top of that. "I had better go in and see him. Just me, you understand? I think he needs to see a familiar face."

Thomas looked relieved. "Yes, miss. And I'll wait out here, just for now. You just let me know when you want me to summon the others."

Tessa nodded and moved past Thomas to push the door open. The drawing room was dim, the only illumination the gray afternoon light that spilled through the tall windows. In the shadows the sofas and armchairs scattered about the room looked like crouched beasts. In one of the larger armchairs by the fire sat Nate. He had found the bloodstained shirt and trousers he had been wearing at de Quincey's, and had put them on. His feet were bare. He sat with his elbows on his knees, his face in his hands. He looked wretched.

"Nate?" Tessa said softly.

At that he looked up—and sprang to his feet, a look of incredulous happiness on his face. "Tessie!"

With a little cry Tessa rushed across the room and threw her arms around her brother, hugging him fiercely. She heard him give a little whimper of pain, but his arms went around her too, and for a moment, embracing him, Tessa was back in her aunt's little kitchen in New York, with the smell of cooking all around her and her aunt's soft laughter as she scolded them for making so much noise.

Nate pulled away first, and looked down at her. "God, Tessie, you look so different. . . ."

A shudder went through her. "What do you mean?"

He patted her cheek, almost absently. "Older," he said. "Thinner. You were a round-faced little girl when I left New York, weren't you? Or is that just the way I remember you?"

Tessa reassured her brother that she was still the same little sister he'd always known, but her mind was only partly engaged with his question. She couldn't help staring at him worriedly; he no longer looked as gray as he had, but he was still pale, and bruises stood out in blue, black, and yellow patches on his face and neck. "Nate . . ."

"It's not as bad as it looks," he said, reading the anxiety on her face.

"Yes, it is. You should be in bed, resting. What are you doing in here?"

"I was trying to find *you*. I knew you were here. I saw you, before that bald bastard with the missing eyes got at me. I figured they'd imprisoned you, too. I was going to try to get us out."

"Imprisoned? Nate, no, it's not like that." She shook her head. "We're safe here."

He narrowed his eyes at her. "This is the Institute, isn't it? I was warned about this place. De Quincey said it was run by madmen, monsters who called themselves Nephilim. He said they keep the damned souls of men penned up in some kind of box of theirs, screaming—"

"What, the Pyxis? It holds bits of demon energy, Nate, not men's souls! It's perfectly harmless. I'll show it to you later, in the weapons room, if you don't believe me."

Nate looked no less grim. "He said that if the Nephilim got their hands on me, they'd take me apart, piece by piece, for breaking their Laws."

A cold shiver went up Tessa's spine; she drew away from her brother, and saw that one of the drawing room windows was open, the curtains fluttering in the breeze. So her shiver had been more than just nerves. "Did you open the window? It's so cold in here, Nate."

Nate shook his head. "It was open when I came in."

Shaking her head, Tessa went across the room and drew the window down. "You'll catch your death—"

"Never mind my death," Nate said irritably. "What about the Shadowhunters? Are you saying they haven't kept you imprisoned here?"

"No." Tessa turned away from the window. "They haven't. They're strange people, but the Shadowhunters have been kind to me. I *wanted* to stay here. They've been generous enough to let me."

Nate shook his head. "I don't understand."

Tessa felt a spark of anger, which surprised her; she pushed it back. It wasn't Nate's fault. There was so much he didn't know. "Where else was I going to go, Nate?" she asked, crossing the room to him and taking his arm. She led him back over to the armchair. "Sit down. You're exhausting yourself."

Nate sat obediently, and looked up at her. There was a distant look in his eyes. Tessa knew that look. It meant he was plotting, hatching some mad plan, dreaming a ridiculous dream. "We can still get away from this place," he said. "Get to Liverpool, get on a steamer. Go back to New York."

"And do what?" Tessa said as gently as she could. "There's nothing there for us. Not with Aunt dead. I had to sell all our things to pay for the funeral. The apartment's gone. There was no rent money. There's no place for us in New York, Nate."

"We'll make a place. A new life."

Tessa looked at her brother sadly. There was pain in seeing him like this, his face full of hopeless pleading, bruises blossoming on his cheekbones like ugly flowers, his fair hair still matted in places with blood. Nate was not like other people, Aunt Harriet had always said. He had a beautiful innocence about him that had to be protected at all costs.

And Tessa had tried. She and her aunt had hidden Nate's own weaknesses from him, the consequences of his own flaws and failings. Never telling him of the work Aunt Harriet had had to do to make up the money he had lost gambling, of the taunts Tessa had endured from other children, calling her brother a drunk, a wastrel. They had hidden these things from him to keep him from being hurt. But he had been hurt anyway, Tessa thought. Maybe Jem was right. Maybe the truth was always best.

Sitting down on the ottoman opposite her brother, she

looked at him steadily. "It can't be like that, Nate. Not yet. This mess we're both in now, it will follow us even if we run. And if we run, we'll be alone when it does find us. There will be no one to help or protect us. We need the Institute, Nate. We need the Nephilim."

Nate's blue eyes were dazed. "I guess so," he said, and the phrase struck Tessa, who had heard nothing but British voices for nearly two months, as so American that she felt homesick. "It's because of me that you're here. De Quincey tortured me. Made me write those letters, send you that ticket. He told me he wouldn't hurt you once he had you, but then he never let me see you, and I thought—I thought—" He raised his head and looked at her dully. "You ought to hate me."

Tessa's voice was firm. "I could never hate you. You're my brother. You're my blood."

"Do you think when all this is over, we can go back home?" Nate asked. "Forget all this ever happened? Live normal lives?"

Live normal lives. The words conjured up an image of herself and Nate in some small, sunny apartment. Nate could get another job, and in the evening she could cook and clean for him, while on weekends they could walk in the park or take the train to Coney Island and ride the carousel, or go to the top of the Iron Tower and watch the fireworks explode at night over the Manhattan Beach Hotel. There would be real sunshine, not like this gray watery version of summer, and Tessa could be an ordinary girl, with her head in a book and her feet planted firmly on the familiar pavement of New York City.

But when she tried to hold this mental picture in her head, the vision seemed to crumble and fall away from her, like a cobweb when you tried to lift it whole in your hands. She saw Will's face, and Jem's, and Charlotte's, and even Magnus's as he said, *Poor thing. Now that you know the truth, you can never go back.*

"But we are not normal," said Tessa. "I am not normal. And you know that, Nate."

He looked down at the floor. "I know." He gave a helpless little wave of his hand. "So it's true. You are what de Quincey said you were. Magical. He said you had the power to change shape, Tessie, to become anything you wanted to be."

"Did you even believe him? It's true—well, almost true—but I barely believed it myself at first. It's so strange—"

"I've seen stranger things." His voice was hollow. "God, it ought to have been me."

Tessa frowned. "What do you mean?"

But before he could answer, the door swung open. "Miss Gray." It was Thomas, looking apologetic. "Miss Gray, Master Will is—"

"Master Will is right here." It was Will, ducking nimbly around Thomas, despite the other boy's bulk. He was still in the clothes he'd changed into the night before, and they looked rumpled. Tessa wondered if he'd slept in the chair in Jem's room. There were blue-gray shadows under his eyes, and he looked tired, though his eyes brightened—with relief? amusement? Tessa couldn't tell—as his gaze fell on Nate.

"Our wanderer, found at last," he said. "Thomas tells me you were hiding behind the curtains?"

Nate looked at Will dully. "Who are you?"

Quickly Tessa made the introductions, though neither boy seemed all that happy to meet the other. Nate still looked as if he were dying, and Will was regarding Nate as if he were a new scientific discovery, and not a very attractive one at that.

"So you're a Shadowhunter," Nate said. "De Quincey told me that you lot were monsters."

"Was that before or after he tried to eat you?" Will inquired.

Tessa rose quickly to her feet. "Will. Might I speak to you in the corridor for a moment, please?"

If she had expected resistance, she didn't get it. After a last hostile look at Nate, Will nodded and went with her silently out into the hall, closing the drawing room door behind him.

The illumination in the windowless corridor was variable, the witchlight casting discrete bright pools of light that didn't quite touch one another. Will and Tessa stood in the shadows between two of the pools, looking at each other—warily, Tessa thought, like angry cats circling in an alley.

It was Will who broke the silence. "Very well. You have me alone in the corridor—"

"Yes, yes," said Tessa impatiently, "and thousands of women all over England would pay handsomely for the privilege of such an opportunity. Can we put aside the display of your wit for a moment? This is important."

"You want me to apologize, do you?" Will said. "For what happened in the attic?"

Tessa, caught off guard, blinked. "The *attic*?"

"You want me to say I'm sorry that I kissed you."

At the words, the memory rose up again in Tessa with an unexpected clarity—Will's fingers in her hair, the touch of his hand on her glove, his mouth on hers. She felt herself flush and hoped furiously that it wouldn't be visible in the dimness. "What—no. No!"

"So you don't want me to be sorry," Will said. He was smiling very slightly now, the sort of smile a small child might bend upon the castle he has just built out of toy blocks, before he destroys it with a wave of his arm.

"I don't care whether you're sorry or not," Tessa said. "That's not what I wanted to talk to you about. I wanted to tell you to be kind to my brother. He's been through an awful ordeal. He doesn't need to be interrogated like some sort of criminal."

Will replied more quietly than Tessa would have thought. "I understand that. But if he's hiding anything—"

"Everyone hides things!" Tessa burst out, surprising herself. "There are things I know he's ashamed of, but that doesn't mean they need to matter to you. It's not as if you tell everyone everything, do you?"

Will looked wary. "What are you on about?"

What about your parents, Will? Why did you refuse to see them? Why do you have nowhere to go but here? And why, in the attic, did you send me away? But Tessa said none of those things. Instead she said, "What about Jem? Why didn't you tell me he was ill the way he is?"

"*Jem?*" Will's surprise seemed genuine. "He didn't want me to. He considers it his business. Which it is. You might recall, I wasn't even in favor of him telling you himself. He thought he owed you an explanation, but he didn't. Jem owes nothing to anyone. What happened to him wasn't his fault, and yet he carries the burden of it and is ashamed—"

"He has nothing to be ashamed of."

"*You* might think so. Others see no difference between his illness and an addiction, and they despise him for being weak. As if he could just stop taking the drug if he had enough willpower." Will sounded surprisingly bitter. "They've said as much, sometimes to his face. I didn't want him to have to hear you say it too."

"I would never have said that."

"How would I have guessed what you might say?" Will said. "I don't really know you, Tessa, do I? Any more than you know me."

"You don't want anyone to know you," Tessa snapped. "And very well, I won't try. But don't pretend that Jem is just like you. Perhaps he'd rather people knew the truth of who he is."

"Don't," Will said, his blue eyes darkening. "Don't think you know Jem better than I do."

"If you care about him so much, why aren't you doing anything to help him? Why not look for a cure?"

"Do you think we *haven't*? Do you think Charlotte hasn't looked, Henry hasn't looked, that we haven't hired warlocks, paid for information, called in favors? Do you imagine Jem's death is just something we have all accepted without ever fighting against it?"

"Jem told me that he had asked you all to stop looking," Tessa said, calm in the face of his anger, "and that you had. Haven't you?"

"He told you that, did he?"

"*Have* you stopped?"

"There is nothing to find, Tessa. There is no cure."

"You don't know that. You could keep looking and not ever tell him you were looking. There might be something. Even the littlest chance—"

Will raised his eyebrows. The flickering corridor light deepened the shadows under his eyes, the angular bones of his cheeks. "You think we should disregard his wishes?"

"I think that you should do whatever you can, even if it means you must lie to him. I think I don't understand your acceptance of his death."

"And I think that *you* do not understand that sometimes the only choice is between acceptance and madness."

Behind them in the corridor someone cleared their throat. "What's going on here, then?" asked a familiar voice. Both Tessa and Will had been so caught up in their conversation that they had not heard Jem approaching. Will gave a guilty start before turning to look at his friend, who was regarding them both with calm interest. Jem was fully dressed but looked as if he had just woken from a feverish sleep, his hair mussed and his cheeks burning with color.

Will looked surprised, and not entirely pleased, to see him. "What are you doing out of bed?"

"I ran into Charlotte in the hall. She said we were all meeting in the drawing room to talk with Tessa's brother." Jem's tone was mild, and it was impossible to tell from his expression how much of Tessa and Will's conversation he had overheard. "I'm well enough to listen, at least."

"Oh, good, you're all here." It was Charlotte, hurrying up the corridor. Behind her strode Henry, and on either side of him, Jessamine and Sophie. Jessie had changed into one of her nicest dresses, Tessa observed, a sheer blue muslin, and she was carrying a folded blanket. Sophie, beside her, held a tray with tea and sandwiches on it.

"Are those for Nate?" Tessa asked, surprised. "The tea, and the blankets?"

Sophie nodded. "Mrs. Branwell thought he'd likely be hungry—"

"And I thought he might be cold. He was shivering so last night," Jessamine put in eagerly. "Should we bring these things in to him, then?"

Charlotte looked to Tessa for her approval, which disarmed her. Charlotte would be kind to Nate; she couldn't help it. "Yes. He's waiting for you."

"Thank you, Tessa," Charlotte said softly, and then she pushed the drawing room door open and went in, followed by the others. As Tessa moved to go after them, she felt a hand on her arm, a touch so light she almost might not have noticed it.

It was Jem. "Wait," he said. "Just a moment."

She turned to look at him. Through the open doorway she could hear a murmur of voices—Henry's friendly baritone, Jessamine's eager falsetto rising as she said Nate's name. "What is it?"

He hesitated. His hand on her arm was cool; his fingers felt like thin stems of glass against her skin. She wondered if the skin over the bones of his cheeks, where he was flushed and feverish, would be warmer to the touch.

"But my sister—" Nate's voice floated into the hallway, sounding anxious. "Is she joining us? Where is she?"

"Never mind. It's nothing." With a reassuring smile Jem dropped his hand. Tessa wondered, but turned and went into the drawing room, Jem behind her.

Sophie was kneeling by the grate, building up the fire; Nate was still in the armchair, where he sat with Jessamine's blanket thrown over his lap. Jessamine, upright on a stool nearby, was beaming proudly. Henry and Charlotte sat on the sofa opposite Nate—Charlotte clearly bursting with curiosity—and Will, as usual, was holding up the nearest wall by leaning against it and looking both irritable and amused at the same time.

As Jem went to join Will, Tessa fixed her attention on her brother. Some of the tension had gone out of him when she'd come back into the room, but he still looked miserable. He was plucking at Jessamine's blanket with his fingertips. She crossed the room and sank down onto the ottoman at his feet, resisting the urge to ruffle his hair or pat his shoulder. She could feel all the eyes in the room on her. Everyone was watching her and her brother, and she could have heard a pin drop.

"Nate," she said softly. "I assume everyone has introduced themselves?"

Nate, still picking at the blanket, nodded.

"Mr. Gray," said Charlotte, "we have spoken to Mr. Mortmain already. He has told us a great deal about you. About your fondness for Downworld. And gambling."

"*Charlotte,*" Tessa protested.

Nate spoke heavily. "It's true, Tessie."

"No one blames your brother for what happened, Tessa." Charlotte made her voice very gentle as she turned back to Nate. "Mortmain says you already knew he was involved in occult practices when you arrived in London. How did you know that he was a member of the Pandemonium Club?"

Nate hesitated.

"Mr. Gray, we simply need to understand what happened to you. De Quincey's interest in you—I know you aren't well, and we have no wish to cruelly interrogate you, but if you could offer us even a little information, it might be of the most invaluable assistance—"

"It was Aunt Harriet's sewing notions," Nate said in a low voice.

Tessa blinked. "It was what?"

Nate continued, in a low voice. "Our aunt Harriet always kept mother's old jewelry box on the nightstand by her bed. She said she kept sewing notions in it, but I—" Nate took a deep breath, looking at Tessa as he spoke. "I was in debt. I'd made a few rash bets, had lost some money, and I was in a bad way. I didn't want you or Aunt to know. I remembered there was a gold bracelet Mother used to wear when she was alive. I got it into my head that it was still in that jewelry box and that Aunt Harriet was just too stubborn to sell it. You know how she is—how she *was*. Anyway, I couldn't let the idea go. I knew that if I could pawn the bracelet, I could get the money to pay off my debts. So one day when you and Aunt were out, I got hold of the box and searched it.

"Of course the bracelet wasn't in it. But I did find a false bottom to the case. There was nothing in it of any worth, just a wadded-up bunch of old papers. I snatched them when I heard you coming up the stairs, and took them back to my room."

Nate paused. All eyes were on him. After a moment Tessa, no longer able to hold her questions in, said, "*And?*"

"They were Mother's diary pages," Nate said. "Torn out of their original binding, with quite a few missing, but it was enough for me to put together a strange story.

"It began when our parents were living in London. Father was gone often, working in Mortmain's offices down at the docks, but mother had Aunt Harriet to keep her company, and me to keep her occupied. I had just been born. That was, until Father began to come home night after night increasingly distressed. He reported odd doings on the factory floor, bits of machinery malfunctioning in strange ways, noises heard at all hours, and even the night watchman gone missing one night. There were rumors, too, that Mortmain was involved in occult practices." Nate sounded as if he were remembering as much as reciting the tale. "Father shrugged the rumors off at first but eventually repeated them to Mortmain, who admitted everything. I gather he managed to make it sound rather harmless, as if he were just having a bit of a lark with spells and pentagrams and things. He called the organization he belonged to the Pandemonium Club. He suggested that Father come to one of their meetings, and bring Mother."

"Bring Mother? But he couldn't possibly have wanted to do that—"

"Probably not, but with a new wife and a new baby, Father would have been eager to please his employer. He agreed to go, and to bring Mother with him."

"Father should have gone to the police—"

"A rich man like Mortmain would have had the police in his pocket," interrupted Will. "Had your father gone to the police, they would have laughed at him."

Nathaniel pushed the hair back off his forehead; he was sweating now, strands of hair sticking to his skin. "Mortmain arranged a carriage to come for both of them late at night, when no one would be watching. The carriage brought them to Mortmain's town house. After that there were many missing pages, and no details about what happened that night. It was the first time they went, but not, I learned, the last. They met with the Pandemonium Club several times over the course of the next few months. Mother, at least, hated going, but they continued to attend the meetings until something changed abruptly. I don't know what it was; there were few pages after that. I was able to discern that when they left London, they did it under cover of night, that they told no one where they were going, and they left no forwarding address. They might as well have vanished. Nothing in the diary, though, said anything about why—"

Nathaniel broke off his story with a fit of dry coughing. Jessamine scrambled for the tea that Sophie had left on the side table, and a moment later was pressing a cup into Nate's hand. She gave Tessa a superior expression as she did so, as if to point out that Tessa really ought to have thought of it first.

Nate, having quieted his coughing with tea, continued. "Having found the diary pages, I felt as if I'd stumbled across a gold mine. I'd heard of Mortmain. I knew the man was as rich as Croesus, even if he was evidently a bit mad. I wrote to him and told him I was Nathaniel Gray, the son of Richard and Elizabeth Gray, that my father was dead, and so was my mother, and in among her papers I had found evidence of his occult activities. I intimated that I was eager to meet him and discuss possible employment, and that if he proved less eager to meet me, there were several newspapers that I imagined would be interested in my mother's diary."

"That was enterprising." Will sounded nearly impressed.

Nate smiled. Tessa shot him a furious look. "Don't look pleased with yourself. When Will says 'enterprising,' he means 'morally deficient.'"

"No, I mean enterprising," said Will. "When I mean morally deficient, I say, 'Now, that's something I would have done.'"

"That's enough, Will," Charlotte interrupted. "Let Mr. Gray finish his story."

"I thought perhaps he'd send me a bribe, some money to

shut me up," Nate went on. "Instead I got a first-class steamer ticket to London and the official offer of a job once I arrived. I figured I was onto a good thing, and for the first time in my life, I didn't plan on messing it up.

"When I got to London, I went straight to Mortmain's house, where I was ushered into the study to meet him. He greeted me with great warmth, telling me how glad he was to see me and how I looked just like my dear dead mother. Then he grew serious. He sat me down and told me he had always liked my parents and had been saddened when they had left England. He had not known they were dead until he received my letter. Even if I were to go public with what I knew about him, he claimed he would happily give me a job and do whatever he could for me, for my parents' sake.

"I told Mortmain that I would keep his secret—*if* he brought me with him to attend a meeting of the Pandemonium Club, that he owed it to me to show me what it was he had shown my parents. The truth was, the mentioning of gambling in my mother's diary had sparked my interest. I imagined a meeting of a group of men silly enough to believe in magic and devils. Surely it wouldn't be difficult to win a bit of money off such fools." Nate closed his eyes.

"Mortmain agreed, reluctantly, to take me. I suppose he had no choice. That night the meeting was at de Quincey's town house. The moment the door opened, I knew I was the fool. This was no group of amateurs dabbling in spiritualism. This was the real thing, the Shadow World my mother had made only glancing reference to in her diary. It was *real*. I can barely describe my sense of shock as I stared around me— creatures of indescribable grotesqueness filled the room. The

Dark Sisters were there, leering at me from behind their whist cards, their nails like talons. Women with their faces and shoulders powdered white smiled at me with blood running out the corners of their mouths. Little creatures whose eyes changed color scuttled across the floor. I had never imagined such things were real, and I said as much to Mortmain.

"'There are more things in Heaven and earth, Nathaniel, than are dreamt of in your philosophy,' he said.

"Well, I knew the quote because of you, Tessa. You were always reading Shakespeare at me, and I even paid attention some of the time. I was about to tell Mortmain not to make fun of me, when a man came up to us. I saw Mortmain go stiff as a board, as if this were someone he was frightened of. He introduced me as Nathaniel, a new employee, and told me the man's name. De Quincey.

"De Quincey smiled. I knew immediately he wasn't human. I'd never seen a vampire before, with that death white skin of theirs, and of course when he smiled, I saw his teeth. I think I just stared. 'Mortmain, you're keeping things from me again,' he said. 'This is more than just a new employee. This is Nathaniel Gray. Elizabeth and Richard Gray's son.'

"Mortmain stammered something, looking baffled. De Quincey chuckled. 'I do hear things, Axel,' he said. Then he turned to me. 'I knew your father,' he told me. 'I liked him quite a bit. Perhaps you'd join me for a game of cards?'

"Mortmain shook his head at me, but I'd seen the card room when I'd come into the house, of course. I was drawn to the gaming tables like a moth to light. I sat playing faro all night with a vampire, two werewolves, and a wild-haired warlock. I made my jack that night—won a great deal of money, and drank a great deal of the colorful sparkling drinks that were passed around the room on silver trays. At some point Mortmain left, but I didn't care. I emerged in the dawn light feeling exultant, on top of the world—and with an invitation from de Quincey to return to the club whenever I liked.

"I was a fool, of course. I was having such a high old time of it because the drinks were mixed with warlock potions, addictive ones. And I had been *allowed* to win that evening. I went back of course, without Mortmain, night after night. At first I won—won steadily, which was how I was able to send money back to you and Aunt Harriet, Tessie. It certainly wasn't from working at Mortmain's. I went into the office irregularly, but I could barely concentrate even on the simple tasks I was assigned. All I thought about was getting back to the club, drinking more of those drinks, winning more money.

"Then I started to lose. The more I lost, the more obsessed I became with winning it back. De Quincey suggested I start playing on tick, so I borrowed money; I stopped coming into the office at all. I slept all day, and gambled all night. I lost everything." His voice was remote. "When I got your letter that Aunt had died, Tessa, I thought it was a judgment on me. A punishment for my behavior. I wanted to rush out and buy a ticket to return to New York that day—but I had no money. Desperate, I went to the club—I was unshaved, miserable, red-eyed. I must have looked like a man at his lowest ebb, because it was then that de Quincey approached me with a proposition. He drew me into a back room and pointed out that I had lost more money to the club than any one man could ever pay back. He seemed amused by it all, the devil, flicking invisible dust off his cuffs, grinning at me with those needle teeth. He asked me what I'd be willing to give to pay off my debts. I said, 'Anything.' And he said, 'What about your sister?'"

Tessa felt the hairs on her arms rise, and was uncomfortably aware of the eyes of everyone in the room on her. "What— what did he say about me?"

"I was utterly taken off guard," said Nate. "I didn't recall having discussed you with him, ever, but I had been drunk so many times at the club, and we had spoken very freely. . . ." The teacup in his hand rattled in its saucer; he set them both down, hard. "I asked him what he could possibly want with my sister. He told me that he had reason to know that one of my mother's children was . . . special. He had thought it might be me, but having had leisure to observe me, the only thing unusual about me was my foolishness." Nate's tone was bitter. "'But your sister, your sister is something else again,' he told me. 'She has all the power you do not. I have no intention of harming her. She is far too important.'

"I spluttered and begged for more information, but he was unyielding. Either I procured Tessa for him, or I would die. He even told me what it was I had to do."

Tessa exhaled slowly. "De Quincey told you to write me that letter," she said. "He had you send me the tickets for the *Main*. He had you bring me here."

Nate's eyes pleaded with her to understand. "He swore he wouldn't hurt you. He told me all he wanted was to teach you to use your power. He told me you'd be honored and wealthy beyond imagining—"

"Well, that's just fine, then," interrupted Will. "It's not as if there are more important things than money." His eyes were blazing with indignation; Jem looked no less disgusted.

"It's not Nate's fault!" Jessamine snapped. "Didn't you hear him? De Quincey would have killed him. And he knew who Nate was, where he came from; he would have found Tessa eventually anyway, and Nate would have died for no reason."

"So that's your objective ethical opinion, is it, Jess?" Will said. "And I suppose it has nothing to do with the fact that you've been drooling over Tessa's brother since he arrived. Any mundane will do, I suppose, no matter how useless—"

Jessamine let out an indignant squawk, and rose to her feet. Charlotte, her voice rising, tried to quiet them both as they shouted at each other, but Tessa had stopped listening; she was looking at Nate.

She had known for some time her brother was weak, that what her aunt had called innocence was really spoiled pettish childishness; that being a boy, the firstborn, and beautiful, Nate had always been the prince of his own tiny kingdom. She had understood that, while it had been his job as older brother to protect her, really it had always been she, and her aunt, who had protected him.

But he was her brother; she loved him; and the old protectiveness rose in her, as it always did where Nate was concerned, and probably always would. "Jessamine's right," she said, raising her voice to cut through the angry voices in the room. "It wouldn't have done him any good to refuse de Quincey, and there's no point arguing about it now. We still need to know what de Quincey's plans are. Do you know, Nate? Did he tell you what he wanted with me?"

Nate shook his head. "Once I agreed to send for you, he kept me trapped in his town house. He had me send a letter to Mortmain, of course, resigning from his employment; the poor man must have thought I was throwing his generosity back in his face. De Quincey wasn't planning on taking his eyes off me until he had you in hand, Tessie; I was his insurance. He gave the Dark Sisters my ring to prove to you that I was in their power. He promised me over and over that he wouldn't hurt you, that he was simply having the Sisters teach you to use your power. The Dark Sisters reported on your progress every day, so I knew you were still alive.

"Since I was there in the house anyway, I found myself observing the workings of the Pandemonium Club. I saw that there was an organization to the ranks. There were those who were very low down, clinging to the fringes, like Mortmain and his ilk. De Quincey and the higher-ups mostly kept them around because they had money, and they teased them with little glimpses of magic and the Shadow World to keep them coming back for more. Then there were those such as the Dark Sisters and others, those who had more power and responsibility in the club. They were all supernatural creatures, no humans. And then, at the top, was de Quincey. The others called him the Magister.

"They often held meetings to which the humans and those lower down weren't invited. That was where I first heard about Shadowhunters. De Quincey despises Shadowhunters," Nate said, turning to Henry and Charlotte. "He has a grudge against them—against you. He kept talking about how much better things would be when Shadowhunters were destroyed and Downworlders could live and trade in peace—"

"What tosh." Henry looked genuinely offended. "Don't know what kind of peace he thinks there'd be, without Shadow-hunters."

"He talked about how there'd never been a way to defeat Shadowhunters before because their weapons were so superior. He said the legend was that God had meant the Nephilim to be superior warriors, so no living creature could destroy them. So, apparently he thought, 'Why not a creature who *wasn't* living at all?'"

"The automatons," said Charlotte. "His machine army."

Nate looked puzzled. "You've seen them?"

"A few of them attacked your sister last night," said Will. "Fortunately, we Shadowhunter monsters were around to save her."

"Not that she was doing too badly by herself," Jem murmured.

"Do you know anything about the machines?" Charlotte demanded, leaning forward eagerly. "Anything at all? Did de Quincey ever talk about them in front of you?"

Nate shrank back in his chair. "He did, but I didn't understand most of it. I don't have a mechanical mind, really—"

"It's simple." It was Henry, using the tone of someone trying to calm a frightened cat. "Right now these machines of de Quincey's just run on mechanisms. They have to be wound up, like clocks. But we found a copy of a spell in his library that indicates that he's trying to find a way to make them *live*, a way to bind demon energy to the clockwork shell and bring it to life."

"Oh, that! Yes, he talked about *that*," Nathaniel replied, like a child pleased to be able to give the right answer in a schoolroom. Tessa could practically see the ears of the Shadowhunters pricking up with excitement. This was what they really wanted to know. "That's what he hired the Dark Sisters for—not just for training Tessa. They're warlocks, you know, and they were meant to be figuring out how it could be done. And they did. It wasn't long ago—a few weeks—but they did."

"They did?" Charlotte looked shocked. "But, then why hasn't de Quincey done it yet? What's he waiting for?"

Nate looked from her anxious face to Tessa's, and all around the room. "I—I thought you knew. He said the binding charm could only be generated at the full moon. When that happens, the Dark Sisters will get to work, and then—he's got dozens of the things stored in his hideaway, and I know he plans to make many more—hundreds, thousands, perhaps. I suppose he'll animate them, and . . ."

"The full moon?" Charlotte, glancing toward the window, bit her lip. "That will be very soon—tomorrow night, I think."

Jem straightened up like a shot. "I can check the lunar tables in the library. I'll be right back." He vanished through the door.

Charlotte turned to Nate. "You're quite sure about this?"

Nate nodded, swallowing hard. "When Tessa escaped from the Dark Sisters, de Quincey blamed me, even though I hadn't known anything about it. He told me he was going to let the Night Children drain my blood as a punishment. He kept me imprisoned for days before the party. He didn't care what he said in front of me then. He knew I was going to die. I heard him talking about how the Sisters had mastered the binding spell. That it wasn't going to be long before the Nephilim were destroyed, and all the members of the Pandemonium Club could rule London in their stead."

Will spoke, his voice harsh. "Have you any idea where de Quincey might be hiding now that his house has burned?"

Nate looked exhausted. "He has a hideaway in Chelsea. He would have gone to ground there with those who are loyal to him—there are still probably a hundred vampires of his clan who weren't at the town house that night. I know exactly where the place is. I can show you on a map—" He broke off as Jem burst into the room, his eyes very wide.

"It's not tomorrow," Jem said. "The full moon. It's tonight."

17

CALL THE
DARKNESS DOWN

The old church tower and garden wall
Are black with autumn rain,
And dreary winds foreboding call
The darkness down again.
—Emily Brontë, "The Old Church Tower"

While Charlotte dashed to the library to notify the Enclave that emergency action would need to be taken that evening, Henry remained in the drawing room with Nathaniel and the others. He was surprisingly patient as Nate painstakingly indicated on a map of London the spot where he believed de Quincey's hideaway to be—a house in Chelsea, near the Thames. "I don't know which one it is exactly," Nate said, "so you'll have to be careful."

"We are always careful," Henry said, ignoring Will's wry

look in his direction. Not long after that, however, he sent Will and Jem to the weapons room with Thomas to ready a stock of seraph blades and other armaments. Tessa remained in the drawing room with Jessamine and Nate while Henry hurried off to the crypt to retrieve some of his more recent inventions.

As soon as the others had gone, Jessamine commenced fluttering around Nate—building up the fire for him, going to fetch another blanket to wrap around his shoulders, and offering to find a book to read aloud to him, which he declined. If Jessamine was hoping to win Nate's heart by fussing over him, Tessa thought, she would be in for a disappointment. Nate expected to be fussed over and would hardly notice her special attentions.

"So what's going to happen now?" he asked finally, half-buried under a mound of blankets. "Mr. and Mrs. Branwell—"

"Oh, call them Henry and Charlotte. Everyone does," Jessamine said.

"They'll be notifying the Enclave—that's all the rest of London's Shadowhunters—of the location of de Quincey's hideaway, so they can plan an attack," said Tessa. "But really, Nate, you shouldn't be worrying about these things. You should be resting."

"So it'll just be us." Nate's eyes were closed. "In this big old place. Seems strange."

"Oh, Will and Jem won't be going with them," said Jessamine. "I heard her talking to them in the weapons room when I went to get the blanket."

Nate's eyes opened. "They *won't*?" He sounded astonished. "Why not?"

"They're too young," said Jessamine. "Shadowhunters are

considered adults at eighteen, and for this kind of undertaking—something dangerous that the whole Enclave is participating in—they tend to leave the younger ones at home."

Tessa felt a strange little pang of relief, which she covered by asking hurriedly, "But that's so odd. They let Will and Jem go to de Quincey's—"

"And that's why they can't go now. Apparently, Benedict Lightwood is arguing that the raid on de Quincey's turned out as badly as it did because Will and Jem are insufficiently trained, though how any of it was meant to be Jem's fault, I'm not sure. If you ask me, he wants an excuse to make Gabriel stay at home, even though he's already eighteen. He babies him horribly. Charlotte said he told her that there have been whole Enclaves wiped out in a single night before, and the Nephilim have an obligation to leave the younger generation standing, to carry on, as it were."

Tessa's stomach twisted. Before she could say anything, the door opened and Thomas came in. He was carrying a stack of folded clothes. "These are old things of Master Jem's," he said to Nate, looking slightly embarrassed. "It looks like you might be about the same size, and, well, you ought to have something to wear. If you'll accompany me back to your room, we can see if they fit."

Jessamine rolled her eyes. Tessa wasn't sure why. Perhaps she thought castoffs weren't good enough for Nate.

"Thank you, Thomas," Nate said, rising to his feet. "And I must tender my apologies for my earlier behavior, when I, ah, hid from you. I must have been feverish. That's the only explanation."

Thomas flushed. "Just doing my job, sir."

"Perhaps you should get some sleep," Tessa said, noting the dark rings of exhaustion around her brother's eyes. "There won't be much for us to do now, not until they return."

"Actually," Nate said, looking from Jessamine to Tessa, "I think I've had enough of rest. A fellow ought to get back on his feet eventually, oughtn't he? I could stand to eat a bite of something, and I wouldn't mind some company. If you wouldn't mind my joining you here once I'm dressed?"

"Of course not!" Jessamine looked delighted. "I'll ask Agatha to prepare something light. And perhaps a game of cards to keep us occupied after we eat. Sandwiches and tea, I think." She clapped her hands together as Thomas and Nate left the room, and turned to Tessa, her eyes bright. "Won't that be fun?"

"Cards?" Tessa, who had been shocked nearly speechless by Jessamine's suggestion, found her voice. "You think we ought to play *cards*? While Henry and Charlotte are off fighting de Quincey?"

Jessamine tossed her head. "As if our moping around would help them! I'm sure they'd rather we were cheerful and active in their absence rather than idle and morose."

Tessa frowned. "I really don't think," she said, "that suggesting cards to Nate was a kind idea, Jessamine. You know perfectly well he has . . . trouble . . . with gambling."

"We're not going to *gamble*," Jessamine said airily. "Just a friendly game of cards. Really, Tessa, must you be such a wet blanket?"

"A *what*? Jessamine, I know you're only trying to keep Nate happy. But this isn't the way—"

"And I suppose *you've* mastered the art of winning men's affections?" Jessamine snapped, her brown eyes sparking with anger. "You think I haven't seen you looking at Will with puppy-dog eyes? As if he were even— Oh!" She threw up her hands. "Never mind. You make me sick. I'm going to talk to Agatha without you." With that, she rose to her feet and flounced out of the room, pausing in the doorway only to say "And I know you don't care how you look, but you ought to at least fix your hair, Tessa. It looks like birds are living in it!" before the door slammed shut behind her.

Silly as Tessa knew it was, Jessamine's words stung. She hastened back to her room to splash water on her face and run a hairbrush through her tangled hair. Looking at her own white face in the mirror, she tried not to wonder if she still looked like the sister Nate remembered. Tried not to imagine how she might have changed.

Finished, she hurried out into the corridor—and nearly walked directly into Will, who was leaning against the corridor wall opposite her door, examining his nails. With his usual disregard for manners, he was in shirtsleeves, and over the shirt was a series of leather straps crisscrossing his chest. Across his back hung a long, thin blade; she could see the hilt of it just over his shoulder. Thrust through his belt were several long, thin white seraph blades.

"I—" Jessamine's voice echoed in Tessa's head: *You think I haven't seen you looking at Will with puppy-dog eyes?* The witchlight was burning low. Tessa hoped it was too dim in the corridor for him to see her blush. "I thought you weren't going with the Enclave tonight," she said finally, more to have something to say than anything else.

"I'm not. I'm bringing these down to Charlotte and Henry

in the courtyard. Benedict Lightwood is sending his carriage for them. It's faster. It should be here shortly." It was dark in the corridor, dark enough that though Tessa thought that Will was smiling, she wasn't sure. "Concerned about my safety, are you? Or had you planned to gift me with a favor so I could wear it into battle like Wilfred of *Ivanhoe*?"

"I never liked that book," Tessa said. "Rowena was such a ninny. Ivanhoe should have chosen Rebecca."

"The dark-haired girl, not the blonde? Really?" Now she was almost sure he was smiling.

"Will—?"

"Yes?"

"Do you think the Enclave will actually manage to kill him? De Quincey, that is?"

"Yes." He spoke without hesitation. "The time for negotiation has passed. If you've ever seen terriers in a rat-baiting pit—well, I don't suppose you would have. But that's what it will be like tonight. The Clave will dispatch the vampires one by one until they are wiped out utterly."

"You mean there will be no more vampires in London?"

Will shrugged. "There are always vampires. But de Quincey's clan will be gone."

"And once it's over—once the Magister is gone—I suppose there will be no more reason for Nate and me to stay in the Institute, will there?"

"I—" Will seemed genuinely taken aback. "I suppose— Yes, well, that's true. I imagine that you would prefer to stay in a less . . . violent locale. Perhaps you could even see some of the nicer parts of London. Westminster Abbey—"

"I would prefer to go home," Tessa said. "To New York."

Will said nothing. The witchlight in the corridor had faded; in the shadows she couldn't clearly see his face.

"Unless there were a reason for me to stay," she went on, half-wondering what she herself even meant by that. It was easier to talk to Will like this, when she couldn't see his face, and could only sense his presence near hers in the dark corridor.

She didn't see him move, but she felt his fingers touch the back of her hand lightly. "Tessa," he said. "Please don't worry. Soon it will all be settled."

Her heart thumped painfully against her ribs. Soon *what* would be settled? He couldn't mean what she thought he did. He had to mean something else. "Don't *you* wish to go home?"

He didn't move, his fingers still brushing her hand. "I can't ever go home."

"But why not?" she whispered, but it was too late. She felt him retreating from her. His hand drew back from hers. "I know your parents came to the Institute when you were twelve and you refused to see them. Why? What did they do to you that was so dreadful?"

"They did nothing." He shook his head. "I must go. Henry and Charlotte are waiting."

"Will," she said, but he was already walking away, a slim dark shadow moving toward the stairs. "Will," she called after him. "Will, who is Cecily?"

But he was already gone.

By the time Tessa returned to the drawing room, Nate and Jessamine were there, and the sun had begun to set. She went immediately to the window and looked out. In the courtyard below, Jem, Henry, Will, and Charlotte were gathered, their shadows cast long and dark across the Institute's steps. Henry was putting a last *iratze* rune on his arm while Charlotte seemed to be giving Jem and Will instructions. Jem was nodding, but Tessa could tell even at this distance that Will, whose arms were crossed over his chest, was being recalcitrant. *He wants to go with them,* she thought. *He doesn't want to stay here.* Jem probably wanted to go as well, but he wouldn't complain about it. That was the difference between the two boys. One of the differences, at any rate.

"Tessie, are you sure you don't want to play?" Nate turned to look at his sister. He was back in his armchair, a rug over his legs, cards laid out on a small table between him and Jessamine beside a silver tea service and a small plate of sandwiches. His hair looked slightly damp, as if he had washed it, and he was wearing Jem's clothes. Nathaniel had lost weight, Tessa could tell, but Jem was slender enough that his shirt was still a little tight on Nate at the collar and cuffs—though Jem's shoulders were still broader, and Nate looked a little slighter of frame in Jem's jacket.

Tessa was still looking out the window. A great black carriage had drawn up, with a design on the door of two burning torches, and Henry and Charlotte were getting into it. Will and Jem had vanished from view.

"She's sure." Jessamine sniffed when Tessa didn't answer. "Just look at her. She looks so disapproving."

Tessa tore her gaze from the window. "I'm not disapproving. It just seems wrong to play games while Henry and Charlotte and others are out risking their lives."

"Yes, I know, you said that before." Jessamine set her cards down. "Really, Tessa. This happens all the time. They go off to battle; they come back. There's nothing worth getting worked up over."

Tessa bit her lip. "I feel I ought to have said good-bye or good luck, but with all the rushing about—"

"You needn't worry," Jem said, coming into the drawing room, Will just behind him. "Shadowhunters don't say good-bye, not before a battle. Or good luck. You must behave as if return is certain, not a matter of chance."

"We don't require luck," said Will, throwing himself into a chair beside Jessamine, who shot him an angry look. "We have a heavenly mandate, after all. With God on your side, what does luck matter?" He sounded surprisingly bitter.

"Oh, stop being so depressing, Will," said Jessamine. "We're playing cards. You can either join the game or be quiet."

Will raised an eyebrow. "What are you playing?"

"Pope Joan," said Jessamine coolly, dealing out cards. "I was just explaining the rules to Mr. Gray."

"Miss Lovelace says you win by ridding yourself of all your cards. That seems backward to me." Nate grinned across the table at Jessamine, who dimpled annoyingly.

Will poked at the steaming cup that sat beside Nathaniel's elbow. "Is there any tea in this," he inquired, "or is it simply *pure* brandy?"

Nate flushed. "Brandy is restorative."

"Yes," said Jem, a little edge to his voice. "It often restores men right to the poorhouse."

"Really! The two of you! Such hypocrites. It isn't as if Will doesn't drink, and Jem—" Jessamine broke off, biting her lip. "You two are just fussing because Henry and Charlotte wouldn't take you along with them," she said finally. "Because you're too *young*." She smiled at Nate across the table. "I prefer the company of a more mature gentleman, myself."

Nate, Tessa thought disgustedly, *is exactly two years older than Will. Hardly a century. Nor is he by any stretch of the imagination "mature."* But before she could say anything, a great, echoing boom sounded through the Institute.

Nate raised his eyebrows. "I thought this wasn't a real church. I thought there were no bells."

"There aren't. That sound isn't church bells ringing." Will rose to his feet. "That's the summoning bell. It means someone is downstairs and demands conference with the Shadowhunters. And since James and I are the only ones here . . ."

He looked at Jessamine, and Tessa realized he was waiting for Jessamine to contradict him, to say that she was a Shadowhunter too. But Jessamine was smiling at Nate, and he was leaning in to say something in her ear; neither of them was paying attention to what else was going on in the room.

Jem looked at Will and shook his head. They both turned toward the door; as they went out, Jem looked at Tessa and gave her a little shrug. *I wish you were a Shadowhunter,* she thought his eyes were saying, but maybe it was simply what she hoped they were saying. Perhaps he was merely smiling at her kindly and there was no meaning in it.

Nate poured himself another hot water and brandy. He and Jessamine had abandoned the pretense that they were playing cards and were leaning close to each other, murmuring in low voices. Tessa felt a dull thump of disappointment. Somehow she had expected that Nate's ordeal would have made him more thoughtful—more inclined to understand that there were larger things at work in the world, more important things than his own immediate pleasures. She expected nothing better of Jessamine, but what had once seemed charming in Nate now grated on her nerves in a way that surprised her.

She leaned toward the window again. There was a carriage in the courtyard. Will and Jem were on the front steps. With them was a man in evening dress—elegant black tailcoat, high silk hat, a white waistcoat that shone under the witchlight torches. He looked like a mundane to Tessa, though at this distance it was difficult to tell. As she watched, he raised his arms and made a broad gesture. She saw Will look at Jem, and Jem nod, and wondered what on earth they were talking about.

She looked past the man to the coach behind him—and froze. Instead of a coat of arms, the name of a business enterprise was painted across one of the doors: MORTMAIN AND COMPANY.

Mortmain. The man her father had worked for, whom Nathaniel had blackmailed, who had introduced her brother to the Shadow World. What was he doing here?

She looked at Nate again, her feeling of annoyance washed away by a wave of protectiveness. If he knew Mortmain was here, he would doubtless be upset. It would be better if she found out what was going on before he did. She slid off the windowsill and made her way quietly to the door; deep in conversation with Jessamine, Nate hardly seemed to notice as she left the room.

It was surprisingly easy for Tessa to find her way to the huge stone-bound spiral stairway that speared through the center of the Institute. She must have been learning her way around the place at last, she decided as she made her way down the steps to the ground floor, and found Thomas standing in the entryway.

He was holding a massive sword, point down, his face very serious. Behind him the massive double doors of the Institute were open on a rectangle of blue-black London twilight, lit by the blaze of the courtyard's witchlight torches. He looked taken aback at the sight of Tessa. "Miss Gray?"

She pitched her voice low. "What's going on out there, Thomas?"

He shrugged. "Mr. Mortmain," he said. "He wanted to speak with Mr. and Mrs. Branwell, but since they're not here—"

Tessa started toward the door.

Thomas, startled, moved to prevent her. "Miss Gray, I don't think—"

"You'll have to use that sword on me to stop me, Thomas," Tessa said in a cold voice, and Thomas, after a moment's hesitation, moved aside. Tessa, with a twinge, hoped she hadn't hurt his feelings, but he looked more astonished than anything else.

She moved past him, onto the steps outside the Institute, where Will and Jem were standing. A hard breeze was coming up, ruffling her hair and making her shiver. At the foot of the stairs stood the man she had seen from the window. He was shorter than she would have imagined: small and wiry-looking, with a tanned, friendly face beneath the brim of his tall hat. Despite the elegance of his clothes, he had the bluff, natural bearing of a sailor or tradesman.

"Yes," he was saying, "Mr. and Mrs. Branwell were kind enough to call on me last week. And were even kinder, I understand, in keeping our meeting something of a secret."

"They didn't tell the Enclave about your occult experimentations, if that is what you mean," Will said a bit shortly.

Mortmain reddened. "Yes. It was a favor. And I had thought to return the favor in kind—" He broke off, looking past Will at Tessa. "And who is this? Another Shadowhunter?"

Will and Jem both turned at the same time and saw Tessa. Jem looked pleased to see her; Will, of course, looked exasperated, and perhaps a touch amused. "Tessa," he said. "Couldn't keep your nose out, could you?" He turned back to Mortmain. "This is Miss Gray, of course. Nathaniel Gray's sister."

Mortmain looked appalled. "Oh, good God. I should have realized. You look like him. Miss Gray—"

"I don't think she does, actually," Will said, but rather quietly, so Tessa doubted Mortmain could hear him.

"You can't see Nate," Tessa said. "I don't know if that's why you've come here, Mr. Mortmain, but he isn't well enough. He needs to recover from his ordeal, not be reminded of it."

The lines deepened at the corners of Mortmain's mouth. "I'm not here to see the boy," he said. "I recognize that I failed him, failed him abominably. Mrs. Branwell made that clear—"

"You should have looked for him," Tessa said. "My brother. You let him sink into the Shadow World without a trace." Some small part of Tessa's mind was amazed she was being so bold, but she went on, regardless. "When he told you he'd gone to work for de Quincey, you should have done something. You knew what kind of man de Quincey was—if you can even call him a man."

"I know." Mortmain looked gray beneath his hat. "That is why I am here. To try to make up for what I've done."

"And how do you propose to do that?" asked Jem, in his clear, strong voice. "And why *now*?"

Mortmain looked at Tessa. "Your parents," he said, "were good, kind people. I have always regretted introducing them to the Shadow World. At the time, I thought it all a delightful game and a bit of a joke. I have learned otherwise since. To assuage that guilt, I will tell you what I know. Even if it means I must flee England to escape de Quincey's wrath." He sighed. "Some time ago, de Quincey ordered from me a number of mechanical parts—cogs, cams, gears, and the like. I never asked what he needed them for. One does not inquire such things of the Magister. Only when you Nephilim came to see me did it occur to me that his need for them might be connected to a nefarious purpose. I investigated, and an informant within the club told me that de Quincey intended to build an army of mechanical monsters meant to destroy the ranks of Shadowhunters." He shook his head. "De Quincey and his ilk may despise Shadowhunters, but I do not. I am only a human man. I know they are all that stand between me and a world in which I and my kind are the playthings of demons. I cannot stand behind what de Quincey is doing."

"That is all very well," Will said, a hint of impatience in his voice, "but you are not telling us anything we do not already know."

"Did you also know," Mortmain said, "that he paid a pair of warlocks called the Dark Sisters to create a binding spell that would animate these creatures not with mechanics but with demonic energies?"

"We did," said Jem. "Though I believe there is only one Dark Sister remaining. Will destroyed the other one."

"But her sister brought her back via a necromantic charm," said Mortmain, a hint of triumph in his tone, as if he were relieved to at last have a piece of information that they did not. "Even now the two of them are ensconced in a mansion in Highgate—it used to belong to a warlock, until de Quincey had him killed—working on the binding spell. If my sources are correct, the Dark Sisters will attempt to implement the spell tonight."

Will's blue eyes were dark and thoughtful. "Thank you for the information," he said, "but de Quincey will soon be no more of a threat to us, or his mechanical monsters, either."

Mortmain's eyes widened. "Is the Clave to move against the Magister? Tonight?"

"Goodness," said Will. "You really do know all the terms, don't you. It's very disconcerting in a mundane." He smiled pleasantly.

"You mean you're not going to tell me," said Mortmain ruefully. "I suppose you wouldn't. But you should know that de Quincey has at his disposal hundreds of those clockwork creatures. An army. The moment the Dark Sisters work their spell, the army will rise and join with de Quincey. If the Enclave is to defeat him, it would be wise to ensure that that army does not rise, or they will be nearly impossible to defeat."

"Are you aware of the Dark Sisters' location, beyond the fact that it is in Highgate?" asked Jem.

Mortmain nodded. "Most certainly," he said, and rattled off a street name and house number.

Will nodded. "Well, we'll certainly take all this under advisement. Thank you."

"Indeed," said Jem. "Good evening, Mr. Mortmain."

"But—" Mortmain looked taken aback. "Are you going to do something about what I've told you, or not?"

"I said we'd take it under advisement," Will told him. "As for you, Mr. Mortmain, you look like a man with somewhere to be."

"What?" Mortmain glanced down at his evening dress, and chuckled. "I suppose so. It's just—if the Magister finds out that I've told you all this, my life could be in danger."

"Then perhaps it is time for a holiday," Jem suggested. "I've heard Italy is very pleasant this time of year."

Mortmain looked from Will to Jem and back again, and then seemed to give up. His shoulders sagged. He raised his eyes to Tessa. "If you could pass along my apologies to your brother . . ."

"I don't think so," Tessa said, "but thank you, Mr. Mortmain."

After a long pause he nodded, then turned away. The three of them watched as he climbed back into his carriage. The sound of the horses' hooves was loud in the courtyard as the carriage pulled away and rattled through the Institute gates.

"What are you going to do?" Tessa asked the moment the carriage was out of sight. "About the Dark Sisters?"

"Go after them, of course." Will's color was high, his eyes glittering. "Your brother said de Quincey had dozens of those creatures at his disposal; Mortmain says there are hundreds. If Mortmain's correct, we must get to the Dark Sisters before they work their spell, or the Enclave may well be walking into a slaughter."

"But—perhaps it would be better to warn Henry and Charlotte and the others—"

"How?" Will managed to make the one word sound cutting. "I suppose we could send Thomas to warn the Enclave, but there is no guarantee he will get there in time, and if the Dark Sisters manage to raise the army, he could simply be killed with the rest. No, we must manage the Dark Sisters on our own. I killed one of them before; Jem and I ought to be able to manage two."

"But perhaps Mortmain is wrong," Tessa said. "You have only his word; he might have faulty information."

"He might," Jem acknowledged, "but can you imagine if he doesn't? And we ignored him? The consequence to the Enclave could be utter destruction."

Tessa, knowing he was right, felt her heart sink. "Maybe I could help. I fought the Dark Sisters with you once before. If I could accompany you—"

"No," Will said. "It's out of the question. We have so little time to prepare that we must rely on our fighting experience. And you have none."

"I fought off de Quincey at the party—"

"I said no." Will's tone was final. Tessa looked at Jem, but he gave only an apologetic shrug as if to say that he was sorry but Will was right.

She turned her gaze back to Will. "But what about Boadicea?"

For a moment she thought he'd forgotten what he'd said to her in the library. Then the glimmer of a smile tugged at the corner of his mouth, as if he'd tried to fight it and couldn't. "You will be Boadicea someday, Tessa," he said, "but not tonight." He turned to Jem. "We ought to get Thomas and tell him to ready the carriage. Highgate's not close; we'd best get started."

Full night had descended on the city by the time Will and Jem stood out by the carriage, preparing to depart. Thomas was checking the fastenings on the horses while Will, his stele a white flash in the dimness, scrawled a Mark on Jem's bare forearm. Tessa, having registered her disapproval, stood on the steps and watched them, a hollow feeling in her stomach.

After satisfying himself that the harnesses were secure, Thomas turned and ran lightly up the steps, stopping when Tessa raised a hand to halt him. "Are they going now?" she asked. "Is that all?"

He nodded. "All ready to go, miss." He had tried to get Jem and Will to take him along, but Will was concerned that Charlotte would be angry at Thomas for participating in their exploit and had told him not to come.

"Besides," Will had said, "we ought to have a man in the house—someone to protect the Institute while we're gone. Nathaniel doesn't count," he'd added, with a sideways glance at Tessa, who had ignored him.

Will slid Jem's sleeve down, covering the Marks he had made. As he returned his stele to his pocket, Jem stood looking up at him; their faces were pale smudges in the torchlight. Tessa raised her hand, then lowered it slowly. What was it he had said? *Shadowhunters don't say good-bye, not before a battle. Or good luck. You must behave as if return is certain, not a matter of chance.*

The boys, as if alerted by her gesture, looked up toward her. She thought she could see the blue of Will's eyes, even from where she stood. He wore a strange look as their eyes locked, the look of someone who has just woken up and wonders if what they are looking at is real or a dream.

It was Jem who broke away and ran up the stairs to her. As he reached her, she saw that he had high color in his face, and his eyes were bright and hot. She wondered how much of the drug Will had let him take, so that he would be ready to fight.

"Tessa—," he said.

"I didn't mean to say good-bye," she said quickly. "But—it seems odd to let you leave without saying anything at all."

He looked at her curiously. He did something that surprised her then, and took her hand, turning it over. She looked down at it, at her bitten fingernails, the still-healing scratches along the backs of her fingers.

He kissed the back of it, just a light touch of his mouth, and his hair—as soft and light as silk—brushed her wrist as he lowered his head. She felt a shock go through her, strong enough to startle her, and she stood speechless as he straightened, his mouth curving into a smile.

"*Mizpah*," he said.

She blinked at him, a little dazed. "What?"

"A sort of good-bye without saying good-bye," he said. "It is a reference to a passage in the Bible. '*And Mizpah, for he said, the Lord watch between me and thee when we are absent one from another.*'"

There was no chance for Tessa to say anything in response, for he had turned and run down the steps to join Will, who was as motionless as a statue, his face upturned, at the foot of the steps. His hands, sheathed in black gloves, were in fists at his sides, Tessa thought. But perhaps it was a trick of the light, for when Jem reached him and touched him on the shoulder, he turned with a laugh, and without another look at Tessa, he swung himself up into the driver's seat, Jem following him. He cracked the whip, and the carriage rattled through the gate, which slammed shut behind it as if pushed by invisible hands. Tessa heard the lock catch, a hard click in the silence, and then the sound of church bells ringing somewhere in the city.

Sophie and Agatha were waiting in the entryway for Tessa when she came back inside; Agatha was saying something to Sophie, but Sophie didn't appear to be listening. She looked over at Tessa as she came in, and something about the way she looked, for a moment, reminded Tessa of the way Will had looked at her in the courtyard. But that was ridiculous; there were no two people in the world more unalike than Sophie and Will.

Tessa stepped aside as Agatha went to close the great, heavy double doors. She had just pushed them shut, panting slightly, when the knob of the leftmost door, untouched, began to turn.

Sophie frowned. "They can't be back so soon, can they?"

Agatha gazed down, perplexed, at the turning knob, her hands still braced against the door—then stood back as the doors swung wide before her.

A figure stood on the doorstep, backlit by the light outside. For a moment all Tessa could tell was that he was tall and clad in a frayed jacket. Agatha, her head tipping back as she gazed upward, said in a startled voice, "Oh, my Lor'—"

The figure moved. Light flashed on metal; Agatha screamed and staggered. She seemed to be trying to back away from the stranger, but something was preventing her.

"Dear God in Heaven," Sophie whispered. *What is that?*

For a moment Tessa saw the whole scene frozen, as if it were a painting—the open door, the clockwork automaton, the one with the stripped bare hands, still in the same worn gray jacket. And still, dear God, with Jem's blood on its hands, dried red-black on the dull gray flesh, and the strips of copper showing through where the skin had been scraped or pulled away.

One bloodstained hand gripped Agatha's wrist; clamped in the other was a long, thin knife. Tessa moved forward, but it was already too late. The creature swung the blade with blinding speed, and buried it in Agatha's chest.

Agatha choked, her hands going to the blade. The creature stood, ragged and terrifying and unmoving as she clawed at the knife hilt; then, with appalling swiftness, it yanked the blade back, letting her crumple to the ground. Nor did the automaton remain to watch her fall, but turned and walked back out the door through which it had come.

Galvanized, Sophie screamed "Agatha!" and ran to her side. Tessa dashed to the door. The clockwork creature was walking down the steps, into the empty courtyard. She stared after it. What on earth had it come for, and why was it leaving now? But there was no time to dwell on that. She reached for the rope of the summoning bell and pulled it, hard. As the sound clanged through the building, she slammed the door shut, dropping the lock bar into place, then turned to help Sophie.

Together they managed to lift Agatha and half-carry, half-drag her across the room, where they fell to their knees beside her. Sophie, ripping strips of fabric from her white apron and pressing them over Agatha's wound, said in a tone of wild panic, "I don't understand, miss. Nothing should be able to touch that door—none but one with Shadowhunter blood should be able to turn the doorknob."

But he had Shadowhunter blood, Tessa thought with a sudden horror. Jem's blood, staining its metal hands like paint. Could that be why it had bent over Jem that night after the bridge? Could that be why it had fled, once it had gotten what it wanted—his blood? And didn't that mean it could come back whenever it wanted?

She began to rise to her feet, but it was already too late. The bar that held the door closed cracked with a noise like a gunshot, and tumbled to the ground in two pieces. Sophie looked up and screamed again, though she didn't move away from Agatha as the door burst open, a window onto the night.

The steps of the Institute were no longer empty; they were teeming, but not with people. Clockwork monsters swarmed up them, their movements jerky, their faces blank and staring. They were not quite like the ones Tessa had seen before. Some looked as though they had been put together so hastily that they had no faces at all, just smooth ovals of metal patched here and there with uneven bits of human skin. Even more horrible, quite a few of them had bits of machinery in place of arms or legs. One automaton had a scythe where his arm ought to have been; another sported a saw that stuck out of the hanging sleeve of his shirt like a parody of a real arm.

Tessa rose and flung herself against the open door, trying to heave it shut. It was heavy, and seemed to move agonizingly slowly. Behind her, Sophie was screaming, helplessly, over and over; Agatha was horribly silent. With a ragged gasp Tessa pushed at the door one more time—

And jerked her hands back as the door was torn out of her grasp, ripped from its hinges like a handful of weeds ripped out of the earth. She fell back as the automaton who had seized the door flung it aside and heaved itself forward, its metal feet clanking against the stone as it lurched over the threshold— followed by another and then another of its mechanical brethren, at least a dozen of them, advancing toward Tessa with their monstrous arms outstretched.

By the time Will and Jem reached the mansion in Highgate, the moon had begun to rise. Highgate was on a hill in the north part of London, commanding an excellent view of the city below, pale under the moon's light, which turned the fog and coal smoke that hung over the city into a silvery cloud. *A dream city*, Will thought, *floating in the air*. A bit of poetry hung at the edges of his mind, something about the terrible wonder of London, but his nerves were tight with the jangling tension of impending battle, and he could not remember the words.

The house was a great Georgian pile, set in abundant parkland. A high brick wall ran around it, the slanting dark mansard roof just visible above it from the street. A shiver of cold passed over Will as they drew near it, but he was unsurprised to feel such a thing in Highgate. They were near what Londoners called the Gravel Pit Woods at the city's edge, where thousands of bodies had been dumped during the Great Plague. Lacking a proper burial, their angry shades haunted the neighborhood even now, and Will had been sent up here more than once, thanks to their activities.

A black metal gate set into the mansion's wall kept out intruders, but Jem's Open rune made short work of the lock. After leaving the carriage just inside the gate, the two Shadowhunters found themselves on the curving drive that led up to the house's front entrance. The path was weed-ridden and overgrown, and the gardens stretched out around it, dotted with crumbling outbuildings and the blackened stumps of dead trees.

Jem turned to Will, eyes feverish. "Shall we get on with it?"

Will drew a seraph blade from his belt. "*Israfel*," he whispered, and the weapon blazed up like a fork of contained lightning. Seraph blades burned so brightly that Will always expected them to give off heat, but their blades were ice cold to the touch. He remembered Tessa telling him that Hell was cold, and he fought back the odd urge to smile at the memory. They'd been running for their lives, she ought to have been terrified, and there she had been, telling him about the *Inferno* in precise American tones.

"Indeed," he said to Jem. "It's time."

They ascended the front steps and tried the doors. Though Will had expected them to be locked, they were open, and gave way at the touch with a resonant creaking. He and Jem edged inside the house, the light of their seraph blades illuminating the way.

They found themselves in a grand foyer. The arched windows behind them had probably once been magnificent. Now they alternated whole panes with broken ones. Through the spiderwebbing cracks in the glass, a view of the tangled and overgrown parkland beyond was visible. The marble underfoot was cracked and broken, weeds growing up through it as they had been growing through the stones of the drive. Before Will and Jem, a great curving staircase swept upward, toward the shadowy first floor.

"This can't be right," Jem whispered. "It's as if no one's been here in fifty years."

Barely had he finished speaking when a sound rose on the night air, a sound that lifted the hairs on Will's neck and made the Marks on his shoulders burn. It was singing—but not pleasant singing. It was a voice capable of reaching notes no human voice could reach. Overhead, the chandelier's crystal pendants rattled like wineglasses set to vibrating at the touch of a finger.

"*Someone's* here," Will muttered back. Without another word he and Jem turned so that their backs were to each other. Jem faced the open front doorway; Will, the vast curving stairs.

Something appeared at the head of the stairs. At first Will saw only an alternating pattern of black and white, a shadow that moved. As it drifted downward, the singing sound grew louder, and the hairs on Will's neck prickled more. Sweat dampened the hair at his temples and ran down the small of his back, despite the chill air.

She was halfway down the stairs before he recognized her— Mrs. Dark, her long, bony body clad in a sort of nun's habit, a shapeless dark robe that fell from her neck to her feet. A lightless lantern swung from one clawed hand. She was alone— though not quite, Will realized as she paused on the landing, for the thing she was clutching in her hand was not a lantern after all. It was her sister's severed head.

"By the Angel," Will whispered. "Jem, look."

Jem looked, and swore too. Mrs. Black's head dangled from a plait of gray hair, which Mrs. Dark clutched as if it were a priceless artifact. The head's eyes were open, and perfectly white, like boiled eggs. Its mouth hung open too, a line of dried black blood threading from one corner of the lips.

Mrs. Dark stopped her song and giggled, like a schoolgirl. "Naughty, naughty," she said. "Breaking into my house like this. Bad little Shadowhunters."

"I thought," Jem said under his breath, "that the other sister was alive."

"Maybe this one brought her sister back to life and then chopped her head off again?" Will muttered. "Seems a lot of work for no real gain, but then . . ."

"Murdering Nephilim," Mrs. Dark snarled, fixing her gaze on Will. "Not content with killing my sister once, are you? You must return and prevent me even from giving her a second life. Do you know—have you any idea—what it's like to be entirely *alone?*"

"More than you can ever imagine," Will said tightly, and saw Jem glance at him sideways, puzzled. *Stupid*, Will thought. *I shouldn't say such things.*

Mrs. Dark swayed on her feet. "You are mortal. You are alone for a moment of time, a single breath of the universe. I am alone forever." She clutched the head to her tightly. "What difference does it make to you? Surely there are darker crimes in London that more urgently require the attention of the Shadowhunters than my poor attempts to bring back my sister."

Will's gaze met Jem's. The other boy shrugged. Clearly he was as confused as Will was. "It's true that necromancy is against the Law," Jem said, "but so is binding demon energies. And that does require our attention, quite urgently."

Mrs. Dark stared at them. "Binding demon energies?"

"There is no point in pretending. We know your plans exactly," said Will. "We know of the automatons, the binding spell, your service to the Magister—whom the rest of our Enclave is, right now, tracking to his hiding place. By tonight's end he will be utterly erased. There is no one for you to call on, nowhere for you to hide."

At that, Mrs. Dark paled markedly. "The Magister?" she whispered. "You have found the Magister? But how . . ."

"That's right," Will said. "De Quincey escaped us once, but not this time. We know where he is, and—"

But his words were drowned out—by laughter. Mrs. Dark was bent over the staircase railing, howling with mirth. Will and Jem stared in confusion as she straightened up. Blackish tears of hilarity streaked her face. "De Quincey, the Magister!" she cried. "That poncing, preening vampire! Oh, what a joke! You fools, you stupid little fools!"

18

THIRTY PIECES
OF SILVER

Blot out his name, then, record one lost soul more,
One task more declin'd, one more foot-path untrod,
One more devil's-triumph and sorrow for angels,
One wrong more to man, one more insult to God!
—Robert Browning, "The Lost Leader"

Tessa staggered back from the door. Behind her, Sophie was frozen, kneeling over Agatha, her hands pressed to the older woman's chest. Blood soaked through the pitiful cloth bandage under her fingers; Agatha had gone a horrible putty color and was making a noise like a teakettle boiling. When she saw the clockwork automatons, her eyes widened and she tried to push Sophie away with her bloody hands, but Sophie, still screaming, clung tenaciously to the older woman, refusing to move.

"Sophie!" There was a clatter of footsteps on the stairs, and Thomas burst into the entryway, his face very white. In his hand he gripped the massive sword Tessa had seen him holding earlier. With him was Jessamine, parasol in hand. Behind her was Nathaniel, looking absolutely terrified. "What on earth—?"

Thomas broke off, staring from Sophie, Tessa, and Agatha to the door and back again. The automatons had come to a halt. They stood in a line just inside the doorway, as still as puppets whose strings were no longer being pulled. Their blank faces stared straight ahead.

"Agatha!" Sophie's voice rose to a wail. The older woman was still, her eyes wide open but unfocused. Her hands hung limply at her sides.

Though it made her skin prickle to turn her back on the machines, Tessa bent and put her hand on Sophie's shoulder. The other girl shook her off; she was making little whimpering noises, like a kicked dog. Tessa darted a glance behind her toward the automatons. They were still as motionless as chess pieces, but how long could that last? "Sophie, please!"

Nate was breathing in pants, his eyes fixed on the door, his face as white as chalk. He looked as if he wanted nothing more than to turn and run. Jessamine glanced at him once, a look of surprise and disdain, before turning to Thomas. "Get her on her feet," she said. "She'll listen to you."

After a single startled glance at Jessamine, Thomas bent down and, gently but firmly, pried Sophie's hands from Agatha, raising her to her feet. She clung to him. Her hands and arms were as red as if she had come from a slaughter-house, and her apron was nearly ripped in half and was printed with bloodied handprints. "Miss Lovelace," he said in a low voice, keeping Sophie close against him with the hand not holding the sword. "Take Sophie and Miss Gray to the Sanctuary—"

"No," said a drawling voice from behind Tessa, "I don't think so. Or rather, certainly, take the servant girl and go where you like with her. But Miss Gray will be remaining here. As will her brother."

The voice was familiar—shockingly so. Very slowly Tessa turned.

Standing among the frozen machines as if he had simply appeared there by magic was a man. Just as ordinary-looking as Tessa had thought he was before, though his hat was gone now, and his graying head was bare under the witchlight.

Mortmain.

He was smiling. Not as he had been smiling earlier, with affable cheerfulness. His smile now was almost sickening in its glee. "Nathaniel Gray," he said. "Excellently done. I admit that my faith in you was tested—tested sorely—but you have recovered admirably from your past missteps. I'm proud of you."

Tessa whirled to look at her brother, but Nate seemed to have forgotten she was there—that anyone else was there. He was staring past her at Mortmain, the oddest expression—a mix of fear and worship—stamped on his face. He moved forward, pushing past Tessa; she reached to hold him back, but he shook off her reaching hand with a flick of annoyance. At last he was standing directly in front of Mortmain.

With a cry he went to his knees and clasped his hands in front of him, almost as if he were praying.

"It was only ever my desire," he said, "to serve you, Magister."

* * *

Mrs. Dark was still laughing.

"But what is it?" Jem said in bewilderment, raising his voice to be heard over her peals of laughter. "What do you mean?"

Despite her ragged appearance Mrs. Dark managed an air of triumph. "De Quincey isn't the Magister," she sneered. "He's just a stupid bloodsucker, no better than the others. That you were so easily fooled proves you have no idea who the Magister is—or what you're facing. You're dead, little Shadowhunters. Little walking dead men."

That was too much for Will's temper. With a snarl he lunged toward the steps, his seraph blade outstretched. Jem called for him to stop, but it was too late. Mrs. Dark, her lips drawn back from her teeth like a hissing cobra's, swung her arm forward and flung her sister's severed head toward Will. With a yell of disgust he ducked aside, and she took the opportunity to charge down the steps, past Will, and through the arched doorway at the west side of the foyer, into the shadows beyond.

Mrs. Black's head, meanwhile, bumped down several stairs and came to rest gently against the toe of Will's boot. He looked down, and winced. One of her eyelids had drooped closed, and her tongue hung, gray and leathery, out of her mouth, for all the world as if she were leering at him.

"I may be sick," he announced.

"There's no time for you to be sick," said Jem. "Come on—"

And he dashed through the archway after Mrs. Dark. Nudging the warlock's severed head out of the way with the toe of his boot, Will followed after his friend at a run.

* * *

"Magister?" Tessa repeated blankly. *But that's impossible. De Quincey is the Magister. Those creatures on the bridge, they said they served him. Nate said . . .* She stared at her brother. "Nate?"

Speaking aloud was a mistake. Mortmain's gaze fell on Tessa, and he grinned. "Seize the shape-changer," he said to the clockwork creatures. "Don't let her go."

"Nate!" Tessa cried, but her brother did not so much as turn to look at her, as the creatures, brought back to sudden life, lurched forward, whirring and clicking, moving toward Tessa. One of them seized her, its metal arms like a vise as they encircled her chest, crushing the breath out of her.

Mortmain grinned at Tessa. "Don't be too hard on your brother, Miss Gray. He really is cleverer than I gave him credit for. It was his idea that I lure young Carstairs and Herondale out of the place with a far-fetched tale, that I might enter unmolested."

"What's going on?" Jessamine's voice trembled as she looked from Nate, to Tessa, to Mortmain, and back again. "I don't understand. Who is this, Nate? Why are you kneeling to him?"

"He is the Magister," said Nate. "If you were wise, you would kneel too."

Jessamine looked incredulous. "This is de Quincey?"

Nate's eyes flashed. "De Quincey is a peon, a serf. He *answers* to the Magister. Few even know the Magister's true identity; I am one of the chosen. The favored."

Jessamine made a rude noise. "Chosen to kneel on the ground, are you?"

Nate's eyes flashed, and he scrambled to his feet. He shouted something at Jessamine, but Tessa could not hear it.

The metal mannequin had tightened its grip on her to the point where she could barely breathe, and dark spots were beginning to float in front of her eyes. She was dimly aware of Mortmain shouting at the creature to loosen its grip on her, but it did not obey. She clawed at its metal arms with weakening fingers, barely aware of something fluttering at her throat, a fluttering that felt as if a bird or a butterfly were trapped beneath the collar of her dress. The chain around her neck was vibrating and twitching. She managed to look down, her vision blurred, and saw to her amazement that the little metal angel had emerged from beneath the collar of her dress; it soared upward, lifting the chain over her head. Its eyes seemed to glow as it flew upward. For the first time its metallic wings were spread, and Tessa saw that each wing was edged with something shimmering and razor-sharp. As she watched in amazement, the angel dived like a hornet, slashing with the edges of its wings at the head of the creature holding her—slicing through copper and metal, sending up a shower of red sparks.

The sparks stung Tessa's neck like a shower of hot cinders, but she barely noticed; the creature's arms loosened around her, and she wrenched herself away as it spun and staggered, its arms jerking blindly in front of it. She couldn't help but be reminded somehow of a sketch she'd seen of an angry gentleman at a garden party waving off bees. Mortmain, noticing a beat too late what was going on, shouted, and the other creatures lurched into motion, surging toward Tessa. She looked around wildly, but could no longer see the tiny angel. It seemed to have vanished.

"Tessa! Get out of the way!" A cold little hand caught at her wrist. It was Jessamine, yanking her backward as Thomas, having released Sophie, dived in front of her. Jessamine thrust Tessa behind her, toward the stairs at the back of the entryway, and moved forward with her parasol whirling. Her face was set with determination. It was Thomas who struck the first blow. Lunging forward with his sword, he sheared through the chest of a creature who was lurching toward him, hands outstretched. The machine man staggered backward, whirring loudly, red sparks spraying from its chest like blood. Jessamine laughed at the sight and laid about her with her parasol. The whirling edge of it sliced through the legs of two of the creatures, sending them toppling forward to flop on the ground like landed fish.

Mortmain looked vexed. "Oh, for goodness' sake. You—" He snapped his fingers, pointing at an automaton, one that had something that looked like a metal tube welded to its right wrist. "Get rid of her. The Shadowhunter."

The creature raised its arm jerkily. A bolt of streaky red fire shot from the metal tube. It hit Jessamine square in the chest, knocking her backward. Her parasol skittered from her hand as she struck the ground, her body twitching, her eyes open and glassy.

Nathaniel, who had moved to stand beside Mortmain on the sidelines of the melee, laughed.

A sizzling bolt of hatred went through Tessa, shocking her with its intensity. She wanted to throw herself at Nate and rip her nails down his cheek, kick him until he screamed. It wouldn't take much, she knew. He'd always been a coward where pain was concerned. She started forward, but the creatures, having dealt with Jessamine, had already swung back around toward her. Thomas, his hair plastered to his face with sweat and a long bloody rent slashed across the front of his shirt, moved to place himself in front of her. He was laying about himself magnificently with the sword, with great, sweeping strokes. It was hard to believe he wasn't slashing the creatures to ribbons—and yet they proved surprisingly dexterous. Ducking out of his way, they kept coming, their eyes fixed on Tessa. Thomas spun to look at her, his gaze wild. "Miss Gray! Now! Take Sophie!"

Tessa hesitated. She did not want to run. She wanted to stand her ground. But Sophie was huddling, transfixed behind her, her eyes full of terror.

"Sophie!" Thomas cried, and Tessa could hear what was in his voice, and knew she had been right about his feelings for Sophie. "The Sanctuary! *Go!*"

"No!" Mortmain shouted, turning to the clockwork creature that had attacked Jessamine. As it raised its arm, Tessa caught hold of Sophie's wrist and began to drag her toward the stairs. A bolt of red fire hit the wall beside them, scorching the stone. Tessa shrieked but didn't slow, yanking Sophie up the spiral staircase, the smell of smoke and death following them as they ran.

Will dashed through the archway that separated the foyer from the room beyond—and came up short. Jem was already there, staring around him in bewilderment. Though there were no exits from the room other than the one they had just come through, Mrs. Dark was nowhere to be seen.

The room, though, was far from empty. It had most likely been a dining room once, and huge portraits adorned the walls, though they had been ripped and slashed to unrecognizability.

A great crystal chandelier hung overhead, fronded with strings of gray cobweb that drifted in the disturbed air like ancient lace curtains. It had probably once hung over a grand table. Now it swung over a bare marble floor that had been painted with a series of necromantic patterns—a five-pointed star inside a circle inside a square. Inside the pentagram stood a repulsive stone statue, the figure of some hideous demon, with twisted limbs and clawed hands. Horns rose from its head.

All around the room were scattered the remains of dark magic—bones and feathers and strips of skin, pools of blood that seemed to bubble like black champagne. There were empty cages lying on their sides, and a low table on which was spread an array of bloody knives and stone bowls filled with unpleasant dark liquids.

In all the gaps between the pentagram's five points were runes and squiggles that hurt Will's eyes when he looked at them. They were the opposite of the runes in the Gray Book, which seemed to speak of glory and peace. These were necromantic symbols that spoke of ruin and death.

"Jem," Will said, "these are not the preparations for a binding spell. This is the work of necromancy."

"She was trying to bring back her sister, isn't that what she said?"

"Yes, but she was doing nothing else." A dreadful dark suspicion had begun to blossom in the back of Will's mind.

Jem did not reply; his attention seemed to be fixed on something across the room. "There's a cat," he said in a low whisper, pointing. "In one of those cages over there."

Will glanced where his friend pointed. Indeed, a bristling

gray cat was huddled in one of the locked animal cages along the wall. "And?"

"It's still alive."

"It's a cat, James. We have bigger things to worry about—"

But Jem was already walking away. He reached the animal's cage and scooped it up, holding the cage at eye level. The cat looked to be a gray Persian, with a squashed-in face and yellow eyes that regarded Jem malevolently. Suddenly it arched its back and hissed loudly, its eyes fixed on the pentagram. Jem looked up—and stared.

"*Will,*" he said in a warning tone. "Look."

The statue in the middle of the pentagram had moved. Instead of crouching, it had straightened until it was standing upright. Its eyes burned with a sulfuric glow. It was only when its triple row of mouths smiled that Will realized it was not stone after all, just a creature of hard gray stonelike skin. A demon.

Will ducked back and flung Israfel reflexively, not really expecting the gesture to do much good. It didn't. As it sailed near the pentagram, the blade bounced off an invisible wall and clattered to the marble floor. The demon in the pentagram cackled. "You attack me here?" it demanded in a high, thin voice. "You could bring the host of Heaven against me and they could do nothing! No angelic power can breach this circle!"

"Mrs. Dark," Will said between his teeth.

"So you recognize me now, do you? No one ever claimed you Shadowhunters were clever." The demon bared its greenish fangs. "This is my true form. An ugly surprise for you, I suppose."

"I daresay it's an improvement," said Will. "You weren't much to look at before, and at least the horns are dramatic."

"What are you, then?" Jem demanded, setting the cage, the cat still in it, down on the floor at his feet. "I thought you and your sister were warlocks."

"My sister was a warlock," hissed the creature that had been Mrs. Dark. "I am a full-blood demon—*Eidolon*. A shape-changer. Like your precious Tessa. But unlike her I cannot *become* what I transform into. I cannot touch the minds of the living or the dead. So the Magister did not want me." Thin hurt was in the creature's voice. "He enlisted me to train her. His precious little protégée. My sister as well. We know the ways of the Change. We were able to force it on her. But she was never grateful."

"That must have hurt you," Jem said in his most soothing voice. Will opened his mouth, but seeing Jem's warning look, closed it again. "Seeing Tessa get what you wanted, and not appreciating it."

"She never understood. The honor that was being done her. The glory that would be hers." The yellow eyes burned. "When she fled, the Magister's rage fell on me—I had disappointed him. He swore out a bounty on me."

That jolted Jem, or seemed to. "You mean de Quincey wanted you dead?"

"How many times must I tell you that de Quincey is not the Magister? The Magister is—" The demon broke off with a growl. "You try to trick me, little Shadowhunter, but your trick will not work."

Jem shrugged. "You cannot remain in that pentagram forever, Mrs. Dark. Eventually the rest of the Enclave will come. We will starve you out. And then you will be ours, and you know how the Clave deals with those who break the Law."

Mrs. Dark hissed. "Perhaps he has forsaken me," she said, "but I still fear the Magister more than I fear you, or your Enclave."

More than I fear the Enclave. She should have been afraid, Will thought. What Jem had said to her was true. She ought to be afraid, but she wasn't. In Will's experience, when someone who ought to be afraid wasn't, the reason was rarely bravery. Usually it meant that they knew something you didn't.

"If you will not tell us who the Magister is," said Will, his voice edged with steel, "perhaps you can answer a simple question instead. Is Axel Mortmain the Magister?"

The demon let out a wail, then clapped its bony hands over its mouth and sank, burning-eyed, to the ground. "The Magister. He will think I told you. I will never earn his forgiveness now—"

"Mortmain?" echoed Jem. "But he is the one who warned us—Ah." He paused. "I see." He had gone very white; Will knew his thoughts were chasing down the same winding road Will's just had. He would probably have gotten there first—Will suspected Jem was in fact cleverer than he was himself—but he lacked Will's tendency to assume the absolute worst about people and proceed from there. "Mortmain lied to us about the Dark Sisters and the binding spell," he added, thinking out loud. "In fact, it was Mortmain who put the idea in Charlotte's head in the first place that de Quincey was the Magister. If it were not for him, we would never have suspected the vampire. But why?"

"De Quincey is a loathsome beast," wailed Mrs. Dark, still crouched inside her pentagram. She seemed to have decided there was no more point in concealment. "He disobeyed

Mortmain at every turn, wishing to be the Magister himself. Such insubordination must be punished."

Will's gaze met Jem's. He could tell they were both thinking the same thing. "Mortmain saw an opportunity to throw suspicion on a rival," Jem said. "That is why he chose de Quincey."

"He could have hidden those plans for automatons in de Quincey's library," agreed Will. "It is not as if de Quincey ever admitted they were his, or even seemed to recognize them when Charlotte showed them to him. And Mortmain could have told those automatons on the bridge to claim they were working for the vampire. In fact, he could have etched de Quincey's seal into that clockwork girl's chest and left her in the Dark House for us to find, as well—all to divert suspicion from himself."

"But Mortmain is not the only one who ever pointed the finger at de Quincey," said Jem, and his voice was heavy. "Nathaniel Gray, Will. Tessa's brother. When two people tell the same lie . . ."

"They are working together," Will finished. He felt, for a moment, something almost like satisfaction, which quickly faded. He had disliked Nate Gray, had hated the way Tessa had treated him as if he could do no wrong, and then he'd despised himself for his own jealousy. To know that he had been correct about Nate's character was one thing, but at what price?

Mrs. Dark laughed, a high, whining sound. "Nate Gray," she spat. "The Magister's little human lapdog. He sold his sister to Mortmain, you know. Just for a handful of silver, he did it. Just for a few sops to his vanity. I would never have treated my own sister so. And you say it is demons who are evil, and the humans who need protecting from us!" Her voice rose to a cackle.

Will ignored her; his mind was whirling. Dear God, that whole story of Nathaniel's about de Quincey had been a trick, a lie to set the Clave off on a false track. Then why have Mortmain appear as soon as they had gone? *To get rid of us, Jem and I,* Will thought grimly. *Nate couldn't have known we two wouldn't be going with Charlotte and Henry. He had to improvise something quickly when we stayed behind.* Thus Mortmain and this extra trickery. Nate had been in it with Mortmain since the beginning.

And now Tessa is in the Institute with him. Will felt sick to his stomach. He wanted to turn and run out the door, race back to the Institute, and beat Nathaniel's head against a wall. Only years of training, and fear for Henry and Charlotte, kept him where he was.

Will whirled on Mrs. Dark. "What is his plan? What will the Enclave find when they reach Carleton Square? Certain slaughter? *Answer me!*" he shouted. Fear made his voice crack. "Or by the Angel, I will make sure that the Clave tortures you before you die. What is his plan for them?"

Mrs. Dark's yellow eyes flashed. "What does the Magister care about?" she hissed. "What has he ever cared about? He despises the Nephilim, but what is it that he wants?"

"Tessa," said Jem immediately. "But she is safe in the Institute, and even his blasted clockwork army can't break inside. Even without us there—"

In a wheedling voice Mrs. Dark said, "Once, when I was in the Magister's confidence, he spoke to me of a plan he had to invade the Institute. He planned to paint the hands of his mechanical creatures with the blood of a Shadowhunter, thus allowing him to open the doors."

"The blood of a Shadowhunter?" Will echoed. "But—"

"Will." Jem had his hand at his chest, where the clockwork creature had torn the skin that night on the steps of the Institute. "*My* blood."

For a moment Will stood perfectly still, staring at his friend. Then, without a word, he turned and raced for the dining room doors; Jem, pausing only to seize the cat's cage, followed. As they reached them, the doors slammed shut as if pushed, and Will came to a skidding halt. He spun to see Jem behind him, looking baffled.

In her pentagram Mrs. Dark was howling with laughter. "Nephilim," she gasped between peals. "Stupid, stupid Nephilim. Where is your angel now?"

As they stared, enormous flames leaped up around the walls, licking up the curtains covering the windows, shimmering along the edges of the floor. The flames burned with a weird blue-green color, and the smell was thick and ugly—a demon smell. Inside its cage the cat was going wild, throwing itself against the bars again and again and howling.

Will drew a second seraph blade from his belt and cried, "*Anael!*" Light burst from the blade, but Mrs. Dark only laughed.

"When the Magister sees your charred corpses," she cried, "then he will forgive me! Then he will welcome me back!"

Her laughter rose, high and horrible. Already the room was dim with smoke. Jem, raising his sleeve to cover his mouth, said to Will in a choking voice, "Kill her. Kill her, and the fire will die."

Will, his grip tight on the hilt of Anael, growled, "Don't you think I would if I could? She's in the pentagram."

"I *know*." Jem's eyes were full of meaning. "Will, cut it *down*."

Because it was Jem, Will knew what he meant immediately,

without being told explicitly. Spinning to face the pentagram, he raised the shining Anael, took aim, and flung the blade—not toward the demon but up toward the thick metal chain that supported the massive chandelier. The blade sheared through the chain like a knife through paper, there was a rending sound, and the demon had time only to scream once before the massive chandelier descended, a crashing comet of twisting metal and shattering glass. Will threw his arm across his eyes as debris rained over them all—smashed bits of stone, fragments of crystal, and chunks of rust. The floor shook underneath him as if the earth were quaking.

When all was quiet at last, he opened his eyes. The chandelier lay like the wreck of some immense ship twisted and destroyed at the bottom of the sea. Dust rose like smoke from the wreckage, and from one corner of the pile of smashed glass and metal a trickle of greenish black blood threaded across the marble. . . .

Jem had been right. The flames were gone. Jem himself, still gripping the handle of the cat's cage, was gazing at the wreckage. His already pale hair had whitened further with plaster dust, and his cheeks were streaked with ash. "Nicely done, William," he said.

Will did not reply; there was no time for it. Throwing the doors—which opened easily under his hands now—wide, he raced out of the room.

Tessa and Sophie flew up the Institute's steps together until Sophie gasped, "Here! This door!" and Tessa flung it open and burst into the corridor beyond. Sophie pulled her wrist out of Tessa's grasp and spun to slam the door shut behind them and slide the bolt closed. She leaned against it for a moment, breathing hard, her face streaked with tears.

"Miss Jessamine," she whispered. "Do you think—"

"I don't know," Tessa said. "But you heard Thomas. We must get to the Sanctuary, Sophie. It's where we'll be safe." *And Thomas wants me to make sure you stay safe.* "You're going to have to show me where it is. I can't find my way there by myself."

Slowly Sophie nodded and drew herself upright. In silence she led Tessa through a winding mass of corridors until they reached the one corridor she remembered from the night when she had met Camille. After taking a lamp from a holder on the wall, Sophie lit it, and they hurried on, until they finally reached the great iron doors with their pattern of Cs. Brought up sharply in front of the doors, Sophie put a hand to her mouth. "The key!" she whispered. "I've forgotten the bloody—pardon me, miss—key!"

Tessa felt a wave of frustrated anger, but pushed it back. Sophie had just had a friend die in her arms; she could hardly be blamed for forgetting a key. "But you know where Charlotte keeps it?"

Sophie nodded. "I'll run and fetch it. You wait here, miss."

She hurried off down the corridor. Tessa watched her go until her white cap and sleeves faded into the shadows, leaving Tessa alone in the darkness. The only light in the corridor came from the illumination that seeped beneath the doors to the Sanctuary. She pressed herself back against the wall as the shadows gathered thickly around her, as if she could disappear into the wall. She kept seeing the blood pouring out of Agatha's chest, staining Sophie's hands; kept hearing the brittle sound of Nate's laugher as Jessamine collapsed—

It came again, harsh and as brittle as glass, echoing out of the darkness behind her.

Sure she was imagining things, Tessa whirled, her back toward the Sanctuary doors. Before her in the hallway, where a moment before there had been empty air, someone was standing. Someone with fair hair and a grin plastered across his face. Someone carrying a long, thin knife in his right hand.

Nate.

"My Tessie," he said. "That was very impressive. I wouldn't have thought either you or the servant could run that fast." He twirled the knife between his fingers. "Unfortunately for you, my master has gifted me with certain . . . powers. I can move faster than you can think." He smirked. "Probably much faster, to judge by how long it took you to catch on to what was going on downstairs."

"Nate." Tessa's voice shook. "It's not too late. You can stop this."

"Stop *what?*" Nate looked directly at her, for the first time since he had knelt to Mortmain. "Stop acquiring incredible power and immense knowledge? Stop being the favored acolyte of the most powerful man in London? I'd be a fool to stop all this, little sister."

"Favored acolyte? Where was he when de Quincey was about to drain your blood?"

"I had disappointed him," Nate said. "*You* disappointed him. You ran from the Dark Sisters, knowing what it would cost me. Your sisterly affection leaves something to be desired, Tessie."

"I let the Dark Sisters torture me for your sake, Nate. I did *everything* for you. And you—you let me believe de Quincey was the Magister. All the things you claimed de Quincey did were done by Mortmain, weren't they? He's the one who wanted me brought here. He's the one who employed the Dark Sisters. All that rubbish about de Quincey was just to lure the Enclave away from the Institute."

Nate smirked. "What was it Aunt Harriet used to say, that cleverness that comes too late is hardly cleverness at all?"

"And what will the Enclave find when they go to the address you claimed was de Quincey's nest? Nothing? An empty house, a burned-out ruin?" She began to retreat from him, until her back struck the cold iron doors.

Nate followed, his eyes gleaming like the blade in his hand. "Oh, dear me, no. That bit was true. It wouldn't do to have the Enclave realize so soon that they'd been made fools of, would it? Better to keep them busy, and cleaning out de Quincey's little hiding place will keep them quite busy indeed." He shrugged. "You're the one who gave me the idea to let the blame for everything fall on the vampire, you know. After what happened the other night, he was a dead man, anyway. The Nephilim had their sights set on him, which made him useless to Mortmain. Sending the Enclave off to get rid of him and Will and Jem off to rid my master of that pestiferous Mrs. Dark—well, it's three birds with one stone, really, isn't it? And quite a clever plan of mine, if I do say so myself."

He was preening, Tessa thought in disgust. Proud of himself. Most of her wanted to spit in his face, but she knew she should keep him talking, give herself a chance to think of a way out of the situation. "You certainly fooled us," she said, hating herself. "How much of that story you told was the truth? How much was lies?"

"Quite a bit was the truth, if you really want to know. The

best lies are based on the truth, at least in part," he bragged. "I came to London thinking I was going to blackmail Mortmain with my knowledge of his occult activities. The fact was, he couldn't have cared less about that. He wanted to get a look at me because he wasn't sure, you see. Wasn't sure if I was our parents' first child or their second. He thought I might be *you*." He grinned. "He was as pleased as punch when he realized I wasn't the child he was looking for. He wanted a girl, you see."

"But why? What does he want with me?"

Nate shrugged. "I don't know. Nor do I care. He told me that if I procured you for him, and you turned out to be all he hoped you would be, he would make me his disciple. After you fled, he gave me to de Quincey in revenge. When you brought me here, to the heart of the Nephilim, it was a second chance to offer the Magister what I'd lost for him before."

"You contacted him?" Tessa felt sick. She thought of the open window in the drawing room, Nate's flushed face, his claim that he hadn't opened it. Somehow, she knew, he had sent Mortmain a message. "You let him know you were here? That you were willing to betray us? But you could have stayed! You would have been safe!"

"Safe, and powerless. Here I'm an ordinary human, weak and contemptible. But as Mortmain's disciple, I will stand at his right hand when he rules the British Empire."

"You're mad," Tessa said. "The whole thing's ridiculous."

"I assure you it isn't. By this time next year Mortmain will be ensconced in Buckingham Palace. The Empire will bow before his rule."

"But you won't be beside him. I see how he looks at you. You're not a disciple; you're a tool to be used. When he gets what he wants, he will throw you aside like rubbish."

Nate's grip tightened on the knife. "Not true."

"It is true," Tessa said. "Aunt always said you were too trusting. It's why you're such an awful gambler, Nate. You're such a liar yourself, but you never can tell when you're being lied to. Aunt said—"

"Aunt Harriet." Nate laughed softly. "So unfortunate the way she died." He grinned. "Didn't you think it was a bit odd that I'd sent you a box of chocolates? Something I knew *you* wouldn't eat? Something I knew she would?"

Nausea gripped Tessa, a pain in her stomach as if Nate's knife were twisting there. "Nate—you wouldn't—Aunt Harriet loved you!"

"You have no idea what I would do, Tessie. No idea at all." He spoke rapidly, almost fevered in his intensity. "You think of me as a fool. Your foolish brother who needs to be protected from the world. So easily duped and taken advantage of. I heard you and Aunt discussing me. I know neither of you ever thought I'd make anything of myself, ever do anything you could be proud of me for. But now I have. *Now I have*," he snarled, as if completely unaware of the irony in his words.

"You've made a murderer of yourself. And you think I ought to be proud? I'm ashamed to be related to you."

"Related to me? You're not even human. You are some *thing*. You are no part of me. From the moment Mortmain told me what you really are, you were dead to me. I have no sister."

"Then why," said Tessa in a voice so quiet she could barely hear it herself, "do you keep calling me Tessie?"

He looked at her for a moment in stark confusion. And as she looked back at her brother—the brother she had thought was all she had left in the world—something moved beyond Nate's shoulder, and Tessa wondered if she was seeing things, if perhaps she was going to faint.

"I wasn't calling you Tessie," he said. He sounded baffled, almost lost.

A feeling of unbearable sadness gripped her. "You're my brother, Nate. You'll always be my brother."

His eyes narrowed. For a moment Tessa thought perhaps he had *heard* her. Perhaps he would reconsider. "When you belong to Mortmain," he said, "I shall be bound to him forever. For I am the one who made it possible for him to have you."

Her heart sank. The thing beyond Nate's shoulder moved again, a disturbance of the shadows. It was real, Tessa thought. Not her imagination. There was something behind Nate. Something moving toward them both. She opened her mouth, then closed it again. *Sophie,* she thought. She hoped the other girl would have the sense to run away before Nate came for her with the knife.

"Come along, then," he said to Tessa. "There's no reason to make a fuss. The Magister isn't going to hurt you—"

"You cannot be sure of that," Tessa said. The figure behind Nate was almost upon him. There was something pale and glimmering in its hand. Tessa fought to keep her eyes locked on Nate's face.

"I am sure." He sounded impatient. "I am not a fool, Tessa—"

The figure exploded into movement. The pale and glimmering object rose above Nate's head and came down with a heavy crash. Nate pitched forward, crumpling to the ground. The blade rolled from his hand as he struck the carpet and lay still, blood staining his pale blond hair.

Tessa looked up. In the dim light she could see Jessamine standing over Nate, a furious expression on her face. The remains of a shattered lamp were still clutched in her left hand.

"Not a fool, perhaps." She prodded Nate's recumbent form with a disdainful toe. "But not your most shining moment, either."

Tessa could only stare. "*Jessamine?*"

Jessamine looked up. The neckline of her dress was torn, her hair had come down out of its pins, and there was a purpling bruise on her right cheek. She dropped the lamp, which narrowly missed hitting Nate once again in the head, and said, "I'm quite all right, if that's what you're so pop-eyed about. It wasn't me they wanted, after all."

"Miss Gray! Miss Lovelace!" It was Sophie, out of breath from running up and down stairs. In one hand she held the slender iron Sanctuary key. She looked down at Nate as she reached the end of the corridor, her mouth opening in surprise. "Is he all right?"

"Oh, who cares if he's all right?" Jessamine said, bending to pick up the knife that Nate had dropped. "After all the lies he told! He lied to *me*! I really thought—" She flushed dark red. "Well, it doesn't matter now." She straightened and whirled on Sophie, her chin held high. "Now, don't just stand there staring, Sophie, do let us into the Sanctuary before God knows what comes after us all and tries to kill us again."

Will burst out of the mansion and onto the front steps, Jem just behind him. The lawn ahead of them was stark in the moonlight; their carriage was where they had left it in the center of the drive. Jem was relieved to see that the horses hadn't spooked despite all the noise, though he supposed that Balios and Xanthos, belonging to Shadowhunters as they did, had probably seen much worse.

"Will." Jem came to a stop beside his friend, trying to conceal the fact that he needed to catch his breath. "We must get back to the Institute as soon as possible."

"You will get no disagreement from me on that front." Will gave Jem a keen look; Jem wondered if his face was as flushed and feverish-looking as he feared. The drug, which he had taken in a great quantity before they'd left the Institute, was wearing off faster than it should have been; at another time the realization would have prickled Jem with anxiety. Now he put it aside.

"Do you think Mortmain expected us to kill Mrs. Dark?" he asked, less because he felt the question was an urgent one than because he needed a few more moments to catch his breath before he climbed into the carriage.

Will had his jacket open and was rummaging in one of the pockets. "I imagine so," he said, almost absently, "or probably he hoped we'd all kill one another, which would have been ideal for him. Clearly he wants de Quincey dead as well and has decided to use the Nephilim as his own band of personal assassins." Will drew a folding knife from his inner pocket and looked at it with satisfaction. "A single horse," he observed, "is much faster than a carriage."

Jem gripped the cage he was holding tighter. The gray cat, behind its bars, was looking around with wide yellow interested eyes. "Please tell me you aren't going to do what I suspect you're going to do, Will."

Will flipped the knife open and started up the drive.

"There's no time to lose, James. And Xanthos can pull the carriage perfectly well by himself, if you're the only one in it."

Jem went after him, but the heavy cage, as well as his own fevered exhaustion, slowed his progress. "What are you doing with that knife? You're not going to murder the horses, are you?"

"Of course not." Will raised the blade and began to slash at the harness fastening Balios, his favored of the two animals, to the carriage.

"Ah," said Jem. "I see. You're going to ride off on that horse like Dick Turpin and leave me here. Have you gone mad?"

"Someone's got to look after that cat." The girth and traces fell away, and Will swung himself up onto Balios.

"But—" Really alarmed now, Jem set the cage down. "Will, you can't—"

It was too late. Will dug his heels into the horse's sides. Balios reared and neighed, Will clinging on resolutely—Jem could have sworn he was *grinning*—and then the horse wheeled and pounded toward the gates. Inside of a moment, horse and rider were out of sight.

19

BOADICEA

Seal'd her mine from her first sweet breath.
Mine, mine by a right, from birth till death
Mine, mine—our fathers have sworn.
—Alfred, Lord Tennyson, "Maud"

As the doors of the Sanctuary closed behind them, Tessa looked around apprehensively. The room was darker than it had been when she had come here to meet Camille. There were no candles burning in the great candelabras, only flickering witchlight that emanated from sconces on the walls. The angel statue continued to weep its endless tears into the fountain. The air in the room was bone-chillingly cold, and she shivered.

Sophie, having slipped the key back into her pocket, looked as nervous as Tessa felt. "Here we are, then," she said. "It's awful cold in this place."

"Well, we won't be here long, I'm sure," said Jessamine. She was still holding Nate's knife, which glittered in her hand. "*Someone* will come back to rescue us. Will, or Charlotte—"

"And find the Institute full of clockwork monsters," Tessa reminded her. "And Mortmain." She shuddered. "I'm not sure it'll be quite so simple as you make it out to be."

Jessamine looked at Tessa with cold dark eyes. "Well, you needn't sound as if it's my fault. If it weren't for you, we wouldn't be in this mess."

Sophie had moved to stand among the massive pillars, and was looking very small. Her voice echoed off the stone walls. "That's not very kind, miss."

Jessamine perched herself on the edge of the fountain, then rose to her feet again, frowning. She brushed at the back of her dress, now stained with damp, in an exasperated manner. "Perhaps not, but it's true. The only reason the Magister is here is because of Tessa."

"I told Charlotte all this was my fault." Tessa spoke quietly. "I told her to send me away. She wouldn't."

Jessamine tossed her head. "Charlotte's softhearted, and so is Henry. And Will—Will thinks he's Galahad. Wants to save everyone. Jem, too. None of them are practical."

"I suppose," Tessa said, "if it had been your decision to make . . ."

"You'd have been out the door with nothing but the key of the street to your name," Jessamine said, and sniffed. Seeing the way Sophie was looking at her, she added, "Oh, really! Don't be such a mush-mouth, Sophie. Agatha and Thomas would still be alive if I'd been in charge, wouldn't they?"

Sophie went pale, her scar standing out along her cheek like the mark of a slap. "Thomas is dead?"

Jessamine looked as if she knew she'd made a mistake. "I didn't mean that."

Tessa looked at her, hard. "What happened, Jessamine? We saw you injured—"

"And precious little any of you did about it either," Jessamine said, and sat down with a flounce on the fountain wall, apparently forgetting to worry about the state of her dress. "I was unconscious . . . and when I awoke, I saw that all of you had gone but Thomas. Mortmain was gone too, but those creatures were still there. One of them began to come after me, and I looked for my parasol, but it had been trampled to shreds. Thomas was surrounded by those creatures. I went toward him, but he told me to run, so . . . I ran." She tilted her chin up defiantly.

Sophie's eyes flashed. "You left him there? Alone?"

Jessamine set the knife down on the wall with an angry clatter. "I'm a lady, Sophie. It is expected that a man sacrifice himself for a lady's safety."

"That's *rubbish!*" Sophie's hands were tight little fists at her sides. "You're a *Shadowhunter!* And Thomas is just a mundane! You could have helped him. You just wouldn't—because you're selfish! And—and awful!"

Jessamine gaped at Sophie, her mouth wide open. "How dare you speak to me like—"

She broke off as the door of the Sanctuary resounded with the noise of the heavy knocker falling. It sounded again, and then a familiar voice, raised, called out to them, "Tessa! Sophie! It's Will."

"Oh, thank God," Jessamine said—clearly just as relieved to be free of her conversation with Sophie as she was to be rescued—and hurried toward the door. "Will! It's Jessamine. I'm in here too!"

"And you're all three all right?" Will sounded anxious in a way that tightened Tessa's chest. "What happened? We raced here from Highgate. I saw the door of the Institute open. How in the Angel's name did Mortmain get in?"

"He evaded the wards somehow," Jessamine said bitterly, reaching for the door handle. "I've no idea how."

"It hardly matters now. He's dead. The clockwork creatures are destroyed."

Will's tone was reassuring—so why, Tessa thought, did she not feel reassured? She turned to look at Sophie, who was staring at the door, a sharp vertical frown line between her eyes, her lips moving very slightly as if she were whispering something under her breath. Sophie had the Sight, Tessa remembered— Charlotte had said so. Tessa's sense of unease rose and crested like a wave.

"Jessamine," she called. "Jessamine, don't open the door—"

But it was too late. The door had swung wide. And there on the threshold stood Mortmain, flanked by clockwork monsters.

Thank the Angel for glamours, Will thought. The sight of a boy riding bareback on a charging black horse down Farringdon Road would normally be enough to raise eyebrows even in a metropolis as jaded as London. But as Will went by—the horse kicking up great puffs of London dust as it reared and snorted its way through the streets—no one turned a hair or batted the lash of an eye. Yet even as they seemed not to see him, they found reasons to move out of his way—a dropped pair of eye-glasses, a step to the side to avoid a puddle in the road—and avoid being trampled.

It was almost five miles from Highgate to the Institute; it had taken them three-quarters of an hour to cover the distance in the carriage. It took Will and Balios only twenty minutes to make the return trip, though the horse was panting and lath-ered with sweat by the time Will pounded through the Institute gates and drew up in front of the steps.

His heart sank immediately. The doors were open. Wide open, as if inviting in the night. It was strictly against Covenant Law to leave the doors of an Institute standing ajar. He had been correct; something was terribly wrong.

He slid from the horse's back, boots clattering loudly against the cobblestones. He looked for a way to secure the ani-mal, but as he'd cut its harness, there was none, and besides, Balios looked inclined to bite him. He shrugged and made for the steps.

Jessamine gasped and leaped back as Mortmain stepped into the room. Sophie screamed and ducked behind a pillar. Tessa was too shocked to move. The four automatons, two on either side of Mortmain, stared straight ahead with their shining faces like metal masks.

Behind Mortmain was Nate. A makeshift bandage, stained with blood, was tied around his head. The bottom of his shirt—Jem's shirt—had a ragged strip torn from it. His baleful gaze fell on Jessamine.

"You stupid whore," he snarled, and started forward.

"Nathaniel." Mortmain's voice cracked like a whip; Nate

froze. "This is not an arena in which to enact your petty revenges. There is one more thing I need from you; you know what it is. Retrieve it for me."

Nate hesitated. He was looking at Jessamine like a cat with its gaze fixed on a mouse.

"Nathaniel. To the weapons room. Now."

Nate dragged his gaze from Jessie. For a moment he looked at Tessa, the rage in his expression softening into a sneer. Then he turned on his heel and stalked from the room; two of the clockwork creatures peeled themselves from Mortmain's side and followed him.

The door closed behind him, and Mortmain smiled pleasantly. "The two of you," he said, looking from Jessamine to Sophie, "get out."

"No." The voice was Sophie's, small but stubborn, though to Tessa's surprise, Jessamine showed no inclination to leave either. "Not without Tessa."

Mortmain shrugged. "Very well." He turned to the clockwork creatures. "The two girls," he said. "The Shadowhunter and the servant. Kill them both."

He snapped his fingers and the clockwork creatures sprang forward. They had the grotesque speed of skittering rats. Jessamine turned to run, but she had gone only a few steps when one of them seized her, lifting her off the ground. Sophie darted among the pillars like Snow White fleeing into the woods, but it did her little good. The second creature caught up to her swiftly and bore her to the ground as she screamed. In contrast Jessamine was utterly silent; the creature holding her had one metal hand clamped across her mouth and the other around her waist, fingers digging in cruelly. Her feet kicked uselessly in the air like the feet of a criminal dangling at the end of a hangman's rope.

Tessa heard her own voice as it emerged from her throat as if it were a stranger's. "Stop it. Please, please, stop it!"

Sophie had broken away from the creature holding her and was scrambling across the floor on her hands and knees. Reaching out, it caught her by the ankle and jerked her backward across the floor, her apron tearing as she sobbed.

"*Please,*" Tessa said again, fixing her eyes on Mortmain.

"*You* can stop it, Miss Gray," he said. "Promise me you won't try to run." His eyes burned as he looked at her. "Then I'll let them go."

Jessamine's eyes, visible above the metal arm clamping her mouth, pleaded with Tessa. The other creature was on its feet, holding Sophie, who dangled limply in its grip.

"I'll stay," Tessa said. "You have my word. Of course I will. Just let them go."

There was a long pause. Then, "You heard her," Mortmain said to his mechanical monsters. "Take the girls out of this room. Bring them downstairs. Don't harm them." He smiled then, a thin, crafty smile. "Leave Miss Gray alone with me."

Even before he passed through the front doors, Will felt it—the jangling sense that something dreadful was happening here. The first time he'd ever felt this sensation, he'd been twelve years old, holding that blasted box—but he'd never imagined feeling it in the fastness of the Institute.

He saw Agatha's body first, the moment he stepped over the threshold. She lay on her back, her glassy eyes staring up at the ceiling, the front of her plain gray dress soaked with blood.

A wave of almost overwhelming rage washed over Will, leaving him light-headed. Biting his lip hard, he bent to close her eyes before he rose and looked around.

The signs of a melee were everywhere—torn scraps of metal, bent and broken gears, splashes of blood mixing with pools of oil. As Will moved toward the stairs, his foot came down on the shredded remains of Jessamine's parasol. He gritted his teeth and moved on to the staircase.

And there, slumped across the lowest steps, lay Thomas, eyes closed, motionless in a widening pool of scarlet. A sword rested on the ground beside him, a little ways away from his hand; its edge was chipped and dented as if he had been using it to hack apart rocks. A great jagged piece of metal protruded from his chest. It looked a little like the torn blade of a saw, Will thought as he crouched down by Thomas's side, or like a sharp bit of some larger metal contraption.

There was a dry burning in the back of Will's throat. His mouth tasted of metal and rage. He rarely grieved during a battle; he saved his emotions for afterward—those he had not already learned to bury so deeply that he barely felt them at all. He had been burying them since he was twelve years old. His chest knotted with pain now, but his voice was steady when he spoke. "Hail and farewell, Thomas," he said, reaching to close the other boy's eyes. "*Ave—*"

A hand flew up and gripped his wrist. Will stared down, dumbfounded, as Thomas's glassy eyes slid toward him, pale brown under the whitish film of death. "Not," he said, with a clear effort to get the words out, "a Shadowhunter."

"You defended the Institute," Will said. "You did as well as any of us would have done."

"No." Thomas closed his eyes, as if exhausted. His chest rose, barely; his shirt was soaked almost black with blood. "You'd've fought 'em off, Master Will. You know you would."

"Thomas," Will whispered. He wanted to say, *Be quiet, and you'll be all right when the others get here.* But Thomas manifestly would not be all right. He was human; no healing rune could help him. Will wished that Jem were here, instead of himself. Jem was the one you wanted with you when you were dying. Jem could make anyone feel that things were going to be all right, whereas Will privately suspected that there were few situations that his presence did not make worse.

"She's alive," Thomas said, not opening his eyes.

"What?" Will was caught off guard.

"The one you come back for. Her. Tessa. She's with Sophie." Thomas spoke as if it were a fact obvious to anyone that Will would have come back for Tessa's sake. He coughed, and a great mass of blood poured out of his mouth and down his chin. He didn't seem to notice. "Take care of Sophie, Will. Sophie is—"

But Will never found out what Sophie was, because Thomas's grip went suddenly slack, and his hand fell away and struck the stone floor with an ugly thump. Will drew back. He had seen death enough times, and knew when it had come. There was no need to close Thomas's eyes; they were closed already. "Sleep, then," he said, not quite knowing where the words came from, "good and faithful servant of the Nephilim. And thank you."

It wasn't enough, not nearly enough, but it was all there was. Will scrambled to his feet and dashed up the staircase.

* * *

The doors had closed behind the clockwork creatures; the Sanctuary was very silent. Tessa could hear the water splashing in the fountain behind her.

Mortmain stood regarding her calmly. He still wasn't frightening to look at, Tessa thought. A small, ordinary man, with dark hair going gray at his temples, and those odd light eyes. "Miss Gray," he said, "I had hoped our first time alone together would be a more pleasant experience for us both."

Tessa's eyes burned. She said, "What are you? A warlock?"

His smile was swift, and without feeling. "Merely a human being, Miss Gray."

"But you did magic," she said. "You spoke in Will's voice—"

"Anyone can learn to imitate voices, with the proper training," he said. "A simple trick, like sleight of hand. No one ever expects them. Certainly not Shadowhunters. They believe humans are good at nothing, as well as being good for nothing."

"No," Tessa whispered. "They don't think that."

His mouth twisted. "How quickly you have grown to love them, your natural enemies. We will soon train you out of that." He moved forward, and Tessa shrank back. "I will not hurt you," he said. "I merely want to show you something." He reached into the pocket of his coat and drew out a gold watch, very fine-looking, on a thick gold chain.

Is he wondering what *time* it is? The mad urge to giggle rose up in the back of Tessa's throat. She forced it down.

He held the watch out to her. "Miss Gray," he said, "please take this."

She stared at him. "I don't want it."

He moved toward her again. Tessa retreated until the back

of her skirts brushed the low wall of the fountain. "Take the watch, Miss Gray."

Tessa shook her head.

"Take it," he said. "Or I will recall my clockwork servants and have them crush the throats of your two friends until they are dead. I need only go to the door and call to them. It is your choice."

Bile rose in the back of Tessa's throat. She stared at the watch he held out to her, dangling on its gold chain. It was clearly unwound. The hands had long ago stopped spinning, the time seemingly frozen at midnight. The initials J. T. S. were carved on the back in elegant script.

"Why?" she whispered. "Why do you want me to take it?"

"Because I want you to Change," Mortmain said.

Tessa's head jerked up. She stared at him incredulously. "*What?*"

"This watch used to belong to someone," he said. "Someone I very much want to meet again." His voice was even, but there was a sort of undercurrent beneath it, an eager hunger that terrified Tessa more than any rage might have. "I know the Dark Sisters taught you. I know you know your power. You are the only one in the world who can do what you do. I know this because *I made you.*"

"You *made* me?" Tessa stared. "You're not saying—you can't be my father—"

"Your father?" Mortmain laughed shortly. "I am a human, not a Downworlder. There is no demon in me, nor do I consort with demons. There is no blood shared between the two of us, Miss Gray. And yet if it were not for me, you would not exist."

"I don't understand," Tessa whispered.

"You don't need to understand." Mortmain's temper was visibly fraying. "You need to do as I tell you. And I am telling you to Change. *Now*."

It was like standing in front of the Dark Sisters again, frightened and alert, her heart pounding, being told to access a part of herself that terrified her. Being told to lose herself in that darkness, that nothingness between self and other. Perhaps it would be easy to do as he told her—to reach out and take the watch as commanded, to abandon herself in someone else's skin as she had done before, with no will or choice of her own.

She looked down, away from Mortmain's searing gaze, and saw something glittering on the fountain wall just behind her. A splash of water, she thought for a moment—but no. It was something else. She spoke then, almost without meaning to.

"No," she said.

Mortmain's eyes narrowed. "What was that?"

"I said no." Tessa felt as if she were outside herself somehow, watching herself face down Mortmain as if she were watching a stranger. "I won't do it. Not unless you tell me what you mean when you say you made me. Why am I like this? Why is it that you need my power so badly? What do you plan to force me to do for you? You are doing more than just building an army of monsters. I can see that. I'm not a fool like my brother."

Mortmain slid the watch back into his pocket. His face was an ugly mask of rage. "No," he said. "You are not a fool like your brother. He is a fool and a coward. You are a fool who has some courage. Though it will do you little good. And it is your friends who will suffer for it. While you watch." He turned on his heel then and strode toward the door.

Tessa bent down and seized up the object that had glittered behind her. It was the knife Jessamine had put there, the blade gleaming in the Sanctuary witchlight. "Stop," she cried. "Mr. Mortmain. *Stop.*"

He turned then, and saw her holding the knife. A look of disgusted amusement spread across his face. "Really, Miss Gray," he said. "Do you honestly think you can harm me with that? Did you think I came entirely unarmed?" He moved his jacket aside slightly, and she saw the butt of a pistol, gleaming at his belt.

"No," she said. "No, I don't think I can hurt you." She turned the knife around then, so that the hilt was away from her, the blade pointing directly at her own chest. "But if you take one more step toward that door, I promise you, I'll put this knife through my heart."

Repairing the mess Will had made of the carriage harnesses took Jem longer than he would have liked, and the moon was worryingly high in the sky by the time he rattled through the gates of the Institute and pulled Xanthos up at the foot of the steps.

Balios, untethered, was standing by the newel post at the foot of the stairs, looking exhausted. Will must have ridden like the devil, Jem thought, but at least he had arrived safely. It was a small bit of reassurance, considering that the doors of the Institute stood wide, sending a dart of horror through him. It was a sight that seemed so wrong that it was like looking at a face missing eyes or a sky with no stars. It was something that simply should not be.

Jem raised his voice. "Will?" he called. "Will, can you hear me?" When there was no answer, he leaped down from the driver's seat of the carriage and reached up to pull his jade-headed cane down after him. He held it lightly, balancing the weight. His wrists had begun to ache, which concerned him. Usually withdrawal from the demon powder began as pain in his joints, a dull ache that spread slowly until his whole body burned like fire. But he could not afford that pain now. There was Will to think about, and Tessa. He could not rid himself of the image of her on the steps, looking down at him as he spoke the ancient words. She had looked so worried, and the thought that she might have been worried about him had given him an unexpected pleasure.

He turned to start up the steps, and paused. Someone was already coming down them. More than one person—a crowd. They were backlit by the light of the Institute, and for a moment he blinked at them, seeing only silhouettes. A few seemed strangely misshapen.

"Jem!" The voice was high, desperate. Familiar.

Jessamine.

Galvanized, Jem darted up the stairs, and then paused. In front of him stood Nathaniel Gray, his clothes torn and spotted with blood. A makeshift bandage was wound around his head and was soaked with blood by his right temple. His expression was grim.

On either side of him moved clockwork automatons, like obedient servants. One flanked his right side, one his left. Behind were two more. One held a struggling Jessamine; the other a limp, half-insensible Sophie.

"Jem!" Jessamine shrieked. "Nate's a liar. He was helping

Mortmain all this time—Mortmain's the Magister, not de Quincey—"

Nathaniel whirled. "Silence her," he barked at the clockwork creature behind him. Its metal arms tightened around Jessamine, who choked and fell silent, her face white with pain. Her eyes darted toward the automaton on Nathaniel's right. Following her gaze, Jem saw that the creature held the familiar golden square of the Pyxis in its hands.

At the look on his face, Nate smiled. "None but a Shadowhunter can touch it," he said. "No *living creature*, that is. But an automaton is not alive."

"That is what all this was about?" Jem demanded, astounded. "The Pyxis? What possible use could it be to you?"

"My master wants demon energies, and demon energies he shall have," said Nate pompously. "Nor will he forget that I am the one who provided them for him."

Jem shook his head. "And what will he give you then? What did he give you to betray your sister? Thirty pieces of silver?"

Nate's face twisted, and for a moment Jem thought he could see through the blandly handsome mask to what was really underneath—something malignant and repellent that made Jem want to turn away and retch. "That thing," he said, "is not my sister."

"It is hard to believe, isn't it," said Jem, making no effort to hide his loathing, "that you and Tessa share anything at all, even a single drop of blood. She is so much finer than you."

Nathaniel's eyes narrowed. "She is not my concern. She belongs to Mortmain."

"I don't know what Mortmain has promised you," Jem said, "but I can promise you that if you hurt Jessamine or Sophie—"

and if you take the Pyxis from these premises—the Clave will hunt you. And find you. And kill you."

Nathaniel shook his head slowly. "You don't understand," he said. "None of the Nephilim understand. The most you can offer is to let me live. But the Magister can promise me that *I won't ever die.*" He turned to the clockwork creature on his left, the one not holding the Pyxis. "Kill him," he said.

The automaton sprang toward Jem. It was faster by far than the creatures Jem had faced on Blackfriars Bridge. He barely had time to flip the catch that released the blade at the end of his cane and raise it, before the thing was on him. The creature squealed like a braking train when Jem drove the blade directly into its chest and sawed it from side to side, tearing the metal wide open. The creature spun away, spraying a Catherine wheel of red sparks.

Nate, caught by the spray of fire, yelled and jumped back, beating at the sparks burning holes into his clothes. Jem took the opportunity to leap up two of the steps and slam Nate across the back with the flat of his blade, knocking him to his knees. Nate twisted around to look for his clockwork protector, but it was staggering from side to side across the steps, sparks fountaining from its chest; it seemed evident that Jem had severed one of its central mechanisms. The automaton holding the Pyxis stood stock-still; clearly Nate was not its first priority.

"Drop them!" Nate cried to the clockwork creatures holding Sophie and Jessamine. "Kill the Shadowhunter! Kill him, do you hear?"

Jessamine and Sophie, released, tumbled to the ground, both gasping but clearly still alive. Jem's relief was short-lived, though, as the second pair of automatons lurched toward him, moving with incredible speed. He slashed out at one with his cane. It leaped back, out of range, and the other raised a hand— not a hand, really, more a square block of metal, its side edged with ragged teeth like a saw—

A yell came from behind Jem, and Henry charged past him, wielding a massive broadsword. He swung it hard, slashing through the automaton's raised arm and sending its hand flying. It skidded across the cobblestones, sparking and hissing, before bursting into flames.

"Jem!" It was Charlotte's voice, raised in warning. Jem spun, and saw the other automaton reaching for him from behind. He drove his blade into the creature's throat, sawing at the copper tubes inside, while Charlotte slashed at its knees with her whip. With a high whine, it collapsed to the ground, legs severed. Charlotte, her pale face set, brought the whip down again, while Jem turned to see that Henry, his ginger hair pasted to his forehead with sweat, was lowering his broadsword. The automaton he had attacked was now a heap of scrap metal on the ground.

In fact, bits of clockwork were scattered across the courtyard, some of it still burning, like a field of fallen stars. Jessamine and Sophie were clinging to each other; Jessamine supporting the other girl, whose throat was necklaced with dark bruises. Jessamine met Jem's eyes across the steps. He thought it might have been the first time she'd really ever looked like she was glad to see him.

"He's gone," she said. "Nathaniel. He vanished with that creature—and the Pyxis."

"I don't understand." Charlotte's bloodied face was a mask of shock. "Tessa's brother . . ."

"Everything he said to us was a lie," said Jessamine. "The whole business with sending you off after the vampires was a diversion."

"Dear God," said Charlotte. "So de Quincey wasn't lying—" She shook her head, as if to clear it of cobwebs. "When we reached his house in Chelsea, we found him there with just a few vampires, no more than six or seven—certainly not the hundred Nathaniel had warned about, and no clockwork creatures that anyone could find. Benedict slew de Quincey, but not before the vampire laughed at us for calling him the Magister—said we had let Mortmain make fools of us. *Mortmain*. And I'd thought he was just—just a mundane."

Henry sank down on the top step, his broad sword clanking. "This is a disaster."

"Will," Charlotte said dazedly, as if in a dream. "And Tessa. Where are they?"

"Tessa's in the Sanctuary. With Mortmain. Will—" Jessamine shook her head. "I didn't realize he was here."

"He's inside," Jem said, raising his gaze to the Institute. He remembered his poison-racked dream—the Institute in flames, a haze of smoke over London, and great clockwork creatures striding to and fro among the buildings like monstrous spiders. "He would have gone after Tessa."

Mortmain's face had drained of blood. "What are you doing?" he demanded, striding toward her.

Tessa set the tip of the blade to her chest and pushed. The pain was sharp, sudden. Blood bloomed on the bosom of her dress. "Don't come any closer."

Mortmain stopped, his face contorted with fury. "What

makes you think I care if you live or die, Miss Gray?"

"As you said, you made me," said Tessa. "For whatever reason, you desired that I exist. You valued me enough that you would not have wanted the Dark Sisters to harm me in any permanent way. Somehow, I am significant to you. Oh, not my *self*, of course. My power. That is what matters to you." She could feel blood, warm and wet, trickling down her skin, but the pain was nothing compared to her satisfaction at seeing the look of fear on Mortmain's face.

He spoke through gritted teeth. "What is it you want from me?"

"No. What is it you want from *me*? Tell me. Tell me why you created me. Tell me who my true parents are. Was my mother really my mother? My father, my father?"

Mortmain's smile was twisted. "You are asking the wrong questions, Miss Gray."

"Why am I . . . what I am, and Nate is only human? Why is he not like me?"

"Nathaniel is only your half brother. He is nothing more than a human being, and not a very good example of that. Do not mourn that you are not more like him."

"Then . . ." Tessa paused. Her heart was racing. "My mother could not have been a demon," she said quietly. "Or anything supernatural, because Aunt Harriet was her sister, and she was only human. So it must have been my father. My father was a demon?"

Mortmain grinned, a sudden ugly grin. "Put down the knife and I will give you your answers. Perhaps we can even summon up the thing that fathered you, if you are so desperate to meet him—or should I say 'it'?"

"Then I am a warlock," Tessa said. Her throat felt tight. "That is what you are saying."

Mortmain's pale eyes were full of scorn. "If you insist," he said, "I suppose that is the best word for what you are."

Tessa heard Magnus Bane's clear voice in her head: *Oh, you're a warlock. Depend on it.* And yet—

"I don't believe any of this," Tessa said. "My mother, she would never have—not with a demon."

"She had no idea." Mortmain sounded almost pitying. "No idea that she was being unfaithful to your father."

Tessa's stomach lurched. This was nothing she hadn't thought might be possible, nothing she hadn't wondered about. Still, to hear it spoken aloud was something else. "If the man I thought was my father, was not my father, and my true father was a demon," she said, "then why am I not marked like a warlock is marked?"

Mortmain's eyes sparkled with malevolence. "Indeed, why are you not? Perhaps because your mother had no idea what she was, any more than you do."

"What do you mean? My mother was human!"

Mortmain shook his head. "Miss Gray, you continue to ask the wrong questions. What you must understand is that much was planned so that you would someday come to be. The planning began even before me—and I carried it forward, knowing I was overseeing the creation of something unique in the world. Something unique that would belong to me. I knew that I would one day marry you, and you would be mine forever."

Tessa looked at him in horror. "But why? You don't *love* me. You don't know me. You didn't even know what I looked like! I could have been hideous!"

"It would not have mattered. You can appear as hideous or as beautiful as you like. The face you wear now is only one of a thousand possible faces. When will you learn that there is no *real* Tessa Gray?"

"Get out," Tessa said.

Mortmain looked at her with his pale eyes. "What did you say to me?"

"Get out. Leave the Institute. Take your monsters with you. Or I will stab myself in the heart."

For a moment he hesitated, his hands clenching and unclenching at his sides. This must have been what he was like when forced to make a lightning-swift business decision—to buy or to sell? To invest or to expand? He was a man used to sizing up the situation in an instant, Tessa thought. And she was only a girl. What chance did she have to outmaneuver him?

Slowly he shook his head. "I don't believe you'll do it. You may be a warlock, but you're still a young girl. A delicate female." He took a step toward her. "Violence is not in your nature."

Tessa gripped the handle of the knife tightly. She could feel everything—the hard slick surface under her fingers, the pain where it pierced her skin, the beat of her own heart. "Don't come a step closer," she said in a shaking voice, "or I'll do it. I'll drive the knife in."

The tremble in her voice seemed to give him conviction; his jaw firmed, and he moved toward her with a confident stride. "No, you won't."

Tessa heard Will's voice in her head. *She took poison rather than let herself be captured by the Romans. She was braver than any man.*

"Yes," she said. "I will."

Something in her face must have changed, for the confidence went from his expression and he lunged toward her, his arrogance gone, reaching desperately for the knife. Tessa spun away from Mortmain, turning to face the fountain. The last thing she saw was the silvery water splashing high above her as she drove the knife toward her chest.

Will was breathless as he approached the doors of the Sanctuary. He had fought two of the clockwork automatons in the stairwell and had thought he was done for, until the first one—having been run through several times with Thomas's sword—began to malfunction and pushed the second creature out a window before collapsing and crashing down the stairs in a whirlwind of crumpling metal and shooting sparks.

Will had cuts on his hands and arms from the creatures' jagged metal hides, but he had not slowed down for an *iratze*. He drew out his stele as he ran, and hit the Sanctuary doors at a dead run. He slashed the stele across the doors' surface, creating the fastest Open rune of his life.

The doors' lock slid back. Will took a split second of time to switch his stele for one of the seraph blades on his belt. *"Jerahmeel,"* he whispered, and as the blade blazed up with white fire, he kicked the Sanctuary doors open.

And froze in horror. Tessa lay crumpled by the fountain, whose water was stained with red. The front of her blue and white dress was a sheet of scarlet, and blood spread from beneath her body in a widening pool. A knife lay by her limp right hand, its hilt smeared with blood. Her eyes were closed.

Mortmain knelt by her side, his hand on her shoulder. He

glanced up as the doors burst open, and then staggered to his feet, backing away from Tessa's body. His hands were red with blood, and his shirt and jacket were stained with it.

"I . . . ," he began.

"You killed her," Will said. His voice sounded stupid to his own ears, and very far away. He saw again in his mind's eye the library of the house he had lived in with his family as a child. His own hands on the box, curious fingers unclasping the catch that held it closed. The library filled with the sound of screaming. The road to London, silver in the moonlight. The words that had gone through his head, over and over, as he'd walked away from everything he had ever known, forever. *I have lost everything. Lost everything.*

Everything.

"No." Mortmain shook his head. He was fiddling with something—a ring on his right hand, made of silver. "I didn't touch her. She did this to herself."

"You lie." Will moved forward, the shape of the seraph blade beneath his fingers comforting and familiar in a world that seemed to shift and change around him like the landscape of a dream. "Do you know what happens when I drive one of these into human flesh?" he rasped, raising Jerahmeel. "It will burn as it cuts you. You will die in agony, burning from the inside out."

"You think you grieve her loss, Will Herondale?" Mortmain's voice was full of torment. "Your grief is nothing to mine. Years of work—dreams—more than you could ever imagine, wasted."

"Then be comforted, for your pain will be of short duration," said Will, and he lunged forward, blade outstretched.

He felt it graze the cloth of Mortmain's jacket—and meet no further resistance. He stumbled forward, righted himself, and stared. Something clinked to the floor at his feet, a brass button. His blade must have severed it from Mortmain's jacket. It winked at him from the ground like a mocking eye.

Shocked, Will dropped the seraph blade. Jerahmeel fell to the floor, still burning. Mortmain was gone—entirely gone. He had vanished like a warlock might vanish, a warlock who had trained in the practice of magic for years. For a human, even a human with occult knowledge, to accomplish such a thing . . .

But that didn't matter; not now. Will could think of only one thing. *Tessa.* Half in dread, half in hope, he crossed the room to where she lay. The fountain made its wretched soothing noises as he knelt down and lifted her into his arms.

He had held her like this only once before, in the attic, the night they had burned de Quincey's town house. The memory of it had come to him, unbidden, often enough since. Now it was torture. Her dress was soaked in blood; so was her hair, and her face was streaked with it. Will had seen enough injuries to know that no one could lose blood like this and live.

"Tessa," he whispered. He crushed her against him; it didn't matter now what he did. He buried his face in the crook of her neck, where her throat met her shoulder. Her hair, already beginning to stiffen with blood, scratched his cheek. He could feel the beat of her pulse through her skin.

He froze. Her *pulse?* His heart leaped; he drew away, meaning to lower her to the ground, and found her looking at him with wide gray eyes.

"Will," she said. "Is it really you, Will?"

Relief crashed over him first, followed instantly by a boiling terror. To have Thomas die before his eyes, and now this, too. Or perhaps she could be saved? Though not with Marks. How were Downworlders healed? It was knowledge only the Silent Brothers had. "Bandages," Will said, half to himself. "I must get bandages."

He began to loosen his grip on her, but Tessa caught at his wrist with her hand. "Will, you must be careful. Mortmain— he's the Magister. He was here—"

Will felt as if he were choking. "Hush. Save your strength. Mortmain's gone. I must get help—"

"No." She tightened her grip on him. "No, you needn't do that, Will. *It's not my blood.*"

"What?" he said, staring. Perhaps she was delirious, he thought, but her grip and her voice were surprisingly strong for someone who should have been dead. "Whatever he did to you, Tessa—"

"*I* did it," she said in the same firm little voice. "I did it to myself, Will. It was the only way I knew to make him go away. He would never have left me here. Not if he'd thought I was alive."

"But—"

"I *Changed*. When the knife touched me, I Changed, just in that moment. It was something that Mortmain had said that gave me the idea—that sleight of hand is a simple trick and that no one ever expects it."

"I don't understand. The blood?"

She nodded, her small face alight with relief, with her pleasure in telling him what she had done. "There was a woman, once, that the Dark Sisters made me Change into, who had died of a gunshot wound, and when I Changed her blood poured all over me. Did I tell you that? I thought perhaps I had, but it doesn't matter—I remembered it, and I Changed into her, just for that moment, and the blood came, as it had before. I turned away from Mortmain so he couldn't see me change, and crumpled forward as if the knife had truly gone in—and indeed, the force of the Change, doing it so quickly, made me quite sincerely faint. The world went dark, and then I heard Mortmain calling my name. I knew I must have come back to myself, and I knew I must pretend to be dead. I fear he would have certainly found me out had you not arrived." She looked down at herself, and Will could have sworn there was a faintly smug tone to her voice as she said, "I tricked the Magister, Will! I would not have thought it possible—he was so confident of his superiority over me. But I recalled what you had said about Boadicea. If it had not been for your words, Will . . ."

She looked up at him with a smile. The smile broke what was left of his resistance—shattered it. He had let the walls down when he'd thought she was gone, and there was no time to build them back up. Helplessly he pulled her against him. For a moment she clung to him tightly, warm and alive in his arms. Her hair brushed his cheek. The color had come back into the world; he could breathe again, and for that moment he breathed her in—she smelled of salt, blood, tears, and Tessa.

When she drew back from his embrace, her eyes were shining. "I thought when I heard your voice that it was a dream," she said. "But you are real." Her eyes searched his face, and, as if satisfied at what they found there, she smiled. "You are real."

He opened his mouth. The words were there. He was about to say them when a jolt of terror went through him, the terror of someone who, wandering in a mist, pauses only to realize that they have stopped inches from the edge of a gaping abyss. The way she was looking at him—she could read what was in his eyes, he realized. It must have been written plainly there, like words on the page of a book. There had been no time, no chance, to hide it.

"Will," she whispered. "Say something, Will."

But there was nothing to say. There was only the emptiness, as there had been before her. As there always would be.

I have lost everything, Will thought. *Everything.*

20

AWFUL WONDER

Yet each man kills the thing he loves,
By each let this be heard,
Some do it with a bitter look,
Some with a flattering word,
The coward does it with a kiss,
The brave man with a sword!
—Oscar Wilde, "The Ballad of Reading Gaol"

The Marks that denoted mourning were red for Shadow-hunters. The color of death was white.

Tessa had not known that, had not read it in the *Codex*, and so had been startled to see the five Shadowhunters of the Institute going out to the carriage dressed all in white like a wedding party as she and Sophie had watched from the windows of the library. Several members of the Enclave had been killed cleaning out de Quincey's vampire nest. In name the funeral was for them, though they were also burying Thomas and Agatha. Charlotte had explained that Nephilim burials were generally for Nephilim only, but an exception could be made for those who had died in the service of the Clave.

Sophie and Tessa, though, had been forbidden to go. The ceremony itself was still closed to them. Sophie had told Tessa it was better anyway, that she did not want to see Thomas burn and his ashes scattered in the Silent City. "I would rather remember him as he was," she'd said, "and Agatha, too."

The Enclave had left a guard behind them, several Shadowhunters who had volunteered to stay and watch over the Institute. It would be a long time, Tessa thought, before they ever left it unguarded again.

She had passed the time while they were gone reading in the window alcove—nothing to do with Nephilim or demons or Downworlders, but a copy of *A Tale of Two Cities* that she'd found on Charlotte's shelf of Dickens books. She had resolutely tried to force herself not to think about Mortmain, about Thomas and Agatha, about the things Mortmain had said to her in the Sanctuary—and most especially, not about Nathaniel or where he might be now. Any thought of her brother made her stomach tighten and the backs of her eyes prickle.

Nor was that all that was on her mind. Two days before, she had been forced to appear before the Clave in the library of the Institute. A man the others called the Inquisitor had questioned her about her time with Mortmain, over and over, alert for any changes in her story, until she was exhausted. They had questioned her about the watch he had wanted to give her, and whether she knew who it had belonged to, or what the initials

J. T. S. might stand for. She did not, and as he had taken it with him when he'd vanished, she pointed out, that was unlikely to change. They had questioned Will, too, about what Mortmain had said to him before he'd disappeared. Will had borne the inquest with surly impatience, to no one's surprise, and had eventually been dismissed with sanctions, for rudeness and insubordination.

The Inquisitor had even demanded that Tessa strip off her clothes, that she might be searched for a warlock's mark, but Charlotte had put a quick stop to that. When Tessa had at last been allowed to go, she had hurried out into the corridor after Will, but he had gone. It had been two days since then, and in that time she had hardly seen him, nor had they spoken beyond the occasional polite exchange of words in front of others. When she had looked at him, he had looked away. When she had left the room, hoping he would follow, he hadn't. It had been maddening.

She couldn't help but wonder if she was alone in thinking that something significant had passed between them there on the floor of the Sanctuary. She had woken out of a darkness more profound than any she had encountered during a Change before, to find Will holding her, the most plainly distraught look she could have envisioned on his face. And surely she couldn't have imagined the way he'd said her name, or looked at her?

No. She could not have imagined that. Will cared for her, she was sure of it. Yes, he had been rude to her almost since he had met her, but then, that happened in novels all the time. Look how rude Darcy had been to Elizabeth Bennet before he'd proposed, and really, quite rude during as well. And

Heathcliff was never anything but rude to Cathy. Though she had to admit that in *A Tale of Two Cities*, both Sydney Carton and Charles Darnay had been very kind to Lucie Manette. *And yet I have had the weakness, and have still the weakness, to wish you to know with what a sudden mastery you kindled me, heap of ashes that I am, into fire. . . .*

The troubling fact was that since that night in the Sanctuary, Will had neither looked at her nor said her name again. She thought she knew the reason for it—had guessed at it in the way Charlotte had looked at her, the way everyone was being so quiet around her. It was evident. The Shadowhunters were going to send her away.

And why shouldn't they? The Institute was for Nephilim, not Downworlders. She had brought death and destruction down on the place in the short time she'd been here; God only knew what would happen if she remained. Of course, she had nowhere to go, and no one to go *to*, but why should that matter to them? Covenant Law was Covenant Law; it could not be changed or broken. Maybe she would wind up living with Jessamine after all, in some town house in Belgravia. There were worse fates.

The rattle of carriage wheels on the cobblestones outside, signaling the return of the others from the Silent City, brought her out of her glum reverie. Sophie hurried down the stairs to greet them while Tessa watched through the window as they left the carriage, one by one.

Henry had his arm around Charlotte, who was leaning against him. Then came Jessamine, with pale flowers wound through her fair hair. Tessa would have admired how she looked, had she not held the sneaking suspicion that Jessamine probably enjoyed funerals because she knew she appeared especially pretty in white. Then came Jem, and then Will, looking like two chess pieces from some odd game, both Jem's silver hair and Will's tangled black locks set off by the pallor of their clothes. White Knight and Black Knight, Tessa thought as they went up the steps and vanished into the Institute.

She had only just set her book down on the seat beside her when the library door opened and Charlotte came in, still pulling off her gloves. Her hat was gone, and her brown hair stood out around her face in humidity-frizzed curls.

"I rather thought I'd find you in here," she said, crossing the room to sink into a chair opposite Tessa's window seat. She dropped the white kid gloves on the nearby table and sighed.

"Was it . . . ?" Tessa began.

"Awful? Yes. I hate funerals, though the Angel knows I've been to dozens." Charlotte paused and bit her lip. "I sound like Jessamine. Forget that I said that, Tessa. Sacrifice and death are part of the Shadowhunting life, and I have always accepted that."

"I know." It was very quiet. Tessa imagined she could feel her heart beating hollowly, like the tick of a grandfather clock in a great empty room.

"Tessa . . . ," Charlotte began.

"I already know what you are going to say, Charlotte, and it is quite all right."

Charlotte blinked. "You do? It . . . is?"

"You want me to go," Tessa said. "I know that you met with the Clave before the funeral. Jem told me. I can't imagine they would think you should allow me to remain. After all the trouble and the dreadfulness I've brought down on you. Nate. Thomas and Agatha—"

"The Clave does not care about Thomas and Agatha."

"The Pyxis, then."

"Yes," Charlotte said slowly. "Tessa, I think you have entirely the wrong idea. I didn't come to ask you to leave; I came to ask you to stay."

"To stay?" The words seemed disconnected from any meaning. Surely Charlotte could not have meant what she'd said. "But the Clave . . . They must be angry. . . ."

"They *are* angry," said Charlotte. "With Henry and me. We were utterly taken in by Mortmain. He used us as his instruments, and we allowed it. I was so proud of the clever and handy way I had taken charge of him that I never stopped to think that perhaps he was the one taking charge. I never stopped to think that not a single living creature other than Mortmain and your brother had ever confirmed that de Quincey was the Magister. All the other evidence was circumstantial, and yet I let myself be convinced."

"It was very convincing." Tessa hastened to reassure Charlotte. "The seal we found on Miranda's body. The creatures on the bridge."

Charlotte made a bitter sound. "All characters in a play that Mortmain put on for our benefit. Do you know that, search as we have, we have not been able to find a scrap of evidence as to what other Downworlders controlled the Pandemonium Club? None of the mundane members have a clue, and since we destroyed de Quincey's clan, the Downworlders are more distrustful of us than ever."

"But it's only been a few days. It took Will six weeks to find the Dark Sisters. If you keep looking . . ."

"We don't have that much time. If what Nathaniel said

to Jem was true, and Mortmain plans to use the demon energies inside the Pyxis to animate his clockwork mannequins,
we have only the time it will take him to learn to open the
box." She shrugged a little. "Of course, the Clave believes that
is impossible. The Pyxis can be opened only with runes, and
only a Shadowhunter can draw them. But then again, only a
Shadowhunter ought to have been able to gain access to the
Institute."

"Mortmain is very clever."

"Yes." Charlotte's hands were tightly knotted in her lap.
"Did you know that Henry is the one who told Mortmain about
the Pyxis? What it was called, and what it did?"

"No . . ." Tessa's reassuring words had deserted her.

"You couldn't. No one knows that. Only I do, and Henry. He
wants me to tell the Clave, but I won't. They already treat him
so badly, and I . . ." Charlotte's voice shook, but her small face
was set. "The Clave is convening a tribunal. My conduct, and
Henry's, will be examined and voted upon. It is possible that we
will lose the Institute."

Tessa was appalled. "But you're wonderful at running the
Institute! The way you keep everything organized and in place,
the way you manage it all."

Charlotte's eyes were wet. "Thank you, Tessa. The fact is
that Benedict Lightwood has always wanted the place of head
of the Institute for himself, or for his son. The Lightwoods have
a great deal of family pride and despise taking orders. If not for
the fact that Consul Wayland himself named my husband and
me as the successors to my father, I am sure Benedict *would* be
in charge. All I have ever wanted is to run the Institute, Tessa. I
will do anything to keep it. If you would only help me—"

"Me? But what can I do? I know nothing of Shadowhunter politics."

"The alliances we forge with Downworlders are some of our most priceless assets, Tessa. Part of the reason I am still where I am is my affiliation with warlocks such as Magnus Bane and vampires such as Camille Belcourt. And you, you are a precious commodity. What you can do has already helped the Enclave once; the aid you could offer us in future could be incalculable. And if you are known to be a firm ally of mine, it will only help me."

Tessa held her breath. In her mind she saw Will—Will as he had looked in the Sanctuary—but, almost to her surprise, he was not all that her thoughts contained. There was Jem, with his kindness and gentle hands; and Henry making her laugh with his odd clothes and funny inventions; and even Jessamine, with her peculiar fierceness and occasional surprising bravery.

"But the Law," she said in a small voice.

"There is no Law against you remaining here as our guest," said Charlotte. "I have searched the archives and have found nothing that would prevent you from staying, if you consented. So do you consent, Tessa? Will you stay?"

Tessa dashed up the steps to the attic; for the first time in what felt like forever, her heart was almost light. The attic itself was much as she remembered, the high small windows letting in a little sunset light, for it was almost twilight now. There was a tipped-over pail on the floor; she maneuvered around it on her way to the narrow steps that led up to the roof.

He is often to be found there when he is troubled, Charlotte had said. *And I have rarely seen Will so troubled. The loss of*

Thomas and Agatha has been more difficult for him than I foresaw.

The steps ended in a square overhead door, hinged on one side. Tessa pushed the trapdoor open, and climbed out onto the Institute's roof.

Straightening, she looked around. She stood in the wide, flat center of the roof, which was surrounded by a waist-high wrought iron railing. The bars of the railing ended in finials shaped like sharpened fleur-de-lis. At the far end of the roof stood Will, leaning against the railing. He did not turn, even as the trapdoor swung shut behind her and she took a step forward, rubbing her scratched palms against the fabric of her dress.

"Will," she said.

He did not move. The sun had begun to set in a torrent of fire. Across the Thames, factory smokestacks belched smoke that trailed dark fingers across the red sky. Will was leaning on the railing as if he were exhausted, as if he intended to fall forward across the javelin-sharp finials and end it all. He gave no sign of hearing Tessa as she approached and moved to stand beside him. From here the steeply pitched roof fell away to a dizzying view of the cobblestones below.

"Will," she said again. "What are you doing?"

He did not look at her. He was staring out at the city, a black outline against the reddened sky. The dome of St. Paul's shone through the mucky air, and the Thames ran like dark strong tea below it, bracketed here and there with the black lines of bridges. Dark shapes moved by the river's edge—mudlarks, searching through the filth thrown up by the water, hoping to find something valuable to sell.

"I remember now," Will said without looking at her, "what it was I was trying to remember the other day. It was Blake. '*And I behold London, a Human awful wonder of God.*'" He stared out over the landscape. "Milton thought Hell was a city, you know. I think maybe he had it half-right. Perhaps London is just Hell's entrance, and we are the damned souls refusing to pass through, fearing that what we will find on the other side will be worse than the horror we already know."

"Will." Tessa was bewildered. "Will, what is it, what's wrong?"

He gripped the railing with both hands, his fingers whitening. His hands were covered with cuts and scratches, his knuckles scraped red and black. There were bruises on his face, too, darkening the line of his jaw, purpling the skin under his eye. His lower lip was split and swollen, and he had done nothing to heal any of it. She could not imagine why.

"I should have known," he said. "That it was a trick. That Mortmain was lying when he came here. Charlotte so often vaunts my skill at tactics, but a good tactician is not blindly trusting. I was a fool."

"Charlotte believes it's her fault. Henry believes it's his fault. I believe it's *my* fault," Tessa said impatiently. "We can't all have the luxury of blaming ourselves, now, can we?"

"Your fault?" Will sounded puzzled. "Because Mortmain is obsessed with you? That hardly seems—"

"For bringing Nathaniel here," Tessa said. Just saying it out loud made her feel as if her chest were being squeezed. "For urging you to trust him."

"You loved him," said Will. "He was your brother."

"He still is," Tessa said. "And I still love him. But I know what he is. I always did know what he was. I just didn't want to believe it. I suppose we all lie to ourselves sometimes."

"Yes." Will sounded tight and distant. "I suppose we do."

Quickly Tessa said, "I came up here because I have good news, Will. Won't you let me tell you what it is?"

"Tell me." His voice was dead.

"Charlotte says I can stay here," Tessa said. "At the Institute." Will said nothing.

"She said there's no Law against it," Tessa went on, a little bewildered now. "So I won't need to leave."

"Charlotte would never have made you leave, Tessa. She cannot bear to abandon even a fly caught in a spider's web. She would not have abandoned you." There was no life in Will's voice and no feeling. He was simply stating a fact.

"I thought . . ." Tessa's elation was fading quickly. "That you would be at least a little pleased. I thought we were becoming friends." She saw the line of his throat move as he swallowed, hard, his hands tensing again on the rail. "As a friend," she went on, her voice dropping, "I have come to admire you, Will. To care for you." She reached out, meaning to touch his hand, but she drew back, startled by the tension in his posture, the whiteness of the knuckles that gripped the metal railing. The red mourning Marks stood out, scarlet against the whitened skin, as if they had been cut there with knives. "I thought perhaps . . ."

At last Will turned to look directly at her. Tessa was shocked at the expression on his face. The shadows under his eyes were so dark, they looked hollow.

She stood and stared at him, willing him to say what the hero in a book would say now, at this moment. *Tessa, my feel-*

*ings for you have grown beyond mere feelings of friendship. They
are so much more rare and precious than that. . . .*

"Come here," he said instead. There was nothing welcoming in his voice, or in the way he stood. Tessa fought back her
instinct to shy away, and moved toward him, close enough
for him to touch her. He reached out his hands and touched
her hair lightly, brushing back the stray curls around her face.
"Tess."

She looked up at him. His eyes were the same color as
the smoke-stained sky; even bruised, his face was beautiful.
She wanted to be touching him, wanted it in some inchoate,
instinctive way she could neither explain nor control. When
he bent to kiss her, it was all she could do to hold herself back
until his lips met hers. His mouth brushed hers and she tasted
salt on him, the tang of bruised and tender skin where his lip
was cut. He took her by the shoulders and pulled her closer to
him, his fingers knotting in the fabric of her dress. Even more
than in the attic, she felt caught in the eddy of a powerful wave
that threatened to pull her over and under, to crush and break
her, to wear her down to softness as the sea might wear down
a piece of glass.

She reached to lay her hands on his shoulders, and he drew
back, looking down at her, breathing very hard. His eyes were
bright, his lips red and swollen now from kissing as well as
injuries.

"Perhaps," he said, "we should discuss our arrangements,
then."

Tessa, still feeling as if she were drowning, whispered,
"Arrangements?"

"If you are going to be staying," he said, "it would be to our advantage to be discreet. It might perhaps be better to use your room. Jem tends to come in and out of mine as if he lives in the place, and he might be puzzled to find the door locked. Your quarters, on the other hand—"

"Use my room?" she echoed. "Use it for what?"

Will's mouth quirked up at the corner; Tessa, who had been thinking about how beautifully shaped his lips were, took a moment to realize with a sense of distant surprise that the smile was a very cold one. "You cannot pretend you don't know. . . . You are not entirely ignorant of the world, I think, Tessa. Not with that brother of yours."

"Will." The warmth was going out of Tessa like the sea drawing back from the land; she felt cold, despite the summer air. "I am not like my brother."

"You care for me," Will said. His voice was cool and sure. "And you know that I admire you, the way that all women know when a man admires them. Now you have come to tell me you will be here, available to me, for as long as I might wish it. I am offering you what I thought you wanted."

"You cannot mean that."

"And you cannot have imagined I meant anything more," Will said. "There is no future for a Shadowhunter who dallies with warlocks. One might befriend them, employ them, but not . . ."

"Marry them?" Tessa said. There was a clear picture in her head of the sea. It had drawn back entirely from the shore, and she could see the small creatures it had left gasping in its wake, flapping and dying on the bare sand.

"How forward." Will smirked; she wanted to slap the expression off his face. "What did you really expect, Tessa?"

"I did not expect you to insult me." Tessa's voice threatened to shake; somehow, she kept it firm.

"It cannot be the unwanted consequences of a dalliance that concern you," Will mused. "Since warlocks are unable to have children—"

"What?" Tessa stepped back as if he had pushed her. The ground felt unsteady under her feet.

Will looked at her. The sun was nearly completely gone from the sky. In the near darkness the bones of his face looked prominent and the lines at the corners of his mouth were as harsh as if he were racked by physical pain. But his voice when he spoke was even. "You didn't know that? I thought someone would have told you."

"No," Tessa said softly. "No one told me."

His gaze was steady. "If you are not interested in my offer . . ."

"Stop," she said. This moment, she thought, was like the edge of a broken bit of glass, clear and sharp and painful. "Jem says you lie to make yourself look bad," she said. "And perhaps that is true, or perhaps he simply wishes to believe that about you. But there is no reason or excuse for cruelty like this."

For a moment he looked actually unnerved, as if she had truly startled him. The expression was gone in an instant, like the shifting shape of a cloud. "Then there is nothing more for me to say, is there?"

Without another word she spun on her heel and walked away from him, toward the steps that led back down into the Institute. She did not turn to see him looking after her, a still black silhouette against the last embers of the burning sky.

* * *

*Lilith's Children, known also by the name warlocks, are,
in the manner of mules and other crossbreeds, sterile. They
cannot produce offspring. No exceptions to this rule have
been noted....*

Tessa looked up from the *Codex* and stared, unseeing, out
the window of the music room, though it was too dark outside
for much of a view. She had taken refuge here, not wanting to
return to her own room, where she would eventually be discovered moping by Sophie or, worse, Charlotte. The thin layer of
dust over everything in this room reassured her that she was
much less likely to be found here.

She wondered how she had missed this fact about warlocks
before. To be fair, it was not in the *Codex*'s section on warlocks,
but rather in the later section on Downworld crossbreeds
such as half faeries and half werewolves. There were no half
warlocks, apparently. Warlocks could not have children. Will
hadn't been lying to hurt her; he'd been telling the truth. Which
seemed worse, in a way. He would have known that his words
weren't a light blow, easily resolved.

Perhaps he had been correct. What else had she really
thought would happen? Will was Will, and she should not have
expected him to be anything else. Sophie had warned her, and
still she hadn't listened. She knew what Aunt Harriet would
have said about girls who didn't listen to good advice.

A faint rustling sound broke into her brown study. She
turned, and at first saw nothing. The only light in the room
came from a single witchlight sconce. Its flickering light
played over the shape of the piano, the curving dark mass of
the harp covered with a heavy drop cloth. As she stared, two

bright points of light resolved themselves, close to the floor, an odd green-yellow color. They were moving toward her, both at the same pace, like twin will-o'-the-wisps.

Tessa expelled her held breath suddenly. *Of course.* She leaned forward. "Here, kitty." She made a coaxing noise. "Here, kitty, kitty!"

The cat's answering meow was lost in the noise of the door opening. Light streamed into the room, and for a moment the figure in the doorway was just a shadow. "Tessa? Tessa, is that you?"

Tessa knew the voice immediately—it was so near to the first thing he had ever said to her, the night she had walked into his room: *Will? Will, is that you?*

"Jem," she said resignedly. "Yes, it's me. Your cat seems to have wandered in here."

"I can't say that I'm surprised." Jem sounded amused. She could see him clearly now as he came into the room; witchlight from the corridor flooded in, and even the cat was clearly visible, sitting on the floor and washing its face with a paw. It looked angry, the way Persian cats always did. "He seems to be a bit of a gadabout. It's as if he demands to be introduced to everyone—" Jem broke off then, his eyes on Tessa's face. "What's wrong?"

Tessa was so taken off guard that she stammered. "W-why would you ask me that?"

"I can see it on your face. Something's happened." He sat down on the piano stool opposite her. "Charlotte told me the good news," he said as the cat rose to its feet and slunk across the room to him. "Or at least, I thought it was good news. Are you not pleased?"

"Of course I'm pleased."

"Hm." Jem looked unconvinced. Bending down, he held out his hand to the cat, who rubbed its head against the back of his fingers. "Good cat, Church."

"Church? Is that the cat's name?" Tessa was amused despite herself. "Goodness, didn't it used to be one of Mrs. Dark's familiars or some such thing? Perhaps Church isn't the best name for it!"

"*He*," Jem corrected with mock severity, "was not a familiar but a poor creature she planned to sacrifice as part of her necromantic spell casting. I wouldn't be surprised if he was now immortal, considering all the magic practiced on him. If nothing else, he ought to live a very long time. And Charlotte's been saying that we ought to keep him because it's good luck to have a cat in a church. So we started calling him "the church cat," and from that . . ." He shrugged. "Church. And if the name helps keep him out of trouble, so much the better."

"I do believe he's looking at me in a superior manner."

"Probably. Cats think they're superior to everyone." Jem scratched Church behind the ears. "What are you reading?"

Tessa showed him the *Codex*. "Will gave it to me. . . ."

Jem reached out and took it from her, with such deftness that Tessa had no time to draw her hand back. It was still open to the page she'd been studying. Jem glanced down at it, and then back up at her, his expression changing. "Did you not know this?"

She shook her head. "It is not so much that I dreamed of having children," she said. "I had not thought so far ahead in my life. It's more that this seems yet another thing that separates me from humanity. That makes me a monster. Something set apart."

Jem was silent for a long moment, his long fingers stroking the gray cat's fur. "Perhaps," he said, "it is not such a bad
thing to be set apart." He leaned forward. "Tessa, you know
that although it seems you are a warlock, you have an ability
we have never seen before. You carry no warlock's mark. With
so much about you uncertain, you cannot allow this one piece
of information to drive you to despair."

"I am not despairing," Tessa said. "It's just— I have been
lying awake these past few nights. Thinking about my parents.
I barely remember them, you see. And yet I cannot help but
wonder. Mortmain said my mother did not know that my father
was a demon, but was he lying? He said she did not know what
she was, but what does that mean? Did she ever know what I
was, that I was not human? Is that why they left London as they
did, so secretively, under cover of darkness? If I am the result of
something—something hideous—that was done to my mother
without her knowing, then how could she ever have loved me?"

"They hid you from Mortmain," said Jem. "They must have
known he wanted you. All those years he searched for you, and
they kept you safe—first your parents, then your aunt. That is
not the act of an unloving family." His gaze was intent on her
face. "Tessa, I do not want to make you promises I cannot keep,
but if you truly wish to know the truth about your past, we
can seek it out. After all you have done for us, we owe you that
much. If there are secrets to be learned about how you came to
be what you are, we can learn them, if that is what you desire."

"Yes. That is what I want."

"You may not," said Jem, "like what you discover."

"It is better to know the truth." Tessa was surprised by the
conviction in her own voice. "I know the truth about Nate,

now, and painful as it is, it is better than being lied to. It is better than going on loving someone who cannot love me back. Better than wasting all that feeling." Her voice shook.

"I think he did," said Jem, "and does love you, in his way, but you cannot concern yourself with that. It is as great a thing to love as it is to be loved. Love is not something that can be wasted."

"It is hard. That is all." Tessa knew she was being self-pitying, but she could not seem to shake it off. "To be so alone."

Jem leaned forward and looked at her. The red Marks stood out like fire on his pale skin, making her think of the patterns that traced the edges of the Silent Brothers' robes. "My parents, like yours, are dead. So are Jessie's, and even Henry's and Charlotte's. Will's might as well be. I am not sure there is anyone in the Institute who is not without family. Otherwise we would not be here."

Tessa opened her mouth, and then closed it again. "I know," she said. "I am sorry. I was being perfectly selfish not to think—"

He held up a slender hand. "I am not blaming you," he said. "Perhaps you are here because you are otherwise alone, but so am I. So is Will. So is Jessamine. And even, to an extent, Charlotte and Henry. Where else could Henry have his laboratory? Where else would Charlotte be allowed to put her brilliant mind to work the way she can here? And though Jessamine pretends to hate everything, and Will would never admit to needing anything, they have both made homes for themselves here. In a way, we are not here just because we have nowhere else; we need nowhere else, because we have the Institute, and those who are in it are our family."

"But not *my* family."

"They could be," said Jem. "When I first came here, I was twelve years old. It most decidedly did not feel like home to me then. I saw only how London was not like Shanghai, and I was homesick. So Will went down to a shop in the East End and bought me this." He drew out the chain that hung around his neck, and Tessa saw that the flash of green she'd noticed before was a green stone pendant in the shape of a closed hand. "I think he liked it because it reminded him of a fist. But it was jade, and he knew jade came from China, so he brought it back to me and I hung it on a chain to wear it. I still wear it."

The mention of Will made Tessa's heart contract. "I suppose it is good to know he can be kind sometimes."

Jem looked at her with keen silver eyes. "When I came in—that look on your face—it wasn't just because of what you read in the *Codex*, was it? It was about Will. What did he say to you?"

Tessa hesitated. "He made it very clear that he didn't want me here," she said at last. "That my remaining at the Institute is not the happy chance I thought it was. Not in his view."

"And after I just finished telling you why you should consider him family," Jem said, a bit ruefully. "No wonder you looked as if I'd just told you something awful had happened."

"I'm sorry," Tessa whispered.

"Don't be. It's Will who ought to be sorry." Jem's eyes darkened. "We shall throw him out onto the streets," he proclaimed. "I promise you he'll be gone by morning."

Tessa started and sat upright. "Oh—no, you can't mean that—"

He grinned. "Of course I don't. But you felt better for a moment there, didn't you?"

"It was like a beautiful dream," Tessa said gravely, but she smiled when she said it, which surprised her.

"Will is . . . difficult," Jem said. "But family is difficult. If I didn't think the Institute was the best place for you, Tessa, I would not say that it was. And one can build one's own family. I know you feel inhuman, and as if you are set apart, away from life and love, but . . ." His voice cracked a little, the first time Tessa had heard him sound unsure. He cleared his throat. "I promise you, the right man won't care."

Before Tessa could reply, there was a sharp tapping against the glass of the window. She looked toward Jem, who shrugged. He heard it too. Crossing the room, she saw that indeed there was something outside—a dark winged shape, like a small bird struggling to get inside. She tried to lift the window sash, but it seemed stuck.

She turned, but Jem had already appeared at her side, and he pushed the window open. As the dark shape fluttered inside, it flew straight for Tessa. She raised her hands and caught it out of the air, feeling the sharp metal wings flutter against her palms. As she held it, they closed, and its eyes closed too. Once more it held its metal sword quietly, as if waiting to be wakened again. *Tick-tick* went its clockwork heart against her fingers.

Jem turned from the open window, the wind ruffling his hair. In the yellow light, it shone like white gold. "What is it?"

Tessa smiled. "My angel," she said.

EPILOGUE

It had grown late, and Magnus Bane's eyelids were drooping with exhaustion. He set Horace's *Odes* down upon the end table and gazed thoughtfully at the rain-streaked windows that looked out onto the square.

This was Camille's house, but tonight she was not in it; it seemed to Magnus unlikely that she would be home again for many more nights, if not for longer. She had left the city after that disastrous night at de Quincey's, and though he had sent her a message telling her it was safe to return, he doubted she would. He could not help but wonder if, now that she had exacted revenge on her vampire clan, she would still desire his company. Perhaps he had only ever been something to throw in de Quincey's face.

He could always depart—pack up and go, leave all this borrowed luxury behind him. This house, the servants, the books, even his clothes, were hers; he had come to London with nothing. It wasn't as if Magnus couldn't earn his own money. He had been quite wealthy in the past, on occasion, though having too much money usually bored him. But remaining here, however annoying, was still the most likely path to seeing Camille again.

A knock on the door broke him out of his reverie, and he turned to see Archer, the footman, standing in the doorway. Archer had been Camille's subjugate for years, and regarded Magnus with loathing, likely because he felt that a liaison with a warlock wasn't the right sort of attachment for his beloved mistress.

"There's someone to see you, sir." Archer lingered over the word "sir" just long enough for it to be insulting.

"At this hour? Who is it?"

"One of the Nephilim." A faint distaste colored Archer's words. "He says his business with you is urgent."

So it wasn't Charlotte, the only one of the London Nephilim that Magnus might have expected to see. For several days now he had been assisting the Enclave, watching while they questioned terrified mundanes who had been members of the Pandemonium Club, and using magic to remove the mundanes' memories of the ordeal when it was over. An unpleasant job, but the Clave always paid well, and it was wise to remain in their favor.

"He is," Archer added, with deepening distaste, "also very wet."

"Wet?"

"It is raining, sir, and the gentleman is not wearing a hat. I offered to dry his clothes, but he declined."

"Very well. Send him in."

Archer's lips thinned. "He is waiting for you in the parlor. I thought he might wish to warm himself by the fire."

Magnus sighed inwardly. He could, of course, demand that Archer show the guest into the library, a room he preferred. But it seemed like a great deal of effort for little return, and besides, if he did, the footman would sulk for the next three days. "Very well."

Gratified, Archer melted away, leaving Magnus to make his own way to the parlor. The door was closed, but he could see from the light that gleamed beneath the door that there was a fire, and light, inside the room. He pushed the door open.

The parlor had been Camille's favorite room and bore her decorating touches. The walls were painted a lush burgundy, the rosewood furniture imported from China. The windows that otherwise would have looked out onto the square were covered with velvet curtains that hung straight from floor to ceiling, blocking out any light. Someone was standing in front of the fireplace, his hands behind his back—a slender someone with dark hair. When he turned, Magnus recognized him immediately.

Will Herondale.

He was, as Archer had said, wet, in the manner of someone who did not care one way or another whether it rained on him or not. His clothes were drenched, his hair hanging in his eyes. Water streaked his face like tears.

"William," Magnus said, honestly surprised. "What on earth are you doing here? Has something happened at the Institute?"

"No." Will's voice sounded as if he were choking. "I'm here on my own account. I need your help. There is—there is absolutely no one else that I can ask."

"Really." Magnus looked at the boy more closely. Will was beautiful; Magnus had been in love many times throughout the years, and normally beauty of any sort moved him, but Will's never had. There was something dark about the boy, something hidden and strange that was hard to admire. He seemed to show nothing real to the world. Yet now, under his dripping black hair, he was as white as parchment, his hands clenched at his sides so tightly that they were shaking. It seemed clear that some terrible turmoil was ripping him apart from the inside out.

Magnus reached behind himself and locked the parlor door. "Very well," he said. "Why don't you tell me what the problem is?"

A NOTE ON TESSA'S LONDON

The London of *Clockwork Angel* is, as much as I could make it, an admixture of the real and the unreal, the famous and the forgotten. The geography of real Victorian London is preserved as much as possible, but there were times that wasn't possible. For those wondering about the Institute: There was indeed a church called All-Hallows-the-Less that burned in the Great Fire of London in 1666; it was located, however, in Upper Thames Street, not where I have placed it, just off Fleet Street. Those familiar with London will recognize the location of the Institute, and the shape of its spire, as that of the famous St. Bride's Church, beloved of newspapermen and journalists, which goes unmentioned in *Clockwork* as the Institute has taken its place. There is no Carleton Square in reality, though there is a Carlton Square; Blackfriars Bridge, Hyde Park, the Strand—even Gunther's ice cream shop—all existed and are presented to the best of my researching abilities. Sometimes I think all cities have a shadow self, where the memory of great events and great places lingers after those places themselves are gone. To that end, there *was* a Devil Tavern on Fleet Street and Chancery, where Samuel Pepys and Dr. Samuel Johnson drank, but though it was demolished in 1787, I like to think Will can visit its shadow self in 1878.

A NOTE ON THE POETRY

The poetry quotations at the beginning of each chapter are by and large taken from poetry Tessa would be familiar with, either of her era, or a staple from before it. The exceptions are the poems by Wilde and Kipling—still Victorian poets, but dating later than the 1870s—and the poem by Elka Cloke at the beginning of the volume, "Thames River Song," which was written specifically for this book. A longer version of the poem can be found at the author's website: ElkaCloke.com.

Acknowledgments

Much thanks for familial support from my mother and father, as well as Jim Hill and Kate Connor; Nao, Tim, David, and Ben; Melanie, Jonathan, and Helen Lewis; Florence and Joyce. To those who read and critiqued and pointed out anachronisms—Clary, Eve Sinaiko, Sarah Smith, Delia Sherman, Holly Black, Sarah Rees Brennan, Justine Larbalestier—tons of thanks. And thanks to those whose smiling faces and snarky remarks keep me going another day: Elka Cloke, Holly Black, Robin Wasserman, Maureen Johnson, Libba Bray, and Sarah Rees Brennan. Thanks to Margie Longoria for her support of Project Book Babe. Thanks to Lisa Gold: Research Maven (http://lisagoldresearch.wordpress.com) for her help in digging up hard-to-find primary sources. My always-gratitude to my agent, Barry Goldblatt; my editor, Karen Wojtyla; and the teams at Simon & Schuster and Walker Books for making it all happen. And lastly, my thanks to Josh, who did a lot of laundry while I was doing revisions on this book, and only complained some of the time.

Continue Tessa, Will, and Jem's adventures in

Clockwork Prince,

BOOK TWO OF THE INFERNAL DEVICES.

PROLOGUE:
The Outcast Dead

The fog was thick, muffling sound and sight; where it parted, Will Herondale could see the street rising ahead of him, slick and wet and black with rain, and hear the voices of the dead.

Not all Shadowhunters could hear ghosts, unless the ghosts chose to be heard, but Will was one of the few who could. As he approached the old cemetery, their voices rose in a ragged musical chorus: wails and pleading, cries and snarls. This was not a peaceful burial ground, but Will knew that; it was not his first visit to the Cross Bones Graveyard near London Bridge. He did his best to block out the noises, hunching his shoulders so that his collar covered his ears, his head down, a fine mist of rain dampening his black hair.

The entrance was halfway down the block: a pair of wrought iron gates set into a high stone wall. Any mundane passing by could see the thick chain that bound the gates shut, and the sign declaring the premises closed—it had been fifteen years since a body was buried here. As Will neared the gates, something no mundane would have seen materialized out of the fog: a great bronze knocker in the shape of a hand, the fingers bony and skeletal. With a grimace, Will reached out one of his own gloved hands and lifted the knocker, letting it fall once, twice, three times, the hollow clank resounding through the night like the rattling chains of Marley's ghost.

Beyond the gates, mist rose like steam from the ground, obscuring the grave markers and long, uneven plots of earth between them. Slowly the mist began to coalesce, taking on an eerie blue glow. Will put his hands to the bars of the gate; the cold of the metal seeped through his gloves, into his bones, and he shivered. It was a more than ordinary cold—when ghosts rose, they drew energy from their surroundings, depriving the air and space around them of heat. The hairs of the back of Will's neck prickled and stood up as the blue mist formed slowly into the shape of an old woman in a ragged dress and white apron, her head bent.

"Hallo, Mol," said Will. "You're looking particularly fine this evening, if I do say so."

The ghost raised her head. Old Molly was a strong spirit, one of the stronger Will had encountered. Even as moonlight speared through a gap in the clouds, she hardly looked transparent: her body was solid, her hair twisted in a thick yellow-gray coil over one shoulder, her rough, red hands braced on her hips. Only her eyes were hollow, twin blue flames flickering in their depths.

"William Herondale," she said. "Back again so soon?"

She moved toward the gate with that gliding motion peculiar to ghosts. Her feet were bare and filthy, despite the fact that they never touched the ground.

Will leaned against the gate. "You know I missed your pretty face."

She grinned, her eyes flickering, and he caught a glimpse of the skull beneath the half-transparent skin. Overhead, the clouds had closed in on each other again, black and roiling, blocking out the moon. Idly, Will wondered what Old Molly had done to get herself buried here, far from consecrated ground. Most of the whispering voices of the dead belonged to prostitutes, suicides, and stillbirths—those outcast dead who could not be buried in a churchyard. Although Molly had managed to make the situation quite profitable for herself, so perhaps she didn't mind.

She chortled. "What d'you want then, young Shadowhunter? Malphas venom? I 'ave the talon of a Morax demon, polished very fine, the poison at the tip entirely invisible—"

"No," Will said. "That's not what I need. I need Foraii demon powders, ground fine."

Molly turned her head to the side and spat a tendril of blue fire. "Now what's a fine young man like you want with stuff like that?"

Will just sighed inwardly; Molly's protests were part of the bargaining process. Magnus had already sent Will to Old Mol several times now, once for black stinking candles that stuck to his skin like tar, once for the bones of an unborn child, and once for a bag of faeries' eyes which had dripped blood on his shirt. Foraii demon powder sounded pleasant by comparison.

"You think I'm a fool," Molly went on. "This is a trap, innit?

You Nephilim catch me selling that sort of stuff, an' it's the stick for Old Mol, it is."

"You're *already* dead." Will did his best not to sound irritable. "I don't know what you think the Clave could do to you now."

"Pah." Her hollow eyes flamed. "The prisons of the Silent Brothers, beneath the earth, can 'old either the living or the dead; you know that, Will Herondale."

Will held his hands up. "No tricks, old one. Surely you must have heard the rumors running about Downworld. The Clave has other things on its mind than tracking down ghosts who traffic in demon powders and faerie blood." He leaned forward. "I'll give you a good price." He drew a cambric bag from his pocket and dangled it in the air. It clinked like coins rattling together. "They all fit your description, Mol."

An eager look came over her dead face, and she solidified enough to take the bag from him. She plunged one hand into it and brought her palm out full of rings—gold wedding rings, each tied in a lover's knot at the top. Old Mol, like many ghosts, was always looking for that talisman, than lost piece of her past that would finally allow her to die, the anchor that kept her trapped in the world. In her case, it was her wedding ring. It was common belief, Magnus had told Will, that the ring was long gone, buried under the silty bed of the Thames, but in the meantime she'd take any bag of found rings on the hope one would turn out to be hers. So far it hadn't happened.

She dropped the rings back into the bag, which vanished somewhere on her undead person, and handed him a folded sachet of powder in return. He slipped it into his jacket pocket just as the ghost began to shimmer and fade. "Hold up, there, Mol. That isn't all I have come for, tonight."

The spirit flickered while greed warred with impatience and the effort of remaining visible. Finally, she grunted. "Very well. What else d'you want?"

Will hesitated. This was not something Magnus had sent him for; it was something he wanted to know for himself. "Love potions—"

Old Mol screeched with laughter. "*Love potions? For Will Herondale?* T'aint my way to turn down payment, but any man who looks like you has got no need of love potions, and that's a fact."

"No," Will said, a little desperation in his voice, "I was looking for the opposite, really—something that might put an end to being in love."

"An 'atred potion?" Mol still sounded amused.

"I was hoping for something more akin to indifference? Toleration . . . ?"

She made a snorting noise, astonishingly human for a ghost. "I 'ardly like to tell you this, Nephilim, but if you want a girl to 'ate you, there's easy enough ways of making it 'appen. You don't need *my* help with the poor thing."

And with that, she vanished, spinning away into the mists among the graves. Will, looking after her, sighed. "Not for her," he said, under his breath, though there was no one to hear him, "for *me* . . ." and he leaned his head against the cold iron gate.

See where the adventure begins in

City of Bones,

BOOK ONE OF THE MORTAL INSTRUMENTS.

PANDEMONIUM

"You've got to be kidding me," the bouncer said, folding his arms across his massive chest. He stared down at the boy in the red zip-up jacket and shook his shaved head. "You can't bring that thing in here."

The fifty or so teenagers in line outside the Pandemonium Club leaned forward to eavesdrop. It was a long wait to get into the all-ages club, especially on a Sunday, and not much generally happened in line. The bouncers were fierce and would come down instantly on anyone who looked like they were going to start trouble. Fifteen-year-old Clary Fray, standing in line with her best friend, Simon, leaned forward along with everyone else, hoping for some excitement.

"Aw, come on." The kid hoisted the thing up over his head. It looked like a wooden beam, pointed at one end. "It's part of my costume."

The bouncer raised an eyebrow. "Which is what?"

The boy grinned. He was normal-enough-looking, Clary thought, for Pandemonium. He had electric blue dyed hair that stuck up around his head like the tentacles of a startled octopus, but no elaborate facial tattoos or big metal bars through his ears or lips. "I'm a vampire hunter." He pushed down on the wooden thing. It bent as easily as a blade of grass bending sideways. "It's fake. Foam rubber. See?"

The boy's wide eyes were way too bright a green, Clary noticed: the color of antifreeze, spring grass. Colored contact lenses, probably. The bouncer shrugged, abruptly bored. "Whatever. Go on in."

The boy slid past him, quick as an eel. Clary liked the lilt to his shoulders, the way he tossed his hair as he went. There was a word for him that her mother would have used—*insouciant*.

"You thought he was cute," said Simon, sounding resigned. "Didn't you?"

Clary dug her elbow into his ribs, but didn't answer.

Inside, the club was full of dry-ice smoke. Colored lights played over the dance floor, turning it into a multicolored fairyland of blues and acid greens, hot pinks and golds.

The boy in the red jacket stroked the long razor-sharp blade in his hands, an idle smile playing over his lips. It had been so easy—a little bit of a glamour on the blade, to make it look harmless. Another glamour on his eyes, and the moment the bouncer had looked straight at him, he was in. Of course, he could probably have gotten by without all that trouble, but it was part of the fun—fooling the mundies, doing it all out in the open right in front of them, getting off on the blank looks on their sheeplike faces.

Not that the humans didn't have their uses. The boy's green eyes scanned the dance floor, where slender limbs clad in scraps of silk and black leather appeared and disappeared inside the revolving columns of smoke as the mundies danced. Girls tossed their long hair, boys swung their leather-clad hips, and bare skin glittered with sweat. Vitality just *poured* off them, waves of energy that filled him with a drunken dizziness. His lip curled. They didn't know how lucky they were. They didn't know what it was like to eke out life in a dead world, where the sun hung limp in the sky like a burned cinder. Their lives burned as brightly as candle flames—and were as easy to snuff out.

His hand tightened on the blade he carried, and he had begun to step out onto the dance floor when a girl broke away from the mass of dancers and began walking toward him. He stared at her. She was beautiful, for a human—long hair nearly the precise color of black ink, charcoaled eyes. Floor-length white gown, the kind women used to wear when this world was younger. Lace sleeves belled out around her slim arms. Around her neck was a thick silver chain, on which hung a dark red pendant the size of a baby's fist. He only had to narrow his eyes to know that it was real—real and precious. His mouth started to water as she neared him. Vital energy pulsed from her like blood from an open wound. She smiled, passing him, beckoning with her eyes. He turned to follow her, tasting the phantom sizzle of her death on his lips.

It was always easy. He could already feel the power of her evaporating life coursing through his veins like fire. Humans were so stupid. They had something so precious, and they barely safeguarded it at all. They threw away their lives for money, for packets of powder, for a stranger's charming smile. The girl was a pale ghost retreating through the colored smoke. She reached the wall and turned, bunching her skirt up in her hands, lifting it as she grinned at him. Under the skirt, she was wearing thigh-high boots.

He sauntered up to her, his skin prickling with her nearness. Up close she wasn't so perfect: He could see the mascara smudged under her eyes, the sweat sticking her hair to her neck. He could smell her mortality, the sweet rot of corruption. *Got you*, he thought.

A cool smile curled her lips. She moved to the side, and he could see that she was leaning against a closed door. NO ADMITTANCE—STORAGE was scrawled across it in red paint. She reached behind her for the knob, turned it, slid inside. He caught a glimpse of stacked boxes, tangled wiring. A storage room. He glanced behind him—no one was looking. So much the better if she wanted privacy.

He slipped into the room after her, unaware that he was being followed.

"So," Simon said, "pretty good music, eh?"

Clary didn't reply. They were dancing, or what passed for it—a lot of swaying back and forth with occasional lunges toward the floor as if one of them had dropped a contact lens— in a space between a group of teenage boys in metallic corsets, and a young Asian couple who were making out passionately, their colored hair extensions tangled together like vines. A boy with a lip piercing and a teddy bear backpack was handing out free tablets of herbal ecstasy, his parachute pants flapping in the breeze from the wind machine. Clary wasn't paying much attention to their immediate surroundings—her eyes were on the blue-haired boy who'd talked his way into the club. He was prowling through the crowd as if he were looking for something. There was something about the way he moved that reminded her of something . . .

"I, for one," Simon went on, "am enjoying myself immensely."

This seemed unlikely. Simon, as always, stuck out at the club like a sore thumb, in jeans and an old T-shirt that said MADE IN BROOKLYN across the front. His freshly scrubbed hair was dark brown instead of green or pink, and his glasses perched crookedly on the end of his nose. He looked less as if he were contemplating the powers of darkness and more as if he were on his way to chess club.

"Mmm-hmm." Clary knew perfectly well that he came to Pandemonium with her only because she liked it, that he thought it was boring. She wasn't even sure why it was that she liked it—the clothes, the music made it like a dream, someone else's life, not her boring real life at all. But she was always too shy to talk to anyone but Simon.

The blue-haired boy was making his way off the dance floor. He looked a little lost, as if he hadn't found whom he was looking for. Clary wondered what would happen if she went up and introduced herself, offered to show him around. Maybe he'd just stare at her. Or maybe he was shy too. Maybe he'd be grateful and pleased, and try not to show it, the way boys did—but she'd know. Maybe—

The blue-haired boy straightened up suddenly, snapping to attention, like a hunting dog on point. Clary followed the line of his gaze, and saw the girl in the white dress.

Oh, well, Clary thought, trying not to feel like a deflated party balloon. *I guess that's that.* The girl was gorgeous, the kind of girl Clary would have liked to draw—tall and ribbon-slim, with a long spill of black hair. Even at this distance Clary could see the red pendant around her throat. It pulsed under the lights of the dance floor like a separate, disembodied heart.

"I feel," Simon went on, "that this evening DJ Bat is doing a singularly exceptional job. Don't you agree?"

Clary rolled her eyes and didn't answer; Simon hated trance music. Her attention was on the girl in the white dress. Through the darkness, smoke, and artificial fog, her pale dress shone out like a beacon. No wonder the blue-haired boy was following her as if he were under a spell, too distracted to notice anything else around him—even the two dark shapes hard on his heels, weaving after him through the crowd.

Clary slowed her dancing and stared. She could just make out that the shapes were boys, tall and wearing black clothes. She couldn't have said how she knew that they were following the other boy, but she did. She could see it in the way they paced him, their careful watchfulness, the slinking grace of their movements. A small flower of apprehension began to open inside her chest.

"Meanwhile," Simon added, "I wanted to tell you that lately I've been cross-dressing. Also, I'm sleeping with your mom. I thought you should know."

The girl had reached the wall, and was opening a door marked NO ADMITTANCE. She beckoned the blue-haired boy after her, and they slipped through the door. It wasn't anything Clary hadn't seen before, a couple sneaking off to the dark corners of the club to make out—but that made it even weirder that they were being followed.

She raised herself up on tiptoe, trying to see over the crowd. The two guys had stopped at the door and seemed to be conferring with each other. One of them was blond, the other dark-haired. The blond one reached into his jacket and drew out something long and sharp that flashed under the strobing lights. A knife. "Simon!" Clary shouted, and seized his arm.

"What?" Simon looked alarmed. "I'm not really sleeping with your mom, you know. I was just trying to get your attention. Not that your mom isn't a very attractive woman, for her age."

"Do you see those guys?" She pointed wildly, almost hitting a curvy black girl who was dancing nearby. The girl shot her an evil look. "Sorry—sorry!" Clary turned back to Simon. "Do you see those two guys over there? By that door?"

Simon squinted, then shrugged. "I don't see anything."

"There are two of them. They were following the guy with the blue hair—"

"The one you thought was cute?"

"Yes, but that's not the point. The blond one pulled a knife."

"Are you *sure*?" Simon stared harder, shaking his head. "I still don't see anyone."

"I'm sure."

Suddenly all business, Simon squared his shoulders. "I'll get one of the security guards. You stay here." He strode away, pushing through the crowd.

Clary turned just in time to see the blond boy slip through the NO ADMITTANCE door, his friend right on his heels. She looked around; Simon was still trying to shove his way across the dance floor, but he wasn't making much progress. Even if she yelled now, no one would hear her, and by the time Simon got back, something terrible might *already* have happened. Biting hard on her lower lip, Clary started to wriggle through the crowd.

"What's your name?"

She turned and smiled. What faint light there was in the storage room spilled down through high barred windows smeared with dirt. Piles of electrical cables, along with broken bits of mirrored disco balls and discarded paint cans, littered the floor.

"Isabelle."

"That's a nice name." He walked toward her, stepping carefully among the wires in case any of them were live. In the faint light she looked half-transparent, bleached of color, wrapped in white like an angel. It would be a pleasure to make her fall. . . . "I haven't seen you here before."

"You're asking me if I come here often?" She giggled, covering her mouth with her hand. There was some sort of bracelet around her wrist, just under the cuff of her dress—then, as he neared her, he saw that it wasn't a bracelet at all but a pattern inked into her skin, a matrix of swirling lines.

He froze. "You—"

He didn't finish. She moved with lightning swiftness, striking out at him with her open hand, a blow to his chest that would have sent him down gasping if he'd been a human being. He staggered back, and now there was something in her hand, a coiling whip that glinted gold as she brought it down, curling around his ankles, jerking him off his feet. He hit the ground, writhing, the hated metal biting deep into his skin. She laughed, standing over him, and dizzily he thought that he should have *known*. No human girl would wear a dress like the one Isabelle wore. She'd worn it to cover her skin—all of her skin.

Isabelle yanked hard on the whip, securing it. Her smile glittered like poisonous water. "He's all yours, boys."

A low laugh sounded behind him, and now there were hands on him, hauling him upright, throwing him against one of the concrete pillars. He could feel the damp stone under his back. His hands were pulled behind him, his wrists bound with wire. As he struggled, someone walked around the side of the pillar into his view: a boy, as young as Isabelle and just as pretty. His tawny eyes glittered like chips of amber. "So," the boy said. "Are there any more with you?"

The blue-haired boy could feel blood welling up under the too-tight metal, making his wrists slippery. "Any other what?"

"Come on now." The tawny-eyed boy held up his hands, and his dark sleeves slipped down, showing the runes inked all over his wrists, the backs of his hands, his palms. "You know what I am."

Far back inside his skull, the shackled boy's second set of teeth began to grind.

"*Shadowhunter*," he hissed.

The other boy grinned all over his face. "Got you," he said.

Clary pushed the door to the storage room open, and stepped inside. For a moment she thought it was deserted. The only windows were high up and barred; faint street noise came through them, the sound of honking cars and squealing brakes. The room smelled like old paint, and a heavy layer of dust covered the floor, marked by smeared shoe prints.

There's no one in here, she realized, looking around in

bewilderment. It was cold in the room, despite the August heat outside. Her back was icy with sweat. She took a step forward, tangling her feet in electrical wires. She bent down to free her sneaker from the cables—and heard voices. A girl's laugh, a boy answering sharply. When she straightened up, she saw them.

It was as if they had sprung into existence between one blink of her eyes and the next. There was the girl in her long white dress, her black hair hanging down her back like damp seaweed. The two boys were with her—the tall one with black hair like hers, and the smaller, fair one, whose hair gleamed like brass in the dim light coming through the windows high above. The fair boy was standing with his hands in his pockets, facing the punk kid, who was tied to a pillar with what looked like piano wire, his hands stretched behind him, his legs bound at the ankles. His face was pulled tight with pain and fear.

Heart hammering in her chest, Clary ducked behind the nearest concrete pillar and peered around it. She watched as the fair-haired boy paced back and forth, his arms now crossed over his chest. "So," he said. "You still haven't told me if there are any other of your kind with you."

Your kind? Clary wondered what he was talking about. Maybe she'd stumbled into some kind of gang war.

"I don't know what you're talking about." The blue-haired boy's tone was pained but surly.

"He means other demons," said the dark-haired boy, speaking for the first time. "You do know what a demon is, don't you?"

The boy tied to the pillar turned his face away, his mouth working.

"Demons," drawled the blond boy, tracing the word on the

air with his finger. "Religiously defined as hell's denizens, the servants of Satan, but understood here, for the purposes of the Clave, to be any malevolent spirit whose origin is outside our own home dimension—"

"That's enough, Jace," said the girl.

"Isabelle's right," agreed the taller boy. "Nobody here needs a lesson in semantics—or demonology."

They're crazy, Clary thought. *Actually crazy.*

Jace raised his head and smiled. There was something fierce about the gesture, something that reminded Clary of documentaries she'd watched about lions on the Discovery Channel, the way the big cats would raise their heads and sniff the air for prey. "Isabelle and Alec think I talk too much," he said, confidingly. "Do *you* think I talk too much?"

The blue-haired boy didn't reply. His mouth was still working. "I could give you information," he said. "I know where Valentine is."

Jace glanced back at Alec, who shrugged. "Valentine's in the ground," Jace said. "The thing's just toying with us."

Isabelle tossed her hair. "Kill it, Jace," she said. "It's not going to tell us anything."

Jace raised his hand, and Clary saw dim light spark off the knife he was holding. It was oddly translucent, the blade clear as crystal, sharp as a shard of glass, the hilt set with red stones.

The bound boy gasped. "Valentine is back!" he protested, dragging at the bonds that held his hands behind his back. "All the Infernal Worlds know it—I know it—I can tell you where he is—"

Rage flared suddenly in Jace's icy eyes. "By the Angel, every time we capture one of you bastards, you claim you know where Valentine is. Well, we know where he is too. He's in Hell. And you—" Jace turned the knife in his grasp, the edge sparking like a line of fire. "You can *join him there*."

Clary could take no more. She stepped out from behind the pillar. "Stop!" she cried. "You can't do this."

Jace whirled, so startled that the knife flew from his hand and clattered against the concrete floor. Isabelle and Alec turned along with him, wearing identical expressions of astonishment. The blue-haired boy hung in his bonds, stunned and gaping.

It was Alec who spoke first. "What's this?" he demanded, looking from Clary to his companions, as if they might know what she was doing there.

"It's a girl," Jace said, recovering his composure. "Surely you've seen girls before, Alec. Your sister Isabelle is one." He took a step closer to Clary, squinting as if he couldn't quite believe what he was seeing. "A mundie girl," he said, half to himself. "And she can see us."

"Of course I can see you," Clary said. "I'm not blind, you know."

"Oh, but you are," said Jace, bending to pick up his knife. "You just don't know it." He straightened up. "You'd better get out of here, if you know what's good for you."

"I'm not going anywhere," Clary said. "If I do, you'll kill him." She pointed at the boy with the blue hair.

"That's true," admitted Jace, twirling the knife between his fingers. "What do you care if I kill him or not?"

"Be-because—," Clary spluttered. "You can't just go around killing people."

"You're right," said Jace. "You can't go around killing *people*."

Discover Emma and Julian's story in

Lady Midnight,

THE FIRST BOOK IN CASSANDRA CLARE'S

NEW SERIES, THE DARK ARTIFICES.

———◆———

Emma took her witchlight out of her pocket and lit it—and almost screamed out loud. Jules's shirt was soaked with blood and worse, the healing runes she'd drawn had vanished from his skin. They weren't working.

"Jules," she said. "I have to call the Silent Brothers. They can help you. I *have* to."

His eyes screwed shut with pain. "You can't," he said. "You know we can't call the Silent Brothers. They report directly to the Clave."

"So we'll lie to them. Say it was a routine demon patrol. I'm calling," she said, and reached for her phone.

"No!" Julian said, forcefully enough to stop her. "Silent Brothers know when you're lying! They can see inside your head, Emma. They'll find out about the investigation. About Mark—"

"You're not going to bleed to death in the backseat of a car for Mark!"

"No," he said, looking at her. His eyes were eerily blue-green, the only bright color in the dark interior of the car. "You're going to fix me."

Emma could feel it when Jules was hurt, like a splinter lodged under her skin. The physical pain didn't bother her; it was the terror, the only terror worse than her fear of the ocean. The fear of Jules being hurt, of him dying. She would give up anything, sustain any wound, to prevent those things from happening.

"Okay," she said. Her voice sounded dry and thin to her own ears. "Okay." She took a deep breath. "Hang on."

She unzipped her jacket, threw it aside. Shoved the console between the seats aside, put her witchlight on the floorboard. Then she reached for Jules. The next few seconds were a blur of Jules's blood on her hands and his harsh breathing as she pulled him partly upright, wedging him against the back door. He didn't make a sound as she moved him, but she could see him biting his lip, the blood on his mouth and chin, and she felt as if her bones were popping inside her skin.

"Your gear," she said through gritted teeth. "I have to cut it off."

He nodded, letting his head fall back. She drew a dagger from her belt, but the gear was too tough for the blade. She said a silent prayer and reached back for Cortana.

Cortana went through the gear like a knife through melted butter. It fell away in pieces and Emma drew them free, then sliced down the front of his T-shirt and pulled it apart as if she were opening a jacket.

Emma had seen blood before, often, but this felt different. It was Julian's, and there seemed to be a lot of it. It was smeared up and down his chest and rib cage; she could see where the arrow had gone in and where the skin had torn where he'd yanked it out.

"Why did you pull the arrow out?" she demanded, pulling her sweater over her head. She had a tank top on under it. She patted his chest and side with the sweater, absorbing as much of the blood as she could.

Jules's breath was coming in hard pants. "Because when someone—shoots you with an arrow—" he gasped, "your immediate response is not—'Thanks for the arrow, I think I'll keep it for a while.'"

"Good to know your sense of humor is intact."

"Is it still bleeding?" Julian demanded. His eyes were shut.

She dabbed at the cut with her sweater. The blood had slowed, but the cut looked puffy and swollen. The rest of him, though—it had been a while since she'd seen him with his shirt off. There was more muscle than she remembered. Lean muscle pulled tight over his ribs, his stomach flat and lightly ridged. Cameron was much more muscular, but Julian's spare lines were as elegant as a greyhound's. "You're too skinny," she said. "Too much coffee, not enough pancakes."

"I hope they put that on my tombstone." He gasped as she shifted forward, and she realized abruptly that she was squarely in Julian's lap, her knees around his hips. It was a bizarrely intimate position.

"I—am I hurting you?" she asked.

He swallowed visibly. "It's fine. Try with the *iratze* again."

"Fine," she said. "Grab the panic bar."

"The what?" He opened his eyes and peered at her.

"The plastic handle! Up there, above the window!" She pointed. "It's for holding on to when the car is going around curves."

"Are you sure? I always thought it was for hanging things on. Like dry cleaning."

"Julian, *now is not the time to be pedantic.* Grab the bar or I swear—"

"All right!" He reached up, grabbed hold of it, and winced. "I'm ready."

She nodded and set Cortana aside, reaching for her stele. Maybe her previous *iratzes* had been too fast, too sloppy. She'd always focused on the physical aspects of Shadowhunting, not the more mental and artistic ones: seeing through glamours, drawing runes.

She set the tip of it to the skin of his shoulder and drew, carefully and slowly. She had to brace herself with her left hand against his shoulder. She tried to press as lightly as she could, but she could feel him tense under her fingers. The skin on his shoulder was smooth and hot under her touch, and she wanted to get closer to him, to put her hand over the wound on his side and heal it with the sheer force of her will. To touch her lips to the lines of pain beside his eyes and—

Stop. She had finished the *iratze.* She sat back, her hand clamped around the stele. Julian sat up a little straighter, the ragged remnants of his shirt hanging off his shoulders. He took a deep breath, glancing down at himself—and the *iratze* faded back into his skin, like black ice melting, spreading, being absorbed by the sea.

He looked up at Emma. She could see her own reflection in his eyes: she looked wrecked, panicked, with blood on her neck and her white tank top. "It hurts less," he said in a low voice.

The wound on his side pulsed again; blood slid down the side of his rib cage, staining his leather belt and the waistband of his jeans. She put her hands on his bare skin, panic rising up inside her. His skin felt hot, too hot. Fever hot.

"I have to call," she whispered. "I don't care if the whole world comes down around us, Jules, the most important thing is that you *live*."

"Please," he said, desperation clear in his voice. "Whatever is happening, we'll fix it, because we're *parabatai*. We're forever. I said that to you once, do you remember?"

She nodded warily, hand on the phone.

"And the strength of a rune your *parabatai* gives you is special. Emma, you can do it. You can heal me. We're *parabatai* and that means the things we can do together are . . . extraordinary."

There was blood on her jeans now, blood on her hands and her tank top, and he was still bleeding, the wound still open, an incongruous tear in the smooth skin all around it.

"Try," Jules said in a dry whisper. "For me, try?"

His voice went up on the question and in it she heard the voice of the boy he had been once, and she remembered him smaller, skinnier, younger, back pressed against one of the marble columns in the Hall of Accords in Alicante as his father advanced on him with his blade unsheathed.

And she remembered what Julian had done, then. Done to protect her, to protect all of them, because he always would do everything to protect them.

She took her hand off the phone and gripped the stele, so tightly she felt it dig into her damp palm. "Look at me, Jules," she said in a low voice, and he met her eyes with his. She placed the stele against his skin, and for a moment she held still, just breathing, breathing and remembering.

Julian. A presence in her life for as long as she could remember, splashing water at each other in the ocean, digging in the sand together, him putting his hand over hers and them marveling at the difference in the shape and length of their fingers. Julian singing, terribly and off-key, while he drove, his fingers in her hair carefully freeing a trapped leaf, his hands catching her in the training room when she fell, and fell, and fell. The first time after their *parabatai* ceremony when she'd smashed her hand into a wall in rage at not being able to get a sword maneuver right, and he'd come up to her, taken her still-shaking body in his arms and said, "Emma, Emma, don't hurt yourself. When you do, I feel it, too."

Something in her chest seemed to split and crack; she marveled that it wasn't audible. Energy raced along her veins, and the stele jerked in her hand before it seemed to move on its own, tracing the graceful outline of a healing rune across Julian's chest. She heard him gasp, his eyes flying open. His hand slid down her back and he pressed her against him, his teeth gritted.

"Don't *stop*," he said.

Emma couldn't have stopped if she'd wanted to. The stele seemed to be moving of its own accord; she was blinded with memories, a kaleidoscope of them, all of them Julian. Sun in her eyes and Julian asleep on the beach in an old T-shirt and her not wanting to wake him, but he'd woken anyway when the sun went down and looked for her immediately, not smiling till his eyes found her and he knew she was there. Falling asleep talking and waking up with their hands interlocked; they'd been children in the dark together once but now they were something else, something intimate and powerful, something Emma felt she was touching only the very edge of as she finished the rune and the stele fell from her nerveless fingers.

"Oh," she said softly. The rune seemed lit from within by a soft glow.

There were other Herondales before Will. Find out
how Magnus met Will's father in this sneak peek of

Vampires, Scones, and Edmund Herondale,

BY CASSANDRA CLARE

AND SARAH REES BRENNAN,

AN EXCERPT FROM

THE BANE CHRONICLES.

————◆————

AFTER ALL

ATTRACTIVE AND INTERESTING PERSONS DO NOT SIMPLY DROP OUT OF THE SKY.

DEVASTATING ENSEMBLES MADE ON BOND STREET WITH RED BROCADE WAISTCOATS DO NOT SIMPLY DROP OUT OF THE SKY!

I BEG YOUR PARDON?

London, 1857

Ever since the unfortunate events of the French Revolution, Magnus had nursed a slight prejudice against vampires. The undead were always killing one's servants and endangering one's pet monkey. The vampire clan in Paris was still sending Magnus rude messages about their small misunderstanding. Vampires bore a grudge longer than any technically living creatures, and whenever they were in a bad temper, they expressed themselves through murder. Magnus generally wished his companions to be somewhat less—no pun intended—bloodthirsty.

There was also the fact that sometimes vampires committed crimes worse than murder. They committed crimes against fashion. When one was immortal, one tended to forget the passing of time. Still, that was no excuse for wearing a bonnet last fashionable in the era of Napoléon I.

Magnus was beginning, however, to feel as if he might have been a trifle hasty in dismissing *all* vampires.

Lady Camille Belcourt was a terribly charming woman. She was also attired in the absolute height of fashion. Her dress had a darling hoop skirt, and the fall of blue taffeta in seven narrow flounces about her chair made it appear as if she were rising from a cascade of gleaming blue water. There was not very much material at all around her bosom, which was as pale and curved as a pearl. All that broke the perfect pallor of the curve of bosom and the column of neck was a black velvet ribbon and the thick shining ringlets clustered about her face. One gold ringlet was long enough so that it rested in the delicate curve of her collarbone, which led Magnus's eyes back once again to—

Really, all roads led back to Lady Camille's bosom.

It was a wonderfully designed dress. It was also a wonderfully designed bosom.

Lady Camille, as observant as she was beautiful, noticed Magnus noticing, and smiled.

"The marvelous thing about being a creature of the night," she confided in a low voice, "is that one need never wear anything but evening clothes."

"I had never considered that point before," said Magnus, much struck.

"Of course I adore variety, so I do seize any opportunity to change costumes. I find there are many occasions during an adventurous night for a lady to divest herself of her garments." She leaned forward, one pale, smooth elbow resting against the

Shadowhunters' mahogany table. "Something tells me that you are a man who knows something about adventurous nights."

"My lady, with me, every night is an adventure. Pray continue your discourse on fashion," Magnus urged her. "It is one of my favorite subjects."

Lady Camille smiled.

Magnus lowered his voice discreetly. "Or if you choose, pray continue your discourse on disrobing. I believe that is my most favorite subject of all."

They sat side by side at a long table in the Shadowhunters' London Institute. The Consul, a dreary Nephilim heading up the proceedings, was droning on about all the spells they wished warlocks to make available to them at cut-rate prices, and about their notions of proper behavior for vampires and werewolves. Magnus had not heard a single way in which these "Accords" could conceivably benefit Downworlders, but he could certainly see why the Shadowhunters had developed a passionate desire to ratify them.

He began regretting his agreement to make the voyage to London and its Institute so that the Shadowhunters could waste his valuable time. The Consul, who Magnus believed was called Morgwhatsit, seemed passionately in love with his own voice.

Though, actually he had stopped talking.

Magnus glanced away from Camille to find the far less pleasant sight of the Consul—his disapproval writ across his face, as stark as the runes on his skin—staring at him. "If you and the—the vampire woman could cease your flirtation for a moment," he said in acid tones.

"Flirting? We were merely indulging in a little risqué

conversation," Magnus said, offended. "When I begin to flirt, I assure you the entire room will know. My flirtations cause sensations."

Camille laughed. "What a clever rhyme."

Magnus's joke seemed to liberate the restless discontent of all Downworlders at the table.

"What else are we to do but talk amongst ourselves?" asked a werewolf stripling, still young but with the intense green eyes of a fanatic and the thin determined face of a fanatic who was actually competent. His name was Ralf Scott. "We have been here for three hours and have not been given the chance to speak at all. You Nephilim have done all the talking."

"I cannot believe," put in Arabella, a charming mermaid with charmingly placed seashells, "that I swam up the Thames, and consented to be hauled out by pulleys and put in a large glass aquarium, for *this*."

She spoke quite loudly.

Even Morgwhatsit looked taken aback. *Why*, Magnus wanted to know, were Shadowhunter names so long, when warlocks gave themselves elegant family names of one syllable? The long names were sheer self-importance.

"You wretches should be honored to be in the London Institute," snarled a silver-haired Shadowhunter by the name of Starkweather. "I wouldn't allow any of you in my Institute, unless I was carrying one of your filthy heads on a pike. Silence, and let your betters speak for you."

An extremely awkward pause ensued. Starkweather glared around, and his eyes dwelled on Camille, not as if she were a beautiful woman but as if she might be a fine trophy for his wall. Camille's eyes went to her leader and friend, the pale-haired vampire Alexei de Quincey, but he did not respond to her mute appeal. Magnus put out his hand and took hers.

Her skin was cool, but her fingers fit his very neatly. He saw Ralf Scott glance over at them and blanch. He was even younger than Magnus had thought. His eyes were huge and glass green, transparent enough for all his emotions to shine through, in his thin face. They were fixed on Camille.

Interesting, Magnus thought, and filed the observation away.

"These are meant to be peace accords," Scott said, deliberately slowly. "Which means we are all meant to have a chance to have our voices heard. I have heard how peace will benefit Shadowhunters. I wish now to discuss how it will benefit Downworlders. Will we be given seats on the Council?"

Starkweather began to choke. One of the Shadowhunter women stood up hastily. "Gracious, I think my husband was so excited by the chance to deliver a speech that he did not offer refreshments," she said loudly. "I am Amalia Morgenstern." *Oh, that's it*, Magnus thought. *Morgenstern. Awful name.* "And is there anything I can offer you?" the woman continued. "I will ring for the maid in a trice."

"No raw meat for the dog, mind," Starkweather said, and sniggered. Magnus saw another Shadowhunter woman titter silently behind her hand. Ralf Scott sat, pale and still. He had been the moving force behind assembling Downworlders here today, and had been the only werewolf willing to come. Even his own young brother, Woolsey, had stayed away, parting from Ralf on the front steps of the Institute with an insouciant toss of his blond head and a wink at Magnus. (Magnus had thought, *Interesting*, about that, too.)

The faeries had flatly refused to attend, the queen having

set herself against the idea. Magnus was the only warlock who had come, and Ralf had been forced to hunt him down, knowing his connections to the Silent Brothers. Magnus himself had not had high hopes about this attempt to forge a peace with Shadowhunters, but it was a shame to see the boy's airy dreams come to this.

"We are in England, are we not?" asked Magnus, and he bent a charming smile on Amalia Morgenstern, who looked rather flustered. "I would be delighted if we could have some scones."

"Oh, certainly," said Amalia. "With clotted cream, of course."

Magnus gazed upon Camille. "Some of my fondest memories include lashings of cream and beautiful women."

Magnus was enjoying scandalizing the Shadowhunters. Camille rather looked as if she were enjoying it too. Her green eyes were heavy-lidded for a moment with amused satisfaction, as if she were a cat who had already had her fill of cream.

Amalia rang the bell. "While we wait for scones, we can hear the rest of dear Roderick's speech!"

There was an appalled silence, and in the stillness the mutter outside the door rang out, loud and clear.

"Merciful Angel, give me strength to endure. . . ."

Roderick Morgenstern, who Magnus thought truly deserved to have a name that sounded like a goat chewing gravel, stood up happily to continue his speech. Amalia attempted to rise unobtrusively from her seat—Magnus could have told her that hoop skirts and stealth together were a lost cause—and made her way to the door, which she threw open.

Several young Shadowhunters tumbled into the room like puppies falling over one another. Amalia's eyes rounded in comic surprise. "What on earth—"

Despite Shadowhunters having the swiftness of angels, only one managed to land with grace. It was a boy, or rather a young man, who ended his fall on one knee before Amalia, like Romeo proposing to Juliet.

He had hair the color of a coin that was pure gold, no base metal, and the lines of his face were as clean and elegant as a profile etched on one of those princely coins. His shirt had become disarranged at some point during the eavesdropping, the collar pulled open to reveal the edge of a rune drawn on his white skin.

The most remarkable thing about him were his eyes. They were laughing eyes, at once both joyous and tender: they were the radiant pale blue of a sky slipping toward evening in Heaven, when angels who had been sweet all day found themselves tempted to sin.

"I could not bear to be parted from you a moment longer, dear, dearest Mrs. Morgenstern," said the young man, possessing himself of Amalia's hand. "I yearn for you."

He made play with his long golden eyelashes, and Amalia Morgenstern was forthwith reduced to blushes and smiles.

Magnus had always had a decided preference for black hair. It appeared as though fate were determined that he should broaden his horizons. Either that or the blonds of the world had formed some sort of conspiracy to be good-looking all of a sudden.

"Excuse me, Bane?" said Roderick Morgenstern. "Are you attending?"

"I'm so sorry," Magnus said politely. "Somebody incredibly attractive just came into the room, and I ceased to pay attention to a word you were saying."

It was perhaps an ill-judged remark. The Shadowhunter elders, representatives from the Clave, all appeared horrified and dismayed at any Downworlder expressing interest in one of their youths. The Nephilim also had very decided opinions on the subject of inverts and deviant behavior, since as a group their chief occupations were waving large weaponry about and judging everybody they met.

Camille, meanwhile, looked as if she found Magnus even more interesting than she had before. She looked back and forth between him and the young blond Shadowhunter boy, and covered her smile with a gloved hand.

"He *is* delightful," she murmured to Magnus.

Magnus was watching as Amalia shooed out the young Shadowhunters—the blond boy; an older young man with thick brown hair and significant eyebrows; and a dark-eyed, birdlike little girl, barely more than a toddler, who looked over her shoulder and said, "Papa?" in a clear questioning voice to the head of the London Institute, a grave dark man called Granville Fairchild.

"Go, Charlotte. You know your duty," said Fairchild. Duty before all; that was the warrior's way, Magnus reflected. Certainly duty before love.

Little Charlotte, already a dutiful Shadowhunter, trotted obediently away.

Camille's low voice recalled Magnus to attention. "I don't suppose you'd like to share him?"

Magnus smiled back at her. "Not as a meal, no. Was that what you meant?"

Camille laughed. Ralf Scott made an impatient noise, but was shushed by de Quincey, who muttered at him in annoyance;

while over that noise rose the discontented grumblings of Roderick Morgenstern, a man who clearly wished to continue with his speech—and then finally the refreshments arrived, carried in on silver tea trays by a host of maids.

Arabella the mermaid lifted a hand, sloshing energetically in her aquarium.

"If you please," she said. "I would like a scone."

When Morgenstern's interminable speech was finally done, everybody had lost all will to converse and simply wished to go home. Magnus parted from Camille Belcourt with deep reluctance and from the Shadowhunters with deep relief.

It had been some time since Magnus was last in love, and he was beginning to feel the effects. He remembered the glow of love as brighter and the pain of loss as gentler than they had actually been. He found himself looking into many faces for potential love, and seeing many people as shining vessels of possibility. Perhaps this time there would be that indefinable something that sent hungry hearts roving, longing and searching for something, they knew not what, and yet could not give up the quest. Every time a face or a look or a gesture caught Magnus's eye these days, it woke to life a refrain in Magnus's breast, a song in persistent rhythm with his heartbeat. *Perhaps this time, perhaps this one.*

As he walked down Thames Street, he began to plot ways in which to see Camille again. He should pay a call upon the vampire clan in London. He knew de Quincey lived in Kensington.

It was only civil.

"After all," Magnus remarked aloud to himself, swinging

his monkey-headed cane, "attractive and interesting persons do not simply drop out of the sky."

It was then that the fair-haired Shadowhunter that Magnus had spotted at the Institute somersaulted from the top of a wall and landed gracefully in the street before him.

"Devastating ensembles made on Bond Street with red brocade waistcoats do not simply drop out of the sky!" Magnus proclaimed experimentally to the Heavens.

The young man frowned. "I beg your pardon?"

"Oh, nothing, nothing at all," said Magnus. "May I help you? I do not believe I have had the pleasure of making your acquaintance."

The Nephilim stooped and picked up his hat, which had fallen onto the cobblestones when he'd made his leap. He then took it off in order to flourish it in Magnus's direction. The effect of the smile and the eyelashes together was like a small earthquake of attractiveness. Magnus could not blame Amalia Morgenstern for her giggling, even if the boy was far too young for her.

"No fewer than four of my esteemed elders told me I was on no account to ever converse with you, so I vowed that I would know you. My name is Edmund Herondale. May I ask your name? They referred to you only as 'that disgraceful one-warlock show.'"

"I am deeply moved by that tribute," Magnus told Edmund, and made his own bow. "Magnus Bane, at your service."

"Now we are acquainted," Edmund said. "Capital! Do you frequent any low dens of sin and debauchery?"

"Oh, now and then."

"The Morgensterns said you did, while they were throwing

away the plates," Edmund said, with every sign of enthusiasm. "Shall we go?"

Throwing away the plates? It took Magnus a moment to comprehend, and when he did, he felt cold inside. The Shadowhunters had thrown away the very plates Downworlders had touched, afraid their china would be corrupted.

On the other hand, that was not Edmund's fault. The only other place Magnus had to go was the mansion he had perhaps rashly purchased in Grosvenor Square. A recent adventure had caused him to become temporarily wealthy (a state he despised; he usually tried to get rid of his money as soon as he had it), so he had decided to live in style. The *ton* of London were referring to him, he believed, as "Bane the nabob." This meant a great many people in London were anxious to make his acquaintance, and a great many of them seemed tiresome. Edmund, at least, did not.

"Why not?" Magnus decided.

Edmund glowed. "Excellent. Very few people are willing to have real adventures. Haven't you found that out, Bane? Isn't it sad?"

"I have very few rules in life, but one of them is to never decline an adventure. The others are: to avoid becoming romantically entangled with sea creatures; to always ask for what you want, because the worst thing that can happen is embarrassment but the best thing that can happen is nudity; to demand ready money up front; and to never play cards with Catarina Loss."

"What?"

"She cheats," Magnus explained. "Never mind that one."

"I would like to meet a lady who cheats at cards," Edmund

said wistfully. "Aside from Granville's aunt Millicent, who is a terror at piquet."

Magnus had never truly considered that the high-and-mighty Shadowhunters ever played cards, let alone cheated at them. He supposed he had imagined that their leisure activities consisted of weapons training and having discussions about their infinite superiority over everyone else.

Magnus ventured to give Edmund a hint. "Mundane clubs do generally frown upon patrons who have, purely for random example, an abundance of weaponry about their person. So that might be an impediment."

"Absolutely not," Edmund promised him. "Why, I have the most paltry assortment of weapons on me. Only a few miserable daggers, a single stiletto knife, a couple of whips—"

Magnus blinked. "Hardly an armory," he said. "Though, it sounds like a most amusing Saturday."

"Capital!" said Edmund Herondale, apparently taking this for approval of his company on Magnus's excursion. He looked delighted.

White's club, on St. James's Street, had not changed outwardly at all. Magnus regarded the pale stone facade with pleasure: the Greek columns and the arched frames to the higher windows, as if each window were a chapel unto itself; the cast-iron balcony, which bore an intricate swirling pattern that had always made Magnus think of a procession of snail shells; the bow window out of which a famous man had once looked, and bet on a race between raindrops. The club had been established by an Italian, had been the haunt of criminals, and had been the irresistible bane of English aristocrats for more than a hundred years.

Whenever Magnus heard anything described as a "bane," he felt sure he would like it. It was why he had chosen that particular last name for himself, and also why he had joined White's several years before on a flying visit to London, in the main because his friend Catarina Loss had bet him that he could not do it.

Edmund swung around one of the black cast-iron lamps set before the door. The leaping flame behind the glass was dim compared to his eyes.

"This used to be a place where highwaymen drank hot chocolate," Magnus told Edmund carelessly as they walked inside. "The hot chocolate was very good. Being a highwayman is chilly work."

"Did you ever ask someone to stand and deliver?"

"I'll just say this," said Magnus. "I look dashing in a tasteful mask and a large hat."

CASSANDRA CLARE'S

#1 *New York Times* Bestselling Series

THE MORTAL INSTRUMENTS
THE INFERNAL DEVICES
THE DARK ARTIFICES

A thousand years ago, the Angel Raziel mixed his blood with the blood of men and created the race of the Nephilim. Human-angel hybrids, they walk among us, unseen but ever present, our invisible protectors.

They call themselves Shadowhunters.

THE INFERNAL DEVICES

Clockwork PRINCE

Book Two

CASSANDRA CLARE

Margaret K. McElderry Books
NEW YORK LONDON TORONTO SYDNEY NEW DELHI

MARGARET K. McELDERRY BOOKS

An imprint of Simon & Schuster Children's Publishing Division

1230 Avenue of the Americas, New York, New York 10020

MARGARET K. McELDERRY BOOKS is a trademark of Simon & Schuster, Inc.

For information about special discounts for bulk purchases, please contact
Simon & Schuster Special Sales at 1-866-506-1949 or business@simonandschuster.com.

The Simon & Schuster Speakers Bureau can bring authors to your live event.
For more information or to book an event, contact the Simon & Schuster Speakers Bureau
at 1-866-248-3049 or visit our website at www.simonspeakers.com.

Also available in a Margaret K. McElderry Books hardcover edition

Cover design by Russell Gordon

Interior design by Mike Rosamilia

Map illustration by Drew Willis

The text for this book is set in Dolly.

Manufactured in the United States of America

This Margaret K. McElderry Books paperback edition September 2015

12 14 16 18 20 19 17 15 13 11

The Library of Congress has cataloged the hardcover edition as follows:

Clare, Cassandra.

Clockwork prince / Cassandra Clare.

p. cm.—(The infernal devices ; bk. 2)

Summary: As the Council attempts to strip Charlotte of her power,
sixteen-year-old orphaned shapechanger Tessa Gray works with the London
Shadowhunters to find the Magister and destroy his clockwork army, learning the
secret of her own identity while investigating his past.

ISBN 978-1-4169-7588-5 (hardcover)

ISBN 978-1-4424-3134-8 (eBook)

[1. Supernatural—Fiction. 2. Demonology—Fiction. 3. Orphans—Fiction. 4. Secret societies—
Fiction. 5. Identity—Fiction. 6. London (England)—History—19th century—Fiction.
7. Great Britain—History—Victoria, 1837–1901—Fiction.] I. Title.

PZ7.C5265Cp 2011

[Fic]—dc23

2011017869

ISBN 978-1-4814-5601-2 (repackaged pbk)

For Elka

Khalepa ta kala

5 The Argent Rooms

6 Lightwood House   **7** Woolsey's house   **8** Hatchards bookshop   **9** The Devil Tavern

THE DEVIL TAVERN

10 Entrance to the Faerie Courts

ST. JOHN'S WOOD

REGENT'S PARK

MARYLEBONE

SOHO

HOLBORN

SPITALFIELDS

NOTTING HILL

MAYFAIR

HYDE PARK

KENSINGTON

BELGRAVIA

WESTMINSTER

LONDON

SOUTHWARK

LAMBETH

CHELSEA

BATTERSEA PARK

River Thames

FULHAM

CAMBERWELL

BRIXTON

Foreword

For many years during the time I've been a writer, people have asked me if I get inspiration for my books from my dreams.

My response has always been that I wish that I did. It seems like such a fun way to get story ideas—dream something and wake up compelled to put the story to paper. Unfortunately, the only real dreams I ever have about my characters and stories are nonsensical: all my characters are in front of me in line at the grocery store and have too many items in their carts.

Which makes the genesis of the idea I had for the Infernal Devices pretty unusual. It wasn't a dream, but it was a daydream.

I was in London, on a trip to promote *City of Bones*, the first book of the Shadowhunters chronicles. I was crossing Blackfriars Bridge, which is a lovely old bridge in the City of London over the river Thames. It was a gray cloudy day, and mist was drifting along the bridge. I leaned against the parapet and looked down at the water.

I thought about how the bridge had stood for so many years, and of all that it must have witnessed. Slowly the image of a girl with brown hair and a boy dressed in Victorian clothing came into my mind, and as I pictured them there on the bridge, I imagined a strange army of clockwork monsters hidden in the shadows, waiting to pounce.

I went home feeling unsettled and inspired. Slowly the story of Tessa, Jem, and Will began to take shape in my mind—I chose the location of the London Institute for its proximity to Blackfriars Bridge, for I always knew the bridge would be central to the tale.

After much wandering around London (using a map dated 1879, which led to a lot of getting lost) I decided the Institute would be Saint Bride's Church off Fleet Street, a gorgeous church gutted by firebombs during the Blitz.

I chose 1878 because it was a time of transition from an old England to a new England: there was regular train service, there was gas light, there were sewers, and yet the time period retained the graciousness and beauty of the past. It seemed like a wonderful era in which to set a story about three young people learning who they are and all they are capable of, especially when it came to the story of a young girl learning she is destined for more than an arranged marriage—that she is destined for an extraordinary love.

I believe that historical fiction is the closest thing we have to time travel. I wanted to feel as much as I could that I was living and breathing the time period of the Infernal Devices, so I set myself a project: for six months I read nothing but books set in the mid and late Victorian era.

It was research by immersion. Soon I started to imagine that I was seeing horse-drawn carriages instead of cars, that I could smell the Thames River and hear the Bow Bells. I wanted my readers to feel that the past was accessible, so the characters of a bygone time's pain and joy would seem real and true. It was a time obsessed with death, in which diseases which are now cured easily were rife, and sicknesses we now understand seemed as mysterious as the corrupting touch of a demon. The real world as it was then slotted neatly into my already-imagined world of the Shadowhunters, demon-hunters, and magic users and gave it new depth and richness: creating a hero who could see and talk to imploring ghosts and another who was condemned to die young of a fatal demonic illness, no matter how desperate the efforts to save him, just as in reality victims of consumption sickened and died without penicillin. The Brontë family, who produced *Wuthering Heights* and *Jane Eyre*, were decimated by consumption, and to mark my respect for and debt to their work I named the head of the London Institute—Charlotte Branwell—after two of the Brontë siblings. It was a difficult time for a woman to have authority in the Shadowhunter world and the mundane world, but Charlotte manages it. Tessa, Charlotte, Sophie, and Jessamine are all heroines who I adore, coping with the prejudice of a time more difficult for women than our own in a way that I hoped would also resonate with the oppression women still face today.

I immersed myself in books to write this series, and in this series two of the characters also find inspiration and comfort in books. Tessa and Will bond over Charles Dickens's *A Tale of Two Cities*, in which one of the heroes considers himself a soul doomed to wickedness. Will thinks he too is doomed to be corrupt and unloved; over the course of the books he learns how wrong he was. His best friend, James Carstairs, who is dying, believes that he is fated to die without love, like the poet Keats, whom his character is partially based on. Both Will and Jem love each other—they are blood brothers—but despite that love, they have no hope. In Tessa they both find their salvation, because Tessa believes in hope—not just because she is stalwart and a heroine, but also because she has discovered hope in books.

Tessa is a bookworm: she doesn't only love classics by the Brontës and Dickens, but the many novels of her time that I read during my months-long reading project. She reads voraciously, in the same way I did, books considered both high- and lowbrow, and she gains enjoyment from both kinds. She learns she has the power to shapeshift, reflecting our real-life ability to slip inside the skin of fictional characters when we read.

I wanted to write a heroine who was invested in books as much as I was and as I knew my readers were: a girl who learned that adventure was possible from books, that romance was potentially as wonderful as it was painful, that courage and kindness would carry her through, and that she could be marvelously transformed. I wanted every girl reading the Infernal Devices to feel that she could be the heroine of a novel—maybe even this one.

THE INFERNAL DEVICES

Clockwork
PRINCE

"I wish you to know that you have been the last dream of my soul. . . . Since I knew you, I have been troubled by a remorse that I thought would never reproach me again, and have heard whispers from old voices impelling me upward, that I thought were silent for ever. I have had unformed ideas of striving afresh, beginning anew, shaking off sloth and sensuality, and fighting out the abandoned fight. A dream, all a dream, that ends in nothing. . . ."

—Charles Dickens, *A Tale of Two Cities*

PROLOGUE

The Outcast Dead

The fog was thick, muffling sound and sight. Where it parted, Will Herondale could see the street rising ahead of him, slick and wet and black with rain, and he could hear the voices of the dead.

Not all Shadowhunters could hear ghosts, unless the ghosts chose to be heard, but Will was one of those who could. As he approached the old cemetery, their voices rose in a ragged chorus—wails and pleading, cries and snarls. This was not a peaceful burial ground, but Will knew that; it was not his first visit to the Cross Bones Graveyard near London Bridge. He did his best to block out the noises, hunching his shoulders so that his collar covered his ears, head down, a fine mist of rain dampening his black hair.

The entrance to the cemetery was halfway down the block: a pair of wrought iron gates set into a high stone wall, though any mundane passing by would have observed nothing but a plot of overgrown land, part of an unnamed builder's yard. As Will neared the gates, something else no mundane would have seen materialized out of the fog: a great bronze knocker in the shape of a hand, the fingers bony and skeletal. With a grimace Will reached out one of his own gloved hands and lifted the knocker, letting it fall once, twice, three times, the hollow clank resounding through the night.

Beyond the gates mist rose like steam from the ground, obscuring the gleam of bone against the rough ground. Slowly the mist began to coalesce, taking on an eerie blue glow. Will put his hands to the bars of the gate; the cold of the metal seeped through his gloves, into his bones, and he shivered. It was a more than ordinary cold. When ghosts rose, they drew energy from their surroundings, depriving the air around them of heat. The hairs on the back of Will's neck prickled and stood up as the blue mist formed slowly into the shape of an old woman in a ragged dress and white apron, her head bent.

"Hallo, Mol," said Will. "You're looking particularly fine this evening, if I do say so."

The ghost raised her head. Old Molly was a strong spirit, one of the stronger Will had ever encountered. Even as moonlight speared through a gap in the clouds, she hardly looked transparent. Her body was solid, her hair twisted in a thick yellow-gray coil over one shoulder, her rough, red hands braced on her hips. Only her eyes were hollow, twin blue flames flickering in their depths.

"William 'erondale," she said. "Back again so soon?"

She moved toward the gate with that gliding motion peculiar to ghosts. Her feet were bare and filthy, despite the fact that they never touched the ground.

Will leaned against the gate. "You know I missed your pretty face."

She grinned, her eyes flickering, and he caught a glimpse of the skull beneath the half-transparent skin. Overhead the clouds had closed in on one another again, blocking out the moon. Idly, Will wondered what Old Molly had done to get herself buried here, far from consecrated ground. Most of the wailing voices of the dead belonged to prostitutes, suicides, and stillbirths—those outcast dead who could not be buried in a churchyard. Although Molly had managed to make the situation quite profitable for herself, so perhaps she didn't mind.

She chortled. "What d'you want, then, young Shadowhunter? Malphas venom? I 'ave the talon of a Morax demon, polished very fine, the poison at the tip entirely invisible—"

"No," Will said. "That's not what I need. I need Foraii demon powders, ground fine."

Molly turned her head to the side and spat a tendril of blue fire. "Now what's a fine young man like you want with stuff like that?"

Will just sighed inwardly; Molly's protests were part of the bargaining process. Magnus had already sent Will to Old Mol several times now, once for black stinking candles that stuck to his skin like tar, once for the bones of an unborn child, and once for a bag of faeries' eyes, which had dripped blood on his shirt. Foraii demon powder sounded pleasant by comparison.

"You think I'm a fool," Molly went on. "This is a trap, innit?

You Nephilim catch me selling that sort of stuff, an' it's the stick for Old Mol, it is."

"You're *already* dead." Will did his best not to sound irritable. "I don't know what you think the Clave could do to you now."

"Pah." Her hollow eyes flamed. "The prisons of the Silent Brothers, beneath the earth, can 'old either the living or the dead; you know that, Shadowhunter."

Will held up his hands. "No tricks, old one. Surely you must have heard the rumors running about in Downworld. The Clave has other things on its mind than tracking down ghosts who traffic in demon powders and faerie blood." He leaned forward. "I'll give you a good price." He drew a cambric bag from his pocket and dangled it in the air. It clinked like coins rattling together. "They all fit your description, Mol."

An eager look came over her dead face, and she solidified enough to take the bag from him. She plunged one hand into it and brought her palm out full of rings—gold wedding rings, each tied in a lovers' knot at the top. Old Mol, like many ghosts, was always looking for that talisman, that lost piece of her past that would finally allow her to die, the anchor that kept her trapped in the world. In her case it was her wedding ring. It was common belief, Magnus had told Will, that the ring was long gone, buried under the silty bed of the Thames, but in the meantime she'd take any bag of found rings in the hope one would turn out to be hers.

She dropped the rings back into the bag, which vanished somewhere on her undead person, and handed him a folded sachet of powder in return. He slipped it into his jacket pocket just as the ghost began to shimmer and fade. "Hold up, there, Mol. That isn't all I have come for tonight."

The spirit flickered while greed warred with impatience and the effort of remaining visible. Finally she grunted. "Very well. What else d'you want?"

Will hesitated. This was not something Magnus had sent him for; it was something he wanted to know for himself. "Love potions—"

Old Mol screeched with laughter. "*Love potions?* For Will 'erondale? 'Tain't my way to turn down payment, but any man who looks like you 'as got no need of love potions, and that's a fact."

"No," Will said, a little desperation in his voice. "I was looking for the opposite, really—something that might put an end to being in love."

"An 'atred potion?" Mol still sounded amused.

"I was hoping for something more akin to indifference? Tolerance?"

She made a snorting noise, astonishingly human for a ghost. "I 'ardly like to tell you this, Nephilim, but if you want a girl to 'ate you, there's easy enough ways of making it 'appen. You don't need *my* help with the poor thing."

And with that she vanished, spinning away into the mists among the graves. Will, looking after her, sighed. "Not for her," he said under his breath, though there was no one to hear him, "for *me* . . ." And he leaned his head against the cold iron gate.

1

The Council Chamber

Above, the fair hall-ceiling stately set
Many an arch high up did lift,
And angels rising and descending met
With interchange of gift.
—Alfred, Lord Tennyson, "The Palace of Art"

"Oh, yes. It really does look just as I imagined," Tessa said, and turned to smile at the boy who stood beside her. He had just helped her over a puddle, and his hand still rested politely on her arm, just above the crook of her elbow.

James Carstairs smiled back at her, elegant in his dark suit, his silver-fair hair whipped by the wind. His other hand rested on a jade-topped cane, and if any of the great crowd of people milling around them thought that it was odd that someone so young should need a walking stick, or found anything unusual about his coloring or the cast of his features, they didn't pause to stare.

"I shall count that as a blessing," said Jem. "I was beginning to worry, you know, that everything you encountered in London was going to be a disappointment."

A *disappointment*. Tessa's brother, Nate, had once promised her everything in London—a new beginning, a wonderful place to live, a city of soaring buildings and gorgeous parks. What Tessa had found instead was horror and betrayal, and danger beyond anything she could have imagined. And yet . . .

"Not everything has been." She smiled up at Jem.

"I am glad to hear it." His tone was serious, not teasing. She looked away from him up at the grand edifice that rose before them. Westminster Abbey, with its great Gothic spires nearly touching the sky. The sun had done its best to struggle out from behind the haze-tipped clouds, and the Abbey was bathed in weak sunlight.

"This is really where it is?" she asked as Jem drew her forward, toward the Abbey entrance. "It seems so . . ."

"Mundane?"

"I had meant to say crowded." The Abbey was open to tourists today, and groups of them swarmed busily in and out the enormous doors, most clutching Baedeker guidebooks in their hands. A group of American tourists—middle-aged women in unfashionable clothes, murmuring in accents that made Tessa briefly homesick—passed them as they went up the stairs, hurrying after a lecturer who was offering a guided tour of the Abbey. Jem and Tessa melted in effortlessly behind them.

The inside of the Abbey smelled of cold stone and metal. Tessa looked up and around, marveling at the size of the place. It made the Institute look like a village church.

"Notice the triple division of the nave," a guide droned,

going on to explain that smaller chapels lined the eastern and western aisles of the Abbey. There was a hush over the place even though no services were going on. As Tessa let Jem lead her toward the eastern side of the church, she realized she was stepping over stones carved with dates and names. She had known that famous kings, queens, soldiers, and poets were buried in Westminster Abbey, but she hadn't quite expected she'd be standing on top of them.

She and Jem slowed finally at the southeastern corner of the church. Watery daylight poured through the rose window overhead. "I know we are in a hurry to get to the Council meeting," said Jem, "but I wanted you to see this." He gestured around them. "Poets' Corner."

Tessa had read of the place, of course, where the great writers of England were buried. There was the gray stone tomb of Chaucer, with its canopy, and other familiar names: "Edmund Spenser, oh, and Samuel Johnson," she gasped, "and Coleridge, and Robert Burns, and *Shakespeare*—"

"He isn't really buried here," said Jem quickly. "It's just a monument. Like Milton's."

"Oh, I know, but—" She looked at him, and felt herself flush. "I can't explain it. It's like being among friends, being among these names. Silly, I know . . ."

"Not silly at all."

She smiled at him. "How did you know just what I'd want to see?"

"How could I not?" he said. "When I think of you, and you are not there, I see you in my mind's eye always with a book in your hand." He looked away from her as he said it, but not before she caught the slight flush on his cheekbones. He was so pale, he could never hide even the least blush, she thought—and was surprised how affectionate the thought was.

She had become very fond of Jem over the past fortnight; Will had been studiously avoiding her, Charlotte and Henry were caught up in issues of Clave and Council and the running of the Institute—and even Jessamine seemed preoccupied. But Jem was always there. He seemed to take his role as her guide to London seriously. They had been to Hyde Park and Kew Gardens, the National Gallery and the British Museum, the Tower of London and Traitors' Gate. They had gone to see the cows being milked in St. James's Park, and the fruit and vegetable sellers hawking their wares in Covent Garden. They had watched the boats sailing on the sun-sparked Thames from the Embankment, and had eaten things called "door-stops," which sounded horrible but turned out to be butter, sugar, and bread. And as the days went on, Tessa felt herself unfolding slowly out of her quiet, huddled unhappiness over Nate and Will and the loss of her old life, like a flower climbing out of frozen ground. She had even found herself laughing. And she had Jem to thank for it.

"You *are* a good friend," she exclaimed. And when to her surprise he said nothing to that, she said, "At least, I hope we are good friends. You do think so too, don't you, Jem?"

He turned to look at her, but before he could reply, a sepulchral voice spoke out of the shadows,

"'Mortality, behold and fear!
What a change of flesh is here:
Think how many royal bones
Sleep within these heaps of stones.'"

A dark shape stepped out from between two monuments. As Tessa blinked in surprise, Jem said, in a tone of resigned amusement, "Will. Decided to grace us with your presence after all?"

"I never said I wasn't coming." Will moved forward, and the light from the rose windows fell on him, illuminating his face. Even now, Tessa never could look at him without a tightening in her chest, a painful stutter of her heart. Black hair, blue eyes, graceful cheekbones, thick dark lashes, full mouth—he would have been pretty if he had not been so tall and so muscular. She had run her hands over those arms. She knew what they felt like—iron, corded with hard muscles; his hands, when they cupped the back of her head, slim and flexible but rough with calluses . . .

She tore her mind away from the memories. Memories did one no good, not when one knew the truth in the present. Will was beautiful, but he was not hers; he was not anybody's. Something in him was broken, and through that break spilled a blind cruelty, a need to hurt and to push away.

"You're late for the Council meeting," said Jem good-naturedly. He was the only one Will's puckish malice never seemed to touch.

"I had an errand," said Will. Up close Tessa could see that he looked tired. His eyes were rimmed with red, the shadows beneath them nearly purple. His clothes looked crumpled, as if he had slept in them, and his hair wanted cutting. *But that has nothing to do with you,* she told herself sternly, looking away from the soft dark waves that curled around his ears, the back of his neck. *It does not matter what you think of how he looks or how he chooses to spend his time. He has made that very clear.* "And you are not exactly on the dot of the hour yourselves."

"I wanted to show Tessa Poets' Corner," said Jem. "I thought she would like it." He spoke so simply and plainly, no one could ever doubt him or imagine he said anything but the truth. In the face of his simple desire to please, even Will didn't seem to be able to think of anything unpleasant to say; he merely shrugged, and moved on ahead of them at a rapid pace through the Abbey and out into the East Cloister.

There was a square garden here surrounded by cloister walls, and people were walking around the edges of it, murmuring in low voices as if they were still in the church. None of them took notice of Tessa and her companions as they approached a set of double oak doors set into one of the walls. Will, after glancing around, took his stele from his pocket and drew the tip across the wood. The door sparked with a brief blue light and swung open. Will stepped inside, Jem and Tessa following just behind. The door was heavy, and closed with a resounding bang behind Tessa, nearly trapping her skirts; she pulled them away only just in time, and stepped backward quickly, turning around in what was a near pitch-darkness. "Jem?"

Light blazed up; it was Will, holding his witchlight stone. They were in a large stone-bound room with vaulted ceilings. The floor appeared to be brick, and there was an altar at one end of the room. "We're in the Pyx Chamber," he said. "Used to be a treasury. Boxes of gold and silver all along the walls."

"A Shadowhunter treasury?" Tessa was thoroughly puzzled.

"No, the British royal treasury—thus the thick walls and doors," said Jem. "But we Shadowhunters have always had access." He smiled at her expression. "Monarchies down through the ages have tithed to the Nephilim, in secret, to keep their kingdoms safe from demons."

"Not in America," said Tessa with spirit. "We haven't got a monarchy—"

"You've got a branch of government that deals with Nephilim, never fear," said Will, crossing the floor to the altar. "It used to be the Department of War, but now there's a branch of the Department of Justice—"

He was cut off as the altar moved sideways with a groan, revealing a dark, empty hole behind it. Tessa could see faint flickers of light in among the shadows. Will ducked into the hole, his witchlight illuminating the darkness.

When Tessa followed, she found herself in a long downward-sloping stone corridor. The stone of the walls, floors, and ceiling was all the same, giving the impression that the passage had been hewn directly through the rock, though it was smooth instead of rough. Every few feet witchlight burned in a sconce shaped like a human hand pushing through the wall, fingers gripping a torch.

The altar slid shut behind them, and they set off. As they went, the passage began to slope more steeply downward. The torches burned with a blue-green glow, illuminating carvings in the rock—the same motif, repeated over and over, of an angel rising in burning fire from a lake, carrying a sword in one hand and a cup in the other.

At last they found themselves standing before two great silver doors. Each door was carved with a design Tessa had seen before—four interlocking Cs. Jem pointed to them. "They stand for Clave and Council, Covenant and Consul," he said, before she could ask.

"The Consul. He's—the head of the Clave? Like a sort of king?"

"Not quite so inbred as your usual monarch," said Will. "He's elected, like the president or the prime minister."

"And the Council?"

"You'll see them soon enough." Will pushed the doors open.

Tessa's mouth fell open; she closed it quickly, but not before she caught an amused look from Jem, standing at her right side. The room beyond them was one of the biggest she had ever seen, a huge domed space, the ceiling of which was painted with a pattern of stars and constellations. A great chandelier in the shape of an angel holding blazing torches dangled from the highest point of the dome. The rest of the room was set up as an amphitheater, with long, curving benches. Will, Jem, and Tessa were standing at the top of a row of stairs that cut through the center of the seating area, which was three quarters full of people. Down at the bottom of the steps was a raised platform, and on that platform were several uncomfortable-looking high-backed wooden chairs.

In one of them sat Charlotte; beside her was Henry, looking wide-eyed and nervous. Charlotte sat calmly with her hands in her lap; only someone who knew her well would have seen the tension in her shoulders and the set of her mouth.

Before them, at a sort of speaker's lectern—it was broader and longer than the usual lectern—stood a tall man with long, fair hair and a thick beard; his shoulders were broad, and he wore long black robes over his clothes like a judge, the sleeves glimmering with woven runes. Beside him, in a low chair, sat an older man, his brown hair streaked with gray, his face clean-shaven but sunk into stern lines. His robe was dark blue, and gems glittered on his fingers when he moved his hand. Tessa recognized him: the ice-voiced, ice-eyed Inquisitor Whitelaw who questioned witnesses on behalf of the Clave.

"Mr. Herondale," said the blond man, looking up at Will, and his mouth quirked into a smile. "How kind of you to join us. And Mr. Carstairs as well. And your companion must be—"

"Miss Gray," Tessa said before he could finish. "Miss Theresa Gray of New York."

A little murmur ran around the room, like the sound of a wave receding. She felt Will, next to her, tense, and Jem draw a breath as if to speak. *Interrupting the Consul,* she thought she heard someone say. So this was Consul Wayland, the chief officer of the Clave. Glancing around the room, she saw a few familiar faces—Benedict Lightwood, with his sharp, beaky features and stiff carriage; and his son, tousle-haired Gabriel Lightwood, looking stonily straight ahead. Dark-eyed Lilian Highsmith. Friendly-looking George Penhallow; and even Charlotte's formidable aunt Callida, her hair piled on her head in thick gray waves. There were many other faces as well, ones she didn't know. It was like looking at a picture book meant to tell you about all the peoples of the world. There were blond Viking-looking Shadowhunters, and a darker-skinned man who looked like a caliph out of her illustrated *The Thousand and One Nights,* and an Indian woman in a beautiful sari trimmed with silver runes. She sat beside another woman, who had turned her head and was looking at them. She wore an elegant silk dress, and her face was like Jem's—the same delicately beautiful features, the same curves to her eyes and cheekbones, though where his hair and eyes were silver, hers were dark.

"Welcome, then, Miss Tessa Gray of New York," said the Consul, sounding amused. "We appreciate your joining us here today. I understand you have already answered quite a few questions for the London Enclave. I had hoped you would be willing to answer a few more."

Across the distance that separated them, Tessa's eyes met Charlotte's. *Should I?*

Charlotte dropped her a nearly imperceptible nod. *Please.*

Tessa squared her shoulders. "If that is your request, certainly."

"Approach the Council bench, then," said the Consul, and Tessa realized he must mean the long, narrow wooden bench that stood before the lectern. "And your gentleman friends may escort you," he added.

Will muttered something under his breath, but so quietly even Tessa couldn't hear it; flanked by Will on her left and Jem on her right, Tessa made her way down the steps and to the bench before the lectern. She stood behind it uncertainly. This close up, she could see that the Consul had friendly blue eyes, unlike the Inquisitor's, which were a bleak and stormy gray, like a rainy sea.

"Inquisitor Whitelaw," said the Consul to the gray-eyed man, "the Mortal Sword, if you please."

The Inquisitor stood, and from his robes drew a massive blade. Tessa recognized it instantly. It was long and dull silver, its hilt carved in the shape of outspread wings. It was the sword from the *Codex*, the one that the Angel Raziel had risen from the lake carrying, and had given to Jonathan Shadowhunter, the first of them all.

"Maellartach," she said, giving the Sword its name.

The Consul, taking the Sword, looked amused again. "You *have* been studying up," he said. "Which of you has been teaching her? William? James?"

"Tessa picks things up on her own, sir," Will's drawl was bland and cheerful, at odds with the grim feeling in the room. "She's very inquisitive."

"All the more reason she shouldn't be here." Tessa didn't have to turn; she knew the voice. Benedict Lightwood. "This is the Gard Council. We don't bring Downworlders to this place." His voice was tight. "The Mortal Sword cannot be used to make her tell the truth; she's not a Shadowhunter. What use is it, or her, here?"

"Patience, Benedict." Consul Wayland held the Sword lightly, as if it weighed nothing. His gaze on Tessa was heavier. She felt as if he were searching her face, reading the fear in her eyes. "We are not going to hurt you, little warlock," he said. "The Accords would forbid it."

"You should not call me warlock," Tessa said. "I bear no warlock's mark." It was strange, having to say this again, but when she had been questioned before, it had always been by members of the Clave, not the Consul himself. He was a tall, broad-shouldered man, exuding a sense of power and authority. Just that sort of power and authority that Benedict Lightwood so resented Charlotte laying claim to.

"Then, what are you?" he asked.

"She doesn't know." The Inquisitor's tone was dry. "Neither do the Silent Brothers."

"She may be allowed to sit," said the Consul. "And to give evidence, but her testimony will be counted only as half a Shadowhunter's." He turned to the Branwells. "In the meantime, Henry, you are dismissed from questioning for the moment. Charlotte, please remain."

Tessa swallowed back her resentment and went to sit in the front row of seats, where she was joined by a drawn-looking Henry, whose gingery hair was sticking up wildly. Jessamine was there, in a dress of pale brown alpaca, looking bored and annoyed. Tessa sat down next to her, with Will and Jem on her other side. Jem was directly beside her, and as the seats were narrow, she could feel the warmth of his shoulder against hers.

At first the Council proceeded much as had other meetings of the Enclave. Charlotte was called upon to give her recollections of the night when the Enclave attacked the stronghold of the vampire de Quincey, killing him and those of his followers who'd been present, while Tessa's brother, Nate, had betrayed their trust in him and allowed the Magister, Axel Mortmain, entry into the Institute, where he had murdered two of the servants and nearly kidnapped Tessa. When Tessa was called up, she said the same things she had said before, that she did not know where Nate was, that she had not suspected him, that she had known nothing of her powers until the Dark Sisters had shown them to her, and that she had always thought her parents were human.

"Richard and Elizabeth Gray have been thoroughly investigated," said the Inquisitor. "There is no evidence to suggest either was anything but human. The boy, the brother—human as well. It could well be that, as Mortmain hinted, the girl's father is a demon, but if so, there is the question of the missing warlock mark."

"Most curious, everything about you, including this power of yours," said the Consul, looking at Tessa with eyes that were steady and pale blue. "You have no idea what its limits, its constructs are? Have you been tested with an item of Mortmain's? To see if you can access his memories or thoughts?"

"Yes, I—tried. With a button he had left behind him. It should have worked."

"But?"

She shook her head. "I could not do it. There was no spark to it, no—no life. Nothing for me to connect with."

"Convenient," muttered Benedict, almost too low to be heard, but Tessa heard it, and flushed.

The Consul indicated that she might take her seat again. She caught sight of Benedict Lightwood's face as she did so; his lips were compressed into a thin, furious line. She wondered what she could possibly have said to anger him.

"And no one has seen hide nor hair of this Mortmain since Miss Gray's . . . altercation with him in the Sanctuary," the Consul went on as Tessa took her seat.

The Inquisitor flipped some of the papers that were stacked on the lectern. "His houses have been searched and found to be completely emptied of all his belongings. His warehouses were searched with the same result. Even our friends at Scotland Yard have investigated. The man has vanished. Quite literally, as our young friend William Herondale tells us."

Will smiled brilliantly as if complimented, though Tessa, seeing the malice under the smile, thought of light sparking off the cutting edge of a razor.

"My suggestion," said the Consul, "is that Charlotte and Henry Branwell be censured, and that for the next three months their official actions, undertaken on behalf of the Clave, be required to pass through me for approval before—"

"My lord Consul." A firm, clear voice spoke out from the crowd. Heads swiveled, staring; Tessa got the feeling that this—someone interrupting the Consul midspeech—didn't happen very often. "If I might speak."

The Consul's eyebrows went up. "Benedict Lightwood," he said. "You had your chance to speak earlier, during the testimonials."

"I hold no arguments with the testimonials given," said Benedict Lightwood. His beaky, sharp profile looked even sharper in the witchlight. "It is your sentence I take issue with."

The Consul leaned forward on the lectern. He was a big man, thick-necked and deep-chested, and his large hands looked as if he could span Benedict's throat easily with a single one. Tessa rather wished he would. From what she had seen of Benedict Lightwood, she did not like him. "And why is that?"

"I think you have let your long friendship with the Fairchild family blind you to Charlotte's shortcomings as head of the Institute," said Benedict, and there was an audible intake of breath in the room. "The blunders committed on the night of July the fifth did more than embarrass the Clave and lose us the Pyxis. We have damaged our relationship with London's Downworlders by futilely attacking de Quincy."

"There have already been a number of complaints lodged through Reparations," rumbled the Consul. "But those will be dealt with as the Law sees fit. Reparations isn't really your concern, Benedict—"

"*And*," Benedict went on, his voice rising, "worst of all, she has let a dangerous criminal with plans to harm and destroy Shadowhunters escape, and we have no idea where he might be. Nor is the responsibility for finding him being laid where it should be, on the shoulders of those who lost him!"

His voice rose. In fact, the whole room was in an uproar; Charlotte looked dismayed, Henry confused, and Will furious. The Consul, whose eyes had darkened alarmingly when Benedict had mentioned the Fairchilds—they must have been Charlotte's family, Tessa realized—remained silent as the noise died down. Then he said, "Your hostility toward the leader of your Enclave does not do you credit, Benedict."

"My apologies, Consul. I do not believe that keeping Charlotte Branwell as the head of the Institute—for we all know that Henry Branwell's involvement is nominal at most—is in the best interests of the Clave. I believe a woman cannot run an Institute; women do not think with logic and discretion but with the emotions of the heart. I have no doubt that Charlotte is a good and decent woman, but a *man* would not have been fooled by a flimsy spy like Nathaniel Gray—"

"*I* was fooled." Will had leaped to his feet and swung around, eyes blazing. "We all were. What insinuations are you making about myself and Jem and Henry, *Mr.* Lightwood?"

"You and Jem are children," said Benedict cuttingly. "And Henry never looks up from his worktable."

Will started to climb over the back of his chair; Jem tugged him back into his seat with main force, hissing under his breath. Jessamine clapped her hands together, her brown eyes bright.

"This is *finally* exciting," she exclaimed.

Tessa looked at her in disgust. "Are you hearing any of this? He's insulting Charlotte!" she whispered, but Jessamine brushed her off with a gesture.

"And who would you suggest run the Institute instead?" the Consul demanded of Benedict, his voice dripping sarcasm. "Yourself, perhaps?"

Benedict spread his hands wide self-deprecatingly. "If you say so, Consul . . ."

Before he could finish speaking, three other figures had risen of their own accord; two Tessa recognized as members of the London Enclave, though she did not know their names; the third was Lilian Highsmith.

Benedict smiled. Everyone was staring at him now; beside him sat his youngest son Gabriel, who was looking up at his father with unreadable green eyes. His slim fingers gripped the back of the chair in front of him.

"Three to support my claim," Benedict said. "That's what the Law requires for me to formally challenge Charlotte Branwell for the position of head of the London Enclave."

Charlotte gave a little gasp but sat motionless in her seat, refusing to turn around. Jem still had Will by the wrist. And Jessamine continued to look as if she were watching an exciting play.

"No," said the Consul.

"You cannot prevent me from challenging—"

"Benedict, you challenged my appointment of Charlotte the moment I made it. You've always wanted the Institute. Now, when the Enclave needs to work together more than ever, you bring division and contention to the proceedings of the Council."

"Change is not always accomplished peacefully, but that does not make it disadvantageous. My challenge stands." Benedict's hands gripped each other.

The Consul drummed his fingers on the lectern. Beside him the Inquisitor stood, cold-eyed. Finally the Consul said, "You suggest, Benedict, that the responsibility of finding Mortmain should be laid upon the shoulders of those who you claim 'lost him.' You would agree, I believe, that finding Mortmain is our first priority?"

Benedict nodded curtly.

"Then, my proposal is this: Let Charlotte and Henry Branwell have charge of the investigation into Mortmain's whereabouts. If by the end of two weeks they have not located him, or at least some strong evidence pointing to his location, then the challenge may go forward."

Charlotte shot forward in her seat. "Find Mortmain?" she said. "Alone, just Henry and I—with no help from the rest of the Enclave?"

The Consul's eyes when they rested on her were not unfriendly, but neither were they entirely forgiving. "You may call upon other members of the Clave if you have some specific need, and of course the Silent Brothers and Iron Sisters are at your disposal," he said. "But as for the investigation, yes, that is for you to accomplish on your own."

"I don't like this," complained Lilian Highsmith. "You're turning the search for a madman into a game of power—"

"Do you wish to withdraw your support for Benedict, then?" asked the Consul. "His challenge would be ended and there would be no need for the Branwells to prove themselves."

Lilian opened her mouth—and then, at a look from Benedict, closed it. She shook her head.

"We have just lost our servants," said Charlotte in a strained voice. "Without them—"

"New servants will be provided to you, as is standard," said the Consul. "Your late servant Thomas's brother, Cyril, is traveling here from Brighton to join your household, and the Dublin Institute has given up its second cook for you. Both are well-trained fighters—which, I must say, Charlotte, yours should have been as well."

"Both Thomas and Agatha *were* trained," Henry protested.

"But you have several in your house who are not," said Benedict. "Not only is Miss Lovelace woefully behind in her training, but your parlor girl, Sophie, and that Downworlder there—" He pointed at Tessa. "Well, since you seem bent on making her a permanent addition to your household, it would hardly hurt if she—and the maid—were trained in the basics of defense."

Tessa looked sideways at Jem in astonishment. "He means *me?*"

Jem nodded. His expression was somber.

"I can't— I'll chop off my own foot!"

"If you're going to chop off anyone's foot, chop off Benedict's," Will muttered.

"You'll be fine, Tessa. It's nothing you can't do," Jem began, but the rest of his words were drowned out by Benedict.

"In fact," Benedict said, "since the two of you will be so busy investigating Mortmain's whereabouts, I suggest I lend you my sons—Gabriel, and Gideon, who returns from Spain tonight—as trainers. Both are excellent fighters and could use the teaching experience."

"Father!" Gabriel protested. He looked horrified; clearly this was not something Benedict had discussed with him in advance.

"We can train our own servants," Charlotte snapped, but the Consul shook his head at her.

"Benedict Lightwood is offering you a generous gift. Accept it."

Charlotte was crimson in the face. After a long moment she bent her head, acknowledging the Consul's words. Tessa felt dizzy. She was going to be trained? Trained to fight, to throw knives and swing a sword? Of course, one of her favorite heroines had always been Capitola in *The Hidden Hand*, who could fight as well as a man—and dressed like one. But that didn't mean she wanted to *be* her.

"Very well," said the Consul. "This session of the Council is ended, to be reconvened here, in the same location, in a fortnight. You are all dismissed."

Of course, everyone did not depart immediately. There was a sudden clamor of voices as people began to rise from their seats and chatter eagerly with their neighbors. Charlotte sat still; Henry beside her, looked as if he wanted desperately to say something comforting but could think of nothing. His hand hovered uncertainly over his wife's shoulder. Will was glaring across the room at Gabriel Lightwood, who looked coldly in their direction.

Slowly Charlotte rose to her feet. Henry had his hand on her back now, murmuring. Jessamine was already standing, twirling her new white lace parasol. Henry had replaced the old one that had been destroyed in battle with Mortmain's automatons. Her hair was done up in tight bunches over her ears like grapes. Tessa got quickly to her feet, and the group of them headed up the center aisle of the Council room. Tessa caught whispers on each side of her, bits of the same words, over and over:

"Charlotte," "Benedict," "never find the Magister," "two weeks," "challenge," "Consul," "Mortmain," "Enclave," "humiliating."

Charlotte walked with her back straight, her cheeks red, and her eyes gazing straight ahead as if she couldn't hear the gossip. Will seemed about to lunge off toward the whisperers to administer rough justice, but Jem had a firm grip on the back of his *parabatai*'s coat. Being Jem, Tessa reflected, must be a great deal like being the owner of a thoroughbred dog that liked to bite your guests. You had to have a hand on his collar constantly. Jessamine merely looked bored again. She wasn't terribly interested in what the Enclave thought of her, or any of them.

By the time they had reached the doors of the Council chamber, they were nearly running. Charlotte paused a moment to let the rest of their group catch up. Most of the crowd was streaming off to the left, where Tessa, Jem, and Will had come from, but Charlotte turned right, marched several paces down the hall, spun around a corner, and abruptly stopped.

"Charlotte?" Henry, catching up to her, sounded worried. "Darling—"

Without warning Charlotte drew her foot back and kicked the wall, as hard as she could. As the wall was stone, this did little damage, though Charlotte let out a low shriek.

"Oh, my," said Jessamine, twirling her parasol.

"If I might make a suggestion," said Will. "About twenty paces behind us, in the Council room, is Benedict. If you'd like to go back in there and try kicking *him*, I recommend aiming upward and a bit to the left—"

"Charlotte." The deep, gravelly voice was instantly recognizable. Charlotte spun around, her brown eyes widening.

It was the Consul. The runes picked out in silver thread on the hem and sleeves of his cloak glittered as he moved toward the little group from the Institute, his gaze on Charlotte. One hand against the wall, she didn't move.

"Charlotte," Consul Wayland said again, "you know what your father always said about losing your temper."

"He did say that. He also said that he should have had a son," Charlotte replied bitterly. "If he had—if I were a man—would you have treated me as you just did?"

Henry put his hand on his wife's shoulder, murmuring something, but she shook it off. Her large, hurt brown eyes were on the Consul.

"And how did I just treat you?" he asked.

"As if I were a child, a little girl who needed scolding."

"Charlotte, I am the one who named you as head of the Institute and the Enclave." The Consul sounded exasperated. "I did it not just because I was fond of Granville Fairchild and knew he wanted his daughter to succeed him, but because I thought you would accomplish the job well."

"You named Henry, too," she said. "And you even told us when you did it that it was because the Enclave would accept a married couple as their leader, but not a woman alone."

"Well, congratulations, Charlotte. I do not think any members of the London Enclave are under the impression that they are in any way being led by Henry."

"It's true," Henry said, looking at his shoes. "They all know I'm rather useless. It's my fault all this happened, Consul—"

"It isn't," said Consul Wayland. "It is a combination of a generalized complacency on the part of the Clave, bad luck and bad timing, and some poor decisions on your part, Charlotte.

Yes, I am holding you accountable for them—"

"So you agree with Benedict!" Charlotte cried.

"Benedict Lightwood is a blackguard and a hypocrite," said the Consul wearily. "Everyone knows that. But he is politically powerful, and it is better to placate him with this show than it would be to antagonize him further by ignoring him."

"A show? Is that what you call this?" Charlotte demanded bitterly. "You have set me an impossible task."

"I have set you the task of locating the Magister," said Consul Wayland. "The man who broke into the Institute, killed your servants, took your Pyxis, and plans to build an army of clockwork monsters to destroy us all—in short, a man who must be stopped. As head of the Enclave, Charlotte, stopping him *is* your task. If you consider it impossible, then perhaps you should ask yourself why you want the job so badly in the first place."

2

REPARATIONS

Then share thy pain, allow that sad relief;
Ah, more than share it! give me all thy grief.
—Alexander Pope, "Eloisa to Abelard"

The witchlight that illuminated the Great Library seemed to be flickering low, like a candle guttering down in its holder, though Tessa knew that was just her imagination. Witchlight, unlike fire or gas, never seemed to fade or burn away.

Her eyes, on the other hand, were beginning to tire, and from the looks of her companions, she wasn't the only one. They were all gathered around one of the long tables, Charlotte at its head, Henry at Tessa's right. Will and Jem sat farther down, beside each other; only Jessamine had retreated to the very far end of the table, separated from the others. The surface of the table was liberally covered with papers of all sorts—old newspaper articles, books, sheets of parchment covered with fine spidery writing. There were genealogies of various Mortmain families, histories of automatons, endless books of spells of summoning and binding, and every bit of research on the Pandemonium Club that the Silent Brothers had managed to scrape out of their archives.

Tessa had been tasked with the job of reading through the newspaper articles, looking for stories about Mortmain and his shipping company, and her eyes were beginning to blur, the words dancing on the pages. She was relieved when Jessamine at last broke the silence, pushing away the book she had been reading—*On the Engines of Sorcery*—and said, "Charlotte, I think we're wasting our time."

Charlotte looked up with a pained expression. "Jessamine, there is no need for you to remain if you do not wish to. I must say, I doubt any of us was expecting your help in this matter, and since you have never much applied yourself to your studies, I cannot help but wonder if you even know what it is you are looking for. Could you tell a binding spell from a summoning spell if I set the two before you?"

Tessa couldn't help being surprised. Charlotte was rarely so sharp with any of them. "I *want* to help," Jessie said sulkily. "Those mechanical *things* of Mortmain's nearly killed me. I want him caught and punished."

"No, you don't." Will, unrolling a parchment so old that it crackled, squinted down at the black symbols on the page. "You want Tessa's brother caught and punished, for making you think he was in love with you when he wasn't."

Jessamine flushed. "I do *not*. I mean, I did not. I mean— ugh! Charlotte, Will's being vexing."

"And the sun has come up in the east," said Jem, to no one in particular.

"I don't want to be thrown out of the Institute if we can't find the Magister," Jessamine went on. "Is that so difficult to understand?"

"You won't be thrown out of the Institute. Charlotte will. I'm sure the Lightwoods will let you stay. And Benedict has two marriageable sons. You ought to be delighted," said Will.

Jessamine made a face. "Shadowhunters. As if I'd want to marry one of them."

"Jessamine, you *are* one of them."

Before Jessamine could reply, the library door opened and Sophie came in, ducking her white-capped head. She spoke quietly to Charlotte, who rose to her feet. "Brother Enoch is here," Charlotte said to the assembled group. "I must speak with him. Will, Jessamine, do try not to kill each other while I am gone. Henry, if you could . . ."

Her voice trailed off. Henry was gazing down at a book—Al-Jazari's *Book of Knowledge of Ingenious Mechanical Devices*—and paying no attention whatsoever to anything else. Charlotte threw up her hands, and left the room with Sophie.

The moment the door closed behind Charlotte, Jessamine shot Will a poisonous look. "If you think I don't have the experience to help, then why is *she* here?" She indicated Tessa. "I don't mean to be rude, but do you think *she* can tell a binding spell from a summoning one?" She looked at Tessa. "Well, can you? And for that matter, Will, you pay so little attention at lessons, can *you* tell a binding spell from a soufflé recipe?"

Will leaned back in his chair and said dreamily, "'I am but mad north-north-west; when the wind is southerly I know a hawk from a handsaw.'"

"Jessamine, Tessa has kindly offered to help, and we need all the eyes we can get right now," said Jem severely. "Will, don't quote *Hamlet*. Henry . . ." He cleared his throat. "HENRY."

Henry looked up, blinking. "Yes, darling?" He blinked again, looking around. "Where's Charlotte?"

"She went to talk to the Silent Brothers," said Jem, who did not appear put out of temper to have been mistaken by Henry for his wife. "In the meantime I'm afraid . . . that I rather agree with Jessamine."

"And the sun comes up in the *west*," said Will, who had apparently heard Jem's earlier comment.

"But why?" Tessa demanded. "We can't give up now. It would be just like handing the Institute over to that awful Benedict Lightwood."

"I'm not suggesting we do nothing, you understand. But we're trying to decipher what it is that Mortmain is going to *do*. We're trying to predict the future instead of trying to understand the past."

"We know Mortmain's past, *and* his plans." Will waved his hand in the direction of the newspapers. "Born in Devon, was a ship's surgeon, became a wealthy trader, got himself mixed up in dark magic, and now plans to rule the world with his massive army of mechanical creatures by his side. A not atypical story for a determined young man—"

"I don't think he ever said anything about ruling the world," interrupted Tessa. "Just the British Empire."

"Admirably literal," said Will. "My point is, we do know

where Mortmain came from. It's hardly our fault that it isn't very interesting . . ." His voice trailed off. "Ah."

"Ah, what?" Jessamine demanded, looking from Will to Jem in a vexed manner. "I declare, the way you two seem to read each other's minds gives me the shudders."

"Ah," said Will. "Jem was just thinking, and I would tend to agree, that Mortmain's life story is, quite simply, balderdash. Some lies, some truth, but very likely there isn't anything in here that will help us. These are just stories he made up to give the newspapers something to print about him. Besides, we don't care how many ships he owns; we want to know where he learned dark magic, and from whom."

"And why he hates Shadowhunters," said Tessa.

Will's blue eyes slid lazily toward her. "Is it hatred?" he said. "I assumed it was a simple greed for domination. With us out of the way, and a clockwork army on his side, he could take power as he liked."

Tessa shook her head. "No, it is more than that. It is difficult to explain, but—he *hates* the Nephilim. It is something very personal for him. And it has something to do with that watch. It's—it's as if he desires recompense for some wrong or hurt they've done him."

"Reparations," said Jem very suddenly, setting down the pen he was holding.

Will looked at him in puzzlement. "Is this a game? We just blurt out whatever word comes next to mind? In that case mine's 'genuphobia.' It means an unreasonable fear of knees."

"What's the word for a perfectly reasonable fear of annoying idiots?" inquired Jessamine.

"The Reparations section of the archives," said Jem, ignoring them both. "The Consul mentioned it yesterday, and it's been in my head since. We haven't looked there."

"Reparations?" asked Tessa.

"When a Downworlder, or a mundane, alleges that a Shadowhunter has broken the Law in their dealings with them, the Downworlder lodges a complaint through Reparations. There will be a trial, and the Downworlder will be accorded some sort of payment, based on whether they can prove their case."

"Well, it seems a bit silly, looking there," said Will. "It's not like Mortmain's going to lodge a complaint against the Shadowhunters through official channels. 'Very upset Shadowhunters refused to all die when I wanted them to. Demand recompense. Please mail cheque to A. Mortmain, 18 Kensington Road—'"

"Enough persiflage," said Jem. "Maybe he hasn't always hated Shadowhunters. Maybe there was a time when he did attempt to gain compensation through the official system and it failed him. What's the harm in asking? The worst thing that could happen is that we turn up nothing, which is exactly what we're turning up right now." He rose to his feet, pushing his silvery hair back. "I'm off to catch Charlotte before Brother Enoch leaves and ask her to have the Silent Brothers check the archives."

Tessa rose to her feet. She did not relish the idea of being left alone in the library with Will and Jessamine, who were bound to bicker. Of course Henry was there, but he seemed to be taking a gentle nap on a pile of books, and was not much of a buffer in the best of cases. Being around Will was uncomfortable in most circumstances; only with Jem there was it bearable. Somehow Jem was able to whittle down Will's sharp edges and make him nearly human. "I'll go with you, Jem," she said. "There's—there was something I wished to speak to Charlotte about anyway."

Jem seemed surprised but pleased; Will looked from one of them to the other and pushed his chair back. "We've been among these moldering old books for ages," he announced. "Mine beautiful eyes are weary, and I have paper cuts. See?" He spread his fingers wide. "I'm going for a walk."

Tessa couldn't help herself. "Perhaps you could use an *iratze* to take care of them."

He glared at her. His eyes *were* beautiful. "Ever and always helpful, Tessa."

She matched his glare. "My only desire is to be of service."

Jem put his hand on her shoulder, his voice concerned. "Tessa, Will. I don't think—"

But Will was gone, snatching up his coat and banging his way out of the library, with enough force to make the door frame vibrate.

Jessamine sat back in her chair, narrowing her brown eyes. "How interesting."

Tessa's hands shook as she tucked a lock of hair behind her ear. She hated that Will had this effect on her. Hated it. She knew better. She knew what he thought of her. That she was nothing, worth nothing. And still a look from him could make her tremble with mingled hatred and longing. It was like a poison in her blood, to which Jem was the only antidote. Only with him did she feel on steady ground.

"Come." Jem took her arm lightly. A gentleman would not normally touch a lady in public, but here in the Institute the

Shadowhunters were more familiar with one another than were the mundanes outside. When she turned to look at him, he smiled at her. Jem put the full force of himself into each smile, so that he seemed to be smiling with his eyes, his heart, his whole being. "We'll find Charlotte."

"And what am I supposed to do while you're gone?" Jessamine said crossly as they made their way to the door.

Jem glanced back over his shoulder. "You could always wake up Henry. It looks like he's eating paper in his sleep again, and you know how Charlotte hates that."

"Oh, *bother*," said Jessamine with an exasperated sigh. "Why do I always get the silly tasks?"

"Because you don't want the serious ones," said Jem, sounding as close to exasperated as Tessa had ever heard him. Neither of them noticed the icy look she shot them as they left the library behind and headed down the corridor.

"Mr. Bane has been awaiting your arrival, sir," the footman said, and stepped aside to let Will enter. The footman's name was Archer—or Walker, or something like that, Will thought—and he was one of Camille's human subjugates. Like all those enslaved to a vampire's will, he was sickly-looking, with parchment pale skin and thin, stringy hair. He looked about as happy to see Will as a dinner party guest might be to see a slug crawling out from under his lettuce.

The moment Will entered the house, the smell hit him. It was the smell of dark magic, like sulfur mixed with the Thames on a hot day. Will wrinkled his nose. The footman looked at him with even more loathing. "Mr. Bane is in the drawing room." His voice indicated that there was no chance whatsoever that he was going to accompany Will there. "Shall I take your coat?"

"That won't be necessary." Coat still on, Will followed the scent of magic down the corridor. It intensified as he drew nearer to the door of the drawing room, which was firmly closed. Tendrils of smoke threaded out from the gap beneath the door. Will took a deep breath of sour air, and pushed the door open.

The inside of the drawing room looked peculiarly bare. After a moment Will realized that this was because Magnus had taken all the heavy teak furniture, even the piano, and pushed it up against the walls. An ornate gasolier hung from the ceiling, but the light in the room was provided by dozens of thick black candles arranged in a circle in the center of the room. Magnus stood beside the circle, a book open in his hands; his old-fashioned cravat was loosened, and his black hair stood up wildly about his face as if charged with electricity. He looked up when Will came in, and smiled. "Just in time!" he cried. "I really think we may have him this round. Will, meet Thammuz, a minor demon from the eighth dimension. Thammuz, meet Will, a minor Shadowhunter from— Wales, was it?"

"*I will rip out your eyes,*" hissed the creature sitting in the center of the burning circle. It was certainly a demon, no more than three feet high, with pale blue skin, three coal black, burning eyes, and long blood-red talons on its eight-fingered hands. "*I will tear the skin from your face.*"

"Don't be rude, Thammuz," said Magnus, and although his tone was light, the circle of candles blazed suddenly, brightly upward, causing the demon to shrink in on itself with a scream. "Will has questions. You will answer them."

Will shook his head. "I don't know, Magnus," he said. "He doesn't look like the right one to me."

"You *said* he was blue. This one's blue."

"He is blue," Will acknowledged, stepping closer to the circle of flame. "But the demon I need—well, he was really a cobalt blue. This one's more . . . periwinkle."

"*What did you call me?*" The demon roared with rage. "*Come closer, little Shadowhunter, and let me feast upon your liver! I will tear it from your body while you scream.*"

Will turned to Magnus. "He doesn't *sound* right either. The voice is different. And the number of eyes."

"Are you sure—"

"I'm absolutely sure," said Will in a voice that brooked no contradiction. "It's not something I would ever—could ever—forget."

Magnus sighed and turned back to the demon. "Thammuz," he said, reading aloud from the book. "I charge you, by the power of bell and book and candle, and by the great names of Sammael and Abbadon and Moloch, to speak the truth. Have you ever encountered the Shadowhunter Will Herondale before this day, or any of his blood or lineage?"

"*I don't know,*" said the demon petulantly. "*Humans all look alike to me.*"

Magnus's voice rose, sharp and commanding. "Answer me!"

"*Oh, very well. No, I've never seen him before in my life. I'd remember. He looks as if he'd taste good.*" The demon grinned, showing razor-sharp teeth. "*I haven't even been to this world for, oh, a hundred years, possibly more. I can never remember the difference between a hundred and a thousand. Anyway, the last time I was here, everyone was living in mud huts and eating bugs. So I doubt*"

he *was around*"—he pointed a many-jointed finger at Will—
"*unless Earthkind lives much longer than I was led to believe.*"

Magnus rolled his eyes. "You're just determined not to be
any help at all, aren't you?"

The demon shrugged, a peculiarly human gesture. "*You
forced me to tell the truth. I told it.*"

"Well, then, have you ever *heard* of a demon like the one I
was describing?" Will broke in, a tinge of desperation in his
voice. "Dark blue, with a raspy sort of voice, like sandpaper—
and he had a long, barbed tail."

The demon regarded him with a bored expression. "*Do you
have any idea how many kinds of demons there are in the Void,
Nephilim? Hundreds upon hundreds of millions. The great demon city
of Pandemonium makes your London look like a village. Demons of all
shapes and sizes and colors. Some can change their appearance at will—*"

"Oh, be quiet, then, if you're not going to be of any use,"
Magnus said, and slammed the book shut. Instantly the candles
went out, the demon vanishing with a startled cry, leaving
behind only a wisp of foul-smelling smoke.

The warlock turned to Will. "I was so sure I had the right
one this time."

"It's not your fault." Will flung himself onto one of the
divans shoved up against the wall. He felt hot and cold at
the same time, his nerves prickling with a disappointment
he was trying to force back without much success. He pulled
his gloves off restlessly and shoved them into the pockets of
his still buttoned coat. "You're trying. Thammuz was right. I
haven't given you very much to go on."

"I assume," Magnus said quietly, "that you have told me all
you remember. You opened a Pyxis and released a demon. It

cursed you. You want me to find that demon and see if it will remove the curse. And that is all you can tell me?"

"It is all I can tell you," said Will. "It would hardly benefit me to hold anything back unnecessarily, when I know what I'm asking. For you to find a needle in—God, not even a haystack. A needle in a tower full of other needles."

"Plunge your hand into a tower of needles," said Magnus, "and you are likely to cut yourself badly. Are you really sure this is what you want?"

"I am sure that the alternative is worse," said Will, staring at the blackened place on the floor where the demon had crouched. He was exhausted. The energy rune he'd given himself that morning before leaving for the Council meeting had worn off by noon, and his head throbbed. "I have had five years to live with it. The idea of living with it for even one more frightens me more than the idea of death."

"You are a Shadowhunter; you are not afraid of death."

"Of course I am," said Will. "Everyone is afraid of death. We may be born of angels, but we have no more knowledge of what comes after death than you do."

Magnus moved closer to him and sat down on the opposite side of the divan. His green-gold eyes shone like a cat's in the dimness. "You don't know that there is only oblivion after death."

"You don't know that there isn't, do you? Jem believes we are all reborn, that life is a wheel. We die, we turn, we are reborn as we deserve to be reborn, based on our doings in this world." Will looked down at his bitten nails. "I will probably be reborn as a slug that someone salts."

"The Wheel of Transmigration," said Magnus. His lips twitched into a smile. "Well, think of it this way. You must have done something right in your last life, to be reborn as you were. Nephilim."

"Oh, yes," said Will in a dead tone. "I've been very lucky." He leaned his head back against the divan, exhausted. "I take it you'll be needing more . . . ingredients? I think Old Mol over at Cross Bones is getting sick of the sight of me."

"I have other connections," said Magnus, clearly taking pity on him, "and I need to do more research first. If you could tell me the nature of the curse—"

"No." Will sat up. "I can't. I told you before, I took a great risk even in telling you of its existence. If I told you any more—"

"Then what? Let me guess. You don't know, but you're sure it would be bad."

"Don't start making me think coming to you was a mistake—"

"This has something to do with Tessa, doesn't it?"

Over the past five years Will had trained himself well not to show emotion—surprise, affection, hopefulness, joy. He was fairly sure his expression didn't change, but he heard the strain in his voice when he said, "Tessa?"

"It's been five years," said Magnus. "Yet somehow you have managed all this time, telling no one. What desperation drove you to me, in the middle of the night, in a rainstorm? What has changed at the Institute? I can think of only one thing—and quite a pretty one, with big gray eyes—"

Will got to his feet so abruptly, he nearly tipped the divan over. "There are other things," he said, struggling to keep his voice even. "Jem is dying."

Magnus looked at him, a cool, even stare. "He has been dying for years," he said. "No curse laid on you could cause or repair his condition."

Will realized his hands were shaking; he tightened them into fists. "You don't understand—"

"I know you are *parabatai*," said Magnus. "I know that his death will be a great loss for you. But what I don't know—"

"You know what you need to know." Will felt cold all over, though the room was warm and he still wore his coat. "I can pay you more, if it will make you stop asking me questions."

Magnus put his feet up on the divan. "Nothing will make me stop asking you questions," he said. "But I will do my best to respect your reticence."

Relief loosened Will's hands. "Then, you will still help me."

"I will still help you." Magnus put his hands behind his head and leaned back, looking at Will through half-lowered lids. "Though I could help you better if you told me the truth, I will do what I can. You interest me oddly, Will Herondale."

Will shrugged. "That will do well enough as a reason. When do you plan to try again?"

Magnus yawned. "Probably this weekend. I shall send you a message by Saturday if there are . . . developments."

Developments. Curse. Truth. Jem. Dying. Tessa. Tessa, Tessa, Tessa. Her name rang in Will's mind like the chime of a bell; he wondered if any other name on earth had such an inescapable resonance to it. She couldn't have been named something awful, could she, like Mildred. He couldn't imagine lying awake at night, staring up at the ceiling while invisible voices whispered "Mildred" in his ears. But *Tessa*—

"Thank you," he said abruptly. He had gone from being too cold to being too warm; it was stifling in the room, still smelling of burned candle wax. "I will look forward to hearing from you, then."

"Yes, do," said Magnus, and he closed his eyes. Will couldn't tell whether he was actually asleep or simply waiting for Will to leave; either way, it was clearly a hint that he expected Will to depart. Will, not entirely without relief, took it.

Sophie was on her way to Miss Jessamine's room, to sweep the ashes and clean the grate of the fireplace, when she heard voices in the hall. In her old place of employment she had been taught to "give room"—to turn and look at the walls while her employers passed by, and do her best to resemble a piece of furniture, something inanimate that they could ignore.

She had been shocked on coming to the Institute to find that things were not managed that way here. First, for such a large house to have so few servants had surprised her. She had not realized at first that the Shadowhunters did much for themselves that a typical family of good breeding would find beneath them—started their own fires, did some of their own shopping, kept rooms like the training area and the weapons room cleaned and neat. She had been shocked at the familiarity with which Agatha and Thomas had treated their employers, not realizing that her fellow servants had come from families that had served Shadowhunters through the generations—or that they'd had magic of their own.

She herself had come from a poor family, and had been called "stupid" and been slapped often when she'd first begun working as a maid—because she hadn't been used to delicate furniture or real silver, or china so thin you could see the darkness of the tea through the sides. But she had learned, and when it had become clear that she was going to be very pretty, she had been promoted to parlor maid.

A parlor maid's lot was a precarious one. She was meant to look beautiful for the household, and therefore her salary had begun to go down each year that she'd aged, once she had turned eighteen.

It had been such a relief, coming to work at the Institute—where no one minded that she was nearly twenty, or demanded that she stare at the walls, or cared whether she spoke before she was spoken to—that she had almost thought it worth the mutilation of her pretty face at the hands of her last employer. She still avoided looking at herself in mirrors if she could, but the dreadful horror of loss had faded. Jessamine mocked her for the long scar that disfigured her cheek, but the others seemed not to notice, save Will, who occasionally said something unpleasant, but in an almost perfunctory way, as if it were expected of him but his heart were not in it.

But that was all before she had fallen in love with Jem.

She recognized his voice now as he came down the hall, raised in laughter, and answering him was Miss Tessa. Sophie felt an odd little pressure against her chest. Jealousy. She despised herself for it, but it could not be stopped. Miss Tessa was always kind to her, and there was such enormous vulnerability in her wide gray eyes—such a need for a friend—that it was impossible to dislike her. And yet, the way Master Jem looked at her . . . and Tessa did not even seem to notice.

No. Sophie just couldn't bear to encounter the two of them in the hall, with Jem looking at Tessa the way he had been lately. Clutching the sweeping brush and bucket to her chest, Sophie opened the nearest door and ducked inside, closing it most of the way behind her. It was, like most of the rooms in the Institute, an unused bedroom, meant for visiting Shadowhunters. She would give the rooms a turn once a fortnight or so, unless someone was using them; otherwise they stood undisturbed. This one was quite dusty; motes danced in the light from the windows, and Sophie fought the urge to sneeze as she pressed her eye to the crack in the door.

She had been right. It was Jem and Tessa, coming toward her down the hall. They appeared entirely engaged with each other. Jem was carrying something—folded gear, it looked like—and Tessa was laughing at something he had said. She was looking a little down and away from him, and he was gazing at her, the way one did when one felt one was unobserved. He had that look on his face, that look he usually got only when he was playing the violin, as if he were completely caught up and entranced.

Her heart hurt. He was so beautiful. She had always thought so. Most people went on about Will, how handsome he was, but she thought that Jem was a thousand times better-looking. He had the ethereal look of angels in paintings, and though she knew that the silvery color of his hair and skin was a result of the medicine he took for his illness, she couldn't help finding it lovely too. And he was gentle, firm, and kind. The thought of his hands in her hair, stroking it back from her face, made her feel comforted, whereas usually the thought of a man, even a boy, touching her made her feel vulnerable and ill. He had the most careful, beautifully constructed hands. . . .

"I can't quite believe they're coming tomorrow," Tessa was saying, turning her gaze back to Jem. "I feel as if Sophie and I are being tossed to Benedict Lightwood to appease him, like a dog with a bone. He can't *really* mind if we're trained or not. He just wants his sons in the house to bother Charlotte."

"That's true," Jem acknowledged. "But why not take advantage of the training when it's offered? That's why Charlotte is trying to encourage Jessamine to take part. As for you, given your talent, even if—I should say, when—Mortmain is no longer a threat, there will be others attracted to your power. You might do well to learn how to fend them off."

Tessa's hand went to the angel necklace at her throat, a habitual gesture Sophie suspected she was not even aware of. "I know what Jessie will say. She'll say the only thing she needs assistance fending off is handsome suitors."

"Wouldn't she rather have help fending off the unattractive ones?"

"Not if they're mundanes." Tessa grinned. "She'd rather an ugly mundane than a handsome Shadowhunter any day."

"That does put me right out of the running, doesn't it?" said Jem with mock chagrin, and Tessa laughed again.

"It is too bad," she said. "Someone as pretty as Jessamine ought to have her pick, but she's so determined that a Shadowhunter won't do—"

"You are much prettier," said Jem.

Tessa looked at him in surprise, her cheeks coloring. Sophie felt the twist of jealousy in her chest again, though she agreed with Jem. Jessamine was quite traditionally pretty, a pocket Venus if ever there was one, but her habitual sour expression spoiled her charms. Tessa, though, had a warm appeal, with her rich, dark, waving hair and sea gray eyes, that grew on you the longer you knew her. There was intelligence in her face, and humor, which Jessamine did not have, or at least did not display.

Jem paused in front of Miss Jessamine's door, and knocked upon it. When there was no answer, he shrugged, bent down, and placed a stack of dark fabric—gear—in front of the door.

"She'll never wear it." Tessa's face dimpled.

Jem straightened up. "I never agreed to wrestle her into the clothes, just deliver them."

He started off down the hallway again, Tessa beside him. "I don't know how Charlotte can bear to talk to Brother Enoch so often. He gives me the horrors," she said.

"Oh, I don't know. I prefer to think that when they're at home, the Silent Brothers are much like us. Playing practical jokes in the Silent City, making toasted cheese—"

"I hope they play charades," said Tessa dryly. "It would seem to take advantage of their natural talents."

Jem burst out laughing, and then they were around the corner and out of sight. Sophie sagged against the door frame. She did not think she had ever made Jem laugh like that; she didn't think anyone had, except for Will. You had to know someone very well to make them laugh like that. She had loved him for such a long time, she thought. How was it that she did not know him at all?

With a sigh of resignation she made ready to depart her hiding place—when the door to Miss Jessamine's room opened, and its resident emerged. Sophie shrank bank into the dimness. Miss Jessamine was dressed in a long velvet traveling cloak that concealed most of her body, from her neck to her feet. Her hair was bound tightly behind her head, and she carried a gentleman's hat in one hand. Sophie froze in surprise as Jessamine looked down, saw the gear at her feet, and made a face. She kicked it swiftly into the room—giving Sophie a view of her foot, which seemed to be clad in a man's boot—and closed the door soundlessly behind her. Glancing up and down the corridor, she placed the hat on her head, dropped her chin low into the cloak, and slunk off into the shadows, leaving Sophie staring, mystified, after her.

3

Unjustifiable Death

Alas! they had been friends in youth;
But whispering tongues can poison truth;
And constancy lives in realms above;
And life is thorny; and youth is vain;
And to be wroth with one we love
Doth work like madness in the brain.
—Samuel Taylor Coleridge, "Christabel"

After breakfast the next day Charlotte instructed Tessa and Sophie to return to their rooms, dress in their newly acquired gear, and meet Jem in the training room, where they would wait for the Lightwood brothers. Jessamine had not come to breakfast, claiming a headache, and Will, likewise, was nowhere to be found. Tessa suspected he was hiding, in an attempt to avoid being forced to be polite to Gabriel Lightwood and his brother. She could only partly blame him.

Back in her room, picking up the gear, she felt a flutter of nerves in her stomach; it was so very much unlike anything she'd ever worn before. Sophie was not there to help her with the new clothes. Part of the training, of course, was being able to dress and to familiarize oneself with the gear: flat-soled shoes; a loose pair of trousers made of thick black material; and a long, belted tunic that reached nearly to her knees. They were the same clothes she had seen Charlotte fight in before, and had seen illustrated in the *Codex*; she had thought them strange then, but the act of actually wearing them was even stranger. If Aunt Harriet could have seen her now, Tessa thought, she would likely have fainted.

She met Sophie at the foot of the steps that led up to the Institute's training room. Neither she nor the other girl exchanged a word, just encouraging smiles. After a moment Tessa went first up the steps, a narrow wooden flight with banisters so old that the wood had begun to splinter. It was strange, Tessa thought, going up a flight of stairs and *not* having to worry about pulling in your skirts or tripping on the hem. Though her body was completely covered, she felt peculiarly naked in her training gear.

It helped to have Sophie with her, obviously equally uncomfortable in her own Shadowhunter gear. When they reached the top of the stairs, Sophie swung the door open and they made their way into the training room in silence, together.

They were obviously at the top of the Institute, in a room adjacent to the attic, Tessa thought, and nearly twice the size. The floor was polished wood with various patterns drawn here and there in black ink—circles and squares, some of them numbered. Long, flexible ropes hung from great raftered beams overhead, half-invisible in the shadows. Witchlight torches burned along the walls, interspersed with hanging weapons—maces and axes and all sorts of other deadly-looking objects.

"Ugh," said Sophie, looking at them with a shudder. "Don't they look too horrible by half?"

"I actually recognize a few from the *Codex*," said Tessa, pointing. "That one there's a longsword, and there's a rapier, and a fencing foil, and that one that looks like you'd need two hands to hold it is a claymore, I think."

"Close," came a voice, very disconcertingly, from above their heads. "It's an executioner's sword. Mostly for decapitations. You can tell because it doesn't have a sharp point."

Sophie gave a little yelp of surprise and backed up as one of the dangling ropes began to sway and a dark shape appeared over their heads. It was Jem, clambering down the rope with the graceful agility of a bird. He landed lightly in front of them, and smiled. "My apologies. I didn't mean to startle you."

He was dressed in gear as well, though instead of a tunic he wore a shirt that reached only to his waist. A single leather strap went across his chest, and the hilt of a sword protruded from behind one shoulder. The darkness of the gear made his skin look even paler, his hair and eyes more silver than ever.

"Yes, you did," said Tessa with a little smile, "but it's all right. I was beginning to worry Sophie and I were going to be left here to train each other."

"Oh, the Lightwoods will be here," said Jem. "They're simply being late to make a point. They don't have to do what we say, or what their father says either."

"I wish you were the one training us," Tessa said impulsively.

Jem looked surprised. "I couldn't—I haven't completed my

own training yet." But their eyes met, and in another moment of wordless communication, Tessa heard what he was really saying: *I'm not well enough often enough to train you reliably.* Her throat hurt suddenly, and she locked eyes with Jem, hoping he could read her silent sympathy in them. She did not want to look away, and found herself wondering if the way that she had scraped her hair back, carefully pinning it into a bun from which no stray strands escaped, looked horribly unflattering. Not that it mattered, of course. It was just *Jem*, after all.

"We won't be going through a *full* course of training, will we?" Sophie said, her worried voice breaking into Tessa's thoughts. "The Council only said that we needed to know how to defend ourselves a bit. . . ."

Jem looked away from Tessa; the connection broke with a snap. "There's nothing to be frightened of, Sophie," he said in his gentle voice. "And you'll be glad of it; it's always useful for a beautiful girl to be able to fend off the unwanted attentions of gentlemen."

Sophie's face tightened, the livid scar on her cheek standing out as red as if it had been painted there. "Don't make fun," she said. "It isn't kind."

Jem looked startled. "Sophie, I wasn't—"

The door to the training room opened. Tessa turned as Gabriel Lightwood strode into the room, followed by a boy she didn't know. Where Gabriel was slender and dark-haired, the other boy was muscular, with thick sandy-blond hair. They were both dressed in gear, with expensive-looking dark gloves studded with metal across the knuckles. Each wore silver bands around each wrist—knife sheaths, Tessa knew—and had the same elaborate white pattern of runes woven into their sleeves. It was clear not just from the similarity of their clothes but from the shape of their faces and the pale, luminous green of their eyes that they were related, so Tessa was not in the least surprised when Gabriel said, in his abrupt manner:

"Well, we're here as we said we would be. James, I assume you remember my brother, Gideon. Miss Gray, Miss Collins—"

"Pleased to make your acquaintance," Gideon muttered, meeting neither of their eyes with his. Bad moods seemed to run in the family, Tessa thought, remembering that Will had said that next to his brother, Gabriel seemed a sweetheart.

"Don't worry. Will's not here," Jem said to Gabriel, who was glancing around the room. Gabriel frowned at him, but Jem had already turned to Gideon. "When did you get back from Madrid?" he asked politely.

"Father called me back home a short while ago." Gideon's tone was neutral. "Family business."

"I do hope everything's all right—"

"Everything is quite all right, thank you, James," said Gabriel, his tone clipped. "Now, before we move to the training portion of this visit, there are two people you should probably meet." He turned his head and called out, "Mr. Tanner, Miss Daly! Please come up."

There were footfalls on the steps, and two strangers entered, neither in gear. Both wore servants' clothes. One was a young woman who was the very definition of "rawboned"— her bones seemed too big for her skinny, awkward frame. Her hair was a bright scarlet, drawn back into a chignon under a modest hat. Her bare hands were red and scrubbed-looking. Tessa guessed she was about twenty. Beside her stood a young man with dark brown curling hair, tall and muscular—

Sophie took a sharp indrawn breath. She had gone pale. "Thomas . . ."

The young man looked terribly awkward. "I'm Thomas's brother, miss. Cyril. Cyril Tanner."

"These are the replacements the Council promised you for your lost servants," said Gabriel. "Cyril Tanner and Bridget Daly. The Consul asked us if we would bring them from Kings Cross here, and naturally we obliged. Cyril will replace Thomas, and Bridget will replace your lost cook, Agatha. They were both trained in fine Shadowhunter households and come soundly recommended."

Red spots had begun to burn on Sophie's cheeks. Before she could say anything, Jem said quickly, "No one could replace Agatha or Thomas for us, Gabriel. They were friends as well as servants." He nodded toward Bridget and Cyril. "No offense intended."

Bridget only blinked her brown eyes, but, "None taken," said Cyril. Even his voice was like Thomas's, almost eerily so. "Thomas was my brother. No one can replace him for me, either."

An awkward silence descended on the room. Gideon leaned back against one of the walls, his arms crossed, a slight scowl on his face. He was quite good-looking, like his brother, Tessa thought, but the scowl rather spoiled it.

"Very well," Gabriel said finally into the silence. "Charlotte had asked us to bring them up so you could meet them. Jem, if you'd like to escort them back to the drawing room, Charlotte's waiting with instructions—"

"So neither of them needs any extra training?" Jem said.

"Since you'll be training Tessa and Sophie regardless, if Bridget or Cyril—"

"As the Consul said, they have been quite effectively trained in their previous households," said Gideon. "Would you like a demonstration?"

"I don't think that's necessary," Jem said.

Gabriel grinned. "Come along, Carstairs. The girls might as well see that a mundane can fight almost like a Shadowhunter, with the *right* kind of instruction. Cyril?" He stalked over to the wall, selected two longswords, and threw one toward Cyril, who caught it out of the air handily and advanced toward the center of the room, where a circle was painted on the floorboards.

"We already know that," muttered Sophie, in a voice low enough that only Tessa could hear. "Thomas and Agatha were both trained."

"Gabriel is only trying to annoy you," said Tessa, also in a whisper. "Do not let him see that he bothers you."

Sophie set her jaw as Gabriel and Cyril met in the center of the room, swords flashing.

Tessa had to admit there was something rather beautiful about it, the way they circled each other, blades singing through the air, a blur of black and silver. The ringing sound of metal on metal, the way they moved, so fast her vision could barely follow. And yet, Gabriel was better; that was clear even to the untrained eye. His reflexes were faster, his movements more graceful. It was not a fair fight; Cyril, his hair pasted to his forehead with sweat, was clearly giving everything he had, while Gabriel was simply marking time. In the end, when Gabriel swiftly disarmed Cyril with a neat flicking motion of his wrist, sending the other boy's sword rattling to the floor, Tessa couldn't help but feel almost indignant on Cyril's behalf. No human could best a Shadowhunter. Wasn't that the point?

The point of Gabriel's blade rested an inch from Cyril's throat. Cyril raised his hands in surrender, a smile, much like his brother's easy grin, spreading across his face. "I yield—"

There was a blur of movement. Gabriel yelped and went down, his sword skittering from his hand. His body hit the ground, Bridget kneeling atop his chest, her teeth bared. She had slipped up behind him and tripped him while no one was looking. Now she whipped a small dagger from the inside of her bodice and held it against his throat. Gabriel looked up at her for a moment, dazed, blinking his green eyes. Then he began to laugh.

Tessa liked him more in that moment than she ever had before. Not that that was saying much.

"Very impressive," drawled a familiar voice from the doorway. Tessa turned. It was Will, looking, as her aunt would have said, as if he'd been dragged through a hedge backward. His shirt was torn, his hair was mussed, and his blue eyes were rimmed with red. He bent down, picked up Gabriel's fallen sword, and leveled it in Bridget's direction with an amused expression. "But can she *cook*?"

Bridget scrambled to her feet, her cheeks flushing dark red. She was looking at Will the way girls always did—a little openmouthed, as if she couldn't quite believe the vision that had materialized in front of her. Tessa wanted to tell her that Will looked better when less bedraggled, and that being fascinated by his beauty was like being fascinated by a razor-sharp piece of steel—dangerous and unwise. But what was the point? She'd learn it herself soon enough. "I am a fine cook, sir," she said in a lilting Irish accent. "My previous employers had no complaints."

"Lord, you're Irish," said Will. "Can you make things that don't have potatoes in them? We had an Irish cook once when I was a boy. Potato pie, potato custard, potatoes with potato sauce . . ."

Bridget looked baffled. Meanwhile, somehow Jem had crossed the room and seized Will's arm. "Charlotte wants to see Cyril and Bridget in the drawing room. Shall we show them where it is?"

Will wavered. He was looking at Tessa now. She swallowed against her dry throat. He looked as if there were something he wanted to say to her. Gabriel, glancing between them, smirked. Will's eyes darkened, and he turned, Jem's hand guiding him toward the stairway, and stalked out. After a startled moment Bridget and Cyril followed.

When Tessa turned back to the center of the room, she saw that Gabriel had taken one of the blades and handed it to his brother. "Now," he said. "It's about time to start training, wouldn't you say, ladies?"

Gideon took the blade. "*Esta es la idea más estúpida que nuestro padre ha tenido,*" he said. "*Jamás.*"

Sophie and Tessa exchanged a look. Tessa wasn't sure *exactly* what Gideon had said, but "*estúpida*" sounded familiar enough. It was going to be a long remainder of the day.

They spent the next few hours performing balancing and blocking exercises. Gabriel took it upon himself to oversee

Tessa's instruction, while Gideon was assigned to Sophie. Tessa couldn't help but feel that Gabriel had chosen her to annoy Will in some obscure way, whether Will knew about it or not. He wasn't a bad teacher, actually—fairly patient, willing to pick up weapons again and again as she dropped them, until he could show her how to get the grip correct, even praising when she did something right. She was concentrating too fiercely to notice whether Gideon was as adept at training Sophie, though Tessa heard him muttering in Spanish from time to time.

By the time the training was over and Tessa had bathed and dressed for dinner, she was starving in a most unladylike manner. Fortunately, despite Will's fears, Bridget *could* cook, and very well. She served a hot roast with vegetables, and a jam tart with custard, to Henry, Will, Tessa, and Jem for dinner. Jessamine was still in her room with a headache, and Charlotte had gone to the Bone City to look directly through the Reparations archives herself.

It was odd, having Sophie and Cyril coming in and out of the dining room with platters of food, Cyril carving the roast just as Thomas would have, Sophie helping him silently. Tessa could hardly help but think how difficult it had to be for Sophie, whose closest companions in the Institute had been Agatha and Thomas, but every time Tessa tried to catch the other girl's eye, Sophie looked away.

Tessa remembered the look on Sophie's face the last time Jem had been ill, the way she'd twisted her cap in her hands, begging for news of him. Tessa had ached to talk to Sophie about it afterward, but knew she never could. Romances between mundanes and Shadowhunters were forbidden; Will's mother was a mundane, and his father had been forced to leave the Shadowhunters to be with her. He must have been terribly in love to be willing to do it—and Tessa had never had the sense that Jem was fond of Sophie in that way at all. And then there was the matter of his illness. . . .

"Tessa," Jem said in a low voice, "are you all right? You look a million miles away."

She smiled at him. "Just tired. The training—I'm not used to it." It was the truth. Her arms were sore from holding the heavy practice sword, and though she and Sophie had done little beyond balancing and blocking exercises, her legs ached too.

"There's a salve the Silent Brothers make, for sore muscles. Knock on the door of my room before you go to sleep, and I'll give you some."

Tessa flushed slightly, then wondered why she had flushed. The Shadowhunters had their odd ways. She had been in Jem's room before, even alone with him, even alone with him in her night attire, and no fuss had been made over it. All he was doing now was offering her a bit of medicine, and yet she could feel the heat rise in her face—and he seemed to see it, and flushed himself, the color very visible against his pale skin. Tessa looked away hastily and caught Will watching them both, his blue eyes level and dark. Only Henry, chasing mushy peas around his plate with a fork, seemed oblivious.

"Much obliged," she said. "I will—"

Charlotte burst into the room, her dark hair escaping from its pins in a whirl of curls, a long scroll of paper clutched in her hand. "I've found it!" she cried. She collapsed breathlessly into the seat beside Henry, her normally pale face rosy with exertion. She smiled at Jem. "You were quite right—the

Reparations archives—I found it after only a few hours of looking."

"Let me see," said Will, setting down his fork. He had eaten only a very little of his food, Tessa couldn't help noticing. The bird design ring flashed on his fingers as he reached for the scroll in Charlotte's hand.

She swatted his hand away good-naturedly. "No. We shall all look at them at the same time. It was Jem's idea, anyway, wasn't it?"

Will frowned, but said nothing; Charlotte spread the scroll out over the table, pushing aside teacups and empty plates to make room, and the others rose and crowded around her, gazing down at the document. The paper was really more like thick parchment, with dark red ink, like the color of the runes on the Silent Brothers' robes. The handwriting was in English, but cramped and full of abbreviations; Tessa could make neither head nor tail of what she was looking at.

Jem leaned in close to her, his arm brushing hers, reading over her shoulder. His expression was thoughtful.

She turned her head toward him; a lock of his pale hair tickled her face. "What does it say?" she whispered.

"It's a request for recompense," said Will, ignoring the fact that she had addressed her question to Jem. "Sent to the York Institute in 1825 in the name of Axel Hollingworth Mortmain, seeking reparations for the unjustified death of his parents, John Thaddeus and Anne Evelyn Shade, almost a decade before."

"John Thaddeus Shade," said Tessa. "*JTS*, the initials on Mortmain's watch. But if he was their son, why doesn't he have the same surname?"

"The Shades were warlocks," said Jem, reading farther down the page. "Both of them. He couldn't have been their blood son; they must have adopted him, and let him keep his mundane name. It does happen, from time to time." His eyes flicked toward Tessa, and then away; she wondered if he was remembering, as she was, their conversation in the music room about the fact that warlocks could not have children.

"He said he began to learn about the dark arts during his travels," said Charlotte. "But if his parents were warlocks—"

"Adoptive parents," said Will. "Yes, I'm sure he knew just who in Downworld to contact to learn the darker arts."

"Unjustifiable death," Tessa said in a small voice. "What does that mean, exactly?"

"It *means* he believes that Shadowhunters killed his parents despite the fact that they had broken no Laws," said Charlotte.

"What Law were they meant to have broken?"

Charlotte frowned. "It says something here about unnatural and illegal dealings with demons—that could be nearly anything—and that they stood accused of creating a weapon that could destroy Shadowhunters. The sentence for that would have been death. This was before the Accords, though, you must remember. Shadowhunters could kill Downworlders on the mere suspicion of wrongdoing. That's probably why there's nothing more substantive or detailed in the paperwork here. Mortmain filed for recompense through the York Institute, under the aegis of Aloysius Starkweather. He was asking not for money but for the guilty parties— Shadowhunters—to be tried and punished. But the trial was refused here in London on the grounds that the Shades were 'beyond a doubt' guilty. And that's really all there is. This is simply a short record of the event, not the full papers. Those would still be in the York Institute." Charlotte pushed her damp hair back from her forehead. "And yet. It *would* explain Mortmain's hatred of Shadowhunters. You were correct, Tessa. It was—it *is*—personal."

"And it gives us a starting point. The York Institute," said Henry, looking up from his plate. "The Starkweathers run it, don't they? They'll have the full letters, papers—"

"And Aloysius Starkweather is eighty-nine," said Charlotte. "He would have been a young man when the Shades were killed. He may remember something of what transpired." She sighed. "I'd better send him a message. Oh, dear. This will be awkward."

"Why is that, darling?" Henry asked in his gentle, absent way.

"He and my father were friends once, but then they had a falling-out—some dreadful thing, absolutely ages ago, but they never spoke again."

"What's that poem again?" Will, who had been twirling his empty teacup around his fingers, stood up straight and declaimed:

> *Each spake words of high disdain,*
> *And insult to his heart's best brother—"*

"Oh, by the Angel, Will, do be quiet," said Charlotte, standing up. "I must go and write a letter to Aloysius Starkweather that drips remorse and pleading. I don't need you distracting me." And, gathering up her skirts, she hurried from the room.

"No appreciation for the arts," Will murmured, setting his

teacup down. He looked up, and Tessa realized she had been staring at him. She knew the poem, of course. It was Coleridge, one of her favorites. There was more to it as well, about love and death and madness, but she could not bring the lines to mind; not now, with Will's blue eyes on hers.

"And of course, Charlotte hasn't eaten a bit of dinner," Henry said, getting up. "I'll go see if Bridget can't make her up a plate of cold chicken. As for the rest of you—" He paused for a moment, as if he were about to give them an order—send them to bed, perhaps, or back to the library to do more research. The moment passed, and a look of puzzlement crossed his face. "Blast it, I can't remember what I was going to say," he announced, and vanished into the kitchen.

The moment Henry left, Will and Jem fell into an earnest discussion of reparations, Downworlders, Accords, covenants, and laws that left Tessa's head spinning. Quietly she rose and left the table, making her way to the library.

Despite its immense size, and the fact that barely any of the books that lined its walls were in English, it was her favorite room in the Institute. There was something about the smell of books, the ink-and-paper-and-leather scent, the way dust in a library seemed to behave differently from the dust in any other room—it was golden in the light of the witchlight tapers, settling like pollen across the polished surfaces of the long tables. Church the cat was asleep on a high book stand, his tail curled round above his head; Tessa gave him a wide berth as she moved toward the small poetry section along the lower right-hand wall. Church adored Jem but had been known to bite others, often with very little warning.

She found the book she was looking for and knelt down beside the bookcase, flipping until she found the right page, the scene where the old man in "Christabel" realizes that the girl standing before him is the daughter of his once best friend and now most hated enemy, the man he can never forget.

> *Alas! they had been friends in youth;*
> *But whispering tongues can poison truth;*
> *And constancy lives in realms above;*
> *And life is thorny; and youth is vain;*
> *And to be wroth with one we love,*
> *Doth work like madness in the brain.*
>
> *. . .*
>
> *Each spake words of high disdain*
> *And insult to his heart's best brother:*
> *They parted—ne'er to meet again!*

The voice that spoke above her head was as light as it was drawling—instantly familiar. "Checking my quotation for accuracy?"

The book slid out of Tessa's hands and hit the floor. She rose to her feet and watched, frozen, as Will bent to pick it up, and held it out to her, his manner one of utmost politeness.

"I assure you," he told her, "my recall is perfect."

So is mine, she thought. This was the first time she had been alone with him in weeks. Not since that awful scene on the roof when he had intimated that he thought her little better than a prostitute, and a barren one at that. They had never mentioned the moment to each other again. They had gone on as if everything were normal, polite to each other in company, never alone together. Somehow, when they were with other people, she was able to push it to the back of her mind, forget it. But faced with Will, just Will—beautiful as always, the collar of his shirt open to show the black Marks twining his collarbone and rising up the white skin of his throat, the flickering taper light glancing off the elegant planes and angles of his face—the memory of her shame and anger rose up in her throat, choking off her words.

He glanced down at his hand, still holding the little green leather-bound volume. "Are you going to take Coleridge back from me, or shall I just stand here forever in this rather foolish position?"

Silently Tessa reached out and took the book from him. "If you wish to use the library," she said, preparing to depart, "you most certainly may. I found what I was looking for, and as it grows late—"

"Tessa," he said, holding out a hand to stop her.

She looked at him, wishing she could ask him to go back to calling her Miss Gray. Just the way he said her name undid her, loosened something tight and knotted underneath her rib cage, making her breathless. She wished he wouldn't use her Christian name, but knew how ridiculous it would sound if she made the request. It would certainly spoil all her work training herself to be indifferent to him.

"Yes?" she asked.

There was a little wistfulness in his expression as he looked at her. It was all she could do not to stare. Will, wistful? He had to be playacting. "Nothing. I—" He shook his head; a lock of dark hair fell over his forehead, and he pushed it out of his eyes impatiently. "Nothing," he said again. "The first time I showed you the library, you told me your favorite book was *The Wide, Wide World*. I thought you might want to know that I . . . read it." His head was down, his blue eyes looking up at her through those thick dark lashes; she wondered how many times he'd gotten whatever he wanted just by doing that.

She made her voice polite and distant. "And did you find it to your liking?"

"Not at all," said Will. "Drivelly and sentimental, I thought."

"Well, there's no accounting for taste," Tessa said sweetly, knowing he was trying to goad her, and refusing to take the bait. "What is one person's pleasure is another's poison, don't you find?"

Was it her imagination, or did he look disappointed? "Have you any other American recommendations for me?"

"Why would you want one, when you scorn my taste? I think you may have to accept that we are quite far apart on the matter of reading material, as we are on so many things, and find your recommendations elsewhere, Mr. Herondale." She bit her tongue almost as soon as the words were out of her mouth. That had been too much, she knew.

And indeed Will was on it, like a spider leaping onto a particularly tasty fly. *"Mr. Herondale?"* he demanded. "Tessa, I thought . . . ?"

"You thought what?" Her tone was glacial.

"That we could at least talk about books."

"We did," she said. "You insulted my taste. And you should know, *The Wide, Wide World* is not my *favorite* book. It is simply a story I enjoyed, like *The Hidden Hand*, or— You know, perhaps you should suggest something to me, so I can judge *your* taste. It's hardly fair otherwise."

Will hopped up onto the nearest table and sat, swinging his legs, obviously giving the question some thought. "*The Castle of Otranto—*"

"Isn't that the book in which the hero's son is crushed to death by a gigantic helmet that falls from the sky? And you said *A Tale of Two Cities* was silly!" said Tessa, who would have died rather than admit she had read *Otranto* and loved it.

"*A Tale of Two Cities,*" echoed Will. "I read it again, you know, because we had talked about it. You were right. It isn't silly at all."

"No?"

"No," he said. "There is too much of despair in it."

She met his gaze. His eyes were as blue as lakes; she felt as if she were falling into them. "Despair?"

Steadily he said, "There is no future for Sydney, is there, with or without love? He knows he cannot save himself without Lucie, but to let her near him would be to degrade her."

She shook her head. "That is not how I recall it. His sacrifice is noble—"

"It is what is left to him," said Will. "Do you not recall what he says to Lucie? 'If it had been possible . . . that you could have returned the love of the man you see before yourself—flung away, wasted, drunken, poor creature of misuse as you know him to be—he would have been conscious this day and hour, in spite of his happiness, that he would bring you to misery, bring you to sorrow and repentance, blight you, disgrace you, pull you down with him—'"

A log fell in the fireplace, sending up a shower of sparks and startling them both and silencing Will; Tessa's heart leaped, and she tore her eyes away from Will. Stupid, she told herself angrily. So stupid. She remembered how he had treated her, the things he had said, and now she was letting her knees turn to jelly at the drop of a line from Dickens.

"Well," she said. "You have certainly memorized a great deal of it. That was impressive."

Will pulled aside the neck of his shirt, revealing the graceful curve of his collarbone. It took her a moment to realize he was showing her a Mark a few inches above his heart. "*Mnemosyne,*" he said. "The Memory rune. It's permanent."

Tessa looked away quickly. "It is late. I must retire—I am exhausted." She stepped past him, and moved toward the door. She wondered if he looked hurt, then pushed the thought from her mind. This was Will; however mercurial and passing his moods, however charming he was when he was in a good one, he was poison for her, for anyone.

"*Vathek,*" he said, sliding off the table.

She paused in the doorway, realizing she was still clutching the Coleridge book, but then decided she might as well take it. It would be a pleasant diversion from the *Codex.* "What was that?"

"*Vathek,*" he said again. "By William Beckford. If you found *Otranto* to your liking"—though, she thought, she had not admitted she did—"I think you will enjoy it."

"Oh," she said. "Well. Thank you. I will remember that."

He did not answer; he was still standing where she had left him, near the table. He was looking at the ground, his dark hair hiding his face. A little bit of her heart softened, and before she could stop herself, she said, "And good night, Will."

He looked up. "Good night, Tessa." He sounded wistful again, but not as bleak as he had before. He reached out to stroke Church, who had slept through their entire conversation and the sound of the falling log in the fireplace, and was still stretched out on the book stand, paws in the air.

"Will—," Tessa began, but it was too late. Church made a yowling noise at being woken, and lashed out with his claws. Will began to swear. Tessa left, unable to hide the slightest of smiles as she went.

4

A JOURNEY

Friendship is one mind in two bodies.
—Meng-tzu

Charlotte slammed the paper down onto her desk with an exclamation of rage. "Aloysius Starkweather is the most stubborn, hypocritical, obstinate, degenerate—" She broke off, clearly fighting for control of her temper. Tessa had never seen Charlotte's mouth so firmly set into a hard line.

"Would you like a thesaurus?" Will inquired. He was sprawled in one of the wing-back armchairs near the fireplace in the drawing room, his boots up on the ottoman. They were caked with mud, and now so was the ottoman. Normally Charlotte would have been taking him to task for it, but the letter from Aloysius that she had received that morning, and that she had called them all into the drawing room to discuss, seemed to have absorbed all her attention. "You seem to be running out of words."

"And is he really *degenerate?*" Jem asked equably from the depths of the other armchair. "I mean, the old codger's almost ninety—surely past real deviancy."

"I don't know," said Will. "You'd be surprised at what some of the old fellows over at the Devil Tavern get up to."

"Nothing anyone *you* know might get up to would surprise us, Will," said Jessamine, who was lying on the chaise longue, a damp cloth over her forehead. She still had not gotten over her headache.

"Darling," said Henry anxiously, coming around the desk to where his wife was sitting, "are you quite all right? You look a bit—splotchy."

He wasn't wrong. Red patches of rage had broken out over Charlotte's face and throat.

"I think it's charming," said Will. "I've heard polka dots are the last word in fashion this season."

Henry patted Charlotte's shoulder anxiously. "Would you like a cool cloth? What can I do to help?"

"You could ride up to Yorkshire and chop that old goat's head off." Charlotte sounded mutinous.

"Won't that make things rather awkward with the Clave?" asked Henry. "They're not generally very receptive about, you know, beheadings and things."

"Oh!" said Charlotte in despair. "It's all my fault, isn't it? I don't know why I thought I could win him over. The man's a nightmare."

"What did he say *exactly?*" said Will. "In the letter, I mean."

"He refuses to see me, or Henry," said Charlotte. "He says he'll never forgive my family for what my father did. My father . . ." She sighed. "He was a difficult man. Absolutely faithful to the letter of the Law, and the Starkweathers have always interpreted the Law more loosely. My father thought they lived wild up there in the north, like savages, and he wasn't shy about saying so. I don't know what else he did, but old Aloysius seems personally insulted still. Not to mention that he also said if I really cared what he thought about anything, I would have invited him to the last Council meeting. As if I'm in charge of that sort of thing!"

"Why *wasn't* he invited?" inquired Jem.

"He's too old—not meant to be running an Institute at all. He just refuses to step down, and so far Consul Wayland hasn't made him, but the Consul won't invite him to Councils either. I think he hopes Aloysius will either take the hint or simply die of old age. But Aloysius's father lived to be a hundred and four. We could be in for another fifteen years of him." Charlotte shook her head in despair.

"Well, if he won't see you or Henry, can't you send someone else?" asked Jessamine in a bored voice. "You run the Institute; the Enclave members are supposed to do whatever you say."

"But so many of them are on Benedict's side," said Charlotte. "They *want* to see me fail. I just don't know who I can trust."

"You can trust us," said Will. "Send me. And Jem."

"What about me?" said Jessamine indignantly.

"What *about* you? You don't really want to go, do you?"

Jessamine lifted a corner of the damp cloth off her eyes to glare. "On some smelly train all the way up to deadly dull

Yorkshire? No, of course not. I just wanted Charlotte to say she could trust me."

"I can trust you, Jessie, but you're clearly not well enough to go. Which is unfortunate, since Aloysius always had a weakness for a pretty face."

"Even more reason why I should go," said Will.

"Will, Jem . . ." Charlotte bit her lip. "Are you sure? The Council was hardly best pleased by the independent actions you took in the matter of Mrs. Dark."

"Well, they ought to be. We killed a dangerous demon!" Will protested.

"And we saved Church," said Jem.

"Somehow I doubt that counts in our favor," said Will. "That cat bit me three times the other night."

"That probably does count in your favor," said Tessa. "Or Jem's, at least."

Will made a face at her, but didn't seem angry; it was the sort of face he might have made at Jem had the other boy mock insulted him. Perhaps they really could be civil to each other, Tessa thought. He had been quite kind to her in the library the night before last.

"It seems a fool's errand," said Charlotte. The red splotches on her skin were beginning to fade, but she looked miserable. "He isn't likely to tell you anything if he knows I sent you. If only—"

"Charlotte," Tessa said, "there is a way we could make him tell us."

Charlotte looked at her in puzzlement. "Tessa, what do you—" She broke off then, light dawning in her eyes. "Oh, I see. Tessa, what an excellent idea."

"Oh, *what?*" demanded Jessamine from the chaise. "What idea?"

"If something of his could be retrieved," said Tessa, "and given to me, I could use it to Change into him. And perhaps access his memories. I could tell you what he recollects about Mortmain and the Shades, if anything at all."

"Then, you'll come with us to Yorkshire," said Jem.

Suddenly all eyes in the room were on Tessa. Thoroughly startled, for a moment she said nothing.

"She hardly needs to accompany us," said Will. "We can retrieve an object and bring it back to her here."

"But Tessa's said before that she needs to use something that has strong associations for the wearer," said Jem. "If what we select turns out to be insufficient—"

"She also said she can use a nail clipping, or a strand of hair—"

"So you're suggesting we take the train up to York, meet a ninety-year-old man, leap on him, and yank out his hair? I'm sure the Clave will be ecstatic."

"They'll just say you're mad," said Jessamine. "They already think it, so what's the difference, really?"

"It's up to Tessa," said Charlotte. "It's her power you're asking to use; it should be her decision."

"Did you say we'd be taking the train?" Tessa asked, looking over at Jem.

He nodded, his silver eyes dancing. "The Great Northern runs trains out of Kings Cross all day long," he said. "It's only a matter of hours."

"Then, I'll come," said Tessa. "I've never been on a train."

Will threw up his hands. "That's it? You're coming because you've never been on a train before?"

"Yes," she said, knowing how much her calm demeanor drove him mad. "I should like to ride in one, very much."

"Trains are great dirty smoky things," said Will. "You won't like it."

Tessa was unmoved. "I won't know if I like it until I try it, will I?"

"I've never swum naked in the Thames, but I know I wouldn't like it."

"But think how entertaining for sightseers," said Tessa, and she saw Jem duck his head to hide the quick flash of his grin. "Anyway, it doesn't matter. I wish to go, and I shall. When do we leave?"

Will rolled his eyes, but Jem was still grinning. "Tomorrow morning. That way we'll arrive well before dark."

"I'll have to send Aloysius a message saying to expect you," said Charlotte, picking up her pen. She paused, and looked up at them all. "Is this a dreadful idea? I—I feel as if I cannot be sure."

Tessa looked at her worriedly—seeing Charlotte like this, doubting her own instincts, made her hate Benedict Lightwood and his cohorts even more than she already did.

It was Henry who stepped up and put a gentle hand on his wife's shoulder. "The only alternative seems to be doing nothing, dearest Charlotte," he said. "And doing nothing, I find, rarely accomplishes anything. Besides, what could go wrong?"

"Oh, by the Angel, I wish you hadn't asked that," replied Charlotte with fervor, but she bent over the paper and began to write.

That afternoon was Tessa's and Sophie's second training session with the Lightwoods. Having changed into her gear,

Tessa left her room to find Sophie waiting for her in the corridor. She was dressed to train as well, her hair knotted up expertly behind her head, and a dark expression on her face.

"Sophie, what is it?" Tessa inquired, falling into step beside the other girl. "You look quite out of countenance."

"Well, if you must know . . ." Sophie dropped her voice. "It's Bridget."

"Bridget?" The Irish girl had been nearly invisible in the kitchen since she'd arrived, unlike Cyril, who had been here and there about the house, doing errands like Sophie. The last memory Tessa had of Bridget involved her sitting atop Gabriel Lightwood with a knife. She let herself dwell on it pleasantly for a moment. "What's she done?"

"She just . . ." Sophie let out a gusty sigh. "She isn't very amiable. Agatha was my friend, but Bridget—well, we have a way of talking, among us servants, you know, usually, but Bridget just won't. Cyril's friendly enough, but Bridget just keeps to herself in the kitchen, singing those awful Irish ballads of hers. I'd wager she's singing one now."

They were passing not far from the scullery door; Sophie gestured for Tessa to follow her, and together they crept close and peered inside. The scullery was quite large, with doors leading off to the kitchen and pantry. The sideboard was piled with food meant for dinner—fish and vegetables, lately cleaned and prepared. Bridget stood at the sink, her hair standing out around her head in wild red curls, made frizzy by the humidity of the water. She was singing too; Sophie had been quite right about that. Her voice drifting over the sound of the water was high and sweet.

"Oh, her father led her down the stair,
Her mother combed her yellow hair.
Her sister Ann led her to the cross,
And her brother John set her on her horse.
'Now you are high and I am low,
Give me a kiss before ye go.'
She leaned down to give him a kiss,
He gave her a deep wound and did not miss.
And with a knife as sharp as a dart,
Her brother stabbed her to the heart."

Nate's face flashed in front of Tessa's eyes, and she shuddered. Sophie, looking past her, didn't seem to notice. "That's all she sings about," she whispered. "Murder and betrayal. Blood and pain. It's horrid."

Mercifully Sophie's voice covered the end of the song. Bridget had begun drying dishes and started up with a new ballad, the tune even more melancholy than the first.

"Why does your sword so drip with blood,
Edward, Edward?
Why does your sword so drip with blood?
And why so sad are ye?"

"Enough of this." Sophie turned and began hurrying down the hall; Tessa followed. "You do see what I meant, though? She's so dreadfully morbid, and it's awful sharing a room with her. She never says a word in the morning or at night, just moans—"

"You share a room with her?" Tessa was astonished. "But the Institute has so many rooms—"

"For visiting Shadowhunters," Sophie said. "Not for servants." She spoke matter-of-factly, as if it would never have occurred to her to question or complain about the fact that dozens of grand rooms stood empty while she shared a room with Bridget, singer of murderous ballads.

"I could talk to Charlotte—," Tessa began.

"Oh, no. Please don't." They had reached the door to the training room. Sophie turned to her, all distress. "I wouldn't want her to think I'd been complaining about the other servants. I really wouldn't, Miss Tessa."

Tessa was about to assure the other girl that she would say nothing to Charlotte if that was what Sophie really wanted, when she heard raised voices from the other side of the training room door. Gesturing at Sophie to be quiet, she leaned in and listened.

The voices were quite clearly those of the Lightwood brothers. She recognized Gideon's lower, rougher tones as he said, "There will be a moment of reckoning, Gabriel. You can depend upon it. What will matter is where we stand when it comes."

Gabriel replied, his voice tense, "We will stand with Father, of course. Where else?"

There was a pause. Then, "You don't know everything about him, Gabriel. You don't know all that he has done."

"I know that we are Lightwoods and that he is our father. I know he fully expected to be named head of the Institute when Granville Fairchild died—"

"Maybe the Consul knows more about him than you do. And more about Charlotte Branwell. She isn't the fool you think she is."

"Really?" Gabriel's voice was a sneer. "Letting us come

here to train her precious girls, doesn't that make her a fool? Shouldn't she have assumed we'd be spying for our father?"

Sophie and Tessa looked at each other with round eyes.

"She agreed to it because the Consul forced her hand. And besides, we are met at the door here, escorted to this room, and escorted out. And Miss Collins and Miss Gray know nothing of import. What damage is our presence here really doing her, would you say?"

There was a silence through which Tessa could almost hear Gabriel sulking. At last he said, "If you despise Father so much, why did you ever come back from Spain?"

Gideon replied, sounding exasperated, "I came back for *you*—"

Sophie and Tessa had been leaning against the door, ears pressed to the wood. At that moment the door gave way and swung open. Both straightened hastily, Tessa hoping that no evidence of their eavesdropping appeared on their faces.

Gabriel and Gideon were standing in a patch of light at the center of the room, facing off against each other. Tessa noticed something she had not noticed before: Gabriel, despite being the younger brother, was lankily taller than Gideon by some inches. Gideon was more muscular, broader through the shoulders. He swept a hand through his sandy hair, nodding curtly to the girls as they appeared in the doorway. "Good day."

Gabriel Lightwood strode across the room to meet them. He really was quite tall, Tessa thought, craning her neck to look up at him. As a tall girl herself, she didn't often find herself bending her head back to look up at men, though both Will and Jem were taller than she was.

"Miss Lovelace still regrettably absent?" he inquired without bothering to greet them. His face was calm, the only sign of his earlier agitation a pulse hammering just beneath a Courage in Combat rune inked upon his throat.

"She continues to have the headache," said Tessa, following him into the training room. "We don't know how long she'll be indisposed."

"Until these training sessions are over, I suspect," said Gideon, so dryly that Tessa was surprised when Sophie laughed. Sophie immediately composed her features again, but not before Gideon had given her a surprised, almost appreciative glance, as if he weren't used to having his jokes laughed at.

With a sigh Gabriel reached up and freed two long sticks from their holsters on the wall. He handed one to Tessa. "Today," he began, "we shall be working on parrying and blocking . . ."

As usual, Tessa lay awake a long time that night before sleep began to come. Nightmares had plagued her recently—usually of Mortmain, his cold gray eyes, and his colder voice saying measuredly that he had made her, that *There is no Tessa Gray.*

She had come face-to-face with him, the man they sought, and still she did not really know what he wanted from her. To marry her, but why? To claim her power, but to what end? The thought of his cold lizardlike eyes on her made her shiver; the thought that he might have had something to do with her birth was even worse. She did not think anyone—not even Jem, wonderful understanding Jem—quite understood her burning need to know what she *was*, or the fear that she was some sort of monster, a fear that woke her in the middle of the night, leaving her gasping and clawing at her own skin, as if she could peel it away to reveal a devil's hide beneath.

Just then she heard a rustle at her door, and the faint scratch of something being gently pushed against it. After a moment's pause she slid off the bed and padded across the room.

She eased the door open to find an empty corridor, the faint sound of violin music drifting from Jem's room across the hall. At her feet was a small green book. She picked it up and gazed at the words stamped in gold on its spine: "*Vathek*, by William Beckford."

She shut the door behind her and carried the book over to her bed, sitting down so she could examine it. Will must have left it for her. Obviously it could have been no one else. But *why*? Why these odd, small kindnesses in the dark, the talk about books, and the coldness the rest of the time?

She opened the book to its title page. Will had scrawled a note for her there—not just a note, in fact. A poem.

> *For Tessa Gray, on the occasion of being given*
> *a copy of* Vathek *to read:*
>
> *Caliph Vathek and his dark horde*
> *Are bound for Hell, you won't be bored!*
> *Your faith in me will be restored—*
> *Unless this token you find untoward*
> *And my poor gift you have ignored.*
>
> —Will

Tessa burst out laughing, then clapped a hand over her mouth. *Drat* Will, for always being able to make her laugh, even when she didn't want to, even when she knew that opening her heart to him even an inch was like taking a pinch of some deadly addictive drug. She dropped the copy of *Vathek*, complete with Will's deliberately terrible poem, onto her nightstand and rolled onto the bed, burying her face in the pillows. She could still hear Jem's violin music, sweetly sad, drifting beneath her door. As hard as she could, she tried to push thoughts of Will out of her mind; and indeed, when she fell asleep at last and dreamed, for once he made no appearance.

It rained the next day, and despite her umbrella Tessa could feel the fine hat she had borrowed from Jessamine beginning to sag like a waterlogged bird around her ears as they—she, Jem, Will, and Cyril, carrying their luggage—hurried from the coach into Kings Cross Station. Through the sheets of gray rain she was conscious only of a tall, imposing building, a great clock tower rising from the front. It was topped with a weathercock that showed that the wind was blowing due north—and not gently, spattering drops of cold rain into her face.

Inside, the station was chaos: people hurrying hither and thither, newspaper boys hawking their wares, men striding up and down with sandwich boards strapped to their chests, advertising everything from hair tonic to soap. A little boy in a Norfolk jacket dashed to and fro, his mother in hot pursuit. With a word to Jem, Will vanished immediately into the crowd.

"Gone off and left us, has he?" said Tessa, struggling with her umbrella, which was refusing to close.

"Let me do that." Deftly Jem reached over and flicked at the mechanism; the umbrella shut with a decided snap. Pushing her damp hair out of her eyes, Tessa smiled at him, just as Will returned with an aggrieved-looking porter who relieved Cyril of the baggage and snapped at them to hurry up, the train wouldn't wait all day.

Will looked from the porter to Jem's cane, and back. His blue eyes narrowed. "It will wait for *us*," Will said with a deadly smile.

The porter looked bewildered but said "Sir" in a decidedly less aggressive tone and proceeded to lead them toward the departure platform. People—so many people!—streamed about Tessa as she made her way through the crowd, clutching at Jem with one hand and Jessamine's hat with the other. Far at the end of the station, where the tracks ran out into open ground, she could see the steel gray sky, smudged with soot.

Jem helped her up into their compartment; there was much bustling about the luggage, and Will tipping the porter in among shouts and whistling as the train prepared to depart. The door swung shut behind them just as the train pulled forward, steam rushing past the windows in white drifts, wheels clacking merrily.

"Did you bring anything to read on the journey?" asked Will, settling into the seat opposite Tessa; Jem was beside her, his cane leaning up against the wall.

She thought of the copy of *Vathek* and his poem in it; she had left it at the Institute to avoid temptation, the way you might leave behind a box of candies if you were banting and didn't want to put on weight. "No," she said. "I haven't come across anything I particularly wanted to read lately."

Will's jaw set, but he said nothing.

"There is always something so exciting about the start of a

journey, don't you think?" Tessa went on, nose to the window, though she could see little but smoke and soot and hurtling gray rain; London was a dim shadow in the mist.

"No," said Will as he sat back and pulled his hat down over his eyes.

Tessa kept her face against the glass as the gray of London began to fall away behind them, and with it the rain. Soon they were rolling through green fields dotted with white sheep, with here and there the point of a village steeple in the distance. The sky had turned from steel to a damp, misty blue, and small black clouds scudded overhead. Tessa watched it all with fascination.

"Haven't you ever been in the countryside before?" asked Jem, though unlike Will's, his question had the flavor of actual curiosity.

Tessa shook her head. "I don't remember ever leaving New York, except to go to Coney Island, and that isn't really countryside. I suppose I must have passed through some of it when I came from Southampton with the Dark Sisters, but it was dark, and they kept the curtains across the windows, besides." She took off her hat, which was dripping water, and laid it on the seat between them to dry. "But I feel as if I have seen it before. In books. I keep imagining I'll see Thornfield Hall rising up beyond the trees, or Wuthering Heights perched on a stony crag—"

"Wuthering Heights is in Yorkshire," said Will, from under his hat, "and we're nowhere near Yorkshire yet. We haven't even reached Grantham. And there's nothing that impressive about Yorkshire. Hills and dales, no proper mountains like we have in Wales."

"Do you miss Wales?" Tessa inquired. She wasn't sure why she did it; she knew asking Will about his past was like poking a dog with a sore tail, but she couldn't seem to help it.

Will shrugged lightly. "What's to miss? Sheep and singing," he said. "And the ridiculous language. *Fe hoffwn i fod mor feddw, fyddai ddim yn cofio fy enw.*"

"What does that mean?"

"It means 'I wish to get so drunk I no longer remember my own name,' Quite useful."

"You don't sound very patriotic," observed Tessa. "Weren't you just reminiscing about the mountains?"

"Patriotic?" Will looked smug. "I'll tell you what's patriotic," he said. "In honor of my birthplace, I've the dragon of Wales tattooed on my—"

"You're in a *charming* temper, aren't you, William?" interrupted Jem, though there was no edge to his voice. Still, having observed them now for some time, together and apart, Tessa knew it meant something when they called each other by their full first names instead of the familiar shortened forms. "Remember, Starkweather can't stand Charlotte, so if this is the mood you're in—"

"I promise to charm the dickens out of him," said Will, sitting up and readjusting his crushed hat. "I shall charm him with such force that when I am done, he will be left lying limply on the ground, trying to remember his own name."

"The man's eighty-nine," muttered Jem. "He may well have that problem anyway."

"I suppose you're storing up all that charm now?" Tessa inquired. "Wouldn't want to waste any of it on us?"

"That's it exactly." Will sounded pleased. "And it isn't

Charlotte the Starkweathers can't stand, Jem. It's her father."

"Sins of the fathers," said Jem. "They're not inclined to like any Fairchild, or anyone associated with one. Charlotte wouldn't even let Henry come up—"

"That is because every time one lets Henry out of the house on his own, one risks an international incident," said Will. "But yes, to answer your unasked question, I do understand the trust Charlotte has placed in us, and I do intend to behave myself. I don't want to see that squinty-eyed Benedict Lightwood and his hideous sons in charge of the Institute any more than anyone else does."

"They're not hideous," said Tessa.

Will blinked at her. "What?"

"Gideon and Gabriel," said Tessa. "They're really quite good-looking, not hideous at all."

"I spoke," said Will in sepulchral tones, "of the pitch-black inner depths of their souls."

Tessa snorted. "And what color do you suppose the inner depths of *your* soul are, Will Herondale?"

"Mauve," said Will.

Tessa looked over at Jem for help, but he only smiled. "Perhaps we should discuss strategy," he said. "Starkweather hates Charlotte but knows that she sent us. So how to worm our way into his good graces?"

"Tessa can utilize her feminine wiles," said Will. "Charlotte said he enjoys a pretty face."

"How did Charlotte explain my presence?" Tessa inquired, realizing belatedly that she should have asked this earlier.

"She didn't really; she just gave our names. She was quite

curt," said Will. "I think it falls to us to concoct a plausible story."

"We can't say I'm a Shadowhunter; he'll know immediately that I'm not. No Marks."

"And no warlock mark. He'll think she's a mundane," said Jem. "She could Change, but . . ."

Will eyed her speculatively. Though Tessa knew it meant nothing—worse than nothing, really—she still felt his gaze on her like the brush of a finger across the back of her neck, making her shiver. She forced herself to return his look stonily. "Perhaps we could say she's a mad maiden aunt who insists on chaperoning us everywhere."

"My aunt or yours?" Jem inquired.

"Yes, she doesn't really look like either of us, does she? Perhaps she's a girl who's fallen madly in love with me and persists in following me wherever I go."

"My talent is shape-shifting, Will, not acting," said Tessa, and at that, Jem laughed out loud. Will glared at him.

"She had the better of you there, Will," he said. "It does happen sometimes, doesn't it? Perhaps I should introduce Tessa as my fiancée. We can tell mad old Aloysius that her Ascension is underway."

"Ascension?" Tessa remembered nothing of the term from the *Codex*.

Jem said, "When a Shadowhunter wishes to marry a mundane—"

"But I thought that was forbidden?" Tessa asked, as the train slid into a tunnel. It was dark suddenly in their compartment, though she had the feeling nevertheless that Will was looking at her, that shivering sense that his gaze was on her somehow.

"It is. *Unless* the Mortal Cup is used to turn that mundane into a Shadowhunter. It is not a common result, but it does happen. If the Shadowhunter in question applies to the Clave for an Ascension for their partner, the Clave is required to consider it for at least three months. Meanwhile, the mundane embarks on a course of study to learn about Shadowhunter culture—"

Jem's voice was drowned out by the train whistle as the locomotive emerged from the tunnel. Tessa looked at Will, but he was staring fixedly out the window, not looking at her at all. She must have imagined it.

"It's not a bad idea, I suppose," said Tessa. "I do know rather a lot; I've finished nearly all of the *Codex*."

"It would seem reasonable that I brought you with me," said Jem. "As a possible Ascender, you might want to learn about Institutes other than the one in London." He turned to Will. "What do you think?"

"It seems as fine an idea as any." Will was still looking out the window; the countryside had grown less green, more stark. There were no villages visible, only long swathes of gray-green grass and outcroppings of black rock.

"How many Institutes are there, other than the one in London?" Tessa asked.

Jem ticked them off on his hands. "In Britain? London, York, one in Cornwall—near Tintagel—one in Cardiff, and one in Edinburgh. They're all smaller, though, and report to the London Institute, which in turn reports to Idris."

"Gideon Lightwood said he was at the Institute in Madrid. What on earth was he doing there?"

"Faffing about, most likely," said Will.

"Once we finish our training, at eighteen," said Jem, as if Will hadn't spoken, "we're encouraged to travel, to spend time at other Institutes, to experience something of Shadowhunter culture in new places. There are always different techniques, local tricks to be learned. Gideon was away for only a few months. If Benedict called him back so soon, he must think that his acquisition of the Institute is assured." Jem looked troubled.

"But he's wrong," Tessa said firmly, and when the troubled look didn't leave Jem's gray eyes, she cast about for something to change the subject. "Where is the Institute in New York?"

"We haven't memorized all their addresses, Tessa." There was something in Will's voice, a dangerous undercurrent. Jem looked at him narrowly, and said:

"Is everything all right?"

Will took his hat off and laid it on the seat next to him. He looked at them both steadily for a moment, his gaze level. He was beautiful to look at as always, Tessa thought, but there seemed something *gray* about him, almost faded. For someone who so often seemed to burn very brightly, that light in him seemed exhausted now, as if he had been rolling a rock up a hill like Sisyphus. "Too much to drink last night," he said finally.

Really, why do you bother, Will? Don't you realize we both know you're lying? Tessa almost said, but one look at Jem stopped her. His gaze as he regarded Will was worried—very worried indeed, though Tessa knew he did not believe Will about the drinking, any more than she did. But, "Well," was all he said, lightly, "if only there were a Rune of Sobriety."

"Yes." Will looked back at him, and the strain in his expression relaxed slightly. "If we might return to discussing your plan, James. It's a good one, save one thing." He leaned forward. "If she is meant to be affianced to you, Tessa will need a ring."

"I had thought of that," said Jem, startling Tessa, who had imagined he had come up with this Ascendant idea on the spot. He slipped his hand into his waistcoat pocket and drew out a silver ring, which he held out to Tessa on his palm. It was not unlike the silver ring Will often wore, though where Will's had a design of birds in flight, this one had a careful etching of the crenellations of a castle tower around it. "The Carstairs family ring," he said. "If you would . . ."

She took it from him and slipped it onto her left ring finger, where it seemed to magically fit itself. She felt as if she ought to say something like *It's lovely*, or *Thank you*, but of course this wasn't a proposal, or even a gift. It was simply an acting prop. "Charlotte doesn't wear a wedding ring," she said. "I hadn't realized Shadowhunters did."

"We don't," said Will. "It is customary to give a girl your family ring when you become engaged, but the actual wedding ceremony involves exchanging runes instead of rings. One on the arm, and one over the heart."

"'Set me as a seal upon thine heart, as a seal upon thine arm: for love is strong as death; jealousy is cruel as the grave,'" said Jem. "Song of Solomon."

"'Jealousy is cruel as the grave'?" Tessa raised her eyebrows. "That's not . . . very romantic."

"'The coals thereof are coals of fire, which hath a most vehement flame,'" said Will, quirking his eyebrows up. "I always thought females found the idea of jealousy romantic. Men, fighting over you . . ."

"Well, there aren't any *graves* in mundane wedding ceremonies," said Tessa. "Though your ability to quote the Bible is impressive. Better than my aunt Harriet's."

"Did you hear that, James? She just compared us to her aunt Harriet."

Jem, as always, was unruffled. "We must be on familiar terms with all religious texts," he said. "To us they are instruction manuals."

"So you memorize them all in school?" She realized she had seen neither Will nor Jem at their studies since she had been at the Institute. "Or rather, when you are tutored?"

"Yes, though Charlotte's rather fallen off in tutoring us lately, as you might imagine," said Will. "One either has a tutor or one is schooled in Idris—that is, until you attain your majority at eighteen. Which will be soon, thankfully, for the both of us."

"Which one of you is older?"

"Jem," said Will, and "I am," said Jem, at the same time. They laughed in unison as well, and Will added, "Only by three months, though."

"I knew you'd feel compelled to point that out," said Jem with a grin.

Tessa looked from one of them to the other. There could not be two boys who looked more different, or who had more different dispositions. And yet. "Is that what it means to be *parabatai*?" she said. "Finishing each other's sentences and the like? Because there isn't much on it in the *Codex*."

Will and Jem looked at each other. Will shrugged first,

casually. "It is rather difficult to explain," he said loftily. "If you haven't experienced it—"

"I meant," Tessa said, "you cannot—I don't know—read each other's minds, or the like?"

Jem made a spluttering noise. Will's lambent blue eyes widened. "Read each other's minds? Horrors, no."

"Then, what's the point? You swear to guard each other, I understand that, but aren't all Shadowhunters meant to do that for each other?"

"It's more than that," said Jem, who had stopped spluttering and spoke somberly. "The idea of *parabatai* comes from an old tale, the story of Jonathan and David. 'And it came to pass . . . that the soul of Jonathan was knit with the soul of David, and Jonathan loved him as his own soul. . . . Then Jonathan and David made a covenant, because he loved him as his own soul.' They were two warriors, and their souls were knit together by Heaven, and out of that Jonathan Shadowhunter took the idea of *parabatai*, and encoded the ceremony into the Law."

"But it doesn't just have to be two men. It can be a man and a woman, or two women?"

"Of course." Jem nodded. "You have only eighteen years to find and choose a *parabatai*. Once you are older than that, the ritual is no longer open to you. And it is not merely a matter of promising to guard each other. You must stand before the Council and swear to lay down your life for your *parabatai*. To go where they go, to be buried where they are buried. If there were an arrow speeding toward Will, I would be bound by oath to step in front of it."

"Handy, that," said Will.

"And he, of course, is bound to do the same for me," said Jem. "Whatever he may say to the contrary, Will does not break oaths, or the Law." He looked hard at Will, who smiled faintly and stared out the window.

"Goodness," said Tessa. "That's all very touching, but I don't see exactly how it confers any advantages."

"Not everyone has a *parabatai*," said Jem. "Very few of us, actually, find one in the allotted time. But those who do can draw on the strength of their *parabatai* in battle. A rune put on you by your *parabatai* is always more potent than one you put on yourself, or one put on by another. And there are some runes we can utilize that no other Shadowhunter can, because they draw on our doubled power."

"But what if you decide that you don't want to be *parabatai* anymore?" Tessa asked curiously. "Can the ritual be broken?"

"Dear God, woman," said Will. "Are there any questions you *don't* want to know the answer to?"

"I don't see the harm in telling her." Jem's hands were folded atop his cane. "The more she knows, the better she will be able to pretend she plans to Ascend." He turned to Tessa. "The ritual cannot be broken save in a few situations. If one of us were to become a Downworlder or a mundane, then the binding is cut. And of course, if one of us were to die, the other would be free. But not to choose another *parabatai*. A single Shadowhunter cannot take part in the ritual more than once."

"It is like being married, isn't it," said Tessa placidly, "in the Catholic church. Like Henry the Eighth; he had to create a new religion just so he could escape from his vows."

"Till death do us part," said Will, his gaze still fixed on the countryside speeding past outside the window.

"Well, Will won't need to create a new religion just to be rid of me," said Jem. "He'll be free soon enough."

Will looked over sharply, but it was Tessa who spoke. "Don't say that," she admonished Jem. "A cure could still be found. I don't see any reason to abandon all hope."

She almost shrank back at the look Will bent on her: blue, blazing, and furious. Jem seemed not to notice as he replied, calmly and unaffectedly. "I haven't abandoned hope," he said. "I just hope for different things than you do, Tessa Gray."

Hours went by after that, hours during which Tessa nodded off, her head propped against her hand, the dull sound of the train's wheels winding its way into her dreams. She woke at last with Jem shaking her gently by the shoulders, the train whistle blowing, and the guard shouting out the name of York station. In a flurry of bags and hats and porters they descended to the platform. It was nowhere near as crowded as Kings Cross, and covered by a far more impressive arched glass and iron roof, through which could be glimpsed the gray-black sky.

Platforms stretched as far as the eye could see; Tessa, Jem, and Will stood on the one closest to the main body of the station, where great gold-faced railway clocks proclaimed the time to be six o'clock. They were farther north now, and the sky had already begun to darken to twilight.

They had only just gathered beneath one of the clocks when a man stepped out of the shadows. Tessa barely suppressed a start at the sight of him. He was heavily cloaked, wearing a black oilskin-looking hat, and boots like an old sailor. His beard was long and white, his eyes crested with thick white eyebrows. He reached out and laid a hand on Will's shoulder. "Nephilim?" he said, his voice gruff and thickly accented. "Is it you?"

"Dear God," said Will, putting his hand over his heart in a theatrical gesture. "It's the Ancient Mariner who stoppeth one of three."

"Ah'm 'ere at t'bequest of Aloysius Starkweather. Art t'lads he wants or not? Ah've not got all night to stand about."

"Important appointment with an albatross?" Will inquired. "Don't let us keep you."

"What my mad friend means to say," said Jem, "is that we are indeed Shadowhunters of the London Institute. Charlotte Branwell sent us. And you are . . . ?"

"Gottshall," the man said gruffly. "Me family's been serving the Shadowhunters of the York Institute for nigh on three centuries now. I can see through tha' glamours, young ones. Save for this one," he added, and turned his eyes on Tessa. "If there's a glamour on the girl, it's summat I've never seen before."

"She's a mundane—an Ascendant," Jem said quickly. "Soon to be my wife." He took Tessa's hand protectively, and turned it so that Gottshall could see the ring on her finger. "The Council thought it would be beneficial for her to see another Institute besides London's."

"Has Mr. Starkweather been told aught about this?" Gottshall asked, black eyes keen beneath the rim of his hat.

"It depends what Mrs. Branwell told him," said Jem.

"Well, I hope she told him something, for yer sakes," said the old servant, raising his eyebrows. "If there's a man in t' world who hates surprises more than Aloysius Starkweather, Ah've yet to meet the bast— beggar. Begging your pardon, miss."

Tessa smiled and inclined her head, but inside, her stomach

was churning. She looked from Jem to Will, but both boys were calm and smiling. They were used to this sort of subterfuge, she thought, and she was not. She had played parts before, but never as herself, never wearing her own face and not someone else's. For some reason the thought of lying without a false image to hide behind terrified her. She could only hope that Gottshall was exaggerating, though something—the glint in his eye as he regarded her, perhaps—told her that he wasn't.

5

SHADES OF THE PAST

But evil things, in robes of sorrow,
Assailed the monarch's high estate;
(Ah, let us mourn, for never morrow
Shall dawn upon him desolate!)
And round about his home the glory
That blushed and bloomed,
Is but a dim-remembered story
Of the old time entombed.
—Edgar Allan Poe, "The Haunted Palace"

Tessa barely noticed the interior of the station as they followed Starkweather's servant through its crowded entry hall. Hustle and bustle, people bumping into her, the smell of coal smoke and cooking food, blurring signs for the Great Northern Railway company and the York and North Midland lines. Soon enough they were outside the station, under a graying sky that arched overhead, threatening rain. A grand hotel reared up against the twilit sky at one end of the station; Gottshall hurried them toward it, where a black carriage with the four Cs of the Clave painted on the door waited near the entrance. After settling the luggage and clambering inside, they were off, the carriage surging into Tanner Row to join the flow of traffic.

Will was silent most of the way, drumming his slim fingers on his black-trousered knees, his blue eyes distant and thoughtful. It was Jem who did the talking, leaning across Tessa to draw the curtains back on her side of the carriage. He pointed out items of interest—the graveyard where the victims of a cholera epidemic had been interred, and the ancient gray walls of the city rising up in front of them, crenellated across the top like the pattern on his ring. Once they were through the walls, the streets narrowed. It was like London, Tessa thought, but on a reduced scale; even the stores they passed—a butcher's, a draper's—seemed smaller. The pedestrians, mostly men, who hurried by, chins dug into their collars to block the light rain that had begun to fall, were not as fashionably dressed; they looked "country," like the farmers who came into Manhattan on occasion, recognizable by the redness of their big hands, the tough, sunburned skin of their faces.

The carriage swung out of a narrow street and into a huge square; Tessa drew in a breath. Before them rose a magnificent cathedral, its Gothic turrets piercing the gray sky like Saint Sebastian stuck through with arrows. A massive limestone tower surmounted the structure, and niches along the front of the building held sculpted statues, each one different. "Is that the Institute? Goodness, it's so much grander than London's—"

Will laughed. "Sometimes a church is only a church, Tess."

"That's York Minster," said Jem. "Pride of the city. Not the Institute. The Institute's in Goodramgate Street." His words were confirmed as the carriage swung away from the cathedral, down Deangate, and onto the narrow, cobbled lane of Goodramgate, where they rattled beneath a small iron gate between two leaning Tudor buildings.

When they emerged on the other side of the gate, Tessa saw why Will had laughed. What rose before them was a pleasant-enough-looking church, surrounded by enclosing walls and smooth grass, but it had none of the grandeur of York Minster. When Gottshall came around to swing the door of the carriage open and help Tessa down to the ground, she saw that occasional headstones rose from the rain-dampened grass, as if someone had intended to begin a cemetery here and had lost interest halfway through the proceedings.

The sky was nearly black now, silvered here and there with clouds made near-transparent by starlight. Behind her, Jem's and Will's familiar voices murmured; before her, the doors of the church stood open, and through them she could see flickering candles. She felt suddenly bodiless, as if she were the ghost of Tessa, haunting this odd place so far from the life she had known in New York. She shivered, and not just from the cold.

She felt the brush of a hand against her arm, and warm breath stirred her hair. She knew who it was without turning. "Shall we go in, my betrothed?" Jem said softly in her ear. She could feel the laughter in him, vibrating through his bones, communicating itself to her. She almost smiled. "Let us beard the lion in his den together."

She put her hand through his arm. They made their way up the steps of the church; she looked back at the top, and saw Will gazing up after them, apparently unheeding as Gottshall tapped him on the shoulder, saying something into his ear. Her eyes met his, but she looked quickly away; entangling gazes with Will was confusing at best, dizzying at worst.

The inside of the church was small and dark compared to the London Institute's. Pews dark with age ran the length of the walls, and above them witchlight tapers burned in holders made of blackened iron. At the front of the church, in front of a veritable cascade of burning candles, stood an old man dressed all in Shadowhunter black. His hair and beard were thick and gray, standing out wildly around his head, his gray-black eyes half-hidden beneath massive eyebrows, his skin scored with the marks of age. Tessa knew him to be almost ninety, but his back was still straight, his chest as thick around as the trunk of a tree.

"Young Herondale, are you?" he barked as Will stepped forward to introduce himself. "Half-mundane, half-Welsh, and the worst traits of both, I've heard."

Will smiled politely. *"Diolch."*

Starkweather bristled. "Mongrel tongue," he muttered, and turned his gaze to Jem. "James Carstairs," he said. "Another Institute brat. I've half a mind to tell the lot of you to go to blazes. That upstart bit of a girl, that Charlotte Fairchild, foisting you all on me with nary a by-your-leave." He had a little of the Yorkshire accent that his servant had, though much fainter; still, the way he pronounced "I" did sound a bit like "Ah." "None of that family ever had a bit o' manners. I could do without her father, and I can do without—"

His flashing eyes came to rest on Tessa then, and he stopped abruptly, his mouth open, as if he had been slapped in the face midsentence. Tessa glanced at Jem; he looked as startled as she did at Starkweather's sudden silence. But there, in the breach, was Will.

"This is Tessa Gray, sir," he said. "She is a mundane girl, but she is the betrothed of Carstairs here, and an Ascendant."

"A *mundane*, you say?" demanded Starkweather, his eyes wide.

"An Ascendant," said Will in his most soothing, silken voice. "She has been a faithful friend to the Institute in London, and we hope to welcome her into our ranks soon."

"A mundane," the old man repeated, and broke into a fit of coughing. "Well, times have— Yes, I suppose then—" His eyes skipped across Tessa's face again, and he turned to Gottshall, who was looking martyred among the luggage. "Get Cedric and Andrew to help you bring our guests' belongings up to their rooms," he said. "And do tell Ellen to instruct Cook to set three extra places for dinner tonight. I may have forgotten to remind her that we would have guests."

The servant gaped at his master before nodding in a seeming daze; Tessa couldn't blame him. It was clear that Starkweather had meant to send them packing and had changed his mind at the last moment. She glanced at Jem, who looked just as mystified as she felt; only Will, blue eyes wide and face as innocent as a choirboy's, seemed as if he had expected nothing else.

"Well, come along, then," said Starkweather gruffly without looking at Tessa. "You needn't stand there. Follow me and I'll show you to your rooms."

"By the Angel," Will said, scraping his fork through the brownish mess on his plate. "What *is* this stuff?"

Tessa had to admit, it was difficult to tell. Starkweather's servants—mostly bent old men and women and a sour-faced female housekeeper—had done as he'd asked and had set three extra places for supper, which consisted of a dark, lumpy stew ladled out of a silver tureen by a woman in a black dress and white cap, so bent and old that Tessa had to physically prevent herself from leaping up to assist her with the serving. When the woman was done, she turned and shuffled off, leaving Jem, Tessa, and Will alone in the dining room to stare at one another across the table.

A place had been set for Starkweather as well, but he wasn't at it. Tessa had to admit that if she were him, she wouldn't be rushing to eat the stew either. Heavy with overcooked vegetables and tough meat, it was even more unappetizing-looking in the dim light of the dining room. Only a few tapers lit the cramped space; the wallpaper was dark brown, the mirror over the unlit hearth stained and discolored. Tessa felt dreadfully uncomfortable in her evening dress, a stiff blue taffeta borrowed from Jessamine and let out by Sophie, which had turned to the color of a bruise in the unhealthy light.

Still, it was awfully peculiar behavior for a host, to be so insistent that they join him for supper and then not to appear. A servant just as frail and ancient as the one who'd ladled out the stew had led Tessa to her room earlier, a great dim cavern full of heavy carved furniture. It too was dimly lit, as if Starkweather were trying to save money on oil or tapers, though as far as Tessa knew, witchlight cost nothing. Perhaps he simply liked the dark.

She had found her room chilly, dark, and more than slightly ominous. The low fire burning in the grate had done little to warm the room. On either side of the hearth was carved a jagged lightning bolt. The same symbol was on the white pitcher full of chilly water that Tessa had used to wash her hands and face. She had dried off quickly, wondering why she couldn't remember the symbol from the *Codex*. It must mean something important. The whole of the London Institute was decorated with Clave symbols like the Angel rising from the lake, or the interlocked Cs of Council, Covenant, Clave, and Consul.

Heavy old portraits were everywhere as well—in her bedroom, in the corridors, lining the staircase. After changing into evening dress and hearing the dinner bell ring, Tessa had made her way down the staircase, a great carved Jacobean monstrosity, only to pause on the landing to gaze at the portrait of a very young girl with long, fair hair, dressed in an old-fashioned child's dress, a great ribbon surmounting her small head. Her face was thin and pale and sickly, but her eyes were bright—the only bright thing in this dark place, Tessa had thought.

"Adele Starkweather," had come a voice at her elbow, reading off the placard on the portrait's frame. "1842."

She had turned to look at Will, who'd stood with his feet apart, his hands behind his back, gazing at the portrait and frowning.

"What is it? You look as if you don't like her, but I rather do. She must be Starkweather's daughter—no, granddaughter, I think."

Will had shaken his head, looking from the portrait to Tessa. "No doubt. This place is decorated like a family home. It is clear there have been Starkweathers in the York Institute for generations. You've seen the lightning bolts everywhere?"

Tessa had nodded.

"That is the Starkweather family symbol. There is as much of the Starkweathers here as there is of the Clave. It is bad form to behave as if one owns a place like this. One cannot inherit an Institute. The guardian of an Institute is appointed by the Consul. The place itself belongs to the Clave."

"Charlotte's parents ran the London Institute before she did."

"Part of the reason old Lightwood is so tinder-tempered about the whole business," Will had replied. "Institutes aren't necessarily meant to stay in families. But the Consul wouldn't have given Charlotte the post if he hadn't thought she was the right person for it. And it's only one generation. This—" He swept his arm about as if to encompass the portraits, the landing, and odd, lonely Aloysius Starkweather, all in one gesture. "Well, no wonder the old man thinks he has the right to throw us out of the place."

"Mad as hops, my aunt would have said. Shall we go down to dinner?"

In a rare show of gentility, Will had offered his arm. Tessa hadn't looked at him as she'd taken it. Will dressed for dinner was handsome enough to take away her breath, and she'd had the feeling she'd need her wits about her.

Jem had already been waiting in the dining room when they'd arrived, and Tessa had settled herself beside him to await their host. His place had been set, his plate filled with stew, even his wineglass filled with dark red wine, but there had been no sign of him. It was Will who had shrugged first and begun to eat, though he'd soon looked as if he wished he hadn't.

"What *is* this?" he went on now, spearing an unfortunate object on a fork and raising it to eye level. "This . . . this . . . *thing?*"

"A parsnip?" Jem suggested.

"A parsnip planted in Satan's own garden," said Will. He

glanced about. "I don't suppose there's a dog I could feed it to."

"There don't seem to be any pets about," Jem—who loved all animals, even the inglorious and ill-tempered Church—observed.

"Probably all poisoned by parsnips," said Will.

"Oh, dear," Tessa said sadly, laying her fork down. "And I was so hungry too."

"There's always the dinner rolls," said Will, pointing to a covered basket. "Though I warn you, they're as hard as stones. You could use them to kill black beetles, if any beetles bother you in the middle of the night."

Tessa made a face and took a swig of her wine. It was as sour as vinegar.

Will set his fork down and began cheerfully, in the manner of Edward Lear's *Book of Nonsense*:

> *"There once was a lass from New York*
> *Who found herself hungry in York.*
> *But the bread was like rocks,*
> *The parsnips shaped like—"*

"You can't rhyme 'York' with 'York,'" interrupted Tessa. "It's cheating."

"She's right, you know," said Jem, his delicate fingers playing with the stem of his wineglass. "Especially with 'fork' being so obviously the correct choice—"

"Good evening." The hulking shadow of Aloysius Starkweather loomed up suddenly in the doorway; Tessa wondered with a flush of embarrassment how long he'd been standing there. "Mr. Herondale, Mr. Carstairs, Miss, ah—"

"Gray," Tessa said. "Theresa Gray."

"Indeed." Starkweather made no apologies, just settled himself heavily at the head of the table. He was carrying a square, flat box, the sort bankers used to keep their papers in, which he set down beside his plate. With a flash of excitement Tessa saw that there was a year marked on it—1825—and even better, three sets of initials. *JTS, AES, AHM.*

"No doubt your young miss will be pleased to know I've buckled to her demands and searched the archives all day and half last night besides," Starkweather began in an aggrieved tone. It took Tessa a moment to realize that in this case, "young miss" meant Charlotte. "It's lucky, she is, that my father never threw anything out. And the moment I saw the papers, I remembered." He tapped his temple. "Eighty-nine years, and I never forget a thing. You tell old Wayland that when he talks about replacing me."

"We surely will, sir," said Jem, his eyes dancing.

Starkweather took a hearty gulp of his wine and made a face. "By the Angel, this stuff's disgusting." He set the glass down and began pulling papers from the box. "What we have here is an application for Reparations on behalf of two warlocks. John and Anne Shade. A married couple.

"Now, here's the odd bit," the old man went on. "The filing was done by their son, Axel Hollingworth Mortmain, twenty-two years old. Now, of course warlocks are barren—"

Will shifted uncomfortably in his seat, his eyes slanting away from Tessa's.

"This son was adopted," said Jem.

"Shouldn't be allowed, that," said Starkweather, taking another slug of the wine he had pronounced disgusting. His cheeks were beginning to redden. "Like giving a human child to wolves to raise. Before the Accords—"

"If there are any clues to his whereabouts," said Jem, gently trying to steer the conversation back onto its track. "We have very little time—"

"Very well, very well," snapped Starkweather. "There's little information about your precious Mortmain in here. More about the parents. It seems suspicion fell on them when it was discovered that the male warlock, John Shade, was in possession of the Book of the White. Quite a powerful spell book, you understand; disappeared from the London Institute's library under suspicious circumstances back in 1752. The book specializes in binding and unbinding spells—tying the soul to the body, or untying it, as the case may be. Turned out the warlock was trying to animate things. He was digging up corpses or buying them off medical students and replacing the more damaged bits with mechanisms. Then trying to bring them to life. Necromancy—very much against the Law. And we didn't have the Accords in those days. An Enclave group swept in and slaughtered both warlocks."

"And the child?" said Will. "Mortmain?"

"No hide nor hair of him," said Starkweather. "We searched, but nothing. Assumed he was dead, till this turned up, cheeky as you please, demanding reparations. Even his address—"

"His *address*?" Will demanded. That information had *not* been included in the scroll they had seen at the Institute. "In London?"

"Nay. Right here in Yorkshire." Starkweather tapped the page with a wrinkled finger. "Ravenscar Manor. A massive old pile up north from here. Been abandoned now, I think, for decades. Now that I think about it, can't figure how he could've afforded it in the first place. It's not where the Shades lived."

"Still," said Jem. "An excellent starting point for us to go looking. If it's been abandoned since his tenancy, there may be things he left behind. In fact, he may well still be using the place."

"I suppose." Starkweather sounded unenthusiastic about the whole business. "Most of the Shades' belongings were taken for spoils."

"Spoils," Tessa echoed faintly. She remembered the term from the *Codex*. Anything a Shadowhunter took from a Downworlder who had been caught breaking the Law belonged to him. Those were the spoils of war. She looked across the table at Jem and Will; Jem's gentle eyes resting on her with concern, Will's haunted blue ones holding all their secrets. Did she really belong to a race of creatures that was at war with what Jem and Will were?

"Spoils," Starkweather rumbled. He had polished off his wine and started on Will's untouched glass. "Do those interest you, girl? We've quite a collection here in the Institute. Puts the London collection to shame, or so I'm told." He stood up, nearly knocking over his chair. "Come along. I'll show them to you, and tell you the rest of this sorry tale, though there's not that much more to it."

Tessa looked quickly to Will and Jem for a cue, but they were already on their feet, following the old man out of the room. Starkweather spoke as he walked, his voice drifting back over his shoulder, making the rest of them hurry to match his long strides.

"Never thought much of this Reparations business myself,"

he said as they passed down another dimly lit, interminably long stone corridor. "Makes Downworlders uppity, thinking they have a right to get something out of us. All the work we do and no thanks, just hands held out for more, more, more. Don't you think so, gentlemen?"

"Bastards, all of them," said Will, who seemed as if his mind were a thousand miles away. Jem looked at him sideways.

"Absolutely!" barked Starkweather, clearly pleased. "Not that one should use such language in front of a lady, of course. As I was saying, this Mortmain was protesting the death of Anne Shade, the male warlock's wife—said she'd had nothing to do with her husband's projects, hadn't known about them, he claimed. Her death was undeserved. Wanted a trial of those guilty of what he called her 'murder,' and his parents' belongings back."

"Was the Book of the White among what he asked for?" Jem inquired. "I know it's a crime for a warlock to own such a volume . . ."

"It was. It was retrieved and placed in the London Institute library, where no doubt it remains still. Certainly no one was going to give it to *him*."

Tessa did a quick mental calculation in her head. If he was eighty-nine now, Starkweather would have been twenty-six at the time of the Shades' deaths. "Were you there?"

His bloodshot eyes danced over her; she noticed that even now, a little drunk, he didn't seem to want to look at her too directly. "Was I where?"

"You said an Enclave group was sent out to deal with the Shades. Were you among them?"

He hesitated, then shrugged. "Aye," he said, his Yorkshire

accent thickening for a moment. "Dinna take long to get the both of them. They weren't prepared. Not a bit. I remember them lying there in their blood. The first time I saw dead warlocks, I was surprised they bled red. I could have sworn it'd be another color, blue or green or some such." He shrugged. "We took the cloaks off them, like skins off a tiger. I was given the keeping of them, or more rightly, my father was. Glory, glory. Those were the days." He grinned like a skull, and Tessa thought of Bluebeard's chamber where he kept the remains of the wives he had killed. She felt both very hot and very cold all over.

"Mortmain never had a chance, did he," she said quietly. "Filing his complaint like that. He was never going to get his reparations."

"Of course not!" barked Starkweather. "Rubbish, all of it— claiming the wife wasn't involved. What wife isn't neck-deep in her husband's business? Besides, he wasn't even their blood son, couldn't have been. Probably more of a pet to them than anything else. I'd wager the father'd have used him for spare parts if it came down to it. He was better off without them. He should have been thanking us, not asking for a trial—"

The old man broke off as he reached a heavy door at the end of the corridor and put his shoulder to it, grinning down at them from beneath beetling brows. "Ever been to the Crystal Palace? Well, this is even better."

He shouldered the door open, and light blazed up around them as they passed through into the room beyond. Clearly it was the only well-lit room in the place.

The room was full of glass-fronted cabinets, and over each cabinet was mounted a lamp of witchlight, illuminating the contents within. Tessa saw Will's back stiffen, and Jem reached for her, his hand tightening on her arm with an almost bruising grip. "Don't—," he began, but she had pushed forward, and was staring at the contents of the cabinets.

Spoils. A gold locket, open to a daguerreotype of a laughing child. The locket was splattered with dried blood. Behind her Starkweather was talking about digging the silver bullets out of the bodies of freshly killed werewolves and melting them down to recast. There was a dish of such bullets, in fact, in one of the cabinets, filling a bloodstained bowl. Sets of vampire fangs, row on row of them. What looked like sheets of gossamer or delicate fabric, pressed under glass. Only on closer inspection did Tessa realize they were the wings of faeries. A goblin, like the one she had seen with Jessamine in Hyde Park, floating open-eyed in a large jar of preservative fluid.

And the remains of warlocks. Mummified taloned hands, like Mrs. Black's. A stripped skull, utterly de-fleshed, human-looking save that it had tusks instead of teeth. Vials of sludgy-looking blood. Starkweather was now talking about how much warlock parts, especially a warlock's "mark," could be sold for on the Downworld market. Tessa felt dizzy and hot, her eyes burning.

Tessa turned around, her hands shaking. Jem and Will stood, looking at Starkweather with mute expressions of horror; the old man was holding up another hunting trophy—a human-looking head mounted to a backing. The skin had shriveled and gone gray, drawn back against the bones. Fleshless spiral horns protruded from the top of its skull. "Got this off a warlock I killed down by Leeds way," he said. "You wouldn't believe the fight he put up—"

Starkweather's voice hollowed out, and Tessa felt herself suddenly cut free and floating. Darkness rushed up, and then there were arms around her, and Jem's voice. Words floated by her in ragged scraps. "My fiancée—never seen spoils before—can't stand blood—very delicate—"

Tessa wanted to fight free of Jem, wanted to rush at Starkweather and strike the old man, but she knew it would ruin everything if she did. She clenched her eyes shut and pressed her face against Jem's chest, breathing him in. He smelled of soap and sandalwood. Then there were other hands on her, drawing her away from Jem. Starkweather's maidservants. She heard Starkweather telling them to take her upstairs and help her to bed. She opened her eyes to see Jem's troubled face as he looked after her, until the door of the spoils room closed between them.

It took Tessa a long time to fall asleep that night, and when she did, she had a nightmare. In the dream she lay manacled to the brass bed in the house of the Dark Sisters . . .

Light like thin gray soup seeped through the windows. The door opened and Mrs. Dark came in, followed by her sister, who had no head, only the white bone of her spine protruding from her raggedly severed neck.

"Here she is, the pretty, pretty princess," said Mrs. Dark, clapping her hands together. "Just think of what we will get for all the parts of her. A hundred each for her little white hands, and a thousand for the pair of her eyes. We'd get more if they were blue, of course, but one can't have everything."

She chuckled, and the bed began to spin as Tessa screamed and thrashed in the darkness. Faces appeared above her: Mortmain, his narrow features screwed up in amusement. "And they say the worth of a good woman is far above rubies," he said. "What of the worth of a warlock?"

"Put her in a cage, I say, and let the groundlings stare at her for pennies," said Nate, and suddenly the bars of a cage sprang up around her and he was laughing at her from the other side, his pretty face twisted up in scorn. Henry was there too, shaking his head. "I've taken her all apart," he said, "and I can't see what makes that heart of hers beat. Still, it's quite a curiosity, isn't it?" He opened his hand, and there was something red and fleshy on his palm, pulsing and contracting like a fish flipped out of water, gasping for air. "See how it's divided into two quite equal parts—"

"Tess," a voice came, urgently, in her ear. "Tess, you're dreaming. Wake up. Wake up." Hands were on her shoulders, shaking her; her eyes flew open, and she was gasping in her ugly gray dimly lit bedroom at the York Institute. The covers were tangled around her, and her nightgown stuck to her back with sweat. Her skin felt as if it were burning. She still saw the Dark Sisters, saw Nate laughing at her, Henry dissecting her heart.

"It was a dream?" she said. "It felt so real, so utterly real—" She broke off.

"Will," she whispered. He still wore his dinner clothes, though they were rumpled, his black hair tangled, as if he had fallen asleep without changing for bed. His hands remained on her shoulders, warming her cold skin through the material of her nightgown.

"What did you dream?" he said. His tone was calm and ordinary, as if there were nothing unusual about her waking up and finding him sitting on the edge of her bed.

She shuddered at the memory. "I dreamed I was being taken apart—that bits of me were being put on display for Shadowhunters to laugh at—"

"Tess." He touched her hair gently, pushing the tangled locks behind her ears. She felt pulled to him, like iron filings to a magnet. Her arms ached to go around him, her head to rest in the crook of his shoulder. "God damn that devil Starkweather for showing you what he did, but you must know it's not like that anymore. The Accords have forbidden spoils. It was just a dream."

But no, she thought. This is the dream. Her eyes had adjusted to the dark; the gray light in the room made his eyes glow an almost unearthly blue, like a cat's. When she drew a shuddering breath, her lungs felt filled with the scent of him, Will and salt and trains and smoke and rain, and she wondered if he had been out, walking the streets of York as he did in London. "Where have you been?" she whispered. "You smell like nighttime."

"Out kicking over the traces. As usual." He touched her cheek with warm, callused fingers. "Can you sleep now? We're meant to rise early tomorrow. Starkweather is lending us his carriage so that we might investigate Ravenscar Manor. You, of course, are welcome to remain here. You need not accompany us."

She shuddered. "Stay here without you? In this big, gloomy place? I would prefer not to."

"Tess." His voice was ever so gentle. "That must have been quite a nightmare, to have taken the spirit out of you so. Usually you are not afraid of much."

"It was awful. Even Henry was in my dream. He was taking apart my heart as if it were made of clockwork."

"Well, that settles it," Will said. "Pure fantasy. As if Henry is a danger to anyone except himself." When she didn't smile, he added, fiercely, "I would never let anyone touch a hair on your head. You know that, don't you, Tess?"

Their gazes caught and locked. She thought of the wave that seemed to catch at her whenever she was near Will, how she had felt herself drawn over and under, pulled to him by forces that seemed beyond her control—in the attic, on the roof of the Institute. As if he felt the same pull, he bent toward her now. It felt natural, as right as breathing, to lift her head, to meet his lips with hers. She felt his soft exhalation against her mouth; relief, as if a great weight had been taken from him. His hands rose to cup her face. Even as her eyes fluttered shut, she heard his voice in her head, again, unbidden:

There is no future for a Shadowhunter who dallies with warlocks.

She turned her face quickly, and his lips brushed her cheek instead of her mouth. He drew back, and she saw his blue eyes open, startled—and hurt. "No," she said. "No, I don't know that, Will." She dropped her voice. "You have made it very clear," she said, "what kind of use you have for me. You think I am a toy for your amusements. You should not have come in here; it is not proper."

He dropped his hands. "You called out—"

"Not for you."

He was silent except for his ragged breathing.

"Do you regret what you said to me that night on the roof, Will? The night of Thomas's and Agatha's funeral?" It was the first time either of them had made reference to the incident since it had happened. "Can you tell me you did not mean what you said?"

He bent his head; his hair fell forward, hiding his face. She clenched her own hands into fists at her sides to stop herself from reaching out and pushing it back. "No," he said, very low. "No, the Angel forgive me, I can't say that."

Tessa withdrew, curling in on herself, turning her face away. "Please go away, Will."

"Tessa—"

"Please."

There was a long silence. He stood up then, the bed creaking beneath him as he moved. She heard his light tread on the floorboards, and then the door of the bedroom shutting behind him. As if the sound had snapped some cord that held her upright, she fell back against the pillows. She stared up at the ceiling a long time, fighting back in vain against the questions that crowded her mind— What had Will meant, coming to her room like that? Why had he shown her such sweetness when she knew that he despised her? And why, when she knew that he was the worst thing in the world for her, did sending him away seem like such a terrible mistake?

The next morning dawned unexpectedly blue and beautiful, a balm to Tessa's aching head and exhausted body. After dragging herself from the bed, where she had spent most of the night tossing and turning, she dressed herself, unable to bear the thought of assistance from one of the ancient, half-blind maidservants. As she did up the buttons on her jacket, she caught sight of herself in the room's old, splotched mirror.

There were half-moons of shadow under her eyes, as if they had been smudged there with chalk.

Will and Jem had already gathered in the morning room for a breakfast of half-burned toast, weak tea, jam, and no butter. By the time Tessa arrived, Jem had already eaten, and Will was busy cutting his toast into thin strips and forming rude pictographs out of them.

"What *is* that supposed to be?" Jem asked curiously. "It looks almost like a—" He glanced up, saw Tessa, and broke off with a grin. "Good morning."

"Good morning." She slid into the seat across from Will; he glanced up at her once as she sat, but there was nothing in his eyes or expression to indicate that he recalled that anything had passed between them the night before.

Jem looked at her with concern. "Tessa, how are you feeling? After last night—" He broke off then, his voice rising, "Good morning, Mr. Starkweather," he said hastily, jostling Will's shoulder hard so that Will dropped his fork, and the toast bits slid all over his plate.

Mr. Starkweather, who had swept into the room, still wrapped in the dark cloak he had worn the night before, regarded him balefully. "The carriage is waiting for you in the courtyard," he said, his clipped diction as tight as ever. "You'd better cut a stick if you want to get back before dinnertime; I'll be needing the carriage this evening. I've told Gottshall to drop you straight at the station on your return, no need for lingering. I trust you've gotten everything you need."

It wasn't a question. Jem nodded. "Yes, sir. You've been very gracious."

Starkweather's eyes swept over Tessa again, one last time,

before he turned and stalked out of the room, his cloak flapping behind him. Tessa couldn't get the image of a great black bird of prey—a vulture, perhaps—out of her mind. She thought of the trophy cases full of "spoils," and shuddered.

"Eat quickly, Tessa, before he changes his mind about the carriage," Will advised her, but Tessa shook her head.

"I'm not hungry."

"At least have tea." Will poured it out for her, and ladled milk and sugar into it; it was much sweeter than Tessa would have liked, but it was so rare that Will made a kind gesture like that—even if it was just to hurry her along—that she drank it down anyway, and managed a few bites of toast. The boys went for their coats and the baggage; Tessa's traveling cloak, hat, and gloves were located, and they soon found themselves on the front steps of the York Institute, blinking in the watery sunlight.

Starkweather had been as good as his word. His carriage was there, waiting for them, the four Cs of the Clave painted across the door. The old coachman with the long white beard and hair was already in the driver's seat, smoking a cheroot; he tossed it aside when he saw the three of them, and sank down farther in his seat, his black eyes glaring out from beneath his drooping eyelids.

"Bloody hell, it's the Ancient Mariner again," said Will, though he seemed more entertained than anything else. He swung himself up into the carriage and helped Tessa in after him; Jem was last, shutting the door behind him and leaning out the window to call to the coachman to drive on. Tessa, settling herself in beside Will on the narrow seat, felt her shoulder brush his; he tensed immediately, and she moved away, biting her lip. It was as if last night had never happened and he were back to behaving as if she were poison.

The carriage began moving with a jerk that nearly flung Tessa into Will again, but she braced herself against the window and stayed where she was. The three of them were silent as the carriage rolled down narrow, cobbled Stonegate Street, under a wide sign advertising the Old Star Inn. Both Jem and Will were quiet, Will reviving only to tell her with a ghoulish glee that they were passing through the old walls, under the city entrance where once traitors' heads had been displayed on spikes. Tessa made a face at him but gave no reply.

Once they had passed the walls, the city quickly gave way to countryside. The landscape was not gentle and rolling, but harsh and forbidding. Green hills dotted with gray gorse swept up into crags of dark rock. Long lines of mortarless stone walls, meant for keeping in sheep, crisscrossed the green; here and there was dotted the occasional lonely cottage. The sky seemed an endless expanse of blue, brushed with the strokes of long gray clouds.

Tessa could not have said how long they had been traveling when the stone chimneys of a large manor house rose in the distance. Jem stuck his head out the window again and called to the driver; the carriage came to a rolling stop.

"But we're not there yet," said Tessa, puzzled. "If that's Ravenscar Manor—"

"We can't just roll right up to the front door; be sensible, Tess," said Will as Jem leaped out of the carriage and reached up to help Tessa down. Her boots plashed into the wet, muddy ground as she landed; Will dropped down lightly beside her. "We need to get a look at the place. Use Henry's device to register demonic presence. Make sure we're not walking into a trap."

"Does Henry's device actually *work?*" Tessa lifted her skirts to keep them out of the mud as the three of them started down the road. Glancing back, she saw the coachman apparently already asleep, leaning back in the driver's seat with his hat tipped forward over his face. All around them the countryside was a patchwork of gray and green—hills rising starkly; their sides pitted with gray shale; flat sheep-cropped grass; and here and there copses of gnarled, entwined trees. There was a severe beauty to it all, but Tessa shuddered at the idea of living here, so far away from anything.

Jem, seeing her shudder, gave a sideways smile. "City lass."

Tessa laughed. "I *was* thinking how odd it would be to grow up in a place like this, so far from any people."

"Where I grew up was not so different from this," said Will unexpectedly, startling them both. "It's not so lonely as you might think. Out in the countryside, you can be assured, people visit one another a great deal. They just have a greater distance to traverse than they might in London. And once they arrive, they often make a lengthy stay. After all, why make the trip just to stay a night or two? We'd often have house guests who'd remain for weeks."

Tessa goggled at Will silently. It was so rare that he ever referred to anything regarding his early life that she sometimes thought of him as someone with no past at all. Jem seemed to be doing the same thing, though he recovered first.

"I share Tessa's view. I have never lived in anything but a city. I don't know how I could sleep at night, not knowing I was surrounded by a thousand other sleeping, dreaming souls."

"And filth everywhere, and everyone breathing down one another's necks," countered Will. "When I first arrived in London, I so quickly tired of being surrounded by so many people that it was only with great difficulty that I refrained from seizing the next unfortunate who crossed my path and committing violent acts upon their person."

"Some might say you retain that problem," said Tessa, but Will just laughed—a short, nearly surprised sound of amusement—and then stopped, looking ahead of them to Ravenscar Manor.

Jem whistled as Tessa realized why she had been able to see only the tops of the chimneys before. The manor was built in the center of a deep declivity between three hills; their slanting sides rose about it, cradling it as if in the palm of a hand. Tessa, Jem, and Will were poised on the edge of one of the hills, looking down at the manor. The building itself was very grand, a great gray stone pile that gave the impression it had been there for centuries. A large circular drive curved in front of the enormous front doors. Nothing about the place hinted at abandonment or disrepair—no weeds grew over the drive or the paths that led to the stone outbuildings, and no glass was missing from the mullioned windows.

"*Someone's* living here," said Jem, echoing Tessa's thoughts. He began to start down the hill. The grass here was longer, waving almost waist-high. "Perhaps if—"

He broke off as the rattle of wheels became audible; for a moment Tessa thought the carriage driver had come after them, but no, this was quite a different carriage—a sturdy-looking coach that turned into the gate and began rolling toward the manor. Jem crouched down immediately in the grass, and Will and Tessa dropped beside him. They watched as the carriage came to a stop before the manor, and the driver leaped down to open the carriage door.

A young girl stepped out, fourteen or fifteen years old, Tessa guessed—not old enough to have put her hair up, for it blew around her in a curtain of black silk. She wore a blue dress, plain but fashionable. She nodded to the driver, and then, as she started up the manor steps, she paused—paused and looked toward where Jem, Will, and Tessa crouched, almost as if she could see them, though Tessa was sure that they were well hidden by the grass.

The distance was too great for Tessa to make out her features, really—just the pale oval of her face below the dark hair. She was about to ask Jem if he had a telescope with him, when Will made a noise—a noise she had never heard anyone make before, a sick, terrible gasp, as if the air had been punched out of him by a tremendous blow.

But it was not just a gasp, she realized. It was a word; and not just a word, a name; and not just a name, but one she had heard him say before.

"*Cecily*."

6

In Silence Sealed

The human heart has hidden treasures,
In secret kept, in silence sealed;
The thoughts, the hopes, the dreams, the pleasures,
Whose charms were broken if revealed
—Charlotte Brontë, "Evening Solace"

The door of the great house swung open; the girl disappeared inside. The coach rattled off around the side of the manor to the coach house as Will staggered to his feet. He had gone a sickly gray color, like the ashes of a dead fire.

"Cecily," he said again. His voice held wonderment, and horror.

"Who on earth is Cecily?" Tessa scrambled into a standing position, brushing grass and thistles from her dress. "Will—"

Jem was already beside Will, his hand on his friend's shoulder. "Will, you must speak to us. You look as if you've seen a ghost."

Will dragged in a long breath. "Cecily—"

"Yes, you've said that already," said Tessa. She heard the sharpness in her own voice, and softened it with an effort. It was unkind to speak so to someone so obviously distraught, even if he did insist on staring into space and muttering "Cecily" at intervals.

It hardly mattered; Will seemed not to have heard her. "My sister," he said. "Cecily. She was— Christ, she was nine years old when I left."

"Your sister," said Jem, and Tessa felt a loosening of something tight around her heart, and cursed herself inwardly for it. What did it matter whether Cecily was Will's sister or someone he was in love with? It had nothing to do with her.

Will started down the hill, not looking for a path, just tramping blindly among the heather and furze. After a moment Jem went after him, catching at his sleeve. "Will, don't—"

Will tried to pull his arm away. "If Cecily's there, then the rest of them—my family—they must be there as well."

Tessa hurried to catch up with them, wincing as she nearly turned an ankle on a loose rock. "But it doesn't make any sense that your family would be here, Will. This was Mortmain's house. Starkweather said so. It was in the papers—"

"I *know* that," Will half-shouted.

"Cecily could be visiting someone here—"

Will gave her an incredulous look. "In the middle of York-shire, by herself? And that was our carriage. I recognized it. There's no other carriage in the carriage house. No, my family's in this somehow. They've been dragged into this bloody busi-ness and I—I have to warn them." He started down the hill again.

"Will!" Jem shouted, and went after him, catching at the

back of his coat; Will swung around and shoved Jem, not very hard; Tessa heard Jem say something about Will having held back all these years and not wasting it now, and then it all blurred together—Will swearing, and Jem yanking him backward, and Will slipping on the wet ground, and the both of them going over together, a rolling tangle of arms and legs, until they fetched up against a large rock, Jem pinning Will to the ground, his elbow against the other boy's throat.

"Get off me." Will shoved at him. "You don't understand. *Your* family's dead—"

"*Will.*" Jem took his friend by the shirtfront and shook him. "I *do* understand. And unless you want your family dead too, you'll listen to me."

Will went very still. In a choked voice he said, "James, you can't possibly— I've never—"

"Look." Jem raised the hand that wasn't gripping Will's shirt, and pointed. "There. Look."

Tessa looked where he was pointing—and felt her insides freeze. They were nearly halfway down the hill above the manor house, and there, above them, standing like a sort of sentry on the ridge at the hill's top, was an automaton. She knew immediately what it was, though it did not look like the automatons that Mortmain had sent against them before. Those had made some surface pretense of being human. This was a tall, spindly metal creature, with long hinged legs, a twisted metallic torso, and sawlike arms.

It was utterly still, not moving, somehow more frightening for its stillness and silence. Tessa could not even tell if it was watching them. It seemed to be turned toward them, but though it had a head, that head was featureless but for the slash of a mouth; metal teeth gleamed within. It seemed to have no eyes.

Tessa quelled the scream rising in her throat. It was an automaton. She had faced them before. She would *not* scream. Will, propped on his elbow, was staring. "By the Angel—"

"That thing's been following us; I'm sure of it," said Jem in a low, urgent voice. "I saw a flash of metal earlier, from the carriage, but I wasn't sure. Now I am. If you go tearing off down the hill, you risk leading that thing right to your family's door."

"I see," Will said. The half-hysterical tone had gone from his voice. "I won't go near the house. Let me up."

Jem hesitated.

"I swear on Raziel's name," Will ground out, between his teeth. "Now let me up."

Jem rolled away and onto his feet; Will leaped up, pushing Jem aside, and, without a glance at Tessa, took off running— not toward the house but away from it, toward the mechanical creature on the ridge. Jem staggered for a moment, openmouthed, swore, and darted after him.

"*Jem!*" Tessa cried. But he was nearly out of earshot already, racing after Will. The automaton had vanished from view. Tessa said an unladylike word, hiked up her skirts, and gave chase.

It was not easy, running up a wet Yorkshire hill in heavy skirts, brambles tearing at her as she went. Practicing in her training clothes had given Tessa a new appreciation for why it was that men could move so quickly and cleanly, and could run so fast. The material of her dress weighed a ton, the heels on her boots caught on rocks as she ran, and her corset left her uncomfortably short of breath.

By the time she reached the top of the ridge, she was only

just in time to see Jem, far ahead of her, disappear into a dark copse of trees. She looked around wildly but could see neither the road nor the Starkweathers' carriage. With her heart pounding, she dashed after him.

The copse was wide, spreading along the ridgeline. The moment Tessa ducked in among the trees, the light vanished; thick tree branches interweaving above her blocked out the sun. Feeling like Snow White fleeing into the forest, she looked around helplessly for a sign of where the boys had gone— broken branches, trodden leaves—and caught a shimmer of light on metal as the automaton surged out of the dark space between two trees and lunged for her.

She screamed, leaping away, and promptly tripped on her skirts. She went over backward, thumping painfully into the muddy earth. The creature stabbed one of its long insectile arms toward her. She rolled aside and the metal arm sliced into the ground beside her. There was a fallen tree branch near her; her fingers scrabbled at it, closed around it, and lifted it just as the creature's other arm swung toward her. She swept the branch between them, concentrating on the parrying and blocking lessons she'd gotten from Gabriel.

But it was only a branch. The automaton's metal arm sheared it in half. The end of the arm sprang open into a multi-fingered metal claw and reached for her throat. But before it could touch her, Tessa felt a violent fluttering against her collarbone. Her angel. She lay frozen as the creature jerked its claw back, one of its "fingers" leaking black fluid. A moment later it gave a high-pitched whine and collapsed backward, a freshet of more black liquid pouring from the hole that had been sliced clean through its chest.

Tessa sat up and stared.

Will stood with a sword in his hand, its hilt smeared with black. He was bareheaded, his thick dark hair tousled and tangled with leaves and bits of grass. Jem stood beside him, a witchlight stone blazing through his fingers. As Tessa watched, Will slashed out with the sword again, cutting the automaton nearly in half. It crumpled to the muddy ground. Its insides were an ugly, horribly biological-looking mess of tubes and wires.

Jem looked up. His gaze met Tessa's. His eyes were as silver as mirrors. Will, despite having saved her, did not appear to notice she was there at all; he drew back his foot and delivered a savage kick to the metal creature's side. His boot rang against metal.

"Tell us," he said through gritted teeth. "What are you doing here? Why are you following us?"

The automaton's razor-lined mouth opened. Its voice when it spoke sounded like the buzzing and grinding of faulty machinery. "I . . . am . . . a . . . warning . . . from the Magister."

"A warning to who? To the family in the manor? Tell me!" Will looked as if he were going to kick the creature again; Jem laid a hand on his shoulder.

"It doesn't feel pain, Will," he said in a low voice. "And it says it has a message. Let it deliver it."

"A warning . . . to you, Will Herondale . . . and to all Nephilim . . ." The creature's broken voice ground out, "The Magister says . . . you must cease your investigation. The past . . . is the past. Leave Mortmain's buried, or your family will pay the price. Do not dare approach or warn them. If you do, they will be destroyed."

Jem was looking at Will; Will was still ashy-pale, but his

cheeks were burning with rage. "How did Mortmain bring my family here? Did he threaten them? What has he done?"

The creature whirred and clicked, then began to speak again. "*I . . . am . . . a . . . warning . . . from . . .*"

Will snarled like an animal and slashed down with the sword. Tessa remembered Jessamine, in Hyde Park, tearing a faerie creature to ribbons with her delicate parasol. Will cut at the automaton until it was little more than ribbons of metal; Jem, throwing his arms around his friend and yanking him bodily backward, finally stopped him.

"Will," he said. "Will, enough." He glanced up, and the other two followed his gaze. In the distance, through the trees, other shapes moved—more automatons, like this one. "We must go," Jem said. "If we want to draw them off, away from your family, we must leave."

Will hesitated.

"Will, you know you cannot go near them," Jem said desperately. "If nothing else, it is the Law. If we bring danger to them, the Clave will not move to help them in any way. They are not Shadowhunters anymore. *Will.*"

Slowly Will lowered his arm to his side. He stood, with one of Jem's arms still around his shoulders, staring down at the pile of scrap metal at his feet. Black liquid dripped from the blade of the sword that dangled in his hand, and scorched the grass below.

Tessa exhaled. She hadn't realized she'd been holding her breath until that moment. Will must have heard her, for he raised his head and his gaze met hers across the clearing. Something in it made her look away. Agony stripped so raw was not meant for her eyes.

* * *

In the end they hid the remains of the destroyed automaton as swiftly as possible, by burying them in the soft earth beneath a rotting log. Tessa helped as best she could, hampered by her skirts. By the end of it her hands were as black with dirt and mud as Will's and Jem's were.

None of them spoke; they worked in an eerie silence. When they were done, Will led the way out of the copse, guided by the light of Jem's witchlight rune-stone. They emerged from the woods nearly at the road, where the Starkweather carriage waited, Gottshall dozing in the driver's seat as if only a few moments had passed since they had arrived.

If their appearances—filthy, smeared with mud, and with leaves caught in their hair—surprised the old man at all, he didn't show it, nor did he ask them if they had found what they had come looking for. He only grunted a hello and waited for them to climb up into the carriage before he signaled the horses with a click of his tongue to turn around and begin the long journey back to York.

The curtains inside the carriage were drawn back; the sky was heavy with blackish clouds, pressing down on the horizon. "It's going to rain," Jem said, pushing damp silvery hair out of his eyes.

Will said nothing. He was staring out the window. His eyes were the color of the Arctic sea at night.

"Cecily," said Tessa in a much gentler voice than she was used to using with Will these days. He looked so miserable—as bleak and stark as the moors they were passing through. "Your sister—she looks like you."

Will remained silent. Tessa, seated next to Jem on the hard seat, shivered a little. Her clothes were damp from the wet earth and branches, and the inside of the carriage was cold. Jem reached down and, finding a slightly ragged lap rug, settled it over the both of them. She could feel the heat that radiated off his body, as if he were feverish, and fought the urge to move closer to him to get warm.

"Are you cold, Will?" she asked, but he only shook his head, his eyes still staring, unseeing, at the passing countryside. She looked at Jem in desperation.

Jem spoke, his voice clear and direct. "Will," he said. "I thought . . . I thought that your sister was dead."

Will drew his gaze from the window and looked at them both. When he smiled, it was ghastly. "My sister *is* dead," he said.

And that was all he would say. They rode the rest of the way back to the city of York in silence.

Having barely slept the night before, Tessa fell in and out of a fitful doze that lasted until they reached the York train station. In a fog she dismounted from the carriage and followed the others to the London platform; they were late for the train, and nearly missed it, and Jem held the door open for her, for her and Will, as both of them stumbled up the steps and into the compartment after him. Later she would remember the way he looked, hanging on to the door, hatless, calling to both of them, and recall staring out the window of the train as it pulled away, seeing Gottshall standing on the platform looking after them with his unsettling dark eyes, his hat pulled low. Everything else was a blur.

There was no conversation this time as the train puffed its way through countryside increasingly darkened by clouds, only silence. Tessa rested her chin on her palm, cradling her head against the hard glass of the window. Green hills flew by, and small towns and villages, each with their own neat small station, the name of it picked out in gold on a red sign. Church spires rose in the distance; cities swelled and vanished, and Tessa was aware of Jem whispering to Will, in Latin, she thought—"*Me specta, me specta,*" and Will not answering. Later she was aware that Jem had left the compartment, and she looked at Will across the small dimming space between them. The sun had begun to go down, and it lent a rosy flush to his skin, belying the blank look in his eyes.

"Will," she said softly, sleepily. "Last night—" *You were kind to me,* she was going to say. *Thank you.*

The glare from his blue eyes stabbed through her. "There was no last night," he said through his teeth.

At that, she sat up straight, almost awake. "Oh, truly? We just went right from one afternoon on through till the next morning? How odd no one else has remarked on it. I should think it some sort of miracle, a day with no night—"

"Don't test me, Tessa." Will's hands were clenched on his knees, his fingernails, half-moons of dirt under them, digging into the fabric of his trousers.

"Your sister's alive," she said, knowing perfectly well that she was provoking him. "Oughtn't you be glad?"

He whitened. "*Tessa—,*" he began, and leaned forward as if he meant to do she knew not what—strike the window and break it, shake her by the shoulders, or hold her as if he never meant to let her go. It was all one great bewilderment with him, wasn't it? Then the compartment door opened and Jem came in, carrying a damp cloth.

He looked from Will to Tessa and raised his silvery eyebrows. "A miracle," he said. "You got him to speak."

"Just to shout at me, really," said Tessa. "Not quite loaves and fishes."

Will had gone back to staring out the window, and looked at neither of them as they spoke.

"It's a start," said Jem, and he sat down beside her. "Here. Give me your hands."

Surprised, Tessa held her hands out to him—and was horrified. They were filthy, the nails cracked and broken and thick with half-moons of dirt where she had clawed at the Yorkshire earth. There was even a bloody scratch across her knuckles, though she had no memory of having gotten it.

Not a lady's hands. She thought of Jessamine's perfect pink and white paws. "Jessie would be horrified," she said mournfully. "She'd tell me I had charwoman's hands."

"And what, pray tell, is dishonorable about that?" said Jem as he gently cleaned the dirt from her scratches. "I saw you chase after us, and that automaton creature. If Jessamine does not know by now that there is honor in blood and dirt, she never will."

The cool cloth felt good on her fingers. She looked up at Jem, who was intent on his task, his lashes a fringe of lowered silver. "Thank you," she said. "I doubt I was any help at all, and probably a hindrance, but thank you all the same."

He smiled at her, the sun coming out from behind clouds. "That's what we're training you for, isn't it?"

She lowered her voice. "Have you any idea what could have happened? Why Will's family would be living in a house Mortmain once owned?"

Jem glanced over at Will, who was still staring bitterly out the window. They had entered London, and gray buildings were beginning to rise up around them on either side. The look Jem gave Will was a tired, loving sort of look, a familial look, and Tessa realized that, though when she had imagined them as brothers, she had always imagined Will as the older, the caretaker, and Jem as the younger, the reality was far more complicated than that. "I do not," he said, "though it makes me think that the game Mortmain is playing is a long one. Somehow he knew exactly where our investigations would lead us, and he arranged for this—encounter—to shock us as much as possible. He wishes us to be reminded who it is who has the power."

Tessa shuddered. "I don't know what he wants from me, Jem," she said in a low voice. "When he said to me that he made me, it was as if he were saying he could unmake me just as easily."

Jem's warm arm touched hers. "You cannot be unmade," he said just as softly. "And Mortmain underestimates you. I saw how you used that branch against the automaton—"

"It was not enough. If it had not been for my angel—" Tessa touched the pendant at her throat. "The automaton touched it and recoiled. Another mystery I do not understand. It protected me before, and again this time, but in other situations lies dormant. It is as much a mystery as my talent."

"Which, fortunately, you did not need to use to Change into Starkweather. He seemed quite happy simply to give us the Shade files."

"Thank goodness," said Tessa. "I wasn't looking forward to it. He seems such an unpleasant, bitter man. But if it ever turns out to be necessary . . ." She took something from her pocket and held it up, something that glinted in the carriage's dim light. "A button," she said smugly. "It fell from the cuff of his jacket this morning, and I picked it up."

Jem smiled. "Very clever, Tessa. I knew we'd be glad we brought you with us—"

He broke off with a cough. Tessa looked at him in alarm, and even Will was roused out of his silent despondency, turning to look at Jem with narrowed eyes. Jem coughed again, his hand pressed to his mouth, but when he took it away, there was no blood visible. Tessa saw Will's shoulders relax.

"Just some dust in my throat," Jem reassured them. He looked not ill but very tired, though his exhaustion only served to point up the delicacy of his features. His beauty did not blaze like Will's did in fierce colors and repressed fire, but it had its own muted perfection, the loveliness of snow falling against a silver-gray sky.

"Your ring!" She started up suddenly as she remembered that she was still wearing it. She put the button back into her pocket, then reached to draw the Carstairs ring off her hand. "I had meant to give it back to you earlier," she said, placing the silver circlet in his palm. "I forgot . . ."

He curled his fingers around hers. Despite her thoughts of snow and gray skies, his hand was surprisingly warm. "That's all right," he said in a low voice. "I like the way it looks on you."

She felt her cheeks warm. Before she could answer, the train whistle sounded. Voices cried out that they were in London, Kings Cross Station. The train began to slow as the platform came into view. The hubbub of the station rose to assault Tessa's ears, along with the sound of the train braking. Jem said something, but his words were lost in the noise; it sounded like a warning, but Will was already on his feet, his hand reaching for the compartment door latch. He swung it open and leaped out and down. If he were not a Shadowhunter, Tessa thought, he would have fallen, and badly, but as it was, he simply landed lightly on his feet and began to run, pushing his way among the crowding porters, the commuters, the gentility traveling north for the weekend with their massive trunks and hunting hounds on leashes, the newspaper boys and pickpockets and costermongers and all the other human traffic of the grand station.

Jem was on his feet, hand reaching for the door—but he turned back and looked at Tessa, and she saw an expression cross his face, an expression that said that he realized that if he fled after Will, she could not follow. With another long look at her, he latched the door shut and sank into the seat opposite her as the train came to a stop.

"But Will—," she began.

"He will be all right," said Jem with conviction. "You know how he is. Sometimes he just wants to be alone. And I doubt he wishes to take part in recounting today's experiences to Charlotte and the others." When she didn't move her eyes from his, he repeated, gently, "Will can take care of himself, Tessa."

She thought of the bleak look in Will's eyes when he had spoken to her, starker than the Yorkshire moors they had just left behind them. She hoped Jem was right.

7

THE CURSE

An orphan's curse would drag to hell
A spirit from on high;
But oh! more horrible than that
Is the curse in a dead man's eye!
Seven days, seven nights, I saw that curse,
And yet I could not die.
—Samuel Taylor Coleridge,
"The Rime of the Ancient Mariner"

Magnus heard the sound of the front door opening and the following clatter of raised voices, and thought immediately, *Will.* And then was amused that he had thought it. The Shadowhunter boy was becoming like an annoying relative, he thought as he folded down a page of the book he was reading—Lucian's *Dialogues of the Gods*; Camille would be furious he had dog-eared her volume—someone whose habits you knew well but could not change. Someone whose presence you could recognize by the sound of their boots in the hallway. Someone who felt free to argue with the footman when he'd been given orders to tell everyone that you were not at home.

The parlor door flew open, and Will stood on the threshold, looking half-triumphant and half-wretched—quite a feat. "I *knew* you were here," he announced as Magnus sat up straight on the sofa, swinging his boots to the floor. "Now, will you tell this—this overgrown bat to stop hovering over my shoulder?" He indicated Archer, Camille's subjugate and Magnus's temporary footman, who was indeed lurking at Will's side. His face was set in a look of disapproval, but then it was always set in a look of disapproval. "Tell him you want to see me."

Magnus set his book down on the table beside him. "But maybe I don't want to see you," he said reasonably. "I told Archer to let no one in, not to let no one in but you."

"He threatened me," Archer said in his hissing not-quite-human voice. "I shall tell my mistress."

"You do that," said Will, but his eyes were on Magnus, blue and anxious. "Please. I *have* to talk to you."

Drat the boy, Magnus thought. After an exhausting day spent clearing a memory-blocking spell for a member of the Penhallow family, he had wanted only to rest. He had stopped listening for Camille's step in the hall, or waiting for her message, but he still preferred this room to others—this room, where her personal touch seemed to cling to the thorned roses on the wallpaper, the faint perfume that rose from the draperies. He had looked forward to an evening spent by the fire here—a glass of wine, a book, and being left strictly alone.

But now here was Will Herondale, his expression a study in pain and desperation, wanting Magnus's help. He was really going to have to do something about this annoying softhearted impulse to assist the desperate, Magnus thought. That, and his weakness for blue eyes.

"Very well," he said with a martyred sigh. "You may stay and talk to me. But I warn you, I'm not raising a demon. Not before I've had my supper. Unless you have turned up some sort of hard proof..."

"No." Will came eagerly into the room, shutting the door in Archer's face. He reached around and locked it, for good measure, and then strode over to the fire. It *was* chilly out. The visible bit of window not blocked by drapes showed the square outside darkening to a blackish twilight, leaves blown rattling across the pavement by a brisk-looking wind. Will drew off his gloves, laid them on the mantel, and stretched his hands out to the flames. "I don't want you to raise a demon."

"Huh." Magnus put his booted feet up on the small rosewood table before the sofa, another gesture that would have infuriated Camille, had she been there. "That's good news, I suppose—"

"I want you to send me through. To the demon realms."

Magnus choked. "You want me to do *what?*"

Will's profile was black against the flickering fire. "Create a portal to the demon worlds and send me through. You can do that, can't you?"

"That's black magic," said Magnus. "Not quite necromancy, but—"

"No one need know."

"Really." Magnus's tone was acid. "These things have a way of getting out. And if the Clave found out I'd sent one of their own, their most promising, to be rent apart by demons in another dimension—"

"The Clave does not consider me promising." Will's voice was cold. "I am not promising. I am not anything, nor will I ever be. Not without your help."

"I am beginning to wonder if you've been sent to test me, Will Herondale."

Will gave a harsh little bark of laughter. "By God?"

"By the Clave. Who might as well be God. Perhaps they simply seek to find out whether I am willing to break the Law."

Will swung around and stared at him. "I am deadly earnest," he said. "This is not some sort of test. I cannot go on like this, summoning up demons at random, never having them be the correct one, endless hope, endless disappointment. Every day dawns blacker and blacker, and I will lose her forever if you—"

"Lose *her*?" Magnus's mind fastened on the word; he sat up straight, narrowing his eyes. "This *is* about Tessa. I knew it was."

Will flushed, a wash of color across the pallor of his face. "Not just her."

"But you love her."

Will stared at him. "Of course I do," he said finally. "I had come to think I would never love anyone, but I love her."

"Is this curse supposed to be some business about taking away your ability to love? Because that's nonsense if I've ever heard it. Jem's your *parabatai*. I've seen you with him. You love him, don't you?"

"Jem is my great sin," said Will. "Don't talk to me about Jem."

"Don't talk to you about Jem, don't talk to you about Tessa. You want me to open a portal to the demon worlds for you, and you won't talk to me or tell me why? I won't do it, Will." Magnus crossed his arms over his chest.

Will rested a hand on the mantel. He was very still, the flames showing the outlines of him, the clear beautiful profile, the grace of his long slender hands. "I saw my family today," he said, and then amended that quickly. "My sister. I saw my younger sister. Cecily. I knew they lived, but I never thought I would see them again. They cannot be near me."

"Why?" Magnus made his voice soft; he felt he was on the verge of something, some sort of breakthrough with this odd, infuriating, damaged, shattered boy. "What did they do that was so terrible?"

"What did *they* do?" Will's voice rose. "What did *they* do? Nothing. It is me. I am poison. Poison to them. Poison to anyone who loves me."

"Will—"

"I lied to you," Will said, turning suddenly away from the fire.

"Shocking," Magnus murmured, but Will was gone, gone into his memories, which was perhaps for the best. He had begun to pace, scuffing his boots along Camille's lovely Persian carpet.

"You know what I've told you. I was in the library of my parents' house in Wales. It was a rainy day; I was bored, going through my father's old things. He kept a few things from his old life as a Shadowhunter, things he had not wanted, for sentiment I suppose, to give up. An old stele, though I did not know what it was at the time, and a small, engraved box, in a false drawer of his desk. I suppose he assumed that would be enough to keep us out, but nothing is enough to keep out curious children. Of course the first thing I did upon finding the box was open it. A mist poured out of it in a blast, forming almost instantly into a living demon. The moment I saw the creature, I began to scream. I was only twelve. I'd never seen anything like it. Enormous, deadly, all jagged teeth and barbed tail—and I had nothing. No weapons. When it roared, I fell to the carpet. The thing was hovering over me, hissing. Then my sister burst in."

"Cecily?"

"Ella. My elder sister. She had something blazing in her hand. I know what it was now—a seraph blade. I had no idea then. I screamed for her to get out, but she put herself between the creature and me. She had absolutely no fear, my sister. She never had. She was not afraid to climb the tallest tree, to ride the wildest horse—and she had no fear there, in the library. She told the thing to get out. It was hovering there like a great, ugly insect. She said, 'I banish you.' Then it laughed."

It would. Magnus felt a strange stirring of both pity and liking for the girl, brought up to know nothing about demons, their summoning or their banishment, yet standing her ground regardless.

"It laughed, and it swung out with its tail, knocking her to the ground. Then it fixed its eyes on me. They were all red, no whites at all. It said, 'It is your father I would destroy, but as he is not here, you will have to do.' I was so shocked, all I could do was stare. Ella was crawling over the carpet, grabbing for the fallen seraph blade. 'I curse you,' it said. 'All who love you will die. Their love will be their destruction. It may take moments, it may take years, but any who look upon you with love will die of it, unless you remove yourself from them forever. And I shall begin it with *her*.' It snarled in Ella's direction, and vanished."

Magnus was fascinated despite himself. "And did she fall dead?"

"No." Will was still pacing. He took off his jacket, slung it over a chair. His longish dark hair had begun to curl with the heat coming off his body, mixing with the heat of the fire; it stuck to the back of his neck. "She was unharmed. She took me in her arms. *She* comforted *me*. She told me the demon's words meant nothing. She admitted she had read some of the forbidden books in the library, and that was how she knew what a seraph blade was, and how to use it, and that the thing I had opened was called a Pyxis, though she could not imagine why my father would have kept one. She made me promise not to touch anything of my parents' again unless she was there, and then she led me up to bed, and sat reading while I fell asleep. I was exhausted with the shock of it all, I think. I remember hearing her murmur to my mother, something about how I had been taken ill while they had been out, some childish fever. By that point I was enjoying the fuss that was being made over me, and the demon was beginning to seem a rather exciting memory. I recall planning how to tell Cecily about it—without admitting, of course, that Ella had saved me while I had screamed like a child—"

"You *were* a child," Magnus noted.

"I was old enough," said Will. "Old enough to know what it meant when I was woken up the next morning by my mother howling with grief. She was in Ella's room, and Ella was dead in her bed. They did their best to keep me out, but I saw what I needed to see. She was swelled up, greenish-black like something had rotted her from inside. She didn't look like my sister anymore. She didn't look *human* anymore.

"I knew what had happened, even if they didn't. 'All who love you will die. And I shall begin it with her.' It was my curse at work. I knew then that I had to get away from them—from all my family—before I brought the same horror down on them. I left that night, following the roads to London."

Magnus opened his mouth, then closed it again. For once he didn't know what to say.

"So, you see," said Will, "my curse can hardly be called nonsense. I have seen it at work. And since that day I have striven to be sure that what happened to Ella will happen to no one else in my life. Can you imagine it? Can you?" He raked his hands through his black hair, letting the tangled strands fall back into his eyes. "Never letting anyone near you. Making everyone who might otherwise love you, hate you. I left my family to distance myself from them, and that they might forget me. Each day I must show cruelty to those I have chosen to make my home with, lest they let themselves feel too much affection for me."

"Tessa . . ." Magnus's mind was suddenly full of the serious-faced gray-eyed girl who had looked at Will as if he were a new sun dawning on the horizon. "You think she does not love you?"

"I do not think so. I have been foul enough to her." Will's voice was wretchedness and misery and self-loathing all combined. "I think there was a time when she almost— I thought she was dead, you see, and I showed her—I let her see what I felt. I think she might have returned my feelings after that. But I crushed her, as brutally as I could. I imagine she simply hates me now."

"And Jem," said Magnus, dreading the answer, knowing it.

"Jem is dying anyway," Will said in a choked voice. "Jem is

what I have allowed myself. I tell myself, if he dies, it is not my fault. He is dying anyway, and in pain. Ella's death at least was swift. Perhaps through me he can be given a good death." He looked up miserably, met Magnus's accusing eyes. "No one can live with nothing," he whispered. "Jem is all I have."

"You should have told him," said Magnus. "He would have chosen to be your *parabatai* anyway, even knowing the risks."

"I cannot burden him with that knowledge! He would keep it secret if I asked him to, but it would pain him to know it—and the pain I cause others would only hurt him more. Yet if I were to tell Charlotte, to tell Henry and the rest, that my behavior is a sham—that every cruel thing I have said to them is a lie, that I wander the streets only to give the impression that I have been out drinking and whoring when in reality I have no desire to do either—then I have ceased to push them away."

"And thus you have never told anyone of this curse? No one but myself, since you were twelve years old?"

"I could not," Will said. "How could I be sure they would form no attachment to me, once they knew the truth? A story like that might engender pity, pity could become attachment, and then . . ."

Magnus raised his eyebrows. "Are you not concerned about me?"

"That you might *love* me?" Will sounded genuinely startled. "No, for you hate Nephilim, do you not? And besides, I imagine you warlocks have ways to guard against unwanted emotions. But for those like Charlotte, like Henry, if they knew the persona I presented to them was false, if they knew of my true heart . . . they might come to care for me."

"And then they would die," said Magnus.

* * *

Charlotte raised her face slowly from her hands. "And you've absolutely no idea where he is?" she asked for the third time. "Will is simply—gone?"

"Charlotte." Jem's voice was soothing. They were in the drawing room, with its wallpaper of flowers and vines. Sophie was by the fire, using the poker to coax more flames from the coal. Henry sat behind the desk, fiddling with a set of copper instruments; Jessamine was on the chaise, and Charlotte was in an armchair by the fire. Tessa and Jem sat somewhat primly side by side on the sofa, which made Tessa feel peculiarly like a guest. She was full of sandwiches that Bridget had brought in on a tray, and tea, its warmth slowly thawing her insides. "It isn't as if this is unusual. When do we ever know where Will is at nighttime?"

"But this is different. He saw his family, or his sister at least. Oh, poor Will." Charlotte's voice shook with anxiety. "I had thought perhaps he was finally beginning to forget about them . . ."

"No one forgets about their family," said Jessamine sharply. She sat on the chaise longue with a watercolor easel and papers propped before her; she had recently made the decision that she had fallen behind in pursuing the maidenly arts, and had begun painting, cutting silhouettes, pressing flowers, and playing on the spinet in the music room, though Will said her singing voice made him think of Church when he was in a particularly complaining mood.

"Well, no, of course not," said Charlotte hastily, "but perhaps not to live with the memory constantly, as a sort of dreadful weight on you."

"As if we'd know what to do with Will if he didn't have the morbs every day," said Jessamine. "Anyway, he can't have cared about his family that much in the first place or he wouldn't have left them."

Tessa gave a little gasp. "How can you say that? You don't know why he left. You didn't see his face at Ravenscar Manor—"

"Ravenscar Manor." Charlotte was staring blindly at the fireplace. "Of all the places I thought they'd go . . ."

"Pish and tosh," said Jessamine, looking angrily at Tessa. "At least his family's alive. Besides, I'll wager he wasn't sad at all; I'll wager you he was shamming. He always is."

Tessa glanced toward Jem for support, but he was looking at Charlotte, and his look was as hard as a silver coin. "What do you mean," he said, "of all the places you thought they'd go? Did you know that Will's family had moved?"

Charlotte started, and sighed. "Jem . . ."

"It's important, Charlotte."

Charlotte glanced over at the tin on her desk that held her favorite lemon drops. "After Will's parents came here to see him, when he was twelve, and he sent them away . . . I begged him to speak to them, just for a moment, but he wouldn't. I tried to make him understand that if they left, then he could never see them again, and I could never tell him news of them. He took my hand, and he said, 'Please just promise me you'll tell me if they die, Charlotte. Promise me.'" She looked down, her fingers knotting in the material of her dress. "It was such an odd request for a little boy to make. I—I had to say yes."

"So you've been looking into the welfare of Will's family?" Jem asked.

"I hired Ragnor Fell to do it," Charlotte said. "For the first three years. The fourth year he came back to me and told me that the Herondales had moved. Edmund Herondale—that's Will's father—had lost their house gambling. That was all Ragnor was able to glean. The Herondales had been forced to move. He could find no further trace of them."

"Did you ever tell Will?" Tessa said.

"No." Charlotte shook her head. "He had made me promise to tell him if they died, that was all. Why add to his unhappiness with the knowledge that they had lost their home? He never mentioned them. I had grown to hope he might have forgotten—"

"He has never forgotten." There was a force in Jem's words that stopped the nervous movement of Charlotte's fingers.

"I should not have done it," Charlotte said. "I should never have made that promise. It was a contravention of the Law—"

"When Will truly wants something," said Jem quietly, "when he *feels* something, he can break your heart."

There was a silence. Charlotte's lips were tight, her eyes suspiciously bright. "Did he say anything about where he was going when he left Kings Cross?"

"No," said Tessa. "We arrived, and he just up and dusted— sorry, got up and ran," she corrected herself, their blank looks alerting her to the fact that she was using American slang.

"'Up and dusted,'" said Jem. "I like that. Makes it sound like he left a cloud of dust spinning in his wake. He didn't say anything, no—just elbowed his way through the crowd and was gone. Nearly knocked down Cyril coming to get us."

"None of it makes any sense," Charlotte moaned. "Why on earth would Will's family be living in a house that used to belong to Mortmain? In Yorkshire of all places? This is not where I thought this road would lead. We sought Mortmain and we found the Shades; we sought him again and found Will's family. He encircles us, like that cursed *ouroboros* that is his symbol."

"You had Ragnor Fell look into Will's family's welfare before," said Jem. "Can you do it again? If Mortmain is somehow entangled with them . . . for whatever reason . . ."

"Yes, yes, of course," said Charlotte. "I will write to him immediately."

"There is a part of this I do not understand," Tessa said. "The reparations demand was filed in 1825, and the complainant's age was listed as twenty-two. If he was twenty-two then, he'd be seventy-five now, and he doesn't look that old. Maybe forty . . ."

"There are ways," Charlotte said slowly, "for mundanes who dabble in dark magic to prolong their lives. Just the sort of spell, by the way, that one might find in the Book of the White. Which is why possession of the Book by anyone other than the Clave is considered a crime."

"All that newspaper business about Mortmain inheriting a shipping company from his father," Jem said. "Do you think he pulled the vampire trick?"

"The vampire trick?" echoed Tessa, trying in vain to remember such a thing from the *Codex*.

"It's a way vampires have of keeping their money over time," said Charlotte. "When they have been too long in one place, long enough that people have started to notice that they never age, they fake their own death and leave their inheritance to a long-lost son or nephew. Voila—the nephew shows up, bears an uncanny resemblance to his father or uncle, but there he is and he gets the money. And they go on like that for generations sometimes. Mortmain could easily have left the company to himself to disguise the fact that he wasn't aging."

"So he pretended to be his own son," said Tessa. "Which would also have given him a reason to be seen changing the direction of the company—to return to Britain and begin interesting himself in mechanisms, that sort of thing."

"And is probably also why he left the house in Yorkshire," said Henry.

"Though that does not explain why it is being inhabited by Will's family," mused Jem.

"Or where Will is," added Tessa.

"Or where *Mortmain* is," put in Jessamine, with a sort of dark glee. "Only nine more days, Charlotte."

Charlotte put her head back into her hands. "Tessa," she said, "I hate to ask this of you, but it is, after all, why we sent you to Yorkshire, and we must leave no stone unturned. You still have the button from Starkweather's coat?"

Wordlessly Tessa took the button from her pocket. It was round, pearl and silver, strangely cold in her hand. "You want me to Change into him?"

"Tessa," Jem said quickly. "If you do not want to do this, Charlotte—*we*—would never require it."

"I know," Tessa said. "But I offered, and I would not go back on my word."

"Thank you, Tessa." Charlotte looked relieved. "We must know if there is anything he is hiding from us—if he was lying to you about any part of this business. His involvement in what happened to the Shades . . ."

Henry frowned. "It will be a dark day when you cannot trust your fellow Shadowhunters, Lottie."

"It is a dark day already, Henry dear," Charlotte replied without looking at him.

"You won't help me, then," Will said in a flat voice. Using magic, Magnus had built the fire up in the grate. In the glow of the leaping flames, the warlock could see more of the details of Will— the dark hair curling close at the nape of his neck, the delicate cheekbones and strong jaw, the shadow cast by his lashes. He reminded Magnus of someone; the memory tickled at the back of his mind, refusing to come clear. After so many years, it was hard sometimes to pick out individual memories, even of those you had loved. He could no longer remember his mother's face, though he knew she had looked like him, a mixture of his Dutch grandfather and his Indonesian grandmother.

"If your definition of 'help' involves dropping you into the demon realms like a rat into a pit full of terriers, then no, I won't help you," said Magnus. "This is madness, you know. Go home. Sleep it off."

"I'm not drunk."

"You might as well be." Magnus ran both hands through his thick hair and thought, suddenly and irrationally, of Camille. And was pleased. Here in this room, with Will, he had gone nearly two hours without thinking of her at all. Progress. "You think you're the only person who's ever lost anyone?"

Will's face twisted. "Don't make it sound like that. Like some ordinary sort of grief. It's not like that. They say time heals all wounds, but that presumes the source of the grief is finite. Over. This is a fresh wound every day."

"Yes," said Magnus, leaning back against the cushions. "That is the genius of curses, isn't it."

"It would be one thing if I had been cursed so that everyone I loved would die," said Will. "I could keep myself from loving. To keep others from caring for me—it is an odd, exhausting procedure." He *sounded* exhausted, Magnus thought, and dramatic in that way that only seventeen-year-olds could be. He also doubted the truth of Will's statement that he could have kept himself from loving, but understood why the boy would want to tell himself such a story. "I must play the part of another person all day, each day—bitter and vicious and cruel—"

"I rather liked you that way. And don't tell me you don't enjoy yourself at least a little, playing the devil, Will Herondale."

"They say it runs in our blood, that sort of bitter humor," said Will, looking at the flames. "Ella had it. So did Cecily. I never thought I did until I found I needed it. I have learned good lessons in how to be hateful over all these years. But I feel myself losing myself—" He groped for words. "I feel myself diminished, parts of me spiraling away into the darkness, that which is good and honest and true— If you hold it away from yourself long enough, do you lose it entirely? If no one cares for you at all, do you even really exist?"

He said this last so softly that Magnus had to strain to hear him. "What was that?"

"Nothing. Something I read somewhere once." Will turned to him. "You would be doing me a mercy, sending me to the demon realms. I might find what I am looking for. It is my only chance—and without that chance my life is worthless to me anyway."

"Easy enough to say at seventeen," said Magnus, with no small amount of coldness. "You are in love and you think that is all there is in the world. But the world is bigger than you, Will, and may have need of you. You are a Shadowhunter. You serve a greater cause. Your life is not yours to throw away."

"Then nothing is mine," said Will, and pushed himself away from the mantel, staggering a little as if he really were drunk. "If I don't even own my own life—"

"Who ever said we were owed happiness?" Magnus said softly, and in his mind he saw the house of his childhood, and his mother flinching away from him with frightened eyes, and her husband, who was not his father, burning. "What about what we owe to others?"

"I've given them everything I have already," said Will, seizing his coat off the back of the chair. "They've had enough out of me, and if this is what you have to say to me, then so have you—*warlock*."

He spat the last word like a curse. Regretting his harshness, Magnus began to rise to his feet, but Will pushed past him toward the door. It slammed behind him. Moments later Magnus saw him pass by the front window, struggling into his coat as he walked, his head bent down against the wind.

Tessa sat before her vanity table, wrapped in her dressing gown and rolling the small button back and forth in her palm. She had asked to be left alone to do what Charlotte had requested of her. It was not the first time she had transformed into a man; the Dark Sisters had forced her to do it, more than once, and while it was a peculiar feeling, it was not what fueled her reluctance. It was the darkness she had seen in Starkweather's eyes, the slight sheen of madness to his tone when he spoke of the spoils he had taken. It was not a mind she wanted to acquaint herself with further.

She did not have to do it, she thought. She could walk out there and tell them she had tried and it had not worked. But she knew even as the thought flickered through her mind, she could not do that. Somehow she had come to think of herself as bound with loyalty to the Institute's Shadowhunters. They had protected her, shown her kindness, taught her much of the truth of what she was, and they had the same goal she did— find Mortmain and destroy him. She thought of Jem's kind eyes on her, steady and silver and full of faith. With a deep breath she closed her fingers around the button.

The darkness came and enveloped her, wrapping her in its cool silence. The faint sound of the fire crackling in the grate, the wind against the panes of the window, vanished. Blackness and silence. She felt her body Change: Her hands felt large and swollen, shot through with the pains of arthritis. Her back ached, her head felt heavy, her feet were throbbing and painful, and there was a bitter taste in her mouth. Rotting teeth, she thought, and felt ill, so ill that she had to force her mind back to the darkness surrounding her, looking for the light, the connection.

It came, but not as the light usually did, as steady as a beacon. It came in shattered fragments, as if she were watching a mirror break into pieces. Each piece held an image that whipped by her, some at terrifying speed. She saw the image of a horse rearing back, a dark hill covered in snow, the black basalt Council room of the Clave, a cracked headstone. She struggled to seize and catch at a single image. Here was one, a memory: Starkweather dancing at a ball with a laughing woman in an empire-waisted ball gown. Tessa discarded it, reaching for another:

The house was small, nestled in the shadows between one hill and another. Starkweather watched from the darkness of a copse of trees as the front door opened and out came a man. Even in memory Tessa felt Starkweather's heart begin to beat more quickly. The man was tall, broad-shouldered—and as green-skinned as a lizard. His hair was black. The child he held by the hand, by contrast, seemed as normal as a child could be—small, chubby-fisted, pink-skinned.

Tessa knew the man's name, because Starkweather knew it. John Shade.

Shade hoisted the child up onto his shoulders as through the door of the house spilled a number of odd-looking metal creatures, like a child's jointed dolls, but human-size, and with skin made of shining metal. The creatures were featureless. Though, oddly, they wore clothes—the rough workman's coveralls of a Yorkshire farmer on some, and on others plain muslin dresses. The automatons joined hands and began to sway as if they were at a country dance. The child laughed and clapped his hands.

"Look well on this, my son," said the green-skinned man, "for one day I shall rule a clockwork kingdom of such beings, and you shall be its prince."

"John!" came a voice from inside the house; a woman leaned through the window. She had long hair the color of a cloudless sky. "John, come in. Someone will see! And you'll frighten the boy!"

"He's not frightened at all, Anne." The man laughed, and

set the boy down on the ground, ruffling his hair. "My little clockwork prince . . ."

A swell of hatred rose in Starkweather's heart at the memory, so violent that it ripped Tessa free, sending her spinning through the darkness again. She began to realize what was happening. Starkweather was becoming senile, losing the thread that connected thought and memory. What came and went in his mind was seemingly random. With an effort she tried to visualize the Shade family again, and caught the brief edge of a memory—a room torn apart, cogs and cams and gears and ripped metal everywhere, fluid leaking as black as blood, and the green-skinned man and blue-haired woman lying dead among the ruins. Then that, too, was gone, and she saw, again and again, the face of the girl from the portrait on the stairwell—the child with the fair hair and stubborn expression—saw her riding a small pony, her face set determinedly, saw her hair blowing in the wind off the moors—saw her screaming and writhing in pain as a stele was set to her skin and black Marks stained its whiteness. And last, Tessa saw her own face, appearing out of the shadowy gloom of the York Institute's nave, and she felt the wave of his shock ripple through her, so strong that it threw her out of his body and back into her own.

There was a faint thump as the button fell out of her hand and struck the floor. Tessa raised her head and looked into the mirror over her vanity. She was herself again, and the bitter taste in her mouth now was blood where she had bitten her lip.

She rose to her feet, feeling ill, and went over to the window, throwing it open to feel the cool night air on her sweaty skin. The night outside was heavy with shadow; there was little wind, and the black gates of the Institute seemed to loom before her, their motto speaking more than ever of mortality and death. A glimmer of movement caught her eye. She looked down and saw a white shape gazing up at her from the stony courtyard below. A face, twisted but recognizable. Mrs. Dark.

She gasped and jerked back reflexively, out of sight of the window. A wave of dizziness came over her. She shook it off fiercely, her hands gripping the sill, and pulled herself forward again, gazing down with dread—

But the courtyard was empty, nothing moving inside it but shadows. She closed her eyes, then opened them again slowly, and put her hand to the ticking angel at her throat. There had been nothing there, she told herself, just the rags of her wild imagination. Telling herself she'd better rein in her daydreaming or she'd end up as mad as old Starkweather, she slid the window shut.

8

A Shadow on the Soul

Oh, just, subtle, and mighty opium! that to the hearts of poor and rich alike, for the wounds that will never heal, and for "the pangs that tempt the spirit to rebel," bringest an assuaging balm; eloquent opium! that with thy potent rhetoric stealest away the purposes of wrath; and to the guilty man for one night givest back the hopes of his youth, and hands washed pure from blood.

—Thomas De Quincey, *Confessions of an English Opium-Eater*

In the morning when Tessa went down for breakfast, she found to her surprise that Will was not there. She had not realized how completely she had expected him to return during the night, and she found herself pausing in the doorway, scanning the seats around the table as if somehow she had accidentally glanced past him. It was not until her gaze came to rest on Jem, who returned her look with a rueful and worried expression of his own, that she knew that it was true. Will was still gone.

"Oh, he'll be back, for goodness' sake," said Jessamine crossly, banging her teacup down in its saucer. "He always does come crawling home. Look at the two of you. Like you've lost a favorite puppy."

Tessa shot Jem an almost guilty, conspiratorial look as she sat down across from him and took a slice of bread from the toast rack. Henry was absent; Charlotte, at the head of the table, was very clearly trying not to look nervous and worried, and failing. "Of course he will," she said. "Will can take care of himself."

"Do you think he might have gone back to Yorkshire?" said Tessa. "To warn his family?"

"I . . . don't think so," Charlotte responded. "Will has avoided his family for years. And he knows the Law. He knows he cannot speak to them. He knows what he would lose." Her eyes rested briefly on Jem, who was playing industriously with his spoon.

"When he saw Cecily, at the manor, he attempted to rush to her—" Jem said.

"In the heat of the moment," said Charlotte. "But he returned with you to London; I am confident he will return to the Institute as well. He knows you obtained that button, Tessa. He'll want to discover what Starkweather knew."

"Precious little, really," said Tessa. She still felt obscurely guilty that she had not found more useful information in Starkweather's memories. She had tried to explain what it was like to be in the mind of someone whose brain was decaying, but it had been hard to find the words, and she remembered mainly the look of disappointment on Charlotte's face when she'd said she had discovered nothing useful about Ravenscar Manor. She had told them all of Starkweather's memories of the Shade family, and that indeed if their deaths had been the impetus for Mortmain's desire for justice and vengeance, it did seem as if it would be a powerful one. She had kept his shock at seeing her to herself—it was baffling still, and seemed somehow private.

"What if Will chooses to leave the Clave forever?" Tessa said. "Would he return to his family to protect them?"

"No," Charlotte replied a little sharply. "No. I don't think he will do that." *She would miss Will if he were gone,* Tessa thought with surprise. Will was always so unpleasant—and often so to Charlotte—that Tessa sometimes forgot the stubborn love Charlotte seemed to feel for all her charges.

"But if they're in danger—," Tessa protested, then fell silent as Sophie entered the room carrying a pot of hot water, and set it down. Charlotte brightened at the sight of her.

"Tessa, Sophie, Jessamine," she said. "Lest you forget, you all have training this morning with Gabriel and Gideon Lightwood."

"I cannot do it," Jessamine said immediately.

"Why not? I thought you had recovered from your headache—"

"Yes, but I don't want it to come *back*, do I?" Jessamine stood up hurriedly. "I'd prefer to help you, Charlotte."

"I don't need your assistance writing to Ragnor Fell, Jessie. I'd really rather you took advantage of the training—"

"But there's dozens of replies piling up in the library from the Downworlders we've queried about Mortmain's whereabouts," Jessamine argued. "I could help you sort through those."

Charlotte sighed. "Very well." She turned to Tessa and Sophie. "In the meantime you won't say anything to the

Lightwood boys about Yorkshire, or about Will? I could do without having them in the Institute right now myself, but there's no help for it. It's a show of good faith and confidence to continue the training. You must behave in all ways as if nothing is wrong. Can you do that, girls?"

"Of course we can, Mrs. Branwell," said Sophie immediately. Her eyes were bright and she was smiling. Tessa sighed inwardly, not sure how to feel. Sophie adored Charlotte, and would do anything to please her. She also detested Will and was unlikely to be worried about his absence. Tessa looked across the table at Jem. She felt a hollowness in her stomach, the ache of not knowing where Will was, and wondered if he felt it too. His normally expressive face was still and unreadable, though when he caught her glance, he smiled a gentle, encouraging smile. Jem was Will's *parabatai*, his blood brother; surely if there were truly something to be concerned about where Will was involved, Jem would not be able to hide it—would he?

From the kitchen Bridget's voice rolled out in a sweet high warble:

> *"Must I go bound while you go free*
> *Must I love a man who doesn't love me*
> *Must I be born with so little art*
> *As to love a man who'll break my heart?"*

Tessa pushed her chair back from the table. "I think I had better go and get dressed."

Having changed from her day dress into gear, Tessa sat down on the edge of her bed and picked up the copy of *Vathek* Will had given her. It did not bring the thought of Will smiling to her mind, but other images of Will—Will bending over her in the Sanctuary, covered in blood; Will squinting into the sun on the roof of the Institute; Will rolling down the hill in Yorkshire with Jem, splattering himself with mud and not caring; Will falling off the table in the dining room; Will holding her in the dark. *Will, Will, Will.*

She threw the book. It struck the fireplace mantel and bounced off, landing on the floor. If only there were some way to scrape Will out of her mind, like scraping the mud off your shoe. If only she knew where he was. Worry made it worse, and she could not stop herself from worrying. She could not forget the look on his face as he had gazed at his sister.

Distraction made her late to the training room; fortunately, when she arrived, the door was open and there was no one there but Sophie, holding a long knife in her hand and examining it thoughtfully as she might examine a dust mop to decide if there was still use in it or if it was time for it to be thrown away.

She looked up as Tessa came into the room. "Well, you look like a wet weekend, miss," she said with a smile. "Is everything all right?" She cocked her head to the side as Tessa nodded. "Is it Master Will? He's gone off missing for a day or two before. He'll be back, don't you fear."

"That's kind of you to say, Sophie, especially as I know you are not overfond of him."

"I rather thought you weren't either," said Sophie, "leastways not any *more* . . ."

Tessa looked at her sharply. She had not had a real conversation with Sophie about Will since the roof incident, she thought, and besides, Sophie had warned her off him, comparing him to a poisonous snake. Before Tessa could say anything in reply, the door opened and Gabriel and Gideon Lightwood came in, followed by Jem. He winked at Tessa before disappearing, closing the door behind him.

Gideon went straight over to Sophie. "A good choice of blade," he said, faint surprise underlining his words. She blushed, looking pleased.

"So," said Gabriel, who had somehow managed to get behind Tessa without her noticing. After examining the racks of weapons along the walls, he drew down a knife and handed it to her. "Feel the weight of the blade there."

Tessa tried to feel the weight of it, struggling to remember what he had told her about where and how it should balance in her palm.

"What do you think?" Gabriel asked. She looked up at him. Of the two boys he certainly looked more like his father, with his aquiline features and the faint shading of arrogance to his expression. His slim mouth curled up at the corners. "Or are you too busy worrying about Herondale's whereabouts to practice today?"

Tessa nearly dropped the knife. "What?"

"I heard you and Miss Collins when I was coming up the stairs. Disappeared, has he? Not surprising, considering I don't think Will Herondale and a sense of responsibility are even on speaking terms."

Tessa set her chin. Conflicted as she was about Will, there was something about someone *outside* the Institute's small family criticizing him that set her teeth on edge. "It's quite a common occurrence, nothing to fuss about," she said. "Will is a—free spirit. He'll return soon enough."

"I hope not," said Gabriel. "I hope he's dead."

Tessa's hand tightened around the knife. "You mean that, don't you? What did he do to your sister to make you hate him so much?"

"Why don't you ask him?"

"Gabriel." Gideon's voice was sharp. "Shall we get to the instruction, please, and cease wasting time?"

Gabriel glared at his older brother, who was standing quite peaceably with Sophie, but obediently turned his attention from Will to the day's training. They were practicing how to hold blades today, and how to balance them as they swept them through the air without the blade point drooping forward or the handle slipping from the hand. It was harder than it looked, and today Gabriel wasn't patient. She envied Sophie, being taught by Gideon, who was always a careful, methodical instructor, though he did have a habit of slipping into Spanish whenever Sophie did something wrong. "*Ay Dios mio*," he would say, pulling the blade from where it had stuck, point down, in the floor. "Shall we try that again?"

"Stand up straight," Gabriel was saying to Tessa meanwhile, impatiently. "No, *straight*. Like this." He demonstrated. She wanted to snap at him that she, unlike him, had not had a lifetime of being taught how to stand and move; that Shadowhunters were natural acrobats, and she was nothing of the sort.

"Hmph," she said. "I'd like to see *you* learn how to manage sitting and standing up straight in stays and petticoats and a dress with a foot's worth of train!"

"So would I," said Gideon from across the room.

"Oh, by the Angel," said Gabriel, and he took her by the

shoulders, flipping her around so she stood with her back to him. He put his arms around her, straightening her spine, arranging the knife in her hand. She could feel his breath on the back of her neck, and it made her shiver—and filled her with annoyance. If he was touching her, it was only because he presumed he could, without asking, and because he thought it would irritate Will.

"Let me go," she said, under her breath.

"This is part of your training," said Gabriel in a bored voice. "Besides, look at my brother and Miss Collins. She isn't complaining."

She glanced across the room at Sophie, who seemed earnestly engaged in her lesson with Gideon. He was standing behind her, one arm around her from the back, showing her how to hold a needle-tipped throwing knife. His hand was gently cupped around hers, and he appeared to be speaking to the back of her neck, where her dark hair had escaped from its tight chignon and curled becomingly. When he saw Tessa looking at them, he flushed.

Tessa was amazed. Gideon Lightwood, blushing! Had he been *admiring* Sophie? Apart from her scar, which Tessa barely noticed anymore, she *was* lovely, but she was a mundane, and a servant, and the Lightwoods were awful snobs. Tessa's insides felt suddenly tight. Sophie had been treated abominably by her previous employer. The last thing she needed was some pretty Shadowhunter boy taking advantage of her.

Tessa looked around, about to say something to the boy with his arms around her—and stopped. She had forgotten that it was Gabriel beside her, not Jem. She had grown so used to Jem's presence, the ease with which she could converse with him, the comfort of his hand on her arm when they walked, the fact that he was the only person in the world now she felt she could say absolutely anything to. She realized with surprise that though she had just seen him at breakfast, she missed him, with what felt almost like an ache inside.

She was so caught up in this mixture of feelings—missing Jem, and a sense of passionate protectiveness over Sophie—that her next throw went wide by several feet, flying by Gideon's head and bouncing off the windowsill.

Gideon looked calmly from the fallen knife to his brother. Nothing seemed to bother him, not even his own near decapitation. "Gabriel, what is the problem, exactly?"

Gabriel turned his gaze on Tessa. "She won't listen to me," he said spitefully. "I can't instruct someone who won't listen."

"Maybe if you were a better instructor, she'd be a better listener."

"And maybe you would have seen the knife coming," said Gabriel, "if you paid more attention to what's going on around you and less to the back of Miss Collins's head."

So even Gabriel had noticed, Tessa thought, as Sophie blushed. Gideon gave his brother a long, steady look—she sensed there would be words between the two of them at home—then turned to Sophie and said something in a low voice, too low for Tessa to hear.

"What's happened to you?" she said under her breath to Gabriel, and felt him stiffen.

"What do you mean?"

"You're usually patient," she said. "You're a good teacher,

Gabriel, most of the time, but today you're snappish and impatient and . . ." She looked down at his hand on her arm. "Improper."

He had the good grace to release her, looking ashamed of himself. "A thousand pardons. I should not have touched you like that."

"No, you shouldn't. And after the way you criticize Will—"

He flushed along his high cheekbones. "I've apologized, Miss Gray. What more do you want of me?"

"A change in behavior, perhaps. An explanation of your dislike of Will—"

"I've told you! If you wish to know why I dislike him, you can ask him yourself!" Gabriel whirled and stalked out of the room.

Tessa looked at the knives stuck into the wall and sighed. "So ends my lesson."

"Try not to be too put out," said Gideon, approaching her with Sophie by his side. It was very odd, Tessa thought; Sophie usually seemed uneasy around men, any men, even gentle Henry. With Will she was like a scalded cat, and with Jem, blushing and watchful, but beside Gideon she seemed . . .

Well, it was hard to define. But it was most peculiar.

"It is not your fault he is like this today," Gideon went on. His eyes on Tessa were steady. This close up she could see that they were not precisely the same color as his brother's. They were more of a gray-green, like the ocean under a cloudy sky. "Things have been . . . difficult for us at home with Father, and Gabriel is taking it out on you, or, really, anyone who happens to be nearby."

"I'm most sorry to hear that. I hope your father is well," murmured Tessa, praying she would not be stricken down on the spot for this blatant falsehood.

"I suppose I had better go after my brother," said Gideon without answering her question. "If I do not, he will take the carriage and leave me stranded. I hope to have him back to you at our next session in a better humor." He bowed to Sophie, then Tessa. "Miss Collins, Miss Gray."

And he was gone, leaving both girls looking after him in mingled confusion and surprise.

With the training session mercifully over, Tessa found herself hurrying to change back into her ordinary clothes, and then to lunch, eager to see if Will had returned. He hadn't. His chair, between Jessamine and Henry, still sat empty—but there was someone new in the room, someone who made Tessa stop short at the doorway, trying not to stare. A tall man, he sat near the head of the table beside Charlotte, and was green. Not a very dark green—his skin had a faint greenish sheen to it, like light reflecting off the ocean, and his hair was snowy white. From his forehead curled two small elegant horns.

"Miss Tessa Gray," said Charlotte, making the introductions, "this is the High Warlock of London, Ragnor Fell. Mr. Fell, Miss Gray."

After murmuring that she was delighted to meet him, Tessa sat down at the table beside Jem, diagonally from Fell, and tried not to stare at him out of the corner of her eye. As Magnus's cat's eyes were his warlock's mark, Fell's would be his horns and tinted skin. She couldn't help being fascinated by Downworlders still, warlocks in particular. Why were they marked and she wasn't?

"What's on the carpet, then, Charlotte?" Ragnor was saying. "Did you really call me out here to discuss dark doings on the Yorkshire moors? I was under the impression that nothing of great interest ever happened in Yorkshire. In fact, I was under the impression that there *was* nothing in Yorkshire except sheep and mining."

"So you never knew the Shades?" Charlotte inquired. "The warlock population of Britain is not so large . . ."

"I knew them." As Fell sawed into the ham on his plate, Tessa saw that he had an extra joint to each finger. She thought of Mrs. Black, with her elongated taloned hands, and repressed a shudder. "Shade was a little mad, with his obsession with clockwork and mechanisms. Their death was a shock to Downworld. The ripples of it went through the community, and there was even some discussion of vengeance, though none, I believe, was ever taken."

Charlotte leaned forward. "Do you remember their son? Their adopted child?"

"I knew of him. A married warlock couple is rare. One who adopts a human child from an orphanage is rarer still. But I never saw the boy. Warlocks—we live forever. A gap of thirty, even fifty, years between meetings is not unusual. Of course now that I know what the boy grew up to be, I wish I had met him. Do you think there is value in attempting to discover who his true parents were?"

"Certainly, if it can be discovered. Whatever information we can glean about Mortmain could be useful."

"I can tell you he gave himself that name," said Fell. "It sounds like a Shadowhunter name. It is the sort of name someone with a grudge against Nephilim, and a dark sense of humor, would take. *Mort main—*"

"Hand of death," supplied Jessamine, who was proud of her French.

"It does make one wonder," said Tessa. "If the Clave had simply given Mortmain what he wanted—reparations—would he still have become what he did? Would there ever have been a Pandemonium Club at all?"

"Tessa—," Charlotte began, but Ragnor Fell waved her silent. He gazed amusedly down the table at Tessa. "You're the shape-changer, aren't you?" he said. "Magnus Bane told me about you. No mark on you at all, they say."

Tessa swallowed and looked him straight in the eye. They were discordantly human eyes, ordinary in his extraordinary face. "No. No mark."

He grinned around his fork. "I do suppose they've looked *everywhere?*"

"I'm sure Will's tried," said Jessamine in a bored tone. Tessa's silverware clattered to her plate. Jessamine, who had been mashing her peas flat with the side of her knife, looked up when Charlotte let out an aghast, *"Jessamine!"*

Jessamine shrugged. "Well, he's like that."

Fell turned back to his plate with a faint smile on his face. "I remember Will's father. Quite the ladies' man, he was. They couldn't resist him. Until he met Will's mother, of course. Then he threw it all in and went to live in Wales just to be with her. What a case he was."

"He fell in love," said Jem. "It isn't that peculiar."

"'Fell' into it," said the warlock, still with the same faint smile. "Hurtled into it is more like. Headlong-crashed into it.

Still, there are always some men like that—just one woman for them, and only she will do, or nothing."

Charlotte looked over at Henry, but he appeared completely lost in thought, counting something—though who knew what—off on his fingers. He was wearing a pink and violet waistcoat today, and had gravy on his sleeve. Charlotte's shoulders slumped visibly, and she sighed. "Well," she said. "By all accounts they were very happy together—"

"Until they lost two of their three children and Edmund Herondale gambled away everything they had," said Fell. "But I imagine you never told young Will about that."

Tessa exchanged a glance with Jem. *My sister is dead,* Will had said. "They had three children, then?" she said. "Will had two sisters?"

"Tessa. Please." Charlotte looked uneasy. "Ragnor . . . I never hired you to invade the privacy of the Herondales, or Will. I did it because I had promised Will I would tell him if harm came to his family."

Tessa thought of Will—a twelve-year-old Will, clinging to Charlotte's hand, begging to be told if his family died. *Why run?* she thought for the hundredth time. *Why put them behind you?* She had thought perhaps he did not care, but clearly he had cared. Cared still. She could not stop the tightening at her heart as she thought of him calling out for his sister. If he loved Cecily as she had once loved Nate . . .

Mortmain had done something to his family, she thought. As he had to hers. That bound them to each other in a peculiar way, she and Will. Whether he knew it or not.

"Whatever it is that Mortmain has been planning," she heard herself say, "he has been planning it a long time. Since before I was born, when he tricked or coerced my parents into 'making' me. And now we know that years ago he involved himself with Will's family and moved them to Ravenscar Manor. I fear we are like chess pieces he slides about a board, and the outcome of the game is already known to him."

"That is what he desires us to think, Tessa," said Jem. "But he is only a man. And each discovery we make about him makes him more vulnerable. If we were no threat, he would not have sent that automaton to warn us off."

"He knew exactly where we would *be*—"

"There is nothing more dangerous than a man bent on revenge," said Ragnor. "A man who has been bent on it for nearly three score years, who has nurtured it from a tiny, poisonous seed to a living, choking flower. He will see it through, unless you end him first."

"Then, we will end him," said Jem shortly. It was as close to a threat as Tessa had ever heard him make.

Tessa looked down at her hands. They were a paler white than they had been when she lived in New York, but they were her hands, familiar, the index finger slightly longer than the middle one, the half-moons of her nails pronounced. *I could Change them*, she thought. *I could become anything, anyone.* She had never felt more mutable, more fluid, or more lost.

"Indeed." Charlotte's tone was firm. "Ragnor, I want to know why the Herondale family is in that house—that house that belonged to Mortmain—and I want to see to it that they are safe. And I want to do it without Benedict Lightwood or the rest of the Clave hearing about it."

"I understand. You want me to look out for them as quietly as possible while also making inquiries regarding Mortmain in the area. If he moved them there, it must have been for a purpose."

Charlotte exhaled. "Yes."

Ragnor twirled his fork. "That will be expensive."

"Yes," Charlotte said. "I am prepared to pay."

Fell grinned. "Then, I am prepared to endure the sheep."

The rest of the lunch passed in awkward conversation, with Jessamine moodily destroying her food without eating it, Jem unusually quiet, Henry muttering equations to himself, and Charlotte and Fell finalizing their plans for the protection of Will's family. As much as Tessa approved of the idea—and she did—there was something about the warlock that made her uncomfortable in a way Magnus never had, and she was glad when lunch was over and she could escape to her room with a copy of *The Tenant of Wildfell Hall*.

It was not her favorite of the Brontë sisters' books—that honor went to *Jane Eyre*, and then *Wuthering Heights*, with *Tenant* a distant third—but she had read the other two so many times that no surprises lay between the pages, only phrases so familiar to her they had become like old friends. What she really wanted to read was *A Tale of Two Cities*, but Will had quoted Sydney Carton to her enough times that she was afraid that picking it up would make her think of him, and make the weight of her nervousness greater. After all, it was never Darnay he quoted, only Sydney, drunk and wrecked and dissipated. Sydney, who died for love.

It was dark out, and the wind was blowing gusts of light rain against the windowpanes when the knock came at her door. It was Sophie, carrying a letter on a silver tray. "A letter for you, miss."

Tessa put the book down in astonishment. "Mail for *me*?"

Sophie nodded and came closer, holding out the tray. "Yes, but it doesn't say who it's from. Miss Lovelace almost snatched it, but I managed to keep it from her, nosy thing."

Tessa took the envelope. It was addressed to her, indeed, in a slanting, unfamiliar hand, printed on heavy cream-colored paper. She turned it over once, began to open it, and caught sight of Sophie's wide-eyed curious gaze reflected in the window. She turned and smiled at her. "That will be all, Sophie," she said. It was the way she had read heroines dismissing servants in novels, and it seemed to be correct. With a disappointed look Sophie took her salver and retired from the room.

Tessa unfolded the letter and spread it out on her lap.

Dear sensible Miss Gray,

I write to you on behalf of a mutual friend, one William Herondale. I know that it is his habit to come and go—most often go—from the Institute as he pleases, and that therefore it may be some time before any alarm is raised at his absence. But I ask you, as one who holds your good sense in esteem, not to assume this absence to be of the ordinary sort. I saw him myself last night, and he was, to say the least, distraught when he left my residence. I have reason for concern that he might do himself an injury, and therefore I suggest that his whereabouts be sought and his safety ascertained. He is a difficult young man to like, but I believe you see the good in him, as I do, Miss Gray, and that is why I humbly address my letter to you—

Your servant,

Magnus Bane

Postscript: If I were you, I would not share the contents of this letter with Mrs. Branwell. Just a suggestion.
M.B.

Though reading Magnus's letter made her feel as if her veins were full of fire, somehow Tessa survived the rest of the afternoon, and dinner as well, without—she thought—betraying any outward sign of her distress. It seemed to take Sophie an agonizingly long time to help her out of her dress, brush her hair, stoke the fire, and tell her the day's gossip. (Cyril's cousin worked in the Lightwoods' house and had reported that Tatiana—Gabriel and Gideon's sister—was due to return from her honeymoon on the Continent with her new husband any day now. The household was in an uproar as she was rumored to have a most unpleasant disposition.)

Tessa muttered something about how she must take after her father that way. Impatience made her voice a croak, and Sophie was only just prevented from rushing out to get her a tisane of mint by Tessa's insistence that she was exhausted, and needed sleep more than she needed tea.

The moment the door shut behind Sophie, Tessa was on her feet, shimmying out of her nightclothes and into a dress, lacing herself up as best she could and throwing a short jacket on over the top. After a cautious glance out into the corridor, she slipped out of her room and across the hall to Jem's door, where she knocked as quietly as she could. For a moment nothing happened, and she had the fleeting worry that he had already gone to sleep, but then the door flew open and Jem stood on the threshold.

She had clearly caught him in the middle of readying

himself for bed; his shoes and jacket were off, his shirt open at the collar, his hair an adorable rumpled mess of silver. She wanted to reach out and smooth it down. He blinked at her. "Tessa?"

Without a word she handed him the note. He glanced up and down the corridor, then gestured her inside the room. She shut the door behind him as he read Magnus's scrawl once, and then again, before balling it up in his hand, the crackling paper loud in the room. "I *knew* it," he said.

It was Tessa's turn to blink. "Knew what?"

"That this wasn't an ordinary sort of absence." He sat down on the trunk at the foot of his bed and shoved his feet into his shoes. "I felt it. Here." He put his hand over his chest. "I knew there was something strange. I felt it like a shadow on my soul."

"You don't think he'd really hurt himself, do you?"

"Hurt himself, I don't know. Put himself in a situation where he might be hurt—" Jem stood up. "I should go."

"Don't you mean 'we'? You weren't thinking of going looking for Will without me, were you?" she asked archly, and when he said nothing, she said, "That letter was addressed to me, James. I didn't have to show it to you."

He half-closed his eyes for a moment, and when he opened them, he was smiling crookedly. "*James*," he said. "Ordinarily only Will calls me that."

"I'm sorry—"

"No. Don't be. I like the sound of it on your lips."

Lips. There was something strangely, delicately indelicate about the word, like a kiss itself. It seemed to hover in the air between them while they both hesitated. *But it's Jem,* Tessa thought in bewilderment. Jem. Not Will, who could make her feel as if he were running his fingers along her bare skin just by looking at her—

"You're right," Jem said, clearing his throat. "Magnus would not have sent the letter to you had he not intended you to be part of searching for Will. Perhaps he thinks your power will be useful. In either case—" He turned from her, going to his wardrobe and flinging it open. "Wait for me in your room. I will be there momentarily."

Tessa wasn't sure if she nodded—she thought she had—and moments later she found herself back in her bedroom, leaning against the door. Her face felt hot, as if she had stood too close to a fire. She looked around. When had she started to think of this room as *her* bedroom? The big, grand space, with its mullioned windows and softly glowing witchlight tapers, was so unlike the tiny box room she had slept in in the flat in New York, with its puddles of wax on the bedside table, caused by her staying up all night reading by candlelight, and the cheap wooden-framed bed with its thin blankets. In the winter the windows, ill-seated, would rattle in their frames when the wind blew.

A soft knock on the door drew her out of her reverie, and she turned, flinging it open to find Jem on the threshold. He was fully dressed in Shadowhunter gear—the tough leather-looking black coat and trousers, the heavy boots. He put a finger to his lips and gestured for her to follow him.

It was probably ten o'clock at night, Tessa guessed, and the witchlight was burning low. They took a curious, winding path through the corridors, not the one she was used to taking to get to the front doors. Her confusion was answered when they reached a door set at the end of a long corridor. There was a rounded look to the space they stood in, and Tessa guessed they were probably inside one of the Gothic towers that stood at each corner of the Institute.

Jem pushed the door open and ushered her in after him; he closed the door firmly behind them, slipping the key he had used back into his pocket. "This," he said, "is Will's room."

"Gracious," Tessa said. "I've never been in here. I was starting to imagine he slept upside down, like a bat."

Jem laughed and went past her, over to a wooden bureau, and began to rummage through the contents on top of it as Tessa glanced around. Her heart was beating fast, as if she were seeing something she wasn't meant to see—some secret, hidden part of Will. She told herself not to be silly, it was just a room, with the same heavy dark furniture as all the other Institute rooms. It was a mess, too—covers kicked down to the foot of the bed; clothes draped over the backs of chairs, teacups half-full of liquid not yet cleared away, balanced precariously on the nightstand. And everywhere books—books on the side tables, books on the bed, books in stacks on the floor, books double-lined in shelves along the walls. As Jem rummaged, Tessa wandered to the shelves and looked curiously at the titles.

She was not surprised to find that they were almost all fiction and poetry. Some were titles in languages she couldn't read. She recognized Latin and the Greek alphabet. There were also books of fairy tales, *The Arabian Nights*, James Payn's work, Anthony Trollope's *Vicar of Bullhampton*, Thomas Hardy's *Desperate Remedies*, a pile of Wilkie Collins—*The New Magdalen*, *The Law and the Lady*, *The Two Destinies*, and a new Jules Verne novel titled *Child of the Cavern* that she itched to get her hands on. And then, there it was—*A Tale of Two Cities*. With a rueful smile she reached to take it from the shelf. As she lifted it, several scrawled-on papers that had been pressed between the covers fluttered to the floor. She knelt to pick them up—and froze. She recognized the handwriting instantly. It was her own.

Her throat tightened as she thumbed through the pages. *Dear Nate,* she read. *I tried to Change today, and failed. It was a coin they gave me, and I could get nothing from it. Either it was never owned by a person, or my power is weakening. I would not care, but that they whipped me—have you ever been whipped before? No, a silly question. Of course you haven't. It feels like fire being laid in lines across your skin. I am ashamed to say I cried, and you know how I hate to cry . . . And Dear Nate, I missed you so much today, I thought I would die. If you are gone, there is no one in the world who cares if I am dead or alive. I feel myself dissolving, vanishing into nothingness, for if there is no one in the world who cares for you, do you really exist at all?*

These were the letters she had written her brother from the Dark House, not expecting Nate to read them—not expecting anyone to read them. They were more of a diary than letters, the only place where she could pour forth her horror, her sadness, and her fear. She knew that they had been found, that Charlotte had read them, but what were they doing here in Will's room, of all places, hidden between the pages of a book?

"Tessa." It was Jem. She turned quickly, slipping the letters into the pocket of her coat as she did so. Jem stood by the bureau, holding a silver knife in his hand. "By the Angel, this place is such a tip, I wasn't sure I'd be able to find it." He turned it over in his hands. "Will didn't bring much from home when he came here, but he did bring this. It's a dagger his father gave him. It has the Herondale bird markings on the blade. It should have a strong enough imprint of him for us to track him with it."

Despite the encouraging words, he was frowning.

"What's wrong?" Tessa asked, crossing the room to him.

"I found something else," he said. "Will has always been the one to buy my—my medicine for me. He knew I despised the whole transaction, finding Downworlders willing to sell it, paying for the stuff . . ." His chest rose and fell quickly, as if merely talking about it sickened him. "I would give him money, and off he would go. I found a bill, though, for the last transaction. It appears the drugs—the medicine—does not cost what I thought it did."

"You mean Will's been cheating you out of money?" Tessa was surprised. Will could be awful and cruel, she thought, but somehow she had thought his cruelty of a more refined order than that. Less petty. And to do that to Jem, of all people . . .

"Quite the opposite. The drugs cost much more than he said they did. He must have been making up the difference somehow." Still frowning, he slid the dagger into his belt. "I know him better than anyone else in the world," he said matter-of-factly. "And yet still I find that Will has secrets that surprise me."

Tessa thought of the letters stuffed into the Dickens book, and what she intended to say to Will about it when she saw him again. "Indeed," she said. "Though it is not so much a mystery, is it? Will would do anything for you—"

"I'm not sure I would take it quite that far." Jem's tone was wry.

"Of course he would," said Tessa. "Anyone would. You're so kind and so good—"

She broke off, but Jem's eyes had already widened. He looked surprised, as if he were not used to such praise, but surely he must be, Tessa thought in confusion. Surely everyone who knew him knew how lucky they were. She felt her cheeks begin to warm again, and cursed herself. *What* was going on?

A faint rattle came from the window; Jem turned after a moment's pause. "That will be Cyril," he said, and there was a slight, rough undercurrent to his voice. "I—I asked him to bring the carriage around. We had better go."

Tessa nodded, wordless, and followed him from the room.

When Jem and Tessa emerged from the Institute, the wind was still gusting into the courtyard, sending dried leaves skittering in circles like faerie dancers. The sky was heavy with a yellow fog, the moon a gold disk behind it. The Latin words over the Institute's gates seemed to glow, picked out by the moonlight: *We are dust and shadows.*

Cyril, waiting with the carriage and the two horses, Balios and Xanthos, looked relieved to see them; he helped Tessa up into the carriage, Jem following her, and then swung himself up into the driver's seat. Tessa, sitting opposite Jem, watched with fascination as he drew both the dagger and the stele from his belt; holding the dagger in his right hand, he drew a rune on the back of that hand with the tip of his stele. It looked to Tessa like all Marks looked, a ripple of unreadable waving lines, circling around to connect with one another in bold black patterns.

He gazed down at his hand for a long moment, then shut his eyes, his face still with intense concentration. Just as Tessa's nerves began to sing with impatience, his eyes flew open. "Brick Lane, near Whitechapel High Street," he said, half to himself; returning the dagger and stele to his belt, he leaned out the window, and she heard him repeat the words to Cyril. A moment later Jem was back in the carriage, shutting the window against the cold air, and they were sliding and bumping forward over the cobblestones.

Tessa took a deep breath. She had been eager to look for Will all day, worried about him, wondering where he was—but now that they were rolling into the dark heart of London, all she could feel was dread.

9

FIERCE MIDNIGHT

Fierce midnights and famishing morrows,
And the loves that complete and control
All the joys of the flesh, all the sorrows
That wear out the soul.
—Algernon Charles Swinburne, "Dolores"

Tessa kept the curtain on her side of the carriage pulled back, her eyes on the glass of the window, as they rolled along Fleet Street toward Ludgate Hill. The yellow fog had thickened, and she could make out little through it—the dark shapes of people hurrying to and fro, the hazy words of advertising signs painted on the sides of buildings. Every once in a while the fog would part and she would get a clear glimpse of something—a little girl carrying bunches of wilting lavender, leaning against a wall, exhausted; a knife grinder rolling his cart wearily homeward; a sign for Bryant and May's Lucifer Matches looming suddenly out of the gloom.

"Chuckaways," said Jem. He was leaning back against the seat across from her, his eyes bright in the dimness. She wondered if he had taken some of the drug before they left, and if so, how much.

"Pardon?"

He mimed the act of striking a match, blowing it out, and tossing the remainder over his shoulder. "That's what they call matches here—chuckaways, because you toss them aside after one use. It's also what they call the girls who work at the match factories."

Tessa thought of Sophie, who could easily have become one of those "chuckaways," if Charlotte hadn't found her. "That's cruel."

"It's a cruel part of the city we're going into. The East End. The slums." He sat forward. "I want you to be careful, and to stay close by me."

"Do you know what Will's doing there?" Tessa asked, half-afraid of the answer. They were passing by the great bulk of St. Paul's now, looming up above them like a giant's glimmering marble tombstone.

Jem shook his head. "I don't. I only got a sense—a fleeting image of the street—from the tracking spell. I will say, though, that there are few *harmless* reasons for a gentleman to go 'down to Chapel' after dark."

"He could be gambling . . ."

"He could be," Jem agreed, sounding as if he doubted it.

"You said you would sense it. Here." Tessa touched herself over the heart. "If something had happened to him. Is that because you're *parabatai*?"

"Yes."

"So there's more to being *parabatai* than just swearing to look out for each other. There's something—mystical about it."

Jem smiled at her, that smile that was like a light suddenly being turned on in every room of a house. "We're Nephilim. Every one of our life's passages has some mystical component—our births, our deaths, our marriages, everything has a ceremony. There is one as well if you wish to become someone's *parabatai*. First you must ask them, of course. It's no small commitment—"

"You asked Will," Tessa guessed.

Jem shook his head, still smiling. "He asked me," he said. "Or rather he told me. We were training, up in the training room, with longswords. He asked me and I said no, he deserved someone who was going to live, who could look out for him all his life. He bet me he could get the sword away from me, and if he succeeded, I'd have to agree to be his blood brother."

"And he got it away from you?"

"In nine seconds flat." Jem laughed. "Pinned me to the wall. He must have been training without my knowing about it, because I'd never have agreed if I'd thought he was that good with a longsword. Throwing daggers have always been his weapons." He shrugged. "We were thirteen. They did the ceremony when we were fourteen. Now it's been three years and I can't imagine not having a *parabatai*."

"Why didn't you want to do it?" Tessa asked a little hesitantly. "When he first asked you."

Jem ran a hand through his silvery hair. "The ceremony binds you," he said. "It makes you stronger. You have each other's strength to draw on. It makes you more aware of where the other one is, so you can work seamlessly together in a fight. There are runes you can use if you are part of a pair of *parabatai* that you can't use otherwise. But . . . you can choose only one *parabatai* in your life. You can't have a second, even if the first one dies. I didn't think I was a very good bet, considering."

"That seems a harsh rule."

Jem said something then, in a language she didn't understand. It sounded like "*khalepa ta kala.*"

She frowned at him. "That isn't Latin?"

"Greek," he said. "It has two meanings. It means that that which is worth having—the good, fine, honorable, and noble things—are difficult to attain." He leaned forward, closer to her. She could smell the sweet scent of the drug on him, and the tang of his skin underneath. "It means something else as well."

Tessa swallowed. "What's that?"

"It means 'beauty is harsh.'"

She glanced down at his hands. Slim, fine, capable hands, with blunt-cut nails, and scars across the knuckles. Were any of the Nephilim unscarred? "These words, they have a special appeal to you, don't they?" she asked softly. "These dead languages. Why is that?"

He was leaning close enough to her that she felt his warm breath on her cheek when he exhaled. "I cannot be sure," he said, "though I think it has something to do with the clarity of them. Greek, Latin, Sanskrit, they contain pure truths, before we cluttered our languages with so many useless words."

"But what of your language?" she said softly. "The one you grew up speaking?"

His lips twitched. "I grew up speaking English and Mandarin Chinese," he said. "My father spoke English, and Chinese badly. After we moved to Shanghai, it was even worse. The dialect there is barely intelligible by someone who speaks Mandarin."

"Say something in Mandarin," said Tessa with a smile.

Jem said something rapidly, that sounded like a lot of breathy vowels and consonants run together, his voice rising and falling melodically: *"Ni hen piao liang."*

"What did you say?"

"I said your hair is coming undone. Here," he said, and reached out and tucked an escaping curl back behind her ear. Tessa felt the blood spill hot up into her cheeks, and was glad for the dimness of the carriage. "You have to be careful with it," he said, taking his hand back slowly, his fingers lingering against her cheek. "You don't want to give the enemy anything to grab hold of."

"Oh—yes—of course." Tessa looked quickly toward the window—and stared. The yellow fog hung heavy over the streets, but she could see well enough. They were in a narrow thoroughfare—though broad, perhaps, by London's standards. The air seemed thick and greasy with coal dust and fog, and the streets were lined with people. Filthy, dressed in rags, they slumped against the walls of tipsy-looking buildings, their eyes watching the carriage go by like hungry dogs following the progress of a bone. Tessa saw a woman wrapped in a shawl, a basket of flowers drooping from one hand, a baby folded into a corner of the shawl propped against her shoulder. Its eyes were closed, its skin as pale as curd; it looked sick, or dead. Barefoot children, as dirty as homeless cats, played together in the streets; women sat leaning against one another on the stoops of buildings, obviously drunk. The men were worst of all, slumped against the sides of houses, dressed in dirty, patched topcoats and hats, the looks of hopelessness on their faces like etchings on gravestones.

"Rich Londoners from Mayfair and Chelsea like to take midnight tours of districts like these," said Jem, his voice uncharacteristically bitter. "They call it slumming."

"Do they stop and—and help in some way?"

"Most of them, no. They just want to stare so they can go home and talk at their next tea party about how they saw real 'mug-hunters' or 'dollymops' or 'Shivering Jemmys.' Most of them never get out of their carriages or omnibuses."

"What's a Shivering Jemmy?"

Jem looked at her with flat silver eyes. "A freezing, ragged beggar," he said. "Someone likely to die of the cold."

Tessa thought of the thick paper pasted over the cracks in the windowpanes in her New York apartment. But at least she had had a bedroom, a place to lie down, and Aunt Harriet to make her hot soup or tea over the small range. She had been lucky.

The carriage came to a stop at an unprepossessing corner. Across the street the lights of an open public house spilled out onto the street, along with a steady stream of drunkards, some with women leaning on their arms, the women's brightly colored dresses stained and dirty and their cheeks highly rouged. Somewhere someone was singing "Cruel Lizzie Vickers."

Jem took her hand. "I can't glamour you against the glances of mundanes," he said. "So keep your head down and keep close to me."

Tessa smiled crookedly but didn't take her hand out of his. "You said that already."

He leaned close and whispered into her ear. His breath sent

a shiver racing through her whole body. "It's *very* important."

He reached past her for the door and swung it open. He leaped down onto the pavement and helped her down after him, pulling her close against his side. Tessa looked up and down the street. There were some incurious stares from the crowds, but the two of them were largely ignored. They headed toward a narrow door painted red. There were steps around it, but unlike all the other steps in the area, they were bare. No one was sitting on them. Jem took them quickly, pulling her up after him, and rapped sharply on the door.

It was opened after a moment by a woman in a long red dress, fitted so tightly to her body that Tessa's eyes widened. She had black hair piled on her head, kept in place by a pair of gold chopsticks. Her skin was very pale, her eyes rimmed with kohl—but on closer examination Tessa realized she was white, not foreign. Her mouth was a sulky red bow. It turned down at the corners as her gaze came to rest on Jem.

"No," she said. "No Nephilim."

She moved to shut the door, but Jem had raised his cane; the blade shot out from the base of it, holding the door open wide. "No trouble," he said. "We're not here for the Clave. It's personal."

She narrowed her eyes.

"We're looking for someone," he said. "A friend. Take us to him, and we won't bother you further."

At that, she threw her head back and laughed. "I know who you're looking for," she said. "There's only one of your kind here." She turned away from the door with a shrug of contempt. Jem's blade slid back into its casing with a hiss, and he ducked under the low lintel, drawing Tessa after him.

Beyond the door was a narrow corridor. A heavy sweet smell hung on the air, like the smell that hung about Jem's clothing after he had taken his drug. Her hand tightened involuntarily on his. "This is where Will comes to buy the—to buy what I need," he whispered, inclining his head so that his lips nearly touched her ear. "Although why he would be here now . . ."

The woman who had opened the door for them glanced back over her shoulder as she set off down the hall. There was a slit up the back of her dress, showing much of her legs—and the end of a long, slender forked tail, marked with black and white markings like the scales of a snake. *She's a warlock,* Tessa thought with a dull thud at her heart. Ragnor, the Dark Sisters, this woman—why was it that warlocks always seemed so—sinister? With the exception of Magnus perhaps, but she had the feeling Magnus was an exception to many rules.

The corridor widened out into a large room, its walls painted dark red. Great lamps, their sides carved and painted with delicate traceries that threw patterned light against the walls, hung down from the ceiling. Along the walls were ranged beds, in bunks, like the inside of a ship. A large round table dominated the center of the room. At it sat a number of men, their skin the same blood-red as the walls, their black hair clipped close to their heads. Their hands ended in blue-black talons that had also been clipped, probably to allow them to more easily count and sift and mix the various powders and concoctions they had spread out before them. The powders seemed to glimmer and shine under the lamplight, like pulverized jewels.

"Is this an opium den?" Tessa whispered into Jem's ear.

His eyes were raking the room anxiously. She could sense

the tension in him, a thrum just under the skin, like the fast-beating heart of a hummingbird. "No." He sounded distracted. "Not really—mostly demon drugs and faerie powders. Those men at the table, they're ifrits. Warlocks without powers."

The woman in the red dress was leaning over the shoulder of one of the ifrits. Together they looked up and over at Tessa and Jem, their eyes lingering on Jem. Tessa didn't like the way they were looking at him. The warlock woman was smiling; the ifrit's look was calculating. The woman straightened up and swayed over to them, her hips moving like a metronome under the tight satin of her dress.

"Madran says we have what you want, silver boy," said the warlock woman, raking a blood-red nail across Jem's cheek. "No need for pretense."

Jem flinched back from her touch. Tessa had never seen him look so unnerved. "I told you, we're here for a friend," he snapped. "A Nephilim. Blue eyes, black hair—" His voice rose. *"Ta xian zai zai na li?"*

She looked at him for a moment, then shook her head. "You are foolish," she said. "There is little of the *yin fen* left, and when it is gone, you will die. We struggle to obtain more, but lately the demand—"

"Spare us your attempts to sell your merchandise," said Tessa, suddenly angry. She couldn't bear the look on Jem's face, as if each word were the cut of a knife. No wonder Will bought his poisons for him. "Where is our friend?"

The warlock woman hissed, shrugged, and pointed toward one of the bunk beds bolted to the wall. "There."

Jem whitened as Tessa stared. Their occupants were so still that at first she had thought the beds were empty, but she realized now, looking more closely, that each was taken up by a sprawled figure. Some lay on their sides, arms trailing over the edges of the bed, hands splayed; most were on their backs, eyes open, staring at the ceiling or the bunk above them.

Without another word Jem began to stalk across the room, Tessa on his heels. As they drew closer to the beds, she realized that not all the occupants were human. Blue, violet, red, and green skin flashed past; green hair as long and netted as a web of seaweed brushed restlessly against a dirty pillow; taloned fingers gripped the wooden sides of a bunk as someone moaned. Someone else was giggling softly, hopelessly, a sound sadder than weeping; another voice repeated a children's rhyme over and over and over again:

> *"Oranges and lemons*
> *Say the bells of St. Clement's*
> *When will ye pay me?*
> *Ring the bells at Old Bailey*
> *When I grow rich*
> *Say the bells of Shoreditch—"*

"Will," whispered Jem. He had stopped at a bunk halfway down the wall, and leaned against it, as if his legs threatened to give way.

Lying in the bunk was Will, half-tangled in a dark, ragged blanket. He wore nothing but trousers and a shirt; his weapons belt hung on a nail peg inside the bunk. His feet were bare, his eyes half-lidded, their blue only slightly visible beneath the fringe of his dark lashes. His hair was wet with sweat, pasted to his forehead, his cheeks bright red and feverish. His chest rose and fell raggedly, as if he were having trouble drawing breath.

Tessa reached out and put the back of her hand to his forehead. It was burning. "Jem," she said softly. "Jem, we must get him out of here."

The man in the bunk beside them was still singing. Not that he was quite a man, exactly. His body was short and twisted, his shoeless feet ending in cloven hooves.

> *"When will that be?*
> *Say the bells of Stepney*
> *I do not know,*
> *Says the great bell of Bow"*

Jem was still staring down at Will, motionless. He seemed frozen. His face had gone a patchy white and red color.

"Jem!" Tessa whispered. "Please. Help me get him on his feet." When Jem did not move, she reached out, took Will by the shoulder, and shook him. "Will. Will, wake up, please."

Will only groaned and turned away from her, burying his head against his arm. He was a Shadowhunter, she thought, six feet of bone and muscle, far too heavy for her to lift. Unless—

"If you do not help me," Tessa said to Jem, "I swear, I will Change into you, and I will lift him myself. And then everyone here will see what you look like in a dress." She fixed him with a look. "Do you understand?"

Very slowly he raised his eyes to hers. He did not look fazed by the idea of being seen by ifrits in a dress; he did not look as if he saw her at all. It was the first time she could remember seeing those silver eyes without any light behind them. "Do you?" he said, and reached into the bunk, catching Will by the arm and hauling him sideways, taking little care, and bumping Will's head, hard, against the side rail of the bed.

Will groaned and opened his eyes. "Let me go—"

"Help me with him," Jem said without looking at Tessa, and together they wrestled Will out of the bunk. He nearly fell, sliding his arm around Tessa to balance himself as Jem retrieved his weapons belt from the nail it was hanging from.

"Tell me this is not a dream," Will whispered, nuzzling his face into the side of her neck. Tessa jumped. He felt feverishly hot against her skin. His lips grazed her cheekbone; they were as soft as she remembered.

"Jem," Tessa said desperately, and Jem looked over at them; he had been buckling Will's belt over his own, and it seemed clear he hadn't heard a word Will had said. He knelt down to stuff Will's feet into his boots, then rose to take his *parabatai's* arm. Will seemed delighted by this.

"Oh, good," he said. "Now we're all three together."

"Shut up," said Jem.

Will giggled. "Listen, Carstairs, you haven't any of the needful on you, have you? I'd stump up, but I'm flat out."

"*What* did he say?" Tessa was baffled.

"He wants me to pay for his drugs." Jem's voice was stiff. "Come. We'll get him to the carriage, and I'll come back with the money."

As they struggled toward the door, Tessa heard the voice of the cloven-footed man, following them, thin and as high as music piped through reeds, ending in a high-pitched giggle.

"Here comes a candle to light you to bed,
And here comes a chopper to chop off your head!"

* * *

Even the dirty Whitechapel air seemed clear and fresh after the cloying incense stench of the faerie drug den. Tessa almost stumbled going down the stairs. The carriage was thankfully still at the curb, and Cyril was swinging himself down out of the seat, heading over to them, concern on his big, open face.

"Is he all right, then?" he said, taking the arm that Will had draped over Tessa's shoulders and draping it over his own. Tessa slipped aside gratefully; her back had begun to ache.

Will predictably, though, did not like this. "Let me go," he said with sudden irritation. "Let me go. I can stand."

Jem and Cyril exchanged glances, then moved apart. Will staggered, but stayed upright. He raised his head, the cold wind lifting the sweaty hair from his neck and forehead, blowing it across his eyes. Tessa thought of him up on the roof of the Institute: *And I behold London, a human awful wonder of God.*

He looked at Jem. His eyes were bluer than blue, his cheeks flushed, his features angelic. He said, "You did not have to come and fetch me like some child. I was having quite a pleasant time."

Jem looked back at him. "God damn you," he said, and hit Will across the face, sending him spinning. Will didn't lose his footing, but fetched up against the side of the carriage, his hand to his cheek. His mouth was bleeding. He looked at Jem with total astonishment.

"Get him into the carriage," Jem said to Cyril, and turned and went back through the red door—to pay for whatever Will had taken, Tessa thought. Will was still staring after him, the blood reddening his mouth.

"James?" he said.

"Come along, then," said Cyril, not unkindly. He really was awfully like Thomas, Tessa thought as he opened the carriage door and helped Will inside, and then Tessa after him. He gave her a handkerchief from his pocket. It was warm and smelled like cheap eau de cologne. She smiled and thanked him as he shut the door.

Will was slumped in the corner of the carriage, his arms around himself, his eyes half-open. Blood had trickled down his chin. She leaned over and pressed the handkerchief to his mouth; he reached up and put his hand over hers, holding it there. "I've made a mess of things," he said. "Haven't I?"

"Dreadfully, I'm afraid," said Tessa, trying not to notice the warmth of his hand over hers. Even in the darkness of the carriage, his eyes were luminously blue. What was it Jem had said, though, about beauty? *Beauty is harsh.* Would people forgive Will the things he did if he were ugly? And did it help him, in the end, to be forgiven? Though, she could not help but feel he did the things he did not because he loved himself too much but because he hated himself. And she did not know why.

He closed his eyes. "I'm so tired, Tess," he said. "I only wanted pleasant dreams for once."

"That is not the way to get them, Will," she said softly. "You cannot buy or drug or dream your way out of pain."

His hand tightened over hers.

The carriage door opened. Tessa drew back from Will hastily. It was Jem, his face like thunder; he spared a cursory glance at Will, threw himself into a seat, and reached up to rap on the roof. "Cyril, drive home," he called, and after a moment the carriage lurched forward into the night. Jem reached out and drew the curtains across the windows. In the dimness Tessa slipped the handkerchief into her sleeve. It was still damp with Will's blood.

Jem said nothing all the way back from Whitechapel, merely stared stonily ahead of him with his arms folded while Will slept, a faint smile on his face, in the corner of the carriage. Tessa, across from them both, could think of nothing to say to break Jem's silence. This was so utterly unlike him—Jem, who was always sweet, always kind, always optimistic. His expression now was worse than blank, his nails digging into the fabric of his gear, his shoulders stiff and angular with rage.

The moment they drew up in front of the Institute, he threw the door open and leaped out. She heard him shout something to Cyril about helping Will to his room, and then he stalked away, up the steps, without another word to her. Tessa was so shocked, she could only stare after him for a moment. She moved to the carriage door; Cyril was already there, his hand up to help her down. Barely had Tessa's shoes hit the cobblestones than she was hurrying after Jem, calling his name, but he was already inside the Institute. He had left the door open for her, and she dashed in after him, after only a brief glance to confirm that Will was being helped by Cyril. She hurried up the stairs, dropping her voice as she realized that, of course, the Institute was asleep, the witchlight torches dimmed to their lowest glow.

She went to Jem's room first and knocked; when there was no answer, she sought a few of his most commonly visited haunts—the music room, the library—but, finding nothing, she returned, disconsolate, to her own room to ready herself for bed. In her nightgown, her dress brushed and hung up, she crawled between the sheets of her bed and stared at the ceiling. She even picked up Will's copy of *Vathek* from her floor, but for the first time the poem in the front failed to make her smile, and she could not concentrate on the story.

She was startled at her own distress. Jem was angry at Will, not at her. Still, she thought, it was perhaps the first time he had lost his temper in front of her. The first time he had been curt with her, or not attended with kindness to her words, had not seemed to think of her first before himself. . . .

She had taken him for granted, she thought with surprise and shame, watching the flickering candlelight. She had assumed his kindness was so natural and so innate, she had never asked herself whether it cost him any effort. Any effort to stand between Will and the world, protecting each of them from the other. Any effort to accept the loss of his family with equanimity. Any effort to remain cheerful and calm in the face of his own dying.

A rending noise, the sound of something being wrenched apart, tore through the room. Tessa sat bolt upright. What *was* that? It seemed to be coming from outside her door—across the hall—

Jem?

She leaped to her feet and caught her dressing gown down from its peg. Hurriedly slipping into it, she darted out the door and into the corridor.

She had been correct—the noise was coming from Jem's room. She remembered the first night she had met him, the lovely violin music that had poured like water through the doorway. This noise sounded nothing like Jem's music. She could hear the saw of bow against string, yet it sounded like screaming, like a person screaming in awful pain. She both longed to go in and felt terrified to do so; finally she took hold of the knob of the door and swung it open, and then ducked inside and pulled the door closed fast after her.

"Jem," she whispered.

The witchlight torches were burning low on the walls. Jem sat on the trunk at the foot of his bed in just his shirtsleeves and trousers, his silver hair tousled, the violin propped against his shoulder. He was sawing at it viciously with the bow, wringing awful sounds out of it, making it scream. As Tessa watched, one of the violin strings snapped with a shriek.

"*Jem!*" she cried again, and when he did not look up, she strode across the room and wrenched the bow out of his hand. "Jem, *stop*! Your violin—your lovely violin—you'll ruin it."

He looked up at her. His pupils were enormous, the silver of his eyes only a thin ring around the black. He was breathing hard, his shirt open at the neck, sweat standing out on his collarbones. His cheeks were flushed. "What does it matter?" he said in a voice so low it was almost a hiss. "What does any of it matter? I'm dying. I won't outlast the decade. What does it matter if the violin goes before I do?"

Tessa was appalled. He never spoke like this about his illness, never.

He stood up and turned away from her, toward the window. Only a little moonlight found its way into the room through the fog; there seemed to be shapes visible in the white mist pressed against the window—ghosts, shades, mocking faces. "You know it is true."

"Nothing is decided." Her voice shook. "Nothing is inevitable. A cure—"

"There's no cure." He no longer sounded angry, just

detached, which was almost worse. "I will die, and you know it, Tess. Probably within the next year. I am dying, and I have no family in the world, and the one person I trusted more than any other made sport of what is killing me."

"But, Jem, I don't think that's what Will meant to do at all." Tessa leaned the bow against the footboard and moved closer to him, tentatively, as if he were an animal she was fearful of startling. "He was just trying to escape. He is running from something, something dark and awful. You know he is, Jem. You saw how he was after—after Cecily."

She stood just behind him now, close enough to reach out and touch him tentatively on the arm, but she did not. His white shirt was stuck to his shoulder blades with sweat. She could see the Marks on his back through the fabric. He dropped the violin almost carelessly onto the trunk and turned to face her. "He knows what it means to me," he said. "To see him even toy with what has destroyed my life—"

"But he wasn't thinking of you—"

"*I know that.*" His eyes were almost all black now. "I tell myself he's better than he makes himself out to be, but, Tessa, what if he isn't? I have always thought, if I had nothing else, I had Will. If I have done nothing else that made my life matter, I have always stood by him. But perhaps I shouldn't."

His chest was rising and falling so fast, it alarmed her; she put the back of her hand to his forehead and nearly gasped. "You're burning up. You should be resting—"

He flinched away from her, and she dropped her hand, hurt. "Jem, what is it? You don't want me to touch you?"

"Not like that," he flared, and then flushed even darker than before.

"Like what?" She was honestly bewildered; this was behavior she might have expected from Will, but not from Jem—this mysteriousness, this anger.

"As if you were a nurse and I were your patient." His voice was firm but uneven. "You think because I am ill that I am not like—" He drew a ragged breath. "Do you think I do not know," he said, "that when you take my hand, it is only so that you can feel my pulse? Do you think I do not know that when you look into my eyes, it is only to see how much of the drug I have taken? If I were another man, a normal man, I might have hopes, presumptions even; I might—" His words seemed to catch, either because he realized he had said too much or because he had run out of breath; he was gasping, his cheeks flushed.

She shook her head, feeling her plaits tickle her neck. "This is the fever speaking, not you."

His eyes darkened, and he began to turn away from her. "You can't even believe I could want you," he said in a half whisper. "That I am alive enough, healthy enough—"

"No—" Without thinking, she caught at his arm. He stiffened. "James, that isn't at all what I meant—"

He curled his fingers around her hand where it lay on his arm. His own scorched her skin, as hot as fire. And then he turned her and drew her toward him.

They stood face-to-face, chest to chest. His breath stirred her hair. She felt the fever rising off him like mist off the Thames; sensed the pounding of the blood through his skin; saw with a strange clarity the pulse at his throat, the light on the pale curls of his hair where they lay against his paler neck. Prickles of heat ran up and down her skin, bewildering her.

This was Jem—her friend, as steady and reliable as a heartbeat. Jem did not set her skin on fire or make the blood rush fast inside her veins until she was dizzy.

"Tessa," he said. She looked up at him. There was nothing steady or reliable about his expression. His eyes were dark, his cheeks flushed. As she raised her face, he brought his down, his mouth slanting across hers, and even as she froze in surprise, they were kissing. *Jem.* She was kissing Jem. Where Will's kisses were all fire, Jem's were like pure air after a long time of being closed up in the airless dark. His mouth was soft and firm; one of his hands circled the back of her neck gently, guiding her mouth to his. With his other hand he cupped her face, running his thumb gently across her cheekbone. His lips tasted of burned sugar; the sweetness of the drug, she guessed. His touch, his lips, were tentative, and she knew why. Unlike Will, he would *mind* that this was the height of impropriety, that he should not be touching her, kissing her, that she should be pulling away.

But she did not want to pull away. Even as she wondered at the fact that it was Jem she was kissing, Jem making her head swim and her ears ring, she felt her arms rise as if of their own accord, curving around his neck, drawing him closer.

He gasped against her mouth. He must have been so sure she would push him away that for a moment he went still. Her hands glided over his shoulders, urging him with gentle touches, with a murmur against his lips, not to pause. Hesitantly he returned her caress, and then with greater force—kissing her again and again, each time with increasing urgency, cupping her face between his burning hands, his thin violinist's fingers stroking her skin, making her shiver. His hands moved to the small of her back, pressing her against him; her bare feet slipped on the carpet, and they half-stumbled backward onto the bed.

Her fingers wound tightly in his shirt, Tessa drew Jem down onto her, taking the weight of him onto her body with the feeling that she was being given back something that had belonged to her forever, a bit of her that she had missed without knowing she was missing it. Jem was light, hollow-boned like a bird and with the same racing heart; she ran her hands through his hair, and it was as soft as she had always in her most buried dreams thought it would be, like pinfeathers between her fingers. He could not seem to stop running his hands over her in wonder. They traced their way down her body, his breath ragged in her ear as he found the tie of her dressing gown and paused there, with shaking fingers.

His uncertainty made Tessa's heart feel as if it were expanding inside her chest, its tenderness big enough to hold them both inside it. She wanted Jem to *see* her, just as she was, herself, Tessa Gray, with none of the Change on her. She reached down and undid the tie, sliding the dressing gown off her shoulders so that she was revealed before him in only her white batiste nightgown.

She looked up at him, breathless, shaking her loosened hair out of her face. Propping himself over her, he gazed down, and said again, huskily, what he had said in the carriage before, when he had touched her hair. "*Ni hen piao liang.*"

"What does it mean?" she whispered, and this time he smiled and said:

"It means that you are beautiful. I did not want to tell you before. I did not want you to think I was taking liberties."

She reached up and touched his cheek, so close to hers, and then the fragile skin of his throat, where the blood beat hard beneath the surface. His eyelashes fluttered down as he followed the movement of her finger with his eyes, like silvery rain.

"Take them," she whispered.

He bent down to her; their mouths met again, and the shock of sensation was so strong, so overpowering, that she shut her eyes against it as if she could hide in the darkness. He murmured and gathered her against him. They rolled sideways, her legs scissoring around his, their bodies shifting to press each other closer and closer still so it became hard to breathe, and yet they could not stop. She found the buttons on his shirt, but even when she opened her eyes, her hands were shaking almost too hard to undo them. Clumsily she worked them free, tearing the fabric. As he shrugged the shirt free of his shoulders, she saw that his eyes were lightening to a pure silver again. She had only a moment to marvel at that, though; she was too busy marveling at the rest of him. He was so thin, without Will's cording of muscle, but there was something about his fragility that was lovely, like the spare lines of a poem. *Gold to airy thinness beat.* Though a layer of muscle still covered his chest, she could see the shadows between his ribs. The pendant of jade Will had given him lay below his angular collarbones.

"I know," he said, looking down at himself self-consciously. "I am not— I mean, I look—"

"Beautiful," she said, and she meant it. "You are beautiful, James Carstairs."

His eyes went wide as she reached to touch him. Her hands

had stopped shaking. They were exploratory, fascinated now. Her mother had owned a very old copy of a book once, she remembered, its pages so fragile they were liable to turn to dust when you touched them, and she felt that same responsibility of enormous care now as she brushed her fingers over the Marks on his chest, across the hollows between his ribs and the slope of his stomach, which shuddered under her touch; here was something that was as breakable as it was lovely.

He did not seem to be able to stop touching her, either. His skilled musician's hands grazed her sides, skimming up her bare legs beneath her nightdress. He touched her as he usually touched his beloved violin, with a soft and urgent grace that left her breathless. They seemed to share his fever now; their bodies burned, and their hair was wet with sweat, pasted to their foreheads and necks. Tessa didn't care; she wanted this heat, this near-pain. This was not herself, this was some other Tessa, some dream Tessa, who would behave like this, and she remembered her dream of Jem in a bed surrounded by flames. She had just never dreamed she would burn with him. She wanted more of this feeling, she knew, more of this fire, but none of the novels she had read told her what happened now. Did *he* know? Will would know, she thought, but Jem, like her, she sensed, must have been following an instinct that ran as deep as her bones. His fingers slipped into the nonexistent space between them, finding the buttons that held her nightdress closed; he bent to kiss her bared shoulder as the fabric slid aside. No one had ever kissed her bare skin there before, and the feeling was so startling that she put out a hand to brace herself, and knocked a pillow from the bed; it hit the small side table. There was the sound of a crash. A sudden sweet dark scent, as of spices, filled the room.

Jem jerked his hands back, a look of horror on his face. Tessa sat up as well, pulling the front of her nightdress together, suddenly self-conscious. Jem was staring over the side of the bed, and she followed his line of sight. The lacquer box that held his drugs had fallen and broken open. A thick layer of shining powder lay across the floor. A faint silvery mist seemed to rise from it, carrying the sweet, spicy smell.

Jem pulled her back, his arm around her, but there was fear in his grip now rather than passion. "Tess," he said in a low voice. "You can't touch this stuff. To get it on your skin would be—dangerous. Even to breathe it in— Tessa, you must go."

She thought of Will, ordering her out of the attic. Was this how it was always going to be—some boy would kiss her, and then order her away as if she were an unwanted servant? "I won't go," she flared. "Jem, I can help you clean it up. I am—"

Your friend, she was about to say. But what they had been doing was not what friends did. What was she to him?

"Please," he said softly. His voice was husky. She recognized the emotion. It was shame. "I do not want you to see me on my knees, grubbing around on the floor for the drug that I need to live. That is not how any man wants the girl he—" He took a shaking breath. "I'm sorry, Tessa."

The girl he what? But she could not ask; she was overwhelmed—with pity, with sympathy, with shock at what they had done. She leaned forward and kissed his cheek. He didn't move as she slipped from the bed, retrieved her dressing gown, and went quietly out of the room.

* * *

The corridor was the same as it had been when Tessa had crossed it moments—hours—minutes?—before: dim with lowered witchlight stretching far in either direction. She had just slipped into her own bedroom and was about to shut the door when her eye caught a flicker of movement down at the end of the hall. Some instinct held her in place, the door almost shut, her eye pressed to the barely open crack.

The movement was someone walking down the hall. A fair-haired boy, she thought for a moment, in confusion, but no—it was *Jessamine*, Jessamine dressed in boys' clothes. She wore trousers and a jacket open over a waistcoat; a hat was in her hand, and her long fair hair was tied back behind her head. She glanced behind her as she hurried down the hall, as if afraid of being followed. A few moments later she had vanished around the corner, out of sight.

Tessa slid the door shut, her mind racing. What on earth was that about? What was Jessamine doing, wandering the Institute in the dead of night, dressed like a boy? After hanging up her dressing gown, Tessa went to lie down on her bed. She felt tired down in the marrow of her bones, the sort of tired she had felt the night her aunt died, as if she had exhausted her body's capacity to feel emotion. When she closed her eyes, she saw Jem's face, and then Will's, his hand to his bloody mouth. Thoughts of the two of them swirled together in her head until she fell asleep finally, not sure if she was dreaming of kissing one of them, or the other.

10

THE VIRTUE OF ANGELS

The virtue of angels is that they cannot deteriorate;
their flaw is that they cannot improve. Man's
flaw is that he can deteriorate; and his virtue is
that he can improve.
—Hasidic saying

"I suppose you all know by now," Will remarked at breakfast the next morning, "that I went to an opium den last night."

It was a subdued morning. It had dawned rainy and gray, and the Institute felt leadenly weighted down, as if the sky were pressing on it. Sophie passed in and out of the kitchen carrying steaming platters of food, her pale face looking pinched and small; Jessamine slumped tiredly over her tea; Charlotte looked weary and unwell from her night spent in the library; and Will's eyes were red-rimmed, his cheek bruised where Jem had hit him. Only Henry, reading the paper with one hand while he stabbed at his eggs with the other, seemed to have any energy.

Jem was conspicuous mainly by his absence. When Tessa had woken up that morning, she had floated for a moment in a blissful state of forgetfulness, the events of the night before a dim blur. Then she had sat bolt upright, absolute horror crashing over her like a wave of scalding water.

Had she really done all those things with *Jem?* His bed—his hands on her—the spilled drugs. She had raised her hands and touched her hair. It fell free over her shoulders, where Jem had tugged it out of its plaits. *Oh, God,* she thought. *I really did all that; that was me.* She had pressed her hands to her eyes, feeling an overwhelming mix of confusion, terrified happiness—for she could not deny that it had been wonderful in its way—horror at herself, and hideous and total humiliation.

Jem would think she had utterly lost control of herself. No wonder he couldn't face her at breakfast. She could barely face herself in the mirror.

"Did you hear me?" Will said again, clearly disappointed at the reception of his announcement. "I said I went to an opium den last night."

Charlotte looked up from her toast. Slowly she folded her newspaper, set it on the table beside her, and pushed her reading glasses down her upturned nose. "No," she said. "That undoubtedly glorious aspect of your recent activities was unknown to us, in fact."

"So is that where you've been all this time?" Jessamine asked listlessly, taking a sugar cube from the bowl and biting into it. "Are you quite a hopeless addict now? They say it takes only one or two doses."

"It wasn't really an *opium* den," Tessa protested before she could stop herself. "That is to say—they seemed to have more of a trade in magic powders and things like that."

"So perhaps not an opium den precisely," said Will, "but still a den. Of vice!" he added, punctuating this last bit by stabbing his finger into the air.

"Oh, dear, not one of those places that's run by ifrits," sighed Charlotte. "Really, Will—"

"Exactly one of those places," said Jem, coming into the breakfast room and sliding into a chair beside Charlotte— quite as far away from Tessa as it was possible to sit, she noticed, with a pinching feeling in her chest. He didn't look at her either. "Off Whitechapel High Street."

"And how do you and Tessa know so much about it?" asked Jessamine, who appeared revitalized by either her sugar intake or the expectation of some good gossip, or both.

"I used a tracking spell to find Will last night," said Jem. "I was growing concerned at his absence. I thought he might have forgotten the way back to the Institute."

"You worry too much," said Jessamine. "It's silly."

"You're quite right. I won't make that mistake again," said Jem, reaching for the dish of kedgeree. "As it turned out, Will wasn't in need of my assistance at all."

Will looked at Jem thoughtfully. "I seem to have woken up with what they call a Monday mouse," he said, pointing at the bruised skin under his eye. "Any idea where I got it?"

"None." Jem helped himself to some tea.

"Eggs," said Henry dreamily, looking at his plate. "I do love eggs. I could eat them all day."

"Was there really a need to bring Tessa with you to Whitechapel?" Charlotte asked Jem, sliding her glasses off and placing them on the newspaper. Her brown eyes were reproachful.

"Tessa is not made of delicate china," said Jem. "She will not break."

For some reason this statement, though he said it still without looking at her, sent a flood of images through Tessa's mind of the night before—of clinging to Jem in the shadows of his bed, his hands gripping her shoulders, their mouths fierce on each other's. No, he had not treated her as if she were breakable then. A boiling flood of heat seared her cheeks, and she looked down quickly, praying for her blush to go away.

"You might be surprised to know," said Will, "that I saw something rather interesting in the opium den."

"I'm sure you did," said Charlotte with asperity.

"Was it an egg?" Henry inquired.

"Downworlders," said Will. "Almost all werewolves."

"There's nothing interesting about werewolves." Jessamine sounded aggrieved. "We're focusing on finding Mortmain now, Will, if you haven't forgotten, not some drug-addled Downworlders."

"They were buying *yin fen*," said Will. "Buckets of it."

At that Jem's head snapped up and he met Will's eyes.

"They had already begun to change color," said Will. "Quite a few had silver hair, or eyes. Even their skin had started to silver over."

"This is very disturbing." Charlotte frowned. "We should speak to Woolsey Scott as soon as this Mortmain matter is cleared up. If there is an issue of addiction to warlock powders in his pack, he will want to know about it."

"Don't you think he already does?" said Will, sitting back in his chair. He looked pleased to have finally gotten a reaction to his news. "It is his pack, after all."

"His pack is all of London's wolves," objected Jem. "He can't possibly keep real track of them all."

"I'm not sure you want to wait," said Will. "If you can get hold of Scott, I'd speak to him as soon as possible."

Charlotte tilted her head to the side. "And why is that?"

"Because," said Will. "One of the ifrits asked a werewolf why he needed so much *yin fen*. Apparently it works on werewolves as a stimulant. The answer was that it pleased the Magister that the drug kept them working all night long."

Charlotte's teacup crashed into her saucer. "Working on what?"

Will smirked, clearly pleased at the effect he was having. "I've no idea. I lost consciousness about then. I was having a lovely dream about a young woman who had mislaid nearly all her clothes . . ."

Charlotte was white-faced. "Dear God, I hope Scott isn't caught up with the Magister. De Quincey first, now the wolves—all our allies. The Accords . . ."

"I'm sure it will all be all right, Charlotte," said Henry mildly. "Scott doesn't seem the sort to get tangled up with Mortmain's sort."

"Perhaps you should be there when I speak with him," said Charlotte. "Nominally, you *are* the head of the Institute—"

"Oh, no," said Henry with a look of horror. "Darling, you'll be quite all right without me. You're such a genius where these negotiations are concerned, and I'm simply not. And besides, the invention I'm working on now could shatter the whole clockwork army into pieces if I get the formulations right!"

He beamed round the table proudly. Charlotte looked at him for a long moment, then pushed her chair back from the table, stood up, and walked out of the room without another word.

Will regarded Henry from beneath half-lidded eyes. "Nothing ever disturbs your circles, does it, Henry?"

Henry blinked. "What do you mean?"

"Archimedes," Jem said, as usual knowing what Will meant, though not looking at him. "He was drawing a mathematical diagram in the sand when his city was attacked by Romans. He was so intent on what he was doing that he didn't see the soldier coming up behind him. His last words were 'Do not disturb my circles.' Of course, he was an old man by then."

"And he was probably never married," said Will, and he grinned at Jem across the table.

Jem didn't return his grin. Without looking at Will, or Tessa—without looking at any of them—he got to his feet and went out of the room after Charlotte.

"Oh, bother," said Jessamine. "Is this one of those days where we all stalk out in a fury? Because I simply haven't got the energy for it." She put her head down on her arms and closed her eyes.

Henry looked bewilderedly from Will to Tessa. "What is it? What have I done wrong?"

Tessa sighed. "Nothing dreadful, Henry. It's just— I think Charlotte wanted you to come *with* her."

"Then, why didn't she say so?" Henry's eyes were mournful. His joy over his eggs and inventions seemed to have vanished. Perhaps he shouldn't have married Charlotte, Tessa thought, her mood as bleak as the weather. Perhaps, like Archimedes, he would have been happier drawing circles in the sand.

"Because women never say what they think," said Will. His eyes drifted toward the kitchen, where Bridget was clearing up the remains of the meal. Her singing floated lugubriously out into the dining room.

"'I fear you are poisoned, my own pretty boy,
I fear you are poisoned, my comfort and joy!'
'O yes, I am poisoned; mother, make my bed soon,
There's a pain in my heart, and I mean to lie down.'"

"I swear that woman had a previous career as a death-hunter selling tragic ballads down around the Seven Dials," said Will. "And I do wish she wouldn't sing about poisoning just after we've eaten." He looked sideways at Tessa. "Shouldn't you be off putting on your gear? Haven't you training with the lunatic Lightwoods today?"

"Yes, this morning, but I needn't change clothes. We're just practicing knife throwing," said Tessa, somewhat amazed that she was able to have this mild and civil a conversation with Will after the events of last night. Cyril's handkerchief, with Will's blood on it, was still in her dresser drawer; she remembered the warmth of his lips on her fingers, and darted her eyes away from his.

"How fortunate that I am a crack hand at knife throwing." Will got to his feet and held out his arm to her. "Come along; it'll drive Gideon and Gabriel mad if I watch the training, and I could do with a little madness this morning."

Will was correct. His presence during the training session seemed to madden Gabriel at least, though Gideon, as he seemed to do with everything, took this intrusion in a stolid manner. Will sat on a low wooden bench that ran along one of the walls, and ate an apple, his long legs stretched out before him, occasionally calling out bits of advice that Gideon ignored and that Gabriel took like blows to the chest.

"*Must* he be here?" Gabriel growled to Tessa the second time he had nearly dropped a knife while handing it to her. He put a hand on her shoulder, showing her the sight line for the target she was aiming at—a black circle drawn on the wall. She knew how much he would rather she were aiming at Will. "Can't you tell him to go away?"

"Now, why would I do that?" Tessa asked reasonably. "Will is my friend, and you are someone whom I do not even like."

She threw the knife. It missed its target by several feet, striking low in the wall near the floor.

"No, you're still weighting the point too much—and what do you mean, you don't like me?" Gabriel demanded, handing her another knife as if by reflex, but his expression was very surprised indeed.

"Well," Tessa said, sighting along the line of the knife, "you behave as if you dislike *me*. In fact, you behave as if you dislike us all."

"I don't," Gabriel said. "I just dislike *him*." He pointed at Will.

"Dear me," said Will, and he took another bite of his apple. "Is it because I'm better-looking than you?"

"Both of you be quiet," Gideon called from across the room. "We're meant to be working, not snapping at each other over years-old petty disagreements."

"Petty?" Gabriel snarled. "He *broke* my *arm*."

Will took another bite out of his apple. "I can hardly believe you're still upset about that."

Tessa threw the knife. This throw was better. It landed inside the black circle, if not in the center itself. Gabriel looked around for another knife and, not seeing one, let out an exhalation of annoyance. "When *we* run the Institute," he said, pitching his voice loud enough for Will to hear, "this training room will be far better kept up and supplied."

Tessa looked at him angrily. "Amazing that I don't like you, isn't it?"

Gabriel's handsome face crumpled into an ugly look of contempt. "I don't see what this has to do with you, little warlock; this Institute isn't your home. You don't belong in this place. Believe me, you'd be better off with my family running things here; we could find uses for your . . . talent. Employment that would make you rich. You could live where you liked. And Charlotte can go run the Institute in York, where she'll do considerably less harm."

Will was sitting upright now, apple forgotten. Gideon and Sophie had ceased their practicing and were watching the conversation—Gideon wary, Sophie wide-eyed. "If you hadn't noticed," Will said, "someone already runs the York Institute."

"Aloysius Starkweather is a senile old man." Gabriel dismissed him with a wave of his hand. "And he has no descendants he can beg the Consul to appoint in his place. Since the business with his granddaughter, his son and daughter-in-law packed up and went to Idris. They won't come back here for love or money."

"What business with his granddaughter?" Tessa demanded,

flashing back to the portrait of the sickly-looking little girl on the staircase of the York Institute.

"Only lived to be ten or so," said Gabriel. "Never was very healthy, by all accounts, and when they first Marked her— Well, she must have been improperly trained. She went mad, turned Forsaken, and died. The shock killed old Starkweather's wife, and sent his children scurrying to Idris. It wouldn't be much trouble to get him replaced by Charlotte. The Consul must see he's no good—far too married to the old ways."

Tessa looked at Gabriel in disbelief. His voice had retained its cool indifference as he'd told the story of the Starkweathers, as if it were a fairy tale. And she—she didn't want to pity the old man with the sly eyes and the bloody room full of dead Downworlders' remains, but she couldn't help it. She pushed Aloysius Starkweather from her mind. "Charlotte runs *this* Institute," she said. "And your father will not take it from her."

"She deserves to have it taken from her."

Will tossed his apple core into the air, at the same time drawing a knife from his belt and throwing it. The knife and the apple sailed across the room together, somehow managing to stick into the wall just beside Gabriel's head, the knife driven cleanly through the core and into the wood. "Say that again," said Will, "and I'll darken your daylights for you."

Gabriel's face worked. "You have no idea what you're talking about."

Gideon took a step forward, warning in every line of his posture. "Gabriel—"

But his brother ignored him. "You don't even know what your precious Charlotte's father did to mine, do you? I only just learned it myself a few days ago. My father finally broke down and told us. He'd protected the Fairchilds till then."

"Your father?" Will's tone was incredulous. "Protected the *Fairchilds*?"

"He was protecting us as well." Gabriel's words tumbled over themselves. "My mother's brother—my uncle Silas—was one of Granville Fairchild's closest friends. Then Uncle Silas broke the Law—a tiny thing, a minor infraction—and Fairchild discovered it. All he cared about was the Law, not friendship, not loyalty. He went straight to the Clave." Gabriel's voice rose. "My uncle *killed* himself in shame, and my mother died of the grief. The Fairchilds don't care about anyone but themselves and the Law!"

For a moment the room was silent; even Will was speechless, looking utterly taken aback. It was Tessa who spoke at last, "But that is the fault of Charlotte's father. Not of Charlotte."

Gabriel was white with rage, his green eyes standing out against his pale skin. "You don't understand," he said viciously. "You're not a Shadowhunter. We have blood pride. Family pride. Granville Fairchild wanted the Institute to go to his daughter, and the Consul made it happen. But even though Fairchild is dead, we can still take that away from him. He was hated—so hated that no one would have married Charlotte if he hadn't paid off the Branwells to hand Henry over. Everyone knows it. Everyone knows he doesn't really love her. How could he—"

There was a crack, like the sound of a rifle shot, and Gabriel fell silent. Sophie had slapped him across the face. His pale skin was already beginning to redden. Sophie was staring at him, breathing hard, an incredulous look on her face, as if she could not believe what she had done.

Gabriel's hands tightened at his sides, but he didn't move. He couldn't, Tessa knew. He could not strike a girl, a girl who was not even a Shadowhunter or a Downworlder but merely a mundane. He looked to his brother, but Gideon, expressionless, met his eyes and shook his head slowly; with a choked sound Gabriel spun on his heel and stalked from the room.

"Sophie!" Tessa exclaimed, reaching for her. "Are you all right?"

But Sophie was looking anxiously up at Gideon. "I'm so sorry, sir," she said. "There's no excuse—I lost my head, and I—"

"It was a well-placed blow," Gideon said calmly. "I see you've been paying attention to my training."

Will was sitting up on the bench, his blue eyes lively and curious. "Was it true?" he said. "That story Gabriel just told us."

Gideon shrugged. "Gabriel worships our father," he said. "Anything Benedict says is like a pronouncement from on high. I knew my uncle had killed himself, but not the circumstances, until the day after we first came back from training you. Father asked us how the Institute seemed to be run, and I told him it seemed in fine condition, no different from the Institute in Madrid. In fact, I told him I could see no evidence that Charlotte was doing a lax job. That was when he told us this story."

"If you don't mind my asking," said Tessa, "what was it that your uncle had done?"

"Silas? Fell in love with his *parabatai*. Not, actually, as Gabriel says, a minor infraction but a major one. Romantic relationships between *parabatai* are absolutely forbidden. Though even the best-trained Shadowhunter can fall prey to emotion. The Clave would have separated the two of them, though, and that Silas couldn't face. That's why he killed himself. My mother was consumed with rage and grief. I can well believe that her dying wish was that we would take the Institute from the Fairchilds. Gabriel was younger than I when our mother died—only five years old, clinging to her skirts still—and it seems to me his feelings are too overwhelming for him now to quite understand them. Whereas I—I feel that the sins of the fathers should not be visited on the sons."

"Or the daughters," said Will.

Gideon looked at him and gave him a crooked smile. There was no dislike in it; in fact, it was jarringly the look of someone who understood Will, and why he behaved as he did. Even Will looked a bit surprised. "There is the problem that Gabriel will never come back here, of course," said Gideon. "Not after this."

Sophie, whose color had started to return, paled again. "Mrs. Branwell will be furious—"

Tessa waved her back. "I'll go after him and apologize, Sophie. It will be all right."

She heard Gideon call after her, but she was already hurrying from the room. She hated to admit it, but she'd felt a spark of sympathy for Gabriel when Gideon had been telling his story. Losing a mother when you were so young you could barely remember her later was something she had familiarity with. If someone had told her that her mother had had a dying wish, she wasn't sure she wouldn't have done everything in her power to execute it . . . whether it made sense or not.

"Tessa!" She was partway down the corridor when she heard Will calling after her. She spun and saw him striding down the hall in her direction, a half smile on his face.

Her next words wiped his smile away. "*Why* are you following me? Will, you shouldn't have left them alone! You must go back to the training room, right away."

Will planted his feet. "Why?"

Tessa threw up her hands. "Don't men notice anything? Gideon has designs on Sophie—"

"On *Sophie*?"

"She's a very beautiful girl," flared Tessa. "You're an idiot if you haven't noticed the way he looks at her, but I don't want him taking advantage of her. She's had enough such trouble in her life—and besides, if you're with me, Gabriel won't talk to me. You know he won't."

Will muttered something under his breath and seized her wrist. "Here. Come with me."

The warmth of his skin against hers sent a jolt up her arm. He pulled her into the drawing room and across to the great windows that looked down over the courtyard. He released her wrist just in time for her to lean forward and see the Lightwoods' carriage rattling furiously across the stone yard and under the iron gates.

"There," Will said. "Gabriel's gone anyway, unless you want to chase after the carriage. And Sophie's perfectly sensible. She's not going to let Gideon Lightwood have his way with her. Besides, he's about as charming as a postbox."

Tessa, surprising even herself, let out a gasp of laughter. She put her hand up to cover her mouth, but it was too late; she was already laughing, leaning a little against the window.

Will looked at her, his blue eyes quizzical, his mouth just beginning to quirk up in a grin. "I must be more amusing than I thought. Which would make me very amusing indeed."

"I'm not laughing at you," she told him in between giggles.

"Just— Oh! The look on Gabriel's face when Sophie slapped him. My goodness." She pushed her hair out of her face and said, "I really shouldn't be laughing. Half the reason he was so awful was your goading him. I should be angry with you."

"Oh, *should*," said Will, spinning away to drop into a chair near the fire, and stretching out his long legs toward the flames. Like every room in England, Tessa thought, it was chilly in here except just in front of the fire. One roasted in the front and froze in the back, like a badly cooked turkey. "No good sentences ever include the word 'should.' I *should* have paid the tavern bill; now they're coming to break my legs. I *should* never have run off with my best friend's wife; now she devils me constantly. I *should*—"

"You *should*," Tessa said softly, "think about the way the things you do affect Jem."

Will rolled his head back against the leather of the chair and regarded her. He looked drowsy and tired and beautiful. He could have been some Pre-Raphaelite Apollo. "Is this a serious conversation now, Tess?" His voice still held humor but was edged, like a gold blade edged in razored steel.

Tessa came and sat down in the armchair across from his. "Aren't you worried that he's cross with you? He's your *parabatai*. And he's Jem. He's never cross."

"Perhaps it's better that he's cross with me," said Will. "So much saintlike patience cannot be good for anyone."

"Do not mock him." Tessa's tone was sharp.

"Nothing is beyond mockery, Tess."

"Jem is. He has always been good to you. He is nothing but goodness. That he hit you last night, that only shows how capable you are of driving even saints to madness."

"*Jem* hit me?" Will, fingering his cheek, looked amazed. "I must confess, I remember very little of last night. Only that the two of you woke me, though I very much wanted to stay asleep. I remember Jem shouting at me, and you holding me. I knew it was you. You always smell of lavender."

Tessa ignored this. "Well, Jem hit you. And you deserved it."

"You *do* look scornful—rather like Raziel in all those paintings, as if he were looking down on us. So tell me, scornful angel, what did I do to deserve being hit in the face by James?"

Tessa reached for the words, but they eluded her; she turned to the language she and Will shared—poetry. "You know, in that essay of Donne's, what he says—"

"'License my roving hands, and let them go'?" quoted Will, eyeing her.

"I meant the *essay* about how no man is an island. Everything you do touches others. Yet you never think about it. You behave as if you live on some sort of—of Will island, and none of your actions can have any consequences. Yet they do."

"How does my going to a warlock den affect Jem?" Will inquired. "I suppose he had to come and haul me out, but he's done more dangerous things in the past for me. We protect each other—"

"No, you *don't*," Tessa cried in frustration. "Do you think he cares about the danger? Do you? His whole life has been destroyed by this drug, this *yin fen*, and there you go off to a warlock den and drug yourself up as if it doesn't even matter, as if it's just a game to you. He has to take this foul stuff every day just so he can live, but in the meantime it's killing him. He hates to be dependent on it. He can't even bring himself to buy it; he has *you* do that." Will made a sound of protest, but Tessa held up a hand. "And then *you* swan down to Whitechapel and throw your money at the people who make these drugs and addict other people to them, as if it were some sort of holiday on the Continent for you. What were you thinking?"

"But it had nothing to do with Jem at all—"

"You didn't think about him," said Tessa. "But perhaps you should have. Don't you understand he thinks you made a mockery out of what's killing him? And you're supposed to be his brother."

Will had whitened. "He can't think that."

"He does," she said. "He understands you don't care what other people think about you. But I believe he always expected you'd care what he thought. What he felt."

Will leaned forward. The firelight made odd patterns against his skin, darkening the bruise on his cheek to black. "I do care what other people think," he said with a surprising intensity, staring into the flames. "It's all I think about—what others think, what they feel about me, and I about them; it drives me mad. I wanted escape—"

"You can't mean that. Will Herondale, minding what others think of him?" Tessa tried to make her voice as light as possible. The look on his face startled her. It was not closed but open, as if he were caught half-entangled in a thought he desperately wanted to share, but could not bear to. *This is the boy who took my private letters and hid them in his room,* she thought, but she could work up no anger about it. She had thought she would be furious when she saw him again, but she was not, only puzzled and wondering. Surely it showed a curiosity about other people that was quite un-Will-like, to want to read them in the first place?

There was something raw in his face, his voice. "Tess," he said. "That is *all* I think about. I never look at you without thinking about what you feel about me and fearing—"

He broke off as the drawing room door opened and Charlotte came in, followed by a tall man whose bright blond hair shone like a sunflower in the dim light. Will turned away quickly, his face working. Tessa stared at him. *What* had he been going to say?

"Oh!" Charlotte was clearly startled to see them both. "Tessa, Will—I didn't realize you were in here."

Will's hands were in fists at his sides, his face in shadow, but his voice was level when he replied: "We saw the fire going. It's as chill as ice in the rest of the house."

Tessa stood up. "We'll just be on our way—"

"Will Herondale, excellent to see you looking well. And Tessa Gray!" The blond man broke away from Charlotte and came toward Tessa, beaming as if he knew her. "The shape-changer, correct? Enchanted to meet you. What a curiosity."

Charlotte sighed. "Mr. Woolsey Scott, this is Miss Tessa Gray. Tessa, this is Mr. Woolsey Scott, head of the London werewolf pack, and an old friend of the Clave."

"Very well, then," said Gideon as the door shut behind Tessa and Will. He turned toward Sophie, who was suddenly acutely aware of the largeness of the room, and how small she felt inside it. "Shall we continue with the training?"

He held out a knife to her, shining like a silver wand in the room's dimness. His green eyes were steady. *Everything* about Gideon was steady—his gaze, his voice, the way he held himself. She remembered what it felt like to have those steady arms around her, and shivered involuntarily. She had never been alone with him before, and it frightened her. "I don't think my heart would be in it, Mr. Lightwood," she said. "I appreciate the offer all the same, but . . ."

He lowered his arm slowly. "You think that I don't take training you seriously?"

"I think you're being very generous. But I ought to face facts, oughtn't I? This training was never about me or Tessa. It was about your father and the Institute. And now that I've slapped your brother—" She felt her throat tighten. "Mrs. Branwell would be so disappointed in me if she knew."

"Nonsense. He deserved it. And the little matter of the *blood feud* between our families does come to mind." Gideon spun the silver knife carelessly about his finger and thrust it through his belt. "Charlotte would probably give you a rise in salary if she knew."

Sophie shook her head. They were only a few steps from a bench; she sank down onto it, feeling exhausted. "You don't know Charlotte. She'd feel honor-bound to discipline me."

Gideon settled himself on the bench—not beside her, but against the far side of it, as distant from her as he could get. Sophie couldn't decide whether she was pleased about that or not. "Miss Collins," he said. "There is something you ought to know."

She laced her fingers together. "What is that?"

He leaned forward a little, his broad shoulders hunched. She could see the flecks of gray in his green eyes. "When my father called me back from Madrid," he said, "I did not want to come. I had never been happy in London. Our house has been a miserable place since my mother died."

Sophie just stared at him. She could think of no words. He was a Shadowhunter and a gentleman, and yet he seemed to be unburdening his soul to her. Even Jem, for all his gentle kindness, had never done that.

"When I heard about these lessons, I thought they would be a dreadful waste of my time. I pictured two very silly girls uninterested in any sort of instruction. But that describes neither Miss Gray nor yourself. I should tell you, I used to train younger Shadowhunters in Madrid. And there were quite a few of them who didn't have the same native ability that you do. You're a talented student, and it's a pleasure to teach you."

Sophie felt herself flush scarlet. "You can't be serious."

"I am. I was pleasantly surprised the first time I came here, and again so the next time and the next. I found that I was looking forward to it. In fact, it would be fair to say that since my return home, I have hated everything in London except these hours here, with you."

"But you said 'ay Dios mio' every time I dropped my dagger—"

He grinned. It lit up his face, changed it. Sophie stared at him. He was not beautiful like Jem was, but he was very handsome, especially when he smiled. The smile seemed to reach out and touch her heart, speeding its pace. *He is a Shadowhunter,* she thought. *And a gentleman. This is not the way to think about him. Stop it.* But she could not stop, any more than she had been able to put Jem out of her mind. Though, where with Jem she had felt safe, with Gideon she felt an excitement like lightning that coursed up and down her veins, shocking her. And yet she did not want to let it go.

"I speak Spanish when I'm in a good mood," he said. "You might as well know that about me."

"So it wasn't that you were so weary of my ineptitude that you were wishing to hurl yourself off the roof?"

"Just the opposite." He leaned closer to her. His eyes were the green-gray of a stormy sea. "Sophie? Might I ask you something?"

She knew she should correct him, ask him to call her Miss Collins, but she didn't. "I—yes?"

"Whatever happens with the lessons—might I see you again?"

Will had risen to his feet, but Woolsey Scott was still examining Tessa, his hand under his chin, studying her as if she were something under glass in a natural history exhibit. He was not at all what she would have thought the leader of a pack of werewolves would look like. He was probably in his early twenties, tall but slender to the point of slightness, with blond hair nearly to his shoulders, dressed in a velvet jacket, knee breeches, and a trailing scarf with a paisley print. A tinted monocle obscured one pale green eye. He looked like drawings she'd seen in *Punch* of those who called themselves "aesthetes."

"Adorable," he pronounced finally. "Charlotte, I insist they stay while we talk. What a charming couple they make. See how his dark hair sets off her pale skin—"

"Thank you," said Tessa, her voice shooting several octaves higher than usual, "Mr. Scott, that's very gracious, but there is no attachment between Will and myself. I don't know what you've heard—"

"Nothing!" he declared, throwing himself into a chair and arranging his scarf around him. "Nothing at all, I assure you, though your blushing belies your words. Come along now, everyone, sit down. There's no need to be intimidated by me. Charlotte, ring for some tea. I'm parched."

Tessa looked to Charlotte, who shrugged as if to say there was nothing to be done about it. Slowly Tessa sat back down. Will sat as well. She didn't look at him; she couldn't, with Woolsey Scott grinning at them both as if he knew something she didn't know.

"And where's young Mr. Carstairs?" he inquired. "Adorable boy. Such interesting coloring. And so talented on the violin. Of course, I've heard Garcin himself play at the Paris Opera, and after that, well, everything simply sounds like coal dust scraping the eardrums. Pity about his illness."

Charlotte, who had gone across the room to ring for Bridget, returned and sat down, smoothing her skirts. "In a way, that's what I wanted to speak to you about—"

"Oh, no, no, no." From nowhere Scott had produced a majolica box, which he waved in Charlotte's direction. "No serious discussion, please, until I've had my tea and a smoke. Egyptian cigar?" He offered her the box. "They're the finest available."

"No, thank you." Charlotte looked mildly horrified at the idea of smoking a cigar; indeed, it was hard to picture, and Tessa felt Will, beside her, laugh silently. Scott shrugged and went back to his smoking preparations. The majolica box was a clever little thing with compartments for the cigars, tied in a bundle with a silk ribbon, new matches and old, and a place to tap one's ashes. They watched as the werewolf lit his cigar with evident relish, and the sweet scent of tobacco filled the room.

"Now," he said. "Tell me how you've been, Charlotte, darling. And that abstracted husband of yours. Still wandering around the crypt inventing things that blow up?"

"Sometimes," said Will, "they're even *supposed* to blow up."

There was a rattle, and Bridget arrived with a tea tray, sparing Charlotte the need to answer. She set the tea things down on the inlaid table between the chairs, glancing back and forth anxiously. "I'm sorry, Mrs. Branwell. I thought there was only going to be two for tea—"

"It's quite all right, Bridget," said Charlotte, her tone firmly dismissive. "I will ring for you if we need anything else."

Bridget dropped a curtsy and left, casting a curious eye over her shoulder at Woolsey Scott as she went. He took no notice of her. He had already poured milk into his teacup and was looking reproachfully at his hostess. "Oh, Charlotte."

She looked at him in bewilderment. "Yes?"

"The tongs—the sugar tongs," Scott said sadly, in the voice of someone remarking on the tragic death of an acquaintance. "They're silver."

"Oh!" Charlotte looked startled. Silver, Tessa remembered, was dangerous for werewolves. "I'm so sorry—"

Scott sighed. "It's quite all right. Fortunately, I travel with my own." From another pocket in his velvet jacket—which was buttoned over a silk waistcoat with a print of water lilies that would have put one of Henry's to shame—he produced a rolled-up bit of silk; unrolling it revealed a set of gold tongs and a teaspoon. He set them on the table, took the lid off the teapot, and looked pleased. "Gunpowder tea! From Ceylon, I presume? Have you ever had the tea in Marrakech? They drench it in sugar or honey—"

"Gunpowder?" said Tessa, who had never been able to stop herself from asking questions even when she knew perfectly well it was a bad idea. "There isn't *gunpowder* in the tea, is there?"

Scott laughed and set the lid back down. He sat back while Charlotte, her mouth set in a thin line, poured tea into his cup. "How charming! No, they call it that because the leaves of the tea are rolled into small pellets that resemble gunpowder."

Charlotte said, "Mr. Scott, we really *must* discuss the situation at hand."

"Yes, yes, I read your letter." He sighed. "Downworlder politics. So dull. I don't suppose you'd let me tell you about having my portrait painted by Alma-Tadema? I was dressed as a Roman soldier—"

"Will," said Charlotte firmly. "Perhaps you should share with Mr. Scott what you saw in Whitechapel last night."

Will, somewhat to Tessa's surprise, obediently did as told, keeping the sarcastic observations to a minimum. Scott watched him over the rim of his teacup as Will spoke. His eyes were such a pale green, they were nearly yellow.

"Sorry, my boy," he said when Will was done speaking. "I don't see why this requires an urgent meeting. We're all aware of the existence of these ifrit dens, and I can't be watching every member of my pack at every moment. If some of them choose to partake in vice . . ." He leaned closer. "You do know that your eyes are almost the exact shade of pansy petals? Not quite blue, not quite violet. Extraordinary."

Will widened his extraordinary eyes and smirked. "I think it was the mention of the Magister that concerned Charlotte."

"Ah." Scott turned his gaze on Charlotte. "You're concerned

that I'm betraying you the way you thought de Quincey did. That I'm in league with the Magister—let's just call him by his name, shall we? Mortmain—and I'm letting him use my wolves to do his bidding."

"I had thought," Charlotte said, haltingly, "that perhaps London's Downworlders felt betrayed by the Institute, after what happened with de Quincey. His death—"

Scott adjusted his monocle. As he did, light flashed along the gold band he wore around his index finger. Words gleamed out against it: *L'art pour l'art.* "Was the best surprise I've had since I discovered the Savoy Turkish Baths on Jermyn Street. I despised de Quincey. Loathed him with every fiber of my being."

"Well, the Night Children and the Moon's Children's have never quite—"

"De Quincey had a werewolf killed," Tessa said suddenly, her memories mixing with Camille's, with the recollection of a pair of yellow-green eyes like Scott's. "For his—attachment—to Camille Belcourt."

Woolsey Scott turned a long, curious look on Tessa. "That," he said, "was my brother. My *older* brother. He was pack leader before me, you see, and I inherited the post. Usually one must kill to become pack leader. In my case, it was put to a vote, and the task of avenging my brother in the name of the pack was mine. Only now, you see—" He gestured with an elegant hand. "You've taken care of de Quincey for me. You've no idea how grateful I am." He cocked his head to the side. "Did he die well?"

"He died screaming." Charlotte's bluntness startled Tessa.

"What a beautiful thing to hear." Scott put down his teacup. "For this you have earned a favor. I will tell you what I know, though it isn't much. Mortmain came to me in the early days, wanting me to join with him in the Pandemonium Club. I refused, for de Quincey had already joined, and I would not be part of a club that had him in it. Mortmain let me know there would be a place for me should I change my mind—"

"Did he tell you of his goals?" Will interrupted. "Of the ultimate purpose of the club?"

"The destruction of all Shadowhunters," said Scott. "I rather thought you knew that. It isn't a *gardening* club."

"He has a grudge, we think," said Charlotte. "Against the Clave. Shadowhunters killed his parents some years ago. They were warlocks, deep in the study of the black arts."

"Less of a grudge, more of an idée fixe," said Scott. "An obsession. He would see your kind wiped out, though he seems content to start with England and work his way out from there. A patient, methodical sort of madman. The worst kind." He sat back in his chair and sighed. "News *has* reached me of a group of young wolves, unsworn to any pack, who have been doing some sort of underground work and have been getting paid very well for it. Flashing their tin around among the pack wolves and creating animosities. I did not know about the drug."

"It will keep them working for him, night and day, until they drop from exhaustion or the drug kills them," said Will. "And there is no cure for addiction to it. It is deadly."

The werewolf's yellow-green eyes met his. "This *yin fen*, this silver powder, it is what your friend James Carstairs is addicted to, isn't it? And he's alive."

"Jem survives it because he is a Shadowhunter, and because he uses as little as possible, as infrequently as possible. And even then it will kill him in the end." Will's voice was deadly flat. "As would withdrawing from it."

"Well, well," said the werewolf breezily. "I do hope that the Magister's merrily buying the stuff up doesn't create a shortage, in that case."

Will went white. It was clear the thought hadn't occurred to him. Tessa turned toward Will, but he was already on his feet, moving toward the door. It shut behind him with a bang.

Charlotte frowned. "Lord, he's off to Whitechapel again," she said. "Was that necessary, Woolsey? I think you just terrified the poor boy, and probably for nothing."

"Nothing wrong with a bit of foresight," said Scott. "I took my own brother for granted, until de Quincey killed him."

"De Quincey and the Magister were two of a kind—ruthless," Charlotte said. "If you could help us—"

"The whole situation is certainly beastly," observed Scott. "Unfortunately, lycanthropes who are not members of my pack are not my responsibility."

"If you could simply send out *feelers*, Mr. Scott. Any bit of information about where they are working or what they are doing could be invaluable. The Clave would be grateful."

"Oh, the *Clave*," said Scott, as if deadly bored. "Very well. Now, Charlotte. Let us talk about you."

"Oh, but I am *very* dull," said Charlotte, and she—quite deliberately, Tessa was sure—upset the teapot. It struck the table with a gratifying bang, spilling hot water. Scott jumped up with a cry, flipping his scarf out of the way of danger.

Charlotte rose to her feet, clucking. "Woolsey, dear," she said, placing a hand on his arm, "you've been *such* a help. Let me show you out. There's an antique *keris* that was sent to us from the Bombay Institute I've just been *yearning* to show you. . . ."

11

WILD UNREST

Your woe hath been my anguish; yea, I quail
*   And perish in your perishing unblest.*
And I have searched the highths and depths, the scope
Of all our universe, with desperate hope
*   To find some solace for your wild unrest.*
—James Thomson, "The City of Dreadful Night"

To my dear Mrs. Branwell—

You may be surprised to receive a letter from me so soon after my departure from London, but despite the sleepiness of the countryside, events here have continued apace, and I thought it best to keep you abreast of developments.

The weather continues fine here, allowing me much time for exploring the countryside, especially the area around Ravenscar Manor, which is indeed a fine old building. The Herondale family appears to live alone there: only the father, Edmund; the mother; and the youngest daughter, Cecily, who is near to fifteen and very like her brother in restlessness, in manner, and in looks. I will arrive at how I know all that in a moment.

Ravenscar itself is near a small village. I set myself up at the local inn, the Black Swan, and posed as a gentleman interested in buying property in the area. The locals have been most forthcoming with information, and when they were not, a persuasion spell or two helped them to see the matter from my point of view.

It seems the Herondales mix very little with local society. Despite—or perhaps because of—this tendency, rumor about them abounds. It seems they do not own Ravenscar Manor but are indeed, by way of its custodians, watching over it for its true owner—Axel Mortmain, of course. Mortmain seems no one to these people but a wealthy industrialist who purchased a country manor he rarely visits; I encountered no rumor about any connection of his to the Shades, whose legacy here seems long forgotten. The Herondales themselves are a matter of curious speculation. It is known that they had a child who died, and that Edmund, whom I knew once, turned to drink and to gambling; eventually he gambled away their home in Wales, whereupon, destitute, they were offered the occupation of this house in Yorkshire by its owner. That was two years ago.

I had all this confirmed for me this afternoon when, watching the manor from a distance, I was startled by the appearance of a girl. I knew who she was immediately. I had seen her go in and out of the house, and her resemblance to her brother Will, as I said, is pronounced. She set into me at once, demanding to know why I was spying on her family. She did not seem angry at first but rather hopeful. "Did my brother send you?" she asked. "Have you any word of my brother?"

It was quite heartbreaking, but I know the Law, and could tell her only that her brother was well and wished to know that they were safe. At that she became angry and opined that Will could best ensure his family's safety by returning to them. She also said that it was not the death of her sister (did you know of this sister?) that had undone her father, but rather Will's desertion. I shall leave it up to your discretion whether to pass this on to young Master Herondale, as it seems news that would do more harm than good.

When I spoke to her of Mortmain, she chatted easily to me of him—a family friend, she said, who had stepped in to offer them this home when they had nothing. As she spoke, I began to get a sense of how Mortmain thinks. He knows it is against the Law for Nephilim to interfere with Shadowhunters who have chosen to leave the Clave, and that therefore Ravenscar Manor would be avoided; he knows also that the Herondales' occupancy of it makes the objects in it theirs, and therefore none can be used to track him. And last, he knows that power over the Herondales could translate into power over Will. Does he require power over Will? Not now perhaps, but there may be a time when he desires it, and when he does, it will be to hand. He is a well-prepared man, and men such as that are dangerous.

Were I you, and I am not, I would reassure Master Will that his family is safe and I am watching them; avoid speaking to him of Mortmain until I can gather more information. As far as I can glean from Cecily, the Herondales

do not know where Mortmain is. She said that he was in
Shanghai, and on occasion they receive correspondence from
his company there, all stamped with peculiar stamps. It is
my understanding, however, that the Shanghai Institute
believes him not to be there.

I told Miss Herondale that her brother missed her; it
seemed the least I could do. She appeared gratified. I shall
remain in this area a good while longer, I think; I have
become myself curious as to how the misfortunes of the
Herondales are entwined with Mortmain's plans. There are
still secrets to be unearthed here beneath the peaceful green
of the Yorkshire countryside, and I aim to discover them.
  —Ragnor Fell

Charlotte read the letter over twice, to commit its details
to memory, and then, having folded it small, cast it into the
drawing room fire. She stood wearily, leaning against the
mantel, watching as the flame ate away the paper in lines of
black and gold.

She was not sure if she was surprised, or disturbed, or
simply made bone-weary by the contents of the letter. Trying
to find Mortmain was like reaching to swat a spider, only to
realize that you were helplessly entangled in the sticky strands
of its web. And Will—she hated to speak of this with him.
She looked into the fire with unseeing eyes. Sometimes she
thought Will had been sent to her by the Angel specifically to
try her patience. He was bitter, he had a tongue like the lash of a
whip, and he met her every attempt to show him love and affection with venom or contempt. And still, when she looked at
him, she saw the boy he'd been at twelve, curled in the corner of

his bedroom with his hands over his ears as his parents called his name from the steps below, entreating him to come out, to come back to them.

She had knelt beside him after the Herondales had gone away. She remembered him lifting his face to her—small and white and set, with those blue eyes and dark lashes; he'd been as pretty as a girl then, thin and delicate, before he had thrown himself into Shadowhunter training with such single-mindedness that within two years all that delicacy had been gone, covered over by muscle and scars and Marks. She'd taken his hand then, and he'd let it lie in hers like a dead thing. He'd bitten his lower lip, though he didn't appear to have noticed, and blood covered his chin and dripped onto his shirt. *Charlotte, you'll tell me, won't you? You'll tell me if anything happens to them?*

Will, I can't—

I know the Law. I just want to know if they live. His eyes had pleaded with her. *Charlotte, please...*

"Charlotte?"

She looked up from the fire. Jem stood in the doorway of the drawing room. Charlotte, still half-caught in the web of the past, blinked at him. When he had first arrived from Shanghai, his hair and eyes had been as black as ink. Over time they had silvered, like copper oxidizing to verdigris, as the drugs had worked their way through his blood, changing him, killing him slowly.

"James," she said. "It's late, isn't it?"

"Eleven o'clock." He put his head to the side, studying her. "Are you all right? You look as if your peace of mind has been rather cut up."

"No, I just—" She gestured vaguely. "It is all this business with Mortmain."

"I have a question," Jem said, moving farther into the drawing room and lowering his voice. "Not wholly unrelated. Gabriel said something today, during training—"

"You were there?"

He shook his head. "Sophie told it to me. She didn't like to carry tales, but she was troubled, and I can't blame her. Gabriel asserted that his uncle had committed suicide and that his mother had died of grief because—well, because of your father."

"My father?" Charlotte said blankly.

"Apparently Gabriel's uncle, Silas, committed some infraction of the Law, and your father discovered it. Your father went to the Clave. The uncle killed himself out of shame, and Mrs. Lightwood died of grief. According to Gabriel, 'The Fairchilds don't care about anyone but themselves and the Law.'"

"And you are telling me this because . . . ?"

"I wondered if it was true," said Jem. "And if it is, perhaps it might be useful to communicate to the Consul that Benedict's motive for wanting the Institute is revenge, not selfless desire to see it run better."

"It's not true. It can't be." Charlotte shook her head. "Silas Pangborn did kill himself—because he was in love with his *parabatai*—but not because my father told the Clave about it. The first the Clave knew of it was from Silas's suicide note. In fact, Silas's father asked my father for help in writing Silas's eulogy. Does that sound like a man who blamed my father for his son's death?"

Jem's eyes darkened. "That's interesting."

"Do you think Gabriel's simply being nasty, or do you think his father lied to him to—"

Charlotte never finished her sentence. Jem doubled up suddenly, as if he had been punched in the stomach, with a fit of coughing so severe that his thin shoulders shook. A spray of red blood spattered the sleeve of his jacket as he raised his arm to cover his face.

"Jem—" Charlotte started forward with her arms out, but he staggered upright and away from her, holding his hand out as if to ward her off.

"I'm all right," he gasped. "I'm fine." He wiped blood from his face with the sleeve of his jacket. "Please, Charlotte," he added in a defeated voice as she moved toward him. "Don't."

Charlotte stopped herself, her heart aching. "Is there nothing—"

"You know there's nothing." He lowered his arm, the blood on his sleeve like an accusation, and gave her the sweetest smile. "Dear Charlotte," he said. "You have always been like the best sort of older sister I could have hoped for. You do know that, don't you?"

Charlotte just looked at him, openmouthed. It sounded so much like a good-bye, she could not bear to reply. He turned with his usual light tread and made his way out of the room. She watched him go, telling herself it meant nothing, that he was no worse than he had been, that he still had time. She loved Jem, as she loved Will—as she could not help loving them all—and the thought of losing him shattered her heart. Not only for her own loss, but for Will's. If Jem died, she could not help but feel, he would take all that was still human about Will with him when he went.

* * *

It was nearly midnight when Will returned to the Institute. It had begun raining on him when he'd been halfway down Threadneedle Street. He had ducked under the awning of Dean and Son Publishers to button his jacket and pull his scarf tight, but the rain had already gotten into his mouth—great, icy drops that tasted of charcoal and silt. He had hunched his shoulders against the needlelike sting of it as he'd left the shelter of the awning and headed past the Bank, toward the Institute.

Even after years in London, rain made him think of home. He still remembered the way it had rained in the countryside, in Wales, the green fresh taste of it, the way it felt to roll over and over down a damp hillside, getting grass in your hair and clothes. If he shut his eyes, he could hear his sisters' laughter echo in his ears. *Will, you'll ruin your clothes; Will, Mother will be furious . . .*

Will wondered if you could ever really be a Londoner if you had that in your blood—the memory of great open spaces, the wideness of the sky, the clear air. Not these narrow streets choked with people, the London dust that got everywhere—in your clothes, a thin powdering on your hair and down the back of your neck—the smell of the filthy river.

He had reached Fleet Street. Temple Bar was visible through the mist in the distance; the street was slick with rain. A carriage rattled by as he ducked into an alley between two buildings, the wheels splashing dirty water up against the curb.

He could see the spire of the Institute in the distance now. They had certainly already finished supper, Will thought. Everything would be put away. Bridget would be asleep; he could duck into the kitchen and cobble together a meal from bread and cheese and cold pie. He had been missing a great many meals lately, and if he was truthful with himself, there was only one reason for it: He was avoiding Tessa.

He did not want to avoid her—indeed, he had failed miserably at it that afternoon, accompanying her not just to training but also to the drawing room afterward. Sometimes he wondered if he did these things just to test himself. To see if the feelings had gone. But they had not. When he saw her, he wanted to be with her; when he was with her, he ached to touch her; when he touched even her hand, he wanted to embrace her. He wanted to feel her against him the way he had in the attic. He wanted to know the taste of her skin and the smell of her hair. He wanted to make her laugh. He wanted to sit and listen to her talk about books until his ears fell off. But all these were things he could not want, because they were things he could not have, and wanting what you could not have led to misery and madness.

He had reached home. The door of the Institute swung open under his touch, opening onto a vestibule full of flickering torchlight. He thought of the blur the drugs had brought to him in the den on Whitechapel High Street. A blissful release from wanting or needing anything. He had dreamed he was lying on a hill in Wales with the sky high and blue overhead, and that Tessa had come walking up the hill to him and had sat down beside him. *I love you*, he had said to her, and kissed her, as if it were the most natural thing in the world. *Do you love me?*

She had smiled at him. *You will always come first in my heart*, she had said.

Tell me this is not a dream, he had whispered to her as she'd put her arms around him, and then he'd no longer known what was waking and what was sleeping.

He shrugged out of his coat as he went up the stairs, shaking out his wet hair. Cold water was trickling down the back of his shirt, dampening his spine, making him shiver. The precious packet he had bought from the ifrits was in his trousers pocket. He slipped his hand in, touching his fingers to it, just to be sure.

The corridors burned with low witchlight; he was halfway down the first one when he paused. Tessa's door was here, he knew, across from Jem's. And there, in front of her door, stood Jem—though "stood" was perhaps not the right word. He was pacing back and forth, "wearing a path in the carpet," as Charlotte would have said.

"James," Will said, more surprised than anything else.

Jem's head jerked up, and he backed away from Tessa's door instantly, retreating toward his own. His face went blank. "I suppose I shouldn't be surprised to find you wandering the halls at all hours."

"I think we can agree that the reverse is more out of character," said Will. "Why are you awake? Are you all right?"

Jem cast a last glance at Tessa's door, and then turned to face Will. "I was going to apologize to Tessa," he said. "I think my violin playing was keeping her awake. Where have you been? Assignation with Six-Fingered Nigel again?"

Will grinned, but Jem didn't return the smile. "I've something for you, actually. Come along, let me into your room. I don't want to spend all night standing about in the hall."

After a moment's hesitation Jem shrugged and opened his door. He went in, Will following; Will shut and bolted the door behind them as Jem threw himself into an armchair. There was a fire in the grate, but it had burned down to pale red-gold coals. He looked at Will. "What is it, then—," he began, and bent almost double, convulsed by a hard cough. It passed quickly, before Will could move or speak, but when Jem straightened, and brushed the back of his hand across his mouth, it came away smeared with red. He looked at the blood expressionlessly.

Will felt sick. He approached his *parabatai*, producing a handkerchief, which Jem took, and then the silver powder he'd bought in Whitechapel. "Here," he said, feeling awkward. He hadn't felt awkward around Jem in five years, but there it was. "I went back to Whitechapel, got this for you."

Jem, having cleaned the blood from his hand with Will's handkerchief, took the packet and stared down at the *yin fen*. "I have enough of this," he said. "For at least another month." He looked up then, a sudden flicker in his eyes. "Or did Tessa tell you—"

"Did she tell me what?"

"Nothing. I spilled some of the powder the other day. I managed to retrieve most of it." Jem set the packet down on the table beside him. "This wasn't necessary."

Will sat down on the trunk at the foot of Jem's bed. He hated sitting there—his legs were so long, he always felt like an adult trying to squeeze behind a schoolroom desk—but he wanted to bring his eyes level with Jem's. "Mortmain's minions have been buying up the *yin fen* supply in the East End," he said. "I confirmed it. If you had run out and he was the only one with a supply . . ."

"We would have been put in his power," said Jem. "Unless

you were willing to let me die, of course, which would be the sensible course of action."

"I would *not* be willing." Will sounded sharp. "You're my blood brother. I've sworn an oath not to let any harm come to you—"

"Leaving aside oaths," said Jem, "and power plays, did any of this have to do with me?"

"I don't know what you mean—"

"I had begun to wonder if you were capable of the desire to spare anyone suffering."

Will rocked back slightly, as if Jem had pushed him. "I . . ." He swallowed, looking for the words. It had been so long since he had searched for words that would earn him forgiveness and not hatred, so long since he had sought to present himself in anything but the worst light, that he wondered for a panicked moment if it were even something he was still able to do. "I spoke to Tessa today," he said finally, not noticing that Jem's face paled even more markedly. "She made me understand— that what I did last night was unforgivable. Though," he added hastily, "I do still hope that you will forgive me." *By the Angel, I'm bad at this.*

Jem raised an eyebrow. "For what?"

"I went to that den because I could not stop thinking about my family, and I wanted—I needed—to stop thinking," said Will. "It did not cross my mind that it would look to you as if I were making a mockery out of your sickness. I suppose I am asking your forgiveness for my lack of consideration." His voice dropped. "Everyone makes mistakes, Jem."

"Yes," said Jem. "You just make more of them than most people."

"I—"

"You hurt everyone," said Jem. "Everyone whose life you touch."

"Not you," Will whispered. "I hurt everyone but you. I never meant to hurt you."

Jem put his hands up, pressing his palms against his eyes. "Will—"

"You can't never forgive me," Will said, hearing the panic tinging his own voice. "I'd be—"

"Alone?" Jem lowered his hands, but he was smiling now, crookedly. "And whose fault is that?" He leaned back against the seat, his eyes half-lidded with tiredness. "I would always have forgiven you," he said. "I would have forgiven you if you hadn't apologized. In fact, I wasn't expecting you would. Tessa's influence, I can only guess."

"I am not here at her request. James, you are all the family I have." Will's voice shook. "I would die for you. You know that. I would die *without* you. If it were not for you, I would be dead a hundred times over these past five years. I owe you everything, and if you cannot believe I have empathy, perhaps you might at least believe I know honor—honor, and debt—"

Jem looked actually alarmed now. "Will, your discomposure is greater than my anger warranted. My temper has cooled; you know I have never had much of one."

His tone was soothing, but something in Will could not be soothed. "I went to get you that medicine because I cannot bear the thought of you dying or in pain, certainly not when I could have done something to prevent it. And I did it because I was afraid. If Mortmain came to us and said he was the only one who had the drug that would save your life, you must know

I would give him whatever he wanted so that I could get it for you. I have failed my family before, James. I would not fail you—"

"*Will.*" Jem rose to his feet; he came across the room to Will and knelt down, looking up into his friend's face. "You begin to concern me. Your regret does you admirable credit, but you must know . . ."

Will looked down at him. He remembered Jem as he had been when he had just come from Shanghai, and had seemed to be all great dark eyes in a pinched white face. It had not been easy to make him laugh then, but Will had set himself to trying. "Know what?"

"That I will die," Jem said. His eyes were wide, and fever-bright; there was a trace of blood, still, at the corner of his mouth. The shadows under his eyes were nearly blue.

Will dug his fingers into Jem's wrist, denting the material of his shirt. Jem did not wince.

"You swore to stay with me," he said. "When we made our oath, as *parabatai*. Our souls are knit. We are one person, James."

"We are two people," said Jem. "Two people with a covenant between us."

Will knew he sounded like a child, but he could not help it. "A covenant that says you must not go where I cannot come with you."

"Until death," Jem replied gently. "Those are the words of the oath. 'Until aught but death part thee and me.' Someday, Will, I will go where none can follow me, and I think it will be sooner rather than later. Have you ever asked yourself why I agreed to be your *parabatai*?"

"No better offers forthcoming?" Will tried for humor, but his voice cracked like glass.

"I thought you needed me," Jem said. "There is a wall you have built about yourself, Will, and I have never asked you why. But no one should shoulder every burden alone. I thought you would let me inside if I became your *parabatai*, and then you would have at least someone to lean upon. I did wonder what my death would mean for you. I used to fear it, for your sake. I feared you would be left alone inside that wall. But now . . . something has changed. I do not know why. But I know that it is true."

"That what is true?" Will's fingers were still digging into Jem's wrist.

"That the wall is coming down."

Tessa could not get to sleep. She lay unmoving on her back, staring up at the ceiling. There was a crack across the plaster of it that looked sometimes like a cloud and sometimes like a razor, depending on the shift of the candlelight.

Dinner had been tense. Apparently Gabriel had told Charlotte that he refused to return and partake in the training anymore, so it was going to be only Gideon working with her and Sophie from now on. Gabriel had refused to say why, but it was clear Charlotte blamed Will; Tessa, seeing how exhausted Charlotte looked at the prospect of more conflict with Benedict, had felt heavy with guilt for having brought Will with her to the training, and for having laughed at Gabriel.

It did not help that Jem had not been at dinner. She had wanted so badly to speak to him today. After he had avoided her eyes at breakfast and then been "ill" at dinner, panic had twisted her stomach. Was he horrified by what had happened between them the night before—or worse, sickened? Maybe in his secret heart of hearts, he felt as Will did, that warlocks were beneath him. Or maybe it had nothing to do with what she was. Maybe he was simply repelled by her wantonness; she had welcomed his embraces, not pushed him away, and hadn't Aunt Harriet always said that men were weak where desire was concerned, and that women were the ones who had to exercise restraint?

She hadn't exercised much last night. She remembered lying beside Jem, his gentle hands on her. She knew with a painful inner honesty that if things had continued, she would have done whatever he wanted. Even now, thinking about it, her body felt hot and restless; she shifted in bed, punching one of the pillows. If she had destroyed the closeness she shared with Jem by allowing what had happened last night, she would never forgive herself.

She was about to bury her face in the pillow, when she heard the noise. A soft rapping at the door. She froze. It came again, insistently. *Jem.* Her hands shaking, she leaped from the bed, ran to the door, and threw it open.

On the threshold stood Sophie. She wore her black house-maid's dress, but her white cap had come askew and her dark curls were tumbling down. Her face was very white and there was a spot of blood on her collar; she looked horrified and almost sick.

"Sophie." Tessa's voice betrayed her surprise. "Are you all right?"

Sophie looked around fearfully. "May I come in, miss?"

Tessa nodded and held the door open for her. When they

were both safely inside, she bolted it and sat down on the edge of her bed, apprehension like a lead weight in her chest. Sophie remained standing, twisting her hands in front of her.

"Sophie, please, what is it?"

"It's Miss Jessamine," Sophie burst out.

"What about Jessamine?"

"She . . . It's just to say, I've seen her . . ." She broke off, looking wretched. "She's been slipping away in the nights, miss."

"Has she? I saw her last night, in the corridor, dressed as a boy and looking quite furtive. . . ."

Sophie looked relieved. She didn't like Jessamine, Tessa knew that well enough, but she was a well-trained maid, and a well-trained maid did not tattle on her mistress. "Yes," she said eagerly. "I've been noticing it for days now. Her bed sometimes not slept in at all, mud on the rugs in the mornings when it weren't there the night before. I would've told Mrs. Branwell, but she's had so dreadful much on her mind, I couldn't bear to."

"So why are you telling me?" Tessa asked. "It sounds as if Jessamine's found herself a suitor. I can't say I approve of her behavior, but"—she swallowed, thinking of her own behavior the night before—"neither of us is responsible for it. And perhaps there is some harmless explanation. . . ."

"Oh, but, miss." Sophie plunged her hand into the pocket of her dress and drew it out with a stiff cream-colored card clamped between her fingers. "Tonight I found this. In the pocket of her new velvet jacket. You know, the one with the ecru stripe."

Tessa did not care about the ecru stripe. Her eyes were fixed on the card. Slowly she reached out and took it, turning it over in her hand. It was an invitation to a ball.

July 20, 1878

Mr. BENEDICT LIGHTWOOD
presents his compliments
to MISS JESSAMINE LOVELACE,
and requests the honor of her company
at a masquerade ball given on Tuesday next,
the 27th of July. RSVP.

The invitation went on to give details of the address and the time the ball would begin, but it was what was written on the back of the invitation that froze Tessa's blood. In a casual hand, as familiar to her as her own, were scrawled the words: *My Jessie. My very heart is bursting at the thought of seeing you tomorrow night at the "great affair." However great it may be, I shall have eyes for nothing and no one but you. Do wear the white dress, darling, as you know how I like it—"in gloss of satin and glimmer of pearls," as the poet said. Yours always, N.G.*

"Nate," Tessa said numbly, staring down at the letter. "*Nate* wrote this. And quoted *Tennyson*."

Sophie drew her breath in sharply. "I feared—but I thought it couldn't be. Not after all he did."

"I know my brother's handwriting." Tessa's voice was grim. "He's planning to meet her tonight at this—this secret ball. Sophie, where is Jessamine? I must speak to her this instant."

Sophie's hands began to twist more rapidly. "See, that's the thing, miss—"

"Oh, God, has she gone already? We'll have to get Charlotte. I don't see another way—"

"She hasn't gone. She's in her room," Sophie interrupted.

"So she doesn't know you found this?" Tessa flapped the card.

Sophie swallowed visibly. "I—she found me with it in my hand, miss. I tried to hide it, but she'd already seen it. She had such a menacing look on her face when she came reaching for it, I couldn't help myself. All the training sessions I've done with Master Gideon, they just took over and, well—"

"Well, *what?* Sophie—"

"I hit her on the head with a mirror," Sophie said hopelessly. "One of those silver-backed ones, so it was quite heavy. She went down just like a stone, miss. So I . . . I tied her to the bed and I came looking for you."

"Let me see if I have this quite correct," said Tessa after a pause. "Jessamine found you with the invitation in your hand, so you struck her over the head with a mirror and tied her to her bed?"

Sophie nodded.

"Good Lord," said Tessa. "Sophie, we're going to need to fetch someone. This ball cannot remain a secret, and Jessamine . . ."

"Not Mrs. Branwell," Sophie moaned. "She'll sack me. She'll have to."

"Jem—"

"No!" Sophie's hand flew to her collar, where the spot of blood was. Jessamine's blood, Tessa realized with a jolt. "I couldn't bear if he thought I could do such a thing—he's so gentle. Please don't make me tell him, miss."

Of course, Tessa thought. Sophie loved Jem. In all the mess of the past few days, she had nearly forgotten. A wave of shame swamped her as she thought of the night before; she fought it back, and said determinedly, "There is only one person, then, Sophie, whom we can go to. You do understand that?"

"Master Will," said Sophie with loathing, and sighed. "Very well, miss. I suppose I don't care what he thinks of me."

Tessa rose and reached for her dressing gown, and wrapped it around herself. "Look upon the bright side, Sophie. At least Will won't be shocked. I doubt Jessamine's the first unconscious female he's ever dealt with, or that she'll be the last either."

Tessa had been wrong about at least one thing: Will *was* shocked.

"*Sophie* did this?" he said, not for the first time. They were standing at the foot of Jessamine's bed. She lay flung upon it, her chest rising and falling slowly like the famous Sleeping Beauty waxwork of Madame du Barry. Her fair hair was scattered on the pillow, and a large, bloody welt ran across her forehead. Each of her wrists was tied to a post of the bed. "*Our* Sophie?"

Tessa glanced over at Sophie, who was sitting in a chair by the door. Her head was down, and she was staring at her hands. She studiously avoided looking at Tessa or Will.

"Yes," Tessa said, "and do stop repeating it."

"I think I may be in love with you, Sophie," said Will. "Marriage could be on the cards."

Sophie whimpered.

"Stop it," Tessa hissed. "I think you're frightening the poor girl more than she's already frightened."

"What's to be frightened of? Jessamine? It looks like Sophie won that little altercation easily." Will was having trouble repressing a grin. "Sophie, my dear, there is nothing to worry about. Many's the time I have wanted to hit Jessamine over the head myself. No one could blame you."

"She's afraid Charlotte will sack her," said Tessa.

"For hitting Jessamine?" Will relented. "Tess, if this invitation is what it looks like, and Jessamine is truly meeting your brother in secret, she may have betrayed us all. Not to mention, what is Benedict Lightwood doing, throwing parties that none of us know about? Parties to which Nate is invited? What Sophie did was heroic. Charlotte will thank her."

At that, Sophie lifted her head. "Do you think so?"

"I know it," said Will. For a moment he and Sophie looked at each other steadily across the room. Sophie looked away first, but if Tessa was not mistaken, there had been—for the first time—no dislike in her eyes when she'd gazed at Will.

From his belt Will drew his stele. He sat down on the bed beside Jessamine and gently brushed aside her hair. Tessa bit her lip, restraining the impulse to ask him what he was doing.

He laid his stele against Jessamine's throat and quickly sketched two runes. "An *iratze*," he said, without Tessa's having to ask. "That is, a healing rune, and a Sleep Now rune. This should keep her quiet at least until morning. Your skill with a hand mirror is to be admired, Sophie, but your knot making could be improved."

Sophie muttered something under her breath in response. The suspension of her dislike of Will appeared to be over.

"The question," said Will, "is what to do now."

"We must tell Charlotte—"

"No," Will said firmly. "We must not."

Tessa looked at him in astonishment. "Why not?"

"Two reasons," said Will. "First, she would be duty-bound

to tell the Clave, and if Benedict Lightwood is hosting this ball, I would make a fair guess that some of his followers will be there. But they might not all be. If the Clave is warned, they may be able to get word to him before anyone can arrive to observe what is truly going on. Second, the ball began an hour ago. We do not know when Nate will arrive, seeking Jessamine, and if he does not see her, he may well depart. He is the best connection to Mortmain we have. We do not have any time to lose or waste, and waking Charlotte to tell her of this will do both."

"Jem, then?"

Something flickered in Will's eyes. "No. Not tonight. Jem is not well enough, but he will say he is. After last night I owe it to him to leave him out of this."

Tessa looked at him hard. "Then what do you propose to do?"

Will's mouth quirked up at both corners. "Miss Gray," he said, "would you be amenable to attending a ball with me?"

"Do you remember the *last* party we went to?" Tessa inquired.

Will's smile remained. He had that look of heightened intensity that he wore when he was strategizing a plan. "Don't tell me that you weren't thinking the same thing I was, Tessa."

Tessa sighed. "Yes," she said. "I shall Change into Jessamine and go in her place. It is the only plan that makes sense." She turned to Sophie. "Do you know the dress Nate spoke of? A white dress of Jessamine's?"

Sophie nodded.

"Get it brushed and ready to be worn," said Tessa. "You will have to do my hair as well, Sophie. Are you calm enough?"

"Yes, miss." Sophie got to her feet and scurried across the room to the wardrobe, which she threw open. Will was still looking at Tessa; his smile widened.

Tessa lowered her voice. "Will, has it crossed your mind that Mortmain might be there?"

The smile vanished from Will's face. "You will go nowhere near him if he is."

"You cannot tell me what to do."

Will frowned. He was not reacting at all in the way Tessa felt he should. When Capitola in *The Hidden Hand* dressed up as a boy and took on the marauding Black Donald to prove her bravery, no one snapped at *her*.

"Your power is impressive, Tessa, but you are in no position to capture a powerful adult magic user like Mortmain. You will leave that to me," he said.

She scowled at him. "And how do *you* plan not to be recognized at this ball? Benedict knows your face, as do—"

Will seized the invitation out of her hand and waved it at her. "It's a *masked* ball."

"And I suppose you just happen to have a mask."

"As a matter of fact I do," said Will. "Our last Christmas party was themed along the lines of the Venetian Carnevale." He smirked. "Tell her, Sophie."

Sophie, who was busy with what looked like a concoction of spiderwebs and moonbeams on the brushing tray, sighed. "It's true, miss. And you let him deal with Mortmain, you hear? It's too dangerous otherwise. And you'll be all the way in Chiswick!"

Will looked at Tessa with triumph. "If even Sophie agrees with me, you can't very well say no."

"I could," Tessa said mutinously, "but I won't. Very well. But you must stay out of Nate's way while I speak with him. He isn't an idiot; if he sees us together, he's quite capable of putting two and two together. I get no sense from his note that he expects Jessamine to be accompanied."

"I get no sense from his note at all," said Will, bounding to his feet, "except that he can quote Tennyson's lesser poetry. Sophie, how quickly can you have Tessa ready?"

"Half an hour," said Sophie, not looking up from the dress.

"Meet me in the courtyard in half an hour, then," said Will. "I'll wake Cyril. And be prepared to swoon at my finery."

The night was a cool one, and Tessa shivered as she passed through the doors of the Institute and stood at the head of the steps outside. This was where she had sat, she thought, that night she and Jem had walked to Blackfriars Bridge together, the night the clockwork creatures had attacked them. It was a clearer night tonight, despite the day of rain; the moon chased stray wisps of cloud across an otherwise unmarked black sky.

The carriage was there, at the foot of the steps, Will waiting in front of it. He glanced up as the doors of the Institute closed behind her. For a moment they simply stood and looked at each other. Tessa knew what he was seeing—she had seen it herself, in the mirror in Jessamine's room. She was Jessamine down to the last inch, clothed in a delicate ivory silk dress. It was low-cut, revealing a great deal of Jessamine's white bosom, with a silk ribbon at the collar to emphasize the shape of her throat. The sleeves were short, leaving her arms vulnerable to the night air. Even if the neckline hadn't been so low, Tessa would have felt naked without her angel, but she couldn't wear it:

Nate would have been sure to notice it. The skirt, with a water-fall train, belled out behind her from a laced, slender waist; her hair was dressed high, with a length of pearls held in place by pearl pins, and she wore a gold domino half mask that set off Jessamine's pale, fair hair to perfection. *I look so delicate,* she had thought with detachment, staring at the mirror's silvered surface as Sophie had fussed about her. *Like a faerie princess.* It was easy to think such thoughts when the reflection was not truly your own.

But Will—Will. He had said she should be ready to swoon at his finery, and she had rolled her eyes, but in his black and white evening dress, he looked more beautiful than she had imagined. The stark and simple colors brought out the angular perfection of his features. His dark hair tumbled over a black half mask that emphasized the blueness of the eyes behind it. She felt her heart contract, and hated herself instantly for it. She looked away from him, at Cyril, in the driver's seat of the carriage. His eyes narrowed in confusion as he saw her; he looked from her to Will, and back again, and shrugged. Tessa wondered what on earth Will had told him they were doing to explain the fact that he was taking Jessamine to Chiswick in the middle of the night. It must have been quite a story.

"Ah," was all Will said as she descended the steps and drew her wrap around herself. She hoped he would put down to the cold the involuntary shiver that went over her as he took her hand. "I see now why your brother quoted that execrable poetry. You are meant to *be* Maud, aren't you? 'Queen rose of the rosebud garden of girls'?"

"You know," Tessa said as he helped her up into the carriage, "I don't care for that poem either."

He swung himself up after her and slammed the carriage door shut. "Jessamine adores it."

The carriage began to rumble across the cobblestones, and through the open doors of the gate. Tessa found that her heart was beating very fast. Fear of being caught by Charlotte and Henry, she told herself. Nothing to do with being alone with Will in the carriage. "I am not Jessamine."

He looked at her levelly. There was something in his eyes, a sort of quizzical admiration; she wondered if it was simply admiration of Jessamine's looks. "No," he said. "No, even though you are the perfect picture of Jessamine, I can see Tessa through it somehow—as if, if I were to scrape away a layer of paint, there would be my Tessa underneath."

"I am not *your* Tessa either."

The light sparkling in his eyes dimmed. "Fair enough," he said. "I suppose you are not. What is it like, being Jessamine, then? Can you sense her thoughts? Read what she feels?"

Tessa swallowed, and touched the velvet curtain of the carriage with a gloved hand. Outside she could see the gaslights going by in a yellow blur; two children were slumped in a doorway, leaning against each other, asleep. Temple Bar flew by overhead. She said, "I tried. Upstairs in her bedroom. But there's something wrong. I—I couldn't feel anything from her."

"Well, I suppose it's hard to meddle in someone's brains if they've got no brains to start with."

Tessa made a face. "Be flippant about it if you like, but there is something wrong with Jessamine. Trying to touch her mind is like trying to touch—a nest of snakes, or a poisonous cloud. I can feel a little of her emotions. A great deal of rage, and longing, and bitterness. But I cannot pick out the individual thoughts among them. It is like trying to hold water."

"That's curious. Have you ever come across anything like it before?"

Tessa shook her head. "It concerns me. I am afraid Nate will expect me to know something and I will not know it or have the right answer."

Will leaned forward. On wet days, which was nearly every day, his normally straight dark hair would begin to curl. There was something about the vulnerable curling of his damp hair against his temples that made her heart ache. "You are a good actress, and you know your brother," he said. "I have every confidence in you."

She looked at him in surprise. "You do?"

"And," he went on without answering her question, "in the event that something goes awry, I will be there. Even if you don't see me, Tess, I'll be there. Remember that."

"All right." She cocked her head to the side. "Will?"

"Yes?"

"There was a third reason you didn't want to wake up Charlotte and tell her what we were doing, wasn't there?"

He narrowed his blue eyes at her. "And what's that?"

"Because you do not yet know if this is simply a foolish flirtation on Jessamine's part, or something deeper and darker. A true connection to my brother and to Mortmain. And you know that if it is the second, it will break Charlotte's heart."

A muscle jumped at the corner of his mouth. "And what do I care if it does? If she is foolish enough to attach herself to Jessamine—"

"You care," said Tessa. "You are no inhuman block of ice,

Will. I have seen you with Jem—I saw you when you looked at Cecily. And you had another sister, didn't you?"

He looked at her sharply. "What makes you think I had—I have—more than one sister?"

"Jem said he thought your sister was dead," she said. "And you said, 'My sister is dead.' But Cecily is clearly very much alive. Which made me think you had a sister who had died. One that wasn't Cecily."

Will let out a long, slow breath. "You're clever."

"But am I clever and right, or clever and wrong?"

Will looked as if he were glad for the mask that hid his expression. "Ella," he said. "Two years older than I. And Cecily, three years younger. My sisters."

"And Ella . . ."

Will looked away, but not before she saw the pain in his eyes. So Ella was dead.

"What was she like?" Tessa asked, remembering how grateful she had been when Jem had asked that of her, about Nate. "Ella? And Cecily, what kind of girl is she?"

"Ella was protective," said Will. "Like a mother. She would have done anything for me. And Cecily was a little mad creature. She was only nine when I left. I can't say if she's still the same, but she was—like Cathy in *Wuthering Heights*. She was afraid of nothing and demanded everything. She could fight like a devil and swear like a Billingsgate fishwife." There was amusement in his voice, and admiration, and . . . love. She had never heard him talk about anyone that way, except perhaps Jem.

"If I might ask—," she began.

Will sighed. "You know you'll ask whether I say it's all right or not."

"You have a younger sister of your own," she said. "So what exactly did you do to *Gabriel's* sister to make him hate you so?"

He straightened. "Are you serious?"

"Yes," she said. "I am forced to spend a great deal of time with the Lightwoods, and Gabriel clearly despises you. And you did break his arm. It would ease my mind if I knew why."

Shaking his head, Will raked his fingers through his hair. "Dear God," he said. "Their sister—her name is Tatiana, by the way; she was named after her mother's dear friend, who was Russian—was twelve years old, I think."

"*Twelve?*" Tessa was horrified.

Will exhaled. "I see you have already decided for yourself what happened," he said. "Would it ease your mind further to know that I myself was twelve? Tatiana, she . . . fancied herself in love with me. In that way that little girls do. She would follow me around and giggle and duck behind pillars to stare at me."

"One does silly things when one is twelve."

"It was the first Christmas party at the Institute that I attended," he said. "The Lightwoods were there in all their finery. Tatiana in silver hair ribbons. She had a little book she carried around with her everywhere. She must have dropped it that night. I found it shoved down the back of one of the chaise longues. It was her diary. Filled with poems about me—the color of my eyes, the wedding we would have. She had written 'Tatiana Herondale' all over it."

"That sounds rather adorable."

"I had been in the drawing room, but I came back into the ballroom with the diary. Elise Penhallow had just finished playing the spinet. I got up beside her and commenced reading from Tatiana's diary."

"Oh, Will—you didn't!"

"I did," he said. "She had rhymed 'William' with 'million,' as in 'You will never know, sweet William / How many are the million / ways in which I love you.' It had to be stopped."

"What happened?"

"Oh, Tatiana ran out of the room in tears, and Gabriel leaped onto the stage and attempted to strangle me. Gideon simply stood there with his arms crossed. You'll notice that's all he ever does."

"I suppose Gabriel didn't succeed," said Tessa. "In strangling you, I mean."

"Not before I broke his arm," said Will with relish. "So there you are. That's why he hates me. I humiliated his sister in public, and what he won't mention is that I humiliated him, too. He thought he could best me easily. I'd had little formal training, and I'd heard him call me 'very nearly a mundane' behind my back. Instead I beat him hollow—snapped his arm, in fact. It was certainly a more pleasant sound than Elise banging away on the spinet."

Tessa rubbed her gloved hands together to warm them, and sighed. She wasn't sure what to think. It was hardly the story of seduction and betrayal she had expected, but neither did it show Will in an admirable light.

"Sophie says she's married now," she said. "Tatiana. She's just getting back from traveling the Continent with her new husband."

"I am sure she is as dull and stupid now as she was then." Will sounded as if he might fall asleep. He thumbed the curtain closed, and they were in darkness. Tessa could hear his breath, feel the warmth of him sitting across from her. She could see why a proper young lady would never ride in a carriage with a gentleman not related to her. There was something oddly intimate about it. Of course, she had broken the rules for proper young ladies what felt like long ago, now.

"Will," she said again.

"The lady has another question. I can hear it in her tone. Will you never have done asking questions, Tess?"

"Not until I get all the answers I want," she said. "Will, if warlocks are made by having one demon parent and one human parent, what happens if one of those parents is a Shadowhunter?"

"A Shadowhunter would never allow that to happen," said Will flatly.

"But in the *Codex* it says that most warlocks are the result of—of a violation," Tessa said, her voice hitching on the ugly word, "or shape-changer demons taking on the form of a loved one and completing the seduction by a trick. Jem told me Shadowhunter blood is always dominant. The *Codex* says the offspring of Shadowhunters and werewolves, or faeries, are always Shadowhunters. So could not the angel blood in a Shadowhunter cancel out that which was demonic, and produce—"

"What it produces is nothing." Will tugged at the window curtain. "The child would be born dead. They always are. Stillborn, I mean. The offspring of a demon and a Shadowhunter parent is death." In the little light he looked at her. "Why do you want to know these things?"

"I want to know what I am," she said. "I believe I am some . . . combination that has not been seen before. Part faerie, or part—"

"Have you ever thought of transforming yourself into one of your parents?" Will asked. "Your mother, or father? It would give you access to their memories, wouldn't it?"

"I have thought of it. Of course I have. But I have nothing of my father's or mother's. Everything that was packed in my trunks for the voyage here was discarded by the Dark Sisters."

"What about your angel necklace?" Will asked. "Wasn't that your mother's?"

Tessa shook her head. "I tried. I—I could reach nothing of her in it. It has been mine so long, I think, that what made it hers has evaporated, like water."

Will's eyes gleamed in the shadows. "Perhaps you are a clockwork girl. Perhaps Mortmain's warlock father built you, and now Mortmain seeks the secret of how to create such a perfect facsimile of life when all he can build are hideous monstrosities. Perhaps all that beats beneath your chest is a heart made of metal."

Tessa drew in a breath, feeling momentarily dizzy. His soft voice was so convincing, and yet— "No," she said sharply. "You forget, I remember my childhood. Mechanical creatures do not change or grow. Nor would that explain my ability."

"I know," said Will with a grin that flashed white in the darkness. "I only wanted to see if I could convince *you*."

Tessa looked at him steadily. "I am not the one who has no heart."

It was too dark in the carriage for her to tell, but she sensed that he flushed, darkly. Before he could say anything in response, the wheels came to a jerking halt. They had arrived.

12

MASQUERADE

So now I have sworn to bury
All this dead body of hate,
I feel so free and so clear
By the loss of that dead weight,
That I should grow light-headed, I fear,
Fantastically merry;
But that her brother comes, like a blight
On my fresh hope, to the Hall to-night.
—Alfred, Lord Tennyson, "Maud"

Cyril had paused the carriage outside the gates of the property, under the shade of a leafy oak tree. The Lightwoods' country house in Chiswick, just outside London proper, was massive, built in the Palladian style, with soaring pillars and multiple staircases. The radiance of the moon made everything pearlescent like the inside of an oyster shell. The stone of the house seemed to gleam silver, while the gate that ran around the property had the sheen of black oil. None of the lights in the house seemed to be illuminated—the place was as dark as pitch and grave-silent, the vast grounds stretching all around it, down to the edge of a meander in the Thames River, unlit and deserted. Tessa began to wonder if they had made a mistake in coming here.

As Will left the carriage, helping her down after him, his head turned, his fine mouth hardening. "Do you smell that? Demonic witchcraft. Its stink is on the air."

Tessa made a face. She could smell nothing unusual—in fact, this far out of the city center, the air seemed cleaner than it had near the Institute. She could smell wet leaves and dirt. She looked over at Will, his face raised to the moonlight, and wondered what weapons lay concealed under his closely fitted frock coat. His hands were sheathed in white gloves, his starched shirtfront immaculate. With the mask, he could have been an illustration of a handsome highwayman in a penny dreadful.

Tessa bit her lip. "Are you certain? The house looks deadly quiet. As if no one were home. Could we be wrong?"

He shook his head. "There is powerful magic at work here. Something stronger than a glamour. A true ward. Someone very much does not want us to know what is happening here tonight." He glanced down at the invitation in her hand, shrugged, and went up to the gate. There was a bell there, and he rang it, the noise jangling Tessa's already stretched nerves. She glared at him. He grinned. "*Caelum denique*, angel," he said, and melted away into the shadows, just as the gate before her opened.

A hooded figure stood before her. Her first thought was of the Silent Brothers, but their robes were the color of parchment, and the figure that stood before her was robed in the color of black smoke. The hood hid its face completely. Wordlessly she held out her invitation.

The hand that took it from her was gloved. For a moment the hidden face regarded the invitation. Tessa could not help but fidget. In any ordinary circumstance, a young lady attending a ball alone would be so improper as to be scandalous. But this was no ordinary circumstance. At last, a voice issued from beneath the hood:

"Welcome, Miss Lovelace."

It was a gritty voice, a voice like skin being scraped over a rough, tearing surface. Tessa's spine prickled, and she was glad she could not see beneath the hood. The figure returned the invitation to her and stepped back, gesturing her inside; she followed, forcing herself not to look around to see if Will was following.

She was led around the side of the house, down a narrow garden path. The gardens extended for a good distance out around the house, silvery-green in the moonlight. There was a circular black ornamental pond, with a white marble bench beside it, and low hedges, carefully clipped, running alongside neat paths. The path she was on ended at a tall and narrow entrance set into the house's side. A strange symbol was carved into the door. It seemed to shift and change as Tessa looked at it, making her eyes hurt. She looked away as her hooded companion opened the door and gestured for her to go inside.

She entered the house, and the door slammed behind her. She turned just as it shut, catching a glimpse, she thought, of the face beneath the hood. She thought she had seen something very like a cluster of red eyes in the center of a dark oval, like the eyes of a spider. She caught her breath as the door clicked shut and she was plunged into darkness.

As she reached, blindly, for the handle of the door, light sprang up all around her. She was standing at the foot of a long, narrow staircase that led upward. Torches burning with a greenish flame—not witchlight—ran up the sides of the stairs.

At the top of the stairs was a door. Another symbol was painted on this one. Tessa felt her mouth go even dryer. It was the *ouroboros*, the double serpent. The symbol of the Pandemonium Club.

For a moment she felt frozen with fear. The symbol brought bleak memories rushing back: the Dark House; the Sisters torturing her, trying to force her to Change; Nate's betrayal. She wondered what Will had said to her in Latin before he had vanished. "Courage," no doubt, or some variant of that. She thought of Jane Eyre, bravely facing down the angry Mr. Rochester; Catherine Earnshaw, who when mauled by a savage dog "did not yell out—no! she would have scorned to do it." And lastly she thought of Boadicea, who Will had told her was "braver than any man."

It's just a ball, Tessa, she told herself, and reached for the knob. *Just a party.*

She had never been to a ball before, of course. She knew only a little of what to expect, and all of that was from books. In Jane Austen's books the characters were constantly waiting for there to be a ball, or arranging a ball, and often an entire village seemed to be involved in the planning and location of the ball. Whereas in other books, such as *Vanity Fair*, they were grand backdrops against which scheming and plotting occurred. She knew that there would be a dressing room for the ladies, where she could leave her shawl, and one for the men, where they could safely dispose of hats, overcoats, and walking sticks. There ought to be a dance card for her, where the names of the men who had asked her to dance could be marked down. It was rude to dance more than a few dances in a row with the same gentleman. There should be a grand, beautifully decorated ballroom, and a smaller refreshment room, where there would be iced drinks and sandwiches and biscuits and tipsy cake . . .

But it was not quite like that. As the door closed behind her, Tessa found no servants hurrying to greet her, to guide her to the ladies' dressing room and offer to take her shawl or assist her with a missing button. Instead a wash of noise and music and light struck her like a wave. She stood at the entrance to a room so grand, it was hard to believe that it fit somehow into the Lightwoods' house. A great crystal chandelier hung from the ceiling; it was only after looking at it for several moments that Tessa realized it was shaped like a spider, with eight dangling "legs," each of which held a collection of massive tapers. The walls, what she could see of them, were a very dark blue, and running all along the side that faced the river were French windows, some propped open to catch the breeze, for the room, despite the cool weather outside, was stifling. Beyond the windows were curved stone balconies, looking out over a view of the city. The walls were largely obscured by great swathes of shimmering fabric, loops and whorls of it hanging over the windows and moving in the faint breeze. The fabric was figured with all manner of patterns, woven in gold; the same shimmering, shifting patterns that had hurt Tessa's eyes downstairs.

The room was crowded with people. Well, not quite *people*,

exactly. The majority looked human enough. She caught sight also of the dead white faces of vampires, and a few of the violet and red-hued ifrits, all dressed in the height of fashion. Most, though not all, of the attendees wore masks—elaborate contraptions of gold and black, beaked Plague Doctor masks with tiny spectacles, red devil masks complete with horns. Some were bare-faced, though, including a group of women whose hair was muted tints of lavender, green, and violet. Tessa did not think they were dyes, either, and they wore their hair loose, like nymphs in paintings. Their clothes were scandalously loose as well. They were clearly uncorseted, dressed in flowing fabrics of velvet, tulle, and satin.

In and among the human guests darted figures of all sizes and shapes. There was a man, far too tall and thin to *be* a man, dressed in topcoat and tails, looming over a young woman in a green cloak whose red hair shone like a copper penny. Creatures that looked like great dogs roamed among the guests, their yellow eyes wide and watchful. They had rows of spikes along their backs, like drawings of exotic animals she had seen in books. A dozen or so little goblin creatures screeched and chattered to one another in an incomprehensible language. They appeared to be fighting over some foodstuff—what looked like a torn-apart frog. Tessa swallowed down bile and turned—

And saw them, where she had not before. Her mind had perhaps dismissed them as decorations, suits of armor, but they were not. Automatons lined the walls, silent and motionless. They were human in shape, like the coachman who had belonged to the Dark Sisters, and wore the livery of the Lightwood household, each with a patterned *ouroboros* over its left breast. Their faces were blank and featureless, like children's sketches that had not been filled in.

Someone caught her by the shoulders. Her heart gave a great leap of fear— *She had been discovered!* As every muscle in her body tightened, a light, familiar voice said:

"I thought you'd never get here, Jessie dear."

She turned and looked up into the face of her brother.

The last time Tessa had seen Nate, he had been bruised and bloodied, snarling at her in a corridor of the Institute, a knife in his hand. He had been a terrible mixture of frightening and pathetic and horrifying all at once.

This Nate was quite different. He smiled down at her— Jessamine was so much shorter than she was; it was odd not to reach to her brother's chin, but rather to his chest—with vivid blue eyes. His fair hair was brushed and clean, his skin unmarked by bruises. He wore an elegant dress coat and a black shirtfront that set off his fair good looks. His gloves were spotlessly white.

This was Nate as he had always dreamed of being—rich-looking, elegant, and sophisticated. A sense of contentment oozed from him—less contentment, Tessa had to admit, than self-satisfaction. He looked like Church did after he had killed a mouse.

Nate chuckled. "What is it, Jess? You look as if you've seen a ghost."

I have. The ghost of the brother I once cared about. Tessa reached for Jessamine, for the imprint of Jessamine in her mind. Again it felt as if she were passing her hands through poisonous water, unable to grasp anything solid. "I—a sudden fear came over me, that you would not be here," she said.

This time his laugh was tender. "And miss a chance to see you? Don't be a foolish girl." He glanced around, smiling. "Lightwood should lay himself out to impress the Magister more often." He held out a hand to her. "Would you do me the honor of favoring me with a dance, Jessie?"

Jessie. Not "Miss Lovelace." Any doubt Tessa might have had that their attachment was serious indeed was gone. She forced her lips into a smile. "Of course."

The orchestra—a collection of small purple-skinned men dressed in silvery netting—was playing a waltz. Nate took her hand and drew her out onto the floor.

Thank God, Tessa thought. Thank God she'd had years of her brother swinging her around the living room of their tiny flat in New York. She knew exactly how he danced, how to fit her movements to his, even in this smaller, unfamiliar body. Of course, he had never looked down at her like this—tenderly, with lips slightly parted. Dear God, what if he kissed her? She had not thought of the possibility. She would be sick all over his shoes if he did. Oh, God, she prayed. Let him not try.

She spoke rapidly, "I had dreadful trouble sneaking out of the Institute tonight," she said. "That little wretch Sophie nearly found the invitation."

Nate's grip tightened on her. "But she didn't, did she?"

There was a warning in his voice. Tessa sensed she was already close to a serious gaffe. She tried a quick glance around the room— Oh, where was Will? What had he said? Even if you don't see me, I'll be there? But she had never felt so much on her own.

With a deep breath she tossed her head in her best imitation of Jessamine. "Do you take me for a fool? Of course not. I rapped her skinny wrist with my mirror, and she dropped it immediately. Besides, she probably can't even read."

"Truly," said Nate, relaxing visibly, "they could have found you a lady's maid who more befits a lady. One who speaks French, can sew . . ."

"Sophie can sew," Tessa said automatically, and could have slapped herself. "Passably," she amended, and batted her eyelashes up at Nate. "And how have you been keeping since the last time we saw each other?" *Not that I have the slightest idea when that might have been.*

"Very well. The Magister continues to favor me."

"He is wise," Tessa breathed. "He recognizes an invaluable treasure when he sees one."

Nate touched her face lightly with a gloved hand. Tessa willed herself not to stiffen. "All down to you, my darling. My veritable little mine of information." He moved closer to her. "I see you wore the dress I asked you to," he whispered. "Ever since you described how you wore it to your last Christmas ball, I have yearned to see you in it. And may I say that you dazzle the eyes?"

Tessa's stomach felt as if it were trying to force its way up into her throat. Her eyes darted around the room again. With a lurch of recognition, she saw Gideon Lightwood, cutting a fine figure in his evening dress, though he stood stiffly against one of the walls as if plastered there. Only his eyes moved around the room. Gabriel was wandering to and fro, a glass of what looked like lemonade in his hand, his eyes glowing with curiosity. She saw him go up to one of the girls with long lavender hair and begin a conversation. *So much for any hope that the boys did not know what their father was up to*, she thought, glancing away from Gabriel in irritation. And then she saw Will.

He was leaning against the wall opposite her, between two empty chairs. Despite his mask she felt as if she could see directly into his eyes. As if he were standing close enough to touch. She would have half-expected him to look amused at her predicament, but he did not; he looked tense, and furious, and . . .

"God, I'm jealous of every other man who looks at you," Nate said. "You should be looked at only by me."

Good Lord, Tessa thought. Did this line of talk really work on most women? If her brother had come to her with the aim of asking her advice on these pearls, she would have told him straight off that he sounded like an idiot. Though perhaps she only thought he sounded like an idiot because he was her brother. And despicable. *Information*, she thought. *I must get information and then get away from him, before I really am sick.*

She looked for Will again, but he was gone, as if he had never been there. Still, she believed him now that he was *somewhere*, watching her, even if she couldn't see him. She plucked up her nerve, and said, "Really, Nate? Sometimes I fear you value me only for the information I can give you."

For a moment he stopped and was stock-still, almost jerking her out of the dance. "Jessie! How can you even think such a thing? You know how I adore you." He looked at her reproachfully as they began to move to the music again. "It is true that your connection to the Nephilim of the Institute has been invaluable. Without you we would never have known they were going to York, for instance. But I thought you knew that you were helping me because we are working toward a future together. When I have become the Magister's right hand, darling, think how I will be able to provide for you."

Tessa laughed nervously. "You're right, Nate. It's only that I get frightened sometimes. What if Charlotte were to find out I was spying for you? What would they do to me?"

Nate swung her around easily. "Oh, nothing, darling; you've said it yourself, they're cowards." He looked past her and raised an eyebrow. "Benedict, up to his old tricks," he said. "Rather disgusting."

Tessa looked around and saw Benedict Lightwood leaning back on a scarlet velvet sofa near the orchestra. He was coatless, a glass of red wine in one hand, his eyes half-lidded. Sprawled across his chest, Tessa saw to her shock, was a woman—or at least it had the form of a woman. Long black hair worn loose, a low-cut black velvet gown—and the heads of little serpents poking out from her eyes, hissing. As Tessa watched, one of them extended a long, forked tongue and licked the side of Benedict Lightwood's face.

"That's a demon," Tessa breathed, forgetting for a moment to be Jessamine. "Isn't it?"

Fortunately Nate seemed to find nothing odd about the question. "Of course it is, silly bunny. That's what Benedict fancies. Demon women."

Will's voice echoed in Tessa's ears, *I would be surprised if some of the elder Lightwood's nocturnal visits to certain houses in Shadwell haven't left him with a nasty case of demon pox.* "Oh, ugh," she said.

"Indeed," said Nate. "Ironic, considering the high-and-mighty manner in which the Nephilim conduct themselves.

I ask myself often why Mortmain favors him so and wishes to see him installed in the Institute so badly." Nate sounded peevish.

Tessa had already guessed as much, but the knowledge that Mortmain was most assuredly behind Benedict's fierce determination to take the Institute from Charlotte still felt like a blow. "I just don't see," she said, trying her best to adopt Jessie's lightly peevish demeanor, "what *use* it will be to the Magister. It's just a big stuffy old building. . . ."

Nate laughed indulgently. "It's not the building, silly thing. It's the position. The head of the London Institute is one of the most powerful Shadowhunters in England, and the Magister controls Benedict as if he were a puppet. Using him, he can destroy the Council from within, while the automaton army destroys them from without." He spun her expertly as the dance required; only Tessa's years of practice dancing with Nate kept her from falling over, so distracted was she by shock. "Besides, it's not *quite* true that the Institute contains nothing of value. Access to the Great Library alone will be invaluable for the Magister. Not to mention the weapons room . . ."

"And Tessa." She clamped down on her voice so it wouldn't tremble.

"Tessa?"

"Your sister. The Magister still wants her, doesn't he?"

For the first time Nate looked at her with a puzzled surprise. "We've been over this, Jessamine," he said. "Tessa will be arrested for illegal possession of articles of dark magic, and sent to the Silent City. Benedict will bring her forth from there and deliver her to the Magister. It is all part of whatever bargain they struck, though what Benedict is getting from it is not clear to me yet. It must be something quite significant, or he would not be so willing to turn on his own."

Arrested? Possession of articles of dark magic? Tessa's head spun.

Nate's hand slipped around the back of her neck. He was wearing gloves, but Tessa couldn't rid herself of the feeling that something slimy was touching her skin. "My little Jessie," he murmured. "You behave almost as if you've forgotten your own part in this. You *did* hide the Book of the White in my sister's room as we asked you to, did you not?"

"Of—of course I did. I was only joking, Nate."

"That's my good girl." He was leaning closer. He was definitely going to kiss her. It was most improper, but then nothing about this place could be considered proper. In a state of absolute horror, Tessa sputtered:

"Nate—I feel dizzy—as if I might faint. I think it's the heat. If you could fetch me a lemonade?"

He looked down at her for a moment, his mouth tight with bottled annoyance, but Tessa knew he could not refuse. No gentleman would. He straightened up, brushed off his cuffs, and smiled. "Of course," he said with a bow. "Let me help you to a seat first."

She protested, but his hand was already on her elbow, guiding her toward one of the chairs lined up along the walls. He settled her into it and vanished into the crowd. She watched him go, trembling all over. *Dark magic.* She felt sick, and angry. She wanted to slap her brother, shake him till he told her the rest of the truth, but she knew she couldn't.

"You must be Tessa Gray," said a soft voice at her elbow. "You look just like your mother."

Tessa nearly jumped out of her skin. At her side stood a tall slender woman with long, unbound hair the color of lavender petals. Her skin was a pale blue, her dress a long and floating confection of gossamer and tulle. Her feet were bare, and in between her toes were thin webs like a spider's, a darker blue than her skin. Tessa's hands went to her face in sudden horror—was she losing her disguise?—but the blue woman laughed.

"I didn't mean to make you fearful of your illusion, little one. It is still in place. It is just that my kind can see through it. All this"—she gestured vaguely at Tessa's blond hair, her white dress and pearls—"is like the vapor of a cloud, and you the sky beyond it. Did you know your mother had eyes just like yours, gray sometimes and blue at others?"

Tessa found her voice. "Who are you?"

"Oh, my kind doesn't like to give our names, but you can call me whatever you like. You can invent a lovely name for me. Your mother used to call me Hyacinth."

"The blue flower," Tessa said faintly. "How did you know my mother? You don't look any older than me—"

"After our youth, my kind does not age or die. Nor will you. Lucky girl! I hope you appreciate the service done you."

Tessa shook her head in bewilderment. "Service? What service? Are you speaking of Mortmain? *Do you know what I am?*"

"Do you know what *I* am?"

Tessa thought of the *Codex*. "A faerie?" she guessed.

"And do you know what a changeling is?"

Tessa shook her head.

"Sometimes," Hyacinth confided, dropping her voice to a whisper, "when our faerie blood has grown weak and thin, we will find our way into a human home, and take the best, the prettiest, and the plumpest child—and, quick as a wink, replace the babe with a sickly one of our own. While the human child grows tall and strong in our lands, the human family will find itself burdened with a dying creature fearful of cold iron. Our bloodline is strengthened—"

"Why bother?" Tessa demanded. "Why not just steal the human child and leave nothing in its place?"

Hyacinth's dark blue eyes widened. "Why, because that would not be *fair*," she said. "And it would breed suspicion among the mundanes. They are stupid, but there are many of them. It does not do to rouse their ire. That is when they come with iron and torches." She shuddered.

"Just a moment," Tessa said. "Are you telling me I'm a *changeling*?"

Hyacinth bubbled over with giggles. "Of course not! What a ridiculous thought!" She held her hands to her heart as she laughed, and Tessa saw that her fingers, too, were bound together with blue webbing. Suddenly she smiled, showing glittering teeth. "There's a very good-looking boy staring over here," she said. "As handsome as a faerie lord! I should leave you to your business." She winked, and before Tessa could protest, Hyacinth melted back into the crowd.

Shaken, Tessa turned, expecting the "good-looking boy" to be Nate—but it was Will, leaning against the wall beside her. The moment her eyes found him, he turned and began studiously examining the dance floor. "What did that faerie woman want?"

"I don't know," Tessa said, exasperated. "To tell me I'm *not* a changeling, apparently."

"Well, that's good. Process of elimination." Tessa had to

admit, Will was doing a good job of somehow blending in with the dark curtains behind him, as if he were not there at all. It must have been a Shadowhunter talent. "And what news from your brother?"

She gripped her hands together, looking at the floor while she spoke. "Jessamine's been spying for Nate all this time. I don't know how long exactly. She's been telling him everything. She thinks he's in love with her."

Will looked unsurprised. "Do *you* think he's in love with her?"

"I think Nate cares only about himself," said Tessa. "There's worse, too. Benedict Lightwood is working for Mortmain. That is why he is scheming to get the Institute. So the Magister can have it. And have *me*. Nate knows all about it, of course. He doesn't care." Tessa looked at her hands again. Jessamine's hands. Small and delicate in their fine white kid gloves. *Oh, Nate*, she thought. *Aunt Harriet used to call him her blue-eyed boy.*

"I expect that was before he killed her," said Will. Only then did Tessa realize she had spoken aloud. "And there he is again," he added, in a mutter, under his breath. Tessa glanced out at the crowd and saw Nate, his fair hair like a beacon, coming toward her. In his hand was a glass of sparkling golden liquid. She turned to tell Will to hurry away, but he had already vanished.

"Fizzy lemonade," said Nate, coming up to her and thrusting the glass into her hand. The ice-cold sides felt good against the heat of her skin. She took a sip; despite everything, it was delicious.

Nate stroked her hair back from her forehead. "Now, you were saying," he said. "You *did* hide the book in my sister's room . . ."

"Yes, just as you told me to do," Tessa fibbed. "She suspects nothing, of course."

"I should hope not."

"Nate . . ."

"Yes?"

"Do you know what the Magister intends to do with your sister?"

"I've told you, she isn't my sister." Nate's voice was clipped. "And I've no idea what he plans to do with her, nor any interest. *My* plans are all for my—*our* future together. I should hope that you are as dedicated?" Tessa thought of Jessamine, sitting sullenly in the room with the other Shadowhunters while they shuffled through papers about Mortmain; Jessamine falling asleep at the table rather than leave when they were discussing plans with Ragnor Fell. And Tessa pitied her even as she hated Nate, hated him so much it felt like fire in her throat. *I've told you, she isn't my sister.*

Tessa let her eyes widen, her lip tremble. "I'm doing the best I can, Nate," she said. "Don't you believe me?"

She felt a faint sense of triumph as she watched him visibly beat back his annoyance. "Of course, darling. Of course." He examined her face. "Are you feeling better? Shall we dance again?"

She clutched the glass in her hand. "Oh, I don't know . . ."

"Of course," Nate chuckled, "they do say a gentleman should dance only the first set or two with his wife."

Tessa froze. It was as if time had stopped: Everything in the room seemed to freeze along with her, even the smirk on Nate's face.

Wife?

He and Jessamine were *married*?

"Angel?" said Nate, his voice sounding as if it were coming from far away. "Are you all right? You've gone white as a sheet."

"Mr. Gray." A dull, mechanical voice spoke from behind Nate's shoulder. It was one of the blank-faced automatons, holding out a silver tray on which was a folded piece of paper. "A message for you."

Nate turned in surprise and plucked the paper from the tray; Tessa watched as he unfolded it, read it, cursed, and stuffed it into his coat pocket. "My, my," he said. "A note from himself." *He must mean the Magister*, Tessa thought. "I'm needed apparently. A dreadful bore, but what can you do?" He took her hand and raised her to her feet, then leaned in for a chaste kiss on the cheek. "Speak to Benedict; he'll make sure you're escorted back out to the carriage, *Mrs. Gray*." He spoke the last two words in a whisper.

Tessa nodded numbly.

"Good girl," Nate said. Then he turned and vanished into the crowd, followed by the automaton. Tessa stared after them both dizzily. It must be the shock, she thought, but everything in the room had begun to look a little—peculiar. It was as if she could see each individual ray of light sparking off the crystals of the chandelier. The effect was beautiful, if strange and a little dizzying.

"Tessa." It was Will, evolving effortlessly into the space beside her. She turned to look at him. He looked flushed, as if he had been running—another beautiful, strange effect, she thought, the black hair and mask, the blue eyes and fair skin, and the flush across his high cheekbones. It was like looking at a painting. "I see your brother got the note."

"Ah." Everything clicked into place. "You sent it."

"I did." Looking pleased with himself, Will plucked the glass of lemonade out of her hand, drained the remainder, and set it on a windowsill. "I had to get him out of here. And we should probably follow suit, before he realizes the note is a falsity and he returns. Though I did direct him to Vauxhall; it'll take him ages to get there and back, so we're likely safe—" He broke off, and she could hear sudden alarm in his voice. "Tess—Tessa? Are you all right?"

"Why do you ask?" Her voice echoed in her own ears.

"Look." He reached out and caught a swinging tendril of her hair, pulling it forward so she could see it. She stared. Dark brown, not fair. Her own hair. Not Jessamine's.

"Oh, God." She put a hand to her face, recognizing the familiar tingles of the Change as they began to wash over her. "How long—"

"Not long. You were Jessamine when I sat down." He caught hold of her hand. "Come along. Quickly." He began to stride toward the exit, but it was a long way across the ballroom, and Tessa's whole body was twitching and shivering with the Change. She gasped as it bit into her like teeth. She saw Will whip his head around, alarmed; felt him catch her as she stumbled, and half-carry her forward. The room swung around her. *I can't faint. Don't let me faint.*

A wash of cool air struck her face. She realized distantly that Will had swung them through a pair of French doors and they were out on a small stone balcony, one of many overlooking the gardens. She moved away from him, tearing the gold mask from her face, and nearly collapsed against the stone balustrade. After slamming the doors behind them, Will turned and hurried over to her, laying a hand lightly on her back. "Tessa?"

"I'm all right." She was glad for the stone railing beneath her hands, its solidity and hardness inexpressibly reassuring. The chilly air was lessening her dizziness too. Glancing down at herself, she could see she had become fully Tessa again. The white dress was now a full few inches too short, and the lacing so tight that her décolletage spilled up and over the low neckline. She knew some women laced themselves tight just to get this effect, but it was rather shocking seeing so much of her own skin on display.

She looked sideways at Will, glad for the cold air keeping her cheeks from flaming. "I just—I don't know what happened. That's never happened to me before, losing the Change without noticing like that. It must have been the surprise of it all. They're married, did you know that? Nate and Jessamine. Married. Nate was never the marrying sort. And he doesn't love her. I can tell. He doesn't love anyone but himself. He never has."

"Tess," Will said again, gently this time. He was leaning against the railing too, facing her. They were only a very little distance apart. Above them the moon swam through the clouds, a white boat on a still, black sea.

She closed her mouth, aware that she had been babbling. "I'm sorry," she said softly, looking away.

Almost hesitantly he laid his hand against her cheek, turning her to face him. He had stripped off his glove, and his skin was bare against hers. "There's nothing to be sorry about," he said. "You were brilliant in there, Tessa. Not a step out of place." She felt her face warm beneath his cool fingers, and was amazed. Was this Will speaking? *Will*, who had spoken to her on the roof of the Institute as if she were so much rubbish? "You did love your brother once, didn't you? I could see your face as he was speaking to you, and I wanted to kill him for breaking your heart."

You broke my heart, she wanted to say. Instead she said, "Some part of me misses him as—as you miss your sister. Even though I know what he is, I miss the brother I thought I had. He was my only family."

"The Institute is your family now." His voice was incredibly gentle. Tessa looked at him in amazement. Gentleness was not something she would ever have associated with Will. But it was there, in the touch of his hand on her cheek, in the softness of his voice, in his eyes when he looked at her. It was the way she had always dreamed a boy would look at her. But she had never dreamed up someone as beautiful as Will, not in all her imaginings. In the moonlight the curve of his mouth looked pure and perfect, his eyes behind the mask nearly black.

"We should go back inside," she said, in a half whisper. She did not want to go back inside. She wanted to stay here, with Will achingly close, almost leaning into her. She could feel the heat that radiated from his body. His dark hair fell around the mask, into his eyes, tangling with his long eyelashes. "We have only a little time—"

She took a step forward—and stumbled into Will, who caught her. She froze—and then her arms crept around him, her fingers lacing themselves behind his neck. Her face was pressed against his throat, his soft hair under her fingers. She closed her eyes, shutting out the dizzying world, the light beyond the French windows, the glow of the sky. She wanted to be here with Will, cocooned in this moment, inhaling the clean sharp scent of him, feeling the beat of his heart against hers, as steady and strong as the pulse of the ocean.

She felt him inhale. "Tess," he said. "Tess, look at me."

She raised her eyes to his, slow and unwilling, braced for anger or coldness—but his gaze was fixed on hers, his dark blue eyes somber beneath their thick black lashes, and they were stripped of all their usual cool, aloof distance. They were as clear as glass and full of desire. And more than desire—a tenderness she had never seen in them before, had never even associated with Will Herondale. That, more than anything else, stopped her protest as he raised his hands and methodically began to take the pins from her hair, one by one.

This is madness, she thought, as the first pin rattled to the ground. They should be running, fleeing this place. Instead she stood, wordless, as Will cast Jessamine's pearl clasps aside as if they were so much paste jewelry. Her own long, curling dark hair fell down around her shoulders, and Will slid his hands into it. She heard him exhale as he did so, as if he had been holding his breath for months and had only just let it out. She stood as if mesmerized as he gathered her hair in his hands, draping it over one of her shoulders, winding her curls between his fingers. "My Tessa," he said, and this time she did not tell him that she was not his.

"Will," she whispered as he reached up and unlocked her hands from around his neck. He drew her gloves off, and they joined her mask and Jessie's pins on the stone floor of the balcony. He pulled off his own mask next and cast it aside, running his hands through his damp black hair, pushing it back from his forehead. The lower edge of the mask had left marks across his high cheekbones, like light scars, but when she reached to touch them, he gently caught at her hands and pressed them down.

"No," he said. "Let me touch you first. I have wanted . . ."

She did not say no. Instead she stood, wide-eyed, gazing up at him as his fingertips traced her temples, then her cheekbones, then—softly despite their rough calluses—outlined the shape of her mouth as if he meant to commit it to memory. The gesture made her heart spin like a top inside her chest. His eyes remained fixed on her, as dark as the bottom of the ocean, wondering, dazed with discovery.

She stood still as his fingertips left her mouth and trailed a path down her throat, stopping at her pulse, slipping to the silk ribbon at her collar and pulling at one end of it; her eyelids fluttered half-closed as the bow came apart and his warm hand covered her bare collarbone. She remembered once, on the *Main*, how the ship had passed through a patch of strangely shining ocean, and how the *Main* had carved a path of fire through the water, trailing sparks in its wake. It was as if Will's hands did the same to her skin. She burned where he touched her, and could feel where his fingers had been even when they had moved on. His hands moved lightly but lower, over the bodice of her dress, following the curves of her breasts. Tessa gasped, even as his hands slid to grip her waist and draw her toward him, pulling their bodies together until there was not a millimeter of space between them.

He bent to put his cheek against hers. His breath against her ear made her shudder with each deliberately spoken word. "I have wanted to do this," he said, "every moment of every hour of every day that I have been with you since the day I met you. But you know that. You *must* know. Don't you?"

She looked up at him, lips parted in bewilderment. "Know what?" she said, and Will, with a sigh of something like defeat, kissed her.

His lips were soft, so soft. He had kissed her before, wildly and desperately and tasting of blood, but this was different. This was deliberate and unhurried, as if he were speaking to her silently, saying with the brush of his lips on hers what he could not say in words. He traced slow, glancing butterfly kisses across her mouth, each as measured as the beat of a heart, each saying she was precious, irreplaceable, wanted. Tessa could no longer keep her hands at her sides. She reached to cup the back of his neck, to tangle her fingers in the dark silky waves of his hair, to feel his pulse hammering against her palms.

His grip on her was firm as he explored her mouth thoroughly with his. He tasted of the sparkling lemonade, sweet and tingling. The movement of his tongue as he flicked it lightly across her lips sent delicious shudders through her whole body; her bones melted and her nerves seared. She yearned to pull him against her—but he was being so gentle with her, so unbelievably gentle, though she could feel how much he wanted her in the trembling of his hands, the hammering of his heart against hers. Surely someone who did not care even a little could not behave with such gentleness. All the pieces inside her that had felt broken and jagged when she had looked at Will these past few weeks began to knit together and heal. She felt light, as if she could float.

"Will," she whispered against his mouth. She wanted him closer to her so badly, it was like an ache, a painful hot ache that spread out from her stomach to speed her heart and knot her hands in his hair and set her skin to burning. "Will, you need not be so careful. I will not break."

"Tessa," he groaned against her mouth, but she could hear the hesitation in his voice. She nipped gently at his lips, teasing him, and his breath caught. His hands flattened against the small of her back, pressing her to him, as his self-control slipped and his gentleness began to blossom into a more demanding urgency. Their kisses grew deeper and deeper still, as if they could breathe each other, consume each other, devour each other whole. Tessa knew she was making whimpering sounds in the back of her throat; that Will was pushing her back, back against the railing in a way that should have hurt but oddly did not; that his hands were at the bodice of Jessamine's dress, crushing the delicate fabric roses. Distantly Tessa heard the knob of the French doors rattle; they opened, and still she and Will clung together, as if nothing else mattered.

There was a murmur of voices, and someone said, "I told you, Edith. That's what happens when you drink the pink drinks," in a disapproving tone. The doors shut again, and Tessa heard footsteps going away. She broke away from Will.

"Oh, my heavens," she said, breathless. "How humiliating—"

"I don't care." He pulled her back to him, nuzzled the side of her neck, his face hot against her cold skin. His mouth glanced across hers. "Tess—"

"You keep saying my name," she murmured. She had one hand on his chest, holding him a little bit away, but had no idea how long she could keep it there. Her body ached for him. Time had snapped and lost its meaning. There was only this moment, only Will. She had never felt anything like it, and she wondered if this was what it was like for Nate when he was drunk.

"I love your name. I love the sound of it." He sounded drunk too, his mouth on hers as he spoke so she could feel the delicious movement of his lips. She breathed his breath, inhaling him. Their bodies fit together perfectly, she couldn't help noticing; in Jessie's white satin heeled shoes, she was but a little shorter than he was, and had only to tilt her head back slightly to kiss him. "I have to ask you something. I have to know—"

"So *there* you two are," came a voice from the doorway. "And quite a spectacular display you're making, if I do say so."

They sprang apart. There, standing in the doorway—though Tessa could not remember the sound of the doors having opened—a long cigar held between his thin brown fingers, was Magnus Bane.

"Let me guess," Magnus said, exhaling smoke. It made a white cloud in the shape of a heart that distorted as it drifted away from his mouth, expanding and twisting until it was no longer recognizable. "You had the lemonade."

Tessa and Will, now standing side by side, glanced at each other. It was Tessa who spoke first. "I—yes. Nate brought me some."

"It has a bit of a warlock powder mixed into it," said Magnus. He was wearing all black, with no other ornamentation save on his hands. Each finger bore a ring set with a huge stone of a different color—lemon yellow citrine, green jade, red ruby, blue topaz. "The kind that lowers your inhibitions and makes you do things you would"—he coughed delicately—"not otherwise do."

"Oh," said Will. And then: "Oh." His voice was low. He

turned away, leaning his hands on the balustrade. Tessa felt her face begin to burn.

"Gracious, that's a lot of bosom you're showing," Magnus went on blithely, gesturing toward Tessa with the burning tip of his cigar. "*Tout le monde sur le balcon*, as they say in French," he added, miming a vast terrace jutting out from his chest. "Especially apt, as we are now, in fact, on a balcony."

"Let her alone," said Will. Tessa couldn't see his face; he had his head down. "She didn't know what she was drinking."

Tessa crossed her arms, realized this only intensified the severity of the bosom problem, and dropped them. "This is Jessamine's dress, and she's half my size," she snapped. "I would never go out like this under ordinary circumstances."

Magnus raised his eyebrows. "Changed back into yourself, did you? When the lemonade took effect?"

Tessa scowled. She felt obscurely humiliated—to have been caught kissing Will; to be standing in front of Magnus in something her aunt would have dropped dead to see her in—yet part of her wished Magnus would go away so she could kiss Will again. "What are you doing here, yourself, if I might ask?" she snapped ungraciously. "How did you know *we* were here?"

"I have sources," said Magnus, trailing smoke airily. "I thought you two might be up against it. Benedict Lightwood's parties have a reputation for danger. When I heard you were here—"

"We're well equipped to handle danger," Tessa said.

Magnus eyed her bosom openly. "I can see that," he said. "Armed to the teeth, as it were." Done with his cigar, he flicked it over the balcony railing. "One of Camille's human subjugates was here and recognized Will. He got a message to me, but if one of you was recognized already, what's the chance it could happen again? It's time to make yourselves scarce."

"What do you care if we get out or not?" It was Will, his head still down, his voice muffled.

"You owe me," Magnus said, his voice steely. "I mean to collect."

Will turned on him. Tessa was startled to see the expression on his face. He looked sick and ill. "I should have known that was it."

"You may choose your friends, but not your unlikely saviors," Magnus said cheerfully. "Shall we go, then? Or would you rather stay here and take your chances? You can start up with the kissing where you left off when you get back to the Institute."

Will scowled. "Get us out of here."

Magnus's cat eyes gleamed. He snapped his fingers, and a shower of blue sparks fell around them in a sudden, startling rain. Tessa tensed, expecting them to burn her skin, but she felt only wind rushing past her face. Her hair lifted as a strange energy crackled through her nerves. She heard Will gasp—and then they were standing on one of the stone paths in the garden, near the ornamental pond, the great Lightwood manor rising, silent and dark, above them.

"There," said Magnus in a bored tone. "That wasn't so difficult, was it?"

Will looked at him with no gratitude. "Magic," he muttered.

Magnus threw his hands up. They still crackled with blue energy, like heat lightning. "And just what do you think your precious runes are? Not magic?"

"Shush," Tessa said. She was bone-weary suddenly. She

ached where the corset crushed her ribs, and her feet, in Jessamine's too-small shoes, were in agony. "Stop spouting off, the both of you. I think someone's coming."

They all paused, just as a chattering group rounded the corner of the house. Tessa froze. Even in the cloudy moonlight, she could see they were not human. They were not Downworlders, either. It was a group of demons—one a shambling corpse-like figure with black holes for eyes; another half again the size of a man, blue-skinned and dressed in a waistcoat and trousers, but with a barbed tail, lizard's features, and a flat snakelike snout; and another that seemed to be a spinning wheel covered in wet red mouths.

Several things happened at once.

Tessa jammed the back of her hand against her mouth before she could scream. There was no point in running. The demons had already seen them and had come to a dead stop on the path. The smell of rot wafted from them, blotting out the scent of the trees.

Magnus raised his hand, blue fire circling his fingers. He was muttering words under his breath. He looked as discomposed as Tessa had ever seen him.

And Will—Will, whom Tessa had expected to reach for his seraph blades—did something entirely unexpected. He raised a trembling finger, pointed at the blue-skinned demon, and breathed, "*You.*"

The blue-skinned demon blinked. All the demons stood stock-still, looking at one another. There must have been some agreement in place, Tessa thought, to keep them from attacking the humans at the party, but she did not like the way the wet red mouths were licking their lips. "Er," the demon Will had addressed said, in a surprisingly ordinary voice. "I don't recall— That is, I don't think I've had the pleasure of your acquaintance?"

"Liar!" Will staggered forward and charged; as Tessa watched in amazement, he barreled past the other demons and threw himself onto the blue demon. It let out a high-pitched shriek. Magnus was watching what was going on with his mouth open. Tessa cried, "Will! *Will!*" but he was rolling over and over on the grass with the blue-skinned creature, which was surprisingly nimble. He had it by the back of its waistcoat, but it tore free and dashed away, streaking across the gardens, Will in hot pursuit.

Tessa took a few steps after them, but her feet were a white-hot agony. Kicking off Jessamine's shoes, she was about to race after Will when she realized the remaining demons were making an angry buzzing noise. They seemed to be addressing Magnus.

"Ah, well, you know," he said, having regained his composure, and he gestured in the direction Will had disappeared in. "Disagreement. Over a woman. It happens."

The buzzing noise increased. It was clear the demons did not believe him.

"Gambling debt?" Magnus suggested. He snapped his fingers, and flame burst up from his palm, bathing the garden in a stark glow. "I suggest you not concern yourselves overmuch with it, gentlemen. Festivities and merriment await you inside." He gestured toward the narrow door that led to the ballroom. "Much more pleasant than what will await you out here if you continue to linger."

That seemed to convince them. The demons moved off,

buzzing and muttering, taking their stench of garbage with them.

Tessa spun around. "Quickly, we have to go after them—"

Magnus reached down and scooped her shoes up off the path. Holding them by their satin ribbons, he said, "Not so quickly, Cinderella. Will's a Shadowhunter. He runs fast. You'll never catch him."

"But you—there must be some magic—"

"*Magic*," Magnus said, mimicking Will's disgusted tone. "Will's where he has to be, doing what he has to do. His purpose is killing demons, Tessa."

"Do you—not like him?" Tessa asked; it was an odd question, perhaps, but there was something in the way Magnus looked at Will, spoke to Will, that she could not put her finger on.

To her surprise, Magnus took the question seriously. "I do like him," he said, "though rather despite myself. I thought him a pretty bit of poison to start with, but I have come around. There is a soul under all that bravado. And he is really *alive*, one of the most alive people I have ever met. When he feels something, it is as bright and sharp as lightning."

"We all *feel*," Tessa said, thoroughly surprised. Will, feeling more strongly than everyone else? Madder than everyone else, perhaps.

"Not like that," said Magnus. "Trust me, I have lived a long time, and I do know." His look was not without sympathy. "And you will find that feelings fade too, the longer you live. The oldest warlock I ever met had been alive nearly a thousand years and told me he could no longer even remember what love felt like, or hatred, either. I asked him why he did not end his life, and he said he still felt one thing, and that was fear—fear of what lies after death. 'The undiscover'd country from whose bourne no traveller returns.'"

"Hamlet," said Tessa automatically. She was trying to push back thoughts of her own possible immortality. The concept of it was too grand and terrifying to truly encompass, and besides . . . it might not even be true.

"We who are immortal, we are chained to this life by a chain of gold, and we dare not sever it for fear of what lies beyond the drop," said Magnus. "Now come along, and don't begrudge Will his moral duties." He started off down the path, Tessa limping quickly after him in an effort to keep up.

"But he behaved as if he knew that demon—"

"Probably tried to kill it before," said Magnus. "Sometimes they get away."

"But how will he get back to the Institute?" Tessa wailed.

"He's a clever boy. He'll find a way. I'm more concerned with getting *you* back to the Institute before someone notices you're missing and there's the devil of a row." They'd reached the front gates, where the carriage awaited, Cyril resting peacefully in the driver's seat, his hat pulled down over his eyes.

She glared mutinously at Magnus as he swung the carriage door open and reached out a hand to help her up into it. "How do you know Will and I didn't have Charlotte's permission to be here tonight?"

"Do give me more credit than that, darling," he said, and grinned in such an infectious manner that Tessa, with a sigh, gave him her hand. "Now," he said, "I'll take you back to the Institute, and on the way you can tell me all about it."

13

THE MORTAL SWORD

"Take my share of a fickle heart,
Mine of a paltry love:
Take it or leave it as you will,
I wash my hands thereof."
—Christina Rosetti, "Maude Clare"

"Oh, my dear merciful heavens!" said Sophie, starting up from her chair as Tessa opened the door to Jessamine's bedroom. "Miss Tessa, what *happened?*"

"Sophie! Shh!" Tessa waved a warning hand as she shut the door behind her. The room was as she had left it. Her nightgown and dressing gown were folded neatly on a chair, the cracked silver mirror was on the vanity table, and Jessamine—Jessamine was still soundly unconscious, her wrists ropebound to the posts of the bed. Sophie, seated in a chair by the wardrobe, had clearly been there since Will and Tessa had left; she clutched a hairbrush in one hand (to hit Jessamine with, should she awaken again, Tessa wondered?), and her hazel eyes were huge.

"But miss . . ." Sophie's voice trailed off as Tessa's gaze went to her reflection in the looking glass. Tessa could not help but stare. Her hair had come down, of course, in a tangled mess all over her shoulders, Jessamine's pearl pins gone where Will had flung them; she was shoeless and limping, her white stockings filthy, her gloves gone, and her dress obviously nearly choking her to death. "Was it very dreadful?"

Tessa's mind went suddenly back to the balcony, and Will's arms around her. *Oh, God.* She pushed the thought away and glanced over at Jessamine, still sleeping peacefully. "Sophie, we are going to have to wake Charlotte. We have no choice."

Sophie looked at her with round eyes. Tessa could not blame her; she dreaded rousing Charlotte. Tessa had even pleaded with Magnus to come in with her to help break the news, but he had refused, on the grounds that internecine Shadowhunter dramas had nothing to do with him, and he had a novel to get back to besides.

"Miss—," Sophie protested.

"We must." As quickly as she could, Tessa told Sophie the gist of what had happened that night, leaving out the part with Will on the balcony. No one needed to know about that. "This is beyond us now. We cannot come in over Charlotte's head any longer."

Sophie made no more sound of protest. She laid the hairbrush down on the vanity, stood up, smoothed her skirts, and said, "I will fetch Mrs. Branwell, miss."

Tessa sank into the chair by the bed, wincing as Jessamine's dress pinched her. "I wish you would call me Tessa."

"I know, miss." Sophie left, closing the door quietly behind her.

Magnus was lying on the sofa in the drawing room with his boots up when he heard the commotion. He grinned without moving at the sound of Archer protesting, and Will protesting. Footsteps neared the door. Magnus flipped a page in his poetry book as the door swung open and Will stalked in.

He was barely recognizable. His elegant evening clothes were torn and stained with mud, his coat ripped lengthwise, his boots encrusted with mud. His hair stood up wildly, and his face was raked by dozens of scratches, as if he had been attacked by a dozen cats simultaneously.

"I'm sorry, sir," said Archer despairingly. "He pushed past me."

"Magnus," Will said. He was grinning. Magnus had seen him grin before, but there was real joy in it this time. It transformed Will's face, took it from beautiful but cold to incandescent. "Tell him to let me in."

Magnus waved a hand. "Let him in, Archer."

The human subjugate's gray face twisted, and the door slammed behind Will. "Magnus!" He half-staggered, half-stalked over to the fireplace, where he leaned against the mantel. "You won't believe—"

"Shh," said Magnus, his book still open on his knees. "Listen to this:

I am tired of tears and laughter,
And men that laugh and weep
Of what may come hereafter

For men that sow to reap:
I am weary of days and hours,
Blown buds of barren flowers,
Desires and dreams and powers
And everything but sleep."

"Swinburne," said Will, leaning against the mantel. "Sentimental and overrated."

"*You* don't know what it is to be immortal." Magnus tossed the book aside and sat up. "So what is it you want?"

Will pulled up his sleeve. Magnus swallowed a sound of surprise. Will's forearm bore a long, deep, and bloody gash. Blood braceleted his wrist and dripped from his fingers. Embedded in the gash, like a crystal sunk into the wall of a cave, was a single white tooth.

"What the—," Magnus began.

"Demon tooth," Will said, his breath a little short. "I chased that blue bastard all around Chiswick, but it got away from me—not before it bit me, though. It left this tooth in me. You can use it, right? To summon the demon?" He took hold of the tooth and yanked it free. Even more blood welled up and spilled down his arm, splattering onto the ground.

"Camille's carpet," Magnus protested.

"It's blood," said Will. "She ought to be thrilled."

"Are you all right?" Magnus looked at Will in fascination. "You're bleeding a great deal. Haven't you a stele on your person somewhere? A healing rune—"

"I don't care about healing runes. I care about this." Will dropped the bloody tooth into Magnus's hand. "Find the demon for me. I know you can do it."

Magnus glanced down with a moue of distaste. "I most likely can, but . . ."

The light in Will's face flickered. "But?"

"But not tonight," said Magnus. "It may take me a few days. You'll have to be patient."

Will took a ragged breath. "I can't be patient. Not after tonight. You don't understand—" He staggered then, and caught himself by seizing the mantel. Alarmed, Magnus rose from the sofa.

"Are you all right?"

The color was coming and going in Will's face. His collar was dark with sweat. "I don't know—," he gasped. "The tooth. It might have been poisonous . . ."

His voice trailed off. He slid forward, his eyes rolling up. With an epithet of surprise Magnus caught Will before he could hit the bloody carpet and, hoisting the boy in his arms, carried him carefully over to the sofa.

Tessa, seated in the chair beside Jessamine's bed, massaged her aching ribs and sighed. The corset was still biting into her, and she had no idea when she'd get a chance to remove it; her feet ached, and she hurt down deep in her soul. Seeing Nate had been like having a knife twisted in a fresh wound. He had danced with "Jessamine"—flirted with her—and had casually discussed the fate of Tessa, his sister, as if it meant nothing to him at all.

She supposed it should not surprise her, that she should be beyond surprise where Nate was concerned. But it hurt just the same.

And Will—those few moments out on the balcony with Will had been the most confusing of her life. After the way

Will had spoken to her on the roof, she had sworn never to entertain romantic thoughts of him again. He was no dark, brooding Heathcliff nursing a secret passion, she had told herself, merely a boy who thought himself too good for her. But the way he had looked at her on the terrace, the way he had smoothed her hair back from her face, even the faint tremble in his hands when he'd touched her—surely those things could not be the product of falsehood.

But then, she had touched him back the same way. In that moment she had wanted nothing but Will. Had felt nothing but Will. Yet just the night before she had touched and kissed Jem; she had felt that she loved him; she had let him see her as no one had ever seen her before. And when she thought of him now, thought of his silence this morning, his absence from dinner, she missed him again, with a physical pain that could not be a lie.

Could you really love two different people at once? Could you split your heart in half? Or was it just that the time with Will on the balcony had been a madness induced by warlock drugs? Would it have been the same with *anyone?* The thought haunted her like a ghost.

"Tessa."

Tessa nearly leaped out of her seat. The voice was almost a whisper. It was Jessamine. Her eyes were half-open, the reflected firelight flickering in their brown depths.

Tessa sat up straight. "Jessamine. Are you . . ."

"What happened?" Jessamine's head rolled fretfully from side to side. "I don't remember." She tried to sit up and gasped, finding her hands bound. "Tessa! Why on earth—"

"It's for your own good, Jessamine." Tessa's voice shook. "Charlotte—she has questions she has to ask you. It would be so much better if you were willing to answer them—"

"The party." Jessamine's eyes flicked back and forth, as if she were watching something Tessa couldn't see. "Sophie, that little monkey, was going through my things. I found her with the invitation in her hands—"

"Yes, the party," said Tessa. "At Benedict Lightwood's. Where you were meeting Nate."

"You read his note?" Jessamine's head whipped to the side. "Don't you know how rude and improper it is to read another person's private correspondence?" She tried to sit up again, and fell back once more against the pillows. "Anyway, he didn't sign it. You can't prove—"

"Jessamine, there is little advantage in falsehood now. I can prove it, for I went to the party, and I spoke with my brother there."

Jessamine's mouth opened in a pink O. For the first time she seemed to note what Tessa was wearing. "My dress," she breathed. "You disguised yourself as me?"

Tessa nodded.

Jessamine's eyes darkened. "Unnatural," she breathed. "Disgusting creature! What did you do to Nate? What did you say to him?"

"He made it very clear you have been spying for Mortmain," said Tessa, wishing that Sophie and Charlotte would return. What on earth was taking them so long? "That you have betrayed us, reporting on all our activities, carrying out Mortmain's commands—"

"Us?" Jessamine screamed, struggling upright as much as the ropes would allow her. "You are not a Shadowhunter! You owe them no loyalty! They do not care about you, any more than they care about me. Only Nate cares for me—"

"My brother," Tessa said in a barely controlled voice, "is a lying murderer, incapable of feeling. He may have married you, Jessamine, but he does not love you. The Shadowhunters have helped and protected me, as they have done for you. And yet you turn on them like a dog the moment my brother snaps his fingers. He will abandon you, if he does not kill you first."

"Liar!" Jessamine screamed. "You don't understand him. You never did! His soul is pure and fine—"

"Pure as ditch water," Tessa said. "I understand him better than you do; you are blinded by his charm. He cares nothing for you."

"Liar—"

"I saw it in his eyes. *I saw the way he looks at you.*"

Jessamine gasped. "How can you be so cruel?"

Tessa shook her head. "You can't see it, can you?" she said wonderingly. "For you it is all play, like those dolls in your dollhouse—moving them about, making them kiss and marry. You wanted a mundane husband, and Nate was good enough. You cannot see what your traitorous behavior has cost those who have always cared for you."

Jessamine bared her teeth; in that moment she looked enough like a trapped, cornered animal that Tessa almost shrank back. "I love Nate," she said. "And he loves me. You are the one who does not understand love. 'Oh, I cannot decide between Will and Jem. Whatever shall I do?'" she said in a high-pitched voice, and Tessa flushed hotly. "So what if Mortmain wants to destroy the Shadowhunters of Britain. I say let them burn."

Tessa gaped at her, just as the door behind her was flung

open, and Charlotte marched in. She looked drawn and hollow with exhaustion, in a gray dress that matched the shadows beneath her eyes, but her carriage was erect, her eyes clear. Behind her came Sophie, scuttling as if frightened—and a moment later Tessa saw why, for bringing up the rear of the party was an apparition in parchment-colored robes, his face hidden beneath the shadow of his hood, and a deadly bright blade in his hand. It was Brother Enoch, of the Silent Brothers, carrying the Mortal Sword.

"Let us burn? Is that what you said, Jessamine?" said Charlotte in a bright, hard voice so unlike her that Tessa stared.

Jessamine gasped. Her eyes were fixed on the blade in Brother Enoch's hand. Its great hilt was carved in the shape of an angel with outspread wings.

Brother Enoch flicked the Sword toward Jessamine, who flinched back, and the ropes binding her wrists to the bedposts unraveled. Her hands fell limply into her lap. She stared at them, and then at Charlotte. "Charlotte, Tessa's a liar. She's a lying Downworlder—"

Charlotte paused at the side of the bed and looked down at Jessamine dispassionately. "That has not been my experience of her, Jessamine. And what of Sophie? She has always been a most honest servant."

"She struck me! With a mirror!" Jessamine's face was red.

"Because she found this." Charlotte drew the invitation, which Tessa had given over to Sophie, from her pocket. "Can you explain this, Jessamine?"

"There's nothing against the Law about going to a party." Jessamine sounded equal parts sulky and frightened. "Benedict Lightwood is a Shadowhunter—"

"This is Nathaniel Gray's writing." Charlotte's voice never seemed to lose its even edge, Tessa thought. There was something about that fact that made it seem even more inexorable. "He is a spy, wanted by the Clave, and you have been meeting with him in secret. Why is that?"

Jessamine's mouth opened slightly. Tessa waited for excuses—*It's all lies, Sophie invented the invitation, I was only meeting Nate to gain his confidence*—but instead tears came. "I love him," she said. "And he loves me."

"So you betrayed us to him," said Charlotte.

"I didn't!" Jessamine's voice rose. "Whatever Tessa says, it isn't true! She's lying. She's always been jealous of me, and she's lying!"

Charlotte gave Tessa a measured look. "Is she, now. And Sophie?"

"Sophie hates me," Jessamine sobbed. This at least was true. "She ought to be put out on the street—without references—"

"Do cease turning on the taps, Jessamine. It accomplishes nothing." Charlotte's voice cut through Jessamine's sobs like a blade. She turned to Enoch. "The true story will be easy enough to get. The Mortal Sword, please, Brother Enoch."

The Silent Brother stepped forward, the Mortal Sword leveled at Jessamine. Tessa stared in horror. Was he going to *torture* Jessamine in her own bed, in front of them all?

Jessamine cried out. "No! No! Get him away from me! *Charlotte!*" Her voice rose to a terrible wailing scream that seemed to go on and on, splitting Tessa's ears, her head.

"Put out your hands, Jessamine," said Charlotte coldly.

Jessamine shook her head wildly, her fair hair flying.

"Charlotte, no," Tessa said. "Don't hurt her."

"Don't interfere in what you don't understand, Tessa," said Charlotte in a clipped voice. "Put your hands out, Jessamine, or it will go very badly for you."

With tears running down her face, Jessamine thrust her hands forward, palms up. Tessa tensed all over. She felt suddenly sick and sorry she had had anything to do with this plan. If Jessamine had been fooled by Nate, then so had she. Jessie did not deserve this—

"It's all right," said a soft voice at her shoulder. It was Sophie. "He won't hurt her with it. The Mortal Sword makes Nephilim tell the truth."

Brother Enoch laid the blade of the Mortal Sword flat across Jessamine's palms. He did it without either force or gentleness, as if he were hardly aware of her as a person at all. He let the blade go and stepped back; even Jessamine's eyes rounded in surprise; the blade seemed to balance perfectly across her hands, utterly immobile.

"It is not a torture device, Jessamine," said Charlotte, her hands folded in front of her. "We must employ it only because you cannot be trusted to tell the truth otherwise." She held up the invitation. "This is yours, is it not?"

Jessamine did not answer. She was looking at Brother Enoch, her eyes wide and black with terror, her chest rising and falling fast. "I cannot think, not with that monster in the room—" Her voice trembled.

Charlotte's mouth thinned, but she turned to Enoch and spoke a few words. He nodded, then glided silently from the room. As the door shut behind him, Charlotte said, "There. He is waiting in the corridor. Do not think he will not catch you should you try to run, Jessamine."

Jessamine nodded. She seemed to droop, broken like a toy doll.

Charlotte fluttered the invitation in her hand. "This is yours, yes? And it was sent to you by Nathaniel Gray. This writing is his."

"Y-yes." The word seemed pulled from Jessamine against her will.

"How long have you been meeting him in secret?"

Jessamine set her mouth, but her lips were trembling. A moment later a torrent of words burst from her mouth. Her eyes darted round in shock as if she could not believe she was speaking. "He sent me a message only a few days after Mortmain invaded the Institute. He apologized for his behavior toward me. He said he was grateful for my nursing of him and that he had not been able to forget my graciousness or my beauty. I—I wanted to ignore him. But a second letter came, and a third. . . . I agreed to meet him. I left the Institute in the middle of the night and we met in Hyde Park. He kissed me—"

"Enough of that," said Charlotte. "How long did it take him to convince you to spy on us?"

"He said that he was only working for Mortmain until he could put together enough of a fortune to live comfortably. I said we could live together on my fortune, but he wouldn't have it. It had to be his money. He said he would not live off his wife. Is that not noble?"

"So by this point he had already proposed?"

"He proposed the second time we met." Jessamine sounded breathy. "He said he knew there would never be another woman for him. And he promised that once he had enough money, I would have just the life I had always wanted, that we would never worry about money, and that there would be ch-children." She sniffled.

"Oh, Jessamine." Charlotte sounded almost sad.

Jessamine flushed. "It was true! He loved me! He has more than proved it. We are married! It was done most properly in a church with a minister—"

"Probably a deconsecrated church and some flunky dressed to look like a minister," said Charlotte. "What do you know of mundane weddings, Jessie? How would you know what a proper wedding *was*? I give you my word that Nathaniel Gray does not consider you his wife."

"He does, he does, he *does*!" Jessamine shrieked, and tried to pull away from the Sword. It stuck to her hands as if it had been nailed there. Her wails went up an octave. "I am Jessamine Gray!"

"You are a traitor to the Clave. What else did you tell Nathaniel?"

"Everything," Jessamine gasped. "Where you were looking for Mortmain, which Downworlders you had contacted in your attempt to find him. That was why he was never anywhere you searched. I warned him about the trip to York. That is why he sent the automatons to Will's family's home. Mortmain wanted to terrify you into ceasing the search. He considers you all pestilential annoyances. But he is not afraid of you." Her chest was heaving up and down. "He will win out over you all. He knows it. So do I."

Charlotte leaned forward, her hands on her hips. "But he did not succeed in terrifying us into ceasing the search," she said. "The automatons he sent tried to snatch Tessa but failed—"

"They weren't sent to try to snatch Tessa. Oh, he still plans to take her, but not like that, not yet. His plan is close to realization, and that is when he will move to take the Institute, to take Tessa—"

"How close is he? Has he managed to open the Pyxis?" Charlotte snapped.

"I—I don't know. I don't think so."

"So you told Nate everything and he told you nothing. What of Benedict? Why has he agreed to work hand in glove with Mortmain? I always knew he was an unpleasant man, but it seems unlike him to betray the Clave."

Jessamine shook her head. She was sweating, her fair hair stuck to her temples. "Mortmain is holding something over him, something he wants. I don't know what it is. But he will do anything to get it."

"Including handing me over to Mortmain," said Tessa. Charlotte looked at her in surprise when she spoke, and seemed about to interrupt her, but Tessa hurtled on. "What is this about having me falsely accused of possessing articles of dark magic? How was that to be accomplished?"

"The Book of the White," Jessamine gasped. "I—took it from the locked case in the library. Hid it in your room while you were out."

"Where in my room?"

"Loose floorboard—near the fireplace." Jessamine's pupils were enormous. "Charlotte . . . please . . ."

But Charlotte was relentless. "Where is Mortmain? Has he spoken to Nate of his plans for the Pyxis, for his automatons?"

"I—" Jessamine took a shuddering gasp. Her face was dark red. "I can't—"

"Nate wouldn't have told her," said Tessa. "He would have

known she might have been caught, and he would have thought she'd crack under torture and spill everything. *He* would."

Jessamine gave her a venomous look. "He hates you, you know," she said. "He says that all his life you looked down on him, you and your aunt with your silly provincial morality, judging him for everything he did. Always telling him what to do, never wanting him to get ahead. Do you know what he calls you? He—"

"I don't care," Tessa lied; her voice shook slightly. Despite everything, hearing that her brother hated her hurt more than she had thought it could. "Did he say what I am? Why I have the power I do?"

"He said that your father was a demon." Jessamine's lips twitched. "And that your mother was a Shadowhunter."

The door opened softly, so softly that had Magnus not already been drifting in and out of sleep, the noise would not have woken him.

He looked up. He was sitting in an armchair near the fire, as his favorite place on the sofa was taken up by Will. Will, in bloody shirtsleeves, was sleeping the heavy sleep of the drugged and healing. His forearm was bandaged to the elbow, his cheeks flushed, his head pillowed on his unhurt arm. The tooth Will had pulled from his arm sat on the side table beside him, gleaming like ivory.

The door to the drawing room stood open behind him. And there, framed in the archway, was Camille.

She wore a black velvet traveling cloak open over a brilliant green dress that matched her eyes. Her hair was dressed high on her head with emerald combs, and as he watched, she drew off her white kid gloves, deliberately slowly, one by one, and laid them on the table by the door.

"Magnus," she said, and her voice, as always, sounded like silvery bells. "Did you miss me?"

Magnus sat up straight. The firelight played over Camille's shining hair, her poreless white skin. She was extraordinarily beautiful. "I did not realize you would be favoring me with your presence tonight."

She looked at Will, asleep on the sofa. Her lips curled upward. "Clearly."

"You sent no message. In fact, you have sent me no messages at all since you left London."

"Are you reproaching me, Magnus?" Camille sounded amused. Gliding behind the sofa, she leaned over the back, looking down into Will's face. "Will Herondale," she said. "He is lovely, isn't he? Is he your newest amusement?"

Instead of answering, Magnus crossed his long legs in front of him. "Where have you been?"

Camille leaned forward farther; if she had had breath, it would have stirred the curling dark hair on Will's forehead. "Can I kiss him?"

"No," said Magnus. "Where have you been, Camille? Every night I lay here on your sofa and I waited to hear your step in the hall, and I wondered where you were. You might at least tell me."

She straightened, rolling her eyes. "Oh, very well. I was in Paris, having some new dresses fitted. A much-needed holiday from the dramas of London."

There was a long silence. Then, "You're lying," Magnus said.

Her eyes widened. "Why would you say such a thing?"

"Because it's the truth." He took a crumpled letter from his pocket and threw it onto the floor between them. "You cannot track a vampire, but you can track a vampire's subjugate. You took Walker with you. It was easy enough for me to track him to Saint Petersburg. I have informants there. They let me know that you were living there with a human lover."

Camille watched him, a little smile playing about her mouth. "And that made you jealous?"

"Did you want me to be?"

"*Ça m'est égal,*" said Camille, dropping into the French she used when she truly wanted to annoy him. "It's all the same to me. He had nothing to do with you. He was a diversion while I was in Russia, nothing more."

"And now he is . . ."

"Dead. So he hardly represents competition for you. You must let me have my little diversions, Magnus."

"Otherwise?"

"Otherwise I shall become extremely cross."

"As you became cross with your human lover, and murdered him?" Magnus inquired. "What of pity? Compassion? Love? Or do you not feel that emotion?"

"I *love*," Camille said indignantly. "You and I, Magnus, who endure forever, love in such a manner as cannot be conceived of by mortals—a dark constant flame to their brief, sputtering light. What do they matter to you? Fidelity is a human concept, based upon the idea that we are here but for a short time. You cannot demand my faithfulness for *eternity*."

"How foolish of me. I thought I could. I thought I could at least expect you not to lie to me."

"You are being ridiculous," she said. "A child. You expect me to have the morals of some mundane when I am not human, and neither are you. Regardless, there is precious little you can do about it. I will not be dictated to, certainly not by some half-breed." It was the Downworlders' own insulting term for warlocks. "You are devoted to me; you have said so yourself. Your devotion will simply have to suffer my diversions, and then we shall rub along quite pleasantly. If not, I shall drop you. I cannot imagine you want *that*."

There was a little sneer in her voice as she spoke, and it snapped something inside Magnus. He recalled the sick feeling in his throat when the letter had come from Saint Petersburg. And yet he had waited for her return, hoping she had an explanation. That she would apologize. Ask him to love her again. Now that he realized he was not worth that to her—that he never had been—a red mist passed before his eyes; he seemed to go mad momentarily, for it was the only explanation for what he did next.

"It doesn't matter." He rose to his feet. "I have Will now."

Her mouth opened. "You can't be serious. A *Shadowhunter*?"

"You may be immortal, Camille, but your feelings are vapid and shallow. Will's are not. He understands what it is to love." Magnus, having delivered this insane speech with great dignity, stepped across the room and shook Will's shoulder. "Will. William. Wake up."

Will's hazy blue eyes opened. He was lying on his back, looking upward, and the first thing he saw was Camille's face as she bent over the back of the sofa, regarding him. He jerked upright. "By the Angel—"

"Oh, shush," said Camille lazily, smiling just enough to

show the tips of baby fangs. "I won't hurt you, Nephilim."

Magnus hauled Will to his feet. "The lady of the house," he said, "has returned."

"I see that." Will was flushed, the collar of his shirt dark with sweat. "Delightful," he said to no one in particular, and Magnus wasn't sure whether he meant he was delighted to see Camille, delighted with the effects of the painkilling spell Magnus had used on him—certainly a possibility—or simply rambling.

"And therefore," said Magnus, squeezing Will's arm with a meaning pressure, "we must go."

Will blinked at him. "Go where?"

"Don't worry about that right now, my love."

Will blinked again. "Pardon?" He glanced around, as if he half-expected people to be watching. "I—where's my coat?"

"Ruined with blood," said Magnus. "Archer disposed of it." He nodded toward Camille. "Will's been hunting demons all night. So brave."

Camille's expression was a mixture of amazement and annoyance.

"I *am* brave," Will said. He looked pleased with himself. The painkilling tonics had enlarged his pupils, and his eyes looked very dark.

"Yes, you are," Magnus said, and kissed him. It wasn't the most dramatic kiss, but Will flailed his free arm as if a bee had landed on him; Magnus had to hope Camille would assume this was passion. When they broke apart, Will looked stunned. So did Camille, for that matter.

"*Now*," Magnus said, hoping that Will would recollect that he was indebted to him. "We must go."

"I—but—" Will swung sideways. "The tooth!" He dashed across the room, retrieved it, and tucked it into Magnus's waistcoat pocket. Then, with a wink at Camille that, Magnus thought, God alone knew how she would interpret, he sauntered out of the room.

"Camille," Magnus began.

She had her arms crossed over her chest and was looking at him venomously. "Carrying on with Shadowhunters behind my back," she said icily, and with no apparent regard for the hypocrisy of her position. "And in my own house! Really, Magnus." She pointed toward the door. "Please leave my residence and do not return. I trust I shall not have to ask you twice."

Magnus was only too pleased to oblige. A few moments later he had joined Will on the pavement outside the house, shrugging on his coat—all he now owned in the world besides what was in his pockets—and fastening the buttons against the chilly air. It would not be long, Magnus thought, before the first gray flush of morning lightened the sky.

"Did you just kiss me?" Will inquired.

Magnus made a split-second decision. "No."

"I thought—"

"On occasion the aftereffects of the painkilling spells can result in hallucinations of the most bizarre sort."

"Oh," Will said. "How peculiar." He looked back at Camille's house. Magnus could see the window of the drawing room, the red velvet curtains drawn tight. "What are we going to do now? About summoning the demon? Have we somewhere to go?"

"*I've* got somewhere to go," said Magnus, saying a prayer of silent thanks for Will's single-minded fixation on demon summoning. "I have a friend I can stop with. You go along back to the Institute. I'll get to work on your blasted demon tooth as soon as I possibly can. I'll send a message to you when I know anything."

Will nodded slowly, then looked up at the black sky. "The stars," he said. "I have never seen them so bright. The wind has blown off the fog, I think."

Magnus thought of the joy on Will's face as he had stood bleeding in Camille's living room, clutching the demon tooth in his hand. *Somehow, I don't think it's the stars that have changed.*

"A *Shadowhunter?*" Tessa gasped. "That's not possible." She whirled around and looked at Charlotte, whose face mirrored her own shock. "It isn't possible, is it? Will told me that the offspring of Shadowhunters and demons are stillborn."

Charlotte was shaking her head. "No. No, it isn't possible."

"But if Jessamine has to tell the truth—" Tessa's voice wavered.

"She has to tell the truth as she believes it," said Charlotte. "If your brother lied to her but she believed him, she will speak it as if it were the truth."

"Nate would never lie to me," Jessamine spat.

"If Tessa's mother was a Shadowhunter," said Charlotte coldly, "then Nate is also a Shadowhunter. Shadowhunter blood breeds true. Did he ever mention *that* to you? That he was a Shadowhunter?"

Jessamine looked revolted. "*Nate* isn't a Shadowhunter!" she cried. "I would have known! I would never have married—" She broke off, biting down on her lip.

"Well, it's one or the other, Jessamine," said Charlotte.

"Either you married a Shadowhunter, a truly supreme irony, or, more likely, you married a liar who used and discarded you. He must have known you'd be caught eventually. And what did he think would happen to you then?"

"Nothing." Jessamine looked shaken. "He said you were weak. That you would not punish me. That you could not bring yourself to truly harm me."

"He was wrong," said Charlotte. "You are a traitor to the Clave. So is Benedict Lightwood. When the Consul hears of all this—"

Jessamine laughed, a thin, broken sound. "Tell him," she said. "That's *exactly* what Mortmain wants." She sputtered. "D-don't bother asking me why. I don't know. But I know he wants it. So tattle all you like, Charlotte. It will only put you in his power."

Charlotte gripped the footboard of the bed, her hands whitening. "Where is Mortmain?"

Jessamine shuddered, shaking her head, her hair whipping back and forth. "No . . ."

"Where is Mortmain?"

"H-he," she gasped. "He—" Jessamine's face was almost purple, her eyes bugging out of her head. She was clutching the Sword so tightly that blood welled around her fingers. Tessa looked at Charlotte in horror. *"Idris,"* Jessamine gasped at last, and slumped back against the pillow.

Charlotte's face froze. "Idris?" she echoed. "Mortmain is in Idris, our homeland?"

Jessamine's eyelids fluttered. "No. He is not there."

"Jessamine!" Charlotte looked as if she were going to leap on the girl and shake her till her teeth rattled. "How can he be in Idris and not be? Save yourself, you stupid girl. Tell us where he is!"

"Stop!" Jessamine cried out. "Stop, it hurts. . . ."

Charlotte gave her a long, hard look. Then she went to the door of the room; when she returned, it was with Brother Enoch in tow. She crossed her arms over her chest and indicated Jessamine with a jerk of her chin. "There is something wrong, Brother. I asked her where Mortmain was; she said Idris. When I asked again, she denied it." Her voice hardened. "Jessamine! Has Mortmain breached the wards of Idris?"

Jessamine made a choking sound; her breath wheezed in and out of her chest. "No, he has not. . . . I swear . . . Charlotte, please . . ."

Charlotte. Brother Enoch spoke firmly, his words echoing in Tessa's mind. *Enough. There is some sort of block in the girl's mind, something placed there by Mortmain. He taunts us with the idea of Idris, yet she confesses he is not there. These blocks are strong. Continue to question her in this manner, and her heart may well fail her.*

Charlotte sagged back. "Then what . . ."

Let me take her to the Silent City. We have our ways of seeking out the secrets locked in the mind, secrets even the girl herself may not be aware she knows.

Brother Enoch withdrew the Sword from Jessamine's grasp. She seemed barely to notice. Her gaze was on Charlotte, her eyes wide and panicked. "The City of Bones?" she whispered. "Where the dead lie? No! I will not go there! I cannot bear that place!"

"Then tell us where Mortmain is," said Charlotte, her voice like ice.

Jessamine only began to sob. Charlotte ignored her. Brother

Enoch lifted the girl to her feet; Jessamine struggled, but the Silent Brother held her in an iron grip, his other hand on the hilt of the Mortal Sword.

"Charlotte!" Jessamine shrieked piteously. "Charlotte, please, not the Silent City! Lock me in the crypt, give me to the Council, but please do not send me alone to that—that grave-yard! I shall die of fear!"

"You should have thought of that before you betrayed us," said Charlotte. "Brother Enoch, take her, please."

Jessamine was still shrieking as the Silent Brother lifted her and threw her over his shoulder. As Tessa stared, wide-eyed, he strode from the room carrying her. Her cries and gasps echoed down the corridor long after the door closed behind them— and then were cut off suddenly.

"Jessamine—," Tessa began.

"She is quite all right. He has probably put a Rune of Quietude on her. That is all. There is nothing to worry about," said Charlotte, and she sat down on the edge of the bed. She looked down at her own hands, wonderingly, as if they did not belong to her. "Henry . . ."

"Shall I rouse him for you, Mrs. Branwell?" Sophie asked gently.

"He is in the crypt, working. . . . I could not bear to get him." Charlotte's voice was distant. "Jessamine has been with us since she was a little girl. It would have been too much for him, too much. He does not have it in him to be cruel."

"Charlotte." Tessa touched her shoulder gently. "Charlotte, you are not cruel either."

"I do what I must. There is nothing to worry about," Charlotte said again, and burst into tears.

14

THE SILENT CITY

She howl'd aloud, "I am on fire within.
  There comes no murmur of reply.
What is it that will take away my sin,
  And save me lest I die?"
—Alfred, Lord Tennyson, "The Palace of Art"

"Jessamine," Henry said again, for what must have been the fifth or sixth time. "I still can't believe it. Our Jessamine?"

Every time he said it, Tessa noticed, Charlotte's mouth grew a little tighter. "Yes," she said again. "Jessamine. She has been spying on us and reporting our every move to Nate, who has been passing the information to Mortmain. Must I say it again?"

Henry blinked at her. "I'm sorry, darling. I have been listening. It is only that—" He sighed. "I knew she was unhappy here. But I did not think Jessamine hated us."

"I don't think she did—or does." This was Jem, who was

standing near the fire in the drawing room, one arm upon the mantel. They had not gathered for breakfast as they usually did; there had been no formal announcement as to why, but Tessa guessed that the idea of going on with breakfast, with Jessamine's place empty, as if nothing had happened, had been too dreadful for Charlotte to bear.

Charlotte had wept for only a short time that night before she had regained her composure; she had waved away Sophie's and Tessa's attempts to help with cold cloths or tea, shaking her head stiffly and saying over and over that she should not allow herself to break down like this, that now was the time for planning, for strategy. She had marched to Tessa's room, with Sophie and Tessa hurrying at her heels, and pried feverishly at the floorboards until she'd turned up a small chapbook, like a family Bible, bound in white leather and wrapped in velvet. She had slipped it into her pocket with a determined expression, waving away Tessa's questions, and risen to her feet. The sky outside the windows had already begun to brighten with the wan light of dawn. Looking exhausted, she had told Sophie to instruct Bridget to serve a simple cold breakfast in the drawing room, and to let Cyril know so that the menfolk might be informed. Then she had left.

With Sophie's help Tessa had finally and gratefully fought her way free of Jessamine's dress; she had bathed, and put on her yellow dress, the one Jessamine had bought her. She thought the color might brighten her mood, but she still felt wan and tired.

She found the same look reflected on Jem's face when she came into the drawing room. His eyes were shadowed, and he looked quickly away from her. It hurt. It also made her think of the night before, with Will, on the balcony. But that had been different, she told herself. That had been a result of warlock powders, a temporary madness. Nothing like what had happened between her and Jem.

"I don't think she hates us," Jem said again now, correcting his use of the past tense. "She has always been someone so full of *wanting*. She has always been so desperate."

"It is my fault," Charlotte said softly. "I should not have tried to force being a Shadowhunter upon her when it was something she so clearly despised."

"No. No!" Henry hurried to reassure his wife. "You were never anything but kind to her. You did everything you could. There are some mechanisms that are so—so broken that they cannot be repaired."

"Jessamine is not a watch, Henry," Charlotte said, her tone remote. Tessa wondered if she were still angry with Henry for not seeing Woolsey Scott with her, or if she were simply angry at the world. "Perhaps I should just parcel up the Institute with a bow and give it to Benedict Lightwood. This is the second time that we have had a spy under our roof and not known about it until significant damage was done. Clearly I am incompetent."

"In a way it was really just the one spy," Henry began, but fell silent as Charlotte gave him a look that could have melted glass.

"If Benedict Lightwood is working for Mortmain, he cannot be allowed to have custody of the Institute," said Tessa. "In fact, that ball he threw last night ought to be enough to disqualify him."

"The problem will be proving it," said Jem. "Benedict will

deny everything, and it will be his word against yours—and you are a Downworlder—"

"There's Will," said Charlotte, and frowned. "Speaking of, where *is* Will?"

"Having a lie-in, no doubt," said Jem, "and as for him being a witness, well, everyone thinks Will is a lunatic as it is—"

"Ah," said a voice from the doorway, "having your annual everyone-thinks-Will-is-a-lunatic meeting, are you?"

"It's biannual," said Jem. "And no, this is not that meeting."

Will's eyes sought Tessa across the room. "They know about Jessamine?" he said. He looked tired, but not as tired as Tessa would have thought; he was pale, but there was a suppressed excitement about him that was almost like—happiness. She felt her stomach drop as memories of the previous night—the stars, the balcony, the *kissing*—swept over her.

When had he gotten home last night? she thought. How had he? And why did he look so—excited? Was he horrified by what had happened on the balcony between them last night, or did he find it amusing? And dear God, had he told *Jem*? Warlock powders, she told herself desperately. She had not been herself, acting of her own will. Surely Jem would understand that. It would break her heart to hurt him. If he even cared . . .

"Yes, they know all about Jessamine," she said hastily. "She was questioned with the Mortal Sword and taken to the Silent City, and right now we're having a meeting about what to do next, and it's dreadfully important. Charlotte's very upset."

Charlotte looked at her in puzzlement.

"Well, you *are*," Tessa said, nearly out of breath from speaking so quickly. "And you were asking for Will—"

"And here I am," said Will, throwing himself down into a

chair near Jem. One of his arms had been bandaged, his sleeve pulled down partway over it. The nails of his hand were crusted with dried blood. "Glad to hear Jessamine's in the Silent City. Best place for her. What's the next step?"

"*That's* the meeting we were trying to have," said Jem.

"Well, who knows she's there?" Will asked practically.

"Just us," said Charlotte, "and Brother Enoch, but he's agreed not to inform the Clave for another day or so. Until we decide what to do. Which reminds me, I shall have some choice words for you, Will, haring off to Benedict Lightwood's without informing me, and dragging Tessa with you."

"There was no time to lose," said Will. "By the time we'd have roused you and made you agree to the plan, Nathaniel could have been and gone. And you can't say it was a dreadful idea. We've learned a great deal about Nathaniel and Benedict Lightwood—"

"Nathaniel Gray and Benedict Lightwood aren't Mortmain."

Will traced a pattern on the air with his long, elegant fingers. "Mortmain is the spider at the heart of the web," he said. "The more we learn, the more we know how far his reach extends. Before last night we had no clue he had any connection to Lightwood; now we know the man is his puppet. I say we go to the Clave and report Benedict and Jessamine. Let Wayland take care of them. See what Benedict spills under the Mortal Sword."

Charlotte shook her head. "No, I—I don't think we can do that."

Will tilted his head back. "Why not?"

"Jessamine said it was exactly what Mortmain wanted us to do. And she said it under the influence of the Mortal Sword. She wasn't lying."

"But she could have been *wrong*," said Will. "Mortmain could have foreseen just this circumstance and have had Nate plant the thought in her head for us to discover."

"D'you think he would have thought ahead like that?" said Henry.

"Assuredly," said Will. "The man's a strategist." He tapped his temple. "Like me."

"So you think we should go to the Clave?" asked Jem.

"Bloody hell, no," said Will. "What if it is the truth? Then we'll feel like right fools."

Charlotte threw her hands up. "But you said—"

"I know what I *said*," said Will. "But you have to look at consequences. If we go to the Clave and we're wrong, then we've played into Mortmain's hands. We still have a few days before the deadline is up. Going to the Clave early gains us nothing. If we investigate, and can proceed on a surer footing . . ."

"And how do you propose to investigate?" Tessa inquired.

Will swiveled his head to look at her. There was nothing in his cool blue eyes to recall the Will of the night before, who had touched her with such tenderness, who had whispered her name like a secret. "The problem with questioning Jessamine is that even when forced to tell the truth, there is a limit to her knowledge. We do, however, have one more connection to the Magister. Someone who is likely to know a great deal more. That is your brother, Nate, through Jessamine. He still trusts her. If she summons him to a meeting, then we will be able to capture him there."

"Jessamine would never agree to do it," said Charlotte. "Not now—"

Will gave her a dark look. "You *are* all in a lather, aren't you?" he said. "Of course she wouldn't. We will be asking Tessa to reprise her starring role as Jessamine, A Traitorous Young Lady of Fashion."

"That sounds dangerous," Jem said in a subdued voice. "For Tessa."

Tessa looked at him quickly, and caught a flash of his silvery eyes. It was the first time he had looked at her since she had left his room that night. Was she imagining the concern in his voice when he spoke of danger to her, or was it simply the concern Jem had for *everyone*? Not wishing for her horrible demise was mere kindness, not—not what it was she hoped he felt.

Whatever that might be. Let him at least not despise her. . . .

"Tessa is fearless," said Will. "And there will be little danger to her. We will send him a note arranging a meeting in a place where we might fall upon him easily and immediately. The Silent Brothers can torture him until he gives up the information that we need."

"Torture?" said Jem. "This is Tessa's brother—"

"Torture him," said Tessa. "If that is what is necessary. I give you my permission."

Charlotte looked up at her, shocked. "You can't mean that."

"You said there was a way to dig through his mind for secrets," Tessa said. "I asked you not to do that, and you didn't. I thank you for that, but I will not hold you to that promise. Dig through his mind if you must. There is more to all of this for me than there is for you, you know. For you this is about the Institute and the safety of Shadowhunters. I care about those things too, Charlotte. But Nate—he is working with Mortmain. Mortmain, who wants to trap me and use me, and for what we still do not know. Mortmain, who may know *what I am*. Nate told Jessamine my father was a demon and my mother was a Shadowhunter—"

Will sat up straight. "That's impossible," he said. "Shadowhunters and demons—they cannot procreate. They cannot produce living offspring."

"Then maybe it was a lie, like the lie about Mortmain being in Idris," said Tessa. "That doesn't mean *Mortmain* doesn't know the truth. I must know what I am. If nothing else, I believe it is the key to why he wants me."

There was sadness in Jem's eyes as he looked at her, and then away. "Very well," he said. "Will, how do you propose we lure him to a meeting? Don't you think he knows Jessamine's handwriting? Isn't it likely they have some secret signal between them?"

"Jessamine must be convinced," said Will. "To help us."

"Please don't suggest we torture her," said Jem irritably. "The Mortal Sword has already been used. She has told us all she can—"

"The Mortal Sword did not give us their meeting places or any codes or pet names they might have used," said Will. "Don't you understand? This is Jessamine's last chance. Her last chance to cooperate. To get leniency from the Clave. To be forgiven. Even if Charlotte keeps the Institute, do you think they will leave Jessamine's fate in our hands? No, it will be left to the Consul and the Inquisitor. And they will not be kind. If she does this for us, it could mean her life."

"I am not sure she cares about her life," said Tessa softly.

"Everyone cares," said Will. "Everyone wants to live."

Jem turned away from him abruptly, and stared into the fire.

"The question is, who can we send to persuade her?" said Charlotte. "I cannot go. She hates and blames me most of all."

"I could go," Henry said, his gentle face troubled. "I could perhaps reason with the poor girl, speak with her of the folly of young love, how swiftly it fades in the face of life's harsh reality—"

"No." Charlotte's tone was final.

"Well, I highly doubt she wishes to see *me*," said Will. "It will have to be Jem. He's impossible to hate. Even that devil cat likes him."

Jem exhaled, still staring into the fire. "I will go to the Silent City," he said. "But Tessa should come with me."

Tessa looked up, startled. "Oh, no," she said. "I do not think Jessamine likes me much. She feels I have betrayed her terribly by disguising myself as her, and I cannot say I blame her."

"Yes," said Jem. "But you are Nate's sister. If she loves him as you say she does . . ." His eyes met hers across the room. "You know Nate. You can speak of him with authority. You may be able to make her believe what I cannot."

"Very well," Tessa said. "I will try."

This seemed to signal the end of breakfast; Charlotte darted off to call for a carriage to come for them from the Silent City; it was how the Brothers liked to do things, she explained. Henry returned to his crypt and his inventions, and Jem, after a murmured word to Tessa, went to gather his hat and coat. Only Will remained, staring into the fire, and Tessa, seeing that he was not moving, waited until the door shut behind Jem and came around to stand between Will and the flames.

He raised his eyes to her slowly. He was still wearing the clothes he had been wearing the night before, though his white shirtfront was stained with blood and there was a long, jagged rent in his frock coat. There was a cut along his cheek, too, under his left eye. "Will," she said.

"Aren't you meant to be leaving with Jem?"

"And I shall," she replied. "But I need a promise from you first."

His eyes moved to the fire; she could see the dancing flames reflected in his pupils. "Then tell me what it is quickly. I have important business to get to. I plan to sulk all afternoon, followed, perhaps, by an evening of Byronic brooding and a nighttime of dissipation."

"Dissipate all you like. I only want your assurance that you will tell no one what transpired between us last night on the balcony."

"Oh, that was *you*," said Will, with the air of someone who has just recollected a surprising detail.

"Spare me," she snapped, stung despite herself. "We were under the influence of warlock powders. It meant nothing. Even I do not blame you for what happened, however tedious you are being about it now. But there is no need for anyone else to know, and if you were a gentleman—"

"But I am not."

"But you are a Shadowhunter," she said venomously. "And there is no future for a Shadowhunter who dallies with warlocks."

His eyes danced with fire. He said, "You have become boring to tease, Tess."

"Then give me your word you will tell no one, not even Jem, and I will go away and cease to bore you."

"You have my word on the Angel," he said. "It was not

something I had planned to brag of in the first place. Though why you are so keen that no one here suspect you of a lack of virtue, I do not know."

Jem's face flashed across her inner eye. "No," she said. "You truly don't." And with that she turned on her heel and stalked from the room, leaving him staring after her in confusion.

Sophie hurried down Piccadilly, her head bent, her eyes on the pavement beneath her feet. She was used to hushed murmurs and the occasional stare when she went out and eyes fell upon her scar; she had perfected a way of walking that hid her face beneath the shadow of her hat. She was not ashamed of the scar, but she hated the pity in the eyes of those who saw it.

She was wearing one of Jessamine's old dresses. It was not out of fashion yet, but Jessamine was one of those girls who dubbed any dress she had worn more than three times "historical" and either cast it off or had it made over. It was a striped watered silk in green and white, and there were waxy white flowers and green leaves on her hat. All together, she thought, she could pass for a girl of good breeding—if she were not out on her own, that was—especially with her work-roughened hands covered in a pair of white kid gloves.

She saw Gideon before he saw her. He was leaning against a lamppost outside the great pale-green porte cochere of Fortnum & Mason. Her heart skipped a little beat as she looked at him, so handsome in his dark clothes, checking the time on a gold watch affixed to his waistcoat pocket by a thin chain. She paused for a moment, watching the people stream around him, the busy life of London roaring around him, and Gideon as calm as a rock in the middle of a churning river. All Shadowhunters had something of that to them, she thought, that stillness, that dark aura of separateness that set them apart from the current of mundane life.

He looked up then, and saw her, and smiled that smile that changed his whole face. "Miss Collins," he said, coming forward, and she moved forward to meet him as well, feeling as she did so as if she were stepping into the circle of his separateness. The steady noise of city traffic, pedestrian and otherwise, seemed to dim, and it was just her and Gideon, facing each other on the street.

"Mr. Lightwood," she said.

His face changed, only a little, but she saw it. She saw too that he was holding something in his left hand, a woven picnic basket. She looked at it, and then at him.

"One of Fortnum & Mason's famous hampers," he said with a sideways smile. "Stilton cheese, quails' eggs, rose petal jam—"

"Mr. Lightwood," she said again, interrupting him, to her own amazement. A servant *never* interrupted a gentleman. "I have been most distressed—most distressed in my own mind, you understand, as to whether I should come here at all. I finally decided that I should, if only to tell you to your own face that I cannot see you. I thought you deserved that much, though I am not sure of it."

He looked at her, stunned, and in that moment she saw not a Shadowhunter but an ordinary boy, like Thomas or Cyril, clutching a picnic basket and unable to hide the surprise and hurt on his face. "Miss Collins, if there is something I have done to offend—"

"I cannot see you. That is all," Sophie said, and turned

away, meaning to hurry back the way she had come. If she was quick, she could catch the next omnibus back to the City—

"Miss Collins. Please." It was Gideon, at her elbow. He did not touch her, but he was walking alongside her, his expression distraught. "Tell me what I've done."

She shook her head mutely. The look on his face—perhaps it had been a mistake to come. They were passing Hatchards bookshop, and she considered ducking inside; surely he would not follow her, not into a place where they'd likely be overheard. But then again, perhaps he would.

"I know what it is," he said abruptly. "Will. He told you, didn't he?"

"The fact that you say that informs me that there was something to tell."

"Miss Collins, I can explain. Just come with me—this way." He turned, and she found herself following him, warily. They were in front of St. James's Church; he led her around the side and down a narrow street that bridged the gap between Piccadilly and Jermyn Street. It was quieter here, though not deserted; several passing pedestrians gave them curious looks—the scarred girl and the handsome boy with the pale face, carefully setting his hamper down at his feet.

"This is about last night," he said. "The ball at my father's house in Chiswick. I thought I saw Will. I had wondered if he would tell the rest of you."

"You confess it, then? That you were there, at that depraved—that unsuitable—"

"Unsuitable? It was a sight more than unsuitable," said Gideon, with more force than she had ever heard him use. Behind them the bell of the church tolled the hour; he seemed not to hear it. "Miss Collins, all I can do is swear to you that until last night I had no idea with what low company, what destructive habits, my father had engaged himself. I have been in Spain this past half-year—"

"And he was not like this before that?" Sophie asked, disbelieving.

"Not quite. It is difficult to explain." His eyes strayed past her, their gray-green stormier than ever. "My father has always been one to flout convention. To bend the Law, if not to break it. He has always taught us that this is the way that everyone goes along, that all Shadowhunters do it. And we—Gabriel and I—having lost our mother so young, had no better example to follow. It was not until I arrived in Madrid that I began to understand the full extent of my father's . . . incorrectness. Everyone does not flout the Law and bend the rules, and I was treated as if I were some monstrous creature for believing it to be so, until I changed my ways. Research and observation led me to believe I had been given poor principles to follow, and that it had been done with deliberation. I could think only of Gabriel and how I might save him from the same realization, or at least from having it delivered so shockingly."

"And your sister—Miss Lightwood?"

Gideon shook his head. "She has been sheltered from it all. My father thinks that women have no business with the darker aspects of Downworld. No, it is I who he believes must know of his involvements, for I am the heir to the Lightwood estate. It was with an eye to that that my father brought me with him to the event last night, at which, I assume, Will saw me."

"You knew he was there?"

"I was so disgusted by what I saw inside that room that I

eventually fought my way free and went out into the gardens for some fresh air. The stench of demons had made me nauseated. Out there, I saw someone familiar chasing a blue demon across the parkland with an air of determination."

"Mr. Herondale?"

Gideon shrugged. "I had no idea what he was doing there; I knew he could not have been invited, but could not fathom how he had found out about it, or if his pursuit of the demon was unrelated. I wasn't sure until I saw the look on your face when you beheld me, just now . . ."

Sophie's voice rose and sharpened. "But did you tell your father, or Gabriel? Do they know? About Master Will?"

Gideon shook his head slowly. "I told them nothing. I do not think they expected Will there in any capacity. The Shadowhunters of the Institute are meant to be in pursuit of Mortmain."

"They are," said Sophie slowly, and when his only look was one of incomprehension, she said: "Those clockwork creatures at your father's party—where did you think they came from?"

"I didn't—I assumed they were demon playthings of some sort—"

"They can only have come from Mortmain," said Sophie. "You haven't seen his automatons before, but Mr. Herondale and Miss Gray, they have, and they were sure."

"But why would my father have anything of Mortmain's?"

Sophie shook her head. "It may be that you should not ask me questions you don't want the answer to, Mr. Lightwood."

"Miss Collins." His hair fell forward over his eyes; he tossed it back with an impatient gesture. "Miss Collins, I know that whatever you tell me, it will be the truth. In many ways, of all those I have met in London, I find you the most trustworthy—more so than my own family."

"That seems to me a great misfortune, Mr. Lightwood, for we have known each other only a little time indeed."

"I hope to change that. At least walk to the park with me, Soph—Miss Collins. Tell me this truth of which you speak. If then you still desire no further connection with me, I will respect your wishes. I ask only for an hour or so of your time." His eyes pleaded with her. "Please?"

Sophie felt, almost against her will, a rush of sympathy for this boy with his sea-storm eyes, who seemed so alone. "Very well," she said. "I will come to the park with you."

An entire carriage ride alone with Jem, Tessa thought, her stomach clenching as she drew on her gloves and cast a last glance at herself in the pier glass in her bedroom. Just two nights ago the prospect had precipitated in her no new or unusual feelings; she had been worried about Will, and curious about Whitechapel, and Jem had gently distracted her as they'd rolled along, speaking of Latin and Greek and *parabatai*.

And now? Now she felt like a net of butterflies was loose in her stomach at the prospect of being shut up in a small, close space alone with him. She glanced at her pale face in the mirror, pinched her cheeks and bit her lips to bring color into them, and reached for her hat on the stand beside the vanity. Settling it on her brown hair, she caught herself wishing she had golden curls like Jessamine, and thought—Could I? Would it be possible to Change just that one small part of herself, give herself shimmering hair, or perhaps a slimmer waist or fuller lips?

She whirled away from the glass, shaking her head. How

had she *not* thought of that before? And yet the mere idea seemed like a betrayal of her own face. Her hunger to know what she was still burned inside her; if even her own features were no longer the ones she'd been born with, how could she justify this demand, this need to know her own nature? *Don't you know there is no Tessa Gray?* Mortmain had said to her. If she used her power to turn her eyes sky blue or to darken her lashes, wouldn't she be proving him right?

She shook her head, trying to cast the thoughts off as she hurried from her room and down the steps to the Institute's entryway. Waiting in the courtyard was a black carriage, unmarked by any coat of arms and driven by a pair of matched horses the color of smoke. In the driver's seat sat a Silent Brother; it was not Brother Enoch but another of his brethren that she didn't recognize. His face was not as scarred as Enoch's, from what she could see beneath the hood.

She started down the steps just as the door opened behind her and Jem came out; it was chilly, and he wore a light gray coat that made his hair and eyes look more silver than ever. He looked up at the equally gray sky, heavy with black-edged clouds, and said, "We'd better get into the carriage before it starts to rain."

It was a perfectly ordinary thing to say, but Tessa was struck speechless all the same. She followed Jem silently to the carriage and allowed him to help her in. As he climbed in after her, and swung the door shut behind them, she noticed he was not carrying his sword-cane.

The carriage started forward with a lurch. Tessa, her hand at the window, gave a cry. "The gates—they're locked! The carriage—"

"Hush." Jem put his hand on her arm. She couldn't help a gasp as the carriage rumbled up to the padlocked iron gates—and passed *through* them, as if they had been made of no more substance than air. She felt the breath go out of her in a whoosh of surprise. "The Silent Brothers have strange magic," said Jem, and dropped his hand.

At that moment it began to rain, the sky opening up like a punctured hot water bottle. Through the sheets of silver Tessa stared as the carriage rolled through pedestrians as if they were ghosts, slipped into the narrowest cracks between buildings, rattled through a courtyard and then a warehouse, boxes all about them, and emerged finally on the Embankment, itself slick and wet with rain beside the heaving gray water of the Thames.

"Oh, dear God," Tessa said, and drew the curtain shut. "Tell me we aren't going to roll into the river."

Jem laughed. Even through her shock, it was a welcome sound. "No. The carriages of the Silent City travel only on land, as far as I know, though that travel *is* peculiar. It's a bit sickening the first time or two, but you get used to it."

"Do you?" She looked at him directly. This was the moment. She had to say it, before their friendship suffered further. Before there could be more awkwardness. "Jem," she said.

"Yes?"

"I—you must know—how very much your friendship means to me," she began, awkwardly. "And—"

A look of pain flashed across his face. "Please don't."

Thrown off her stride, Tessa could only blink. "What do you mean?"

"Every time you say that word, 'friendship,' it goes into me like a knife," he said. "To be friends is a beautiful thing, Tessa, and I do not scorn it, but I have hoped for a long time now that we might be more than friends. And then I had thought after the other night that perhaps my hopes were not in vain. But now—"

"Now I have ruined everything," she whispered. "I am so sorry."

He looked toward the window; she could sense that he was fighting some strong emotion. "You should not have to apologize for not returning my feelings."

"But *Jem*." She was bewildered, and could think only of taking his pain away, of making him feel less hurt. "I was apologizing for my behavior that other night. It was forward and inexcusable. What you must think of me . . ."

He looked up in surprise. "Tessa, you can't think that, can you? It is I who have behaved inexcusably. I have barely been able to look at you since, thinking how much you must despise me—"

"I could never despise you," she said. "I have never met anyone as kind and good as you are. I thought it was you who were dismayed by me. That you despised me."

Jem looked shocked. "How could I despise you when it was my own distraction that led to what happened between us? If I had not been in such a desperate state, I would have shown more restraint."

He means he would have had enough restraint to stop me, Tessa thought. *He does not expect propriety of me. He assumes it would not be in my nature.* She stared fixedly at the window again, or the bit of it she could see. The river was visible, black boats bobbing on the tide, the rain mixing with the river.

"Tessa." He scrambled across the carriage so that he was sitting beside her rather than across from her, his anxious, beautiful face close to hers. "I know that mundane girls are taught that it is their responsibility not to tempt men. That men are weak and women must restrain them. I assure you, Shadowhunter mores are different. More equal. It was our equal choice to do—what we did."

She stared at him. He was so kind, she thought. He seemed to read the fears in her heart and move to dispel them before she could speak them aloud.

She thought then of Will. Of what had transpired between them the previous evening. She pushed away the memory of the cold air all around them, the heat between their bodies as they clung together. She had been drugged, as had he. Nothing they had said or done meant anything more than an opium addict's babbling. There was no need to tell anyone; it had meant nothing. Nothing.

"Say something, Tessa." Jem's voice shook. "I fear that you think that I regret that night. I do not." His thumb brushed over her wrist, the bare skin between the cuff of her dress and her glove. "I only regret that it came too soon. I—I would have wanted to—to court you first. To take you driving, with a chaperon."

"A chaperon?" Tessa laughed despite herself.

He went on determinedly. "To *tell* you of my feelings first, before I showed them. To write poetry for you—"

"You don't even like poetry," Tessa said, her voice catching on a half laugh of relief.

"No. But you make me want to write it. Does that not count for anything?"

Tessa's lips curled into a smile. She leaned forward and looked up into his face, so close to hers that she could make out each individual silvery eyelash on his lids, the faint white scars on his pale throat where once there had been Marks. "That sounds almost practiced, James Carstairs. How many girls have you made swoon with that observation?"

"There is only one girl I care to make swoon," he said. "The question is, does she?"

She smiled at him. "She does."

A moment later—she did not know how it had happened—he was kissing her, his lips soft on hers, his hand rising to cup her cheek and chin, holding her face steady. Tessa heard a light crinkling and realized it was the sound of the silk flowers on her hat being crushed against the side of the carriage as his body pressed hers back. She clutched at his coat lapels, as much to keep him close as to stop herself from falling over.

The carriage came to a jerking halt. Jem drew back from her, looking dazed. "By the Angel," he said. "Perhaps we do need a chaperon."

Tessa shook her head. "Jem, I . . ."

Jem still looked stunned. "I think I'd better sit over here," he said, and moved to the seat across from hers. Tessa glanced toward the window. Through the gap in the curtains she saw that the Houses of Parliament loomed above them, towers framed darkly against the lightening sky. It had stopped raining. She was not sure why the carriage had stopped; indeed, it rumbled into life a moment later, rolling directly into what seemed a pit of black shadow that had opened up before them. She knew enough not to gasp in surprise this time; there was darkness, and then they rolled out into the great room of black basalt lit with torches that she remembered from the Council meeting.

The carriage stopped and the door flew open. Several Silent Brothers stood on the other side. Brother Enoch was at their head. Two Brothers flanked him, each holding a burning torch. Their hoods were back. Both were blind, though only one, like Enoch, seemed to have missing eyes; the others had eyes that were shut, with runes scrawled blackly across them. All had their lips stitched shut.

Welcome again to the Silent City, Daughter of Lilith, said Brother Enoch.

For a moment Tessa wanted to reach behind herself for the warm pressure of Jem's hand on hers, let him help her out of the carriage. She thought of Charlotte then. Charlotte, so small and strong, who leaned on no one.

She emerged from the carriage on her own, the heels of her boots ringing on the basalt floor. "Thank you, Brother Enoch," she said. "We are here to see Jessamine Lovelace. Will you take us to her?"

The prisons of the Silent City were beneath its first level, past the pavilion of the Speaking Stars. A dark staircase led down. The Silent Brothers went first, followed by Jem and Tessa, who had not spoken to each other since they'd left the carriage. It was not an awkward silence, though. There was something about the haunting grandeur of the City of Bones, with its great mausoleums and soaring arches, that made her feel as if she were in a museum or a church, where hushed voices were required.

At the bottom of the stairs, a corridor snaked in two

directions; the Silent Brothers turned to the left, and led Jem and Tessa nearly to the end of the hall. As they went, they passed row after row of small chambers, each with a barred, padlocked door. Each contained a bed and washstand, and nothing else. The walls were stone, and the smell was of water and dampness. Tessa wondered if they were under the Thames, or somewhere else altogether.

At last the Brothers stopped at a door, the second to the last on the hall, and Brother Enoch touched the padlock. It clicked open, and the chains holding the door shut fell away.

You are welcome to enter, said Enoch, stepping back. *We will be waiting for you outside.*

Jem put his hand to the door handle and hesitated, looking at Tessa. "Perhaps you should talk to her for a moment alone. Woman to woman."

Tessa was startled. "Are you sure? You know her better than I do—"

"But you know Nate," said Jem, and his eyes flicked away from her briefly. Tessa had the feeling there was something he was not telling her. It was such an unusual feeling when it came to Jem that she was not sure how to react. "I will join you in a moment, once you have put her at ease."

Slowly Tessa nodded. Brother Enoch swung the door open, and she walked inside, flinching a little as the heavy door crashed to behind her.

It was a small room, like the others, stone-bound. There was a washstand and what had probably once been a ceramic jug of water; now it was in pieces on the floor, as if someone had thrown it with great force against the wall. On the narrow bed sat Jessamine in a plain white gown, a rough blanket wrapped around her. Her hair fell around her shoulders in tangled snakes, and her eyes were red.

"Welcome. Nice place to live out of, isn't this?" Jessamine said. Her voice sounded rough, as if her throat were swollen from crying. She looked at Tessa, and her lower lip began to tremble. "Did—did Charlotte send you to bring me back?"

Tessa shook her head. "No."

"But—" Jessamine's eyes began to fill. "She can't *leave* me here. I can hear them, all night." She shuddered, pulling the blanket closer around her.

"You can hear what?"

"The dead," she said. "Whispering in their tombs. If I stay down here long enough, I will join them. I know it."

Tessa sat down on the edge of the bed and carefully touched Jessamine's hair, stroking the snarls lightly. "That won't happen," she said, and Jessamine began to sob. Her shoulders shook. Helplessly Tessa looked around the room, as if something in the miserable cell might give her inspiration. "Jessamine," she said. "I brought you something."

Jessamine very slowly raised her face. "Is it from Nate?"

"No," Tessa answered gently. "It's something of yours." She reached into her pocket and drew it out, extending her hand toward Jessamine. In her palm lay a tiny baby doll that she had taken from its crib inside Jessamine's doll's house. "Baby Jessie."

Jessamine made an "oh" sound low in her throat, and plucked the doll from Tessa's grasp. She held it tightly, against her chest. Her eyes spilled over, her tears making tracks in the grime on her face. She really was a most pitiful sight, Tessa thought. If only . . .

"Jessamine," Tessa said again. She felt as if Jessamine were an animal in need of gentling, and that repeating her name in a kind tone might somehow help. "We need your help."

"In betraying Nate," Jessamine snapped. "But I don't know anything. I don't even know why I'm here."

"Yes, you do." It was Jem, coming into the cell. He was flushed and a little out of breath, as if he had been hurrying. He shot Tessa a conspiratorial glance and closed the door behind him. "You know exactly why you're here, Jessie—"

"Because I fell in love!" Jessamine snapped. "You ought to know what that's like. I see how you look at Tessa." She shot Tessa a poisonous look as Tessa's cheeks flamed. "At least Nate is human."

Jem didn't lose his composure. "I haven't betrayed the Institute for Tessa," he said. "I haven't lied to and endangered those who have cared for me since I was orphaned."

"If you wouldn't," said Jessamine, "you don't really love her."

"If she asked me to," said Jem, "I would know she did not really love *me*."

Jessamine sucked in a breath and turned away from him, as if he had slapped her face. "You," she said in a muffled voice. "I always thought you were the nicest one. But you're horrible. You're all horrible. Charlotte *tortured* me with that Mortal Sword until I told everything. What more could you possibly want from me? You've already forced me to betray the man I love."

At the very corner of Tessa's vision, she saw Jem roll his eyes. There was a certain theatricality to Jessamine's despair, as there was to everything she did, but under it—under the role of wronged woman Jessamine had cast herself in—Tessa felt she was genuinely afraid.

"I know you love Nate," Tessa said. "And I know that I will not be able to convince you that he does not return your sentiment."

"You're jealous—"

"Jessamine, Nate cannot love you. There is something wrong with him—some piece missing from his heart. God knows my aunt and I tried to ignore it, to tell each other it was boyish high-jinks and thoughtlessness. But he murdered our aunt—did he tell you that?—murdered the woman who brought him up, and laughed to me about it later. He has no empathy, no capacity for gratitude. If you shield him now, it will win you nothing in his eyes."

"Nor is it likely you will ever see him again," said Jem. "If you do *not* help us, the Clave will never let you go. It will be you and the dead down here for eternity, if you are not punished with a curse."

"Nate said you would try to frighten me," said Jessamine in a sliver of a voice.

"Nate also said the Clave and Charlotte would do nothing to you because they were weak," said Tessa. "That has not proven true. He said to you only what he had to say, to get you to do what he wanted you to. He is my brother, and I tell you, he is a cheat and a liar."

"We need you to write a letter to him," said Jem. "Telling him you have knowledge of a secret Shadowhunter plot against Mortmain, and to meet you tonight—"

Jessamine shook her head, plucking at the rough blanket. "I will not betray him."

"Jessie." Jem's voice was soft; Tessa did not know how Jessamine could hold out against him. "Please. We are only asking you to save yourself. Send this message; tell us your usual meeting place. That is all we ask."

Jessamine shook her head. "Mortmain," she said. "Mortmain will yet win out over you. Then the Silent Brothers will be defeated and Nate will come to claim me."

"Very well," said Tessa. "Imagine that does happen. You say Nate loves you. Then, he would forgive you anything, wouldn't he? Because when a man loves a woman, he understands that she is weak. That she cannot hold out against, for instance, torture, in the manner in which he could."

Jessamine made a whimpering sound.

"He understands that she is frail and delicate and easily led," Tessa went on, and gently touched Jessamine's arm. "Jessie, you see your choice. If you do not help us, the Clave will know it, and they will not be lenient with you. If you do help us, Nate will understand. If he loves you . . . he has no choice. For love means forgiveness."

"I . . ." Jessamine looked from one of them to the other, like a frightened rabbit. "Would you forgive Tessa, if it were her?"

"I would forgive Tessa anything," Jem said gravely.

Tessa could not see his expression, she was facing Jessamine, but she felt her heart skip a beat. She could not look at Jem, too afraid her expression would betray her feelings.

"Jessie, please," she said instead.

Jessamine was silent for a long time. When she spoke, finally, her voice was as thin as a thread. "You will be meeting him, I suppose, disguised as me."

Tessa nodded.

"You must wear boys' clothes," she said. "When I meet him at night, I am always dressed as a boy. It is safer for me to traverse the streets alone like that. He will expect it." She looked up, pushing her matted hair out of her face. "Have you a pen and paper?" she added. "I will write the note."

She took the proffered items from Jem and began to scribble. "I ought to get something in return for this," she said. "If they will not let me out—"

"They will not," said Jem, "until it is determined that your information is good."

"Then they ought to at least give me better food. It's dreadful here. Just gruel and hard bread." Having finished scribbling the note, she handed it to Tessa. "The boys' clothes I wear are behind the doll's house in my room. Take care moving it," she added, and for a moment again she was Jessamine, her brown eyes haughty. "And if you must borrow some of my clothes, do. You've been wearing the same four dresses I bought you in June over and over. That yellow one is practically ancient. And if you don't want anyone to know you've been kissing in carriages, you should refrain from wearing a hat with easily crushed flowers on it. People aren't blind, you know."

"So it seems," said Jem with great gravity, and when Tessa looked over at him, he smiled, just at her.

15

THOUSANDS MORE

There is something horrible about a flower;
This, broken in my hand, is one of those
He threw it in just now; it will not live another hour;
There are thousands more; you do not miss a rose.
—Charlotte Mew, "In Nunhead Cemetery"

The rest of the day at the Institute passed in a mood of great tension, as the Shadowhunters prepared for their confrontation with Nate that night. There were no formal meals again, only a great deal of rushing about, as weapons were readied and polished, gear was prepared, and maps consulted while Bridget, warbling mournful ballads, carried trays of sandwiches and tea up and down the halls.

If it hadn't been for Sophie's invitation to "come and have a pickle" Tessa probably wouldn't have eaten anything all day; as it was, her knotted throat would allow only a few bites of sandwich to slide down before she felt as if she were choking.

I'm going to see Nate tonight, she thought, staring at herself in the pier glass as Sophie knelt at her feet, lacing up her boots—boys' boots from Jessamine's hidden trove of male clothing.

And then I am going to betray him.

She thought of the way Nate had lain in her lap in the carriage on the way from de Quincey's, and the way he had shrieked her name and held on to her when Brother Enoch had appeared. She wondered how much of that had been show. Probably at least part of him had been truly terrified—abandoned by Mortmain, hated by de Quincey, in the hands of Shadowhunters he had no reason to trust.

Except that she had told him they were trustworthy. And he had not cared. He had wanted what Mortmain was offering him. More than he had wanted her safety. More than he had cared about anything else. All the years between them, the time that had knitted them together so closely that she had thought them inseparable, had meant nothing to him.

"You can't brood on it, miss," said Sophie, rising to her feet and dusting off her hands. "He aren't—I mean, he isn't worth it."

"Who isn't worth it?"

"Your brother. Wasn't that what you were thinking on?"

Tessa squinted suspiciously. "Can you tell what I'm thinking because you have the Sight?"

Sophie laughed. "Lord, no, miss. I can read it on your face like a book. You always have the same look when you think of Master Nathaniel. But he's a bad hat, miss, not worth your thoughts."

"He's my brother."

"That doesn't mean you're like him," said Sophie decisively. "Some are just born bad, and that's all there is to it."

Some imp of the perverse made Tessa ask: "And what of Will? Do you still think he was born bad? Lovely and poisonous like a snake, you said."

Sophie raised her delicately arched eyebrows. "Master Will is a mystery, no doubt."

Before Tessa could reply the door swung open, and Jem stood in the doorway. "Charlotte sent me to give you—," he began, and broke off, staring at Tessa.

She looked down at herself. Trousers, shoes, shirt, waistcoat, all in order. It was certainly a peculiar feeling, wearing men's clothes—they were tight in places she was not used to clothes being tight, and loose in others, and they itched—but that hardly explained the look on Jem's face.

"I . . ." Jem had flushed all over, red spreading up from his collar to his face. "Charlotte sent me to tell you we're waiting in the drawing room," he said. Then he turned around and left the room hurriedly.

"Goodness," Tessa said, perplexed. "What was that about?"

Sophie chuckled softly. "Well, look at yourself." Tessa looked. She was flushed, she thought, her hair tumbling loose over her shirt and waistcoat. The shirt had clearly been made with something of a feminine figure in mind, since it did not strain over the bosom as much as Tessa had feared it would; still, it was tight, thanks to Jessie's smaller frame. The trousers were tight as well, as was the fashion, molding themselves to her legs. She cocked her head to the side. There *was* something indecent about it, wasn't there? A man was not supposed to be able to see the shape of a lady's upper legs, or so much of the curve of her hips. There was something about the men's clothing that made her look not masculine but . . . undressed.

"My goodness," she said.

"Indeed," said Sophie. "Don't worry. They'll fit better once you Change, and besides . . . he fancies you anyway."

"I—you know—I mean, you think he fancies me?"

"Quite," said Sophie, sounding unperturbed. "You should see the way he looks at you when he doesn't think you see. Or looks up when a door opens, and is always disappointed when it isn't you. Master Jem, he isn't like Master Will. He can't hide what he's thinking."

"And you're not . . ." Tessa searched for words. "Sophie, you're not—put out with me?"

"Why would I be put out with you?" A little of the amusement had gone out of Sophie's voice, and now she sounded carefully neutral.

You're in for it now, Tessa, she thought. "I thought perhaps that there was a time when you looked at Jem with a certain admiration. That is all. I meant nothing improper, Sophie."

Sophie was silent for such a long time that Tessa was sure she was angry, or worse, terribly hurt. Instead she said, finally, "There was a time when I—when I admired him. He was so gentle and so kind, not like any man I'd known. And so lovely to look at, and the music he makes—" She shook her head, and her dark ringlets bounced. "But he never cared for me. Never by a word or a gesture did he lead me to believe he returned my admiration, though he was never unkind."

"Sophie," Tessa said softly. "You have been more than a maidservant since I have come here. You have been a good friend. I would not do anything that might hurt you."

Sophie looked up at her. "Do you care for him?"

"I think," Tessa said with slow caution, "that I do."

"Good." Sophie exhaled. "He deserves that. To be happy. Master Will has always been the brighter burning star, the one to catch attention—but Jem is a steady flame, unwavering and honest. He could make you happy."

"And you would not object?"

"Object?" Sophie shook her head. "Oh, Miss Tessa, it is kind of you to care what I think, but no. I would not object. My fondness for him—and that is all it was, a girlish fondness—has quite cooled into friendship. I wish only his happiness and yours."

Tessa was amazed. All the worrying she had done about Sophie's feelings, and Sophie didn't mind at all. What *had* changed since Sophie had wept over Jem's illness the night of the Blackfriars Bridge debacle? Unless . . . "Have you been walking out with someone? Cyril, or . . ."

Sophie rolled her eyes. "Oh, Lord have mercy on us all. First Thomas, now Cyril. When *will* you stop trying to marry me off to the nearest available man?"

"There must be someone—"

"There's no one," Sophie said firmly, rising to her feet and turning Tessa toward the pier glass. "There you are. Twist up your hair under your hat and you'll be the model of a gentleman."

Tessa did as she was told.

When Tessa came into the library, the small band of Institute Shadowhunters—Jem, Will, Henry, and Charlotte, all in gear now—were grouped around a table on which a small oblong device made of brass was balanced. Henry was gesturing at it animatedly, his voice rising. "This," he was saying, "is what

I have been working on. For just this occasion. It is specifically calibrated to function as a weapon against clockwork assassins."

"As dull as Nate Gray is," Will said, "his head is not actually filled with gears, Henry. He's a human."

"He may bring one of those creatures with him. We don't know he'll be there unaccompanied. If nothing else, that clockwork coachman of Mortmain's—"

"I think Henry is right," said Tessa, and they all whirled to face her. Jem flushed again, though more lightly this time, and offered her a crooked smile; Will's eyes ran up and down her body once, not briskly.

He said, "You don't look like a boy at all. You look like a girl in boys' clothes."

She couldn't tell if he was approving, disapproving, or neutral on the subject. "I'm not trying to fool anyone but a casual observer," she replied crossly. "Nate *knows* Jessamine's a girl. And the clothes will fit me better once I've Changed into her."

"Maybe you should do it now," said Will.

Tessa glared at him, then shut her eyes. It was different, Changing into someone you had been before. She did not need to be holding something of theirs, or to be near them. It was like closing her eyes and reaching into a wardrobe, detecting a familiar garment by touch, and drawing it out. She reached for Jessamine inside herself, and let her free, wrapping the Jessamine disguise around herself, feeling the breath pushed from her lungs as her rib cage contracted, her hair slipping from its twist to fall in light corn silk waves against her face. She pushed it back up under the hat and opened her eyes.

They were all staring at her. Jem was the only one to offer a smile as she blinked in the light.

"Uncanny," said Henry. His hand rested lightly on the object on the table. Tessa, uncomfortable with the eyes on her, moved toward it. "What is that?"

"It's a sort of . . . infernal device that Henry's created," Jem said. "Meant to disrupt the internal mechanisms that keep the clockwork creatures running."

"You twist it, like this"—Henry mimed twisting the bottom half of the thing in one direction and the top half in another—"and then throw it. Try to lodge it into the creature's gears or somewhere that it will stick. It is meant to disrupt the mechanical currents that run through the creature's body, causing them to wrench apart. It could do you some damage too, even if you aren't clockwork, so don't hang on to it once it's activated. I've only two, so . . ."

He handed one to Jem, and another to Charlotte, who took it and hung it from her weapons belt without a word.

"The message has been sent?" Tessa asked.

"Yes. We're only waiting for a reply from your brother now," said Charlotte. She unrolled a paper across the surface of the table, weighting down the corners with copper gears from a stack Henry must have left there. "Here," she said, "is a map that shows where Jessamine claims she and Nate usually meet. It's a warehouse on Mincing Lane, down by Lower Thames Street. It used to be a tea merchant's packing factory until the business went bankrupt."

"Mincing Lane," said Jem. "Center of the tea trade. Also the opium trade. Makes sense Mortmain might keep a warehouse there." He ran a slender finger over the map, tracing the names of the nearby streets: Eastcheap, Gracechurch Street, Lower Thames Street, St. Swithin's Lane. "Such an odd place for Jessamine, though," he said. "She always dreamed of such glamour—of being introduced at Court and putting her hair up for dances. Not of clandestine meetings in some sooty warehouse near the wharves."

"She did do what she set out to do," Tessa said. "She married someone who isn't a Shadowhunter."

Will's mouth quirked into a half smile. "If the marriage were valid, she'd be your sister-in-law."

Tessa shuddered. "I—it's not that I hold a grudge against Jessamine. But she deserves better than my brother."

"Anyone deserves better than that." Will reached under the table and drew out a rolled-up bunch of fabric. He spread it across the table, avoiding the map. Inside were several long, thin weapons, each with a gleaming rune carved into the blade. "I'd nearly forgotten I had Thomas order these for me a few weeks ago. They've only just arrived. Misericords—good for getting in between the jointure of those clockwork creatures."

"The question is," Jem said, lifting one of the misericords and examining the blade, "once we get Tessa inside to meet Nate, how do the rest of us watch their meeting without being noticed? We must be ready to intervene at any moment, especially if it appears that his suspicions have been aroused."

"We must arrive first, and hide ourselves," said Will. "It is the only way. We listen to see if Nate says anything useful."

"I dislike the idea of Tessa being forced to speak with him at all," muttered Jem.

"She can well hold her own; I have seen it. Besides, he is more likely to speak freely if he thinks himself safe. Once captured, even if the Silent Brothers do explore his mind, Mortmain may have thought to put blocks in it to protect his knowledge, which can take time to dismantle."

"I think Mortmain has put in blocks in Jessamine's case," said Tessa. "For whatever it is worth, I cannot touch her thoughts."

"Even more likely he will have done it in Nate's, then," said Will.

"That boy is as weak as a kitten," said Henry. "He will tell us whatever we want to know. And if not, I have a device—"

"Henry!" Charlotte looked seriously alarmed. "Tell me you have not been working on a torture device."

"Not at all. I call it the Confuser. It emits a vibration that directly affects the human brain, rendering it incapable of telling between fiction and fact." Henry, looking proud, reached for his box. "He will simply spill everything that is in his mind, with no attention to the consequences . . ."

Charlotte held up a warning hand. "Not right now, Henry. If we must utilize the . . . Confuser on Nate Gray, we will do so when we have brought him back here. At the moment we must concentrate on reaching the warehouse before Tessa. It is not *that* far; I suggest Cyril takes us there, then returns for Tessa."

"Nate will recognize the Institute's carriage," Tessa objected. "When I saw Jessamine leaving for a meeting with Nate, she was most decidedly going on foot. I shall walk."

"You will get lost," said Will.

"I won't," said Tessa, indicating the map. "It's a simple walk.

I could turn left at Gracechurch Street, go along Eastcheap, and cut through to Mincing Lane."

An argument ensued, with Jem, to Tessa's surprise, siding with Will against the idea of her walking the streets alone. Eventually it was decided that Henry would drive the carriage to Mincing Lane, while Tessa would walk, with Cyril following her at a discreet distance, lest she lose herself in the crowded, dirty, noisy city. With a shrug she agreed; it seemed less trouble than arguing, and she didn't mind Cyril.

"I don't suppose anyone's going to point out," said Will, "that once again we are leaving the Institute without a Shadowhunter to protect it?"

Charlotte rolled up the map with a flick of her wrist. "And which of us would you suggest stay home, then, instead of helping Tessa?"

"I didn't say anything about anyone staying home." Will's voice dropped. "But Cyril will be with Tessa, Sophie's only half-trained, and Bridget . . ."

Tessa glanced over at Sophie, who was sitting quietly in the corner of the library, but the other girl gave no sign of having heard Will. Meanwhile, Bridget's voice was wafting faintly from the kitchen, another miserable ballad:

> "So John took out of his pocket
> A knife both long and sharp,
> And stuck it through his brother's heart,
> And the blood came pouring down.
> Says John to William, 'Take off thy shirt,
> And tear it from gore to gore,

And wrap it round your bleeding heart,
And the blood will pour no more.'"

"By the Angel," said Charlotte, "we really *are* going to have to do something about her before she drives us all to madness, aren't we?"

Before anyone could reply, two things happened at once: Something tapped at the window, startling Tessa so much that she took a step back, and a great, echoing noise sounded through the Institute—the sound of the summoning bell. Charlotte said something to Will—lost in the noise of the bell—and he left the room, while Charlotte crossed it, slid the window up and open, and captured something hovering outside.

She turned away from the window, a fluttering piece of paper in her hand; it looked a bit like a white bird, edges flapping in the breeze. Her hair blew about her face too, and Tessa was reminded how young Charlotte was. "From Nate, I suppose," said Charlotte. "His message for Jessamine." She brought it to Tessa, who tore the creamy parchment lengthwise in her eagerness to get it open.

Tessa glanced up. "It is from Nate," she confirmed. "He has agreed to meet Jessie in the usual place at sundown—" She gave a little gasp as, recognizing itself somehow as having been read, the note burst into quick, heatless flames, consuming itself until it was only a film of black ash on her fingers.

"That gives us only a little time," said Henry. "I will go and tell Cyril to ready the carriage." He looked to Charlotte, as if for approval, but she only nodded without meeting his eyes. With a sigh Henry left the room—nearly bumping into Will, who was on his way back in, followed by a figure in a traveling cloak. For a moment Tessa wondered in confusion if it was a Silent Brother—until the visitor drew his hood back and she saw the familiar sandy-blond curling hair and green eyes.

"Gideon Lightwood?" she said in surprise.

"There." Charlotte slipped the map she was holding into her pocket. "The Institute will not be Shadowhunterless."

Sophie got hastily to her feet—then froze, as if, outside the atmosphere of the training room, she was not sure what to do or say in front of the eldest Lightwood brother.

Gideon glanced around the room. As always his green eyes were calm, unruffled. Will, behind him, seemed to burn with bright energy by contrast, even when he was simply standing still. "You called on me?" Gideon said, and she realized that of course, looking at her, he was seeing Jessamine. "And I am here, though I know not why, or what for."

"To train Sophie, ostensibly," said Charlotte. "And also to look after the Institute while we're gone. We need a Shadow-hunter of age to be present, and you qualify. In fact, it was Sophie who suggested you."

"And how long will you be gone?"

"Two hours, three. Not all night."

"All right." Gideon began to unbutton his cloak. There was dust on his boots, and his hair looked as if he had been out in the cold wind, hatless. "My father would say it was good prac-tice for when I run the place."

Will muttered something under his breath that sounded like "bloody cheek." He looked at Charlotte, who shook her head at him minutely.

"It may be that the Institute will be yours one day," she said to Gideon quite mildly. "In any case, we're grateful for your assistance. The Institute is the responsibility of all Shadowhunters, after all. These are our dwelling places—our Idris away from home."

Gideon turned to Sophie. "Are you ready to train?"

She nodded. They left the room together in a group, Gideon and Sophie turning right to make their way to the training room, the rest of them heading for the stairs. Bridget's mournful yowl was even louder out here, and Tessa heard Gideon say something to Sophie about it, and Sophie's soft voice in response, before they were too far away for her to hear them anymore.

It seemed natural to fall into step beside Jem as they went downstairs and through the nave of the cathedral. She was walking close enough to him that though they did not speak, she could feel the warmth of him against her side, the brush of his bare hand against hers as they stepped outside. Sunset was coming. The sky had begun to take on the bronze sheen that came just before twilight. Cyril was waiting on the front stairs, looking so much like Thomas that it hurt one's heart to look at him. He was carrying a long, thin dagger, which he handed off to Will without a word; Will took it and put it through his belt.

Charlotte turned and put her hand against Tessa's cheek. "We shall see you at the warehouse," she said. "You will be perfectly safe, Tessa. And thank you, for doing this for us." Charlotte dropped her hand and went down the steps, Henry following her, and Will just after. Jem hesitated, just for a moment, and Tessa—remembering a night like this one, when he had run up the steps to bid her good-bye—pressed her fingers lightly against his wrist.

"*Mizpah*," she said.

She heard him suck in his breath. The Shadowhunters were getting into the carriage; he turned and kissed her quickly on the cheek, before spinning and running down the steps after the others; none of them seemed to have noticed, but Tessa put her hand to her face as Jem climbed, last, into the carriage and Henry made his way up to the driver's seat. The gates of the Institute swung open, and the carriage clattered out into the darkening afternoon.

"Shall we go, then, miss?" Cyril inquired. Despite how much he looked like Thomas, Tessa thought, he had a less diffident demeanor. He looked her directly in the eye when he spoke, and the corners of his mouth always seemed to be about to crinkle into a smile. She wondered if there was always one calmer and one more high-strung brother, like Gabriel and Gideon.

"Yes, I think we—" Tessa stopped suddenly, one foot about to descend the steps. It was ridiculous, she knew, and yet—she had taken off the clockwork angel to dress herself in Jessamine's clothes. She had not put it back on. She couldn't *wear* it—Nate would recognize it immediately—but she had meant to put it into her pocket for luck, and she had forgotten. She hesitated now. It was more than silly superstition; twice now the angel had literally saved her life.

She turned. "I have forgotten something. Wait here for me, Cyril. I'll be only a moment."

The door to the Institute was still open; she charged back through it and up the stairs, through the halls and into the corridor that led to Jessamine's room—where she froze.

Jessamine's hall was the same hall that led to the steps to

the training room. She had seen Sophie and Gideon disappear down it minutes ago. Only, they had not disappeared; they were still there. The light was low, and they were only shadows in the dimness, but Tessa could see them plainly: Sophie, standing against the wall, and Gideon pressing her hand.

Tessa took a step backward, her heart jerking inside her chest. Neither of them saw her. They seemed entirely concentrated on each other. Gideon leaned in then, murmuring something to Sophie; gently he brushed a stray strand of hair from her face. Tessa's stomach tensed, and she turned and crept away, as soundlessly as she could.

The sky had turned a shade darker when she came back out onto the steps. Cyril was there, whistling off-key; he broke off abruptly when he saw Tessa's expression. "Is everything all right, miss? Did you get what you wanted?"

Tessa thought of Gideon moving Sophie's hair away from her face. She remembered Will's hands gentle on her waist and the softness of Jem's kiss on her cheek, and felt as if her mind were whirling. Who was she to tell Sophie to be careful, even silently, when she was so lost herself?

"Yes," she lied. "I got what I wanted. Thank you, Cyril."

The warehouse was a great limestone building surrounded by a black wrought iron fence. The windows had been boarded over, and a stout iron padlock held closed the front gates, over which the blackening name of Mortmain and Co. could barely be seen below layers of soot.

The Shadowhunters left the carriage drawn up to the curb, with a glamour on it to prevent it from being stolen or molested by passing mundanes, at least until Cyril arrived to wait with it. A closer inspection of the padlock showed Will that it had been oiled recently and opened; a rune took care of the lack of a key, and he and the others slipped inside, closing the gate behind them.

Another rune unlocked the front door, leading them into a suite of offices. Only one was still furnished, with a desk, a green-shaded lamp, and a floral sofa with a high carved back. "Doubtless where Jessamine and Nate accomplished the majority of their courtship," Will observed cheerfully.

Jem made a noise of disgust and poked at the couch with his cane. Charlotte was bending over the desk, hastily going through the drawers.

"I didn't realize you'd taken up such a strong anti-courtship stance," Will observed to Jem.

"Not on principle. The thought of Nate Gray touching anyone—" Jem made a face. "And Jessamine is so convinced he loves her. If you could see her, I think even you might pity her, Will."

"I would not," said Will. "Unrequited love is a ridiculous state, and it makes those in it behave ridiculously." He tugged at the bandage on his arm as if it were paining him. "Charlotte? The desk?"

"Nothing." She slid the drawers shut. "Some papers listing the prices of tea and the times of tea auctions, but other than that, nothing but dead spiders."

"How romantic," murmured Will. He ducked behind Jem, who had already wandered ahead into the adjacent office, using his cane to sweep away cobwebs as he went. The next few rooms were empty, and the last opened out onto what had once been a warehouse floor. It was a great shadowy cavernous space, its ceiling disappearing up into darkness. Rickety wooden steps led up to a second-floor gallery. Burlap bags were propped against the walls on the first floor, looking for all the world, in the shadows, like slumped bodies. Will raised his witchlight rune-stone in one hand, sending out spokes of light through the room as Henry went to investigate one of the sacks. He was back in a moment, shrugging his shoulders.

"Broken bits of loose-leaf tea," he said. "Orange pekoe, from the looks of it."

But Jem was shaking his head, glancing about. "I am perfectly willing to accept that this was an active tea-trading office at one point, but it's clearly been shuttered for years, ever since Mortmain decided to interest himself in mechanisms instead. And yet the floor is clear of dust." He took Will's wrist, guiding the beam of witchlight over the smooth wooden floor. "There has been activity here—more than simply Jessamine and Nate's meeting in a disused office."

"There are more offices that way," said Henry, pointing to the far end of the room. "Charlotte and I will search them. Will, Jem, you examine the second floor."

It was a rare and novel thrill when Henry gave orders; Will looked at Jem and grinned, and commenced making his way up the rickety wooden stairs. The steps creaked under the pressure, and under Jem's slighter weight behind Will. The witchlight stone in Will's hand threw sharp patterns of light against the wall as he reached the top step.

He found himself on a gallery, a platform where perhaps trunks of tea had been stored, or a foreman had watched the floor below. It was empty now, save for a single figure, lying on the ground. The body of a man, slim and youthful, and as Will came closer, his heart began to pound crazily, because he had seen this before—had had this vision before—the limp body, the silver hair and dark clothes, the closed bruised-looking eyes, fringed with silver lashes.

"Will?" It was Jem, behind him. He looked from Will's silent, stunned face to the body on the floor and pushed past him to kneel down. He took the man by the wrist just as Charlotte reached the top of the steps. Will looked at her in surprise for a moment; her face was sheened with sweat and she looked slightly ill. Jem said, "He has a pulse. Will?"

Will came closer, and knelt down beside his friend. At this distance it was easy to see that the man on the floor was not Jem. He was older, and Caucasian; he had a growth of silver stubble on his chin and cheeks, and his features were broader and less defined. Will's heartbeat slowed as the man's eyes fluttered open.

They were silver discs, like Jem's. And in that moment Will recognized him. He smelled the sweet-sour tang of burning warlock drugs, felt the heat of them in his veins, and knew that he had seen this man before, and knew where.

"You're a werewolf," he said. "One of the packless ones, buying *yin fen* off the ifrits down the Chapel. Aren't you?"

The werewolf's eyes roamed over them both, and fastened on Jem. His lids narrowed, and his hand shot out, grabbing Jem by the lapels. "You," he wheezed. "You're one of us. 'ave you got any of it on you—any of the stuff—"

Jem recoiled. Will seized the werewolf by the wrist and yanked his hand free. It wasn't difficult; there was very little strength in his nerveless fingers. "Don't touch him." Will heard his own voice as if from a distance, clipped and cold. "He doesn't have any of your filthy powder. It doesn't work on us Nephilim like it does on you."

"Will." There was a plea in Jem's voice: *Be kinder.*

"You work for Mortmain," said Will. "Tell us what you do for him. Tell us where he is."

The werewolf laughed. Blood splashed up over his lips and dribbled down his chin. Some of it splattered onto Jem's gear. "As if—I'd know—where the Magister was," he wheezed. "Bloody fools, the pair of you. Bloody useless Nephilim. If I 'ad—me strength—I'd chop yer into bloody rags—"

"But you don't." Will was remorseless. "And maybe we *do* have some *yin fen.*"

"You don't. You think—I don't know?" The werewolf's eyes wandered. "When 'e gave it to me first, I saw things—such things as yer can't imagine—the great crystal city—the towers of Heaven—" Another spasming cough racked him. More blood splattered. It had a silvery sheen to it, like mercury. Will exchanged a look with Jem. *The crystal city.* He couldn't help thinking of Alicante, though he had never been there. "I thought I were going ter live forever—work all night, all day, never get tired. Then we started dying off, one by one. The drug, it kills ya, but 'e never said. I came back here to see if maybe there was still any of it stashed somewhere. But there's none. No point leavin'. I'm dyin' now. Might as well die 'ere as anywhere."

"He knew what he was doing when he gave you that drug," said Jem. "He knew it would kill you. He doesn't deserve your secrecy. Tell us what he was doing—what he was keeping you working on all night and day."

"Putting those *things* together—those metal men. They don't 'arf give you the willies, but the money were good and the drugs were better—"

"And a great deal of good that money will do you now," said Jem, his voice uncharacteristically bitter. "How often did he make you take it? The silver powder?"

"Six, seven times a day."

"No wonder they're running out of it down the Chapel," Will muttered. "Mortmain's controlling the supply."

"You're not supposed to take it like that," said Jem. "The more you take, the faster you die."

The werewolf fixed his gaze on Jem. His eyes were shot through with red veins. "And you," he said. "'Ow much longer 'ave *you* got left?"

Will turned his head. Charlotte was motionless behind him at the top of the stairs, staring. He raised a hand to gesture her over. "Charlotte, if we can get him downstairs, perhaps the Silent Brothers can do something to help him. If you could—"

But Charlotte, to Will's surprise, had turned a pale shade of green. She clapped her hand over her mouth and dashed downstairs.

"Charlotte!" Will hissed; he didn't dare shout. "Oh, bloody hell. All right, Jem. You take his legs, I'll take his shoulders—"

"There's no point, Will." Jem's voice was soft. "He's dead."

Will turned back. Indeed, the silver eyes were wide open, glassy, fixed on the ceiling; the chest had ceased to rise and fall. Jem reached to close his eyelids, but Will caught his friend by the wrist.

"Don't."

"I wasn't going to give him the blessing, Will. Just close his eyes."

"He doesn't deserve that. He was working with the Magister!" Will's whisper was rising to a shout.

"He is like me," said Jem simply. "An addict."

Will looked at him over their joined hands. "He is *not like you*. And you will not die like that."

Jem's lips parted in surprise. "Will . . ."

They both heard the sound of a door opening, and a voice calling out Jessamine's name. Will released Jem's wrist, and both of them dropped flat to the ground, inching to the edge of the gallery to see what was happening on the warehouse floor.

16

MORTAL RAGE

When I have seen by Time's fell hand defac'd
The rich-proud cost of outworn buried age;
When sometime lofty towers I see down-raz'd,
And brass eternal slave to mortal rage
—Shakespeare, "Sonnet 64"

It was a peculiar experience walking the streets of London as a boy, Tessa thought as she made her way along the crowded pavement of Eastcheap. The men who crossed her path spared her barely a glance, just pushed past her toward the doors of public houses or the next turn in the street. As a girl, walking alone through these streets at night in her fine clothes, she would have been the object of stares and jeers. As a boy she was—invisible. She had never realized what it was like to be invisible before. How light and free she felt—or would have felt, had she not felt like an aristocrat from *A Tale of Two Cities* on his way to the guillotine in a tumbrel.

She caught sight of Cyril only once, slipping between two buildings across the road from 32 Mincing Lane. It was a great stone building, and the black iron fence surrounding it, in the vanishing twilight, looked like rows of jagged black teeth. From the front gates dangled a padlock, but it had been left open; she slipped through, and then up the dusty steps to the front door, which was also unlocked.

Inside she found that the empty offices, their windows looking out onto Mincing Lane, were still and dead; a fly buzzed in one, hurling itself over and over against the plated glass panes until it fell, exhausted, to the sill. Tessa shuddered and hurried on.

In each room she walked into, she tensed, expecting to see Nate; in each room, he was not there. The final room had a door that opened out onto the floor of a warehouse. Dim blue light filtered in through the cracks in the boarded-up windows. She looked around uncertainly. "Nate?" she whispered.

He stepped out of the shadows between two flaking plaster pillars. His blond hair shone in the bluish light, under a silk top hat. He wore a blue tweed frock coat, black trousers, and black boots, but his usually immaculate appearance was disheveled. His hair hung lankly in his eyes, and there was a smear of dirt across his cheek. His clothes were wrinkled and creased as if he had slept in them. "Jessamine," he said, relief evident in his tone. "My darling." He opened his arms.

She came forward slowly, her whole body tensed. She did not want Nate touching her, but she could see no way to avoid his embrace. His arms went around her. His hand caught the brim of her hat and pulled it free, letting her fair curls tumble down her back. She thought of Will pulling the pins from her hair, and her stomach involuntarily tightened.

"I need to know where the Magister is," she began in a shaking voice. "It's terribly important. I overheard some of the Shadowhunters' plans, you see. I know you didn't wish to tell me, but . . ."

He pushed her hair back, ignoring her words. "I see," he said, and his voice was deep and husky. "But first—" He tipped her head up with a finger under her chin. "Come and kiss me, sweet-and-twenty."

Tessa wished he wouldn't quote Shakespeare. She'd never be able to hear that sonnet again without wanting to be sick. Every nerve in her body wanted to leap screaming through her skin in revulsion as he leaned toward her. She prayed for the others to burst in as she let him tilt her head up, up—

Nate began to laugh. With a jerk of his wrist, he sent her hat sailing into the shadows; his fingers tightened on her chin, the nails digging in. "My apologies for my impetuous behavior," he said. "I couldn't help but be curious to see how far you'd go to protect your Shadowhunter friends . . . little sister."

"Nate." Tessa tried to jerk backward, out of his grasp, but his grip on her was too strong. His other hand shot out like a snake, spinning her around, pinning her against him with his forearm across her throat. His breath was hot against her ear. He smelled sour, like old gin and sweat.

"Did you really think I didn't know?" he spat. "After that note arrived at Benedict's ball, sending me off on that wild goose chase to Vauxhall, I realized. It all made sense. I should have known it was you from the beginning. Stupid little girl."

"Stupid?" she hissed. "I got you to spill your secrets, Nate. You told me everything. Did Mortmain find out? Is that why you look like you haven't slept in days?"

He jerked his arm tighter around her, making her gasp with pain. "You couldn't leave well enough alone. You had to pry into my business. Delighted to see me brought low, are you? What kind of sister does that make you, Tessie?"

"You would have killed me if you had the chance. There is no game you can play, nothing you can say to make me think I've betrayed you, Nate. You earned every bit of it. Allying yourself with Mortmain—"

He shook her, hard enough to make her teeth rattle. "As if my alliances are any of your business. I was doing well for myself until you and your Nephilim friends came and meddled. Now the Magister wants my head on a block. Your fault. All your fault. I was almost in despair, till I got that ridiculous note from Jessamine. I knew you were behind it, of course. All the trouble you must have gone through too, torturing her to get her to write me that ridiculous missive—"

"We didn't torture her," Tessa ground out. She struggled, but Nate only held her more tightly, the buttons on his waistcoat digging into her back. "She wanted to do it. She wanted to save her own skin."

"I don't believe you." The hand that wasn't across her throat gripped her chin; his nails dug in, and she yelped with pain. "She loves me."

"No one could love you," Tessa spat. "You're my brother— I loved you—and you have killed even that."

Nate leaned forward and growled, *"I am not your brother."*

"Very well, my half brother, if you must have it—"

"You're not my sister. Not even by half." He said the words with a cruel pleasure. "Your mother and my mother were not the same woman."

"That's not possible," Tessa whispered. "You're lying. Our mother was Elizabeth Gray—"

"*Your* mother was Elizabeth Gray, born Elizabeth Moore," said Nate. "Mine was Harriet Moore."

"Aunt Harriet?"

"She was engaged once. Did you know that? After our parents—your parents—were married. The man died before the wedding could take place. But she was already with child. Your mother raised the baby as hers to spare her sister the shame of the world knowing she had consummated her marriage before it had taken place. That she was a whore." His voice was as bitter as poison. "I'm not your brother, and I never was. Harriet—she never told me she was my mother. I found out from your mother's letters. All those years, and she never said a word. She was too ashamed."

"You killed her," Tessa said numbly. "Your own mother."

"Because she was my mother. Because she'd disowned me. Because she was ashamed of me. Because I'll never know who my father was. Because she was a whore." Nate's voice was empty. *Nate* had always been empty. He had never been anything but a pretty shell, and Tessa and her aunt had dreamed into him empathy and compassion and sympathetic weakness because they had wanted to see it there, not because it was.

"Why did you tell Jessamine that my mother was a Shadowhunter?" Tessa demanded. "Even if Aunt Harriet was your mother, she and my mother were sisters. Aunt Harriet would have been a Shadowhunter, too, and so would you. Why tell such a ridiculous lie?"

He smirked. "Wouldn't you like to know?" His grip tightened on her neck, choking her. She gasped and thought suddenly of Gabriel, saying, *Aim your kicks at the kneecaps; the pain is agonizing.*

She kicked up and backward, the heel of her boot colliding with Nate's knee, making a dull cracking sound. Nate yelled, and his leg went out from under him. He kept his grip on Tessa as he fell, rolling so that his elbow jammed into her stomach as they tumbled to the ground together. She gasped, the air punched from her lungs, her eyes filling with tears.

She kicked out at him again, trying to scramble backward, and caught him a glancing blow on the shoulder, but he lunged at her, seizing her by the waistcoat. The buttons popped off it in a rain as he dragged her toward him; his other hand gripped her hair as she flailed out at him, raking her nails down his cheek. The blood that sprang immediately to the surface was a savagely satisfying sight.

"Let me go," she panted. "You can't kill me. The Magister wants me alive—"

"'Alive' is not 'unhurt,'" Nate snarled, blood running down his face and off his chin. He knotted his hand in her hair and dragged her toward him; she screamed at the pain and lashed out with her boots, but he was nimble, dodging her flailing feet. Panting, she sent up a silent call: *Jem, Will, Charlotte, Henry—where are you?*

"Wondering where your friends are?" He hauled her to her

feet, one hand in her hair, the other fisted in the back of her shirt. "Well, here's one of them, at least."

A grinding noise alerted Tessa to a movement in the shadows. Nate dragged her head around by the hair, shaking her. "Look," he spat. "It's time you knew what you are up against."

Tessa stared. The thing that emerged from the shadows was gigantic—twenty feet tall, she guessed, made of iron. There was barely any jointure. It appeared to move as one single fluid mechanism, seamless and almost featureless. Its bottom half did split into legs, each one ending in a foot tipped with metal spikes. Its arms were the same, finishing in clawlike hands, and its head was a smooth oval broken only by a wide jagged-toothed mouth like a crack in an egg. A pair of twisting silvery horns spiraled up from its "head." A thin line of blue fire crackled between them.

In its enormous hands it carried a limp body, dressed in gear. Against the bulk of the gigantic automaton, she looked even smaller than ever.

"Charlotte!" Tessa screamed. She redoubled her attempts to get away from Nate, whipping her head to the side. Some of her hair tore free and fluttered to the ground—Jessamine's fair hair, stained now with blood. Nate retaliated by slapping her hard enough that she saw stars; when she sagged, he caught her around the throat, the buttons on his cuffs digging into her windpipe.

Nate chuckled. "A prototype," he said. "Abandoned by the Magister. Too large and cumbersome for his purposes. But not for mine." He raised his voice. "Drop her."

The automaton's metal hands opened. Charlotte tumbled free and struck the ground with a sickening thump. She lay unmoving. From this distance Tessa could not tell if her chest was rising and falling or not.

"Now crush her," said Nate.

Ponderously the thing raised its spiked metal foot. Tessa clawed at Nate's forearms, ripping his skin with her nails.

"Charlotte!" For a moment Tessa thought the voice screaming was her own, but it was too low-pitched for that. A figure darted out from behind the automaton, a figure all in black, topped by a shock of blazing ginger hair, a thin-bladed misericord in hand.

Henry.

Without even a glance at Tessa and Nate, he launched himself at the automaton, bringing his blade down in a long curving arc. There was the clang of metal on metal. Sparks flew, and the automaton staggered back. Its foot came down, slamming into the floor, inches from Charlotte's supine body. Henry landed, then threw himself at the creature again, slashing out with his blade.

The blade shattered. For a moment Henry simply stood and looked at it with stupid shock. Then the creature's hand whipped forward and seized him by the arm. He shouted out as it lifted him and threw him with incredible force against one of the pillars; he struck it, crumpled, and fell to the floor, where he lay still.

Nate laughed. *"Such* a display of matrimonial devotion," he said. "Who would have thought it? Jessamine always said she thought Branwell couldn't stand his wife."

"You're a pig," Tessa said, struggling in his grasp. "What do you know about the things people do for each other? If Jessamine were burning to death, you wouldn't look up from your card game. You care for nothing but yourself."

"Be quiet, or I'll loosen your teeth for you." Nate shook her again, and called out, "Come! Over here. You must hold her till the Magister arrives."

With a grinding of gears the automaton moved to obey. It was not as swift as its smaller brethren, but its size was such that Tessa could not help but follow its movements with an icy fear. And that was not all. The Magister was coming. Tessa wondered if Nate had summoned him yet, if he was on his way. Mortmain. Even the memory of his cold eyes, his icy, controlling smile, made her stomach turn. "Let me go," she cried, jerking away from her brother. "Let me go to Charlotte—"

Nate shoved her forward, hard, and she sprawled on the ground, her elbows and knees connecting with force with the hard wooden floor. She gasped and rolled sideways, under the shadow of the second-floor gallery, as the automaton lumbered toward her. She cried out—

And they leaped from the gallery above, Will and Jem, each landing on a shoulder of the creature. It roared, a sound like bellows being fed with coal, and staggered back, allowing Tessa to roll out of its path and launch herself to her feet. She glanced from Henry to Charlotte. Henry was pale and still, crumpled beside the pillar, but Charlotte, lying where the automaton had dropped her, was in imminent danger of being crushed by the rampaging machine.

Taking a deep breath, Tessa dashed across the room to Charlotte and knelt down, laying her fingers to Charlotte's throat; there was a pulse there, fluttering weakly. Putting her hands under Charlotte's arms, she began to drag her toward the wall, away from the center of the room, where the automaton was spinning and spitting sparks, reaching up with its pincered hands to claw at Jem and Will.

They were too quick for it, though. Tessa laid Charlotte down among the burlap sacks of tea and gazed across the room, trying to determine a path that might lead her to Henry. Nate was dashing back and forth, shouting and cursing at the mechanical creature; in answer Will sawed off one of its horns and threw it at Tessa's brother. It bounced across the floor, skittering and sparking, and Nate jumped back. Will laughed. Jem meanwhile was clinging on to the creature's neck, doing something that Tessa could not see. The creature itself was turning in circles, but it had been designed for reaching out and grabbing what was in front of it, and its "arms" did not bend properly. It could not reach what clung to the back of its neck and head.

Tessa almost wanted to laugh. Will and Jem were like mice scurrying up and down the body of a cat, driving it to distraction. But hack and slash as they might at the metal creature with their blades, they were inflicting few injuries. Their blades, which she had seen shear through iron and steel as if they were paper, were leaving only dents and scratches on the surface of the mechanical creature's body.

Nate, meanwhile, was screaming and cursing. "Shake them off!" he yelled at the automaton. "Shake them off, you great metal bastard!"

The automaton paused, then shook itself violently. Will slipped, catching on to the creature's neck at the last moment to keep himself from falling. Jem was not so lucky; he stabbed forward with his sword-cane, as if he meant to drive it into the creature's body to arrest his fall, but the blade merely skidded down the creature's back. Jem fell, gracelessly, his weapon clattering, his leg bent under him.

"*James!*" Will shouted.

Jem dragged himself painfully to his feet. He reached for the stele at his belt, but the creature, sensing weakness, was already on him, reaching out its clawed hands. Jem took several staggering steps backward and fumbled something out of his pocket. It was smooth, oblong, metallic—the object Henry had given him in the library.

He reached back a hand to throw it—and Nate was behind him suddenly, kicking out at his injured, likely broken, leg. Jem didn't make a sound, but the leg went out from under him with a snapping noise and he hit the ground for a second time, the object rolling from his hand.

Tessa scrambled to her feet and ran for it just as Nate did the same. They collided, his greater weight and height bearing her to the floor. She rolled as she fell, as Gabriel had taught her to, to absorb the impact, though the shock still left her breathless. She reached for the device with shaking fingers, but it skittered away from her. She could hear Will screaming her name, calling to her to throw it to him. She stretched her hand out farther, her fingers closing around the device—and then Nate seized her by one leg and dragged her back toward him, mercilessly.

He is bigger than I am, she thought. *Stronger than I am. More ruthless than I am. But there is one thing I can do that he cannot.*

She Changed.

She reached out with her mind for the grip of his hand on her ankle, his skin touching her own. She reached out for the intrinsic, inborn *Nate* that she had always known, that spark inside him that flickered the way it did inside everyone, like a candle in a dark room. She heard him suck in his breath, and then the Change took her, rippling her skin, melting her bones. The buttons at her collar and cuffs snapped as she grew in size, convulsions thrashing through her limbs, ripping her leg free of Nate's grasp. She rolled away from her brother, staggering to her feet, and saw his eyes widen as he looked at her.

She was now, other than her clothes, an exact mirror image of himself.

She whirled on the automaton. It was frozen, waiting for instructions, Will still clinging to its back. He raised his hand, and Tessa threw the device, silently thanking Gabriel and Gideon for the hours of knife throwing instruction. It flew through the air in a perfect arc, and Will caught it out of the sky.

Nate was on his feet. "Tessa," he snarled. "What in the bloody hell do you possibly think you're—"

"Seize him!" she shouted at the automaton, pointing at Nate. "Catch him and hold him!"

The creature did not move. Tessa could hear nothing but Nate's harsh breathing beside her, and the sound of clanking from the metal creature; Will had vanished behind it and was doing something, though she could not see what.

"Tessa, you're a fool," Nate hissed. "This cannot work. The creature is obedient only to—"

"I am Nathaniel Gray!" Tessa shouted up at the metal giant. "And I order you in the name of the Magister to *seize this man and hold him!*"

Nate whirled on her. "Enough of your games, you stupid little—"

His words were cut off suddenly as the automaton bent and seized him in its pincered grasp. It lifted him up, up, level with its slash of a mouth clicking and whirring inquisitively. Nate began to scream, and kept screaming, witlessly, his arms flailing as Will, finished with whatever he was doing, dropped to the ground in a crouch. He shouted something at Tessa, his blue eyes wide and wild, but she couldn't hear him over her brother's screams. Her heart was slamming against her chest; she felt her hair tumble down, hitting her shoulders with a soft, heavy weight. She was herself again, the shock of what was happening too great for her to hold on to the Change. Nate was still screaming—the thing had him in a terrible pincer grip. Will had begun to run, just as the creature, staring at Tessa, reared up with a roar—and Will struck her, knocking her to the ground and covering her with his body as the automaton blew apart like an exploding star.

The cacaphony of bursting, clattering metal was incredible. Tessa tried to cover her ears, but Will's body was pinning her firmly to the ground. His elbows dug into the floor on either side of her head. She felt his breath on the back of her neck, the pounding of his heart against her spine. She heard her brother cry out, a terrible gurgling cry. She turned her head, pressing her face into Will's shoulder as his body jerked against hers; the floor shuddered beneath them—

And it was over. Slowly Tessa opened her eyes. The air was cloudy with plaster dust and floating splinters and tea from torn burlap sacks. Huge chunks of metal lay scattered haphazardly about the floor, and several of the windows had burst open, letting in foggy evening light. Tessa's glance darted about the room. She saw Henry, cradling Charlotte, kissing her pale face as she gazed up at him; Jem, struggling to his feet, stele in hand and plaster dust coating his clothes and hair—and Nate.

At first she thought he was leaning against one of the pillars. Then she saw the spreading red stain across his shirt, and realized. A jagged chunk of metal had gone through him like a spear, pinning him upright to the pillar. His head was down, his hands clawing weakly at his chest.

"Nate!" she screamed. Will rolled sideways, freeing her, and she was on her feet in seconds, racing across the room to her brother. Her hands were shaking with horror and revulsion, but she managed to close them around the metal spear in his chest and pull it free. She threw it aside and barely succeeded in catching him as he slumped forward, his sudden dead weight bearing her to the ground. Somehow she found herself on the ground, Nate's limp body stretched awkwardly across her lap.

A memory rose in her mind—her crouching on the floor at de Quincey's town house, holding Nate in her arms. She had loved him then. Trusted him. Now, as she held him and his blood soaked into her shirt and trousers, she felt as if she were watching actors on a stage, playing parts, acting out grief.

"Nate," she whispered.

His eyes fluttered open. A pang of shock went through her. She had thought he was already dead.

"Tessie . . ." His voice sounded thick, as if it were coming through layers of water. His eyes roamed her face, then the blood on her clothes, and then, finally, came to rest on his own chest, where blood pumped steadily through a massive rent in his shirt. Tessa shrugged off her jacket, wadded it up, and pressed it hard against the wound, praying it would be enough to make the blood stop.

It wasn't. The jacket was soaked through instantly, thin wet streams of blood running down Nate's sides. "Oh, God," Tessa whispered. She raised her voice. "Will—"

"Don't." Nate's hand seized her wrist, his nails digging in.

"But, Nate—"

"I'm dying. I know." He coughed, a loose, wet, rattling sound. "Don't you understand? I've failed the Magister. He'll kill me anyway. And he'll make it slow." He made a hoarse, impatient noise. "Leave it, Tessie. I'm not being noble. You know I'm not that."

She took a ragged breath. "I should leave you here to die alone in your own blood. That's what you'd do if it were me."

"Tessie—" A stream of blood spilled from the corner of his mouth. "The Magister was never going to hurt you."

"Mortmain," she whispered. "Nate, where is he? Please. Tell me where he is."

"He—" Nate choked, heaving in a breath. A bubble of blood appeared on his lips. The jacket in Tessa's hand was a sodden rag. His eyes went wide, starkly terrified. "Tessie . . . I—I'm dying. I'm really dying—"

Questions still exploded through her head. *Where is Mortmain? How could my mother be a Shadowhunter? If my father was a demon, how is it that I am still alive when all the offspring of Shadowhunters and demons are stillborn?* But the terror in Nate's eyes silenced her; despite everything, she found her hand slipping into his. "There's nothing to be afraid of, Nate."

"Not for you, maybe. You were always—the good one. I'm going to burn, Tessie. Tessie, where's your angel?"

She put her hand to her throat, a reflexive gesture. "I couldn't wear it. I was pretending to be Jessamine."

"You—must—wear it." He coughed. More blood. "Wear it always. You swear?"

She shook her head. "Nate . . ." *I can't trust you, Nate.*

"I know." His voice was a bare rattle. "There's no forgiveness for—the kinds of things I've had to do."

She tightened her grip on his hand, her fingers slippery with his blood. "I forgive you," she whispered, not knowing, or caring, if it was true.

His blue eyes widened. His face had gone the color of old yellow parchment, his lips almost white. *"You don't know everything I've done, Tessie."*

She leaned over him anxiously. "Nate?"

But there was no reply. His face went slack, his eyes wide, half-rolled-back in his head. His hand slid out of hers and struck the floor.

"Nate," she said again, and put her fingers to the place where his pulse should have beat in his throat, already knowing what she would find.

There was nothing. He was dead.

Tessa stood up. Her torn waistcoat, her trousers, her shirt, even the ends of her hair, were soaked with Nate's blood. She felt as numb as if she had been dipped in ice-cold water. She turned, slowly, only now, and for the first time, wondering if the others had been watching her, overhearing her conversation with Nate, wondering—

They weren't even looking in her direction. They were kneeling—Charlotte, Jem, and Henry—in a loose circle around a dark shape on the floor, just where she had been lying before, with Will on top of her.

Will.

Tessa had had dreams before in which she'd been walking down a long, darkened corridor toward something dreadful—something she could not see but knew was terrifying and deadly. In the dreams, with each step, the corridor had gotten longer, stretching farther into darkness and horror. That same feeling of dread and helplessness overwhelmed her now as she moved forward, each step feeling like a mile, until she had joined the circle of kneeling Shadowhunters and was looking down at Will.

He lay on his side. His face was white, his breathing shallow. Jem had one hand on his shoulder and was speaking to him in a low, soothing voice, but Will gave no sign of being able to hear him. Blood had pooled under him, smearing the floor, and for a moment Tessa just stared, unable to fathom where it had come from. Then she moved closer and saw his back. His gear had been shredded all along his spine and shoulder blades, the thick material torn by flying shards of razored metal. His skin swam with blood; his hair was soaked with it.

"Will," Tessa whispered. She felt peculiarly dizzy, as if she were floating.

Charlotte looked up. "Tessa," she said. "Your brother . . ."

"He's dead," Tessa said through her daze. "But Will—?"

"He knocked you down and covered you to protect you from the explosion," Jem said. There was no blame in his voice. "But there was nothing to protect him. You two were the closest to the blast. The metal fragments shredded his back. He's losing blood quickly."

"But isn't there anything you can do?" Tessa's voice rose, even as dizziness threatened to envelop her. "What about your healing runes? The *iratzes*?"

"We used an *amissio*, a rune that slows blood loss, but if we attempt a healing rune, his skin will heal over the metal, driving it farther into the soft tissue," said Henry flatly. "We need to get him back home to the infirmary. The metal must be removed before he can be healed."

"Then, we must go." Tessa's voice was shaking. "We must—"

"Tessa," said Jem. He still had his hand on Will's shoulder, but he was looking at her, his eyes wide. "Did you know you're hurt?"

She gestured impatiently at her shirt. "This isn't my blood. This is Nate's. Now we must— Can he be carried? Is there anything—"

"No," Jem interrupted, sharply enough to surprise her. "Not the blood on your clothes. You've a gash on your head. Here." He touched his temple.

"Don't be ridiculous," Tessa said. "I'm perfectly all right." She put her hand up to touch her temple—and felt her hair, thick and stiff with blood, and the side of her face sticky with it, before her fingertips touched the ragged flap of torn skin that ran from the corner of her cheek to her temple. A searing bolt of pain shot through her head.

It was the last straw. Already weak from blood loss and dizzy from repeated shocks, she felt herself begin to crumple. She barely felt Jem's arms go around her as she fell into the darkness.

17

IN DREAMS

Come to me in my dreams, and then
By day I shall be well again.
For then the night will more than pay
The hopeless longing of the day.
—Matthew Arnold, "Longing"

Consciousness came and went in a hypnotic rhythm, like the sea appearing and disappearing on the deck of a boat in a storm. Tessa knew she lay in a bed with crisp white sheets in the center of a long room; that there were other beds, all the same, in the room; and that there were windows high above her letting in shadows and then the bloody light of dawn. She closed her eyes against it, and the darkness came again.

She woke to whispering voices, and faces hovering over her, anxious. Charlotte, her hair knotted back neatly, still in her gear, and beside her Brother Enoch. His scarred face was no longer a terror. She could hear his voice in her mind. *The wound to her head is superficial.*

"But she fainted," said Charlotte. To Tessa's surprise there was real fear in her voice, real anxiety. "With a blow to the head—"

She fainted from repeated shocks. Her brother died in her arms, you said? And she may have thought Will was dead as well. You said he covered her with his body when the explosion occurred. If he had died, he would have given his life for her. That is quite a burden to bear.

"But you do think she'll be well again?"

When her body and spirit have rested, she will wake. I cannot say when that will be.

"My poor Tessa." Charlotte touched Tessa's face lightly. Her hands smelled of lemon soap. "She has no one in the world at all now. . . ."

The darkness returned, and Tessa fell into it, grateful for the respite from light and thought. She wrapped herself in it like a blanket and let herself float, like the icebergs off the coast of Labrador, cradled in the moonlight by icy black water.

A guttural cry of pain cut through her dream of darkness. She was curled on her side in a tangle of sheets, and a few beds away from her lay Will, on his stomach. She realized, though in her state of numbness it was only a faint shock, that he was probably naked; the sheets had been drawn up to his waist, but his back and chest were bare. His arms were folded on the pillows in front of him, his head resting on them, his body tensed like a bowstring. Blood spotted the white sheets beneath him.

Brother Enoch stood at one side of his bed, and beside him Jem, at Will's head, wearing an anxious expression. "Will," Jem said urgently. "Will, are you sure you won't have another pain-killing rune?"

"No—more," Will ground out, between his teeth. "Just—get it over with."

Brother Enoch raised what looked like a wickedly sharp pair of silver tweezers. Will gulped and buried his head in his arms, his dark hair startling against the white of the sheets. Jem shuddered as if the pain were his own as the tweezers dug deep into Will's back and his body tautened on the bed, muscles tensing under the skin, his cry of agony short and muffled. Brother Enoch drew back the tool, a blood-smeared shard of metal gripped in its teeth.

Jem slid his hand into Will's. "Grip my fingers. It will help the pain. There are only a few more."

"Easy—for you to say," Will gasped, but the touch of his *parabatai*'s hand seemed to relax him slightly. He was arched up off the bed, his elbows digging into the mattress, his breath coming in short pants. Tessa knew she ought to look away, but she couldn't. She realized she had never seen so much of a boy's body before, not even Jem's. She found herself fascinated by the way the lean muscle slid under Will's smooth skin, the flex and swell of his arms, the hard, flat stomach convulsing as he breathed.

The tweezers flashed again, and Will's hand bore down on Jem's, both their fingers whitening. Blood welled and spilled down his bare side. He made no sound, though Jem looked sick and pale. He moved his hand as if to touch Will's shoulder, then drew it back, biting down on his lip.

All this because Will covered my body with his to protect me, Tessa thought. As Brother Enoch had said, it was a burden to bear indeed.

She lay on her narrow bed in her old room in the New York flat. Through the window she could see gray sky, the rooftops of Manhattan. One of her aunt's colorful patchwork quilts was on the bed, and she clutched it to her as the door opened and her aunt herself came in.

Knowing what she knew now, Tessa could see the resemblance. Aunt Harriet had blue eyes, faded fair hair; even the shape of her face was like Nate's. With a smile she came and bent over Tessa, putting a hand on her forehead, cool against Tessa's hot skin.

"I'm so sorry," Tessa whispered. "About Nate. It's my fault he's dead."

"Hush," her aunt said. "It isn't your fault. It is his and mine. I always felt such guilt, you see, Tessa. Knowing I was his mother but not being able to bear telling him. I let him get away with anything he wanted, until he was spoiled beyond saving. If I had told him that I was really his mother, he would not have felt so betrayed when he discovered the truth, and would not have turned against us. Lies and secrets, Tessa, they are like a cancer in the soul. They eat away what is good and leave only destruction behind."

"I miss you so much," Tessa said. "I have no family now. . . ."

Her aunt leaned forward to kiss her on the forehead. "You have more family than you think."

"We will almost certainly forfeit the Institute now," said Charlotte. She did not sound brokenhearted, but distant and detached. Tessa was hovering like a ghost over the infirmary, looking down at where Charlotte stood with Jem at the foot of Tessa's own bed. Tessa could see herself, asleep, her dark hair spread like a fan across her pillows. Will lay asleep a few beds over, his back striped with bandages, an *iratze* black against the back of his neck. Sophie, in her white cap and dark dress, was dusting the windowsills. "We have lost Nathaniel Gray as a source, one of our own has turned out to be a spy, and we are no closer to finding Mortmain than we were a fortnight ago."

"After all that we have done, have learned? The Clave will understand—"

"They will not. They are already at the end of their tether where I am concerned. I might as well march over to Benedict Lightwood's house and make over the Institute paperwork in his name. Have done with it."

"What does Henry say about all this?" asked Jem. He was no longer in gear, and neither was Charlotte; he wore a white shirt and brown cloth trousers, and Charlotte was in one of her drab dark dresses. As Jem turned his hand over, though, Tessa saw that it was still spotted with Will's dried blood.

Charlotte snorted in an unladylike manner. "Oh, Henry," she said, sounding exhausted. "I think he's just so shocked that one of his devices actually worked that he doesn't know what to do with himself. And he can't bear to come in here. He thinks it's his fault that Will and Tessa are hurt."

"Without that device we might all be dead, and Tessa in the hands of the Magister."

"You are welcome to explain that to Henry. I have given up the attempt."

"Charlotte . . ." Jem's voice was soft. "I know what people say. I know you've heard the cruel gossip. But Henry does love you. When he thought you were hurt, at the tea warehouse, he went almost mad. He threw himself against that machine—"

"James." Charlotte clumsily patted Jem's shoulder. "I do appreciate your attempt to console me, but falsehoods never do anyone any good in the end. I long ago accepted that Henry loves his inventions first, and me second—if at all."

"Charlotte," Jem said wearily, but before he could say another word, Sophie had moved to stand beside them, dust cloth in hand.

"Mrs. Branwell," she said in a low voice. "If I might speak to you for just a moment."

Charlotte looked surprised. "Sophie . . ."

"Please, ma'am."

Charlotte placed a hand on Jem's shoulder, said something softly into his ear, and then nodded toward Sophie. "Very well. Come with me to the drawing room."

As Charlotte left the room with Sophie, Tessa realized to her surprise that Sophie was actually taller than her mistress. Charlotte's presence was such that one often forgot how very small she was. And Sophie was as tall as Tessa herself, as slender as a willow. Tessa saw her again in her mind with Gideon Lightwood, pressed up against the corridor wall, and Tessa worried.

As the door closed behind the two women, Jem leaned forward, his arms crossed over the foot of Tessa's brass bed. He was looking at her, smiling a little, though crookedly, his hands hanging loose—dried blood across the knuckles, and under the nails.

"Tessa, my Tessa," he said in his soft voice, as lulling as his violin. "I know you cannot hear me. Brother Enoch says you're not hurt badly. I can't say I find that enough to comfort me. It's rather like when Will assures me that we're only a little bit lost somewhere. I know it means we won't be seeing a familiar street again for hours."

He dropped his voice, so low that Tessa wasn't sure if what he said next was real or part of the dream darkness rising to claim her, though she fought against it.

"I've never minded it," he went on. "Being lost, that is. I had always thought one could not be truly lost if one knew one's own heart. But I fear I may be lost without knowing yours." He closed his eyes as if he were bone-weary, and she saw how thin his eyelids were, like parchment paper, and how tired he looked. "Wo ai ni, Tessa," he whispered. "Wo bu xiang shi qu ni."

She knew, without knowing how she knew, what the words meant.

I love you.

And I don't want to lose you.

I don't want to lose you, either, she wanted to say, but the words wouldn't come. Lassitude rose up instead, in a dark wave, and covered her in silence.

Darkness.

It was dark in the cell, and Tessa was conscious first of a feeling of great loneliness and terror. Jessamine lay in the narrow bed, her fair hair hanging in lank ropes over her shoulders. Tessa both hovered over her and felt somehow as if she were touching her mind. She could feel a great aching sense of loss. Somehow Jessamine knew that Nate was dead. Before, when Tessa had tried to touch the other girl's mind, she had met resistance, but now she felt only a growing sadness, like the stain of a drop of black ink spreading through water.

Jessie's brown eyes were open, staring up into the darkness. *I have nothing. The words were as clear as a bell in Tessa's mind. I chose Nate over the Shadowhunters, and now he is dead, and Mortmain will want me dead as well, and Charlotte despises me. I have gambled and lost everything.*

As Tessa watched, Jessamine reached up and drew a small cord from her neck over her head. At the end of the cord was a gold ring with a glittering white stone—a diamond. Clasping it between her fingers, she began to use the diamond to scratch letters into the stone wall.

JG.

Jessamine Gray.

There might have been more to the message, but Tessa would never find out; as Jessamine pressed down on the gemstone, it shattered, and her hand slammed against the wall, scraping her knuckles.

Tessa did not need to touch Jessamine's mind to know what she was thinking. Even the diamond had not been real. With a low cry Jessamine rolled over and buried her face in the rough blankets of the bed.

When Tessa woke again, it was dark. Faint starlight streamed through the high infirmary windows, and there was a witchlight lamp lit on the table near her bed. Beside it was a cup of tisane, steam rising from it, and a small plate of biscuits. She rose to a sitting position, about to reach for the cup—and froze.

Will was seated on the bed beside hers, wearing a loose shirt and trousers and a black dressing gown. His skin was pale in the starlight, but even the light's dimness couldn't wash out the blue of his eyes. "Will," she said, startled, "what are you doing awake?" Had he been watching her *sleep*, she wondered? But what an odd and un-Will-like thing to do.

"I brought you a tisane," he said, a little stiffly. "But you sounded as if you were having a nightmare."

"Did I? I don't even remember what I dreamed." She drew the covers up over herself, though her modest nightgown more than covered her. "I thought I had been escaping into sleep—that real life was the nightmare and that sleep was where I could find peace."

Will picked up the mug and moved to sit beside her on the bed. "Here. Drink this."

She took the cup from him obediently. The tisane had a bitter but appealing taste, like the zest of a lemon. "What will it do?" she asked.

"Calm you," said Will.

She looked at him, the taste of lemon in her mouth. There seemed a haze across her vision; seen through it, Will looked like something out of a dream. "How are your injuries? Are you in pain?"

He shook his head. "Once all the metal was out, they were able to use an *iratze* on me," he said. "The wounds are not completely healed, but they are healing. By tomorrow they will be scars."

"I am jealous." She took another sip of the tisane. It was beginning to make her feel light-headed. She touched the bandage across her forehead. "I believe it will be a good while before this comes off."

"In the meantime you can enjoy looking like a pirate."

She laughed, but it was shaky. Will was close enough to her that she could feel the heat emanating from his body. He was furnace-hot. "Do you have a fever?" she asked before she could stop herself.

"The *iratze* raises our body temperatures. It's part of the healing process."

"Oh," she said. Having him so close to her was sending little shivers through her nerves, but she felt too light-headed to draw away.

"I am sorry about your brother," he said softly, his breath stirring her hair.

"You couldn't be." She spoke bitterly. "I know you think he deserved what he got. He probably did."

"My sister died. She died, and there was nothing I could do about it," he said, and there was raw grief in his voice. "I *am* sorry about your brother."

She looked up at him. His eyes, wide and blue, that perfect face, the bow-shape of his mouth, turned down at the corners in concern. Concern for *her*. Her skin felt hot and tight, her head light and airy, as if she were floating. "Will," she whispered. "Will, I feel very odd."

Will leaned across her to put the mug down on the table, and his shoulder brushed hers. "Do you want me to get Charlotte?"

She shook her head. She was dreaming. She was nearly sure of it now; she had the same feeling of being in her body and yet not in it as she had had when she was dreaming of Jessamine. The knowledge that it was a dream made her bolder. Will was still leaning forward, his arm extended; she curled against him, her head on his shoulder, closing her eyes. She felt him jerk with surprise.

"Did I hurt you?" she whispered, belatedly remembering his back.

"I don't care," he said fervently. "I don't care." His arms went around her, and he held her; she rested her cheek against the warm juncture of his neck and shoulder. She heard the echo of his pulse and smelled the scent of him, blood and sweat and soap and magic. It was not like it had been on the balcony, all fire and desire. He held her carefully, laying his cheek against her hair. He was shaking, even as his chest rose and fell, even as he hesitantly slid his fingers beneath her chin, lifting her face . . .

"Will," Tessa said. "It's all right. It doesn't matter what you do. We're dreaming, you know."

"Tess?" Will sounded alarmed. His arms tightened about her. She felt warm and soft and dizzy. If only Will really were like this, she thought, not just in dreams. The bed rolled under her like a boat set adrift on the sea. She closed her eyes and let the darkness take her.

The night air was cold, the fog thick and yellowish-green under the intermittent pools of gaslight as Will made his way down King's Road. The address Magnus had given him was on Cheyne Walk, down near the Chelsea Embankment, and Will could already smell the familiar scent of the river, silt and water and dirt and rot.

He had been trying to keep his heart from beating its way out of his chest ever since he had found Magnus's note, neatly folded on a tray on the table beside his bed. It had said nothing beyond a curtly scrawled address: *16 Cheyne Walk*. Will was familiar with the Walk and the area around it. Chelsea, near the river, was a popular haunt for artists and literary types, and the windows of the public houses he passed glowed with welcoming yellow light.

He drew his coat around him as he turned a corner, making

his way south. His back and legs still ached from the injuries he had sustained, despite the *iratzes*; he was sore, as if he'd been stung by dozens of bees. And yet he hardly felt it. His mind was full of possibilities. What had Magnus discovered? Surely he would not summon Will if there were no reason? And his body was full of Tessa, the feel and scent of her. Strangely, what pierced his heart and mind most sharply was not the memory of her lips under his at the ball, but the way she had leaned into him tonight, her head on his shoulder, her breath soft against his neck, as if she trusted him utterly. He would have given everything he had in the world and everything he would ever have, just to lie beside her in the narrow infirmary bed and hold her while she slept. Pulling away from her had been like pulling his own skin off, but he'd had to do it.

The way he always had to. The way he always had to deny himself what he wanted.

But maybe—after tonight—

He cut the thought off before it bloomed in his mind. Better not to think about it; better not to hope and be disappointed. He looked around. He was on Cheyne Walk now, with its fine houses with their Georgian fronts. He stopped in front of number 16. It was tall, with a wrought iron fence about it and a prominent bay window. Set into the fence was an ornately worked gate; it was open, and he slipped inside and made his way up to the front door, where he rang the bell.

To his great surprise it was opened not by a footman but by Woolsey Scott, his blond hair in tangles to his shoulders. He wore a dark green dressing gown of Chinese brocade over a pair of dark trousers and a bare chest. A gold-rimmed monocle perched in one eye. He carried a pipe in his left hand, and as he examined Will at his leisure, he exhaled, sending out a cloud of sweet-smelling, cough-inducing smoke. "Finally broken down and admitted you're in love with me, have you?" he inquired of Will. "I do enjoy these surprise midnight declarations." He leaned against the door frame and waved a languid ringed hand. "Go along, have at it."

For once Will was speechless. It was not a position he found himself in often, and he was forced to admit that he did not like it.

"Oh, leave him be, Woolsey," said a familiar voice from inside the house—Magnus, hurrying along the corridor. He was fastening his shirt cuffs as he came forward, and his hair was a thicket of mussed black tangles. "I told you Will would be coming by."

Will looked from Magnus to Woolsey. Magnus was barefoot; so was the werewolf. Woolsey had a glimmering gold chain around his neck. From it hung a pendant that said *Beati Bellicosi*, "Blessed Are the Warriors." Beneath it was an imprint of a wolf's paw. Scott noticed Will staring at it and grinned. "Like what you see?" he inquired.

"*Woolsey*," said Magnus.

"Your note to me *did* have something to do with demon summoning, didn't it?" Will asked, looking at Magnus. "This isn't you . . . calling in your favor, is it?"

Magnus shook his rumpled head. "No. This is business, nothing else. Woolsey's been kind enough to let me lodge with him while I decide what to do next."

"I say we go to Rome," said Scott. "I adore Rome."

"All well and fine, but first I need the use of a room. Preferably one with little or nothing in it."

Scott removed his monocle and stared at Magnus. "And you're going to do *what* in this room?" His tone was more than suggestive.

"Summon the demon Marbas," said Magnus, flashing a grin.

Scott choked on his pipe smoke. "I suppose we all have our ideas about what constitutes an enjoyable evening . . ."

"Woolsey." Magnus ran his hands through his rough black hair. "I hate to bring this up, but you do owe me. Hamburg? 1863?"

Scott threw his hands up. "Oh, very well. You may utilize my brother's room. No one's used it since he died. Enjoy. I'll be in the drawing room with a glass of sherry and some rather naughty woodcuts I had imported from Romania."

With that, he turned and padded off down the hall. Magnus gestured Will inside, and he entered gladly, the warmth of the house enveloping him like a blanket. Since there was no footman, he slid off his blue wool frock coat and draped it over his arm as Magnus watched him with a curious gaze. "Will," he said. "I see you wasted no time after you got my note. I wasn't expecting you until tomorrow."

"You know what this means to me," said Will. "Did you really think I'd delay?"

Magnus's eyes searched his face. "You are prepared," he said. "For this to fail? For the demon to be the incorrect one? For the summoning not to work?"

For a long moment Will could not move. He could see his own face in the mirror that hung by the door. He was horrified to see how raw he looked—as if there were no longer any wall between the world and his own heart's desires. "No," he said. "I am not prepared."

Magnus shook his head. "Will . . ." He sighed. "Come with me."

He turned with catlike grace and made his way down the hall and up the curving wooden steps. Will followed, up through the shadowed staircase, the thick Persian stair runner muffling his footsteps. Niches set back in the walls contained polished marble statues of entwined bodies. Will looked away from them hastily, and then back. It wasn't as if Magnus seemed to be paying attention to what Will was doing, and he'd honestly never imagined two people could *get* themselves into a position like that, much less make it look artistic.

They reached the second landing, and Magnus padded off down the corridor, opening doors as he went and muttering to himself. Finally finding the correct room, he threw the door open and gestured for Will to follow him.

The bedroom of Woolsey Scott's dead brother was dark and cold, and the air smelled of dust. Automatically Will fumbled for his witchlight, but Magnus waved a dismissing hand at him, blue fire sparking from his fingertips. A fire roared up suddenly in the grate, lighting the room. It *was* furnished, though everything had been draped with white cloths—the bed, the wardrobe and dressers. As Magnus stalked through the room, rolling up his shirtsleeves and gesturing with his hands, the furniture began to slide back from the center of the room. The bed swung around and lay flat against the wall; the chairs and bureaus and washstand flew into the corners of the room.

Will whistled. Magnus grinned. "Easily impressed," Magnus said, though he sounded slightly out of breath. He knelt down in the now denuded center of the room and hastily drew a pentagram. In each point of the occult symbol, he scrawled a rune, though none were runes Will knew from the Gray Book. Magnus raised his arms and held them out over the star; he began to chant, and gashes opened up in his wrists, spilling blood into the pentagram's center. Will tensed as the blood struck the floor and began to burn with an eerie blue glow. Magnus backed out of the pentagram, still chanting, reached into his pocket, and produced the demon's tooth. As Will watched, Magnus tossed it into the now flaming center of the star.

For a moment nothing happened. Then, out of the burning heart of the fire, a dark shape began to take form. Magnus had stopped chanting; he stood, his narrowed eyes focused on the pentagram and what was happening within it, the gashes on his arms closing swiftly. There was little sound in the room, just the crackle of the fire and Will's harsh breathing, loud in his own ears, as the dark shape grew in size—coalesced, and, finally, took a solid, recognizable shape.

It was the blue demon from the party, no longer dressed in evening wear. Its body was covered in overlapping blue scales, and a long yellowish tail with a stinger on the end switched back and forth behind it. The demon looked from Magnus to Will, its scarlet eyes narrowed.

"*Who summons the demon Marbas?*" it demanded in a voice that sounded as if its words were echoing from the bottom of a well.

Magnus jerked his chin toward the pentagram. The message was clear: This was Will's business now.

Will took a step forward. "You don't remember me?"

"*I remember you,*" the demon growled. "*You chased me through the grounds of the Lightwood country house. You tore out one of my*" teeth." It opened its mouth, showing the gap. "*I tasted your blood.*" Its voice was a hiss. "*When I escape this pentagram, I will taste it again, Nephilim.*"

"No." Will stood his ground. "I'm asking you *if you remember me.*"

The demon was silent. Its eyes, dancing with fire, were unreadable.

"Five years ago," said Will. "A box. A Pyxis. I opened it, and you emerged. We were in my father's library. You attacked, but my sister fended you off with a seraph blade. *Do you recollect me now?*"

There was a long, long silence. Magnus kept his cat's eyes fixed on the demon. There was an implied threat in them, one that Will couldn't read. "Speak the truth," Magnus said finally. "Or it will go badly for you, Marbas."

The demon's head swung toward Will. "*You,*" it said reluctantly. "*You are that boy. Edmund Herondale's son.*"

Will sucked in a breath. He felt suddenly light-headed, as if he were going to pass out. He dug his nails into his palms, hard, gashing the skin, letting the pain clear his head. "You remember."

"*I had been trapped for twenty years in that thing,*" Marbas snarled. "*Of course I remember being freed. Imagine it, if you can, idiot mortal, years of blackness, darkness, no light or movement— and then the break, the opening. And the face of the man who imprisoned you hovering just above your gaze.*"

"I am not the man who imprisoned you—"

"*No. That was your father. But you look just like him to my eyes.*" The demon smirked. "*I remember your sister. Brave girl, fending me off with that blade she could hardly use.*"

"She used it well enough to keep you away from us. That's why you cursed us. Cursed *me*. Do you remember that?"

The demon chuckled. "'*All who love you will find only death. Their love will be their destruction. It may take moments, it may take years, but any who look upon you with love will die of it. And I shall begin it with her.*'"

Will felt as if he were breathing fire. His whole chest burned. "Yes."

The demon cocked its head to the side. "*And you summoned me that we might reminisce about this shared event in our past?*"

"I called you up, you blue-skinned bastard, to get you to take the curse off me. My sister—Ella—she died that night. I left my family to keep them safe. It's been five years. It's enough. *Enough!*"

"*Do not try to engage my pity, mortal,*" said Marbas. "*I was twenty years tortured in that box. Perhaps you too should suffer for twenty years. Or two hundred—*"

Will's whole body tensed. Before he could fling himself toward the pentagram, Magnus said, in a calm tone, "Something about this story strikes me as odd, Marbas."

The demon's eyes flicked toward him. "*And what is that?*"

"A demon, upon being let out of a Pyxis, is usually at its weakest, having been starved for as long as it was imprisoned. Too weak to cast a curse as subtle and strong as the one you claim to have cast on Will."

The demon hissed something in a language Will didn't know, one of the more uncommon demon languages, not Cthonic or Purgatic. Magnus's eyes narrowed.

"But she died," Will said. "Marbas said my sister would die, and she did. That night."

Magnus's eyes were still fixed on the demon's. Some kind of battle of wills was taking place silently, outside Will's range of understanding. Finally Magnus said, softly, "Do you really wish to disobey me, Marbas? Do you wish to anger my father?"

Marbas spat a curse, and turned to Will. Its snout twitched. *"The half-caste is correct. The curse was false. Your sister died because I struck her with my stinger."* It swished its yellowish tail back and forth, and Will remembered Ella knocked to the ground by that tail, the blade skittering from her hand. *"There has never been a curse on you, Will Herondale. Not one put there by me."*

"No," Will said softly. "No, it isn't possible." He felt as if a great storm were blowing through his head; he remembered Jem's voice saying *the wall is coming down*, and he envisioned a great wall that had surrounded him, isolated him, for years, crumbling away into sand. He was free—and he was alone, and the icy wind cut through him like a knife. "No." His voice had taken on a low, keening note. *"Magnus . . ."*

"Are you lying, Marbas?" Magnus snapped. "Do you swear on Baal that you are telling the truth?"

"I swear," said Marbas, red eyes rolling. *"What benefit would it be to me to lie?"*

Will slid to his knees. His hands were locked across his stomach as if they were keeping his guts from spilling out. *Five years,* he thought. Five years wasted. He heard his family screaming and pounding on the doors of the Institute and himself ordering Charlotte to send them away. And they had never known why. They had lost a daughter and a son in a matter of days, and they had never known why. And the others—Henry and Charlotte and Jem—and Tessa—and the things he had done—

Jem is my great sin.

"Will is right," said Magnus. "Marbas, you *are* a blue-skinned bastard. *Burn and die!*"

Somewhere at the edge of Will's vision, dark red flame soared toward the ceiling; Marbas screamed, a howl of agony cut off as swiftly as it had begun. The stench of burning demon flesh filled the room. And still Will crouched on his knees, his breath sawing in and out of his lungs. *Oh God, oh God, oh God.*

Gentle hands touched his shoulders. "Will," Magnus said, and there was no humor in his voice, only a surprising kindness. "Will, I am sorry."

"Everything I've done," Will said. His lungs felt as if he couldn't get enough air. "All the lying, the pushing people away, the abandonment of my family, the unforgivable things I said to Tessa—a waste. A bloody waste, and all because of a lie I was stupid enough to believe."

"You were twelve years old. Your sister was dead. Marbas was a cunning creature. He has fooled powerful magicians, never mind a child who had no knowledge of the Shadow World."

Will stared down at his hands. "My whole life wrecked, destroyed . . ."

"You're seventeen," Magnus said. "You can't have wrecked a life you've barely lived. And don't you understand what this means, Will? You've spent the last five years convinced that no one could possibly love you, because if they did, they would be dead. The mere fact of their continued survival proved their indifference to you. But you were wrong. Charlotte, Henry, Jem—your family—"

Will took a deep breath, and let it out. The storm in his head was ebbing slowly.

"Tessa," he said.

"Well." Now there was a touch of humor to Magnus's voice. Will realized the warlock was kneeling beside him. *I am in a werewolf's house,* Will thought, *with a warlock comforting me, and the ashes of a dead demon mere feet away. Who could ever have imagined?* "I can give you no assurance of what Tessa feels. If you have not noticed, she is a decidedly independent girl. But you have as much a chance to win her love as any man does, Will, and isn't that what you wanted?" He patted Will on the shoulder and withdrew his hand, standing up, a thin dark shadow looming over Will. "If it's any consolation, from what I observed on the balcony the other night, I do believe she rather likes you."

Magnus watched as Will made his way down the front walk of the house. Reaching the gate, he paused, his hand on the latch, as if hesitating on the threshold of the beginning of a long and difficult journey. The moon had come out from behind the clouds and shone on his thick dark hair, the pale white of his hands.

"Very curious," said Woolsey, appearing behind Magnus in the doorway. The warm lights of the house turned Woolsey's dark blond hair into a pale gold tangle. He looked as if he'd been sleeping. "If I didn't know better, I'd say you were fond of that boy."

"Know better in what sense, Woolsey?" Magnus asked, absently, still watching Will, and the light sparking off the Thames behind him.

"He's Nephilim," said Woolsey. "And you've never cared for them. How much did he pay you to summon Marbas for him?"

"Nothing," said Magnus, and now he was not seeing anything that was there, not the river, not Will, only a wash of memories—eyes, faces, lips, receding into memory, love that he could no longer put a name to. "He did me a favor. One he doesn't even remember."

"He's very pretty," said Woolsey. "For a human."

"He's very broken," said Magnus. "Like a lovely vase that someone has smashed. Only luck and skill can put it back together the way it was before."

"Or magic."

"I've done what I can," Magnus said softly as Will pushed the latch, at last, and the gate swung open. He stepped out onto the Walk.

"He doesn't look very happy," Woolsey observed. "Whatever it was you did for him . . ."

"At the moment he is in shock," said Magnus. "He has believed one thing for five years, and now he has realized that all this time he has been looking at the world through a faulty mechanism—that all the things he sacrificed in the name of what he thought was good and noble have been a waste, and that he has only hurt what he loved."

"Good God," said Woolsey. "Are you quite sure you've helped him?"

Will stepped through the gate, and it swung shut behind him. "Quite sure," said Magnus. "It is always better to live the truth than to live a lie. And that lie would have kept him alone forever. He may have had nearly nothing for five years, but now he can have everything. A boy who looks like that . . ."

Woolsey chuckled.

"Though he had already given his heart away," Magnus

said. "Perhaps it is for the best. What he needs now is to love and have that love returned. He has not had an easy life for one so young. I only hope she understands."

Even from this distance Magnus could see Will take a deep breath, square his shoulders, and set off down the Walk. And—Magnus was quite sure he was not imagining it—there seemed to be almost a spring in his step.

"You cannot save every fallen bird," said Woolsey, leaning back against the wall and crossing his arms. "Even the handsome ones."

"One will do," said Magnus, and, as Will was no longer within his sight, he let the front door fall shut.

18

UNTIL I DIE

My whole life long I learn'd to love.
This hour my utmost art I prove
And speak my passion—heaven or hell?
She will not give me heaven? 'Tis well!
—Robert Browning, "One Way of Love"

"Miss. Miss!" Tessa woke slowly, Sophie shaking her shoulder. Sunlight was streaming through the windows high above. Sophie was smiling, her eyes alight. "Mrs. Branwell's sent me to bring you back to your room. You can't stay here forever."

"Ugh. I wouldn't want to!" Tessa sat up, then closed her eyes as dizziness washed through her. "You might have to help me up, Sophie," she said in an apologetic voice. "I'm not as steady as I could be."

"Of course, miss." Sophie reached down and briskly helped Tessa out of the bed. Despite her slenderness, she was quite strong. She'd have to be, wouldn't she, Tessa thought, from years of carrying heavy laundry up and down stairs, and coal from the coal scuttle to the grates. Tessa winced a bit as her feet struck the cold floor, and couldn't help glancing over to see if Will was in his infirmary bed.

He wasn't.

"Is Will all right?" she asked as Sophie helped her slide her feet into slippers. "I woke for a bit yesterday and saw them taking the metal out of his back. It looked dreadful."

Sophie snorted. "Looked worse than it was, then. Mr. Herondale barely let them *iratze* him before he left. Off into the night to do the devil knows what."

"*Was* he? I could have sworn I spoke to him last night." They were in the corridor now, Sophie guiding Tessa with a gentle hand on her back. Images were starting to take shape in Tessa's head. Images of Will in the moonlight, of herself telling him that nothing mattered, it was only a dream—and it had been, hadn't it?

"You must have dreamed it, miss." They had reached Tessa's room, and Sophie was distracted, trying to get the doorknob turned without letting go of Tessa.

"It's all right, Sophie. I can stand on my own."

Sophie protested, but Tessa insisted firmly enough that Sophie soon had the door open and was stoking the fire in the grate while Tessa sank into an armchair. There was a pot of tea and a plate of sandwiches on the table beside the bed, and she helped herself to it gratefully. She no longer felt dizzy, but she did feel tired, with a weariness that was more spiritual than physical. She remembered the bitter taste of the tisane she'd drunk, and the way it had felt to be held by Will—but that had been a dream. She wondered how much else of what she'd seen last night had been a dream—Jem whispering at the foot of her bed, Jessamine sobbing into her blankets in the Silent City . . .

"I was sorry to hear about your brother, miss." Sophie was on her knees by the fire, the rekindling flames playing over her lovely face. Her head was bent, and Tessa could not see her scar.

"You don't have to say that, Sophie. I know it was his fault, really, about Agatha—and Thomas—"

"But he was your brother." Sophie's voice was firm. "Blood mourns blood." She bent farther over the coals, and there was something about the kindness in her voice, and the way her hair curled, dark and vulnerable, against the nape of her neck, that made Tessa say:

"Sophie, I saw you with Gideon the other day."

Sophie stiffened immediately, all over, without turning to look at Tessa. "What do you mean, miss?"

"I came back to get my necklace," Tessa said. "My clockwork angel. For luck. And I saw you with Gideon in the corridor." She swallowed. "He was . . . pressing your hand. Like a suitor."

There was a long, long silence, while Sophie stared into the flickering fire. At last she said, "Are you going to tell Mrs. Branwell?"

Tessa recoiled. "What? Sophie, no! I just—wanted to warn you."

Sophie's voice was flat. "Warn me against what?"

"The Lightwoods . . ." Tessa swallowed. "They are not nice people. When I was at their house—with Will—I saw dreadful things, awful—"

"That's Mr. Lightwood, not his sons!" The sharpness in Sophie's voice made Tessa flinch. "They're not like him!"

"How different could they be?"

Sophie stood up, the poker clattering into the fire. "You think I'm such a fool that I'd let some half-hour gentleman make a mockery of me after all I been through? After all Mrs. Branwell's taught me? Gideon's a good man—"

"It's a question of upbringing, Sophie! Can you picture him going to Benedict Lightwood and saying he wants to marry a mundane, and a parlor maid to boot? Can you see him doing that?"

Sophie's face twisted. "You don't know anything," she said. "You don't know what he'd do for us—"

"You mean the *training*?" Tessa was incredulous. "Sophie, really—"

But Sophie, shaking her head, had gathered up her skirts and stalked from the room, letting the door slam shut behind her.

Charlotte, her elbows on the desk in the drawing room, sighed and balled up her fourteenth piece of paper, and tossed it into the fireplace. The fire sparked up for a moment, consuming the paper as it turned black and fell to ashes.

She picked up her pen, dipped it into the inkwell, and began again.

I, Charlotte Mary Branwell, daughter of Nephilim, do hereby and on this date tender my resignation as the director of the London Institute, on behalf of myself and of my husband, Henry Jocelyn Branwell—

"Charlotte?"

Her hand jerked, sending a blot of ink sprawling across the page, ruining her careful lettering. She looked up and saw Henry hovering by the desk, a worried look on his thin, freckled face. She set her pen down. She was conscious, as she always was with Henry and rarely at any other times, of her physical appearance—that her hair was escaping from its chignon, that her dress was not new and had an ink blot on the sleeve, and that her eyes were tired and puffy from weeping.

"What is it, Henry?"

Henry hesitated. "It's just that I've been— Darling, what are you writing?" He came around the desk, glancing over her shoulder. "*Charlotte!*" He snatched the paper off the desk; though ink had smeared through the letters, enough of what she had written was left for him to get the gist. "Resigning from the Institute? How can you?"

"Better to resign than to have Consul Wayland come in over my head and force me out," Charlotte said quietly.

"Don't you mean 'us'?" Henry looked hurt. "Should I have at least a say in this decision?"

"You've never taken an interest in the running of the Institute before. Why would you now?"

Henry looked as if she had slapped him, and it was all Charlotte could do not to get up and put her arms around him and kiss his freckled cheek. She remembered, when she had fallen in love with him, how she had thought he reminded her of an adorable puppy, with his hands just a bit too large for the rest of him, his wide hazel eyes, his eager demeanor. That the mind behind those eyes was as sharp and intelligent as her own was something she had always believed, even when others had laughed at Henry's eccentricities. She had always thought it would be enough just to be near him always, and love him whether he loved her or not. But that had been before.

"Charlotte," he said now. "I know why you're angry with me."

Her chin jerked up in surprise. Could he truly be that perceptive? Despite her conversation with Brother Enoch, she had thought no one had noticed. She had barely been able to think about it herself, much less how Henry would react when he knew. "You do?"

"I wouldn't go with you to meet with Woolsey Scott."

Relief and disappointment warred in Charlotte's breast. "Henry," she sighed. "That is hardly—"

"I didn't realize," he said. "Sometimes I get so caught up in my ideas. You've always known that about me, Lottie."

Charlotte flushed. He so rarely called her that.

"I would change it if I could. Of all the people in the world, I did think you understood. You know—you know it isn't just tinkering for me. You know I want to create something that will make the world better, that will make things better for the Nephilim. Just as you do, in directing the Institute. And though I know I will always come second for you—"

"Second for *me*?" Charlotte's voice shot up to an incredulous squeak. "*You* come second for *me*?"

"It's all right, Lottie," Henry said with incredible gentleness. "I knew when you agreed to marry me that it was because you needed to be married to run the Institute, that no one would accept a woman alone in the position of director—"

"Henry." Charlotte rose to her feet, trembling. "How can you say such terrible things to me?"

Henry looked baffled. "I thought that was just the way it was—"

"Do you think I don't know why you married me?" Charlotte cried. "Do you think I don't know about the money your father owed my father, or that my father promised to forgive the debt if you'd marry me? He always wanted a boy, someone to run the Institute after him, and if he couldn't have that, well, why not *pay* to marry his unmarriageable daughter—too plain, too headstrong—off to some poor boy who was just doing his duty by his family—"

"CHARLOTTE." Henry had turned brick red. She had never seen him so angry. "WHAT ON EARTH ARE YOU TALKING ABOUT?"

Charlotte braced herself against the desk. "You know very well," she said. "It is why you married me, isn't it?"

"You've never said a word about this to me before today!"

"Why would I? It's nothing you didn't know."

"It is, actually." Henry's eyes were blazing. "I know nothing of my father's owing yours anything. I went to your father in good faith and asked him if he would do me the honor of allowing me to ask for your hand in marriage. There was never any discussion of money!"

Charlotte caught her breath. In the years they had been married, she had never said a word about the circumstances of her betrothal to Henry; there had never seemed a reason, and she had never before wanted to hear any stammered denials of what she knew was true. Hadn't her father said it to her when he had told her of Henry's proposal? *He is a good enough man, better than his father, and you need some sort of a husband, Charlotte, if you are going to direct the Institute. I've forgiven his father's debts, so that matter is closed between our families.*

Of course, he had never said, not in so many words, that that was *why* Henry had asked to marry her. She had assumed . . .

"You are not plain," Henry said, his face still blazing. "You are beautiful. And I didn't ask your father if I could marry you out of duty; I did it because I loved you. I've always loved you. I'm your *husband*."

"I didn't think you wanted to be," she whispered.

Henry was shaking his head. "I know people call me eccentric. Peculiar. Even mad. All of those things. I've never minded. But for you to think I'd be so weak-willed— Do you even love me at all?"

"Of course I love you!" Charlotte cried. "That was never in question."

"Wasn't it? Do you think I don't hear what people say? They speak about me as if I weren't there, as if I were some sort of half-wit. I've heard Benedict Lightwood say enough times that you married me only so that you could pretend a man was running the Institute—"

Now it was Charlotte's turn to be angry. "And you criticize me for thinking you weak-willed! Henry, I'd never marry you for that reason, never in a thousand years. I'd give up the Institute in a moment before I'd give up . . ."

Henry was staring at her, his hazel eyes wide, his ginger hair bristling as if he had run his hands madly through it so many times that he was in danger of pulling it out in chunks. "Before you'd give up what?"

"Before I'd give *you* up," she said. "Don't you know that?"

And then she said nothing else, for Henry put his arms around her and kissed her. Kissed her in such a way that she no longer felt plain, or conscious of her hair or the ink spot on her dress or anything but Henry, whom she had always loved. Tears welled up and spilled down her cheeks, and when he drew away, he touched her wet face wonderingly.

"Really," he said. "You love me, too, Lottie?"

"Of course I do. I didn't marry you so I'd have someone to run the Institute with, Henry. I married you because—because I knew I wouldn't mind how difficult directing this place was, or how badly the Clave treated me, if I knew yours would be the last face I saw every night before I went to sleep." She hit him lightly on the shoulder. "We've been married for years, Henry. What did you *think* I felt about you?"

He shrugged his thin shoulders and kissed the top of her head. "I thought you were fond of me," he said gruffly. "I thought you might come to love me, in time."

"That's what I thought about you," she said wonderingly. "Could we really both have been so stupid?"

"Well, I'm not surprised about *me*," said Henry. "But honestly, Charlotte, you ought to have known better."

She choked back a laugh. "Henry!" She squeezed his arms. "There's something else I have to tell you, something very important—"

The door to the drawing room banged open. It was Will. Henry and Charlotte drew apart and stared at him. He looked exhausted—pale, with dark rings about his eyes—but there was a clarity in his face Charlotte had never seen before, a sort of brilliance in his expression. She braced herself for a sarcastic remark or cold observation, but instead he just smiled happily at them.

"Henry, Charlotte," he said. "You haven't seen Tessa, have you?"

"She's likely in her room," said Charlotte, bewildered. "Will, is something the matter? Oughtn't you be resting? After the injuries you sustained—"

Will waved this away. "Your excellent *iratzes* did their

work. I don't require rest. I only wish to see Tessa, and to ask you—" He broke off, staring at the letter on Charlotte's desk. With a few strides of his long legs, he had reached the desk and snatched it up, and read it with the same look of dismay Henry had worn. "Charlotte—no, you can't give up the Institute!"

"The Clave will find you another place to live," Charlotte said. "Or you may stay here until you turn eighteen, though the Lightwoods—"

"I wouldn't want to live here without you and Henry. What d'you think I stay for? The ambiance?" Will shook the piece of paper till it crackled. "I even bloody miss Jessamine— Well, a bit. And the Lightwoods will sack our servants and replace them with their own. Charlotte, you can't let it happen. This is our home. It's Jem's home, Sophie's home."

Charlotte stared. "Will, are you sure you haven't a fever?"

"Charlotte." Will slammed the paper back down onto the desk. "I *forbid* you to resign your directorship. Do you understand? Over all these years you've done everything for me as if I were your own blood, and I've never told you I was grateful. That goes for you as well, Henry. But I am grateful, and because of it I shall not let you make this mistake."

"Will," said Charlotte. "It is over. We have only three days to find Mortmain, and we cannot possibly do so. There simply is not time."

"Hang Mortmain," said Will. "And I mean that literally, of course, but also figuratively. The two-week limit on finding Mortmain was in essence set by Benedict Lightwood as a ridiculous test. A test that, as it turns out, was a cheat. He is working for Mortmain. This test was his attempt to leverage the Institute out from under you. If we but expose Benedict for what he is—Mortmain's puppet—the Institute is yours again, and the search for Mortmain can continue."

"We have Jessamine's word that to expose Benedict is to play into Mortmain's hands—"

"We cannot do nothing," Will said firmly. "It is worth at least a conversation, don't you think?" Charlotte couldn't think of a word to say. This Will was not a Will she knew. He was firm, straightforward, intensity shining in his eyes. If Henry's silence was anything to go by, he was just as surprised. Will nodded as if taking this for agreement.

"Excellent," he said. "I'll tell Sophie to round up the others."

And he darted from the room.

Charlotte stared up at her husband, all thoughts of the news she had wished to tell him driven from her mind. "Was that *Will?*" she said finally.

Henry arched one ginger eyebrow. "Perhaps he's been kidnapped and replaced by an automaton," he suggested. "It seems possible . . ."

For once Charlotte could only find herself in agreement.

Glumly Tessa finished the sandwiches and the rest of the tea, cursing her inability to keep her nose out of other people's business. Once she was done, she put on her blue dress, finding the task difficult without Sophie's assistance. *Look at yourself,* she thought, *spoiled after just a few weeks of having a lady's maid. Can't dress yourself, can't stop nosing about where you're not wanted. Soon you'll be needing someone to spoon gruel into your mouth or you'll starve.* She made a horrible face at herself in the mirror and sat down at her vanity table, picking up the silver-backed hairbrush and pulling the bristles through her long brown hair.

A knock came at the door. *Sophie*, Tessa thought hopefully, back for an apology. Well, she would get one. Tessa dropped the hairbrush and rushed to throw the door open.

Just as once before she had expected Jem and been disappointed to find Sophie on her threshold, now, in expecting Sophie, she was surprised to find Jem at her door. He wore a gray wool jacket and trousers, against which his silvery hair looked nearly white.

"Jem," she said, startled. "Is everything all right?"

His gray eyes searched her face, her long, loose hair. "You look as if you were waiting for someone else."

"Sophie." Tessa sighed, and tucked a stray curl behind her ear. "I fear I have offended her. My habit of speaking before I think has caught me out again."

"Oh," said Jem, with an uncharacteristic lack of interest. Usually he would have asked Tessa what she had said to Sophie, and either reassured her or helped her plot a course of action to win Sophie's forgiveness. His customary vivid interest in everything seemed oddly missing, Tessa thought with alarm; he was quite pale as well, and seemed to be glancing behind her as if checking to see whether she was quite alone. "Is now— that is, I would like to speak to you in private, Tessa. Are you feeling well enough?"

"That depends on what you have to tell me," she said with a laugh, but when her laugh brought no answering smile, apprehension rose inside her. "Jem—you promise everything's all right? Will—"

"This is not about Will," he said. "Will is out wandering and no doubt perfectly all right. This is about— Well, I suppose you might say it's about me." He glanced up and down the corridor. "Might I come in?"

Tessa briefly thought about what Aunt Harriet would say about a girl who allowed a boy she was not related to into her bedroom when there was no one else there. But then Aunt Harriet herself had been in love once, Tessa thought. Enough in love to let her fiancé do—well, whatever it was exactly that left one with child. Aunt Harriet, had she been alive, would have been in no position to talk. And besides, etiquette was different for Shadowhunters.

She opened the door wide. "Yes, come in."

Jem came into the room, and shut the door firmly behind him. He walked over to the grate and leaned an arm against the mantel; then, seeming to decide that this position was unsatisfactory, he came over to where Tessa was, in the middle of the room, and stood in front of her.

"Tessa," he said.

"Jem," she replied, mimicking his serious tone, but again he did not smile. "Jem," she said again, more quietly. "If this is about your health, your—illness, please tell me. I will do whatever I can to help you."

"It is not," he said, "about my illness." He took a deep breath. "You know we have not found Mortmain," he said. "In a few days, the Institute may be given to Benedict Lightwood. He would doubtless allow Will and me to remain here, but not you, and I have no desire to live in a house that he runs. And Will and Gabriel would kill each other inside a minute. It would be the end of our little group; Charlotte and Henry would find a house, I have no doubt, and Will and I perhaps would go to Idris until we were eighteen, and Jessie—I suppose it depends what sentence the Clave passes on her. But we could not bring you to Idris with us. You are not a Shadowhunter."

Tessa's heart had begun to beat very fast. She sat down, rather suddenly, on the edge of her bed. She felt faintly sick. She remembered Gabriel's sneering jibe about the Lightwoods' finding "employment" for her; having been to the ball at their house, she could imagine little worse. "I see," she said. "But where should I go— No, do not answer that. You hold no responsibility toward me. Thank you for telling me, at least."

"Tessa—"

"You all have already been as kind as propriety has allowed," she said, "given that allowing me to live here has done none of you any good in the eyes of the Clave. I shall find a place—"

"Your place is with me," Jem said. "It always will be."

"What do you mean?"

He flushed, the color dark against his pale skin. "I mean," he said, "Tessa Gray, will you do me the honor of becoming my wife?"

Tessa sat bolt upright. *"Jem!"*

They stared at each other for a moment. At last he said, trying for lightness, though his voice cracked, "That was not a no, I suppose, though neither was it a yes."

"You can't mean it."

"I do mean it."

"You can't—I'm not a Shadowhunter. They'll expel you from the Clave—"

He took a step closer to her, his eyes eager. "You may not be precisely a Shadowhunter. But you are not a mundane either, nor provably a Downworlder. Your situation is unique, so I do not know what the Clave will do. But they cannot forbid something that is not forbidden by the Law. They will have to take your—our—individual case into consideration, and that could take months. In the meantime they cannot prevent our engagement."

"You *are* serious." Her mouth was dry. "Jem, such a kindness on your part is indeed incredible. It does you credit. But I cannot let you sacrifice yourself in that way for me."

"*Sacrifice?* Tessa, I love you. I *want* to marry you."

"I . . . Jem, it is just that you are kind, so selfless. How can I trust that you are not doing this simply for my sake?"

He reached into the pocket of his waistcoat and drew out something smooth and circular. It was a pendant of whitish-green jade, with Chinese characters carved into it that she could not read. He held it out to her with a hand that trembled ever so slightly.

"I could give you my family ring," he said. "But that is meant to be given back when the engagement is over, exchanged for runes. I want to give you something that will be yours forever."

She shook her head. "I cannot possibly—"

He interrupted her. "This was given to my mother by my father, when they married. The writing is from the I Ching, the Book of Changes. It says, *When two people are at one in their inmost hearts, they shatter even the strength of iron or bronze.*"

"And you think we are?" Tessa asked, shock making her voice small. "At one, that is?"

Jem knelt down at her feet, so that he was gazing up into her face. She saw him as he had been on Blackfriars Bridge, a lovely silver shadow against the darkness. "I cannot explain love," he said. "I could not tell you if I loved you the first moment I saw you, or if it was the second or third or fourth. But I remember the first moment I looked at you walking toward me and realized that somehow the rest of the world seemed to vanish when I was with you. That you were the center of everything I did and felt and thought."

Overwhelmed, Tessa shook her head slowly. "Jem, I never imagined—"

"There is a force and strength in love," he said. "That is what that inscription means. It is in the Shadowhunter wedding ceremony, too. *For love is as strong as death.* Have you not seen how much better I have been these past weeks, Tessa? I have been ill less, coughing less. I feel stronger, I need less of the drug—because of you. Because my love for you sustains me."

Tessa stared. Was such a thing even possible, outside of fairy tales? His thin face glowed with light; it was clear he believed it, absolutely. And he *had* been better.

"You speak of sacrifice, but it is not my sacrifice I offer. It is yours I ask of you," he went on. "I can offer you my life, but it is a short life; I can offer you my heart, though I have no idea how many more beats it shall sustain. But I love you enough to hope that you will not care that I am being selfish in trying to make the rest of my life—whatever its length—happy, by spending it with you. I want to be married to you, Tessa. I want it more than I have ever wanted anything else in my life." He looked up at her through the veil of silvery hair that fell over his eyes. "That is," he said shyly, "if you love me, too."

Tessa looked down at Jem, kneeling before her with the pendant in his hands, and understood at last what people meant when they said someone's heart was in their eyes, for Jem's eyes, his luminous, expressive eyes that she had always found beautiful, were full of love and hope.

And why should he *not* hope? She had given him every reason to believe she loved him. Her friendship, her trust, her confidence, her gratitude, even her passion. And if there was some small locked away part of herself that had not quite given up Will, surely she owed it to herself as much as to Jem to do whatever she could to destroy it.

Very slowly she reached down and took the pendant from Jem. It slipped around her neck on a gold chain, as cool as water, and rested in the hollow of her throat above the spot where the clockwork angel lay. As she lowered her hands from its clasp, she saw the hope in his eyes light to an almost unbearable blaze of disbelieving happiness. She felt as if someone had reached inside her chest and unlocked a box that held her heart, spilling tenderness like new blood through her veins. Never had she felt such an overwhelming urge to fiercely protect another person, to wrap her arms around someone else and curl up tightly with them, alone and away from the rest of the world.

"Then, yes," she said. "Yes, I will marry you, James Carstairs. Yes."

"Oh, thank God," he said, exhaling. "Thank God." And he buried his face in her lap, wrapping his arms around her waist. She bent over him, stroking his shoulders, his back, the silk of his hair. His heart pounded against her knees. Some small inner part of her was reeling with amazement. She had never imagined she had the power to make someone else so happy. And not a magical power either—a purely human one.

A knock came at the door; they sprang apart. Tessa hastily rose to her feet and made her way to the door, pausing to smooth down her hair—and, she hoped, calm her expression—before opening it. This time it really *was* Sophie. Though, her mutinous expression showed she had not come of her own accord. "Charlotte is summoning you to the drawing room, miss," she said. "Master Will has returned, and she wishes to have a meeting." She glanced past Tessa, and her expression soured further. "You, too, Master Jem."

"Sophie—," Tessa began, but Sophie had already turned and was hurrying away, her white cap bobbing. Tessa tightened her grip on the doorknob, looking after her. Sophie had said that she did not mind Jem's feelings for Tessa, and Tessa knew now that Gideon was the reason why. Still . . .

She felt Jem come up behind her and slip his hands into hers. His fingers were slender; she closed her own around them, and let out her held breath. Was this what it meant to love someone? That any burden was a burden shared, that they could give you comfort with a word or a touch? She leaned her head back against his shoulder, and he kissed her temple. "We'll tell Charlotte first, when there's a chance," he said, "and then the others. Once the fate of the Institute is decided . . ."

"You sound as if you don't mind what happens to it," said Tessa. "Won't you miss it here? This place has been your home."

His fingers stroked her wrist lightly, making her shiver. "You are home for me now."

19

IF TREASON DOTH PROSPER

Treason doth never prosper: what's the reason?
Why, if it prosper, none dare call it treason.
—Sir John Harrington

Sophie was tending a blazing fire in the drawing room grate, and the room was warm, almost stuffy. Charlotte sat behind her desk, Henry in a chair beside her. Will was sprawled in one of the flowered armchairs beside the fire, a silver tea service at his elbow and a cup in his hand. When Tessa walked in, he sat upright so abruptly that some of the tea spilled on his sleeve; he set the cup down without taking his eyes off her.

He looked exhausted, as if he had been walking all night. He still wore his overcoat, of dark blue wool with a red silk lining, and the legs of his black trousers were splattered with mud. His hair was damp and tangled, his face pale, his jaw dark with the shadow of stubble. But the moment he saw Tessa, his eyes glowed like lanterns at the touch of the lamplighter's match. His whole face changed, and he gazed upon her with such an inexplicable delight that Tessa, astonished, stopped in her tracks, causing Jem to bump into her. For that moment, she could not look away from Will; it was as if he held her gaze to him, and she remembered again the dream she had had the night before, that she was being comforted by him in the infirmary. Could he read the memory of it on her face? Was that why he was staring?

Jem peered around her shoulder. "Hallo, Will. Sure it was a good idea to spend all night out in the rain when you're still healing?"

Will tore his eyes away from Tessa. "I am quite sure," he said firmly. "I had to walk. To clear my head."

"And is your head clear now?"

"Like crystal," Will said, returning his gaze to Tessa, and the same thing happened again. Their gazes seemed to lock together, and she had to tear her eyes away and move across the room to sit on the sofa near the desk, where Will was not in her direct line of sight. Jem came and sat down beside her, but did not reach for her hand. She wondered what would happen if they announced what had just happened now, casually: *The two of us are going to be married.*

But Jem had been correct; it was not the right time for that. Charlotte looked as if, like Will, she had been awake all night; her skin was a sickly yellow color, and there were dark auburn bruises beneath her eyes. Henry sat beside her at the desk, his hand protectively over hers, watching her with a worried expression.

"We are all here, then," Charlotte said briskly, and for a moment Tessa wanted to remark that they were not, for Jessamine was not with them. She stayed silent. "As you probably know, we are near the end of the two-week period granted to us by Consul Wayland. We have not discovered the whereabouts of Mortmain. According to Enoch, the Silent Brothers have examined Nathaniel Gray's body and learned nothing from it, and as he is dead, we can learn nothing from him."

And as he is dead. Tessa thought of Nate as she remembered him, when they had been very young, chasing dragonflies in the park. He had fallen in the pond, and she and Aunt Harriet—his mother—had helped to pull him out; his hand had been slippery with water and green-growing underwater plants. She remembered his hand sliding out of hers in the tea warehouse, slippery with blood. *You don't know everything I've done, Tessie.*

"We can certainly report what we know about Benedict to the Clave," Charlotte was saying when Tessa forcibly snapped her mind back to the conversation at hand. "It would seem to be the sensible course of action."

Tessa swallowed. "What about what Jessamine said? That we'd be playing into Mortmain's hands by doing so."

"But we cannot do nothing," said Will. "We cannot sit back and hand over the keys to the Institute to Benedict Lightwood and his lamentable offspring. They *are* Mortmain. Benedict is his puppet. We must *try.* By the Angel, haven't we enough evidence? Enough to earn him a trial by the Sword, at least."

"When we tried the Sword on Jessamine, there were blocks in her mind put there by Mortmain," Charlotte said wearily. "Do you think Mortmain would be so unwise as to not take the same precaution with Benedict? We will look like fools if the Sword can get nothing out of him."

Will ran his hands through his black hair. "Mortmain expects us to go to the Clave," he said. "It would be his first assumption. He is also used to cutting free associates for whom he no longer has a use. De Quincey, for instance. Lightwood is not irreplaceable to him, and knows it." He drummed his fingers on his knees. "I think that if we went to the Clave, we could certainly get Benedict taken out of the running for leadership of the Institute. But there is a segment of the Clave that follows his lead; some are known to us, but others are not. It is a sad fact, but we do not know whom we can trust beyond ourselves. The Institute is secure with us, and we cannot allow it to be taken away. Where else will Tessa be safe?"

Tessa blinked. "Me?"

Will looked taken aback, as if startled by what he had just said. "Well, you are an integral part of Mortmain's plan. He has always wanted *you*. He has always needed you. We must not let him have you. Clearly you would be a powerful weapon in his hands."

"All of that is true, Will, and of course I will go to the Consul," said Charlotte. "But as an ordinary Shadowhunter, not as head of the Institute."

"But why, Charlotte?" Jem demanded. "You excel at your work—"

"Do I?" she demanded. "For the second time I have not noted a spy under my own roof; Will and Tessa easily evaded my guardianship to attend Benedict's party; our plan to capture Nate, which we never shared with the Consul, went awry, leaving us with a potentially important witness dead—"

"Lottie!" Henry put his hand on his wife's arm.

"I am not fit to run this place," said Charlotte. "Benedict was right. . . . I will of course try to convince the Clave of his guilt. Someone else will run the Institute. It will not be Benedict, I hope, but it will not be me, either—"

There was a clatter. "Mrs. Branwell!" It was Sophie. She had dropped the poker and turned away from the fire. "You can't resign, ma'am. You—you simply can't."

"Sophie," Charlotte said very kindly. "Wherever we go after this, wherever Henry and I set up our household, we will bring you—"

"It isn't that," Sophie said in a small voice. Her eyes darted around the room. "Miss Jessamine— She were—I mean, she was telling the truth. If you go to the Clave like this, you'll be playing into Mortmain's plans."

Charlotte looked at her, perplexed. "What makes you say that?"

"I don't—I don't know exactly." Sophie looked at the floor. "But I know it's true."

"Sophie?" Charlotte's tone was querulous, and Tessa knew what she was thinking: Did they have another spy, another serpent in their garden? Will, too, was leaning forward with narrowed eyes.

"Sophie's not lying," Tessa said abruptly. "She knows because—because we overheard Gideon and Gabriel speaking of it in the training room."

"And you only now decided to mention it?" Will arched his brows.

Suddenly, unreasonably furious with him, Tessa snapped, "Be quiet, Will. If you—"

"I've been stepping out with him," Sophie interrupted loudly. "With Gideon Lightwood. Seeing him on my days off." She was as pale as a ghost. "He told me. He heard his father laughing about it. They knew Jessamine was found out. They were hoping you'd go to the Clave. I should've said something, but it seemed like you didn't want to go to them anyways, so I . . ."

"Stepping out?" said Henry incredulously. "With *Gideon Lightwood?*"

Sophie kept her attention on Charlotte, who was gazing at her, round-eyed. "I know what Mortmain is holding over Mr. Lightwood too," she said. "Gideon only just found out. His father doesn't know he knows."

"Well, dear God, girl, don't just stand there," said Henry, who looked as poleaxed as his wife. "Tell us."

"Demon pox," said Sophie. "Mr. Lightwood's got it, has had for years, and it'll kill him in a right couple of months if he doesn't get the cure. And Mortmain said he can get it for him."

The room exploded in a hubbub. Charlotte raced over to Sophie; Henry called after her; Will leaped from his chair and was dancing in a circle. Tessa stayed where she was, stunned, and Jem remained beside her. Meanwhile, Will appeared to be singing a song about how he had been right about demon pox all along.

"Demon pox, oh, demon pox,
Just how is it acquired?
One must go down to the bad part of town
Until one is very tired.

Demon pox, oh, demon pox
I had it all along—
No, not the pox, you foolish blocks,
I mean this very song—
For I was right, and you were wrong!"

"Will!" Charlotte shouted over the noise. "Have you LOST YOUR MIND? CEASE THAT INFERNAL RACKET! Jem—"

Jem, rising to his feet, clapped his hands over Will's mouth. "Do you promise to be quiet?" he hissed into his friend's ear.

Will nodded, blue eyes blazing. Tessa was staring at him in amazement; they all were. She had seen Will many things— amused, bitter, condescending, angry, pitying—but never *giddy* before.

Jem let him go. "All right, then."

Will slid to the floor, his back against the armchair, and threw his arms up. "A demon pox on all your houses!" he announced, and yawned.

"Oh God, weeks of pox jokes," said Jem. "We're for it now."

"It can't be true," said Charlotte. "It's simply—*demon pox?*"

"How do we know Gideon did not lie to Sophie?" asked Jem, his tone mild. "I am sorry, Sophie. I hate to have to say it, but the Lightwoods are not trustworthy. . . ."

"I've seen Gideon's face when he looks at Sophie," said Will. "It was Tessa who told me first that Gideon fancied our Miss Collins, and I thought back, and I realized it was true. And a man in love—a man in love will tell anything. Betray anyone." He was staring at Tessa as he spoke. She stared back; she could not help it. Her gaze felt pulled to him. The way he looked at her, with those blue eyes like pieces of sky, as if trying to communicate something to her silently. But what on earth . . . ?

She did owe him her life, she realized with a start. Perhaps he had been waiting for her to thank him. But there had been no time, no chance! She resolved to thank him at the first opportunity that presented itself. "Besides, Benedict was holding a demon woman on his lap at that party of his, kissing her," Will went on, glancing away. "She had snakes for eyes. Each man to his own, I suppose. Anyway, the only way you can contract demon pox is by having improper relations with a demon, so . . ."

"Nate told me Mr. Lightwood preferred demon women," said Tessa. "I don't suppose his wife ever knew about *that*."

"Wait." It was Jem, who had suddenly gone very still. "Will—what are the symptoms of demon pox?"

"Quite nasty," said Will with relish. "It begins with a shield-shaped rash on one's back, and spreads over the body, creating cracks and fissures in the skin—"

Jem expelled a gasp of breath. "I—I shall return," he said, "in just a moment. By the Angel—"

And he vanished out the door, leaving the others staring after him.

"You don't think he has demon pox, do you?" Henry inquired of no one in particular.

I hope not, since we just got engaged, Tessa had the urge to say—just to see the looks on their faces—but repressed it.

"Oh, shut up, Henry," said Will, and looked as if he were about to say something else, but the door banged open and Jem was back in the room, panting, and holding a piece of parchment. "I got this," he said, "from the Silent Brothers—when Tessa and I went to see Jessamine." He gave Tessa a slightly guilty look from under his fair hair, and she remembered him leaving Jessamine's cell and returning moments later, looking preoccupied. "It is the report on Barbara Lightwood's death. After Charlotte told us that her father had never turned Silas Pangborn over to the Clave, I thought I would inquire of the Silent Brothers if there was another manner in which Mrs. Lightwood had died. To see if Benedict had also lied that she had died of grief."

"And had he?" Tessa leaned forward, fascinated.

"Yes. In fact, she cut her own wrists. But there was more." He looked down at the paper in his hand. "*A shield-shaped rash, indicative of the heraldic marks of astriola, upon the left shoulder.*" He held it out to Will, who took it and scanned it, his blue eyes widening.

"*Astriola,*" he said. "That *is* demon pox. You had evidence that demon pox existed and you didn't mention it to me! *Et tu, Brute!*" He rolled up the paper and hit Jem over the head with it.

"Ouch!" Jem rubbed his head ruefully. "The words meant nothing to me! I assumed it a minor sort of ailment. It hardly seemed as if it were what killed her. She slit her wrists, but if Benedict wanted to protect his children from the fact that their mother had taken her own life—"

"By the Angel," said Charlotte softly. "No wonder she killed herself. *Because her husband gave her demon pox. And she knew it.*" She whirled on Sophie, who made a little gasping noise. "Does Gideon know of this?"

Sophie shook her head, saucer-eyed. "No."

"But wouldn't the Silent Brothers be obligated to tell

someone if they discovered this?" Henry demanded. "It seems—well, dash it, irresponsible to say the least—"

"Of course they would tell someone. They would tell *her husband*. And no doubt they did, but what of it? Benedict probably already knew," said Will. "There would have been no need to tell the children; the rash appears when one has first contracted the disease, so they were too old for her to have passed it on to them. The Silent Brothers doubtless told Benedict, and he said 'Horrors!' and promptly concealed the whole thing. One cannot prosecute the dead for improper relations with demons, so they burned her body, and that was that."

"So how is it that Benedict is still alive?" Tessa demanded. "Should the disease not have killed him by now?"

"Mortmain," said Sophie. "He's been giving him drugs to slow the progress of the disease all this time."

"Slow it, not stop it?" asked Will.

"No, he's still dying, and faster now," said Sophie. "That's why he's so desperate, and he'll do anything Mortmain wants."

"Demon pox!" Will whispered, and looked at Charlotte. Despite his clear excitement, there was a steady light flickering behind his blue eyes, a light of sharp intelligence, as if he were a chess player examining his next move for potential advantages or drawbacks. "We must contact Benedict immediately," said Will. "Charlotte must play on his vanity. He is too sure of getting the Institute. She must tell him that though the Consul's official decision is not scheduled until Sunday, she has realized that it is he who will come out ahead, and she wishes to meet with him and make peace before it happens."

"Benedict is stubborn—," Charlotte began.

"Not as much as is he is proud," said Jem. "Benedict has always wanted control of the Institute, but he also wants to humiliate you, Charlotte. To prove that a woman cannot run an Institute. He believes that Sunday the Consul will rule to take the Institute away from you, but that does not mean he will be able to pass up a chance to see you grovel in private."

"To what end?" Henry demanded. "Sending Charlotte to confront Benedict accomplishes what, exactly?"

"Blackmail," said Will. His eyes were burning with excitement. "Mortmain may not be in our grasp, but Benedict is, and for now that may be enough."

"You think he will walk away from trying to get the Institute? Won't that simply leave the business for one of his followers to take up?" Jem asked.

"We're not trying to get rid of him. We want him to throw his full support behind Charlotte. To withdraw his challenge and to declare her fit to run the Institute. His followers will be at a loss; the Consul will be satisfied. We hold the Institute. And more than that, we can force Benedict to tell us what he knows of Mortmain—his location, his secrets, everything."

Tessa said dubiously, "But I am almost certain he is more afraid of Mortmain than he is of us, and he certainly needs what Mortmain provides. Otherwise he will die."

"Yes, he will. But what he did—having improper relations with a demon, then infecting his wife, causing her death—is the knowing murder of another Shadowhunter. It would not be considered only murder, either, but murder accomplished through demonic means. That would call down the worst of all punishments."

"What is worse than death?" asked Tessa, and immediately

regretted saying it as she saw Jem's mouth tighten almost imperceptibly.

"The Silent Brothers will remove that which makes him Nephilim. He will become Forsaken," said Will. "His sons will become mundane, their Marks stripped. The name of Lightwood will be stricken from the rolls of Shadowhunters. It will be the end of the Lightwood name among Nephilim. There is no greater shame. It is a punishment even Benedict will fear."

"And if he does not?" said Jem in a low voice.

"Then, we are no worse off, I suppose." It was Charlotte, whose expression had hardened as Will had spoken; Sophie was leaning against the mantel, a dejected figure, and Henry, his hand on his wife's shoulder, looked unusually subdued. "We will call on Benedict. There is no time to send a proper message ahead; it will have to be something of a surprise. Now, where are the calling cards?"

Will sat upright. "You've decided on my plan, then?"

"It's my plan now," said Charlotte firmly. "You may accompany me, Will, but you will follow my lead, and there will be no talk of demon pox until I say so."

"But—but . . ." Will sputtered.

"Oh, leave it," said Jem, kicking Will, not without affection, lightly on the ankle.

"She's *annexed* my plan!"

"Will," Tessa said firmly. "Do you care more about the plan being enacted or about getting credit for it?"

Will pointed a finger at her. "That," he said. "The second one."

Charlotte rolled her eyes skyward. "William, this will be either on my terms or not at all."

Will took a deep breath, and looked at Jem, who grinned at him; Will let the air out of his lungs with a defeated sigh and said, "All right, then, Charlotte. Do you intend for all of us to go?"

"You and Tessa, certainly. We need you as witnesses regarding the party. Jem, Henry, there is no need for you to go, and we require at least one of you to remain and guard the Institute."

"Darling . . ." Henry touched Charlotte's arm with a quizzical look on his face.

She looked up at him in surprise. "Yes?"

"You're sure you don't want me to come with you?"

Charlotte smiled at him, a smile that transformed her tired, pinched face. "Quite sure, Henry; Jem isn't technically an adult, and to leave him here alone—not that he isn't capable—will only add fuel to Benedict's fire of complaints. But thank you."

Tessa looked at Jem; he gave her a regretful smile and, hidden behind the spread of her skirts, pressed her hand with his. His touch sent a warm rush of reassurance through her, and she rose to her feet, amid Will rising to go, while Charlotte sought for a pen to scribble a note to Benedict on the back of a flossed calling card, which Cyril would deliver while they waited in the carriage.

"I'd best fetch my hat and gloves," Tessa whispered to Jem, and made her way to the door. Will was just behind her, and a moment later, the drawing room door swinging shut behind them, they found themselves alone in the corridor. Tessa was about to hurry down the hall toward her room, when she heard Will's footsteps behind her.

"Tessa!" he called, and she swung around. "Tessa, I need to speak with you."

"Now?" she said, surprised. "I gathered from Charlotte that she wanted us to hurry—"

"Damn hurrying," said Will, coming closer to her. "Damn Benedict Lightwood and the Institute and all this business. I want to talk to *you*." He grinned at her. There had always been a reckless energy to him, but this was different—the difference between the recklessness of despair and the abandonment of happiness. But what an odd time to be happy!

"Have you gone quite mad?" she asked him. "You say 'demon pox' the way someone else might say 'massive surprise inheritance.' Are you really that pleased?"

"Vindicated, not happy, and anyway, this isn't about the demon pox. This is about you and me—"

The drawing room door opened, and Henry emerged, Charlotte just behind him. Knowing Jem would be next, Tessa stepped away from Will hastily, though nothing improper had transpired between them at all. *Except in your thoughts*, said a little voice in the back of her mind, which she ignored. "Will, not now," she said under her breath. "I believe I know what it is you want to say, and you're quite right to wish to say it, but this isn't the time or place, is it? Believe me, I am as eager for the talk as you, for it has been weighing heavily on my mind—"

"You are? It has?" Will looked dazed, as if she had hit him with a rock.

"Well—yes," said Tessa, looking up to see Jem coming toward them. "But not *now*."

Will followed her gaze, swallowed, and nodded reluctantly. "Then, when?"

"Later, after we go to the Lightwoods'. Meet me in the drawing room."

"In the drawing room?"

She frowned at him. "Really, Will," she said. "Are you going to repeat everything I say?"

Jem had reached them, and heard this last remark; he grinned. "Tessa, do let poor Will gather his wits about him; he's been out all night and looks as if he can barely remember his own name." He put his hand on his *parabatai*'s arm. "Come along, Herondale. You seem as if you need an energy rune—or two or three."

Will tore his eyes away from Tessa's and let Jem lead him off down the corridor. Tessa watched them, shaking her head. *Boys*, she thought. She would never understand them.

Tessa had gone only a few steps into her bedroom when she stopped in surprise, staring at what was on the bed. A stylish walking suit of cream and gray striped India silk, trimmed with delicate braid and silver buttons. Gray velvet gloves lay beside it, figured with a pattern of leaves in silver thread. At the foot of the bed were bone-colored buttoned boots, and fashionable patterned stockings.

The door opened, and Sophie came in, holding a pale gray hat with trimmings of silver berries. She was very pale, and her eyes were swollen and red. She avoided Tessa's gaze. "New clothing, miss," Sophie said. "The fabric was part of Mrs. Branwell's trousseau, and, well, a few weeks ago she thought of having it made into a dress for you. I think she thought you ought to have some clothes that Miss Jessamine didn't buy for you. She thought it might make you more—comfortable. And these were just delivered this morning. I asked Bridget to lay them out for you."

Tessa felt tears sting the backs of her eyes and sat down hastily on the edge of the bed. The thought that Charlotte, with everything else that was going on, would think of Tessa's comfort at all made her want to cry. But she stifled the urge, as she always did. "Sophie," she said, her voice uneven. "I ought—no, I *wanted*—to apologize to you."

"Apologize to me, miss?" Sophie said tonelessly, laying the hat on the bed. Tessa stared. Charlotte wore such plain clothes herself. She never would have thought of her as having the inclination or taste to choose such lovely things.

"I was entirely wrong to speak to you about Gideon as I did," said Tessa. "I put my nose in where it was decidedly not wanted, and you are quite correct, Sophie. One cannot judge a man for the sins of his family. And I should have told you that, though I saw Gideon at the ball that night, I cannot say he was partaking of the festivities; in fact, I cannot see into his head to determine what he thinks at all, and I should not have behaved as if I could. I am no more experienced than you, Sophie, and where it comes to gentlemen, I am decidedly uninformed. I apologize for acting superior; I shan't do it again, if only you'll forgive me."

Sophie went to the wardrobe and opened it to reveal a second dress—this one of a very dark blue, trimmed with a golden velvet braid, the polonaise slashed down the right side to reveal pale faille flounces beneath. "So lovely," she said a little wistfully, and touched it lightly with her hand. Then she turned to Tessa. "That were—that was a very pretty apology, miss, and I do forgive you. I forgave you in the drawing room, I did, when you lied for me. I don't approve of lying, but I know you meant it out of kindness."

"It was very brave, what you did," said Tessa. "Telling the truth to Charlotte. I know how you feared she'd be angry."

Sophie smiled sadly. "She isn't angry. She's disappointed. I know. She said she couldn't talk to me now but she would later, and I could see it, on her face. It's worse in a way, somehow."

"Oh, Sophie. She's disappointed in Will all the time!"

"Well, who isn't."

"That's not what I meant. I meant she loves you, like you were Will or Jem or—well, you know. Even if she's disappointed, you must stop fearing she'll sack you. She won't. She thinks you're wonderful, and so do I."

Sophie's eyes widened. "Miss Tessa!"

"Well, I do," said Tessa mutinously. "You are brave and selfless and lovely. Like Charlotte."

Sophie's eyes shone. She wiped at them hastily with the edge of her apron. "Now, that's enough of that," she said briskly, still blinking hard. "We must get you dressed and ready, for Cyril's coming round with the carriage, and I know Mrs. Branwell doesn't want to waste any time."

Tessa came forward obediently, and with Sophie's help she changed into the gray and white striped dress. "And do be careful, is all I have to say," said Sophie as she deftly wielded her buttonhook. "The old man is a nasty piece of work, and don't forget it. Very harsh, he is, on those boys."

Those boys. The way she said it made it sound like Sophie had sympathy for Gabriel as well as Gideon. Just what did Gideon think of his younger brother, Tessa wondered, and the sister, too? But she asked nothing as Sophie brushed and curled her hair, and daubed her temples with lavender water.

"Now, don't you look lovely, miss," she said proudly when

she was done at last, and Tessa had to admit that Charlotte had done a fine job in selecting just the right cut to flatter her, and gray suited her well. Her eyes looked bigger and blue, her waist and arms more slender, her bosom fuller. "There's just one other thing . . ."

"What is it, Sophie?"

"Master Jem," said Sophie, startling Tessa. "Please, whatever else you do, miss . . ." The other girl glanced at the chain of the jade pendant tucked down the front of Tessa's dress and bit her lip. "Don't break his heart."

20

THE BITTER ROOT

But now, you are twain, you are cloven apart,
Flesh of his flesh, but heart of my heart;
And deep in one is the bitter root,
  And sweet for one is the lifelong flower.
—Algernon Charles Swinburne,
"The Triumph of Time"

Tessa was just drawing on her velvet gloves as she ducked through the front doors of the Institute. A sharp wind had come up off the river and was blowing armfuls of leaves through the courtyard. The sky had gone thunderous and gray. Will stood at the foot of the stairs, hands in his pockets, looking up at the church steeple.

He was hatless, and the wind lifted his black hair and blew it back from his face. He did not seem to see Tessa, and for a moment she stood and looked at him. She knew it was not right to do; Jem was hers, she was his now, and other men might as well not exist. But she could not stop herself from

comparing the two—Jem with his odd combination of delicacy and strength, and Will like a storm at sea, slate blue and
black with brilliant flashes of temper like heat lightning. She
wondered if there would ever be a time when the sight of him
didn't move her, make her heart flutter, and if that feeling
would subside as she grew used to the idea of being engaged to
Jem. It was new enough still that it did not seem real.

There was one thing that was different, though. When she
looked at Will now, she no longer felt any pain.

Will saw her then, and smiled through the hair that blew
across his face. He reached up to push it back. "That's a new
dress, isn't it?" he said as she came down the stairs. "Not one
of Jessamine's."

She nodded, and waited resignedly for him to say something sarcastic, about her, Jessamine, the dress, or all three.

"It suits you. Odd that gray would make your eyes look blue,
but it does."

She looked at him in astonishment, but before she could do
more than open her mouth to ask him if he was feeling all right,
the carriage came rattling around the corner of the Institute
with Cyril at the reins. He pulled up in front of the steps, and
the door of the carriage opened; Charlotte was inside, wearing
a wine-colored velvet dress and a hat with a sprig of dried flowers in it. She looked as nervous as Tessa had ever seen her. "Get
in quickly," she called, holding her hat on as she leaned out the
door. "I think it's going to rain."

To Tessa's surprise, Cyril drove her, Charlotte, and Will not
to the manor house in Chiswick but to an elegant house in
Pimlico, which was apparently the Lightwoods' weekday resi-

dence. It *had* begun to rain, and their wet things—gloves, hats, and coats—were taken from them by a sour-faced footman before they were ushered down many polished corridors and into a large library, where a roaring fire burned in a deep grate.

Behind a massive oak desk sat Benedict Lightwood, his sharp profile made even sharper by the play of light and shadow inside the room. The drapes were pulled across the windows, and the walls were lined with heavy tomes bound in dark leather, gold printing across the spines. On either side of him stood his sons—Gideon at his right, his blond hair falling forward to hide his expression, his arms crossed over his broad chest. On the other side was Gabriel, his green eyes alight with a superior amusement, his hands in the pockets of his trousers. He looked as if he were about to start whistling.

"Charlotte," said Benedict. "Will. Miss Gray. Always a pleasure." He gestured for them to seat themselves in the chairs set before the desk. Gabriel grinned nastily at Will as he sat. Will looked at him, his face a careful blank, and then looked away. *Without a sarcastic remark*, Tessa thought, baffled. Without even a cold glare. *What* was going on?

"Thank you, Benedict." Charlotte, tiny, her spine straight, spoke with perfect poise. "For seeing us on such short notice."

"Of course." He smiled. "You do know that there's nothing you can do that's going to change the outcome of this. It isn't up to me what the Council rules. It is their decision entirely."

Charlotte tilted her head to the side. "Indeed, Benedict. But it is you who are making this happen. If you had not forced Consul Wayland into making a show of disciplining me, there would be no ruling."

Benedict shrugged his narrow shoulders. "Ah, Charlotte.

I remember you when you were Charlotte Fairchild. You were such a delightful little girl, and believe it or not as you will, I am fond of you even now. What I am doing is in the best interests of the Institute and the Clave. A woman cannot run the Institute. It is not in her nature. You'll be thanking me when you're home with Henry raising the next generation of Shadowhunters, as you should be. It might sting your pride, but in your heart you know I'm correct."

Charlotte's chest rose and fell rapidly. "If you abdicated your claim on the Institute before the ruling, do you truly think it would be such a disaster? Me, running the Institute?"

"Well, we'll never find out, will we?"

"Oh, I don't know," Charlotte said. "I think most Council members would choose a woman over a dissolute reprobate who fraternizes not just with Downworlders but with demons."

There was a short silence. Benedict didn't move a muscle. Neither did Gideon.

Finally Benedict spoke, though now there were teeth in the smooth velvet of his voice. "Rumors and innuendo."

"Truth and observation," said Charlotte. "Will and Tessa were at your last gathering, in Chiswick. They observed a great deal."

"That demon woman you were lounging with on the divan," said Will. "Would you call her a friend, or more of a business associate?"

Benedict's dark eyes hardened. "Insolent puppy—"

"Oh, I'd say she was a friend," said Tessa. "One doesn't usually let one's business associates lick one's face. Although I could be wrong. What do I know about these things? I'm only a silly woman."

Will's mouth quirked up at the corner. Gabriel was still staring; Gideon had his eyes on the floor. Charlotte sat perfectly composed, hands in her lap.

"All three of you are quite foolish," said Benedict, gesturing contemptuously toward them. Tessa caught a glimpse of something on his wrist, a shadow, like the coils of a woman's bracelet, before his sleeve fell back to cover it. "That is, if you think the Council will believe any of your lies. You"—he cast a dismissive look at Tessa—"are a Downworlder; your word is worthless. And you"—he flung an arm at Will—"are a certifiable lunatic who fraternizes with warlocks. Not just this chit here but Magnus Bane as well. And when they test me under the Mortal Sword and I refute your claims, who do you think will be believed, you or me?"

Will exchanged a quick look with Charlotte and Tessa. He had been right, Tessa thought, that Benedict did not fear the Sword. "There is other evidence, Benedict," he said.

"Oh?" Lightwood's lip curled upward in a sneer. "And what is that?"

"The evidence of your own poisoned blood," said Charlotte. "Just now, when you gestured at us, I saw your wrist. How far has the corruption spread? It begins on the torso, does it not, and spreads down the arms and legs—"

"What is he talking about?" Gabriel's voice was a mixture of fury and terror. "Father?"

"Demon pox," said Will with the satisfaction of the truly vindicated.

"What a disgusting accusation—," began Benedict.

"Refute it, then," said Charlotte. "Pull up your sleeve. Show us your arm."

The muscle by the side of Benedict's mouth twitched again. Tessa watched him in fascination. He did not terrify her, as Mortmain had, but rather disgusted her, the way the sight of a fat worm wriggling across a garden might. She watched as he whirled on his eldest son.

"You," he snarled. "*You* told them. You betrayed me."

"I did," said Gideon, raising his head and uncurling his arms at last. "And I would again."

"Gideon?" It was Gabriel, sounding bewildered. "Father? What are you talking about?"

"Your brother has betrayed us, Gabriel. He has told our secrets to the Branwells." Benedict spat his words out like poison. "Gideon Arthur Lightwood," Benedict went on. His face looked older, the lines at the sides of his mouth more severe, but his tone was unchanged. "I suggest you think very carefully about what you have done, and what you will do next."

"I *have* been thinking," said Gideon in his soft, low voice. "Ever since you called me back from Spain, I have been thinking. As a child I assumed all Shadowhunters lived as we did. Condemning demons by the light of day, yet fraternizing with them under cover of darkness. I now realize that is not true. It is not our way, Father; it is *your* way. You have brought shame and filth upon the name of Lightwood."

"There is no need to be melodramatic—"

"Melodramatic?" There was terrible contempt in Gideon's normally flat tone. "Father, I fear for the future of the Enclave if you get your hands on the Institute. I am telling you now, I will witness against you at the Council. I will hold the Mortal Sword in my hands and I will tell Consul Wayland why I think Charlotte is a thousand times more fit than you are to run the

Institute. I will reveal what goes on here at night to every member of the Council. I will tell them that you are working for Mortmain. I will tell them *why*."

"Gideon!" It was Gabriel, his voice sharp, cutting across his brother's. "You know our custodianship of the Institute was mother's dying wish. And it is the fault of the Fairchilds that she died—"

"That is a lie," said Charlotte. "She took her own life, but not because of anything my father did." She looked directly at Benedict. "It was, rather, because of something *your* father did."

Gabriel's voice rose. "What do you mean? Why would you say such a thing? Father—"

"Be quiet, Gabriel." Benedict's voice had gone hard and commanding, but for the first time there was fear in his voice, his eyes. "Charlotte, what are you saying?"

"You know very well what I am saying, Benedict," said Charlotte. "The question is whether you wish me to share my knowledge with the Clave. And with your children. You know what it will mean for them."

Benedict sat back. "I know blackmail when I hear it, Charlotte. What do you want from me?"

It was Will who responded, too eager to hold himself back any longer. "Withdraw your claim on the Institute. Speak out for Charlotte in front of the Council. Tell them why you think the Institute should be left in her keeping. You are a well-spoken man. You'll think of something, I'm sure."

Benedict looked from Will to Charlotte. His lip curled. "Those are your terms?"

Before Will could speak, Charlotte said, "Not all our terms.

We need to know how you have been communicating with Mortmain, and where he is."

Benedict chuckled. "I communicated with him through Nathaniel Gray. But, since you've killed him, I doubt he will be a forthcoming source of information."

Charlotte looked appalled. "You mean no one else knew where he was?"

"I certainly don't," said Benedict. "Mortmain is not that stupid, unfortunately for you. He wished me to be able to take the Institute that he might strike at it from its heart. But it was only one of his many plans, a strand of his web. He has been waiting for this a long time. He will have the Clave. And he will have *her*." His eyes rested on Tessa.

"What does he intend to do with me?" Tessa demanded.

"I don't know," Benedict said with a sly smile. "I do know he was consistently asking after your welfare. Such concern, so touching in a potential bridegroom."

"He says he created me," said Tessa. "What does he mean by that?"

"I haven't the vaguest idea. You are mistaken if you think he made me his confidant."

"Yes," said Will, "you two don't seem to have much in common, save a penchant for demon women and evil."

"Will!" snapped Tessa.

"I didn't mean *you*," said Will, looking surprised. "I meant the Pandemonium Club—"

"If you are quite done with your byplay," said Benedict, "I wish to make one thing very clear to my son. Gideon, understand that if you support Charlotte Branwell in this, you will no longer be welcome under my roof. It is not for nothing that they say a man should never hang all his bells on one horse."

In answer Gideon raised his hands in front of him, almost as if he meant to pray. But Shadowhunters did not pray, and Tessa realized quickly what he was doing—slipping the silver ring from his finger. The ring that was like Jem's Carstairs ring, only this one had a pattern of flames about the band. The Lightwood family ring. He set it down on the edge of his father's desk, and turned to his brother.

"Gabriel," he said. "Will you come with me?"

Gabriel's green eyes were brilliant with anger. "You know I cannot."

"Yes, you can." Gideon held his hand out to his brother. Benedict stared between the two of them. He had paled slightly, as if suddenly realizing that he might lose not just one son, but both. His hand gripped the edge of the desk, his knuckles whitening. Tessa could not help staring at the expanse of the wrist that was revealed as his sleeve rose. It was very pale, banded with black circular striations. Something about the sight nauseated her, and she rose from her seat. Will, beside her, was already standing. Only Charlotte was still sitting, as prim and expressionless as ever.

"Gabriel, please," Gideon said. "Come with me."

"Who will take care of father? What will people say about our family if we both abandon him?" Gabriel said, bitterness and desperation coloring his tone. "Who will manage the estates, the Council seat—"

"I don't know," said Gideon. "But it does not need to be you. The Law—"

Gabriel's voice shook. "Family before Law, Gideon." His eyes locked with his brother's for a moment; then he looked away, chewing his lip, and went to stand behind Benedict, his hand on the back of his father's chair.

Benedict smiled; in this one thing, at least, he was triumphant. Charlotte rose to her feet, her chin held high. "I trust we will see you tomorrow, in the Council chamber, Benedict. I trust you will know what to do," she said, and swept from the room, Gideon and Tessa on her heels. Only Will hesitated a moment, in the doorway, his eyes on Gabriel, but when the other boy did not look at him, he shrugged at last and went out after the others, shutting the door behind him.

They rode back to the Institute in silence, rain lashing against the windows of the carriage. Charlotte attempted several times to speak to Gideon, but he was silent, staring at the blurred view of streets as they rolled by. Tessa could not tell if he was angry, or regretted his actions, or might even be relieved. He was as impassive as always, even as Charlotte explained to him that there would always be a room for him at the Institute, and that they could hardly express their gratitude for what he had done. At last, as they rattled down the Strand, he said, "I had really thought Gabriel would come with me. Once he knew about Mortmain . . ."

"He does not understand yet," said Charlotte. "Give him time."

"How did you know?" Will looked at Gideon keenly. "We only just discovered what happened to your mother. And Sophie said you had no idea—"

"I had Cyril deliver two notes," said Charlotte. "One for Benedict and one for Gideon."

"He slipped it into my hand while my father was not looking," Gideon said. "I had only just time to read it before you came in."

"And you chose to believe it?" Tessa said. "So quickly?"

Gideon looked toward the rain-washed window. His jaw was set in a hard line. "Father's story about Mother's death never made sense to me. This made sense."

Crowded into the damp carriage, with Gideon only a few feet from her, Tessa felt the oddest urge to reach out to him, to tell him that she too had had a brother whom she had loved and had lost to what was worse than death, that she understood. She could see now what Sophie liked in him—the vulnerability under the impassive countenance, the solid honesty beneath the handsome bones of his face.

She said nothing, however, sensing it would not be welcome. Will, meanwhile, sat beside her, a bundle of coiled energy. Every once in a while she would catch a flash of blue as he looked at her, or the edge of a smile—a surprisingly *sweet* smile, something like giddiness, which she had never associated with Will before. It was as if he were sharing a private joke with her, only she was not entirely sure she knew what that joke *was*. Still, she felt his tension so keenly that her own calm, or what there was of it, was entirely cut up by the time they finally reached the Institute and Cyril—soaked to the skin, but friendly as always—came around the carriage to open the doors.

He helped Charlotte out first, and then Tessa, and then Will was beside her, having jumped down from the carriage and narrowly skirted a puddle. It had stopped raining. Will glanced up at the sky and took hold of Tessa's arm. "Come along," he whispered, steering her toward the front door of the Institute.

Tessa glanced back over her shoulder, to where Charlotte

stood at the foot of the steps, having succeeded, it seemed, in finally getting Gideon to speak to her. She was gesturing animatedly, using her hands.

"We ought to wait for them, oughtn't we—," Tessa began.

Will shook his dark head determinedly. "Charlotte will be blathering at him for ages about what room he wants to stay in, and how grateful she is for his help, and all I want is to talk to you."

Tessa stared at him as they entered the Institute. Will wanted to talk to her. He had said so before, true, but to speak so straightforwardly was very unlike him.

A thought seized her. Had Jem told him of their engagement? Was he angry, thinking her not worthy of his friend? But when would Jem have had a *chance*? Perhaps while she was dressing—but, then, Will did not *look* angry.

"I can't wait to tell Jem about our meeting," he said as they mounted the stairs. "He'll never believe that scene—for Gideon to turn on his father like that! It's one thing to tell secrets to Sophie, another to renounce your whole allegiance to your family. Yet he cast away his family ring."

"It is as you said," Tessa said as they turned at the top of the stairs and made their way down the corridor. Will's gloved hand was warm on her arm. "Gideon's in love with Sophie. People will do anything for love."

Will looked at her as if her words had jolted him, then smiled, that same maddeningly sweet smile he had given her in the carriage. "Amazing, isn't it?"

Tessa made as if to answer, but they had reached the drawing room. It was bright inside; the witchlight torches were high, and there was a fire in the grate. The curtains were drawn back, showing squares of leaden sky. Tessa took off her hat and gloves and was just laying them on a small Moroccan table when she saw that Will, who had followed her in, was drawing closed the bolt on the door.

Tessa blinked. "Will, why are you locking—"

She never finished her sentence. Covering the space between them in two long strides, Will reached her and caught her up in an embrace. She gasped in surprise as he took her by the arms, walking her backward until they half-collided with the wall, her crinolette protesting.

"*Will*," she said in surprise, but he was pinning her to the wall with his body, his hands sliding up her shoulders, into her damp hair, his mouth sudden and hot on hers. She fell and spun and drowned in the kiss; his lips were soft and his body was hard against her, and he tasted like rain. Heat spread through the pit of her stomach as his mouth moved urgently on hers, willing her response.

Jem's face flashed against the back of her closed eyelids. She put her hands flat against Will's chest and shoved him away from her, as hard as she could. Her breath came out on a violent exhalation: "*No*."

Will took a surprised step backward. His voice, when he spoke, was throaty and low. "But last night? In the infirmary? I—you embraced me—"

I did? With an acute shock she realized that what she had taken for a dream had been no dream after all. Or was he lying? But no. There was no manner in which he could have known what she had dreamed.

"I . . ." Her words stumbled over themselves. "I thought I was dreaming . . ."

The hazy look of desire was fast vanishing from his eyes, replaced by hurt and confusion. He almost stammered: "But even today. I thought you—you said you were as eager to be alone with me as I was—"

"I imagined you wanted an apology! You saved my life at the tea warehouse, and I *am* grateful, Will. I thought you wanted me to tell you that—"

Will looked as if she had slapped him. "I didn't save your life so you'd be *grateful!*"

"Then, what?" Her voice rose. "You did it because it's your mandate? Because the Law says—"

"*I did it because I love you!*" he half-shouted, and then, as if registering the shocked look on her face, he said in a more subdued voice, "I love you, Tessa, and I have loved you, almost since the moment I met you."

Tessa laced her hands together. They were icy cold. "I thought you couldn't be crueler than you were on the roof that day. I was wrong. This is crueler."

Will stood motionless. Then he shook his head slowly, from side to side, like a patient denying the deadly diagnosis of a physician. "You . . . don't believe me?"

"Of course I don't believe you. After the things you said, the way you've treated me—"

"I *had* to," he said. "I had no choice. Tessa, listen." She began to move toward the door; he scrambled to block her way, his blue eyes burning. "Please listen. *Please.*"

Tessa hesitated. The way he said "please"—the catch in his voice—this was not like it had been on the roof. Then he had barely been able to look at her. Now he was staring at her desperately, as if he could will her to remain with desire alone.

The voice that cried within her that he would hurt her, that he was not sincere, grew softer, buried under an ever loudening treacherous voice that told her to stay. To hear him out.

"Tessa." Will pushed his hands through his black hair, his slim fingers trembling with agitation. Tessa remembered what it was like to touch that hair, to have her fingers wound through it, like rough silk against her skin. "What I am going to tell you I have never told another living soul but Magnus, and that was only because I needed his help. I have not even told Jem." Will took a deep breath. "When I was twelve, living with my parents in Wales, I found a Pyxis in my father's office."

She was not sure what she had expected Will to say, but this was not it. "A *Pyxis*? But why would your father keep a Pyxis?"

"A memento from his Shadowhunting days? Who can guess? But do you recall the *Codex* discussing curses and how they can be cast? Well, when I opened the box, I released a demon—Marbas—who cursed me. He swore that anyone who loved me was doomed to die. I might not have believed it—I was not well schooled in magic—but my elder sister died that night, horribly. I thought it was the beginning of the curse. I fled my family and came here. It seemed to me the only way to keep them safe, not to bring them death on death. I did not realize at first that I was walking into a second family. Henry, Charlotte, even bloody Jessamine—I had to make sure that no one here could ever love me. To do so, I thought, would be to put them into deadly danger. For years I have held everyone at arm's length—everyone I could not push away entirely."

Tessa stared at him. The words echoed in her head. *Held everyone at arm's length—pushed everyone away—* She thought of his lies, his hiding, the unpleasantness to Charlotte and

Henry, the cruelties that seemed forced, even the story of Tatiana, who had only loved him the way little girls did, and whose affections he had crushed. And then there was ... "Jem," she whispered.

He looked at her miserably. "Jem is different," he whispered.

"Jem is *dying*. You let Jem in because he was already near death? You thought the curse wouldn't affect him?"

"And with every year that passed, and he survived, that seemed more likely. I thought I could learn to live like this. I thought when Jem was gone, after I turned eighteen, I'd go live by myself, not inflict myself or my curse on anyone—and then everything changed. Because of you."

"Me?" said Tessa in a quiet, stunned voice.

The ghost of a smile touched his mouth. "When I first met you, I thought you were unlike anyone else I had ever known. You made me laugh. No one but Jem has made me laugh in, good God, five years. And you did it like it was nothing, like breathing."

"You did not even know me. Will—"

"Ask Magnus. He'll tell you. After that night on the roof, I went to him. I had pushed you away because I thought you had begun to realize how I felt about you. In the Sanctuary that day, when I thought you were dead, I realized you must have been able to read it on my face. I was terrified. I had to make you hate me, Tessa. So I tried. And then I wanted to die. I had thought I could bear it if you hated me, but I could not. I realized you would be staying in the Institute, and that every time I saw you it would be like standing on that roof all over again, making you despise me and feeling as if I were choking down poison. I went to Magnus and demanded that he help me find the demon who had cursed me in the first place, that the curse might be lifted. If it was, I thought, I could try again. It might be slow and painful and nearly impossible, but I thought I could make you care for me again, if only I could tell you the truth. That I could gain your trust back—build something with you, slowly."

"Are—are you saying the curse is lifted? That it's *gone*?"

"There is no curse on me, Tessa. The demon tricked me. There never was a curse. All these years, I've been a fool. But not so much a fool that I didn't know that the first thing I needed to do once I had learned the truth was tell you how I really felt." He took another step forward, and this time she did not move back. She was staring at him, at the pale, almost translucent skin under his eyes, at the dark hair curling at his temples, the nape of his neck, at the blue of his eyes and the curve of his mouth. Staring at him the way she might stare at a beloved place she was not sure she would ever see again, trying to commit the details to memory, to paint them on the backs of her eyelids that she might see it when she shut her eyes to sleep.

She heard her own voice as if from very far away. "Why me?" she whispered. "Why me, Will?"

He hesitated. "After we brought you back here, after Charlotte found your letters to your brother, I—I read them."

Tessa heard herself say, very calmly, "I know you did. I found them in your room when I was there with Jem."

He looked startled. "You said nothing to me about it."

"At first I was angry," she admitted. "But that was the night we found you in the ifrit den. I felt for you, I suppose. I told myself you had only been curious, or Charlotte had asked you to read them."

"She didn't," he said. "I pulled them out of the fire myself. I read them all. Every word you wrote. You and I, Tess, we're alike. We live and breathe words. It was books that kept me from taking my own life after I thought I could never love anyone, never be loved by anyone again. It was books that made me feel that perhaps I was not completely alone. They could be honest with me, and I with them. Reading your words, what you wrote, how you were lonely sometimes and afraid, but always brave; the way you saw the world, its colors and textures and sounds, I felt—I felt the way you thought, hoped, felt, dreamed. I felt I was dreaming and thinking and feeling *with* you. I dreamed what you dreamed, wanted what you wanted—and then I realized that truly I just wanted *you*. The girl behind the scrawled letters. I loved you from the moment I read them. I love you still."

Tessa had begun to tremble. This was what she had always wanted someone to say. What she had always, in the darkest corner of her heart, wanted *Will* to say. Will, the boy who loved the same books she did, the same poetry she did, who made her laugh even when she was furious. And here he was standing in front of her, telling her he loved the words of her heart, the shape of her soul. Telling her something she had never imagined anyone would ever tell her. Telling her something she would never be told again, not in this way. And not by him.

And it did not matter.

"It's too late," she said.

"Don't say that." His voice was half a whisper. "I love you, Tessa. I love you."

She shook her head. "Will . . . stop."

He took a ragged breath. "I knew you would be reluctant to trust me," he said. "Tessa, please, is it that you do not believe me, or is it that you cannot imagine ever loving me back? Because if it is the second—"

"Will. It doesn't *matter*—"

"Nothing matters more!" His voice grew in strength. "I *know* that if you hate me it is because I forced you to. I *know* that you have no reason to give me a second chance to be regarded by you in a different light. But I am begging you for that chance. I will do anything. *Anything*."

His voice cracked, and she heard the echo of another voice inside it. She saw Jem, looking down at her, all the love and light and hope and expectancy in the world caught up in his eyes.

"No," she whispered. "It isn't possible."

"It is," he said desperately. "It must be. You cannot hate me as much as all that—"

"I don't hate you at all," she said, with great sadness. "I tried to hate you, Will. But I could never manage it."

"Then, there's a chance." Hope flared in his eyes. She should not have spoken so gently—oh, God, was there nothing that would make this less awful? She had to tell him. Now. Quickly. Cleanly. "Tessa, if you don't hate me, then there's a chance that you might—"

"Jem has proposed to me," she blurted out. "And I have said yes."

"*What?*"

"I said that Jem proposed to me," she whispered. "He asked if I would marry him. And I said I would."

Will had gone shockingly white. He said, "Jem. *My* Jem?"

She nodded, without words to say.

Will staggered and put his hand on the back of a chair

for balance. He looked like someone who had been suddenly, viciously kicked in the stomach. "When?"

"This morning. But we have been growing closer, much closer, for a long time."

"You—and Jem?" Will looked as if he were being asked to believe in something impossible—snow in summertime, a London winter without rain.

In answer, Tessa touched with her fingertips the jade pendant Jem had given her. "He gave me this," she said. Her voice was very quiet. "It was his mother's bridal gift."

Will stared at it, at the Chinese characters on it, as if it were a serpent curled about her throat. "He never told me anything. He never said a word about you to me. Not that way." He pushed his hair back from his face, that characteristic gesture she had seen him make a thousand times, only now his hand was visibly shaking. "Do you love him?"

"Yes, I love him," she said, and she saw Will flinch. "Don't you?"

"But he would understand," he said dazedly. "If we explained it to him. If we told him . . . he would understand."

For just a moment Tessa imagined herself drawing the pendant off, going down the hallway, knocking on Jem's door. Giving it back to him. Telling him she had made a mistake, that she could not marry him. She could tell him, tell him everything about herself and about Will—how she was not sure, how she needed time, how she could not promise him all of her heart, how some part of her belonged to Will and always would.

And then she thought of the first words she had ever heard Jem speak, his eyes closed, his back to her, his face to the moonlight. *Will? Will, is that you?* The way Will's voice, his face, softened for Jem as it did for no one else; the way Jem had gripped Will's hands in the infirmary while he'd bled, the way Will had called out *James!* when the warehouse automaton had knocked Jem down.

I cannot sever them, one from the other, she thought. *I cannot be responsible for such a thing.*

I cannot tell either of them the truth.

She imagined Jem's face if she called off the engagement. He would be kind. Jem was always kind. But she would be breaking something precious inside him, something essential. He would not be the same afterward, and there would be no Will to comfort him. And he had so little time.

And Will? What would he do then? Whatever he might think now, she knew that if she broke things off with Jem, even then, he would not touch her, would not be with her, no matter how much he loved her. How could he parade his love for her in front of Jem, knowing his happiness came at the cost of his best friend's pain? Even if Will told himself he could manage it, to him she would always be the girl Jem loved, until the day Jem died. Until the day *she* died. He would not betray Jem, even after death. If it had been anyone else, anyone else in the world—but she did not love anyone else in the world. These were the boys she loved. For better. And for worse.

She made her voice as cold as she could. As calm. "Told him *what?*"

Will only looked at her. There had been light in his eyes on the stairs, as he'd locked the door, when he'd kissed her—a brilliant, joyous light. And it was going now, fading like the last breath of someone dying. She thought of Nate, bleeding to death in her arms. She had been powerless then, to help him.

As she was now. She felt as if she were watching the life bleed out of Will Herondale, and there was nothing she could do to stop it.

"Jem would forgive me," Will said, but there was hopelessness in his face, his voice, already. He had given up, Tessa thought; Will, who never gave up on any fight before it had started. "He . . ."

"He would," she said. "He could never stay angry at you, Will; he loves you too well for that. I do not even think he would hold anger toward me. But this morning he told me he thought he would die without ever loving anyone as his father loved his mother, without ever being loved like that in return. Do you want me to go down the hallway and knock on his door and take that away from him? And would you love me still, if I did?"

Will looked at her for a long moment. Then he seemed to crumple inside, like paper; he sat down in the armchair, and put his face into his hands. "You promise me," he said. "That you love him. Enough to marry him and make him happy."

"Yes," she said.

"Then, if you love him," he said quietly, "please, Tessa, don't tell him what I just told you. Don't tell him that I love you."

"And the curse? He doesn't know—"

"Please don't tell him about that either. Nor Henry, nor Charlotte—no one. I must tell them in my own time, in my own way. Pretend I said nothing to you. If you care about me at all, Tessa . . ."

"I will tell no one," she said. "I swear it. I promise it, on my angel. My mother's angel. And, Will . . ."

He had lowered his hands, but he still could not seem to

look at her. He was gripping the sides of the armchair, his knuckles white. "I think you had better go, Tessa."

But she could not bear to. Not when he was looking like that, like he was dying on the inside. More than anything else, she wanted to go and put her arms around him, to kiss his eyes closed, to make him smile again. "What you have endured," she said, "since you were twelve years old—it would have killed most people. You have always believed that no one loved you, that no one *could* love you, as their continued survival was proof to you that they did not. But Charlotte loves you. And Henry. And Jem. And your family. They all have always loved you, Will Herondale, for you cannot hide what is good about yourself, however hard you try."

He lifted his head and looked at her. She saw the flame of the fire reflected in his blue eyes. "And you? Do you love me?"

Her nails dug into her palms. "Will," she said.

He looked at her, almost through her, blindly. *"Do you love me?"*

"I . . ." She took a deep breath. It hurt. "Jem has been right about you all this time. You were better than I gave you credit for being, and for that I am sorry. Because if this is you, what you are truly like, and I think that it is—then you will have no difficulty finding someone to love you, Will, someone for whom you come first in their heart. But I . . ."

He made a sound halfway between a choking laugh and a gasp. "'First in your heart,'" he said. "Would you believe that is not the only time you have said that to me?"

She shook her head, bewildered. "Will, I have not—"

"You can never love me," he said flatly, and when she did not respond, when she said nothing, he shuddered—a shudder that ran through his whole body—and pushed away from the armchair without looking at her. He stood up stiffly and crossed the room, groping for the bolt on the door; she watched with her hand across her mouth as, after what seemed like an age, he found it, fumbled it open, and went out into the corridor, slamming the door behind him.

Will, she thought. *Will, is that you?* The backs of her eyes ached. Somehow she found that she was sitting on the floor in front of the grate of the fire. She stared at the flames, waiting for the tears to come. Nothing happened. After such a long time of forcing them back, it seemed, she had lost the ability to cry.

She took the poker from the fireplace iron holder and drove the tip of it into the heart of the burning coals, feeling the heat on her face. The jade pendant around her throat warmed, almost burning her skin.

She drew the poker out of the fire. It glowed as red as a heart. She closed her hand around the tip.

For a moment she felt absolutely nothing. And then, as if from a very great distance, she heard herself cry out, and it was like a key turned inside her heart, freeing the tears at last. The poker clattered to the ground.

When Sophie came dashing in, having heard her scream, she found Tessa on her knees by the fire, her burned hand pressed to her chest, sobbing as if her heart would break.

It was Sophie who took Tessa to her room, and Sophie who put her in her nightgown and then in bed, and Sophie who washed her burned hand with a cool flannel and bound it up with a salve that smelled like herbs and spices, the same salve, she told Tessa, that Charlotte had used on Sophie's cheek when she had first come to the Institute.

"Do you think I'll have a scar?" Tessa asked, more out of curiosity than because she cared one way or the other. The burn, and the weeping that had followed it, seemed to have seared and flooded all the emotion out of her. She felt as light and hollow as a shell.

"Probably a bit of a one, not like I've got," said Sophie frankly, securing the bandage around Tessa's hand. "Burns hurt worse than they are, if you catch my meaning, and I got to you quickly with the salve. You'll be all right."

"No, I won't be," said Tessa, looking at her hand, and then over at Sophie. Sophie, lovely as always, calm and patient in her black dress and white cap, her curls clustering around her face. "I'm sorry again, Sophie," she said. "You were right about Gideon, and I was wrong. I should have listened to you. You're the last person on earth inclined to be foolish over men. The next time you say someone is worth trusting, I will believe you."

Sophie's smile flashed out, the smile that made even strangers forget her scar. "I understand why you said it."

"I should have trusted you—"

"I shouldn't have got so angry," Sophie said. "The truth is, I wasn't sure myself what he was going to do. I wasn't sure till he came back in the carriage with you all that he would side with us in the end."

"It must be nice, though," Tessa said, playing with the bedclothes, "that he's going to live here. He'll be so close to you—"

"It will be the worst thing in the world," Sophie said, and suddenly her eyes were full of tears. Tessa froze in horror, wondering what she could have said so wrong. The tears stood in Sophie's eyes, without falling, making their green shimmer. "If he lives here, he'll see me as I really am. A servant." Her voice cracked. "I knew I should never have gone to see him when he asked me. Mrs. Branwell's not the type to punish her servants for having followers and the like, but I knew it was wrong anyway, because he's himself and I'm me, and we don't belong together." She reached up a hand and wiped at her eyes, and then the tears did fall, spilling down both her cheeks, the whole and the scarred one. "I could lose everything if I let myself— and what's he stand to lose? Nothing."

"Gideon's not like that."

"He's his father's son," Sophie said. "Who says that doesn't matter? It's not as if he was going to marry a mundane as it was, but to see me building up his fire, doing the washing-up—"

"If he loves you, he won't mind all that."

"People *always* mind all that. They are not so noble as you think."

Tessa thought of Will with his face in his hands, saying, *If you love him, please, Tessa, don't tell him what I just told you.* "One finds nobility in the oddest places, Soph. Besides, would you really *want* to be a Shadowhunter? Wouldn't you rather—"

"Oh, but I do want it," said Sophie. "More than anything in the world. I always have."

"I never knew," Tessa said, marveling.

"I used to think if I married Master Jem—" Sophie picked at the blanket, then looked up and smiled bleakly. "You haven't broken his heart yet, have you?"

"No," Tessa said. *Just torn my own in two.* "I haven't broken his heart at all."

21

COALS OF FIRE

O brother, the gods were good to you.
Sleep, and be glad while the world endures.
Be well content as the years wear through;
Give thanks for life, and the loves and lures;
Give thanks for life, O brother, and death,
For the sweet last sound of her feet, her breath,
For gifts she gave you, gracious and few,
Tears and kisses, that lady of yours.
—Algernon Charles Swinburne,
"The Triumph of Time"

Music poured out from under Jem's door, which was partly cracked open. Will stood with his hand on the knob, his shoulder against the wall. He felt profoundly exhausted, more tired than he ever had in his life. A terrible burning energy had kept him alert since he had left Cheyne Walk, but it was gone now, drained away, and there was only an exhausted darkness.

He had waited for Tessa to call after him once he had

slammed the drawing room door, but she had not. He could still see her, looking at him, with her eyes like great gray storm clouds. *Jem has proposed to me, and I have said yes.*

Do you love him?

I love him.

And yet here he was, standing in front of Jem's door. He did not know if he had come here to try to talk Jem out of Tessa—if such a thing could be accomplished—or, more likely, if this was where he had learned to go for comfort and he could not unlearn the habit of years. He pushed the door open; witchlight poured out into the hallway, and he stepped into Jem's room.

Jem was sitting on the trunk at the foot of his bed, his violin balanced on his shoulder. His eyes were closed as the bow sawed over the string, but the corners of his lips quirked up as his *parabatai* came into the room, and he said: "Will? Is that you, Will?"

"Yes," Will said. He was standing just inside the room, feeling as if he could go no farther.

Jem stopped playing and opened his eyes. "Telemann," he said. "Fantasia in E-flat major." He set the violin and bow down. "Well, come in, then. You're making me nervous, standing there."

Will took a few more steps inside. He had spent so much time in this room, he knew it as well as his own. Jem's collection of music books; the case in which his violin lived when he was not playing it; the windows that let in square patches of sunlight. The trunk that had come all the way from Shanghai. The cane with its jade top, leaning against the wall. The box with Kwan Yin on it, that held Jem's drugs. The armchair in which Will had spent countless nights, watching Jem sleep, counting his breaths and praying.

Jem looked up at him. His eyes were luminous; no suspicion colored them, only a simple happiness at seeing his friend. "I am glad you're here."

"So am I," said Will gruffly. He felt awkward, and wondered if Jem could sense it. He had never felt awkward around his *parabatai* before. It was the words, he thought, there on the tip of his tongue, pleading to be said.

You see it, don't you, James? Without Tessa there is nothing for me—no joy, no light, no life. If you loved me, you would let me have her. You can't love her as I do. No one could. If you are truly my brother, you would do this for me.

But the words remained unspoken, and Jem leaned forward, his voice low and confiding. "Will. There was something I wanted to say to you, and not when everyone else was around."

Will braced himself. This was it. Jem was going to tell him about the engagement, and he was going to have to pretend to be happy, and not be sick out the window, which he desperately wanted to be. He stuffed his hands into his pockets. "And what's that?"

The sun glittered off Jem's hair as he ducked his head. "I should have talked to you before. But we never have discussed the subject of love, have we, and with you being such a cynic . . ." He grinned. "I thought you'd mock me for it. And besides, I never thought there was a chance she'd return my feelings."

"Tessa," said Will. Her name was like knives in his mouth.

Jem's smile was luminous, lighting his whole face, and any hope that Will had harbored in some secret chamber of his heart that perhaps Jem did not really love her, was gone, blown away like mist before a hard wind. "You have never shirked your duties," Jem said. "And I know that you would have done what you could to save Tessa in the tea warehouse, whoever she was. But I could not help thinking that perhaps the reason you were so determined to save her was because you knew what she meant to me." He tipped his head back, his smile incandescent. "Did I guess correctly, or am I a thickheaded idiot?"

"You're an idiot," said Will, and swallowed hard, past his dry throat. "But—you are correct. I know what she means to you."

Jem grinned. His happiness was printed all over his face, his eyes, Will thought; he had never seen him look like this. He had always thought of Jem as a calm and peaceful presence, always thought that joy, like anger, was too extreme and human an emotion for him. He realized now that he had been quite wrong; Jem had simply not been happy like this before. Not since his parents had died, Will imagined. But Will had never considered it. He had dwelled on whether Jem was safe, whether he was surviving, but not if he was *happy*.

Jem is my great sin.

Tessa had been right, he thought. He had wanted her to break things off with Jem, whatever the cost; now he realized he did not, could not. *You might at least believe I know honor— honor, and debt*, he had said to Jem, and he had meant it. He owed Jem his life. He could not take from him the one thing Jem wanted more than anything else. Even if it meant Will's own happiness, for Jem was not only someone to whom he owed a debt that could never be repaid, but, as the covenant said, someone he loved as he loved his own soul.

Jem looked not just happier, but stronger, Will thought,

with healthy color in his cheeks, his back straight. "I ought to apologize," Jem said. "I was too severe regarding the ifrits' den. I know you were merely seeking solace."

"No, you were right to have—"

"I wasn't." Jem stood up. "If I was harsh with you, it was because I cannot bear to see you treat yourself as if you are worth nothing. Whatever part you might act to the contrary, I see you as you really are, my blood brother. Not just better than you pretend to be, but better than most people could hope to be." He placed a hand on Will's shoulder, gently. "You are worth everything, Will."

Will closed his eyes. He saw the black basalt Council room, the two circles burning on the ground. Jem stepping from his circle to Will's, so they inhabited the same space, circumscribed by fire. His eyes had still been black then, wide in his pale face. Will remembered the words of the *parabatai* oath. *Whither thou goest, I will go; where thou diest, will I die, and there will I be buried: the Angel do so to me, and more also, if aught but death part thee and me.* That same voice spoke again to him now. "Thank you for what you did for Tessa," said Jem.

Will could not look at Jem; he looked instead toward the wall, where their shadows blended together in relief, so that one could not tell where one boy ended and the other began. "Thank you for watching Brother Enoch pull shards of metal out of my back afterward," he said.

Jem laughed. "What else are *parabatai* for?"

The Council chamber was draped with red banners slashed with black runes; Jem whispered to Tessa that they were runes of decision and judgment.

They took their seats toward the front, in a row that also contained Henry, Gideon, Charlotte, and Will. Tessa had not spoken to Will since the day before; he had not been at breakfast, and had joined them in the courtyard late, still buttoning his coat as he ran down the stairs. His dark hair was disheveled, and he looked as if he had not slept. He seemed to be trying to avoid looking at Tessa, and she, in turn, avoided returning his gaze, though she could feel it flicking over her from time to time, like hot flecks of ash landing on her skin.

Jem was a perfect gentleman; their engagement was still secret, and other than smiling at her every time she looked at him, he behaved in no way out of the ordinary. As they settled themselves in their seats at the Council, she felt him brush her arm with the knuckles of his right hand, gently, before moving his hand away.

She could feel Will watching them, from the end of the row they sat in. She did not look toward him.

In seats on the raised platform at the chamber's center sat Benedict Lightwood, his eagle profile turned away from the mass of the Council, his jaw set. Beside him sat Gabriel, who, like Will, looked exhausted and unshaven. He glanced once at his brother as Gideon entered the room, and then away as Gideon took his seat, deliberately, among the Shadowhunters of the Institute. Gabriel bit his lip and looked down at his shoes, but did not move from where he sat.

She recognized a few more faces in the audience. Charlotte's aunt Callida was there, as was gaunt Aloysius Starkweather— despite, as he had complained, doubtless not being invited. His eyes narrowed as they fell on Tessa, and she turned back quickly to the front of the room.

"We are here," said Consul Wayland when he had taken his place before the lectern with the Inquisitor seated to his left, "to determine to what extent Charlotte and Henry Branwell have been of assistance to the Clave during the past fortnight in the matter of Axel Mortmain, and whether, as Benedict Lightwood has put in a claim, the London Institute would be better off in other hands."

The Inquisitor rose. He was holding something that gleamed silver and black in his hands. "Charlotte Branwell, please come up to the lectern."

Charlotte got to her feet, and climbed up the stairs to the stage. The Inquisitor lowered the Mortal Sword, and Charlotte wrapped her hands around the blade. In a quiet voice she recounted the events of the past two weeks—searching for Mortmain in newspaper clippings and historical accounts, the visit to Yorkshire, the threat against the Herondales, discovering Jessie's betrayal, the fight at the warehouse, Nate's death. She never lied, though Tessa was conscious of when she left out a detail here or there. Apparently the Mortal Sword could be gotten around, if only slightly.

There were several moments during Charlotte's speech when the Council members reacted audibly: breathing in sharply, shuffling their feet, most notably to the revelation of Jessamine's role in the proceedings. "I knew her parents," Tessa heard Charlotte's aunt Callida saying from the back of the room. "Terrible business—terrible!"

"And the girl is where now?" the Inquisitor demanded.

"She is in the cells of the Silent City," said Charlotte, "awaiting punishment for her crime. I informed the Consul of her whereabouts."

The Inquisitor, who had been pacing up and down the platform, stopped and looked Charlotte keenly in the face. "You say this girl was like a daughter to you," he said, "and yet you handed her over to the Brothers willingly? Why would you do something like that?"

"The Law is hard," said Charlotte, "but it is the Law."

Consul Wayland's mouth flicked up at the corner. "And here you said she'd be too soft on wrongdoers, Benedict," he said. "Any comment?"

Benedict rose to his feet; he had clearly decided to shoot his cuffs today, and they protruded, snowy white, from the sleeves of his tailored dark tweed jacket. "I do have a comment," he said. "I wholeheartedly support Charlotte Branwell in her leadership of the Institute, and renounce my claim on a position there."

A murmur of disbelief ran through the crowd.

Benedict smiled pleasantly.

The Inquisitor turned and looked at him in disbelief. "So you are saying," he echoed, "that *despite* the fact that these Shadowhunters killed Nathaniel Gray—or were responsible for his death—our only link to Mortmain, despite the fact that once again they harbored a spy beneath their roof, *despite* the fact that they still don't know where Mortmain is, you would recommend Charlotte and Henry Branwell to run this Institute?"

"They may not know where Mortmain is," said Benedict, "but they know *who* he is. As the great mundane military strategist Sun Tzu said in *The Art of War*, 'If you know your enemies and know yourself, you can win a hundred battles without a single loss.' We know now who Mortmain really is—a mortal man, not a supernatural being; a man afraid of death; a man bent on revenge for what he considers the undeserved murder of his family. Nor does he have compassion for Downworlders. He utilized werewolves to help him build his clockwork army swiftly, feeding them drugs to keep them working around the clock, knowing the drugs would kill the wolves and ensure their silence. Judging by the size of the warehouse he used and the number of workers he employed, his clockwork army will be sizeable. And judging by his motivations and the years over which he has refined his strategies for revenge, he is a man who cannot be reasoned with, cannot be dissuaded, cannot be stopped. We must prepare for a war. And *that* we did not know before."

The Inquisitor looked at Benedict, thin-lipped, as if he suspected that something untoward was going on but could not imagine what it might be. "Prepare for a war? And how do you suggest we do that—building, of course, on all this supposedly valuable information the Branwells have acquired?"

Benedict shrugged. "Well, that of course will be for the Council to decide over time. But Mortmain has tried to recruit powerful Downworlders such as Woolsey Scott and Camille Belcourt to his cause. We may not know where he is, but we now know his ways, and we can trap him in that manner. Perhaps by allying ourselves with some of Downworld's more powerful leaders. Charlotte seems to have them all well in hand, don't you think?"

A faint laugh ran around the Council, but they were not laughing *at* Charlotte; they were smiling with Benedict. Gabriel was watching his father, his green eyes burning.

"And the spy in the Institute? Would you not call that an example of her carelessness?" said the Inquisitor.

"Not at all," said Benedict. "She dealt with the matter swiftly and without compassion." He smiled at Charlotte, a smile like a razor. "I retract my earlier statement about her softheartedness. Clearly she is as able to deal justice without pity as any man."

Charlotte paled, but said nothing. Her small hands were very still on the Sword.

Consul Wayland sighed gustily. "I wish you had come to this conclusion a fortnight ago, Benedict, and saved us all this trouble."

Benedict shrugged elegantly. "I thought she needed to be tested," he said. "Fortunately, she has passed that test."

Wayland shook his head. "Very well. Let us vote on it." He handed what looked like a cloudy glass vessel to the Inquisitor, who stepped down among the crowd and handed the vial to the woman sitting in the first chair of the first row. Tessa watched in fascination as she bent her head and whispered into the vial, then passed it to the man on her left.

As the vial made its way around the room, Tessa felt Jem slip his hands into hers. She jumped, though her voluminous skirts, she suspected, largely hid their hands. She laced her fingers through his slim, delicate ones and closed her eyes. *I love him. I love him. I love him.* And indeed, his touch made her shiver, though it also made her want to weep—with love, with confusion, with heartbreak, remembering the look on Will's face when she had told him she and Jem were engaged, the happiness going out of him like a fire doused by rain.

Jem drew his hand out of hers to take the vial from Gideon on his other side. She heard him whisper, "Charlotte Branwell," before he passed the vial over her, to Henry on her other side.

She looked at him, and he must have misconstrued the unhappiness in her eyes, because he smiled at her encouragingly. "It will be all right," he said. "They'll choose Charlotte."

When the vial finished its travels, it was handed back to the Inquisitor, who presented it with a flourish to the Consul. The Consul took the vial and, placing it on the lectern before him, drew a rune on the glass with his stele.

The vial trembled, like a kettle on the boil. White smoke poured from its open neck—the collected whispers of hundreds of Shadowhunters. They spelled words out across the air.

CHARLOTTE BRANWELL.

Charlotte dropped her hands from the Mortal Sword, almost sagging in relief. Henry made a whooping noise and threw his hat into the air. The room was filled with chatter and confusion. Tessa couldn't stop herself from glancing down the row at Will. He had slumped down in his seat, his head back, his eyes closed. He looked white and drained, as if this last bit of business had taken the remainder of his energy.

A scream pierced the hubbub. Tessa was on her feet in moments, whirling around. It was Charlotte's aunt Callida screaming, her elegant gray head thrown back and her finger pointing Heavenward. Gasps ran around the room as the other Shadowhunters followed her gaze. The air above them was filled with dozens—scores, even—of buzzing black metal creatures, like enormous steel black beetles with coppery wings, zipping back and forth through the air, filling the room with the ugly sound of metallic buzzing.

One of the metal beetles dipped down and hovered in front of Tessa, just at eye level, making a clicking sound. It was eyeless, though there was a circular plate of glass in the flat front of its head. She felt Jem reach for her arm, trying to pull her away from it, but she jerked away impatiently, seized her hat off her head, and slammed it down on top of the thing, trapping it between her hat and the seat of her chair. It immediately set up an enraged, high-pitched buzzing. "Henry!" she called. "Henry, I've got one of the things—"

Henry appeared behind her, pink-faced, and stared down at the hat. A small hole was opening in the side of the elegant gray velvet where the mechanical creature was tearing at it. With a curse Henry brought his fist down hard, crushing the hat and the thing inside it against the seat. It buzzed and went still.

Jem reached around and lifted the smashed hat gingerly. What was left under it was a scatter of parts—a metal wing, a shattered chassis, and broken-off stumps of copper legs. "Ugh," said Tessa. "It's so very—buglike." She glanced up as another cry went through the room. The insectile creatures had come together in a black swirl in the center of the room; as she stared, they swirled faster and faster and then vanished, like black beetles sucked down a drain.

"Sorry about the hat," said Henry. "I'll get you another."

"Bother the hat," said Tessa as the cries of the angry Council echoed through the room. She looked toward the center of the room; the Consul stood with the glowing Mortal Sword in his hand, and behind him was Benedict, stone-faced, with eyes like ice. "Clearly, we have bigger things to worry about."

"It's a sort of camera," Henry said, holding the bits of the smashed metal beetle creature on his lap as the carriage clopped toward home. "Without Jessamine, Nate, or Benedict,

Mortmain must be out of reliable human spies who can report to him. So he sent these things." He poked at a shard; the bits were gathered together in the wreckage of Tessa's hat, held on his lap as they jounced along.

"Benedict didn't look any too pleased to see those things," said Will. "He must realize Mortmain already knows about his defection."

"It was a matter of time," said Charlotte. "Henry, can those things record sound, like a phonautograph, or simply pictures? They were flying around so quickly—"

"I'm not sure." Henry frowned. "I shall have to examine the parts more closely in the crypt. I can find no shutter mechanism, but that does not mean—" He looked up at the uncomprehending faces focused on him, and shrugged. "In any case," he said, "perhaps it is not the worst thing for the Council to get a look at Mortmain's inventions. It is one thing to hear about them, another to *see* what he is doing. Don't you think, Lottie?"

Charlotte murmured an answer, but Tessa didn't hear it. Her mind was caught up in going over a peculiar thing that had occurred just after she'd left the Council chambers and was waiting for the Branwells' carriage. Jem had just turned away from her to speak to Will, when the flap of a black cloak caught her eye, and Aloysius Starkweather stalked up to her, his grizzled face fierce. "Miss Gray," he'd barked. "That clockwork creature—the way it approached you . . ."

Tessa had stood silently, staring—waiting for him to accuse her of something, though she could not imagine what.

"Thee's all right?" he'd said, abruptly and at last, his Yorkshire accent seeming suddenly very pronounced. "It dinna harm thee?"

Slowly Tessa had shaken her head. "No, Mr. Starkweather. Thank you kindly for your inquiry into my welfare, but no."

By then Jem and Will had turned and were staring. As if aware he was drawing attention, Starkweather had nodded once, sharply, turned, and walked off, his ragged cloak blowing behind him.

Tessa could make neither head nor tail of the whole business. She was just thinking of her brief time in Starkweather's head, and the astonishment he'd felt when he'd first seen her, when the carriage came to a jerking halt before the Institute. Relieved to be free of their cramped quarters, the Shadowhunters and Tessa spilled out, onto the drive.

There was a gap in the gray cloud cover over the city, and lemon yellow sunlight poured down, making the front steps glisten. Charlotte started toward them, but Henry stopped her, pulling her close with the arm that wasn't holding Tessa's destroyed hat. Tessa watched them with the first glimmer of happiness she'd felt since yesterday. She had truly come to care for Charlotte and Henry, she realized, and she wanted to see them happy. "What we should remember is that everything went as well as we could have hoped," Henry said, holding her tightly. "I'm so proud of you, darling."

Tessa would have expected a sarcastic comment from Will at this juncture, but he was staring off toward the gates. Gideon looked embarrassed, Jem as if he were pleased.

Charlotte pulled away from Henry, blushing furiously and straightening her hat, but obviously delighted. "Are you really, Henry?"

"Absolutely! Not only is my wife beautiful, she is brilliant, and that brilliance should be recognized!"

"This," said Will, still looking off toward the gates, "is when Jessamine would have told you to stop because you were making her sick."

The smile vanished from Charlotte's face. "Poor Jessie . . ."

But Henry's expression was uncharacteristically hard. "She shouldn't have done what she did, Lottie. It's not your fault. We can only hope the Council deals with her leniently." He cleared his throat. "And let's have no more talk about Jessamine today, shall we? Tonight is for celebration. The Institute is still ours."

Charlotte beamed at him, with so much love in her eyes that Tessa had to look away, toward the Institute. She blinked. High up in the stone wall, her eyes caught a flicker of movement. A curtain twitched away from the corner of a window, and she saw a pale face peering down. Sophie, looking for Gideon? She couldn't be sure—the face was gone as soon as it had appeared.

Tessa dressed with special care that night, in one of the new gowns Charlotte had provided her: blue satin with a heart-shaped basque and a deeply cut, rounded neckline over which was pinned a chemisette of Mechlin lace. The sleeves were short and ruched, showing her long white arms, and she wore her hair in curls, pinned up and back, a coiffure interlaced with dark blue pansies. It was not until after Sophie had carefully fixed them in her hair that Tessa realized they were the color of Will's eyes, and wanted suddenly to pull them out, but of course she did nothing of the sort, only thanked Sophie for her efforts and complimented her sincerely on how prettily her hair had turned out.

Sophie left before she did, to go and help Bridget in the kitchen. Tessa sat down automatically in front of the mirror to bite her lips and pinch her cheeks. She needed the color, she thought. She was unusually pale. The jade pendant was shoved down under the Mechlin lace, where it could not be seen; Sophie had looked at it as Tessa had dressed, but had not commented. She reached for the clockwork angel pendant and fastened it, too, around her throat. It sat below the other pendant, just under her collarbones, and steadied her with its ticking. There was no reason she could not wear both, was there?

When she emerged into the corridor, Jem was waiting for her. His eyes lit up when he saw her, and after a glance up and down the hall, he drew her toward him and kissed her on the mouth.

She willed herself to melt into the kiss, to dissolve against him as she had done before. His mouth was soft on hers and tasted sweet, and his hand when it cupped her neck was strong and gentle. She moved closer to him, wanting to feel the beat of his heart.

He drew back, breathless. "I didn't mean to do that . . ."

She smiled. "I think you did, James."

"Not before I saw you," he said. "I meant only to ask if I could escort you to dinner. But you look so beautiful." He touched her hair. "I'm afraid too much passion could start you shedding petals like a tree in autumn, though."

"Well, you can," she said. "Escort me to dinner, that is."

"Thank you." He ran his fingertips lightly across her cheekbones. "I thought I would wake up this morning and it would have been a dream, you saying yes to me. But it wasn't. Was it?" His eyes searched her face.

She shook her head. She could taste tears in the back of her throat and was glad for the kid gloves that hid the burn on her left hand.

"I'm sorry you're getting such a bad bargain in me, Tessa," he said. "In years, I mean. Shackling yourself to a dying man when you're only sixteen . . ."

"*You're* only seventeen. Plenty of time to find a cure," she whispered. "And we will. Find one. I will be with you. Forever."

"Now, *that* I believe," he said. "When two souls are as one, they stay together on the Wheel. I was born into this world to love you, and I will love you in the next life, and the one after that."

She thought of Magnus. *We are chained to this life by a chain of gold, and we dare not sever it for fear of what lies beyond the drop.*

She knew what he meant now. Immortality was a gift, but not one without its consequences. *For if I am immortal*, she thought, *then I have only this, this one life. I will not turn and change as you do, James. I will not see you in Heaven, or on the banks of the great river, or in whatever life lies beyond this one.*

But she did not say it. It would hurt him, and if there was anything she knew to be true, it was that a fierce unreasoning desire lived in her to protect him from hurt, to stand between him and disappointment, between him and pain, between him and death, and fight them all back as Boadicea had fought back the advancing Romans. She reached up and touched his cheek instead, and he put his face against her hair, her hair full of flowers the color of Will's eyes, and they stood like that, clasped together, until the dinner bell rang a second time.

Bridget, who could be heard singing mournfully in the kitchen, had outdone herself in the dining room, placing candles in silver holders everywhere so the whole place glimmered with light. Cut roses and orchids floated in silver bowls on the white linen tablecloth. Henry and Charlotte presided at the head of the table. Gideon, in evening dress, sat with his eyes fixed on Sophie as she came in and out of the room, though she seemed to be studiously avoiding his glances. And beside him sat Will.

I love Jem. I am marrying Jem. Tessa had repeated it to herself all the way down the hall, but it made little difference; her heart flipped sickeningly in her chest when she saw Will. She had not seen him in evening dress since the night of the ball, and, despite seeming pale and ill, he still looked ridiculously handsome in it.

"Is your cook *always* singing?" Gideon was asking in an awed tone as Jem and Tessa came in. Henry looked up and, on seeing them, smiled all over his friendly, freckled face.

"We were beginning to wonder where you two were—," he began.

"Tessa and I have news," Jem burst out. His hand found Tessa's, and held it; she stood frozen as three curious faces turned toward them—four, if you counted Sophie, who had just walked into the room. Will sat where he was, gazing at the silver bowl in front of him; a white rose was floating in it, and he seemed prepared to stare at it until it went under. In the kitchen Bridget was still singing one of her awful sad songs; the lyrics drifted in through the door:

> "'Twas on an evening fair I went to take the air,
> I heard a maid making her moan;
> Said, 'Saw ye my father? Or saw ye my mother?

Or saw ye my brother John?
Or saw ye the lad that I love best,
And his name it is Sweet William?"'

I may murder her, Tessa thought. *Let her make a song about that.*

"Well, you have to tell us now," said Charlotte, smiling. "Don't leave us dangling in suspense, Jem!"

Jem raised their joined hands and said, "Tessa and I are engaged to be married. I asked her, and—she accepted me."

There was a shocked silence. Gideon looked astonished—Tessa felt rather sorry for him, in a detached sort of way—and Sophie stood holding a pitcher of cream, her mouth open. Both Henry and Charlotte looked startled out of their wits. None of them could have been expecting this, Tessa thought; whatever Jessamine had said about Tessa's mother being a Shadowhunter, she was still a Downworlder, and Shadowhunters did not marry Downworlders. This moment had not occurred to her. She had thought somehow that they would tell everyone separately, carefully, not that Jem would blurt it out in a fever of joyous happiness in the dining room. And she thought, *Oh, please smile. Please congratulate us. Please don't spoil this for him. Please.*

Jem's smile had only just begun to slip, when Will rose to his feet. Tessa drew a deep breath. He *was* beautiful in evening dress, that was true, but he was always beautiful; there was something different about him now, though, a deeper layer to the blue of his eyes, cracks in the hard and perfect armor around himself that let through a blaze of light. This was a new Will, a different Will, a Will she had caught only glimpses of—a Will that perhaps only Jem had ever really known. And now she would never know him. The thought pierced her with a sadness as if she were remembering someone who had died.

He raised his glass of wine. "I do not know two finer people," he said, "and could not imagine better news. May your lives together be happy and long." His eyes sought Tessa's, then slid away from her, fastening on Jem. "Congratulations, brother."

A flood of other voices came after his speech. Sophie set the pitcher down and came to embrace Tessa; Henry and Gideon shook Jem's hand, and Will stood watching it all, still holding the glass. Through the happy babble of voices, only Charlotte was silent, her hand against her chest; Tessa bent worriedly over her. "Charlotte, is everything all right?"

"Yes," Charlotte said, and then more loudly, "*Yes*. It is just—I have news of my own. Good news."

"Yes, darling," said Henry. "We won the Institute back! But everyone does already know—"

"No, not that, Henry. You—" Charlotte made a hiccuping sound, half laughter, half tears. "Henry and I are going to have a child. A boy. Brother Enoch told me. I didn't want to say anything before, but—"

The rest of her words were drowned out by Henry's incredulous whoop of joy. He lifted Charlotte entirely out of her seat and threw his arms around her. "Darling, that's wonderful, wonderful—"

Sophie gave a little shriek and clapped her hands. Gideon looked as if he were so embarrassed that he might conceivably die on the spot, and Will and Jem exchanged bemused smiles. Tessa could not help smiling as well; Henry's delight was infectious. He waltzed Charlotte across the room and then back again before suddenly stopping, horrified that waltzing might be bad for the baby, and sat her down in the nearest chair.

"Henry, I'm perfectly capable of walking," Charlotte said indignantly. "Even of dancing."

"My darling, you are indisposed! You must remain abed for the next eight months. Little Buford—"

"I am *not* naming our child Buford. I don't care if it was your father's name, or if it is a traditional Yorkshire name—," Charlotte began in exasperation, when a knock sounded on the door, and Cyril poked his tousled head in. He stared at the scene of gaiety going on in front of him, and said hesitantly:

"Mr. Branwell, there's someone here to see you all."

Henry blinked. "Someone to see us? But this is a private dinner, Cyril. And I did not hear the bell ring—"

"No, she is Nephilim," said Cyril. "And she says it's very important. She will not wait."

Henry and Charlotte exchanged bewildered glances. "Well, all right, then," said Henry at last. "Let her up, but tell her it will have to be quick."

Cyril vanished. Charlotte rose to her feet, smoothing down her dress and patting her disheveled hair. "Aunt Callida, perhaps?" she said in a puzzled voice. "I can't fathom who else . . ."

The door opened again, and Cyril came in, followed by a young girl of about fifteen. She wore a black traveling cloak over a green dress. Even if Tessa had not seen her before, she would have known who she was instantly—known her by her black hair, by the violet-blue of her eyes, by the graceful curve of her white throat, the delicate angles of her features, the full swoop of her mouth.

She heard Will draw a sudden, violent breath.

"Hello," said the girl, in a voice both surprisingly soft and surprisingly firm. "I apologize for interrupting your dinner hour, but I had nowhere else to go. I am Cecily Herondale, you see. I have come to be trained as a Shadowhunter."

A Note on Tessa's England

As in *Clockwork Angel*, the London of *Clockwork Prince* is, as much as I could make it, an admixture of the real and the unreal, the famous and the forgotten. (For instance, there really is a Pyx Chamber in Westminster Abbey.) The geography of real Victorian London is preserved as much as possible, but there were times that wasn't possible.

For those wondering about the Institute: There was indeed a church called All-Hallows-the-Less that burned in the Great Fire of London in 1666; it was located, however, in Upper Thames Street, not where I have placed it, just off Fleet Street. Those familiar with London will recognize the location of the Institute, and the shape of its spire, as that of the famous St. Bride's Church, beloved of newspapermen and journalists, which goes unmentioned in the Infernal Devices as the Institute has taken its place. For those wondering about the Institute in

York, it is based on Holy Trinity Goodramgate, a church you can still find and tour in York.

As for the Lightwoods' house in Chiswick, during the sixteenth and seventeenth centuries it was believed Chiswick was far enough from London to be a healthy refuge from the city's dirt and disease, and wealthy families did have mansions there. The Lightwoods' is based very sketchily on famous Chiswick House. As for Number 16 Cheyne Walk, where Woolsey Scott lives, it was at the time actually rented together by Algernon Charles Swinburne, Dante Gabriel Rossetti, and George Meredith. They were members of the aesthetic movement, and would have appreciated the motto on Woolsey's ring—"*L'art pour l'art*," or "Art for art's sake."

As for the opium den in Whitechapel, much research has been done on the subject but there is no proof that the opium den, much beloved of Sherlock Holmes fans and enthusiasts of the Gothic, ever existed at all. Here it has been replaced by a den of demonic vice. It has never been proved that those existed either, but then, it has never been proved that they didn't.

For those wondering what Will says to Tessa just outside the mansion in Chiswick, *Caelum denique* was the battle cry of the Crusaders and means "Heaven at last!"

Acknowledgments

Thanks as always to my family: my mother and father; Jim Hill and Kate Connor; Nao, Tim, David, and Ben; Melanie, Jonathan, and Helen Lewis; Florence; and Joyce. Thanks to those who read and critiqued and pointed out anachronisms or inconsistencies: Kelly Link, Clary, Delia Sherman, Holly Black, Sarah Rees Brennan, Justine Larbalestier, Robin Wasserman, Maureen Johnson. Thanks to Lisa Gold, Research Maven (lisagoldresearch.wordpress.com) for her help. Thanks to Joey Yeung and Huan Yu for the Mandarin translations. Thanks to Wayne Miller for Greek and Latin help. My always gratitude to my agent, Barry Goldblatt; my editor, Karen Wojtyla; and the teams at Simon & Schuster and Walker Books for making it all happen. And of course, thanks to my husband, Josh, for keeping Linus and Lucy from eating the manuscript.

Continue Tessa, Will, and Jem's adventures in

Clockwork Princess,

BOOK THREE OF THE INFERNAL DEVICES.

London, 1873.

"Will?" Charlotte Fairchild eased the door of the Institute's training room open. "Will, are you in there?"

A muffled grunt was the only response. The door swung all the way open, revealing the wide, high-ceilinged room on the other side. Charlotte herself had grown up training here, and she knew every warp of the floorboards, the ancient target painted on the north wall, the square-paned windows, so old that they were thicker at the base than the top. In the center of the room stood Will Herondale, a knife held in his right hand.

He turned his head to look at Charlotte, and she thought again what an odd child he was—although at twelve he was barely still a child. He was a very pretty boy, with thick dark hair that waved slightly where it touched his collar—wet now with sweat, and pasted to his forehead. His skin had been tanned by country air and sun when he had first come to the Institute, though six months of city life had drained its color, causing the red flush across his cheekbones to stand out. His eyes were an unusually luminous blue. He would be a handsome man one day, if he could do something about the scowl that perpetually twisted his features.

"What is it, Charlotte?" he snapped.

He still spoke with a slight Welsh accent, a roll to his vowels that would have been charming if his tone hadn't been so sour. He drew his sleeve across his forehead as she came partway through the door, then paused. "I've been looking for you for hours," she said with some asperity, though asperity had little effect on Will. Not much had an effect on Will when he was in a mood, and he was nearly always in a mood. "Didn't you recall what I told you yesterday, that we were welcoming a new arrival to the Institute today?"

"Oh, I remembered." Will threw the knife. It stuck just outside the circle of the target, deepening his scowl. "I just don't care."

The boy behind Charlotte made a stifled noise. A laugh, she would have thought, but certainly he couldn't be laughing? She had been warned the boy coming to the Institute from Shanghai was not well, but she had still been startled when he had stepped from the carriage, pale and swaying like a reed in the wind, his curling dark hair streaked with silver as if he were a man in his eighties, not a boy of twelve. His eyes were wide and silvery-black, strangely beautiful but haunting in such a delicate face. "Will, you *shall* be polite," she said now, and drew the boy out from behind her, ushering him ahead into the room. "Don't mind Will; he's only moody. Will Herondale, may I introduce you to James Carstairs, of the Shanghai Institute."

"Jem," said the boy. "Everyone calls me Jem." He took another step forward into the room, his gaze taking in Will with a friendly curiosity. He spoke without the trace of an accent, to Charlotte's surprise, but then his father was—had been—British. "You can too."

"Well, if everyone calls you that, it's hardly any special favor to me, is it?" Will's tone was acid; for someone so young, he was amazingly capable of unpleasantness. "I think you will find, James Carstairs, that if you keep to yourself and let me alone, it will be the best outcome for both of us."

Charlotte sighed inwardly. She had so hoped that this boy, the same age as Will, would prove a tool to disarm Will of his anger and his viciousness, but it seemed clear that Will had been speaking the truth when he had told her he did not care if another Shadowhunter boy was coming to the Institute. He did not want friends, or want for them. She glanced at Jem, expecting to see him blinking in surprise or hurt, but he was only smiling a little, as if Will were a kitten that had tried to bite him. "I haven't trained since I left Shanghai," he said. "I could use a partner—someone to spar with."

"So could I," said Will. "But I need someone who can keep up with me, not some sickly creature that looks as if he's doddering off to the grave. Although I suppose you might be useful for target practice."

Charlotte, knowing what she did about James Carstairs—a

fact she had not shared with Will—felt a sickly horror come over her. *Doddering off to the grave, oh dear Lord.* What was it her father had said? That Jem was dependent on a drug to live, some kind of medicine that would extend his life but not save it. *Oh, Will.*

She made as if to move in between the two boys, as if she could protect Jem from Will's cruelty, more awfully accurate in this instance that even he knew—but then she paused.

Jem had not even changed expression. "If by 'doddering off to the grave' you mean dying, then I am," he said. "I have about two years more to live, three if I am lucky, or so they tell me."

Even Will could not hide his shock; his cheeks flushed red. "I . . ."

But Jem had set his steps toward the target painted on the wall; when he reached it, he yanked the knife free from the wood. Then he turned and walked directly up to Will. Delicate as he was, they were of the same height, and only inches from each other their eyes met and held. "You may use me for target practice if you wish," said Jem, as casually as if he were talking about the weather. "It seems to me I have little to fear from such an exercise, as you are not a very good shot." He turned, took aim, and let the knife fly. It stuck directly into the heart of the target, quivering slightly. "Or," Jem went on, turning back to Will, "you could allow *me* to teach *you*. For I am a *very* good shot."

Charlotte stared. For half a year she had watched Will push away everyone who'd tried to get near him—tutors; her father; her fiancé, Henry; both the Lightwood brothers—with a combination of hatefulness and precisely accurate cruelty. If it were not that she herself was the only person who had ever seen him cry, she imagined she would have given up hope as well, long ago, that he would ever be any good to anybody. And yet here he was, looking at Jem Carstairs, a boy so fragile-looking that he appeared to be made out of glass, with the hardness of his expression slowly dissolving into a tentative uncertainty. "You are not *really* dying," he said, the oddest tone to his voice, "are you?"

Jem nodded. "So they tell me."

"I am sorry," Will said.

"No," Jem said softly. He drew his jacket aside and took a knife from the belt at his waist. "Don't be ordinary like that. Don't say you're sorry. Say you'll train with me."

He held out the knife to Will, hilt first. Charlotte held her breath, afraid to move. She felt as if she were watching something very important happen, though she could not have said what.

Will reached out and took the knife, his eyes never leaving Jem's face. His fingers brushed the other boy's as he took the weapon from him. It was the first time, Charlotte thought, that she had ever seen him touch any other person willingly.

"I'll train with you," he said.

See where the adventures begin in

City of Bones,

BOOK ONE OF THE MORTAL INSTRUMENTS.

———◆———

PANDEMONIUM

"You've got to be kidding me," the bouncer said, folding his arms across his massive chest. He stared down at the boy in the red zip-up jacket and shook his shaved head. "You can't bring that thing in here."

The fifty or so teenagers in line outside the Pandemonium Club leaned forward to eavesdrop. It was a long wait to get into the all-ages club, especially on a Sunday, and not much generally happened in line. The bouncers were fierce and would come down instantly on anyone who looked like they were going to start trouble. Fifteen-year-old Clary Fray, standing in line with her best friend, Simon, leaned forward along with everyone else, hoping for some excitement.

"Aw, come on." The kid hoisted the thing up over his head. It looked like a wooden beam, pointed at one end. "It's part of my costume."

The bouncer raised an eyebrow. "Which is what?"

The boy grinned. He was normal-enough-looking, Clary thought, for Pandemonium. He had electric blue dyed hair that stuck up around his head like the tentacles of a startled octopus, but no elaborate facial tattoos or big metal bars through his ears or lips. "I'm a vampire hunter." He pushed down on the wooden thing. It bent as easily as a blade of grass bending sideways. "It's fake. Foam rubber. See?"

The boy's wide eyes were way too bright a green, Clary noticed: the color of antifreeze, spring grass. Colored contact lenses, probably. The bouncer shrugged, abruptly bored. "Whatever. Go on in."

The boy slid past him, quick as an eel. Clary liked the lilt to his shoulders, the way he tossed his hair as he went. There was a word for him that her mother would have used—*insouciant*.

"You thought he was cute," said Simon, sounding resigned. "Didn't you?"

Clary dug her elbow into his ribs, but didn't answer.

Inside, the club was full of dry-ice smoke. Colored lights played over the dance floor, turning it into a multicolored fairyland of blues and acid greens, hot pinks and golds.

The boy in the red jacket stroked the long razor-sharp blade in his hands, an idle smile playing over his lips. It had been so easy—a little bit of a glamour on the blade, to make it look harmless. Another glamour on his eyes, and the moment the bouncer had looked straight at him, he was in. Of course, he could probably have gotten by without all that trouble, but it was part of the fun—fooling the mundies, doing it all out in the open right in front of them, getting off on the blank looks on their sheeplike faces.

Not that the humans didn't have their uses. The boy's green eyes scanned the dance floor, where slender limbs clad in scraps of silk and black leather appeared and disappeared inside the revolving columns of smoke as the mundies danced. Girls tossed their long hair, boys swung their leather-clad hips, and bare skin glittered with sweat. Vitality just *poured* off them, waves of energy that filled him with a drunken dizziness. His lip curled. They didn't know how lucky they were. They didn't know what it was like to eke out life in a dead world, where the sun hung limp in the sky like a burned cinder. Their lives burned as brightly as candle flames—and were as easy to snuff out.

His hand tightened on the blade he carried, and he had begun to step out onto the dance floor when a girl broke away from the mass of dancers and began walking toward him. He stared at her. She was beautiful, for a human—long hair nearly the precise color of black ink, charcoaled eyes. Floor-length white gown, the kind women used to wear when this world was younger. Lace sleeves belled out around her slim arms. Around her neck was a thick silver chain, on which hung a dark red pendant the size of a baby's fist. He only had to narrow his eyes to know that it was real—real and precious. His mouth started to water as she neared him. Vital energy pulsed from her like blood from an open wound. She smiled, passing him, beckoning with her eyes. He turned to follow her, tasting the phantom sizzle of her death on his lips.

It was always easy. He could already feel the power of her evaporating life coursing through his veins like fire. Humans were so stupid. They had something so precious, and they barely safeguarded it at all. They threw away their lives for money, for packets of powder, for a stranger's charming smile. The girl was a pale ghost retreating through the colored smoke. She reached the wall and turned, bunching her skirt up in her hands, lifting it as she grinned at him. Under the skirt, she was wearing thigh-high boots.

He sauntered up to her, his skin prickling with her nearness. Up close she wasn't so perfect: He could see the mascara smudged under her eyes, the sweat sticking her hair to her neck. He could smell her mortality, the sweet rot of corruption. *Got you*, he thought.

A cool smile curled her lips. She moved to the side, and he could see that she was leaning against a closed door. NO ADMITTANCE—STORAGE was scrawled across it in red paint. She reached behind her for the knob, turned it, slid inside. He caught a glimpse of stacked boxes, tangled wiring. A storage room. He glanced behind him—no one was looking. So much the better if she wanted privacy.

He slipped into the room after her, unaware that he was being followed.

"So," Simon said, "pretty good music, eh?"

Clary didn't reply. They were dancing, or what passed for it—a lot of swaying back and forth with occasional lunges toward the floor as if one of them had dropped a contact lens—in a space between a group of teenage boys in metallic corsets, and a young Asian couple who were making out passionately, their colored hair extensions tangled together like vines. A boy with a lip piercing and a teddy bear backpack was handing out free tablets of herbal ecstasy, his parachute pants flapping in the breeze from the wind machine. Clary wasn't paying much attention to their immediate surroundings—her eyes were on the blue-haired boy who'd talked his way into the club. He was prowling through the crowd as if he were looking for something. There was something about the way he moved that reminded her of something . . .

"I, for one," Simon went on, "am enjoying myself immensely."

This seemed unlikely. Simon, as always, stuck out at the club like a sore thumb, in jeans and an old T-shirt that said MADE IN BROOKLYN across the front. His freshly scrubbed hair was dark brown instead of green or pink, and his glasses perched crookedly on the end of his nose. He looked less as if he were contemplating the powers of darkness and more as if he were on his way to chess club.

"Mmm-hmm." Clary knew perfectly well that he came to Pandemonium with her only because she liked it, that he thought it was boring. She wasn't even sure why it was that she liked it— the clothes, the music made it like a dream, someone else's life, not her boring real life at all. But she was always too shy to talk to anyone but Simon.

The blue-haired boy was making his way off the dance floor. He looked a little lost, as if he hadn't found whom he was looking for. Clary wondered what would happen if she went up and introduced herself, offered to show him around. Maybe he'd just stare at her. Or maybe he was shy too. Maybe he'd be grateful and pleased, and try not to show it, the way boys did— but she'd know. Maybe—

The blue-haired boy straightened up suddenly, snapping to attention, like a hunting dog on point. Clary followed the line of his gaze, and saw the girl in the white dress.

Oh, well, Clary thought, trying not to feel like a deflated party balloon. *I guess that's that.* The girl was gorgeous, the kind of girl Clary would have liked to draw—tall and ribbon-slim, with a long spill of black hair. Even at this distance Clary could see the red pendant around her throat. It pulsed under the lights of the dance floor like a separate, disembodied heart.

"I feel," Simon went on, "that this evening DJ Bat is doing a singularly exceptional job. Don't you agree?"

Clary rolled her eyes and didn't answer; Simon hated trance music. Her attention was on the girl in the white dress. Through the darkness, smoke, and artificial fog, her pale dress shone out like a beacon. No wonder the blue-haired boy was following her as if he were under a spell, too distracted to notice anything else around him—even the two dark shapes hard on his heels, weaving after him through the crowd.

Clary slowed her dancing and stared. She could just make out that the shapes were boys, tall and wearing black clothes. She couldn't have said how she knew that they were following the other boy, but she did. She could see it in the way they paced him, their careful watchfulness, the slinking grace of their movements. A small flower of apprehension began to open inside her chest.

"Meanwhile," Simon added, "I wanted to tell you that lately I've been cross-dressing. Also, I'm sleeping with your mom. I thought you should know."

The girl had reached the wall, and was opening a door marked NO ADMITTANCE. She beckoned the blue-haired boy after her, and they slipped through the door. It wasn't anything Clary hadn't seen before, a couple sneaking off to the dark corners of the club to make out—but that made it even weirder that they were being followed.

She raised herself up on tiptoe, trying to see over the crowd. The two guys had stopped at the door and seemed to be conferring with each other. One of them was blond, the other dark-haired. The blond one reached into his jacket and drew out something long and sharp that flashed under the strobing lights. A knife. "Simon!" Clary shouted, and seized his arm.

"What?" Simon looked alarmed. "I'm not really sleeping with your mom, you know. I was just trying to get your attention. Not that your mom isn't a very attractive woman, for her age."

"Do you see those guys?" She pointed wildly, almost hitting a curvy black girl who was dancing nearby. The girl shot her an evil look. "Sorry—sorry!" Clary turned back to Simon. "Do you see those two guys over there? By that door?"

Simon squinted, then shrugged. "I don't see anything."

"There are two of them. They were following the guy with the blue hair—"

"The one you thought was cute?"

"Yes, but that's not the point. The blond one pulled a knife."

"Are you *sure*?" Simon stared harder, shaking his head. "I still don't see anyone."

"I'm sure."

Suddenly all business, Simon squared his shoulders. "I'll get one of the security guards. You stay here." He strode away, pushing through the crowd.

Clary turned just in time to see the blond boy slip through the NO ADMITTANCE door, his friend right on his heels. She looked around; Simon was still trying to shove his way across the dance floor, but he wasn't making much progress. Even if she yelled now, no one would hear her, and by the time Simon got back, something terrible might *already* have happened. Biting hard on her lower lip, Clary started to wriggle through the crowd.

"What's your name?"

She turned and smiled. What faint light there was in the storage room spilled down through high barred windows smeared with dirt. Piles of electrical cables, along with broken bits of mirrored disco balls and discarded paint cans, littered the floor.

"Isabelle."

"That's a nice name." He walked toward her, stepping carefully among the wires in case any of them were live. In the faint light she looked half-transparent, bleached of color, wrapped in white like an angel. It would be a pleasure to make her fall. . . . "I haven't seen you here before."

"You're asking me if I come here often?" She giggled, covering her mouth with her hand. There was some sort of bracelet around her wrist, just under the cuff of her dress—then, as he neared her, he saw that it wasn't a bracelet at all but a pattern inked into her skin, a matrix of swirling lines.

He froze. "You—"

He didn't finish. She moved with lightning swiftness, striking out at him with her open hand, a blow to his chest that would have sent him down gasping if he'd been a human being. He staggered back, and now there was something in her hand, a coiling whip that glinted gold as she brought it down, curling around his ankles, jerking him off his feet. He hit the ground, writhing, the hated metal biting deep into his skin. She laughed, standing over him, and dizzily he thought that he should have *known*. No human girl would wear a dress like the one Isabelle wore. She'd worn it to cover her skin—all of her skin.

Discover Emma and Julian's story in

Lady Midnight,

THE FIRST BOOK IN CASSANDRA CLARE'S

NEW SERIES, THE DARK ARTIFICES.

Emma took her witchlight out of her pocket and lit it—and almost screamed out loud. Jules's shirt was soaked with blood and worse, the healing runes she'd drawn had vanished from his skin. They weren't working.

"Jules," she said. "I have to call the Silent Brothers. They can help you. I *have* to."

His eyes screwed shut with pain. "You can't," he said. "You know we can't call the Silent Brothers. They report directly to the Clave."

"So we'll lie to them. Say it was a routine demon patrol. I'm calling," she said, and reached for her phone.

"No!" Julian said, forcefully enough to stop her. "Silent Brothers know when you're lying! They can see inside your head, Emma. They'll find out about the investigation. About Mark—"

"You're not going to bleed to death in the backseat of a car for Mark!"

"No," he said, looking at her. His eyes were eerily blue-green, the only bright color in the dark interior of the car. "You're going to fix me."

Emma could feel it when Jules was hurt, like a splinter lodged under her skin. The physical pain didn't bother her; it was the terror, the only terror worse than her fear of the ocean. The fear of Jules being hurt, of him dying. She would give up anything, sustain any wound, to prevent those things from happening.

"Okay," she said. Her voice sounded dry and thin to her own ears. "Okay." She took a deep breath. "Hang on."

She unzipped her jacket, threw it aside. Shoved the console between the seats aside, put her witchlight on the floorboard. Then she reached for Jules. The next few seconds were a blur of Jules's blood on her hands and his harsh breathing as she pulled him partly upright, wedging him against the back door. He didn't make a sound as she moved him, but she could see him biting his lip, the blood on his mouth and chin, and she felt as if her bones were popping inside her skin.

"Your gear," she said through gritted teeth. "I have to cut it off."

He nodded, letting his head fall back. She drew a dagger from her belt, but the gear was too tough for the blade. She said a silent prayer and reached back for Cortana.

Cortana went through the gear like a knife through melted butter. It fell away in pieces and Emma drew them free, then sliced down the front of his T-shirt and pulled it apart as if she were opening a jacket.

Emma had seen blood before, often, but this felt different. It was Julian's, and there seemed to be a lot of it. It was smeared up and down his chest and rib cage; she could see where the arrow had gone in and where the skin had torn where he'd yanked it out.

"Why did you pull the arrow out?" she demanded, pulling her sweater over her head. She had a tank top on under it. She patted his chest and side with the sweater, absorbing as much of the blood as she could.

Jules's breath was coming in hard pants. "Because when someone—shoots you with an arrow—" he gasped, "your immediate response is not—'Thanks for the arrow, I think I'll keep it for a while.'"

"Good to know your sense of humor is intact."

"Is it still bleeding?" Julian demanded. His eyes were shut.

She dabbed at the cut with her sweater. The blood had slowed, but the cut looked puffy and swollen. The rest of him, though—it had been a while since she'd seen him with his shirt off. There was more muscle than she remembered. Lean muscle pulled tight over his ribs, his stomach flat and lightly ridged. Cameron was much more muscular, but Julian's spare lines were as elegant as a greyhound's. "You're too skinny," she said. "Too much coffee, not enough pancakes."

"I hope they put that on my tombstone." He gasped as she shifted forward, and she realized abruptly that she was squarely in Julian's lap, her knees around his hips. It was a bizarrely intimate position.

"I—am I hurting you?" she asked.

He swallowed visibly. "It's fine. Try with the *iratze* again."

"Fine," she said. "Grab the panic bar."

"The what?" He opened his eyes and peered at her.

"The plastic handle! Up there, above the window!" She pointed. "It's for holding on to when the car is going around curves."

"Are you sure? I always thought it was for hanging things on. Like dry cleaning."

"Julian, *now is not the time to be pedantic*. Grab the bar or I swear—"

"All right!" He reached up, grabbed hold of it, and winced. "I'm ready."

She nodded and set Cortana aside, reaching for her stele. Maybe her previous *iratzes* had been too fast, too sloppy. She'd always focused on the physical aspects of Shadowhunting, not the more mental and artistic ones: seeing through glamours, drawing runes.

She set the tip of it to the skin of his shoulder and drew, carefully and slowly. She had to brace herself with her left hand against his shoulder. She tried to press as lightly as she could, but she could feel him tense under her fingers. The skin on his shoulder was smooth and hot under her touch, and she wanted to get closer to him, to put her hand over the wound on his side and heal it with the sheer force of her will. To touch her lips to the lines of pain beside his eyes and—

Stop. She had finished the *iratze*. She sat back, her hand clamped around the stele. Julian sat up a little straighter, the ragged remnants of his shirt hanging off his shoulders. He took a deep breath, glancing down at himself—and the *iratze* faded back into his skin, like black ice melting, spreading, being absorbed by the sea.

He looked up at Emma. She could see her own reflection in his eyes: she looked wrecked, panicked, with blood on her neck and her white tank top. "It hurts less," he said in a low voice.

The wound on his side pulsed again; blood slid down the side of his rib cage, staining his leather belt and the waistband of his jeans. She put her hands on his bare skin, panic rising up inside her. His skin felt hot, too hot. Fever hot.

"I have to call," she whispered. "I don't care if the whole world comes down around us, Jules, the most important thing is that you *live*."

"Please," he said, desperation clear in his voice. "Whatever is happening, we'll fix it, because we're *parabatai*. We're forever. I said that to you once, do you remember?"

She nodded warily, hand on the phone.

"And the strength of a rune your *parabatai* gives you is special. Emma, you can do it. You can heal me. We're *parabatai* and that means the things we can do together are . . . extraordinary."

There was blood on her jeans now, blood on her hands and her tank top, and he was still bleeding, the wound still open, an incongruous tear in the smooth skin all around it.

"Try," Jules said in a dry whisper. "For me, try?"

His voice went up on the question and in it she heard the voice of the boy he had been once, and she remembered him smaller, skinnier, younger, back pressed against one of the marble columns in the Hall of Accords in Alicante as his father advanced on him with his blade unsheathed.

And she remembered what Julian had done, then. Done to protect her, to protect all of them, because he always would do everything to protect them.

She took her hand off the phone and gripped the stele, so tightly she felt it dig into her damp palm. "Look at me, Jules," she said in a low voice, and he met her eyes with his. She placed the stele against his skin, and for a moment she held still, just breathing, breathing and remembering.

Julian. A presence in her life for as long as she could remember, splashing water at each other in the ocean, digging in the sand together, him putting his hand over hers and them marveling at the difference in the shape and length of their fingers. Julian singing, terribly and off-key, while he drove, his fingers in her hair carefully freeing a trapped leaf, his hands catching her in the training room when she fell, and fell, and fell. The first time after their *parabatai* ceremony when she'd smashed her hand into a wall in rage at not being able to get a sword maneuver right, and he'd come up to her, taken her still-shaking body in his arms and said, "Emma, Emma, don't hurt yourself. When you do, I feel it, too."

Something in her chest seemed to split and crack; she marveled that it wasn't audible. Energy raced along her veins, and the stele jerked in her hand before it seemed to move on its own, tracing the graceful outline of a healing rune across Julian's chest. She heard him gasp, his eyes flying open. His hand slid down her back and he pressed her against him, his teeth gritted.

"Don't *stop*," he said.

Emma couldn't have stopped if she'd wanted to. The stele seemed to be moving of its own accord; she was blinded with memories, a kaleidoscope of them, all of them Julian. Sun in her eyes and Julian asleep on the beach in an old T-shirt and her not wanting to wake him, but he'd woken anyway when the sun went down and looked for her immediately, not smiling till his eyes found her and he knew she was there. Falling asleep talking and waking up with their hands interlocked; they'd been children in the dark together once but now they were something else, something intimate and powerful, something Emma felt she was touching only the very edge of as she finished the rune and the stele fell from her nerveless fingers.

"Oh," she said softly. The rune seemed lit from within by a soft glow.

Turn the page for

An Offering of Moonlight,

A NEW PERSPECTIVE ON

JEM AND TESSA'S FIRST KISS.

————◆————

"I wish to offer you moonlight in a handful."
—Zhang Jiu Ling

The first thing Jem did the moment he entered his room was stride to the *yin fen* box on his nightstand.

He usually took the drug in a solution of water, letting it dissolve and drinking it, but he was too impatient now; he took a pinch between his thumb and forefinger, and sucked it from his fingers. It tasted of burned sugar and left the inside of his mouth feeling numb. He slammed the box shut with a feeling of dark satisfaction.

The second thing he did was retrieve his violin.

The fog was thick against the windows, making them look as if they had been painted over with lead. If it had not been for the witchlight torches burning low, there would not have been enough illumination for him to see what he was doing as he wrenched open the box that held his Guarneri and took the instrument from it. A snatch of one of Bridget's songs played in his head: *It was mirk, mirk night, there was no starlight, and they waded through blood to the knees.*

Mirk, mirk night indeed. The sky had been black as pitch down in Whitechapel. Jem thought of Will, standing on the pavement, dizzy-eyed and grinning. Until Jem had hit him. He had never hit Will before, no matter how maddening his *parabatai* had been. No matter how destructive to other people, no matter his casual cruelty, no matter his wit that was like the edge of a knife, Jem had never hit him. Until now.

The bow was already rosined; he flexed his fingers before he took hold of it, and drew in several deep breaths. He could feel the *yin fen* surging through his veins already, lighting his blood like fire lighting gunpowder. He thought of Will again, asleep on the bed in the opium den. He had been flushed, his face smooth and innocent in sleep, like a child with his cheek pillowed on his hand. Jem remembered when Will had been young like that, though never a time when he had been innocent.

He set the bow to the strings and played. He played softly at first. He played Will lost in dreams, finding solace in a drugged haze that muffled his pain. Jem could only envy him that. The *yin fen* was no balm: He did not find in it whatever opium addicts found in their pipes, or alcoholics in the dregs of a gin bottle. There was only exhaustion and lassitude without it, and with it, energy and fever. But there was no surcease from pain.

Jem's knees gave out, and he sank to the trunk at the foot

of his bed, still playing. He played Will breathing the name *Cecily*, and he played himself watching the glint of his own ring on Tessa's hand on the train from York, knowing it was all a charade, knowing, too, that he wished that it wasn't. He played the sorrow in Tessa's eyes when she had come into the music room after Will had told her she would never have children. Unforgivable, that—what a thing to do—and yet Jem had forgiven him. Love was forgiveness, he had always believed that, and the things Will did, he did out of some bottomless well of pain. Jem did not know the source of that pain, but he knew it existed and was real, knew it as he knew of the inevitability of his own death, knew it as he knew that he had fallen in love with Tessa Gray and that there was nothing he or anyone else could do about it.

He played that now, played all their broken hearts, and the sound of the violin wrapped him and lifted him and he closed his eyes—

His door opened. He heard the sound through the music, but for a moment did not credit it, for it was Tessa's voice he heard saying his name. "Jem?"

Surely she was a dream, conjured up by the music and the drug and his own fevered mind. He played on, played his own rage and anger at Will, for however he had always forgiven Will for his cruelty to others, he could not forgive him for endangering himself.

"*Jem!*" came Tessa's voice again, and suddenly there were hands on his, wrenching the bow out of his grasp. He let go in shock, staring up at her. "Jem, *stop*! Your violin—your lovely violin—you'll ruin it."

She stood over him, a dressing gown thrown over her white

nightgown. He remembered that nightgown: She had been wearing it the first time he had seen her, when she had come into his room and he had thought for one mad moment that she was an angel. She was breathing hard now, her face flushed, his violin gripped in one hand and the bow in the other.

"What does it matter?" he demanded. "What does any of it matter? I'm dying—I won't outlast the decade. What does it matter if the violin goes before I do?" She stared at him, her lips parting in astonishment. He stood up and turned away from her. He could no longer bear to look her in the face, to see her disappointment with him, his weakness. "You know it is true."

"Nothing is decided." Her voice trembled. "Nothing is inevitable. A cure—"

"There's no cure. I will die, and you know it, Tess. Probably within the next year. I am dying, and I have no family in the world, and the one person I trusted more than any other made sport of what is killing me."

"But, Jem, I don't think that's what Will meant to do at all." She had set down his violin and bow, and was moving toward him. "He was just trying to escape. He is running from something, something dark and awful. You know he is, Jem. You saw how he was after—after Cecily."

"He knows what it means to me," he said. She was just behind him. He could smell the faint perfume of her skin: violet water and soap. The urge to turn about and touch her was overwhelming, but he held himself still. "To see him even toy with what has destroyed my life—"

"But he wasn't thinking of you—"

"*I know that.*" How could he say it? How could he explain? How could he tell her that Will was what he had devoted his life to: Will's rehabilitation, Will's innate goodness. Will was the cracked mirror of his own soul that he had spent years trying to repair. He could forgive Will harming anyone but his own self. "I tell myself he's better than he makes himself out to be, but, Tessa, what if he isn't? I have always thought, if I had nothing else, I had Will. If I have done nothing else that made my life matter, I have always stood by him. But perhaps I shouldn't."

"Oh, Jem." Her voice was so soft that he turned. Her dark hair was unbound: It tumbled around her face and he had the most absurd urge to bury his hands in it, to draw her close, his hands cupping the back of her neck. She reached out a soft hand for him, and for a moment, wild hope rose up in him, unstoppable as the tide—but she only laid her hand against his forehead, careful as a nurse. "You're burning up. You should be resting—"

He jerked away from her before he could stop himself. Her gray eyes widened. "Jem, what is it? You don't want me to touch you?"

"Not like that." The words burst out before he could stop them. The night, Will, the music, the *yin fen*, all had unlocked something in him—he barely knew his own self, this stranger who spoke the truth and spoke it harshly.

"Like what?" Her confusion was plain on her face. Her pulse beat at the side of her throat; where her nightgown was open he could see the soft curve of her collarbone. He dug his fingers into the palms of his hands. He could not hold back the words anymore. It was swim or drown.

"As if you were a nurse and I were your patient," he told her. "Do you think I do not know that when you take my hand, it is only so that you can feel my pulse? Do you think I do not know that when you look into my eyes, it is only to see how much of the drug I have taken? If I were another man, a normal man, I might have hopes, presumptions even; I might—" *I might want you*. He broke off before he said it. It could not be said. Words of love were one thing; words of desire were as dangerous as a rocky shore where a ship could founder. It was hopeless, he knew it was hopeless, and yet—

She shook her head. "This is the fever speaking, not you."

Hopeless. The despair cut at him like a dull knife, and he said the next words without thinking: "You can't even believe I could want you. That I am alive enough, healthy enough—"

"No—" She caught at his arm, and it was like having five brands of fire laid across his skin. Desire lanced through him like pain. "James, that isn't at all what I meant—"

He laid his hand over hers, where she held his arm. He heard her indrawn breath—sharp, surprised. But not horrified. She did not pull away. She did not remove his hand. She let him hold her, and turn her, so that they stood face-to-face, close enough to breathe each other in.

"Tessa," he said. She looked up at him. The fever pounded in him like blood, and he no longer knew what was the desire and what was the drug, or if the one simply enhanced the other, and it did not matter, it did not matter because he wanted her, he had wanted her for so long. Her eyes were huge and gray, her pupils dilated, and her lips were parted on a breath as if she were about to speak, but before she could speak he kissed her.

The kiss exploded in his head like fireworks on Guy Fawkes Day. He closed his eyes on a whirl of colors and sensations almost too intense to bear: Her lips were soft and hot under his and he found himself running his fingers over her face, the curves at her cheekbones, the hammering pulse in her throat, the tender skin at the back of her neck. It took every ounce of control he had to touch her gently, not to crush her against him, and when she raised her arms and twined them around his neck, sighing into his mouth, he had to stifle a gasp and for a moment hold himself very still or they would have been on the floor.

Her own hands on him were gentle, but there was no mistaking their encouragement. Her lips murmured against his, whispering his name, her body soft and strong in his arms. He followed the arch of her back with his hands, feeling the curve of it under her nightgown, and he could not stop himself then: He pulled her so tightly against him that they both stumbled, and collapsed backward onto the bed.

Tessa sank into the cushions and he propped himself over her. Her hair tumbled, dark, across the pillows. A flush of blood spread over her face and down to the neckline of her gown, staining her pale skin. The hot press of body to body was dizzying, like nothing he had imagined, more fierce and delicious than the most delirious music. He kissed her again and again, each time harder, savoring the texture of her lips under his, the taste of her mouth, until the intensity of it threatened to tip over from pleasure into pain.

He should stop, he knew. This had gone beyond honor, beyond any bounds of propriety. He had imagined, sometimes, kissing her, carefully cupping her face between his hands, but had never imagined this: that they would be wrapped so tightly around each other that he could hardly tell where he left off and she began. That she would kiss him and stroke him and run her fingers through his hair. That when he hesitated with his fingers on the tie of her dressing gown, the reasonable part of his brain commanding his rebellious and unwilling body to stop, that she would neatly solve the dilemma by undoing the fastening herself and lying back as the material fell away around her and she looked up at him in only her thin nightgown.

Her chin was raised, determination and candor in her eyes, and her lifted arms welcomed him back to her, enfolding him, drawing him in. "Jem, my Jem," she was whispering, and he whispered back, losing his words against her mouth, whispering what was true but what he hoped she wouldn't understand. He whispered in Chinese, worried that if he spoke in English, he would say something profoundly stupid. "*Wo ai ni. Ni hen piao liang, Tessa. Zhe shi jie shang, wo shi zui ai ni de.*"

But he saw her eyes darken; he knew she recalled what he had said to her in the carriage. "What does it mean?" she whispered.

He stilled against her body. "It means that you are beautiful. I did not want to tell you before. I did not want you to think I was taking liberties."

She reached up and touched his cheek. He could feel his heart beating against hers. It felt as if it might beat out of his chest entirely.

"Take them," she whispered.

His heart soared, and he gathered her up against him, something he had never done before, but she did not seem to mind his clumsiness. Her hands were traveling gently over him, learning his body. Her fingers stroked the bone of his hip, the cup of his collar. They tangled in his shirt and it was up and over his head, and he was leaning into her, shaking silvery hair out of his face. He saw her eyes go wide and felt his insides tighten.

"I know," he said, looking down at himself—skin like papier-mâché, ribs like violin strings. I am not— I mean, I look—"

"Beautiful," she said, and the word was a pronouncement. "You are beautiful, James Carstairs."

Breath eased back into his lungs and they were kissing again, her hands warm and smooth against his bare skin. She touched him with hesitant, curious strokes, mapping a body that seemed to flower under her ministrations into something perfect, healthy: no longer a fragile device of swiftly diminishing flesh lashed to a framework of breakable bones. It was only now, while this was happening, that he realized how sincerely he had believed it never would.

He could feel the soft, nervous puffs of her breath against the sensitive skin of his throat as he drew his hands up and over her body. He touched her as he would touch his violin: it was how he knew to touch something that was precious and loved. He had carried the violin in his arms from Shanghai to London and he had carried Tessa, too, in his heart, for longer than he thought he remembered. When had it happened? His hands touched her through the nightgown, the curve and dip of her waist and hips like the curve of the Guarneri, but the violin did not give gratifying gasps when he touched it, did not seek his mouth out for kisses or have fascinating eyelids that fluttered shut just so when he stroked the sensitive skin at the backs of her knees.

Maybe it had been the day he'd run up the stairs to her and kissed her hand. *Mizpah.* May the Lord watch between me and thee when we are parted. It was the first time he had thought that there was something more to his regard than the ordinary regard for a pretty girl he could not have, that it had the aspect of something holy to it.

The pearl buttons of her nightdress were smooth under his fingertips. Her body bowed backward, her throat arched, as the material slipped aside, leaving her shoulder bare. Her breath was quick in her throat, the curls of her brown hair stuck to her flushed cheeks and forehead, the material of her dress crushed between them. He was shaking himself as he bent to kiss her bare skin, skin that most likely no one but herself and perhaps Sophie had ever seen, and her hand came up to cup his head, threading through the hair at the back of his neck. . . .

There was the sound of a crash. And a choking fog of *yin fen* filled the room.

It was as if Jem had swallowed fire; he jerked back and away from Tessa with such force that he nearly overbalanced them both. Tessa sat up as well, pulling the front of her nightdress together, her expression suddenly self-conscious. All Jem's heat was gone; his skin was suddenly freezing—with shame, and with fear for Tessa. He had never dreamed of her being this close to the poisonous stuff that had destroyed his life. But the lacquer box was broken: A thick layer of shining powder lay across the floor, and even as Jem drew in a breath to tell her she must go, that she must leave him if she were to be safe, he did not think of the loss of the precious drug, or of the danger to him if it could not be retrieved. He thought only:

No more.

The yin fen *has taken so much from me: my family, the years of my life, the strength in my body, the breath in my lungs. It will not take from me this, too: the most precious thing we are given by the Angel. The ability to love. I love Tessa Gray.*

And I will make sure that she knows it.

CASSANDRA CLARE'S

#1 *New York Times* Bestselling Series

THE MORTAL INSTRUMENTS
THE INFERNAL DEVICES
THE DARK ARTIFICES

A thousand years ago, the Angel Raziel mixed his blood with the blood of men and created the race of the Nephilim. Human-angel hybrids, they walk among us, unseen but ever present, our invisible protectors.

They call themselves Shadowhunters.

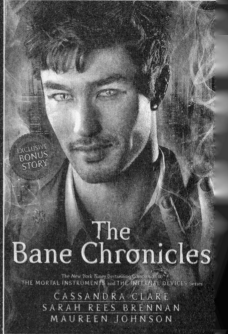

Go deeper into the world of the Shadowhunters with

THE SHADOWHUNTER'S CODEX

the essential guide to becoming one of the Nephilim

PRINT AND EBOOK EDITIONS AVAILABLE

Explore the legends and legacy of Magnus Bane in

THE BANE CHRONICLES

What happens when Magnus meets Marie Antoinette?
And what *really* happened in Peru?
Find out the answers in this illustrated short-story
collection featuring everyone's favorite warlock.

PRINT AND EBOOK EDITIONS AVAILABLE

From Margaret K. McElderry Books | TEEN.SimonandSchuster.com